A Dragonfly in the Sun

An Anthology of Pakistani Writing in English

A Dragonfly in the Sun

An Anthology of Pakistani Writing in English

Selected & Edited by
Muneeza Shamsie

Karachi
Oxford University Press
Oxford New York Delhi
1997

Oxford University Press, Walton Street, Oxford OX2 6DP

Oxford New York
Athens Auckland Bangkok Bombay
Calcutta Cape Town Dar es Salaam Delhi
Florence Hong Kong Istanbul Karachi
Kuala Lumpur Madras Madrid Melbourne
Mexico City Nairobi Paris Singapore
Taipei Tokyo Toronto

and associated companies in

Berlin Ibadan

Oxford is a trade mark of Oxford University Press

ISBN 0 19 577784 0

Printed in Pakistan at
Mas Printers, Karachi.
Published by
Ameena Saiyid, Oxford University Press
5-Bangalore Town, Sharae Faisal
P.O. Box 13033, Karachi-75350, Pakistan.

In memory of my father

Isha'at Habibullah
(1911-1991)

with love

A Dragonfly in the Sun

The afternoon's light is caught
in the dragonfly's wings where
transparency permits no reflections
and yet will not give free passage
to the sun, preserving the surface
brightness of delicate webbing
as a fragile brilliance of gleaming
points which make the wings nearly
invisible and the diagonal markings appear
as tiny irradiations of very faint
pink and blue when the dragonfly
darts up against the sun as if it
plucked colours from the air
and immediately discarded them:
this is the moment of intensity,
of the afternoon's light gathering
in the garden in a brief flickering
of a dragonfly's wings just above
the red blossoms of the pomegranate.

Zulfikar Ghose

THANKS

There are so many people who have given me invaluable help in putting together this book. I would particularly like to thank Ameena Saiyid, the Managing Director of OUP, for her unstinting support throughout; and to my editor, Yasmin Qureshi: she has helped me at every step and taken great pains to locate rare books for me. Source material was often a problem. Pakistani English work has such a low profile in the country that it's often hard to find. I owe a great debt to Zuhra Karim, Asif Farrukhi, Tahmina Ahmed and Majorie Junejo, who were kind enough to lend me books from their personal collections; and to Professor Muhammed Umar Memon at the University of Wisconsin, Madison who introduced me to a whole range of Pakistani writers in America; I thank Moazzam Sheikh and Athar Tahir for their generous co-operation too. I would also like to take this opportunity to express my gratitude to my very first editor at *Dawn,* Muhammed Ali Siddiqi who guided me and gave me faith in myself as a writer; and to Begum Shaista Suhrawardy Ikramullah, Naz Ikramullah Ashraf and Naheed Jafri Azfar for sustaining me through my earliest struggles. None of this would have been possible without my family: my parents, Isha' at and Jahanara Habibullah, who gave me so much; and above all, the interest, encouragement, and patience of my husband, Saleem Shamsie and my daughters, Saman and Kamila, for whom words cannot suffice.

Contents

INTRODUCTION

The tradition of using English for literary purposes in South Asia predates the British Raj. According to Alamgir Hashmi.[1]* the first book in English published in the region was *Travels* (1794) by an Indian Muslim, Sake Deen Mohammed. Hashmi points out that this establishes South Asia as 'one of the first regions outside the United Kingdom and the United States of America to have used English for literary purposes.' In the nineteenth century the British gradually established their hegemony over India. English became the instrument of government and the medium of instruction in schools, which were designed to provide officials who could assist the British Raj. An increasing but select number of Indians took to English. Some started to write English poetry and prose but produced work which was 'more derivative than creative,' as Tariq Rahman[2]* has stated.

The twentieth century saw rapid change. English had become the language of political debate and the bridge between the Raj and the representatives of undivided India. As the country moved towards Independence, Indian writers, including Ahmed Ali,* were determined to forge their own voice in English: they

1 Hashmi, Alamgir, Prolegomena to the study of Pakistani English and Pakistani Literature in English', The International Conference on English in South Asia, University Grants Commission, Islamabad, January 4-9, 1989.

* Writers and creative work marked* appear in this book.

2 Rahman, Tariq, *A History of Pakistani Literature in English*, Vanguard, Lahore, 1991.

explored innovative styles to find a true expression of the subcontinental experience. They are important ancestors to modern South Asian writers, who have evolved exciting new linguistic strategies.

Interestingly, poetry, fiction and drama by Muslim writers in the pre-Partition era addressed nationalist, socialist and social issues but not the political and communal tensions which led to the polarization between the Congress and the Muslim League, culminating in the division of India and the creation of Pakistani as a separate homeland. In 1948 with the benefit of hindsight the Pakistani writer, Mumtaz Shahnawaz*, finished the first draft of her novel *The Heart Divided**, written over five years, about those events and the Pakistan Movement. She died in an air crash before she had time to make revisions; but her work has been included here because of its honesty and its historical importance.

Inevitably, Indian and Pakistani writing cannot be entirely divorced from each other; nor can Pakistani writers be isolated from trends in world literature in English, particularly those of England and America or from the movement of South Asians into the diaspora.

The trans-geographical nature of Muslim philosophy and Pakistan's proximity to Afghanistan, Iran, India, China and Russia; its layers of history dating back to one of the world's earliest civilizations; the contact with the Hindu and Buddhist sages of antiquity and itinerant merchants along the Silk Route; and the encounter with invaders from Persia, Arabia, Central Asia and Greece long before the British came has given Pakistani writers a particularly rich cultural heritage to draw on.

This anthology aims to show that there has been a much greater diversity of interesting creative work published in English by authors of Pakistani origin than most people realize. This is partly because many of these writers have dispersed and live elsewhere; and largely because those living and writing in Pakistan itself have received little encouragement and have had a limited forum. The tyrannical nature of Pakistan's various governments has not been conducive to freedom of expression in any language. In fact many writers have been driven into exile. But there has always been an over-sensitivity to English writing particularly if it is deemed as 'creating a bad impression of the country' internationally. There has also been a deplorable tendency to exclude and to question the 'Pakistani' identity of Pakistani English writers, who may have been born or educated in Pakistan but have migrated, or have Pakistani parents and live elsewhere.

In 1947, when Pakistan was created, it already had a very small number of established writers in English. The most eminent of these were Shahid Suhrawardy* and Ahmed Ali. Suhrawardy was widely regarded as the first modern English poet of undivided India, with the publication of *Essays in Verse* (1937). This is described by Alamgir Hashmi[3] as 'a high water mark of South Asian poetry in the first half of the twentieth century'. The influence of Ezra Pound or T.S. Eliot might be evident, but the poet's own voice became increasingly apparent. As Hashmi points out, Suhrawardy's 'witty, skilful if austere' compositions stand out in marked contrast to the derivative nineteenth century verse of other South Asian writers of that post-World War I period. Hashmi regards him as the forefather of all Pakistani writing in English.

Meanwhile, in the 1930s, the bilingual Ahmed Ali had introduced concepts of European realism into his Urdu stories and revolutionized Urdu literature. He then wrote *Twilight in Delhi**, the first major Muslim novel to emergeg from the sub-continent. He chose English as its literary language to challenge the imperial narrative. By this very act, Ahmed Ali was reaching out to a dual audience: the British who had minimized and destroyed traditional society and also the Indian Muslims whose society had fallen into decay and who refused to change with the times.

This duality embodies almost all writing in English from countries where English was acquired as the direct result of the

3 Hashmi, Alamgir, 'Prolegomena to the Study of Pakistani English and Pakistani Literature in English', The International Conference on English, in South Asia, University Grants Commission, Islamabad, January 4-9.

colonial encounter. One of Pakistan's most significant poets, Maki Kureishi*, decided that she too could write English poetry after she came across the work of Afro-Caribbean writers: this literature expressed experiences and cross cultural influences which approximated her own, more so than the literatures of England and America in which she was steeped and which she used as her grounding. Similarly, other Pakistani English writers have also identified with writing different to the Anglo-Saxon norm.

Aamer Hussein* self-consciously describes himself as 'a product of modern Asia, with its Partition and post-national squabbles' and not 'a child of Empire or English Literature'. He has struggled hard to free himself of stereotypes and labels such as 'colonial and post-colonial'. His influences have been European and black American writers and those of the Middle and Far East, whom he has read in translation, and above all, the contemporary Urdu literature which he teaches. His story *The Lost Cantos of The Silken Tiger*'* is not only unusual in Pakistani English writing because it incorporates both poetry and prose, but is also a dialogue about writing, gender and text. Furthermore, as an expatriate living in Britain, he perceives this story as an imaginary discussion with contemporary Urdu writers about issues of history, migration, exile.

Aamer Hussein states, 'I haven't discarded notions of commitment and belonging. But a modest lack of ideological dogma is crucial to the engaged writer. I claim, with fiction as my only instrument, the native's right to argue and discuss my history with my compatriots. I guess that makes me a Pakistani writer.'

All Pakistani English writers live between East and West, literally or intellectually and express it through their work. Those living in foreign lands have also been irrefutably shaped by their Pakistani heritage. This is evident in the work of the British born Hanif Kureishi.* He had already won The George Devine Award for his play about Asians in Southhall before he made his first trip to Pakistan. The experience of visiting Pakistan provided him with more material for his fertile imagination.

Shortly afterwards he won an Oscar nomination for his screenplay *My Beautiful Laundrette** which deals with racism and unemployment in Britain, but links up and contrasts the lives of British Asians with relatives from Pakistan. His subsequent novel, *The Buddha of Suburbia,* about an Asian boy growing up in Britain received the 1990 Whitbread Award for the best first novel.

Hanif Kureishi is among the three writers of Pakistani origin to win important British awards in this category. One other is Adam Zameenzad* who received the 1987 David Higham Award for his novel *The Thirteenth House*, set in Karachi. The third is Nadeem Aslam*, the youngest writer to be included in this anthology. His novel, *Season of the Rainbirds**, set in the Punjab, won the Betty Trask Award, the Authors' Club Award and was short-listed for three other major prizes. Meanwhile the Pakistani born poet in Britain, Moniza Alvi* received the 1991 Poetry Business Prize; in an earlier time, Adrian A. Husain* received the Guinness Prize for poetry.

A number of Pakistani English writers including Ahmed Ali, Hanif Kureishi and Zulfikar Ghose*, have had their work translated into several languages. Bapsi Sidhwa,* who probably has a wider audience in her own country than any other Pakistani writer in English, has been translated into German. She was given Germany's 1991 Liberature Prize for her novel about Partition, *Ice-Candy-Man**, which is the first Pakistani novel to employ a narrative style written in the multilingual cadences of Pakistani English. Later, Bapsi Sidhwa received the three year $100,000 dollar grant the 1993 Reader Digest's Lila Wallace Award in the United States. Among the most notable English writers to emerge from Pakistan is Sara Suleri*. She won America's 1987 Pushcart Prize for the first chapter of *Meatless Days*, her moving, creative memoir, crafted with a novelist's skill. Other writers featured in this book are Sorayya Y. Khan* and Javaid Qazi* both winners of literary contests in North America.

There are few literary prizes for English creative writing in Pakistan, the most well-known being The Jane Townsend Poetry

Prize for young writers though little has been heard of it lately. The concept of official literary honours and awards for creative work in English is also fairly recent: recipients range from Ahmed Ali and Bapsi Sidhwa to G.F. Riaz* and Alamgir Hashmi. There are glaring omissions however and Pakistani officialdom has yet to recognize the enormous contribution of Shahid Suhrawardy, Maki Kureishi and Zulfikar Ghose to name but a few.

The subject of English in Pakistan has been filled with paradoxes since Independence. Although English has remained the language of Government and the ruling class, English poetry, fiction and drama by Pakistanis in the early years was regarded as a somewhat irrelevant activity and a colonial hangover and it is still excluded from the mainstream of Pakistani writing. The discussion on English as a Pakistani language was nevertheless continued.

The development of English poetry in Pakistan owes much to *The Ravi,* the literary magazine of the Government College, Lahore which provided a platform for many aspiring writers. In the first three decades of Pakistan, there were magazines such as *The Pakistan Quarterly* and *Vision* which published English poetry and fiction regularly. Oxford University Press brought out three anthologies of Pakistani English poetry *First Voices* edited by Shahid Hosain* (1965), *Pieces of Eight* edited by Yunus Said (1971) and *Wordfall* (1975) edited by Kaleem Omar*. Some very fine English poetry has been written in Pakistan, though its practitioners are few. These poets have always had a small but faithful following, but have not received the recognition that is their due though some are now being introduced into school and college syllabi.

As the chronological order of writers in this book shows, English poetry flourished in Pakistan much earlier than prose; it must also be pointed out that while most of the prose writers featured here might live abroad, the poets do not. The towering presence in Pakistani English poetry is Taufiq Rafat. He was the first to introduce a Pakistani idiom into his verse which, according to Waqas Ahmad Khwaja*[4], 'validated' English as a creative medium in Pakistan. Taufiq Rafat played a pivotal role as mentor and guide for others, including Kaleem Omar, Athar Tahir* and Shuja Nawaz.*

In fact the 1970's saw tremendous activity in Pakistani English poetry. Taufiq Rafat and Kaleem Omar held readings and poetry workshops in Lahore's schools and colleges; later they took part in a multi-media event together with Maki Kureishi and in radio programmes when Shahid Hosain was Director General. Kaleem Omar also put together a programme 'The Creative Use of English' with the well-known actor Zia Mohyeddin, which travelled to all the major cities of Pakistan. Alamgir Hashmi taught the first official creative writing workshop in Lahore and compiled the first anthology of Pakistani literature in English in 1978. Further north, Daud Kamal*, the head of the English Department at Peshawar University, was forging his own distinct voice and also published an excellent literary journal which provided a forum for others. In Karachi, Adrian Husain initiated 'Mixed Voices' a multi-lingual literary group. The founders included Maki Kureishi and Salman Tarik Kureshi*. They provided a support system for each other, as well as for younger poets, and encouraged an interchange with writers of other Pakistani languages.

These activities dissipated in the 1980's, but in Islamabad writers were active in a group called 'Margalla Voices'. In Lahore there were readings at The Quaid-e-Azam University Library and in the 'Cactus' group, which led to various anthologies. The most highly acclaimed book of Pakistani verse in this period was an anthology *The Blue Wind* (1984) published in Britain.

At the end of the 1970s, Pakistan saw a new martial law regime, which attempted to do away with English. various draconian laws were introduced in the name of religion, including those which minimized women. The result of these laws was that strong feminist consciousness developed. This

4 Khwaja, Waqas Ahmed, *Morning in The Wilderness*: *Readings in Pakistan Literature*, Lahore: Sang-e-Meel Publications 1987.

permeates the work of Rukhsana Ahmad,* Talat Abbasi,* Bapsi Sidhwa and Hina Faisal Imam.* The debate over English was finally laid to rest because the resistance to abolishing English was such that it became increasingly evident English was in Pakistan to stay, as a link to the outside world and the technology of the 21st century. Some of today's Pakistani English writers are not necessarily products of English medium schools, as they once were, but grew up with Urdu as the language of instruction.

The last two decades coincided with the electronic revolution, the concept of a global village and the West's increasing interest in the new literatures in English. The dialogue on multi-culturalism too, had also given migrant groups a voice through the creative arts. Writers who were challenging the traditional, colonial, patriarchal Anglo-Saxon narrative were increasingly making themselves heard.

In this era, Bapsi Sidhwa emerged as the new voice in Pakistani fiction. She became the first Pakistan-based novelist to receive international recognition since Ahmed Ali, although by this time the expatriate writer Zulfikar Ghose was already well-established in the United States and had received considerable literary acclaim.

In 1989, The Asia Foundation organized The International Conference on English in South Asia in Islamabad. The delegates included writers Anita Desai from India, Edwin Thumboo from Singapore, Chitra Fernando from Sri Lanka, Ahmed Ali, and Bapsi Sidhwa, Alamgir Hashmi, Imran Shirvani and myself* from Pakistan. There were many lively discussions on 'non-native varieties of English', the use of English as a creative medium in Asia and of a Pakistani idiom. After this, conferences and seminars on Pakistani creative writing in English became increasingly popular in different cities.

Thus, Pakistani creative writing in English gained acceptance, but the outlets for English poetry and fiction in the country had dried up. Today there are hardly any Pakistani magazines or newspapers which publish English creative writing regularly except for *She*. Creative writing workshops too are scarce, though a very worthwhile one was held at the American Center in 1992, conducted by David Applefield. He is the editor of *Frank*, a Paris-based literary magazine which had brought out a special section on Pakistani writing, with the help of Tariq Rahman.

Pakistan's publishing industry has been in a deep crisis for numerous reasons, including rising costs and the threat from book pirates. Few publishers are willing to take a risk on Pakistani writing in English which has a limited market. The result is that a plethora of sub-standard, self-published writing in English has proliferated, while collections of quality work have been few and far between. Countries such as America and Britain have their own commercial dynamics too and Pakistani writing, being little known, cannot always fit into a suitable publishing 'slot'.

For this reason the criteria for selecting published work for this book, which is essentially retrospective, was made as flexible as possible: it was decided that it should cover a wide selection of good, representative poetry, fiction and drama which has appeared or been accepted for publication in a book, or literary journals and anthologies. All the contributors have been loosely arranged in chronological order to show the development of Pakistani writing in English.

There has been no attempt to standardize English spellings of ethnic words; nor have italics necessarily been used. The usage varies from author to author. Many new writers deliberately avoid italics and believe that indigenous words should have their own resonance in English. Some of these can also be found in new English dictionaries.

Contrary to popular belief, a great deal of Pakistani English fiction has been written in direct response to political events, as this volume reveals. The writing included here was chosen for its quality, rather than subject matter or geography, but a deliberate attempt was made to use as much prose and poetry about the birth of Pakistan, fifty years ago, which is being commemorated this year. As it happens Bapsi Sidhwa's *Ice-Candy-Man* about the Partition riots is her most powerful and polished work. She skilfully shows how Sikh/Hindu-Muslim tensions arose and religious differences crept into people's lives. Hers is the only Pakistani novel to focus on the bloodbath which irrevocably changed and brutalized South Asian society. Partition also features in Zulfikar Ghose's complex and sophisticated novel *The Triple Mirror of the Self** about migration, exile and prejudice.

Zulfikar Ghose is a writer of considerable distinction, a great stylist, who has consistently produced poetry and fiction of a remarkably high quality. He has written over ten novels. *The Triple Mirror of the Self* is the most recent and revolves around a migrant's need to re-discover roots, to re-define his essential self by going back to the beginning through memory, in order to attain ultimate knowledge.

A man's search for dignity and salvation takes the reader across three continents in Adam Zameenzad's fourth novel *Cyrus Cyrus**. This novel also touches on an event which mirrors Partition: the breakup of Pakistan and the creation of Bangla Desh. Furthermore, both the expatriate Pakistani novelists Tariq Ali* and Zulfikar Ghose have used their experience of Pakistan to breathe life into historical novels set in another time and another age. Tariq Ali has explored Andalusian Islam in his novel *Shadows of the Pomegranate Tree**, which deals with a subject intrinsic to the Pakistani psyche: past Muslim glory and the reasons for Muslim decline. Zulfikar Ghose has set his trilogy *The Incredible Brazilian* in South America, a continent which he knows well and which he has often said has a definite resonance with Pakistan.

A great deal of Pakistani fiction in English which has marked milestones for English writing in Pakistan but was cumbersome or inadequate has not been included here. Instead works by younger writers, who are taking Pakistani writing in English towards new horizons, or who provide an enjoyable and thought-provoking reading, have been used here instead. Anyone interested in an in-depth study of Pakistan's English literary history should refer to Tariq Rahman's invaluable *A History of Pakistani Literature in English* (1991). He has not only analyzed a vast body of work but has provided an excellent bibliography to which I am greatly indebted.

In Pakistan, English drama has had a limited tradition as an art form. It is significant that the few well-known Pakistani English dramatists such as Rukhsana Ahmad, Tariq Ali, and Hanif Kureishi have all established themselves in Britain. Today, few people know that the first South Asian play to have been performed on the London stage was *Daughter of Ind* (1937), by the Bombay-based Fyzee Rahamin. He migrated to Pakistan in 1947 with his literary wife Attiya Begum and is better remembered as a painter.

Otherwise original English plays in Pakistan have been few and far between. Among the most noteworthy is Taufiq Rafat's *The Foothold* which was written entirely in verse and performed by Government College, Lahore some decades ago, but little has been heard of it since. Imran Aslam, now editor of the English newspaper, *The News,* has stated that after the 1970's he and other playwrights made a conscious decision to write plays in Urdu, to reach a wider, more meaningful audience and partly because they were a little embarrassed at the 'elitist' connotations of English. Having established himself as an Urdu playwright, he has started writing short political skits in English for the stage.

Meanwhile there exists a group of young aspiring Pakistani writers who have been writing with dedication from an early age. Some are creative writing majors from the United States—at least three are in MFA programmes there—and several are at colleges in Pakistan, or elsewhere, pursuing other disciplines, but snatching every moment to write. They will determine the future of Pakistani creative writing in English, which is finally coming into its own.

Muneeza Shamsie
Karachi, 1997

Shahid Suhrawardy

Shahid Suhrawardy was born in Midnapur in 1890. His mother, Khujista Akhter Bano, was among the few women of her generation to write both in English and Urdu and was a regular contributor to *Ismat,* the literary Urdu magazine. After Shahid Suhrawardy graduated from Oxford, he became an English lecturer in Moscow, where he produced plays and witnessed the Russian Revolution. He moved to France and finally returned to India after an absence of twenty years. He had a wide social circle, spoke thirteen languages and is mentioned in the letters of D.H. Lawrence, Robert Bridges, and other literary luminaries of his day. He published his first book of poetry *Faded Leaves* in 1910; but it was his *Essays in Verse* (1937) that established him as the first of undivided India's modern poets. He forged his own distinct voice and his work stood out in marked contrast to the sentimental, derivative Indian English poetry of an earlier era. He was the Bhageshwar Professor of Fine Art at Calcutta University for many years and it was during his tenure there that he wrote *Prefaces: Lectures on Art Subjects*. He migrated to Pakistan after Partition. From 1952-4 he was a Professor of Oriental Studies at Columbia University; then he joined the Pakistan Foreign Service and served as Ambassador. His work was reprinted in anthologies of Pakistani writing including *First Voices* (1965). He co-translated a book of Chinese verse, *Poems of Lee Hou Chu*, and a Russian book by V. Bartold, *Mussalman Culture*. He died in Karachi in 1965.

Narcisse: Mallarmeen

Your eyes to me are moonlit seas
where rove my sea-gull dreams like souls,
where coral roses keep their tryst
with large translucent bees,
where sea-weeds held in amber bowls
whisper like eager girls,
where leaves of lily-pearls
wander amongst cold gleaming eyes,
and where the dream-entranced skies
tremble, grape-coloured, starlight-kist.
But in your inmost eyes I see a boy,
a wondrous fair-limbed flower-bodied boy,
gazing into an amethyst.

Letter from O'Ni to E.T. at the Shiffolds a Fu

I lie content in my poor fields
With the young spring sun warming my bones.
The bamboo shoots out its sprays,
Stands like a mighty fishing rod
To catch the new-come birds.
The blue-throated peacock screeches on the lawn;
The oriole sings a love-song on the high branch.
My paper house stands a little on one side
Because of last winter's winds:
The thatch on it has gathered towards the front,
Like a fringe upon a bald man's head.
The heavy dog fat from his wintry sleep
Gradually is regaining his nimbleness,
Noses about the damp earth
And barks at the sun without intent or thought.

While I lie in the little fields
That kindly fate has given me for my banishment
I dream of the great hubbub town of Ch'ang-an,
Where reign the sons of the ungrateful Chu,
And I think on the days
Which not far from Ch' ang-an—
Sixty li in all—
I passed in the pleasant land of Shi-fo,
There in the marble palace
I would lie in bed soft with swan's feathers,
My freezing feet resting on a bottle of Jade,
And in the light softly pouring from the ceiling
The naughty 'Birds' of To-fan flitted through my sleep,
Or the night through I shared in the noble wisdom of Fla-tun;

Or was merged in that most fascinating writing,
Great Ssuma-Kien's Grand Encyclopedia.
In the evening in that lovely palace
(where lacquered boxes are set on tall trees
For tits to home with the first arrival of spring,
Such is the friendly disposition of my noble protectors)
The stately Li-zu, lady of the house,
Reads out in a voice more sweet than ivory flute
The tales of that pale man, Che-ko;
While Bo-bo, more learned than those
Who after travail
And many attempts at suicide
Have passed the civil service,
Pares his scholarly nails,
Thinking of holy Flan-si talking to a ghost
Or mourning o'er Chiao Chung Ching's faithful wife.

Sweet airy noises from abodes unseen
Fill the spacious ceremonial Hall,
And the fire leaps up to devour the cold—
For the sake of that house
I even love the winter.

Away, away, O dreams of roasted golden fowl
And silvered papyrus-scrolls cut from the side of the well-fed hog,
And gaudy fruit soaked in a perfumed cream!
I wish to be content as now I lie,
Waiting for my simple herbal diet
Which the amiable Ma-li and the young Dru-sha
Are preparing amid loud talk
But with great gentleness of mind.

The white cranes of my years
Are circling overhead.
The nose is lengthening,
The empty patch on my head is spreading towards the ears.
The bundle of my pains bows down my back.
Yesterday the rain, driven by the wind,
Was lashing at my windows.
Today I watched the moisture
Gather into whole drops
And softly trickle down the window panes.

To My Dog

When we are old,
And sausages dangling at your nose
Won't raise the ancient appetite,
Nor the keen apprised sight
Of a fleet-limbed female add
To your muscular thighs an iron strain,

And the surly herd of your young foes
Will make you hide beneath my overcoat;
When we'll be sad,
And the warm sun will seem to us cold
As we stumble through the street,
Friend leading friend,
And no more meet
The gladsome sympathy in every eye;
When bent down with all kinds of disease
You will rheumatically trail your wasted limbs,
And I be saddled with a chronic lymph,
Or an eternal coughing choke my throat,
To which you'll gurgle out a bark by rote;
When we'll be tottering to our end—
Shall we not think then of this opalescent sky?

Will not remembrance wake in our endangered brain
Of these green lawns
Where humble flowers broke in bloom on your swift track?
Or will our faculties have grown so slack
That we shall muddle joy with pain?
And at the stroke of ruthless memories
Again you'll disappear,
And I will be searching you in bush and underwood;
The loving names by which I'll call
Intentionally you will not hear,
And for my unshared solitude
You will not care at all.
You might be lying somewhere dead,
Curving your tired head
As in deep sleep.
I shall not weep—
You might be looking for a long-lost ball.
Who knows if in a last obstreperous mood
You might be consummating in a ditch
Your agonizing orgies with a bitch?

FROM *An Old Man's Songs*

II

You make some efforts for my sake,
You part on the side your hair,
You attempt to read Blake:
An old man's whims,
An old man's vanity!
Why do you wish
My heart to swell the pageantry of praise
Which paves your triumphal way?
Old men are not so easily beguiled
By gestures, handmaids of your sanity.
Old men do not allow their hearts to run wild.
Beware, my Love, beware,
Lest in your riotous hair
There might not be a dream of mine that sighs—
Though you don't note the hunger in my eyes.

IV

God has dowered you with all gifts.
Roses and songs and men's hearts
Lie strewn in your path
For you to step upon.
The prowess of your loveliness,
The onward pressure of your youth
Nothing can thwart.
Why should you then redden your mouth,
Grow poisonous flowers on a pale face,
Completing the girlish grace
Of a beauty too complete?
I do not wish your hand to stray, by chance,
Into my hand.
I understand,

An old man's heart is brittle
And cold his hand.
Bowed down I pick the litter of your charms:
Alms of a word,
Blessings of a glance,
Gestures thrown out with squandering ease.
The riverine cadence, Friend,
Might mean an old man's end.

VII

Around your innocence
A net I laid
Pieced out of bits
Of vile experience:
The parenthetic phrase,
Ambiguous words,
Sharp hits,
The undulating gaze,
In short, all the tricks of the trade,
Which in former times had ensnared birds.
Love, today I unloose the strings
To the heavy tumult of your fate,
To the flutter of your anxious wings.
My pride is soothed.
They say, an old man's pride,
When all things go,
Is his sole preoccupation.
Others will hold your hands;
Others will kiss your mouth;
I am content to know
That technical skill
Still
Outbids the insolence of youth.

AHMED ALI

Born in Delhi in 1908, Ahmed Ali was educated at Aligarh Muslim University and Lucknow University. He taught English Literature at various universities in undivided India. He wrote two plays, *The Land of Twilight* (1931), and *Break the Chains* (1932), and was the Listener's Research Director with the BBC, during the Second World War. He was a man who imbibed two cultures and bridged them through his writing. He brought the European traditions of realism and social comment into his fiction: his Urdu short story *Hamari Gali* (*Our Lane*) (1935) proved to be a milestone in Urdu Literature. He was among the four radical contributors to *Angaray* (1932), a collection of stories which scandalized society and revolutionized sub-continental literature. It was banned by the Government of India. The authors gave a statement in its defence and founded the historic Progressive Writers Movement. This became the All-India Progressive Writers Association (1936) which was supported by, and spawned, many literary luminaries. Ahmed Ali soon broke away from the group, amid much acrimony, because he refused to accept the Marxist view 'that only proletarian literature or literature dealing with the proletariat and/or peasantry could be considered progressive.'[1] He chose to write his first novel *Twilight in Delhi* (1940) in English because he wanted to challenge the existing canons of imperial literature and to provide a Muslim view of the colonial encounter. The novel remained Professor Ahmed Ali's classic, though he wrote two more *Ocean of the Night* (1964) and *Rats and Diplomats* (1986). He also published five volumes of Urdu short stories.

An active member of PEN, he also founded the Pakistan Academy of Letters. Among other university appointments that he held in the United States, he was Distinguished Professor of Humanities at Michigan State University in 1975 and a

---

Ali, Ahmed, *The Prison House*, Karachi: Akrash Publishing, 'Afterword: The Progressive Writers Movement'.

Fullbright Visiting Professor from 1978-9. Prior to Partition he was Visiting Professor at Nanking University, and he later established Pakistan's diplomatic relations with China as Pakistan's first envoy. He translated Chinese poetry *The Call of The Trumpet* (unpublished) and Indonesian poetry *The Flaming Earth* (1960). He adopted Chinese imagery as a metaphor in his English poetry which first appeared in *The Purple Gold Mountain: Selected Poems of Ahmed Ali* (1960). He later added over fifty other poems. The collection is unique because it is influenced by triple traditions: Chinese, English and Urdu. He is also well-known for his translations, particularly *The Golden Tradition: An Anthology of Urdu Poetry* (1973) and *Al-Quran: A Contemporary Translation* (1984). He was awarded an honorary doctorate of literature from Karachi University and was decorated by the Government of Pakistan with the Sitara-e-Imtiaz (Star of Distinction). He died in 1994.

Twilight in Delhi is the first major Muslim novel in English to have been written in the sub-continent; it has been translated into Urdu, French, Spanish and Portuguese and was broadcast on All-India Radio. In the novel, Ahmed Ali explored and innovated a style which incorporated the sounds, imagery and poetry of Indo-Muslim culture into the English language. *Twilight in Delhi* initially faced difficulties with the printer who found it subversive, but E.M. Forster, Virginia Woolf, Harold Nicholson and others rallied around the author and the novel was published in London by the Hogarth Press in 1940. The novel was much acclaimed in Britain and India by eminent literary critics and is essentially a portrait of the erstwhile Muslim capital and its dying culture. While the British hold the Coronation Durbar of 1911 and build their new imperial city, New Delhi, as a decadent hybrid culture 'a hodge podge of Indian and Western ways' emerges in the old city. Prefaced by the verses of the last Mughal Emperor, Bahadur Shah Zafar, the novel has been planned on several interconnecting levels: it links up historical events with changes and tensions in the traditional household of Mir Nihal.

FROM *TWILIGHT IN DELHI*

FROM *Part I*

(Mir Nihal and his wife, Begum Nihal, live in a joint family, which includes, their youngest son, Asghar, their daughter, Mehro, their young nephew, Masroor, and their newly married son, Shamsuddin.)

Chapter 3

The world came to consciousness with the resonant voice of Nisar Ahmad calling the morning azaan. Far and wide his golden voice rang calling the faithful to prayer, calling them to leave their beds and arise from sleep, in a rippling voice full of the glory of a summer dawn. As yet it was dark and the stars twinkled in the cool and restful sky. Only on the eastern horizon there was a sense of birth, but as yet far away, hidden from the prying eyes of men. But the azaan carried forth a message of joy and hope, penetrating into the by-lanes and the courtyards, echoing in the silent atmosphere.

Men heard his voice in their sleep, as if far away in a happy dream. Some woke up for a while then turned on their sides and curling once more about themselves fell into a fresh slumber. Or they got up from their beds and, rubbing their eyes, groped for their bowls, and went to attend to the calls of nature.

In response to the azaan, as it were, the sparrows began to twitter one by one, in twos and threes, in dozens and scores, until at last their cries mingled and swelled into a loud and unending chorus. The dogs were awakened from sleep and began a useless search for refuse and offal, going about sniffing the very earth in search of food.

A cool green light crept over the sky. The stars paled, twinkled awhile, then hid their shy faces behind the veil of dawn which opened out gradually and the waxing light of day began to illumine the dark corners of the earth. A forward sun peeped over the world and its light coloured the waters of the

Jamuna, dyed them rose and mauve and pink. Its rays were caught by the tall minarets of the Jama Masjid, glinted across the surface of its marble domes, and flooded the city with a warm and overbearing light.

The sky was covered with the wings of pigeons which flew in flocks. These flocks met other flocks, expanded into a huge, dark patch, flew awhile, then folded their wings, nose-dived, and descended upon a roof. The air was filled with the shouts of the pigeon-fliers who were rending the atmosphere with their cries of 'Aao, Koo, Haa!'

This went on in the air and on the house-tops. Down below on the earth the parched gram vendors cried their loud cries and, dressed in dark and dirty rags, went about the streets and the by-lanes, with their bags slung across their backs, selling gram from door to door. And the beggars began to whine, begging in ones and twos or in a chorus. They stood before the doors and sang a verse or just shouted for bread or pice or, tinkling their bowls together, they waved their heads in a frenzy, beating time with their feet, singing for all they were worth:

Dhum ! Qalandar, God will give,
Dhum ! Qalandar, God alone;
Milk and sugar, God will give,
Dhum! Qalandar, God alone....

They were ever so many, young ones and old ones, fair ones and dark ones, beggars with white flowing beards and beggars with shaved chins. They wore long and pointed caps, round caps and oval caps, or turbans on their heads. And there were beggars in tattered rags and beggars in long robes reaching down to the knees. There were beggars in patched clothes and beggars in white ones. But they had deep and resonant voices and all looked hale and hearty. The house doors creaked, the gunny bag curtains hanging in front of them moved aside, the tender hand of some pale beauty came out and gave a pice or emptied the contents of a plate into their bowls and dishes, and satisfied they went away praying for the souls of those within....

Men went about their work with hurried steps; and from the lanes the peculiar noise of silver-leaf makers beating silver and gold shot forth like so many bottles being opened one after the other. To cap it all the tinsmiths began to hammer away at corrugated iron sheets with all their might. And the city hummed with activity and noise, beginning its life of struggle and care.

Begam Nihal had already got up, and, having finished her prayers, sat on a small wooden couch reading the Koran in rhythmic tones, moving gently to and fro. Mehro had also got up and sat on the platform performing her ablutions; and Masroor was getting ready to go to school. Shams was still asleep; but his wife was in the latrine. From the kotha could be heard the voice of Begam Jamal saying angrily to her widowed sister-in-law who lived with her:

'You have made my life a misery, Bi Anjum. I have neither rest nor peace....'

As the parched gram vendor came near the house Begam Nihal turned round and without opening her lips began to attract Dilchain's attention by muttering something like the dumb. One who was not accustomed to her habit could not have made head or tail of what she said. But Dilchain understood her. She was cleansing the pots sitting in the kitchen, fumbling with her hands in the ashes, then crunching the inside of the pot with the help of hemp string made into a knot. As Begam Nihal mumbled again Dilchain dipped her hands in a bowl of water and grumbled:

'There is no peace for me, O God.'

She got up and came near her mistress, who took out a pice from under her prayer-cloth and gave it to Dilchain, and asked her to buy gram.

Masroor came out of the room, books under his arm, wearing a dirty sherwani, dirt and oil on the lower part of his Turkish cap, and quietly went out by the door. Mehro, having finished her ablutions, was busy at prayer. Shams's wife came out of the latrine and vanished into the bathroom.

The sparrows chattered on the henna tree and on the date palm perched a crow and croaked in a hoarse and heart-rending way his monotonous cries....

Mir Nihal went to the kotha where his flying pigeons were kept. He released the birds, and as they all came out he rushed at them with a flag tied to a bamboo stick in one hand, the other stretched out, and shouted at the birds: 'Haa, koo!' and off they went. They were ever so many, black ones and white ones and blue ones, dappled and grey, beautiful wings stretched out in flight.

The pigeons circled over the roof, then seeing their master's flag pointing towards the east where Khwaja Ashraf Ali's flock of rare, dappled pigeons was circling over the roof, they flew in a straight line shooting like an arrow. As they neared the Khwaja's flock they took a dip and suddenly rose upwards from below the other flock, mixed with the pigeons and took a wide detour. They would have come home, but Mir Nihal put two fingers in his mouth and blew a loud whistle, and the pigeons flew away in one straight line.

Khwaja Ashraf Ali began to rend the air with his cries of 'Aao, aao' (come), but to no purpose. Mir Nihal's flock along with Khwaja Saheb's flew far away, mixing and intermixing with other flocks, forming a huge mass which grew smaller and smaller in the distance. The other pigeon-fliers were also shouting, calling their pigeons home. Many pigeons separated from the flock and, joining their wings together, shot towards the roofs. Only just a few of Khwaja Saheb's pigeons came home in ones and twos; the others were still flying with the rest, far away. Mir Nihal stopped whistling and sat looking in the direction where his flock had flown. Khwaja Ashraf Ali stood there peeping over the parapet, still shouting to his pigeons to come back home.

After a long time a dark patch appeared over the house tops in the distance, growing bigger and bigger as it neared. With its approach the noises increased and became more hysterical. As it drew near Mir Nihal's house Khwaja Ashraf Ali bellowed and howled, calling his pigeons home. He could be seen standing there shouting and waving his hands. He was throwing handfuls of grain in the air instead of water to attract the attention of the birds. But as the flock drew near home from the west it had to pass over Mir Nihal's roof; and he put his hand in an earthen pot which was full of water and grain and threw some water in the air. His pigeons descended on the roof; but many other pigeons, recognizing that it was not their home, separated. A small flock went towards Khwaja Saheb's house, and many others flew away in other directions.

As Mir Nihal's pigeons sat on the roof picking grain he saw that some new pigeons were also there, and a few of them were dappled. Mir Nihal smiled to himself, a smile of satisfaction and victory. He threw a little grain inside the loft and the pigeons rushed in, the new ones included. He shut the door, and catching the new ones he put them in another loft and released his flock.

Khwaja Ashraf Ali stood there and his close-cropped head could be seen peeping over his wall towards Mir Nihal's house. Now and then as some pigeon of his which had gone astray came into sight, he shouted. But Mir Nihal sat there happy beyond measure, giving his pigeons grain mixed with clarified butter. Other pigeon-fliers were shouting, and the sky was full of wings, ever so many….

As the heat became intense and a hot wind began to blow, the voices died down one by one, and the pigeons were not seen in such great numbers. The sky became bronzed and grey, dirty with the dust and sand which floated in the air. The kites shrilly cried, and the grating noise of tram cars far away sounded more dreary. A heartrending monotony and a blinding glare crept over the earth. People went inside the rooms and closed the doors. Drowsiness came upon every living thing. The dogs hid in cool corners, and the sparrows found shelter in the shade of trees or inside their nests in the walls. Only now and then the wild pigeons flew in and out of the veranda, cooed awhile, and added to the feeling of monotony.

Even when the sun stood lower down in the sky, the heat remained intense, and the glare hurt the eyes. The wind moaned through the houses and the by-lanes and rustled heavily through the desolate trees, and the sound of tinsmiths beating iron sheets and the cries of vendors and ice-cream sellers sounded more disquieting and dull. But when the sun went still lower down people came out and went about their work.....

FROM *Part II*

(Mir Nihal's second son, Habibuddin, has come to Delhi. The erstwhile Mughal capital prepares for George V's Coronation Durbar.)

Chapter 8

Delhi awoke very early on the seventh of December, 1911. At four o'clock people were up and ready to go and take their places at the Jama Masjid to see the procession. Mir Nihal was loath to go, but his sons persuaded him to come. The boys dressed up in their best and warmest clothes and their pockets were filled with dried fruits. Even Nasim, Habibuddin's four-year-old son, insisted on accompanying them, for his elder cousins were going; and he was carried by Ghafoor on his shoulder. Asghar and Masroor were put in charge of the boys; and Mir Nihal was there to look after them.

People were already going to take their places in the stands. It was bitterly cold and they walked fast to keep themselves warm.

When they reached the Jama Masjid a pale green light was creeping over the horizon. They took their seats on the steps of the mosque overlooking the maidan and the Fort. Policemen went about and the Tommies paraded on roads, and a noise of talk and laughter filled the air. They made themselves comfortable on their stony seats; and Nasim fell asleep in the lap of Ghafoor who had besmeared himself with more attar and had put a greater quantity of oil in his hair for the occasion.

Gradually a little light appeared in the east, but soon it was smothered by a fog which covered everything up in its grey mantle. When a shivering sun came out it displayed a unique sight of hundreds and thousands of people, dressed in bright and gaudy clothes, all around; and Tommies stood lining the roads, afraid, as it were, lest the crowds rush at their King when he passed.

At last when the sun had risen and the fog had lifted up, a salute of guns announced the arrival of the English King. As they sounded, a shout went up from the crowds, as if the King had come right in their midst.

It was a long time until the procession emerged out of the main gate of the Fort through which once the Mughal kings used to come out. Slowly it crept forward with horses and its show of martial might; and people gazed with wondering eyes, trying to distinguish the King in the crowd. But most failed to see which was the King and which the officials. The English looked all so alike with their white faces and their similar military uniforms. Behind were the carriages of native rajahs and nawabs. As Mir Nihal thought of their slavishness and their treacherous acceptance of the foreign yoke he was filled with shame and disgust.

Here it was, in this very Delhi, he thought, that kings once rode past, Indian kings, his kings, kings who have left a great and glorious name behind. But the Farangis came from across the seven seas, and gradually established their rule. By egging on Indian chiefs to fight each other and by giving them secret and open aid they won concessions for themselves; and established their 'empire....'

The procession passed, one long unending line of generals and governors, the Tommies and the native chiefs with their retinues and soldiery, like a slow unending line of ants. In the background were the guns booming, threatening the subdued people of Hindustan. Right on the road, lining it on either side, and in the procession, were English soldiers, to show, as it seemed to Mir Nihal, that India had been conquered with the force of arms, and at the point of guns will she be retained.

Mir Nihal closed his eyes for a while, but painful thoughts were in his mind which did not allow him any peace. As he tried to forget them, more and more of them swarmed upon him.

Right in front of him was the Red Fort built long ago by Shah Jahan, the greatest of artists in mortar and stone, but which was now being trampled by the ruthless feet of an alien race. On his right, beyond the city wall, was the Khooni Darwaza, the Bloody Gate; and beyond that still was the Old Fort built by Feroz Shah Tughlaq many more centuries ago. Still beyond stretched the remnants of the past Delhis and of the ravished splendour of once mighty Hindustan—a Humayun's tomb or a Qutab Minar. There it was that the Hindu kings had built the early Delhis, Hastinapur or Dilli; and still in Mahroli stands the Iron Pillar as a memory of Asoka; and other ruins of the days of India's golden age, and dynasties greater than history has ever known. Today it was this very Delhi which was being despoiled by a Western race who had no sympathy with India or her sons, thought Mir Nihal. Already they had put the iron chains of slavery round their once unbending necks.

The horses pranced on the road as they walked; and people gazed with curious eyes at the cortege of native chiefs with its vainglorious pomp and show and soldiers in armour and coats of mail and swords and lances, weapons useless in the face of guns. The procession passed by the Jama Masjid whose facade had been vulgarly decorated with a garland of golden writing containing slavish greetings from the Indian Mussalmans to the English King, displaying the treachery of the priestly class to their people and Islam.

It was this very mosque, Mir Nihal remembered with blood in his eyes, which the English had insisted on demolishing or turning into a church during 1857. As he thought of this a most terrible and awe-inspiring picture flashed before his mind. It was on the fourteenth day of September, 1857, that most fateful day when Delhi fell into the hands of the English, that this mosque had seen a different sight. Mir Nihal was ten years of age then, and had seen everything with his own eyes. It was a Friday and thousands of Mussalmans had gathered in the mosque to say their prayers. The invaders had succeeded at last in breaking through the city wall after a battle lasting for four months and four days. Sir Thomas Metcalfe with his army had taken his stand by the hospital on the Esplanade Road, and was contemplating the destruction of the Jama Masjid. The Mussalmans came to know of this fact, and they talked of making an attack on Metcalfe; but they had no guns with them, only swords. One man got up and standing on the pulpit shamed the people, saying that they would all die one day, but it was better to die like men, fighting for their country and Islam. His words still rang in Mir Nihal's ears:

'The time of your trial has come,' the man had shouted. 'I give you the invitation to death. The enemy is standing there right in front of you. Those who wish to prove their mettle should come with me to the northern gate of the mosque. Those who hold life dear should go to the southern gate, for the enemy is not there on that side...'

When they had heard this speech the Mussalmans had cried in unison 'Allah-o-Akbar'; and there was not one soul who went to the southern gate of the mosque. They unsheathed their swords, broke the scabbards into two, and flashing them rushed out of the northern gate. In front stood Metcalfe with his men, and all around lay the corpses of the dead. Already the vultures had settled down to devour the carrion; and the dogs were tearing the flesh of the patriots who lay unburied and unmourned. As Metcalfe saw the people with the swords in their hands he opened fire. Hundreds fell down dead on the steps of the mosque and inside, colouring the stones a deeper red with their blood. But with a resolution to embrace death in the cause of the motherland, the Mussalmans made a sudden rally and before Metcalfe's men could fire a second volley of shots they were at their throats. They began to kill the soldiers, who turned their backs and ran for their lives. The Mussalmans chased them at their heels, killing many more until the English had reached the hill. On the hill was more of the English army and a battle ensued. The Mussalmans had no guns and most of them lost their lives, the rest came away....

As this scene passed before his eyes Mir Nihal could not contain himself and his rage burst out of bounds. There were those men of 1857, and here were the men of 1911, chicken-hearted and happy in their disgrace. This thought filled him with pain, and he sat there, as it were, on the rack, weeping dry tears of blood, seeing the death of his world and of his birth-place. The past, which was his, had gone, and the future was not for him. He was filled with shame and grief, until the tears of helplessness came into his eyes and he wiped them from his cheeks. People were busy looking at the show, and the children were curious and shouted. They did not know yet what it all meant. It all seems a fair to them, thought Mir Nihal; but soon, when they have grown up Time will show them a new and quite a different sight, a peep into the mysteries of life, and give them a full glimpse of the sorrows of subjection. But happy are they who feel not, for they do not know, and miserable are those who see and suffer and can do nothing. A fire burns within their breasts; but the flames do not shoot up. Only the soul is consumed by the internal heat and they feel dead, so dead, alas....

The procession had gone behind the Jama Masjid, and people began to talk loudly, guessing who was who. Nasim was bewildered and began to cry, feeling lonely without his mother, and wanted to go home. Other children were crying and shouting, some wanting to go home, others wanting to urinate. Since there was no place where they could relieve themselves people had brought bottles with them, and made the children urinate in the bottles. As Nasim persisted in crying Mir Nihal took him in his lap and began to console him.

'We shall go home soon,' he said to Nasim. 'See there go the horses and the Farangis,' and he pointed to the riders as the procession had already come out on the northern side and was on the Esplanade Road. 'Don't you see them? Those are the people who have been our undoing, and will be yours too.'

Nasim looked at the procession, unable to understand what his grandfather was telling him.

'But you will be brave, my child, and will fight them one day. Won't you?'

Nasim looked at the horses and the men; and two teardrops hung on his eyelashes and glistened in the sun.

'You will be brave,' Mir Nihal repeated as he wiped the child's tears with his fingers, 'and drive them out of the country...'

FROM *Part III*

(Mir Nihal's youngest son, Asghar, was married to Bilqeece, soon after the Coronation.)

Chapter 4

Bilqeece had become pregnant, and was nearly always ill. Her appetite deserted her, and she only ate dried mangoes or tamarinds. She felt sick all the time and was confined to bed. Her complexion lost its glow and became sallow; and hollows appeared under her eyes. Now and then she looked up at the date palm whose leaves had become thin, for the lower ones had sered and fallen; and it seemed to her drab and full of hopelessness.

But now and then she became conscious of the new life within her. As the child moved inside her womb her heart was filled with a rare joy, and everything looked to her beautiful. The henna tree which had shed its old leaves and had put on new ones, the sparrows twittering on the walls, the breeze that blew, everything brought to her a message of Beauty and sang the paeans of Birth. She covered herself up with a sheet in a protective way, and gently, very tenderly stroked her belly as if caressing the child inside her.

Everyone became more gentle with her, and asked her to take care of herself, and not to walk fast or climb the stairs too often. Asghar was also happy, full of pride and vanity at the prospect of having a son who would not only carry on his father's name, but would be his support in old age. He would give his son a good education and bring him up according to his own ideas; and he would make good his father's failings, realize his frustrated ambitions. They talked a great deal of this son of theirs, made schemes for him together, and even gave him a name.

At these moments Bilqeece looked at Asghar with passionate and loving eyes which seemed to express gratitude and indebtedness for having given her that which she most desired, fulfillment of all her dreams. She even put her hand round his neck one day and caressed his hair; and his heart came well nigh to bursting with love and happiness. He often brought presents for her and gave her a pair of English shoes which, he said, she should wear at Mehro's wedding. All this made her happy beyond measure, and her heart went out to her husband. She just wanted to fall down at his feet and worship him like a god. And Asghar was more than satisfied....

In this mood the date of Mehro's marriage drew near. Bilqeece was better now, and her nausea had almost left her. With happiness she sewed and helped preparing Mehro's trousseau. She went to her parents off and on, because her father had fallen ill. But she came back to get busy with the preparations for the marriage.

The guests arrived again, though not so many as at Asghar's wedding. After the mayun ceremony Mehro was kept inside a room for a week, and was massaged with scented preparations every day.

The marriage party arrived from Bhopal one day before the wedding. On the day of the wedding Mehro was dressed as a bride. Masroor, who had gone to see the bridegroom, came and said to her in a whisper:

'Your bridegroom is ugly, positively ugly.'

'Shut up,' she said to him. 'Don't crack jokes with me.' But in her heart she was filled with dread, and began to weep behind her veil.

The marriage was going to be performed in the evening. When the bridegroom and his party arrived, Mir Nihal saw Meraj for the first time. He was really ugly, with a black bushy beard and the ferocious eyes of a madman. One part of his face was disfigured, and one ear was missing. Meraj was very fond of shooting, and one day his gun had gone off by accident and had disfigured him for life. The bullet had not been extracted from his brain as there was the risk of his losing his life, and this had affected his mind.

Nazrul Hasan had been sent from Delhi to see the bridegroom. They had, however, kept him out of Nazrul Hasan's way, and he came away without seeing him. But it was thought that he had no defect.

When Mir Nihal saw his future son-in-law, he was filled with disgust and said that he would not give his daughter away to a madman. Everyone was shocked at this news. They persuaded him to agree, but he refused to listen to them. Habibuddin was also filled with loathing at the sight of his future brother-in-law. But he had foresight and wisdom.

'What are you doing, father?' he argued with Mir Nihal. 'If the marriage is cancelled it would mean a bad name for our family....'

'I can't give my daughter away to a man who looks like a kazzaq. There is no dearth of boys.'

'But don't you see, if they go away without the marriage taking place, no one will blame them. They will all say that there is some defect in the girl. We shall then have no face to show to anyone....'

It was with difficulty that Habibuddin made his father see the point and persuaded him to agree to Mehro's marriage. It was with trepidation and tears streaming down his face that he gave his consent.

Masroor went and informed Mehro of all the developments. She sat there frightened and mortified, the tears flowing down her cheeks. But she could not say anything. The girls were never consulted about their own marriages and were given away to any men their parents selected.

When after the vida she saw Meraj she felt like a cow under the butcher's knife. But she could not alter her fate, and had to accept it with as much courage as she could muster....

Inside the zenana the women guests did not know much about these difficulties. They had come to attend a marriage and displayed their finest clothes and talked and laughed and made merry. Bilqeece wore her fine bridal clothes and looked charming. Many ladies saw her English shoes and were outraged.

'Hai, hai, sister, have you seen those dirty shoes Asghar's wife is wearing?' said one of the guests. 'We have never seen such a thing before!'

'She looks like a good-as-dead Farangan,' another replied.

'Yes, what else could you expect from Mirza Shahbaz Beg's daughter? They seem to have eaten some Farangi's shit....'

Thus the women whispered to one another. Bilqeece heard these remarks, for they had been said in her hearing, and were meant for her to hear. She felt ashamed and tears rushed to her eyes. But she had to keep her mouth shut, although the insults were obvious and pointed. Had they been directed towards her alone it would not have been so difficult. They were insulting her father; and this cut her to the quick.

When the rush of marriage was over and she was able to see Asghar alone, she told him of all the insults which had been heaped upon her, and burst into tears. Asghar was filled with anger when he heard this. He felt so sorry for her that all the insults seemed to have been showered upon him. He took Bilqeece in his arms and kissed her and said: 'You should forget all about it. I shall take a separate house and we shall live alone as soon as I have got a job....'

FROM *THE PURPLE GOLD MOUNTAIN*

Having become a high official I was sent to preach the Doctrine of No-Famine

Having passed the Examination I donned
The official gown. Collecting taxes like farmers
Grains of corn, I earned a name.
To preach the doctrine of no-famine
The Duke of Keui
Sent me to the Kingdom of Liang

I watched from my window the flowers of Spring;
Under my strides
The T'en Shan was only a mound.
My pride rose like the morning sun.
Watching the snow capped peaks I lost all sense
Of the Wheel of Law in a world of change.

When the Summer came and the red
Of the flowers turned to rust,
The earth caked and cracked and cleft in two
Driving a fissure between South and North,
The Autumn and Spring.

With a heart heavy with sorrow I returned
To a land that was not my own.
Though grown in stature and fame earned
Through merit and sweat of the brow,
I was different for men were not the same.

That which is gone brings grief
To the mind. I remember my house and pine.

I was put into prison for speaking the truth and there wrote this poem on the advent of spring

For speaking the truth
They put me in prison.
I sleep on a handful of straw
And feed on cabbage leaves.
The cell is cold as the Emperor's heart.

Outside the spring comes astride
The vernal clouds.
The plum trees are aglow with silver blossoms;
The daphne bushes are on fire;
The brown thrush calls to his mate.

When shall I see you,
O Purple Gold Mountain?
Magnolia buds recall
My loved one's cream white hands.
I lift sad cups of grief
And drain their wine towards the moon.

The Wheel of Age comes full circle at last

Here I sit amidst Buddhas in stone and bronze
And ancient wood, and treasures of Sung and T'ang,
Thinking upon the days long past
When I had climbed the Nu Sho Shan
And contemplated love in the White Cloud Monastery,
Listening to the orioles in daphne bushes on fire.

But gone are the peonies and roses:
Only memory remains
A niche in the caves at Shih tze Lin,
And dreams of maidens in skirts of gauze
Drinking of emerald wine.

Within my heart nought else but hate remains
For what is past and youth that's gone.

Mumtaz Shahnawaz

Mumtaz 'Tazi' Shahnawaz was born in Lahore in 1912. She accompanied her grandfather, Sir Mohammed Shafi, and her mother, the prominent Muslim League activist Lady Jahanara Shahnawaz, to London in 1930. There she gave readings of her poems, some of which later appeared in *The Spectator*. She also became a socialist, looked to the Congress for leadership, and corresponded with Nehru for many years. According to her brother, Dr Ahmed Shahnawaz[1], Mumtaz's 'first stirrings of doubt' with the Congress began in 1937, when Nehru and Gandhi sided with the party's right wing elements. 'This increased in 1939 with the anti-Muslim actions of Congress Ministries in several Indian provinces.'[2] She broke away from the party in 1942 and 'decided her future lay in organizing Muslim women to demand their rights.'[3] Joining the Muslim League, she played a prominent part in the Pakistan Movement, but after Partition she concentrated on her writing once more. In 1948, she was due to attend a UN session in the United States and to show the first draft of her novel, *The Heart Divided,* to a publisher when she was killed in an air crash over Ireland.

The Heart Divided is Mumtaz Shahnawaz's only novel and was published by her family in 1959, but it has never been edited, though the 1990 edition has removed grammatical errors. Despite its many stylistic and structural shortcomings the novel does provide an authentic account of events which forged the Pakistan Movement. The central character, Zohra is the socialist daughter of an eminent Lahore lawyer. Her brother Habib falls in love with Mohini, Zohra's best friend. Mohini belongs to a prominent Hindu family and is a Congress activist. Mohini and

---

1 Shahnawaz, Dr Ahmed, Introduction to *The Heart Divided* by Mumtaz Shahnawaz, edition published by ASR Publications, Lahore, 1990.

2 ibid.

3 ibid.

Habib resolve to marry despite much family opposition, but Mohini who keeps in poor health, dies. The rest of the novel revolves around Zohra and her elder sister, Sughra. They discard purdah and battle against age-old prejudices to assert themselves as dynamic, intelligent twentieth century women. When Sughra's marriage to a feudal landlord begins to break down she becomes a tireless Muslim League worker. Zohra takes up teaching and becomes involved in the trade union movement, which gradually takes her towards the Muslim League and a radical young man with whom her future lies.

The Heart Divided

FROM *Chapter 3*

In the days when Raja Ranjit Singh ruled the Punjab, there were two young nobles at his court, who were close friends. One was Sheikh Jamaluddin, a Muslim, whose family had migrated to Lahore from Multan, in the days of the Moghul Emperors: and the other was Diwan Kailash Nath Kaul, a Hindu Kashmiri Pandit. An ancestor of the Kauls had come down from Kashmir during the reign of the Emperor Shah Jahan, and had taken up an appointment at the Moghul Court at Delhi. Later, he had been given an appointment at Lahore with a small *jagir* or estate near that town and the title of Diwan.

The two friends, Sheikh Jamaluddin and Diwan Kailash Nath Kaul, had exchanged turbans and taken the vow of brotherhood and the friendship thus established between the two families, had continued from generation to generation until the present day. Sheikh Nizamuddin and Diwan Jawala Prashad Kaul, the present head of the Kaul family, were proud of the old ties that bound their two families together. They met almost every evening. Diwan Jawala Prashad Kaul would come to Nishat Manzil in his smart new gig or Sheikh Nizamuddin would get into his two-horse carriage and drive to Shanti Niwas, a rambling two storied bungalow, on Mozang Road, the home of the Kauls. Here, in the beautiful old library full of rare manuscripts and old pictures, they would sit on a divan smoking the *hooka*, talking about the old days and reciting the verses of Hafiz, Saadi or Ghalib.

(Zohra and Mohini and are the respective daughters of Sheikh Jamaluddin and Diwan Kailash Nanth Kaul. Soon after Zohra's brother Habib comes back from England, Mohini, who has been ill, arrives unexpectedly for the festivities at the wedding of Zohra's elder sister, Sughra.)

FROM ***Chapter 8***

Just then, the door opened and Mohini walked in. Zohra jumped up and rushed forward to meet her. The two friends embraced and then Zohra said, 'Oh I'm so happy to see you. When did you come back to Lahore?'

'This morning. I didn't telephone, because I wanted to give you a surprise.'

'Darling, you look wonderful. Your health must have improved.'

'Oh yes, I'm quite all right now.'

'No fever, or—or anything?'

'No trouble at all.'

Meanwhile, the other girls stopped singing and they all crowded round Mohini. For some minutes, a merry chatter filled the room. Then two maids came in with a table cloth in their hands. This they spread on the floor and then laid plates and dishes upon it, and very soon the girls were busy having their dinner. All through the meal the laughter and the jokes continued and Sughra, who would not eat much, was continually, teased.

Mohini and Zohra sat near each other and talked in whispers. 'Oh Mohini, there are a thousand and one things I want to talk about — but, I cannot talk freely here,' said Zohra.

'Let's go into another room after dinner and have a chat,' suggested Mohini.

'The house is full to over-flowing. There is no privacy anywhere, not even in the garden.'

'Then we must wait until after the wedding.'

'No, I'm too impatient. Listen, we can go into Habib's sitting room. I know he's dining with some friends and will not be home until late tonight, so we can have the room to ourselves.'

'But—but your brother may not like it.'

'Oh, Habib won't mind in the least.'

Having finished dinner they washed their hands and then walked through the courtyard to Habib's rooms. His sitting-room was small, but tastefully furnished and Mohini looked appreciatively at the two good paintings on the walls. Zohra curled herself up in one corner of the sofa and she looked like a little kitten sitting there with her legs tucked under her. Mohini settled down in the other corner and they were soon chatting away. Mohini's health, her stay in Kashmir, Zohra's activities at college, her desire to speak in the debate, her grandfather's anger and his illness, the political situation in the country were all discussed. Time passed: the songs of the girls floating across the courtyard were heard no more, the maids were no longer rushing excitedly to and fro, the shy winter moon sank into the western mist, but the two friends went on talking.

Suddenly, the door opened and Habib walked in. Seeing his sister talking to a friend, who jumped up hurriedly, as she saw him, he murmured an apology and was about to withdraw, when Zohra said, 'Come in Bhaiya. There is no need for you to run away for this is no *purdah* maiden! Surely you know Mohini?'

As he heard the name, Habib looked up with interest. Zohra had told him so much about Mohini, that he had often thought about her and wondered what she was really like. Mohini had read several of Habib's letters to Zohra and she had found in them thoughts so similar to her own that she too had been looking forward to meeting him. And so, it happened, that she raised her eyes just as he turned to look at her and for an instant they stood thus looking into each other's eyes. Then Mohini blushed and lowered her lids, while Habib smiled and said, 'Of course we know each other.'

'Yes of course,' murmured Mohini. 'We met last six—or was it seven years ago?'

'When you invited me to play hide and seek with you...' said Habib.

Mohini blushed again. 'And you considered yourself far too grown-up for such frivolous games,' she retorted: and they all laughed.

Then Mohini looked at her watch. 'Zori do you know, what time it is? It's eleven o'clock! I never realized it was so late. I must go now, as my mother will be waiting for me.'

'Stay a little longer,' said Habib, 'and let me offer you girls a drink. What about some orange squash or some *sherbat*? I have both.'

'I really must be going,' Mohini murmured.

'You can stay another fifteen minutes,' said Zohra and she pulled her down on the sofa besides her. 'After all there's a wedding in this house and you are supposed to stay here until late. Do give us some *sherbat*, Habib I'm thirsty.'

Habib poured out the drinks and handed them to the girls. 'This is really an unsuitable drink for this cold weather,' he said. 'Next time you two honour me by a visit, give me due notice and I shall have coffee and cakes ready for you.'

'Darling Bhaiya!' exclaimed Zohra. 'You are the perfect brother. Do you know Mohini, he takes me out to the pictures and once he actually gave me tea at Lorange, in one of the private cubicles.'

'You are getting on Zori. The *purdah* seems to be disappearing slowly.'

'Not so slowly either,' said Zohra, 'now that I have a brother as an accomplice. You know, the first time I went out without a *burqah*, was just before you went to prison.'

'Mohini,' said Habib and then paused. 'May I call you Mohini?'

'Of course. You always have called me that—Bhaiya,' she said.

'Thank you. I was going to say that I envy you. You took part in the struggle last year and actually went to jail: while I only read about it in the newspapers, though I wished with all my heart to be in it too.'

'You could not help that as you were so far away. But never mind, you can take part in it next time.'

'Next time—then you think there will be another struggle.'

'The struggle never stopped. Although the movement was called off and the prisoners released, although Gandhiji went to London to the Second Round Table Conference, the government repression did not stop. Now as you must have seen arrests and convictions have increased again.'

'I once had hopes from this Round Table Conference.'

'So had I after the Gandhi-Irwin Pact and when Gandhiji finally went to London. But, they kept on diminishing, and I'm not surprised at the result. Nothing has come of it and Gandhiji is coming home again a disappointed man.'

'If only there had been a Hindu-Muslim settlement. Then, I think, we may have wrung something from their unwilling hands.'

'You are right. We all long for a Hindu-Muslim settlement.'

'One day, we read in the papers, that a settlement had been arrived at,' said Zohra, 'and then, it proved to be wrong and I was so dejected that I almost cried.'

'It's a pity that the Hindus and Muslims could not settle their differences even in London,' said Habib. 'I know, of course, that the Englishmen did their best to keep them divided, but our leaders should not have played into their hands. If the Congress and League had come to terms at the Round Table, Britain would have had to give in to their demands.'

'I am told that Gandhiji and the League leaders had come to terms,' said Zohra, 'but the Mahasabha and the Sikhs would not agree.'

'Whatever happened, it was a tragedy.'

'Let us hope, that there will be settlement soon,' sighed Mohini, and she looked at her watch again. 'I really must go now. Goodnight Bhaiya, and thank you for the *sherbat*.'

FROM *Chapter 16*

'What's the matter with Habib?' She [*Sughra*] asked Zohra one day, 'and why is father annoyed with him?'

'There's been quite a rumpus in the family,' Zohra told her. 'Habib has refused to marry Akhtari and uncle Fakhruddin has gone off in a huff.'

'So that's it. Is father very angry?'

'Yes, but he dotes on Habib and will soon forgive him.'

'Then why is Habib so moody and irritable?'

'I don't know.'

'Oh, come on, you must know something.'

'Really Apa, I have no idea.'

Zohra had her suspicions, but she was reticent. Besides, if what she suspected were true, it was such a delicate and serious matter, that, she thought, it best to keep silent about it. She had noticed the growing attraction between Habib and Mohini, but she realized, that a marriage between them, was almost an impossibility. She knew that such things never happened, and that neither custom, nor society, nor the law allowed them. Muslims married Muslims, and Hindus wedded Hindus, so it had been for centuries and so it would always be. True, some of the Moghul emperors, in the days gone-by, had taken Hindu wives, but then they were Emperors and could defy laws and convention, but even in their case, the marriages had been resented both by Hindus and by Muslims. Here and there, through the hundreds of years that they had lived side by side, there had been romantic attachments between young people of the two communities, but they had almost always resulted either in the conversion of one of them to the other faith or in tragedy: and, in each case of conversion, the one who was converted, was ostracised by his or her family and community. Some modern people had recently begun to advocate inter-marriage without conversion, but there had been very few such cases in the whole of India. To begin with, the law of the land did not allow marriage between people of different faiths. True, they could marry by Civil Registration, but before that could be done, they had both to declare that they had no religion. Then Hindus and Muslims equally looked down upon these people and even the best educated families would not tolerate any of their members making such a marriage. Among Muslims, their law allowed a man to marry a Christian or a Jew, as these were spoken of as 'people of the book', but Hindus were considered infidels, and no marriage with a Hindu girl was legal, while a Muslim girl could not marry anyone save a Muslim, the reason given being that the children of such a marriage would follow the father's faith and be lost to Islam. Among Hindus, it was still difficult even to marry out of caste in their own community, and a marriage with a non-Hindu was considered monstrous. Zohra knew all these circumstances, as they had often been discussed at college, and in view of these, she was glad that Mohini had gone away. It would be better for her brother and her friend to forget each other as an attachment between them could only lead to heartbreak. She could see that Habib was suffering, and she would often go and have a chat with him in his room. They never talked of Mohini, but there was an unspoken sympathy between them.

These days, Habib thought long and furiously. He was face to face with the greatest problem of his life and he could not as yet see a solution. The night before Mohini went away, he had paced the lawn in impatience, expecting every moment to see her car drive in. But she did not come, and slowly his ardent expectations had died down leaving a dull ache behind. He had waited long, pacing the garden long after there had been any chance of her coming. He had hoped against hope, pinning his faith upon the light in her eyes and the tender note in her voice, and then dread had entered his heart. Perhaps, she did not care, he thought. Perhaps, he had only imagined she did. Perhaps, the light in her eyes had just been a reflection of the fire in his own. Perhaps, she had merely been kind to him for her nature was sweet and gentle, and he had read more in her words than she had intended. Yes, that was it or she would have come this evening. She did not care, why should she? She was brilliant and lovely and all men, who knew her, must love her, why then should she care for him, an ordinary man belonging to another community? In despair, he had tossed upon his bed all night and fallen into a heavy sleep towards dawn. For the next few days, he had gone about doing his work in a listless and half-hearted manner, and the dull ache in his heart would not leave him, and then a letter had come through the post and seeing the Srinagar post-mark, he had hastily opened it in hope and in dread.

Habib
Try not to misunderstand. It is better thus. I shall try to think over everything with my head as well as with my heart. It will not be easy, just as it is not easy to go away. But I must and you must understand.
Mohini.
P.S.
I know, you will want to come to Kashmir as soon as possible. But I want you to promise not to come or to write to me for four months; this time, we must both try to spend in cool reflection. Promise! Please! For my sake—

He had read the letter again and again. At first, a wave of exultation had swept over him, for now, he knew, that she cared and he had gone out with bright eyes and smiling lips and Zohra had wondered what had happened to him, and then a cold fear had begun to trouble him again. He would not see her for four long months and after? He did not know. She did not promise anything. Supposing she changed? He chided himself for the thought. Mohini could not change, any other woman might, but not she, for she was loyal and true and steadfast. But she talked of cool reflection and there were so many obstacles between them, so many, that even he shuddered at the thought of them. How then could she decide to unite her life with his? She may think the difficulties insurmountable and ask him to give her up, and that he would never do now that he knew that she cared.

(1940. The Muslim League gathers for its Lahore Session. There have been bloody clashes between the militant Khaksar group and the government belonging to the Unionist Party.)

FROM ***Chapter 32***

The momentous day dawned and the historic session began, the session that was to change the destiny of the Muslim people.

Saeed Ahmad told the girls that the programme for the President's procession had been greatly curtailed owing to the disturbed state of the city and advised them to go straight to the *pandal* that had been erected for the meetings.

'Shall we sit behind the *purdah?'* Zohra asked curiously.

'Of course, not,' said Sughra. 'What made you think that?'

'I just wondered.'

'Lots of women sat outside at the Patna session and two of them addressed the open session.'

'Good. But what happens to the *purdah* women?'

'There are separate arrangements for them behind *chicks* and curtains.'

They were still two miles away from the *pandal* when the car began to crawl slowly through the surging sea of humanity. On one side of the road was a stream of cars and on the other a line of tongas and the whole space in between was filled with people, more and more cheering and enthusiastic people, and here and there angry groups that shouted, 'Down with the ministry!' 'Long live the Muslim League!,' 'Long live the Khaksars!' 'Death to the Unionist murderers!'

Arriving at the *pandal* at last they saw that all the roads leading up to it were crowded in the same way and that people from the villages were streaming in from beyond the Ravi river.

'I never expected such a crowd,' said Zohra as they took their seats. 'How may do you think they are?'

'Heaven knows,' said Sughra, 'there are arrangements for a 100,000 in the *pandal* alone and as you can see that is overfull and still they continue to come like an unabating flood.'

Uniformed National Guards led them to the left of the dais where almost all the seats were occupied by lady delegates and visitors. 'It's good to see so many women sitting among the men,' said Zohra.

'And there are thousands more behind the screens,' said Sughra pointing to the curtained enclosure.

The thunderous roars of cheering were heard drawing nearer and nearer and then the President accompanied by his sister entered the *pandal*. The whole audience stood up spontaneously and shouted, 'Quaid-i-Azam *Zindabad*'. Dignified and graceful, he walked up to the platform and took his seat. The Prime Minister of the Punjab was a few steps behind him and his appearance on the platform was a signal for an uproar.

'Down with the Premier!' 'Long live the Muslim League!' 'Long live the Khaksars!' 'Death to the murderers of the people!'

Angry shouts rent the air and the people would not be quietened until at last the President stood up and appealed to them to remain calm.

The session began and Zohra's interest grew apace, for even she could no longer deny that Muslim Punjab was awake at last and that it was the Muslim League that had awakened it.

After the Provincial President's address of welcome, the Quaid-i-Azam rose to speak and again Zohra was struck by the affectionate ovation that greeted him.

The audience listened in spellbound silence interspaced with cheers to his summing up of events past and present and she saw a look of gratification on the faces of the women when he said words of special praise for the Women's Committee.

He referred to the unhappy incident in which some Khaksars had been killed and announced amidst thunderous cheers that he would address a public meeting of the citizens of Lahore and speak to them upon the subject.

That night there were many in Lahore who were apprehensive, for the temper of the people had been roused and they wondered if even the Quaid-i-Azam would be able to control them. In spite of the fact that Saeed Ahmad had warned her that it might be a rowdy affair, Zohra was determined to go to the meeting. She arrived to find a sea of people, a seething angry mass that was shouting for justice and civil liberties, while here and there *lathis* and spades were freely brandished. Would any man be able to control them? she wondered, and then she heard loud cheering and knew that Mr Jinnah had arrived.

Slim and dignified, clad in his smart *achkan* and pyjamas with a Jinnah cap on his head, he walked up to the platform undaunted, while cries of 'Down with the murderous ministry!'

again rent the air. Calm in his demeanour he sat down in a chair, lit a cigarette and chatted with those around him while the loudspeakers were adjusted. Hundreds of thousands of eyes were riveted on him and people sat in an atmosphere of expectancy while shouts demanding justice continued to be heard from every corner.

He stood up and raised his hand and immediately there was a pindrop silence. Then he began to speak and watching the look on the faces around him, Zohra for the first time gauged the measure of the peoples' devotion. He went on speaking and the air was again rent by cheering, but the cries for justice still continued. Then slowly but surely he controlled the whole surging mass of them, until their anger gave place to confidence, for he assured them that he had the cause of his people at heart and would do all in his power, to see justice meted out to the Khaksars, and they knew that they could trust his word. He warned and told them that he would see to it that their civil liberties were restored and they broke into wild cheering.

Zohra sat there and marvelled while the angry crowd was turned into a joyful cheering multitude, and then she knew that here was a leader, who could not only awaken the people but discipline them as well.

Two days later, the League Session passed a resolution declaring their sympathy with the relatives of the Khaksars who had died and demanding an independent and impartial committee of enquiry. It also urged upon the Government to withdraw the ban upon the Khaksar's organization. In the meanwhile, however, an event of far greater importance occurred that overshadowed not only the recent happenings in Lahore, but all that had happened in the country for many years before. For the main resolution of the Lahore Session of the Muslim League demanded 'Independent States' for the Muslims in India.

'Resolved that it is the considered view of this session of the All India Muslim League,' it said, 'that no constitutional plan would be workable in this country or acceptable to the Muslims unless it is designed on the following basic principles, viz., that geographically contiguous units are demarcated into regions which should be so constituted with such territorial readjustments as may be necessary that the areas in which the Muslims are numerically in a majority, as in the north western and western zones of India, should be grouped to constitute 'Independent States' in which the constituent units shall be autonomous and sovereign.'

'Sovereign States for the Muslims!' 'Real independence!' were the whispers heard on every side as the resolution was read out.

'This session further authorizes the Working Committee to frame a scheme of constitution in accordance with these basic principles, providing for the assumption finally by the respective regions of all power such as defence, external affairs, communications and such other matters as may be necessary.'

Speaker after speaker from province after province rose in support of the resolution, and with each speech the enthusiasm of the people mounted higher.

On Sughra's face was the look of a visionary, who sees the land of dreams draw nearer. At last the nation had taken up the cry that her heart had murmured so often and the road to freedom lay before them.

Zohra sick at heart, looked at the faces around her and in their eyes she saw the fading of her dream, the dream of Hindu-Muslim unity in an India free and whole. But she also saw in these very eyes the dawn of a new ideal, an ideal that had already gripped their hearts. It was as if someone had said to them, 'You shall be free! — and this alone is the way…' And they had lifted up their eyes to gaze at new horizons and their minds had raced ahead of them down fresh vistas of thought.

Zaib-un-Nissa Hamidullah

The daughter of an English mother, Zaib-un-Nissa Hamidullah grew up in Calcutta during the 1920s. She was educated at the Loretto Convent. Her father, a judge, Janab Wazed Ali wrote *Babissater Bangali*, a book which provided a vision for Bengali nationalism. Zaib-un-Nissa started writing as a child. Her visits to her father's village in Bengal and, later, her posting in small Punjab towns with her executive husband, brought her into contact with rural life. This strongly influenced her poetry and fiction. Moving to Karachi after Partition, Zaib-un-Nissa became Pakistan's first woman columnist, and wrote a weekly column in *Dawn.* In 1951, she became editor and publisher of her own magazine, *The Mirror,* a popular, social glossy, with fearless political editorials which led to its ban in 1957.[1] She challenged the ban in the Supreme Court and won, becoming the first Pakistani woman to do so. She also represented Pakistan at the UN, and wrote a travelogue, *Sixty Days in America* (1965). Several books of poetry, which she published before and after Partition, include *Lotus Leaves* (1946) and *The Flute of Memory* (1964), but it was her collection of short stories, *The Young Wife* (1958), that brought her critical acclaim. 'The Bull and the She Devil', a story about sexuality, was considered a rare and courageous story for a woman to write in the puritanical Pakistan of that time.

1 Niazi, Zamir, *The Press in Chains,* Karachi: The Royal Book Company, 1986.

The Bull and the She Devil

The well was one only infrequently used. Even so it had water, sweet water, and Ghulam Qadir drank thirstily from the bucket he had just drawn up. For it was a hot day, the hottest of the season, and his throat was parched. Having quenched his thirst he splashed the remaining contents of the bucket over his face and upon his thick crop of unruly black hair. 'This has cooled me,' he told himself, 'cooled me from the outside, but not from the inside. Not from the inside,' he repeated moodily, staring at his bullock resting in the shade.

The cooling water trickled from his face and hair down his neck and on to his long striped shirt, but he did not bother to wipe it. All he did was to brush back the drops that dripped from his bushy eyebrows on to his lashes. Then he put the bucket back in its place on the edge of the well and looked down into its depths. His glance was a casual one, but suddenly, like a man possessed, he bent his whole body forward and peered into the darkness below, his eyes glittering with excitement.

From the depths of the water she stared back at him. Yes, even here, even here on the land she haunted him. He looked with loathing upon her sensitive face, that soft slow smile, those eyes so full of tenderness. Almost he could hear her speak. Speak in those soft, persuasive accents that irritated him so. In a sudden outburst of fury he clenched his fist at the lovely face. '*Shaitan*,' he shouted. 'She Devil! She Devil!! She Devil!!!' Frenziedly he picked up a stone and hurled it into the well, aiming straight at her eyes…

The stone splashed right into the middle of the water, agitated ripples disturbed its tranquillity and her face, that face he hated so, vanished. Ghulam Qadir stood erect once more, tightened his *lungi* around his waist, tethered his bullock and once again set about his ploughing. But even here, even on this field that hailed him victor and gave unto him its abundance, season after season, she haunted him. 'Curse her! Curse her!!' he shouted out aloud, staring full into the face of the summer sun and spitting in disgust upon the brown earth.

She would be sitting by the fire now, he knew, her black hair, newly washed, flowing gracefully around her and reaching to her knees. She would be smiling. Yes, smiling that strange half smile that set his heart beating so furiously. Smiling to herself as she cooked his meal. Yes, it was for him that she cooked, for him that she worked, for him that she existed. For was she not his woman—she his wife and he her master?

Yes, he told himself again and again, thrusting angrily at his bull to give full emphasis to his thoughts, he was her master and would force her to bring forth the fruits of her womb, even the fields gave up to him their abundance. 'She Devil!' He spat out the words once again as the bullock stumbled on a stone, and gave it an angry, vicious twist of its tail. 'She Devil, that's what she is, a She Devil.'

But though he strove to give up his spleen, though he thought of her again and again with hate, she would not give him peace. In spite of himself he found his thoughts turning to the softness and the roundness of her slender form, the fairness of her complexion, the way her lashes curled upon her cheeks and fluttered as frightenedly as the wings of a bird fallen from a bush, when he shouted at her.

To possess her was his one object in life now. And yet, had he not already possessed her a score of times and over? Had he not claimed her again and yet again, night after night? Was she not, without any manner of doubt, his woman? His by every claim that man can have over woman? And yet...And yet there was this doubt that disturbed him and tormented him, this new element in the relationship between man and woman of even the possibility of which he had been oblivious.

He remembered how, when first he had brought her here as a bride, all his ardent young manhood aflame, he had had his fill of her. To him she was, those first few weeks, a body. A body and nothing more. A body beautiful and soft that eased the so long suppressed desires of his senses. But as the weeks passed and he saw her about their mud hut, the way she walked, the way she smiled at others, the tender look in her eyes as she patted the bullock, in his mind a doubt was born. For she remained a separate being, an individual in her own right, a stranger. Yes, a stranger, even though her body grew sweetly familiar.

And he noticed, first with apprehension and then with anger that her face, so expressionless when speaking to him, was soft and sweet when turned towards his nephew, his elder brother or his bullock. He looked with antagonism at the fine beast of burden in front of him, and anger rising high gave the bull another vicious twist of its tail. For even this four legged creature, this *shaitan* of a bull was spoken to in sweeter accents than any she had ever addressed to him. In his annoyance at remembrance of the night before, he picked up a stone and aimed it straight at the animal's head…

For it was all the bull's fault. Yes, none other but this devil incarnate of a beast that had made him do it. Even now, even in mere remembrance of it, he was embarrassed. For he had never intended to raise his hand to her. After all, he was a gentle man and a patient one. The whole village would bear witness to this. Had not Amna, the village match-maker, used this description above all others to win over the She Devil's parents and make them agreeable to the match? At least that is what Amna had told him when she held out her greedy fingers for the fifty rupees that was her fee for arranging this marriage.

He recalled her words: 'You are a fortunate man, Ghulam Qadir,' she had said in her quavering old tones, 'a very fortunate man. For not only is Shirin as sweet as the scent of *champak* flowers, but she is as supple as a reed and will sway to your slightest wishes, for she is a child nurtured to womanhood in an atmosphere of tenderness and affection. One who, they say, has a heart filled to over-flowing with love of everything living. And,' here the old woman's furtive eyes had peered lasciviously into his, 'that over-flowing cup of love will be yours to drink your fill.'

The sun was hotter today than he had ever known it before, and all around him the earth lay hard and parched and barren. Bead upon bead of perspiration trickled down his body, wetting his shirt so that it stuck to him so closely that the hair on his chest showed clearly through it as he worked. He was alone on the field today for Gul Mohammed, his elder brother, had gone to the city to arrange purchase of a new much talked about fertilizer which, people said, would increase the fertility of the soil. And with him he had taken his son, Allah Wasaya. So she must be alone in the hut, all alone, he thought, and hot waves of desire rose within him and he hurried his bullock for he wanted to get home early and be with her…

But he was not at his best today and, in spite of his eagerness, the tilling progressed much slower than usual. 'It's this dull ache in my head,' he thought angrily, 'this dull ache that this She Devil has put there.' And again anger against his young wife infuriated him. 'Curse her,' he said, spitting once again. 'Curse her and that evil old liar Amna.' The heavy, hot beat of anger drummed at his temples as he repeated, 'That old liar Amna. Told me she had a cup of love brimful with tenderness. Liar!' He looked once more full into the face of the blazing morning sun and repeated, 'Liar!'

For she was as cold to his caresses as the pieces of ice they put into the glass of *lassi* he sometimes had at the village shop. True, he held her in his arms and had his way; true her body was soft and sweet to his caresses, but where was her heart? That was the question that tormented him, where was her heart and who was king of it?

Last night, before the regrettable incident outside the hut, he had asked her. Asked her suddenly, himself unaware that such words could come out of his mouth. She had been standing at the window staring up at the stars and, though he was hot with desire and knew that his hunger could easily be assuaged, he had suddenly become aware of another hunger within him; a deeper, more disturbing one. A hunger that he had never known before, but which had emerged even as he had held her in his arms and eased the hunger of his senses. And this new tormenting hunger grew great, the more the one of his senses was satisfied.

He himself knew not what it was, and yet…and yet something within him told him that it stemmed from something far above and beyond sex. He wanted her to desire him, wanted her voice to soften to him as it softened when she spoke to his brother and his nephew and even to his bull. Damn the creature! Again his anger against the animal returned and he prodded it viciously between its legs and felt a passing satisfaction at the way the poor beast winced.

'Are you happy with me?' he had asked. And amazingly his voice had, even to his astonished ears, a tinge of pleading, as if longing to be re-assured, longing to be told that he possessed, not the empty shell of her body alone, but the whole of her.

She had turned away from the window and looked at him. With astonishment he realized that this was the first time in their three months of marriage that they had looked thus into each others eyes. Was it wistfulness in hers, he wondered, was it appeal, was it reproach? He could not tell. Though this much he knew and joyed in it, it was not hate. But neither was it love. Yet even as she looked into his questioning eyes and saw the pleading and the puzzlement within them, a sudden light sparkled and softened hers, as if for the first time she saw him as a man and not as a demanding animal.

'I...' but even as she spoke there was commotion outside and Allah Wasaya came pounding at their door.

'The bull,' he cried excitedly, 'the bull has strayed again. He's in the next house and running wild.' Ghulam Qadir rushed out, for he knew this bull of his was a stubborn creature, capable of doing much damage as he had discovered to his cost only a few weeks previously when made, by the village elders, to pay compensation to his neighbour.

He had run in search of the animal and she had followed him. He knew this, although she kept her distance. And the knowledge brought his hatred of her to the surface again. 'She Devil!' he had thought. 'I'll show her who's owner of the bull, I'll show her whose command it obeys.'

And to do this he was determined. For the bull, the finest in the village and his own precious beast of burden had, ever since his wife's arrival, turned turbulent. This in spite of the fact that it had been the best and the most amenable of animals before.

Instead of answering to his summons, as in the past, it ignored him now. And, as if this were not bad enough, defied him even. Thrice already the animal had turned unruly and wandered around refusing to allow him, Ghulam Qadir, his master to tether it. And on each occasion it was his wife who ultimately, with a few soft words, calmed the creature and led it back as easily as if it had been a baby lamb.

Yet once again Ghulam Qadir gave the animal's tail a vicious twist. He hated the bull now. Hated it as much as he had loved it formerly.

'Faithless creature,' he shouted at the poor, uncomprehending animal. 'Even you have surrendered your soul into this She-Devil's keeping.' He looked from the animal up at the blazing sun and a strange light came into his eyes. 'She's after my soul as well,' he shouted. 'She wants to ensnare me as she has ensnared all the others. She Devil, She Devil, She Devil!' He continued yelling as he tilled the soil, while the perspiration streamed down his back and the deadly noon day sun struck with all its brilliance upon his uncovered head.

At last the morning's work was over and Ghulam Qadir turned his bullock homewards. In spite of himself his heart began to beat excitedly as he neared the little courtyard and caught a glimpse of his wife's sky blue *duppatta*. But anger surged once more within him for his anticipated afternoon alone with his young wife would never materialize. For there, lying full length on a charpoy under the *Neem* tree was his nephew, Allah Wasaya, and beside him sat his elder brother, Gul Mohammed, smoking his *hookah*.

So annoyed did Ghulam Qadir feel that he did not even respond to his brother's greeting and quickly entered the hut, forgetting even to tie the bullock. His wife turned as she saw him and a little half smile of greeting flitted across her face. It was evident that she had forgotten his harsh words and anger of the evening before when, exasperated and humiliated at the fact that she had succeeded in doing what he could not, and had shamed him before the whole village by bringing the bull passively home, he had struck her full in the face. This he had done not so much to hurt her as to proclaim to the village that he was master and this his woman, even as the bull was his animal.

'Lunch is ready,' she said in her sweet, soft voice, 'but would you first like to have a glass of *falsa sherbet* that I made with the fruit your brother brought from the city?'

Without condescending to reply, he brushed past her and went to wash his hands, the anger within him mounting in intensity until it turned the mild headache of the morning into a throbbing, tempestuous one.

As he washed his hands he cursed her again. Cursed her again with every fibre of his being. This She Devil had bewitched not only his bull, but his brother and his nephew as well. His brother, who was as dear to him as a father, indeed had been a father to him all these years, for he was twenty years his senior and had brought him up as his son. Yes, she had bewitched this wise, grey bearded brother of his. Bewitched him so thoroughly that, instead of appreciating his anger against the bull, he was for ever reprimanding him on his treatment of it.

And only last night, after the public slapping of his wife was over and she inside and weeping, his brother had said very gravely and anxiously as they sat outside, 'I don't know what has come over you Ghulam Qadir. Your marriage, I thought would bring added joy into all our lives. For you have never known the tender companionship of a woman and I, ever since Allah Wasaya's mother followed our parents to the grave, have had none but you two to ease my loneliness. Your marriage, I fondly hoped, would bring sweetness into our lives again and, later on, with Allah Wasaya also wed, the family rounded and complete. But,' here he sighed deeply and looked at his brother out of puzzled worried eyes, 'instead of this I find that your entire nature has changed since the arrival of your bride. You've become both rude and callous. Not only do you treat your bull with cruelty, but you beat your wife for being kind to it.'

He had not even condescended to reply. What would have been the use, anyway? Had not his brother been bewitched as well? Did he not heed every one of her soft spoken suggestions about household matters?

And his nephew, Allah Wasaya, how he hated him! That handsome strapping youth on the verge of manhood with something of the weakness of womanhood within him. A something that made him waste his time playing on a flute, gazing up at the moon or planting flowers round the house. Flowers! Ghulam Qadir pushed aside the *lota* with disgust and, seeing a pot of *motia* flowers in a corner on which white waxen blooms had opened up their scented sweetness, with a wild gesture of anger he stretched towards the plant and, with one mighty pull, uprooted it. 'Flowers and flutes,' he muttered angrily to himself, 'just the foolish kind of things that appeal to women…' and continued with the washing of his hands.

But he stopped abruptly and fear flickered in his eyes. For suddenly he remembered, remembered that he had forgotten to tie the bull. By God! That rascal would run off again. Run off and shame him once more! Nervously he threw the *lota* aside and rushed out, followed by the frightened, anxious eyes of his wife.

The bullock was resting quietly under the shade of the tree, chewing the cud. But the sight of Ghulam Qadir rushing towards it unnerved the animal and, with a sudden jerk, the bull turned and ran frenziedly in the opposite direction. Anger almost made Ghulam Qadir's face unrecognizable, as picking up the short stout stick that always stood by the side of their door, he rushed after the animal gesticulating wildly and shouting at it at the top of his voice.

Some children were playing outside the courtyard. At the sound of Ghulam Qadir's shouting they turned and, seeing him running after the bull, came and stood at the fence, watching. Round and round the hut ran the frightened bull, and round and round ran Ghulam Qadir, the veins on his throat swelling out with each angry shout. To the children the sight was comical. First one and then another began to giggle; softly at first and then hilariously.

The young wife winced at the sound of their laughter. She could no longer prevent herself and rushed from the doorway towards her husband and the bull. Nearing the animal she called out to it softly and soothingly. Each time the bull neared her in its frantic circlings it became calmer, until at last it slowed down so much that she could quickly go up and take hold of it.

She did so with gentle, re-assuring fingers and the animal, quieter now, allowed her to lead it to its stall and tie it up. *'Shabash! Shabash!'* shouted the children in great glee. *'Shabash* auntie you have succeeded where uncle could not.'

Ghulam Qadir, who had been standing for the past few minutes watching his wife, was galvanized into action by the words. With a quick lunge of his powerful arm he caught hold of a handful of his wife's long black hair and, with it, dragged her down to the ground before him. Then he hit her with the stick held in his hand. Once twice and thrice the blows fell, each time more forcefully. Yet even so, the woman did not cry out.

'I'll show you, I'll show you!' swore Ghulam Qadir, as he put every ounce of strength he possessed behind the fourth blow. But it never fell. For Gul Mohammed was upon him, twisting his arm in an endeavour to shield the woman. Wild with rage, Ghulam Qadir turned away from the woman and upon his brother, striking out at him with every ounce of concentrated energy. The old man moaned and fell to the ground, blood trickling from his mouth.

Allah Wasaya had been asleep all this while. Awakened by the commotion he watched unbelievingly for a second rubbing his eyes to make certain he was not having a nightmare. Then he rushed towards Ghulam Qadir screaming in horrified accents, 'Have you gone mad, uncle, have you gone mad?'

Ghulam Qadir watched the advancing youth with eyes that had the cunning of a wild animal. As soon as the lad was within striking range he picked up the heavy spade that lay but a few paces away and, even as the youth came remonstrating towards him, he struck, aiming straight at the handsome head. Again and again he hit out, joying in it. Till the lad stumbled and, blood gushing out in streams from his battered head, crumpled in a heap on the ground.

A deathly silence descended. Even the air seemed still as Ghulam Qadir stared around him. First at his brother, down whose grey-bearded face blood and tears made a curious mixture, then at the still, stiffening figure of Allah Wasaya whose life blood dripped all over his father's encircling arms, and lastly, straight into the tear filled eyes of his wife.

A mist seemed to rise in front of him. He was dizzy. Dizzy with he knew not what heart-break and despair. Slowly, ever so carefully, he rubbed his eyes with his hairy, blood stained hands as if trying to wipe out the scene confronting him. Then he looked again. And again he met the large, long lashed eyes of his wife. He gazed fascinated deep down into their depths and saw hate uncoil within them, a deep and deadly hate of him and all that he was…

He reeled. His vision clouded and he would have fallen. But he steadied himself and swaying as if drunk, he walked as quickly as he could out of the courtyard and towards the open fields. Even as he did so his pace quickened and he began to run. On and on he went in the full blaze of the noon day sun, and as he ran tears trickled down his cheeks and again and yet again he brushed them away with his hairy, blood stained hands.

He did not stop running until he reached the well where he had drunk water earlier. Here he stopped, sank to the ground, buried his face in his hands and wailed like some mortally wounded animal. For a long, long while he continued thus, sobs shaking his sturdy frame and mingling with the cawing of curious crows. When he had cried his fill he stood up and, going slowly to the edge of the well, stared once again into its depths.

Her face smiled up at him once again. Smiled up at him sweetly and mockingly, with eyes in which love and hate alternated. 'You devil,' he said, dry-eyed now and curiously tranquil. 'You She Devil.'

And then, with a sudden leap he was over the edge of the well and had plunged deep into its dark depths. A tremendous splash startled the crows and started them crowing interminably, while agitated ripples continued to disturb the surface of the water throughout that torrid afternoon.

TAUFIQ RAFAT

Born in Sialkot, Taufiq Rafat was educated in Dehra Dun, Aligarh, and Lahore. He became a company executive. He also revolutionized Pakistani poetry in English, being the first Pakistani poet to adapt and naturalize English to express the Pakistani experience. His reflections however, transcend issues which are culture specific. In sparse, fluid language, replete with vivid imagery, his poems often build up stories around small every day incidents or rituals. He celebrated the monsoon as Anglo-American writers do spring but wrote of its lurking dangers too. His classic poem 'Wedding in the Flood' is a tragi-comedy on a grand scale. An admirer of Ezra Pound, T.S. Eliot and W.H. Auden, Taufiq Rafat is the one poet whose work has appeared in all three of Pakistan's major anthologies: *First Voices* (1965), *Pieces of Eight* (1971) and *Wordfall* (1975). He also wrote a full-length play in verse, *The Foothold,* which remains unpublished but was performed by The Government College Dramatic Club in Lahore. He has been a guide, mentor and critic to many younger poets, including Kaleem Omar*, Athar Tahir* and Shuja Nawaz*. His major work *The Arrival of the Monsoon: The Collected Poems 1947-1978* (1985), was greeted as a momentous event for Pakistani literature in English. He went on to translate the Punjabi poet Bulleh Shah (1982) and Qadir Yar's Punjabi epic *Puran Bhagat* (1983) into lyrical English. His work has appeared in a large number of international anthologies and is included in the curricula of secondary schools and universities in Pakistan, America and the Commonwealth. He is now bringing out *Taufiq Rafat: A Selection*. Another forthcoming book is *Half Moon* consisting of his new poems.

FROM *THE ARRIVAL OF THE MONSOON*

Circumcision

Having hauled down my pyjamas
they dragged me, all legs and teeth,
that fateful afternoon, to a stool
before which the barber hunkered
with an open cut-throat. He stropped it
on his palm with obvious relish.
I did not like his mustachios, nor
his conciliatory smile. Somehow
they made me sit, and two cousins
held a leg apiece. The barber
looked at me; I stared right back,
defying him to start something.
He just turned aside to whisper
to my cousin who suddenly cried
'Oh look at that golden bird,'
and being only six I looked up;
which was all the time he needed
to separate me from my prepuce.
'Bastard, sonofapig,' I roared,
'sister-ravisher, you pimp
and catamite,' while he applied
salve and bandaged the organ.
Beside myself with indignation
and pain, I forgot the presence
of elders, and cursed and cursed
in the graphic vocabulary
of the lanes, acquired at leap-frog,
marbles, and blindman's buff.
Still frothing at the mouth they fetched
me to bed, where an anxious mother
kissed and consoled me. It was not
till I was alone that I dared
to look down at my naked middle.

When I saw it so foreshortened,
raw, and swathed in lint, I burst
into fresh tears. Dismally
I wondered if I would ever
be able to pee again.

This
was many many years ago.
I have since learnt it was more
than a ritual, for by the act
of a pull and downward slash,
they prepare us for the disappointments
at the absence of golden birds
life will ask us to look at
between our circumcision and death.

The Kingfisher

Bird or Hovercraft, your angling skill
proclaims the confidence
of repeated success; you flash
rainbows, as you plunge to kill.

The luckless minnows in their drifting know
only when the beak is home,
No sound or shadow warns that death
is poised, and pointing below.

But what about tomorrow? Will they hiss
and boo from the sidelines
as you find, pause, fold, and dip towards
the horror of your first miss?

I'll learn to love you then, for lost
causes link all temperaments.
What drains my speech of sap will blunt
your keen iridescent thrust.

Return to Rajagriha

When Gautam reached the spot
                    called Sattapanni,
he was tired, but happy.
He walked further up the hill
and sat down on a boulder
still warm with the sun,
and looked north:
Smoke curled lazily from
a clearing in the grove, below,
where his disciples were busy
preparing the evening meal.
From that eminence
with his perfect vision he could see
the towers of Kapilavastu
where abandoned wife and child
still waited;
the tree in whose shade
he had received intimations
of his destiny;
and the deer-park in Benares,
the place of his first acclaim.
The path from there to here
was clear. All was orderly
on either side. People debouched
from barn and sty to walk that lane.
Gautam smiled. Some he knew
would exaggerate what he had done,
others renege, and a lucky handful
follow to the radiant conclusion.
But he was satisfied
with what had been done.
Then he faced the East:
Here was nothing but wilderness,
jungle piled upon jungle,
and snowy wastes, and not

a track anywhere to be seen.
Undeterred, Gautam rose,
impatient to begin again
what only he could begin.
He judged what light there remained,
and with the sun behind his head,
he began his descent.

Arrival of the Monsoon

Before the thrust of this liberating wind
whatever is not fixed, has a place to go,
strains northwards to the coniferous lands.

And drunk with motion, clothes on the washing-line
are raised above themselves; a flapping sheet
turns a roof corner into a battlement.

Gliding days are over. The birds are tossed
sideways and back, and lifted against their will.
They must struggle to achieve direction.

A welcome darkness descends. Harsh contours
dissolve, lose their prosaic condition.
All the sounds we have loved are restored.

And now the rain! In sudden squalls
it sweeps the street, and equally sudden
are the naked boys paddling in the ditches.

Alive, alive, everything is alive again.
Savour the rain's coolness on lips and eyes.
How madly the electric wire is swinging!

From brown waters eddying round their hooves
the drenched trees rise and shake themselves
and summer ends in a flurry of drops.

Wedding in the Flood

They are taking my girl away forever,
sobs the bride's mother, as the procession
forms slowly to the whine of the clarinet.
She was the shy one. How will she fare
in that cold house, among these strangers?
This has been a long and difficult day.
The rain nearly ruined everything,
but at the crucial time, when lunch was ready,
it mercifully stopped. It is drizzling again
as they help the bride into the palankeen.
The girl has been licking too many pots.
Two sturdy lads carrying the dowry
(a cot, a looking-glass, a tin-trunk,
beautifully painted in grey and blue)
lead the way, followed by a foursome
bearing the palankeen on their shoulders.
Now even the stragglers are out of view.

I like the look of her hennaed hands,
gloats the bridegroom, as he glimpses
her slim fingers gripping the palankeen's side.
If only her face matches her hands,
and she gives me no mother-in-law problems,
I'll forgive her the cot and the trunk
and looking-glass. Will the rain never stop?
It was my luck to get a pot-licking wench.
Everything depends on the ferryman now.
It is dark in the palankeen, thinks the bride,
and the roof is leaking. Even my feet are wet.
Not a familiar face around me

as I peep through the curtains. I'm cold and scared.
The rain will ruin cot, trunk, and looking-glass.
What sort of a man is my husband?
They would hurry, but their feet are slipping,
and there is a swollen river to cross.

They might have given a bullock at least,
grumbles the bridegroom's father; a couple of oxen
would have come in handy at the next ploughing.
Instead, we are landed with
a cot, a tin trunk, and a looking-glass,
all the things that she will use!
Dear God, how the rain is coming down.
The silly girl's been licking too many pots.
I did not like the look of the river
when we crossed it this morning.
Come back before three, the ferryman said,
or you'll not find me here. I hope
he waits. We are late by an hour,
or perhaps two. But whoever heard
of a marriage party arriving on time?
The light is poor, and the paths treacherous,
but it is the river I most of all fear.

Bridegroom and bride and parents and all,
the ferryman waits; he knows you will come,
for there is no other way to cross,
and a wedding party always pays extra.
The river is rising, so quickly aboard
with your cot, tin trunk, and looking-glass,
that the long homeward journey can begin.
Who has seen such a brown and angry river
or can find words for the way the ferry
saws this way and that, and then disgorges
its screaming load? The clarinet fills with water.
Oh what a consummation is here:
The father tossed on the horns of the waves,

and full thirty garlands are bobbing past
the bridegroom heaved on the heaving tide,
and in an eddy, among the willows downstream,
the coy bride is truly bedded at last.

FROM ***Half Moon***

To See Fruit Ripen

To see fruit ripen
By the weather's connivance,
Eyes bud and flower again,
Be scorched in June
And shrunk by the North-East wind,
Is to become complete.

Can we come to terms
With our deciduous love
Until we have seen
The mulberry in its bare
Essentials—trunk, branch
And twig—the X-rayed tree?

A lone ignited leaf
Downsailing from the moment
It takes to air
Till it touches ground
Has a significance
No jet can imitate.

And a flight of geese
Rising from our marshes at dawn
Drives a wedge
Into history more deeply
Than a prophet fleeing to a cave
Or an ultimatum.

Poems for a Younger Brother

II

Flight to London

When you leave the airport lounge for the tarmac
trying to walk unaided with a straight back
I know I am seeing you for the last time,

and try to be brave like you. I rehearse
a smile at a passing stranger, but tears
are knocking hard at the back of the eyes.

I wander off towards the canteen gates
pretending I am out of cigarettes,
and let the tears come. And then I pretend

a mote of dust is making my eyes hurt.
Having no handkerchief, I pull the shirt-
ends from my trousers and use them freely...

Soon, I am a man again. To relatives
return with cheerful talk no one believes
and every one is eager to promote.

Back home, we sit on the lawn, and wait.
When your plane roars overhead, gaining height
rapidly, we follow it over the hills,

till it is a speck, and then nothing.
You are on your way, gaining height rapidly,
to London, return ticket in your pocket.

V

Long-distance Call

The neighbour's servant rings the bell
at three in the afternoon
to tell me I am wanted on the phone.
At three in the afternoon
when everyone is sleeping?
I know what it is about.
Brother, you are gone.

So little is really needed
for preparation
A quick wash, slippers, specs,
and I am ready.

I shall greet the neighbour calmly,
my hand will be steady
when I lift the phone.

VI

Cancer

What was inside you
flowered so intensely
it overtook all
with a springtime swiftness
Brother, you were good
ground. Water and prayer
have done their work.
Sleep sound.

X

Indestructible

Indestructible I thought,
Younger, but tougher,
always bullying your brother.
The uncles called you bulldog.

Lingering
at the gates of my friends
till they called you in.

Showing off your lieutenant's pips
to mother, who kissed them.

Tall just man
with the rough exterior.
Optimist.

Mutual memories.
Now they are mine.

XII

Shirt

His wife gives me
one of his old shirts.
I would like to think
they are being used, she says.

He was tall and heavy.
The shirt hangs loosely
on my smaller frame,
but where it touches the skin
it will not be shaken free.

Lights

The car whispers down
the hill road.
Its lights   gouge out
                                        a shifting
                                        hollow of
                                        brightness
except at the turns
where they wander off
                    into unsure space

But wait!

What lights are those
        pricking
        the distant
        mountaintops
        each
        one
        alone?

Starlight and a thin mist
deepen the mystery.

One is tempted to call them elfin,

for what kind of men
would struggle up those backbreaking slopes
all their maizebread goatmilk days
to achieve such
        loneliness?

Maki Kureishi

Nee Maki Dhunjibhoy, she was born in Calcutta in 1927 and spent her early childhood in Ranchi. She moved to Karachi with her family some years before Partition. She was educated at St. Joseph's Convent, D.J. Science College and did her M.A. from Smith College, Massachusetts. She taught English Literature at Karachi University for over thirty years. She started writing in the 1960s, after reading Afro-Caribbean poetry which, she found, is nearer in content to Pakistani experiences than is British poetry. She admired Dennis Walcott in particular and was very conscious that her use of English as a creative vehicle should reflect the East-West duality of her world. As an Anglicized Parsi married to an Anglicized Muslim she viewed the world with a degree of detachment that heightened her sensibilities as a poet. Her prolonged battle against rheumatoid arthritis made her work very introspective, her later poems showing an increasing pre-occupation with death. Never given to excess she used language cleverly to convey multiple images, and wrote prolifically during the 1960s and 1970s, establishing herself as one of Pakistan's foremost poets writing in English. She was a founder member of 'Mixed Voices', a forum for Karachi's poets initiated by Adrian Husain* in the 1970s. Her poetry was published in various anthologies including *Wordfall* (1975), *Pakistani Literature: The Contemporary English Writers* (1978), *The Worlds of the Muslim Imagination* (1986) and appeared in various American/Commonwealth literary journals. For a long time she wrote very little and then gained momentum once more in the late 1980s. Some of her best poems, included here, were written in her last few years and also appear in her posthumous collection, *The Far Thing* (1997). Maki Kureishi wrote 'A Letter from Chao-Chun' as an exercise; inspired by Arthur Waley, whom she read often, it marks a new departure for her.

Day

Across the garden a koel shouts
and wakes me up to dawn.
From under clouds the sun
rises to the bait of its song. A day
lyric as old Persian glass that snares
the light's intrigue, to celebrate beginnings.

Like a bell God's name shatters the air,
and usurping birds
lose voice. A chameleon
disturbed, the exuberance of grass
evoke a grace I am
wary of; a benediction like

the desert rain, too comforting to last.
Yet light is a holy
thought, until the crow
lifts an assassin beak that stabs and stabs
I think of Omar
absorbed in the quietude of prayer.

The chameleon writhes. I cannot hear
it scream. Its tail loops
like a hangman's noose
around the sun, pulls up a jerking body.
The beak scissors
as God's repeated name dies on the air.

Christmas Letter to my Sister

Each year I decorate a Christmas tree
with trinkets from Bohri Bazaar, Germany, Japan.

You'll send home more from China
and Korea to please my daughter.

Each year I hang the glitter
of our childhood up again.

Mother kept our own tree secret
until Christmas Eve, when, doors thrown wide,

it startled us—a dour
cypress from the garden, now enchanted,

bearing its fragile globes and stars
like goblin fruit. I use

a less dramatic Casurina pine,
as you plant spices in Cologne, but though

your backyard's fertile as a flower-pot,
they'll not grow native; yet are native

to the private landscape where we lived,
alien and homegrown. Often

as a Christmas treat the Raja sent
his official elephant. We were shipwrecked on.

When the haunches rose like a tidal wave
we learned to brace and sway. Still practised in equipoise

I teeter safe, and braced to my uncertainties
survive, Anglo-Indian as a dak bungalow.

You, among buildings that cut down
our elephant to size, play house—never at home.

Always the long, repeated journeys looking for
something you've left behind.

When we meet, all the doors swing open
for this is where you live; but the rooms

are empty, echo to our timid
grown-up voices; and this old child

who lifts a broken-toy face, is she
you or me? Only our scars mark where we built

our personal and nursery planet.
Still, we've kept the knack. I, middle-aged, fidget

with make-believe; you, homesick and not
eager to come home, are foreign everywhere. Live European,

stay haunted by the image of
that makeshift geography we share.

So come December, I wish you peace
with faith in make-believe; and deck my sunny tree

with blobs of cotton-wool. Perhaps you stand
before a frozen pane, indifferent to carols,

snow, your fir-tree; watching that large ghost,
our elephant, lumbering by.

Kittens

There are too many kittens.
Even the cat is dismayed
at this overestimation
of her stock and slinks away.
Kind friends cannot adopt them all.

My relatives say: Take them
to a bazaar and let them go
each to his destiny. They'll live
off pickings. But they are so small
somebody may step on one
like a tomato.

Or too fastidious to soil
a polished shoe will kick it
out of his path. If they survive
the gaunt dogs and battering heels,
they will starve gently, squealing
a little less each day.

The European thing to do
is drown them. Warm water
is advised to lessen the shock.
They are so small it takes only
a minute. You hold them down
and turn your head away.

Then the water shatters. Your hands
are frantic eels. Oddly
like landed fish, their blunt pink mouths
open and shut. Legs strike out.
Each claw, a delicate nail
paring, is bared.

They are blind and will never known
you did this to them. The water
recomposes itself.
                    Snagged
by two cultures, which
shall I choose?

Curfew Summer

Summer clocks in at eight. By now
most plants have dried to a rasping brown,
and the grass burns to its roots.

Only the bougainvillea flags
its violent colours - dissident
in a brutal summer.

No one may walk next door.
Yet from house to house the grapevine runs:
Arrested! Bombed!

Two hundred shot! Long used
to a seasonal withering, each summer
we die nearer the root.

Envy the sparrows! They forage
without a Pass, shrieking all over the city
reckless, uncensored opinions.

Laburnum Tree

This is not your season.
Splotched by passing trucks and slapped
by brutal winds, your branches are
inhospitable to birds. Winter

plucks you to a sparse
rattle of twigs. 'Dead!' think passersby.

Not suspecting when April begins
cautiously to unwind tendril
and modest bud, that every branch
will hang blossoms
like a thousand chandeliers
opulent with light.

If the sky's blue to set off
that elemental yellow. If the wind
blows gently it's to display
the shaping of each floweret. Rooted,
you turn slowly to create
our transient spring. The landscape

Stops at your feet - observing
how you struggle to retrench
your lavishness. But the petals won't
stop falling. So now you wait, desolate
in green, through the long hard-hitting months
your sap still rioting flowers.

Oyster Rocks

Engulfed by waves that tussle and knock,
they stand, have ever stood unimpaired.
Mothering whale and plankton,
the sea losing every tide pulls out;
not a flake nudged off. Lacking definition
we call them the Oyster Rocks.

One a rugged pyramid. One squat.
Keeled flat; the small might be a primeval wreck.
Immune to the wind's sandpaper

rasping, brutally, self sufficient
they breed (if at all) oysters,
clenched inward like themselves. Having done with growth,

begrudge nesting. Their solid irrelevance
dumbfounds the mind. When the moon through black water
draws threads of light; on days of lucid
windblown weather, they are stark. Shadows
avoid them and lost sea-birds.
We cannot ignore such massive absence.

Yet how can we who lapse grief-stricken;
cannot sleep; are ruled by season, define
a point blank perspective? Outside
our timid reach they withdrew from touch
and self enclosed, may have died;
lest flake by flake they should fall to ruin.

For my Grandson

Small shape of our death, with loving care
we nurture you, scanning our own mementos
in your plump tenderness: in your eyes, hair
or hands. Frail little being that must enclose
more than yourself. One day you will grow to be
like me or me or me. Even your allergies
are identified. We shall harass you
with our tall and sacrilegious
gods. This is our final opportunity
to survive. It is my future you will reconstruct

in your grown-up life. Clutching our hungers
we make dreams for you, part love and part
cupidity: inching ownership further
till your mind is patterned to our warped hearts.
Turn from us, child, we are vampires

wailing: Remember. That I may not entirely die.
And forgive us the grasping appetite
that manipulates love to stay undead
for we fade like shadows till our absence
is forgotten, unless you hold us in the light.

Snipers in Karachi

May 1990

Death is everywhere.
Also here at a jerry-built stall
selling vegetables four days old. (The trucks
too frightened to deliver.)
From under onion sacks it scuttles
steel-plated, shiny; its tail
slung over, vindictive as a gun.

Panic. Hard-headed traders
abandon shops. Screaming women pull high
all their draperies, exposing knee, thigh.
In which sack does it silently wait?
Iron pipes, stones, pound smash
until surely it must lie
minced into dust.

Not so.

The next day on a bus
a dozen passengers crumple up.
On kerbs, in doorways, drinking tea…
Death is everywhere.
Scuttling through traffic it rides
a shiny steel-plated roar. The gun
now unslung—and lethal as a sting.

Letter from Chao-Chun

I am surprised you are not here today.
At sunrise I looked for your return.
I wear not a grain of powder, feather-brush of rouge.
If you but come I shall put them all on. Also
my tortoise-shell combs, earrings of jade
and bronze silk gown fragile
as a chrysanthemum. I am ready.
I have been ready twenty years
unconvinced you will not come
riding down from the water-coloured hills.
Fallen peach blossoms cling to your hat.
The flanks of your horse are striped green
with shadows of willow.

I kneel beside the last stream you must cross,
(I go every day pretending
to water my silkworms.)
I am surprised of course.
Quite taken aback.
You hold me in a close embrace. Alas!
How long can such day dreams prevail?
Is it so with you?
A single bed is sleepless and hard.
When will you come?

Postponed for a while, by the Emperor's whim,
our mutual bliss, you write from the Court.

I pluck white hairs from my head.

Arthur Waley. *Translations 170 Chinese Poems.* 'Chao-Chun, a Chinese girl who in 33 B.C. was bestowed upon the Khan of the Hsiang-nu as a mark of Imperial regard. Hers was the only grave in this desolate district on which grass would grow.'

Meantime I have not been negligent
of your concerns. Not a speck of dust escapes.
Your dancing girls grow plump. I have
woven rolls of silk:
sapphire, crimson, amethyst,
for you to choose your wedding robe.
All things are prepared. I keep the wine cool.
I have instructed your servants from an ancient scroll
how to grow the grass thick and green
on my grave even in frozen weather.
So you can find it easily
in case you are a little late.

Shahid Hosain

Born in Aligarh, Khwaja Shahid Hosain was among the earliest Pakistani poets writing in English. He edited the first anthology of Pakistani poetry in English, *First Voices: Six Poets from Pakistan* (1965), in which his own work also appeared. His later poetry was published in *Pieces of Eight* (1971), and *Pakistani Literature: The Contemporary English Writers* (1978). As a civil servant, he was closely associated with the development of films and the electronic media in Pakistan. He moved to London where he set up an antiquarian bookshop, Hosain's. At present, he is Pakistan's Ambassador to UNESCO.

A Speculation

(There is a small rural town in the Punjab whose name means, literally, 'Village of the Assassins'.)

This is a mud-infested town
Lost in a blaze of sun throughout the day,
Untroubled by a road, surrounded
By a quiet profusion of fields
Defiant with stake-high corn.

The women work the fields,
Anklet-burdened, stooping to the grain
Or swaying hungrily to the single well:
The water deep, receding from the light.

No children play in the refuse of the lanes,
No voices stir the silent, dragging day;
The air is left
To the warm drone of flies, to the soft plod
Of buffaloes imposing on the dust.

The houses stoop together at one end,
Sackcloth and straw fall at the entrances;
The smoke works, timid and concentric
Within each courtyard, and the beetles click
In the shaking, rotten beams.

There is an absence and a memory here
Soaked into the deep ink-red
Scattered across the walls, speaking from the scars
Grown dark and age-locked in the green trunks
Of the bending, growing trees.

And at night, when the moon abstains,
The men file, white and silent, on the path:
Hurry, intent and silent, and silently
Return just as the town
Surrenders peace before the growing sun.

Then the women return to the grain,
Bending and scything in a busy arc,
Lost in their work, creating
A rhythm and a pause, until one night,
One moonless, manless and remembered night
Across the treacherous, resuming river
And past the high corn the avengers come.

Regarding the Appearance of Sir Laurence Olivier as Richard III in a Lahore Cinema

Across the hot scootered streets, past
The building mosque ('site for the first air-
conditioned mosque in Asia' says the board).
Through the betel-ruined walls
Up the stairs, beneath the ample-
bosomed, wide-hipped bending beauties, staring
From the posters, eyes wide with collyrium,
Around the green stucco goddess, a hound
Nuzzling her improbable breasts, we came
To the Grand Stalls, 'conditioned climate by Trane'.

Dodging the hard hail of our running world
We come to see that monstrous, glossy head
Stare watchful, devious from a distant screen,
And we have heard the high imperious voice
Beat faintly, without meaning, on our ears:
But these coloured distractions find a home
Here, where the edges of those splendid words
Fall soft, like feathers, on unknowing ears,

But rage and treachery speak loud and clear
When this black scorpion crimps across our eyes.
For the language vaults our senses
But these painted figures bring
Time and reason's sure defences,
We understand this real king
Stalking the tinsel alleys of the screen
In garish anger.

M.K. Hameed

His work has been published in various British, American, and Canadian magazines and in three anthologies: *Young Commonwealth Poets '65, New Voices of the Commonwealth,* and *Pieces of Eight* (1971).

Gold Spot Glow

From the stagnant weight
Of the massive grey clouds
A thin long rain fell
With cold unconcern, insistently—
On the creased leaking roof,
On the ancient boltless door,
On the awry mud-painted walls
Of a very old house.
It fell in resolute strings
Of calloused luminous beads
On the sackcloth curtain,
Modestly concealing, beneath
The gold spot glow of an oil lamp,
A man, a woman and three children,
Bare to the gleaming ribs,
Crouching in one-tone abstract design
Around the damp corner, wherein,
Elusively burning firewood
Sends out thick smoke-signals
To the rain-happy world outside.

Daud Kamal

Born in Abbottabad, in 1935, Daud Kamal was educated at Burn Hall in Srinagar and Abbottabad respectively, Islamia College, Peshawar, and the University of Cambridge. He wrote prolifically, and was one of Pakistan's most significant poets. He published several collections of English poetry including *Compass of Love* (1973), *Recognitions* (1979), *A Remote Beginning* (1985) and *The Unicorn and the Dancing Girl* (1988). He was among the four Pakistani poets whose poetry constituted an anthology, *The Blue Wind* (1984). The poems in all these books were grouped together in a posthumous collection *Before the Carnations Wither: Collected Poems* (1995). He had developed his own distinct style as a poet, using brief visual images which often had inner meaning. He believed that poetry should be multi-layered, and acknowledged the influence of Urdu literature on his English poetry. He loosely translated two great Urdu poets, Ghalib and Faiz into English in *Ghalib, Reverberations* (1970) and *Faiz in English* (1984). As Head of the Department of English at Peshawar University, he also brought out *The Journal of the English Literary Club*, one of Pakistan's best literary journals in English.

His work was read on the BBC. He received gold medals under the aegis of Triton College, USA in 1977, 1978, 1980 and he was invited to the Rockerfeller Foundation's Bellagio Centre. His poems are now appearing in a new book, *The Selected Poems of Daud Kamal*. He died in 1987.

FROM *BEFORE THE CARNATIONS WITHER*

Prayer Beads

Under
the shade
of a willow tree
where the river bends
on a rock-pool
prayer-beads rise
to the surface
from the mouth
of an invisible
fish

An Ancient Indian Coin

Far away, beyond the glaciers of the Himalayas and the snow-roofed home of the negligent gods, was slowly gathering a swarm of hard, hungry savages...

H. G. Keene, *A Sketch of the History of Hindustan.*

Gazelle embossed on a lop-sided moon.
Vasanta had only been rendered insensible
by the outrage in the garden.
A sadhu watches his toe-nails grow
in his Himalayan cave.

Men create their own gods
and a learned Brahmin is exempt
From all taxation.
But a piece of gold
does not take one very far.

Out of the seven jade goblets
they dug up

only one was whole.
The king's hunting-dogs are better fed
than most of his subjects.

Look, the Indus is choked with stars
and the glaciers are beginning to melt.
I try to calm myself
but my tongue is smothered
by its own thickness.

Solitude, silence, stone.

An Ode to Death

Your ode to death is in the lifting
of a single eyebrow. Lift it and see.
Conrad Aiken

Death is more than certain, says e.e. cummings,
but the clocks go on ticking as before
and in every particle of carbon-dust
there lives a diamond dream.
How many galaxies yet to be explored—
how many seeds in the pomegranate of time?
The pine tree blasted by last year's thunderbolt
and the burnt-out match-stick in my ashtray
look so terribly alike.
I have sat by your bedside and felt
your sinking pulse. Are the hair and bones
really indestructible and how long
does it take for the eyes
to dissolve in the grave?
Two streams mingle in a forgotten river.
Between the eye and the tear
there is an archipelago of naked rocks.
Only sleep and silence there—

no anchorage for grief.
I, too, have wandered in a forest of symbols
and clutched at the harlots of memory.
I have seen the 'stars plummet to their dark addresses.'
I have felt your absence around my neck.
But let bygones be bygones.
Who was the deceiver and who the deceived?
Was I on a floating island
and were you on the shore?
Which one of us moved away?

A Street Revisited

A white pigeon comes down a stairway
one step at a time.
Leaning against a stone wall,
an old beggar rearranges his crutches.
Scruffy children (one wipes his nose on his sleeve)
play marbles in a shrinking patch of sunlight.

Quite a bit seems to have changed
in these thirty years.
Tourists stay longer and have more to spend.
Cinema posters are more provocative than ever.
Coke has replaced iced-sherbet
and gas-lamps now are seldom seen.

Beyond this street are other streets —
a forest of anonymous houses —
too many broken windows.
Mothers with sagging breasts go on cooking
the same meagre dinners.
If happiness existed, they were widowed long ago.

The Blue Wind

Imagine how it is
in the mountains —
the sharpness of pine-needles
and valleys green with regret.

Chart the flight of birds
on the night's migratory page.

Clouds melt into one another
and seeds sprout
but the rocks stand apart
asymmetrical in the torrent's rage.

The grey salt of glaciers
and the stars' inviolate beauty.

The Hunt

Rain-inscribed
these rocks record
the primordial scripture
of a people betrayed
by their kings and priests.
The savage wind
claws at them
from generation to generation.
Rusty nails fall out
when the door burns.

In the blood of sunset
my body remembers
past endearments —
the mud-river island
and the otherworld music

of freedom. The sky
has witnessed
my humiliation. The huntsmen
stand on the crest
of the hill.

I spit blood. I have swallowed
my screams.

The Leap

Alexander on horseback
leapt over the Indus here,
or so the storytellers say,

and on the other side
of that hill in a grove
of mango trees he listened

in rapt attention
to a naked sadhu
talking of immortality.

The Gift

I have read
somewhere
that Buddha
gave a handful
of yellow leaves
to Annanda
and told him
that besides those
there were
many thousands

of other truths
scattered
all over the earth.
It was autumn
and from far away
came the sounds
of oxen-bells.
I, too, have tried
to plumb
the depths
of my being
but found nothing—
neither
brittle truths
nor lush green
lies.

Voyage to the Enchanted Island

Barnacles
on a broken
stone-jar
half-buried
in the sand.

A cool gust
of wind.
Frayed curtains
billow in
through the window.

Overlap
of faces. We are
in a moon-boat
and the sea
is our room.

Turquoise

A sky
patched with cobwebs.
Take a deep breath,
she says,
and the past
will come back.

Blind fish
(they don't change colour)
glide between the branches
of submerged trees.
The stars
chronicle our despair.

No matter
how hard you look
things won't relinquish
their opacity.
The wind
has bled the stones white.

Zulfikar Ghose

Born in Sialkot, Zulfikar Ghose moved to Bombay in 1942 and later migrated to England in 1952. After graduating from Keele University he became an English teacher and also worked as a sports correspondent for *The Observer*. He has published several collections of poetry: *The Loss of India* (1964), *Jets from Orange* (1967), *The Violent West* (1972), *A Memory of Asia* (1984) and *Selected Poems* (1991). He is a great stylist, to whom language and imagery are paramount. He dislikes the idea of writers being 'pigeon-holed' into geographical or cultural categories: he has often said that he has simply tried to produce good literature. He has written five books of literary criticism including *Hamlet, Prufrock and Language* (1978), *The Fiction of Reality* (1983), and *Shakespeare's Mortal Knowledge* (1993). He moved to the United States in 1969, and has taught at the University of Texas at Austin since. He is married to the Brazilian artist, Helena de la Fontaine. He has written over ten novels, including *The Murder of Aziz Khan* (1967), a gripping evocative tale about the tussle between a group of industrialists and a small Punjab farmer in early post-independence Pakistan. The leitmotif in many of his books is alienation. He has written much about South America, a continent which has similar landscape and resonance to the subcontinent. His books have been translated into many European languages. His famous trilogy *The Incredible Brazilian*: *The Native* (1972), *The Beautiful Empire* (1975) and *A Different World* (1978), is a historical romance which spans several centuries. It has been acclaimed for its poetic language and mystic dimension. In between he wrote a stream-of-consciousness novel *Crump's Terms* (1975). Later, he wrote *Hulme's Investigations into the Bogart Script* (1981), *A New History of Torments* (1982), *Figures of Enchantment* (1986) and *Don Bueno* (1983). His latest novel *The Triple Mirror of the Self* (1992), a tale of migration and exile, links together the many continents in which he has lived.

The Triple Mirror of the Self is a complex, multi-faceted novel about migration, illusion and reality and a man's search for his soul, his essential core: it begins and ends with the snow clad peaks of the Andes and the Hindu Kush respectively, which mirror each other. In the first section 'The Burial of the Self' the narrator, Urimba—the scattered one—is living among a primitive South American tribe, but his timeless world is shattered by armed, uniformed men. The novel goes back in time to 'Voyager and Pilgrim' which portrays the narrator's life as Jonathan Archibald Pons, an American academic. He is presented with a manuscript which turns out to be the story of Urimba/Pons. At this point the narrator dissociates himself from Pons, an aspect of himself that he cannot accept. As a private joke he reveals he has invented the name Zinalco Shimomura for Pons from Shimmers, the nickname he acquired in England, when he migrated there as Roshan, an Indian Muslim. The novel hammers away at racist myths and stereotypes; it also peels away the narrator's changing identities until in 'The Origins of Self' it goes back to his early years in the land where his life began.

FROM *The Triple Mirror of the Self*

FROM *Voyager and Pilgrim*

8: In the Desert

In that part of the United States, Shimomura's features so resembled a Latin American's that even his neatly groomed appearance and sartorial elegance inspired no more complex a fantasy in the general faculty than that he was a visiting professor from Mexico City or perhaps Caracas come to do some research on Hopi Indians and from whom one might expect to hear a lecture on the seventeenth-century migratory impulse into the northern interior of South America, resulting from the European conquest, of the Carib Indians.

Being Latin American, or mistaken for one, in the Southwest of the USA, with its majority of non-white population of Mexican origin, guaranteed a person's anonymity, and so no one paid much attention to the new wanderer of the corridors of the liberal arts building, and only the Dean of Humanities and a couple of his associates knew that he had done more than to have published a poem in the *Atlantic*. The Latin identification was reinforced when his wife joined him at the end of the semester, by when Shimomura had established his immigrant status, for she was a Peruvian named Maria Isabel Valdivieso. Black hair that she wore in a thick plait which reached the small of her back, slightly protuberant cheekbones and very dark brown eyes, together with her Spanish name, and of course the native fluency with which she spoke Spanish and the accent that coloured her use of English, made her so emphatically a Latin that people simply took it for granted that her husband was of the same racial type, and both no different from the local Chicanos.

Shimomura's anonymity was helped by another factor, that of Isabel's carving out for herself a career at the same university. She succeeded in joining the Sociology Department and became prominent in the university's politics. Because of the domineering image she projected of her own character, the majority of her colleagues assumed that she was one of the new feminist recruits from an ethnic minority whose ideas were to be liberally applauded without investigation if one were not to be damned by their collective vindictiveness. Her spouse seemed to fit neatly into the category of the husbands of the new species of highly motivated and politically aggressive female professors. He appeared meek, obscure and submissive. Though false, the appearance suited Shimomura who did not have the interest in society that Isabel had. He preferred to go unnoticed than to have to endure the boorish talk of a colleague. Isabel, however, was always desperate for company and action.

Her father had served as Minister of the Interior in a government considered by the intellectuals of the time to be repressive, and he had decided that Maria Isabel's university education would be best undertaken outside Peru, fearing that among the liberal agitators who infested the university in Lima she was bound to hear of his own role in the repression. Communist lies, of course, as far as he was concerned, the rumour about institutionalized torture and a secret police, but he wanted to protect his daughter from such representations of his work. He offered to send her to Paris, thinking that the very name of the city would dazzle and increase her affection for him; being at the age when the slightest hint that someone else made decisions for her was to the young girl an outrageous affront, Maria Isabel thought about her father's proposal and made up her mind that if she was to leave Lima it would be only for London. It made little difference to her father, however, who was astute enough to guess that had he proposed London to her she would have insisted upon Paris.

Going to London, she had dropped the Maria from her name, feeling that she needed to shed her alien identity. She struck a deliberately independent pose and avoided becoming attached to groups of South Americans who met in one another's flats in Earls Court and Clapham and listened to records of Violeta Parra or Nara Leáo and talked obsessively about 'the political situation' prevailing back home. After a somewhat lonely first year, she found herself in a crowd of artists and writers — most of them English but several from France, Italy and Spain — among whom, the only allegiance was to the latest trends in the cinema, rock music, fashion, and anything that had the potential to become, however briefly, a passionate obsession. By the time she had taken her degree in sociology, the international set she moved in had split up, regrouped, altered, so that in her fourth year in London the circle Isabel most frequented was made up of young writers and artists who met in Highgate and among whom she was regarded with considerable esteem for having published in a national left-wing weekly a series of articles on the living conditions of immigrants in east London.

Although during these years she twice returned to Lima, once for a Christmas holiday and the second time with the idea that, having got her degree, she ought to settle upon a career, she found that her adoption in London of friends who were almost exclusively European had so altered her thinking that she had become impatient of native customs that were somehow unbearably suffocating. Also, the very reason her father had got her out of Lima now made it difficult to return to it: a change of government had exposed past brutality, and that old rumour about torture had not been a communist lie at all. She could not go to a university and expect to be employed by people who had suffered vicious surveillance, and in some cases personal affliction, at her father's direction. She went back to London, but now with an ambiguous feeling that she was both rejecting her country and had been rejected by it, so that in her new life the more she wanted to think of herself as a European the more she thought of herself as a South American in exile, and where she had earlier attempted to expunge the alien accent from her English speech she began to preserve it so deliberately that she sometimes sounded like a Hollywood caricature of a Spanish senorita.

Zinalco Shimomura was one of the group of people she mixed with in Highgate. There is no documentation that I can draw upon to describe the relationship between them that led to their marriage. I knew the two of them best when they were not together because then they wrote to each other. I have been able to trace only three of the other people who were part of the Highgate crowd, and their recollections have been vague, speculative and sometimes contradictory — though one of them was to give me a small group of important letters, from which I shall quote in the course of this narrative. One thing the Highgate group did agree upon, however, was the idea that Isabel was attracted to the young man from India because his features were indistinguishable from that of a Peruvian while his speech, education and the poems with which his literary career had begun in the same left-wing weekly in which she had published her articles made him, in her eyes, perfectly English. I thought this an absurd conjecture and a piece of idle gossip, but was reminded that while she adopted English habits of thought Isabel never gave up wearing her long black hair in a thick plait which had once made Shimomura say that she looked just like the village girls in Gujarat.

10: You

You are tucked inside a blue eiderdown sleeping bag, upon which are heaped three grey blankets, in the attic room of the flat in Drayton Gardens. Flannel pyjamas finally feel warm. A prickly, coarse woollen vest close to the skin, two pairs of grey socks pulled up to the knees, you are woolly warm inside the sleeping bag, but the stuck-out nose is ticklish in the cold air and the black locks of hair feel the wind of the high mountains blowing through them, in the slate-roofed attic flat. The milkman's dray-horse is already in the street going clippety-clop when the milkman whistles walking to the doorstep of the next house in a tinkling rattle of bottles three pints please two gold tops and one silver clippety-clop whoa there tock-tock stop and a rattling shifting of milk crates with a tinkle-tinkle of empty bottles. You are asleep in London in the dead middle of the twentieth century. The pink-faced schoolboys running in the playground among the soccer games with tennis balls, black blazers flying behind them, stopped and shouted in glee and instantly made up a song *Here comes the sav Here comes the sav Here comes the savage Who lives in the coconut tree* and went wild with malicious joviality. But one, a tall fifth-form Latin prodigy, Brian Humphreys, constant quoter of Catullus who when walking away from people sadly intoned *Omnia qui magni dispexit lumina mundi*, sighed at the foreign sound and then laughed when informed the name could be translated as a brightness, a light, as something that shimmers. *Shimmers! Why, that's splendid!* declared Humphreys and befriended the stranger because he could say to a third person in some future conversation *My luminous friend here*. And even your mother now shouts up the narrow unconstructed wooden staircase to the attic room, *Shimmers!* and you throw the blankets away and stand up in the sleeping bag and hop around the room like in a sack race looking for the school uniform and then let the sleeping bag fall and step out of it quickly grabbing the white shirt with the soiled collar from the chair and the grey trousers from the ground, quickly put them on over the pyjamas, double-quickly grab the school tie hanging from the chair already knotted and slip it over your head and pull it tight, then a green sleeveless sweater and a grey full-sleeved sweater over that and then the black blazer, now treble-quick put on black boots, sprinkle face with cold water, brush hair, munch toast, swallow tea, grab coat and cap and briefcase fat with homework and go running down Drayton Gardens past the Society of Authors, stopping for breath at the corner with Fulham Road where you stand a moment outside the cinema and wake up in a dream looking at the stills of Elizabeth Taylor. The smoggy-smelling cold air sets you marching briskly up the road but your whole life is ruined as you enter the school building because you remember that you have a gym lesson in the morning and you are still wearing your pyjamas. Benson, the school captain and cricket captain and number one scholar bound for Balliol, is with the prefects at the school gate but you have your foot in just before the bell rings, not like last time when you were two minutes late and placed

Benson in a moment's moral dilemma: should he wink and let you pass because you were his best batsman in the summer and super useful come Easter at Rugby fives or should he appear to do no favours and book you for detention with the usual lazy sods, and you are certain he'll take you aside for a private word to give the appearance of conveying a severe warning and then let you go with a wink but are shocked that he clenches his jaw, suppresses any consideration of partiality, and takes down your name. Your name! An hour's detention after school. What a way to treat your best batsman, like any other lazy sod! At four o'clock you go resentfully to detention. You sit there first angry with Benson and then thinking of the English films in which the British officers rose above favouritism and prejudice, the judges were never corrupt, and there was honour even among thieves. It is a long hour. Justice is blind. You sit there and realize come the cricket season you are going to do your damned best for Benson. He's a jolly good fellow. You are never late again. But you are a proper fool keeping your pyjamas on when you have a gym lesson first thing after the milk break. Entering the school, you start limping. You limp past the door where the PT master Mr Clay is standing getting his form, noisy 3B, into order and you say *Good morning, Mr Clay*, so that he sees you limping past. Every term there is a boy who is convinced he is the first to think up the remark that Mr Clay's wife makes a mug of him. *Watch it*, you shout at a boy who has bumped into you, *I got a sprained ankle*, and limp extra hard, glancing back to see if Mr Clay heard that. After registration you limp up to your form master and ask permission to be excused from assembly because it would be hard on your sprained ankle to stand up for the hymn. When the whole school is in assembly and is shouting blood-rousing commands at Christian soldiers marching as to war you slip to the school secretary Mrs Tyndall's office and ask if she has anything you can put on a sprained ankle. She produces a bottle of Sloane's liniment and a bit of cotton wool. You rub some on, thank the kind lady like a good boy, and limp out, having established a useful alibi. But she calls you back. She saw something when you pulled the trouser leg up and the socks down to rub the liniment on your ankle. *Do you have pyjamas on under your clothes*? she asks in a shrilly rising voice. You stare at her, gone totally dumb. *Uh it's uh special winter underwear*, miss, you say at last, and appealing to the Orient's reputation for mystery add hopefully *from Kashmir*. You almost forget to limp, making a second exit. Mr Clay does not even look at you when you ask to be excused from PT but quickly agrees. The boys are changing in the steamy room where many smells from bodies unwashed for weeks are trapped and a strong sweaty odour is rising from the naked chests and thickening the already sickening air. Mr Clay blows his whistle and says it's turning out fine, they'll go and have five-a-side football outside in the playground. You realize Mr Clay has some trouble on his mind, he's not thinking or seeing anything, and doesn't want to work. It's turning out fine, he says. It's miserable cold outside. But the boys give a cheer and go running out with nothing on but shorts, though a few put their shirts back on as they dash out, and are already dividing up into teams. You slip away to the empty form room, take a seat by the hot radiator near the window and get a thrill reading 'Porphyria's Lover' aloud, *her cheek once more blushed bright beneath my burning kiss* and instead of the pink boys giggling at your funny accent there is a respectful silence in the class followed by thunderous applause. Class standing, applauding. Headmaster moved to tears. First prize for declamation. From the window you can see the boys down in the playground, several almost naked in the freezing cold, others with shirt-tails flying, running up and down in two games of five-a-side, what a funny lot the English to think it's turning fine when the clouds are like muddy buffalo hide. When you came on a white ship ten months ago, sailing across the gorgeous blue of the Arabian Sea and the marvellous Mediterranean, under sunlit and moonlit skies, suddenly the world's brilliance was dimmed. Grey the passage into the Channel, grey the mouth of the Thames, grey the docks at Tilbury and dark dark dark the landscape from where the doomed were led manacled to the hulks moored in a perpetual melancholy mist. But O then came April then came

May with the buds on the chestnut trees and the hawthorn bursting in white and pink glory and you knew this was an ambiguous land, its days successively so foul and fair you had not seen such contradictions in the air that alternately so soothed and tormented it seemed the breath now of angels and now of witches…

You come out of Whitechapel Gallery where you had gone to see an exhibition of Pop art and instead of proceeding to the tube station you unthinkingly walk in the direction of the West India Docks, not realizing your mistake until you are in a confusion of streets. There is a pub at the opposite corner from where, remarkably in this ancient part of London, Indian film music can be heard. It is what has arrested you in your thoughtless progress. The exhibition at the Whitechapel disturbed you. Western culture has lately begun to take a gleeful pleasure in applauding the mediocre and to proclaim its delighted approval of the trivial as though it were the astonishing invention of some genius. You spent longer at the gallery than you had planned, slowed down by sadness, and when at last you left a mourning sort of mood overcame you. The world is suddenly full of wrong directions. But the female Indian singer's voice stops you. You look at the sign on the pub. Charrington's. Toby Ale. But there is a picture on the sign of a blue elephant with a dark brown turbaned youth above its head sitting in front of a scarlet and green howdah. Below the picture is the name of the pub. The Howdah. You cross the street and go into the pub. It is one large, curiously shaped room, being a pentagon of unequal proportions: the two walls that meet at the furthest apex are the longest and the two on either side the shortest. The room is poorly lit, but the murmur of voices that can be heard as an undertone to the Indian singer, whose voice is quite shrilly loud, as well as the dense cigarette smoke that fills the room, immediately creates the impression, which you confirm as soon as you become accustomed to the dim light, that groups of people are sitting at the several tables. A long mahogany counter joins the two further walls like the horizontal stroke in the capital letter A. The other walls have large mirrors on them but the surface of each mirror is dulled and tarnished, so that the reflections that appear in them are indistinct and shadowy, especially when seen through the smoke-filled atmosphere which seems to make things remote and insubstantial. You have no desire for a drink and you are about to leave when the song ends. In the brief relative silence from the tape recorder the voices from the tables are suddenly loud and the language that you hear is Hindustani. By now you can see clearly. Mostly men sit at the tables, all of them brown-skinned, some so dark as to be very nearly black. The whites of the men's eyes are conspicuous when they are turned to look at you. Then you see the young woman who looks surprisingly familiar. She too notices you in the same moment. And because your eyes meet neither can pretend not to have seen the other. You take a step towards her remembering where you have seen her. She keeps her eyes on you and begins to smile. You have seen each other at a party at a common friend's flat, in Highgate, but not met, and where you wondered who this girl was with the thick black hair with a long plait, she looked she came from Gujarat. Yes, you say to each other, exchanging names, it was at that party at Highgate. You glance at the two men with whom she has been sitting. They are middle-aged Indians of a somewhat impoverished background. One of them, seeing himself being stared at, quickly picks up his half-pint in which there is less than an inch of beer left and drinks from it as if it were full. A new song commences on the rather loud speakers, a painfully agitated voice lamenting a lost love. You look at the young woman, whose name you have heard as Sybil, and see that she is folding shut her reporter's notebook and saying something to the men. She rises from her chair. You step back to make room for her to come out of the narrow space between the tables and the two of you begin to walk out as if you were close companions and you had come there at a previously fixed time in order to escort her away. Outside, she stares at you with a smile and says, 'Well?' You say you have been convinced she is from Gujarat, or possibly from Bengal, from Calcutta which is so full of sophisticated girls with a refined sense of culture, but *Sybil*, could she be from Goa? She laughs. 'It's *Isabel!* and I'm from *Peru*.' Then what was she doing among all those Indians? Research, she says, for her thesis. And you begin to walk towards Whitechapel, exchanging history and expectations.

FROM *The Origins of the Self*

2: On Forbidden Territory

Baldev Singh from one of the neighbouring buildings was known as Mona because he cut his hair. In the flat below lived Chandrasekhar whom everyone called Chandru. When Roshan had mastered the English alphabet and begun to make his sister mad by reciting nursery rhymes at the top of his shrill voice he was considered qualified to be moved from Miss Nogueira's hillside school for boys of all ages, with its promise 'English coached,' to a high school run by Catholic missionaries from Italy. Even before he changed schools he had become closer friends with Mona and Chandru, who had the double advantage over Mangal and Rusi of being his own age and also his neighbours. Soon a crowd of them assembled after school every day and walked through the rust-coloured iron bridge over the suburban railway line to play cricket on a dusty field at the foot of a forested hill which the boys had named Pavilion Hill.

Bamboos growing wild at the foot of the hill made a wide arch below which fell a permanent area of shade that became known as the changing room in the pavilion. There was nothing to change into, however, since most of the boys wore the same pair of shorts for months at a time. Nor was there any equipment to store in the pavilion. The team possessed only one bat and that had been cut from a piece of flat wood by Chandru's father; another boy, Raman, usually brought a worn tennis ball, making everyone believe he received it from the English soldiers with whom he was on intimate terms when it was common knowledge that he got the balls from a club run by Hindu businessmen where his father worked as a peon. No one questioned Raman's claim to friendship with the English soldiers as long as he provided the team with tennis balls.

From the pavilion they went out into the dusty field with its clump of coarse grass, thin brown legs sticking out of the dirty shorts. Some of them wore no shirt, exposing a narrow, bony rib-cage that made them look more like scrawny chickens than cricketers, especially when they ran after the ball with a competitive fervour. When he walked out of the pavilion, Roshan always held up his head as he had seen Walter Hammond do in British Movietone News when his father had taken him to see *Pinocchio*. What a big man he was, Walter Hammond. Beautiful white flannel trousers, striding across green grass, which you could see was green in the grey black-and-white picture. Ohyessir, he was Walter Hammond, tall, heavy man who was weightless when he stroked the ball and ran an easy single. No, what am I talking about, I am Bradman! Small man with the eyes of a falcon and the strength of a savage in his arms. Here is Larwood pounding up to the wicket. Here is Maurice Tate. What a nice name, Maurice Tate. Roshan Tate, Hammond is nicer. Roshan Hammond. Ohyessir, here comes Roshan Hammond! Mister number one batsman of all India on the green grass at Lord's. Mister perfect all-rounder, medium pace from the Nursery End, and what a fielder, he runs one hundred yards on the leg boundary, dives through the air for ten feet and, whew, what a catch just inside the boundary one inch from the ground. Beautiful white flannels, shirt of cream-coloured viyella, silk cravat, white buckskin boots on the lovely green grass. Mister perfect number one of all India.

The boys around him, from different parts of India, chased the ball in a dusty confusion, fell upon one another, cursed in Hindustani and made up in English. Shake hands on it, old boy. When they chatted while crossing over the iron bridge, their origin would sometimes make one utter a chauvinistic remark that asserted the pre-eminence of his native province. Niran from Dacca was the most assertive about his beloved Bengal, provoking the South Indian Raman to mock him with a mouthful of Telugu. At such moments, Mona, the hair-cutting Sikh from Amritsar, would hold Roshan's hand, and utter some nonsense in Punjabi. And Chandru from Madras would taunt the Goanese Freddie for taking on European airs when he was as dark-skinned as any Maharashtran. But such provincial rivalries were brief, for soon they were on the cricket field and the game had to be played by English rules.

Although their common language Punjabi should have made Roshan and Mona the closest of friends, Roshan and Chandru became more attached to each other. Mona's parents were ambitious for their son and made him study on some evenings with a private tutor, so that he was often obliged to remain away. Sometimes Roshan and Chandru would abandon the game on the cricket field and climb up Pavilion Hill to look at the view from the eastern slope. Far on the horizon were the foothills of the Western Ghats beyond which was the Deccan Plateau. Looking at the Western Ghats reminded Roshan that he was on an island, as if on a separate colony with its own peculiar composition of an exiled but unified humanity, gazing at some real country, that India over there with its continuously bloody history. From the top of Pavilion Hill they could also see out to the harbour of Bombay and get a glimpse of the ships docked there, among them sometimes a beautifully white sparkling P & O ocean liner at which Roshan and Chandru stared in awe and wonder.

The ship to England! Women with milky-white skin in floral dresses and wide-brimmed straw hats, with a little Pekinese dog on a leash, would be embarking. With them, pink-faced men in double-breasted suits or white linen jackets and loose drill trousers, and officers with a polished leather belt coming from the shoulder diagonally across the stomach, a small stick under the arm. Going home. Home leave. Some maharajah among them, some rich nawab, going to London for Ascot, for Wimbledon. But now the war was on. The War. Mostly soldiers came and went. And rulers who had to rule when people were dying. But to the young Indian boys who had only recently slipped into English as their common language the white ocean liners possessed mystery and power. At first it was an envy of the unknown, and they suppressed that envy by imagining themselves as the English going home to a familiar world of beautiful gardens and King George VI riding in his carriage across London town, as they had seen in magazine pictures. Then, as they grew older and began to understand the language heard among their parents' friends, the ocean liners became an object of nationalistic resentment, so that seeing them made Roshan and Chandru feel more Indian, their sense of the ocean liners as a symbol of the ship of enchantment, with its latent promise of taking one to a land of pulsing beauty, being replaced by a sense of the ocean liners as malevolent carriers, as if each were a ship of death come to ferry them to some overwhelming darkness. And in this ambiguity of intuitive knowledge, which rendered the fascinatingly attractive as a pestilence to be avoided and equated desire with the forbidden, they watched the ships with longing and with loathing, looking away at last towards the continental mass and beginning to talk about the great trains running the length and breadth of India.

FROM *12: Incident on the Grand Trunk Road*

'That's correct,' the Sikh answered. 'Indian sailors took over a ship in which they were setting out for the European war and turned the guns on the British.'

'That's what you heard,' the other Sikh said, 'twenty-one pounders smashing a British ship. It sank in the harbour.'

'The tricolour is flying from the Gateway of India,' his friend said.

Several of the other boys and some men in the restaurant shouted nationalist slogans in Hindi and there were two minutes of unrestrained jubilation. The proprietor came out from behind his counter, looked dreamily across the room, walked to the door and went out. He could be seen strolling on the pavement and gazing in. When the noise subsided, he wandered back in and resumed his position behind the counter where he picked up a newspaper and began to read it.

Roshan and his friends sucked the last of the tea from their saucers and lit their second cigarettes. Waves of a distant murmur had been reaching the restaurant and now a distinct commotion could be heard. The boys paid for their tea and went out. The main road that ran as a central artery in the island and became, when connected to the mainland, the Grand Trunk Road, on which one could travel all the way to the Khyber Pass, was three streets down and the boys, hearing the noise coming from there, hurried in that direction.

A long procession of humanity filled the main road. Poor people pushing hand-carts piled with their belongings, families crowded in bullock carts, their eyes staring out in mortal fear, and thousands others on foot seemed to be making a hurried exit from Bombay. They chattered loudly as they walked, some waited or cried aloud and some merely mimed the gestures of lamentation. A cloud of dust had risen in the air which was heavy also with an increasingly disagreeable smell. People stood in doorways of shops and were crowded in the balconies and windows of the buildings that lined the main road which, though its name changed with each district it traversed, was also known as the Delhi Road.

But the procession was not a response to the nationalist cry, 'Let's march together to Delhi!' They were people in flight. The island had exploded in their face. One instant of terror, and they were fleeing to the security of a larger land.

'What's happened, what's going on?' voices called from the doorways. But mostly the watchers of the exodus were silent, being too amazed by what they saw.

'Communal violence?' Roshan heard a voice ask, echoing his own apprehension. Some small misunderstanding sometimes led to Hindus and Muslims killing each other by the hundred followed by one group fleeing to a safer district. But the humanity that was fleeing from Bombay was clearly of mixed religious composition, for he could recognize Sikhs and Hindus and Muslims in the procession. For once, they were all together pursuing a common aim. What were they all running from, what had happened? Nazi submarines, mutiny, who knew the truth? How quickly the Indian had learned to run from the place he had made his home! A rumour in the air, and he was on the road.

Then another apprehension seized Roshan. What if his family also needed to flee? His parents must be waiting anxiously for him, he ought to run home. Whatever catastrophe had struck Bombay remained a mystery, but he must hurry home and be with his family. Bhatia said there could be nothing to worry about. 'Look,' he said, pointing to the human procession, 'these are all poor, illiterate people.' Adi concurred, and said, 'People like us don't take to the road just like that. We don't even know yet what's happened.'

So they waited on the pavement where the crowd had swelled from more curious people coming from the side streets to see the remarkable sight of thousands of people in flight. Roshan noticed that a group of six or seven young men wearing orange-coloured Gandhi caps pressed near them. A new rumour had sprung up concerning the explosions. The British were leaving India. The Viceroy had come down from Delhi secretly in a carriage attached to the Frontier Mail. Overnight, ships of the Royal Navy had filled up with high-ranking English officials and their families. And then, sailing out, they had fired their guns to smash the Gateway of India.

Adi thought it a naïve explanation and dismissed it. 'Just you wait,' said the man in an orange cap who had conveyed the rumour, 'Gandhi-ji will be proclaiming the Hindu Republic of India on All-India Radio any minute now.'

'What rubbish,' Bhatia said. 'Gandhi-ji never talked of a Hindu Republic.'

The other orange-capped men took offence at this assertion, and one remarked aggressively, 'Let's not even say India, let's use the proper native name, Bharat, Bharatmata, Hindustan, land of the Hindus.'

Bhatia looked askance at Roshan to see how his Muslim friend was reacting to this flow of exclusively Hindu nationalism, and instinctively wanting to show his allegiance to him, answered back to the Hindu claim, 'India is for all Indians, whoever they are.' Seeing that the men in the orange caps stared angrily at him only emboldened him, and he went on, 'Look at the National Congress. It has Pandit Nehru-ji and Maulana Abul Kalam Azad, Hindu and Muslim, sitting side by side, leaders of free India for all Indians. No one ever talked of a Hindu India. Least of all Gandhi-ji.'

'Hey, this man's a Muslim!' one of the angered men exclaimed aloud.

'No, damn it, my name's Premchand Bhatia,' Bhatia shouted to declare his Hindu identity.

'He's lying!' charged the other. 'Pull his pants down, and see if it isn't a cut-off one.'

Bhatia, sensing that the group of orange-capped men was on the verge of becoming a violent little mob, attempted to dart out of the crowd. But two of the men sprang on him and threw him to the ground, and in a moment a third had torn off his pants and a circle of orange-capped men stood gazing down upon his uncircumcised penis. Bhatia yelled obscenities in Hindi. Roshan had become terrified. He imagined himself in Bhatia's situation and a wave of cold fear ran down his body. Seeing the men momentarily absorbed in confirming that Bhatia was a Hindu gave Roshan his chance to slip away, but he did not want to abandon his friend. Adi was making a sign to him to leave but he shook his head in refusal.

The men pulled up Bhatia from the ground and pushed him aside. And now they noticed Adi and Roshan. Frustrated by being proven wrong, they had become more enraged. They stood frozen for a moment, surveying the two boys with eyes that looked murderous. 'We're Parsees,' Adi shouted at them. 'I'm Adi and he's Jamshed.' Roshan was unable to utter a word. The men seemed about to accept Adi's word. The two boys were fairer skinned and taller than Bhatia and looked Parsee. But suddenly one of the men cried aloud, 'He's lying!'

The group made no move towards Adi and Roshan. Adi quickly tore at the buttons on his trousers and pulled out his penis and shouted. 'Parsee, Parsee! Can't you see?' The men stopped. One said almost resignedly. 'Go shove it into your sister's cunt,' and turned away. The others began to follow.

But one of them, remained standing, staring with great curiosity at Roshan. The boy seemed vaguely familiar, as if he had seen him before in some shadowy light. Parsee or Muslim. The man moved closer to Roshan. 'Parsee, didn't you hear!' Roshan attempted to shout but the words were stuck in his throat. Adi had rearranged his trousers and now saw the man menacingly step towards Roshan. Bhatia had also composed himself, managing somehow to tie his torn pants across the waist. The man looked grimly at Roshan and suddenly recalled the image he had been seeing. His sister in the little park with a youth while he stood hidden against the trunk of a tree. And then when they left the park, he had hastened out and taken a good look at Roshan's features under a street-light. The very youth! And not a Parsee, but a Muslim, as his sister had declared.

Bhatia and Adi now stood on either side of Roshan. The man looked back to call to his friends but noticed that the gathering crowd had increased the distance between them while they went searching for some other victim. Obliged to act alone, he suddenly struck out at Roshan, his two fists rapidly pounding Roshan's abdomen and, as he staggered forward, the man struck his rib-cage and then his jaw, sending the boy staggering back. The beating was fast and of vicious ferocity. Before Adi and Bhatia could move to their friend's defence, the man was gone, pushing aside people in his way and shouting to his companions in the distance, 'There's a Muslim here, there's a Muslim here!'

Bhatia began to go after him but Adi held his arm and checked him. 'They'll all be back in a minute and finish him off,' Adi said to Bhatia. Stopping, Bhatia looked back at Roshan and saw him helplessly doubled over, his arms across his stomach, blood dribbling down his chin. 'We should take him to safety first,' Adi said, dodging past a man in his way and going to hold Roshan up. 'Maybe we should take him to Ibrahim,' Bhatia said over the head of the man Adi had just side-stepped past and going to join in the rescue. But Adi had another idea. In the huge and noisy procession of humanity that still continued on the Delhi Road a string of bullock carts was at that moment being driven past. 'Let's get him among those women,' Adi said, pointing to a cart on which stood five or six women in bright pink or purple saris over apple green or aquamarine blue blouses of the type that left the midriff exposed.

The two carried Roshan through the crowd on the pavement shouting, 'Fainted, fainted, please step aside, fainted, fainted!' Reaching the front of the bullock cart, Adi held on to Roshan while Bhatia jumped up into the cart, shouting at the women, 'Quick, quick, there's an injured boy, come on, help, quickly!' The man sitting at the front with his legs sticking out and his bare feet rhythmically beating with his big toes the rear sides of the bullocks to drive them on shouted at Bhatia, 'Hey, donkey go bray in your sister's cunt!' One of the women who had seen the injured boy said loudly, in a scolding voice, 'Hey, Desani, what a way to talk!' But another woman, also touched by the boy's plight, spoke to the driver in his own language, 'Listen you, Desani-Pissani, when you go to hell you'll beg the devil for a donkey to lick the sores on your arse, why don't you do a good deed for a change?' But it was a third woman who achieved the desired result. She simply walked up to the front, threw a stinging slap to the back of Desani's head and, bending towards his ear, shouted, 'Stop right now, goddam sodomist!'

Roshan was put aboard the cart, the women making room for him amidst the heaped luggage that consisted of two rolled-up mattresses, large boxes made of tin, several earthen jars and one empty bird cage.

'What happened?' the women asked, and Bhatia quickly answered, 'Got crushed in the crowd.' The women gazed sadly at Roshan and clicked their tongues. 'Poor thing,' one said, and another, 'Hai, what a pretty boy!'

16: But You

But you are not seven years old when in the still pitch-black night long before dawn you are awoken and for some minutes you wander sleepy-eyed among the rooms where familiar voices are ordering do-this-do-that preparations for some undreamed-of journey. There are sacks and bundles beside doorways and your father's voice is broadcasting instructions to the whole house while he himself rearranges the items in an old leather suitcase. 'Do we need blankets?' your mother's voice asks loudly from one room. 'Do we need more towels?' As if in answer, your sister Zakia starts singing. 'Yes, we do, oh yes we do!' and your father shouts back from another room, 'Just two hand towels, the hosts will provide the rest.' But your grandfather says, 'Better take a blanket or two, just in case.' Your grandmother, who is helping Zakia tie up a bundle of her clothes, picks up her nonsense song and sings, 'A blanket or two, oh yes we do!' There is your aunt Faridah in the kitchen, her eyes in tears from the sharp smoke rising from the brazier, who shouts, 'How many boiled eggs you want to take?' From two rooms away your mother shouts back, 'All of them, there are two dozen in the basket.' From another room your grandfather jokes, 'It's your wedding, Faridah, you take all the eggs!' Your father, whose two fists are pulling at the ends of a cord that he is tying around the old leather suitcase, shouts, 'Don't forget the salt and black pepper.' Your Uncle Mansur is chasing a hen round the courtyard where you go to escape the inexplicable confusion in the rooms. A rooster is crowing aloud vigorously while the hen goes cluck-cluck-cluck as she dashes just out of Uncle Mansur's reach. Uncle Mansur is 15 years old and whenever he sees a dog or a cat or a hen he has to chase it. Completing a second circle round the courtyard, the hen dashes into the house where people, seeing its wild dash around the rooms dodging in and out of the chaos of luggage, clap hands or stamp on the ground or yell at her to chase her away so that she comes dashing back just when Uncle Mansur has reached the door and, confronting him, flaps her wings violently, is momentarily airborne, flies over Uncle Mansur's shoulder, lands in the courtyard, hops and dashes for a few yards and takes off again into the air and alights upon a branch of the guava tree. Cluck-cluck-cluck she goes in her irritation and the rooster, looking confused and panic-stricken but continuing to pretend he is in charge, crows vehemently as if welcoming the dawn. But it must be the middle of the night, for the sky is full of brilliant stars. You hear your father calling Uncle Mansur to help with the luggage. A glow from the house is casting a dim light on the pomegranate bush and the round little globes of the ripening pomegranates look like small lanterns hanging in the air. You put your fingers around a pomegranate, first just to touch its shiny leathery skin like a cricket ball's, but then find yourself clasping the fruit. A little saliva spurts from below your tongue and you feel a sharp edge on your lower front teeth. Your hand has tightened over the pomegranate. A trickle had formed at the corner of your mouth and your hand pulls the fruit free from the branch. You run to a further corner of the courtyard and crouch there in the darkness, tearing at the pomegranate's leathery skin with your teeth. A sharp, sour taste of the unripe fruit pierces your gums and sets your teeth on edge, but you bite deeper and harder and rapidly chew the dry seeds in the scarcely moist flesh. Just then you are being called. Your father and your grandfather and Uncle Mansur are all shouting your name. The rooster stops crowing. You chew, swallow and spit double fast. The fruit is so sour it's pinching your gums. Now your mother's voice is calling too. You stuff the remaining pomegranate into your mouth and chew and spit treble fast and run to the house. It is still far from dawn when the family is parading out of the house and walking to the railway station under the eerie light of the street-lamps. Your mother has made you wear a new pair of navy shorts in which you have neatly tucked a clean white shirt. You are thrilled to be wearing new black boots and cannot take your eyes off your feet as you march along with Uncle Mansur, helping him to carry a large sack that contains several small bundles. You regret it is not daytime and your friends are not in the street to see you in your new boots. Left-right left-right, you march. Your father and grandfather are carrying the large suitcase between them, changing sides from time to time. Inside the suitcase is your new dark blue sweater that your mother knitted a month ago. It has a pattern like two snakes wound together. Already long before sunrise it is hot and you are beginning to sweat. The dust is catching in your throat. But you are going where you will be able to wear your new sweater. Your grandmother and Zakia are walking together. The two are always carrying on some nonsense duet. You hurry along with Uncle Mansur, trying to get out of hearing range from Zakia's nonsense that drives you crazy. Your mother and Aunt Faridah are carrying a basket of food between them. Aunt Faridah is big and slow and reminds you of a cow. You always like sitting in her lap and putting your arms round her neck. She sighs as she walks. She has a sad face. But she cannot be really sad. She is wearing new clothes of red satin so bright and shiny you think it is her blood you are seeing in the dimly lit street. She is going to get married and so she sighs and has a sad face. You will be eating sweet rice on her wedding day. The sour, bitter taste of the unripe pomegranate stays in your mouth but because it is your secret it is therefore a sweeter taste than sweet rice with pistachios and cardamom seeds in it. Next thing you are at the railway station, on the platform under the open sky which is still black and full of stars. You look at the arm of the signal with its red eye. The station master walks up the platform. A lantern with a red light in it swings from his hand. It looks like a red pendulum is swinging from the end of his arm. There is a smell from the fields of wheat growing. There must be goats sleeping nearby, you can smell them too. Then you see the big white eye of the engine coming out of the black distance and becoming a piercing light. Clanking and screeching the engine comes to a halt and lets out a long hiss. It is only pulling three carriages and is coming to stop at a small country station but the noise it makes, you think it is pretending to be at the head of the Frontier Mail coming into Peshawar. Your father and grandfather are hurrying to the door of a carriage. Uncle Mansur has already jumped on to the train before it comes to a stop and has claimed a long bench in the third-class compartment, an act that proves unnecessary since the carriage is nearly empty. There are only two men in it. They wear beards and look pious and it is decided that your mother, grandmother, aunt and sister need not travel separately in the women's compartment. You run to a window seat. You plan to put your head out if Zakia and your grandmother start their nonsense duets. You are going to listen to the rushing air instead. Then off you move with a sudden jolt and clank with the engine going chuff-chuff shoo-shoo-shooo. Warm air rushes in. You look out of the window but can see nothing in the darkness. Chukha-chukha chukha-chukha, the engine settles down to a slow rhythm and ticka-tick ticka-tick go the wheels of the carriage. You doze off. The train stops and starts several times. Your father decides to eat a boiled egg although your mother says it is not yet time for breakfast. Everyone wants to eat a boiled egg. The train stops at a station where there is nobody. Then after a long run when the wheels go cutta-cut cutta-cut the train slows down to a crawl while another train goes thundering past. 'That's the Mail, that's the Mail,' Uncle Mansur shouts. It has many carriages. They are brightly lit up. You see hundreds of faces rush past. You think you are looking at the cinema screen in the darkness. The thunder suddenly stops, the train has disappeared and it is blacker dark outside than it was before. Your little train resumes its earlier slower rhythm, chukha-chukha chukha-chukha, and then begins to screech and puff and put on a big show. You arrive at a large station and your father is shouting from the window at a porter and the porter jumps into the carriage before the train stops. Soon everything is being transferred to the longer train on the opposite platform. The train seems full, overflowing with people. It is so long you cannot see its beginning or end. It has one carriage that is painted silver. Uncle Mansur tells you that it is air-conditioned. Always cold inside even when the train is going through the desert in the middle of the day. It is reserved for the English. The Governor of the Punjab travels in it when he goes to Bombay to catch the ship to England. You look at the mysterious silver carriage with its closed windows. Suddenly there is a commotion on the platform. Two English soldiers are marching across the platform. Behind them walks an Englishwoman, followed by four porters carrying brown leather suitcases. Tall and straight she is with a green pill-box hat on her wavy blonde hair and a beautiful white neck like ivory. She wears a light lime-coloured coat over a frock of printed cotton. You can see red and green flowers and leaves as the skirt of her frock swings out and about. Her calves and ankles stand out below the coat. Her green high-heeled shoes match her hat and the green on her frock. She walks quickly, decisively. Her hair bounces up from her shoulders with each step, her chin rises and falls. But her eyes, blue and unblinking, are seeing nothing. Another English soldier marches behind the porters. For a minute or so every eye is upon the Englishwoman. One of the soldiers opens the door of the silver carriage. The Englishwoman enters the compartment. The platform is again busy with Indian families arriving and departing. The Englishwoman's luggage has gone in, her door has been locked, the English soldiers stand outside the next door of the silver carriage where the porters are taking some of the luggage. You are told to go with the women to the women's compartment in which there is more room. You refuse, stamping your foot on the ground. You see dust rise from your new boots, and so stamp both feet hard on the ground. No, you won't travel in the women's compartment. You squeeze in with the men. Some people are still trying to get off while many more are pushing in with their luggage. And some who are staying on the train are calling out to the tea vendors on the platform. The men are tall and lean. Many have beards and turbans and are wearing clothes of coarse cotton. Four of them are sharing a hookah which is filling the compartment with smoke which smells almost sweet but which irritates your eyes. Everyone is talking about the Englishwoman. What is she doing in the middle of the Punjab? She must be the governor's daughter. No, no, an actress. What actress, what are you talking about, where is the studio for the shooting? Your shooting-looting can be done outside too, on location it's called. No, she is the Pindi district commissioner's wife. What, and has an escort of three soldiers? Exactly why she has to be higher up, royalty perhaps. There is not enough room in the carriage for everyone and so you make a deal with Uncle Mansur to take turns to sit down. He wants to stand first so that he can be by the door when the train starts to move. You are staring out at the crowd on the platform when you see the people are slowly passing out of your sight and you realize that the train has begun to move. There is none of the laboured chuff-chuff of the smaller train. This one is imperceptibly easing out and then gliding quite smoothly and just when the platform is about to disappear there is a burst of powerful acceleration. The smoke from the hookah that had been hanging in the compartment and drifting about the ceiling rushes out. You look out in wonder at the dark grey land, amazed to be sitting in the most famous train in all India with an Englishwoman with a neck like ivory three carriages ahead of you. You have never experienced such speed. A thin line of light appears on the eastern horizon. There is a change of sound from the wheels of the carriage before yours and you lean towards the window, trying to get a glimpse out past the crowd of men. '*The Chenab, the Chenab*,' people are saying even before the wheels of your carriage go ctunk-ctunk over the bridge and you manage to see a gleam on the water's surface of the broad, dark river. But soon the sky is lit up and you are racing across the cultivated land, green with cotton and wheat and rice, you are crossing another beautiful river, the Jhelum, and the land is beginning to undulate and tilt, for there far to the east and the north, beyond the horizon, are the great snowy mountains, the Karakoram Range and the Hindu Kush.

FROM *SELECTED POEMS*

The Loss of India

I

Eagles cartwheeled above the illuminations
of Independence Day, the dogs sniffed at
the electric bulbs which sizzled like fat.

The tall grass the monsoons left on the mountains
was aflame like corn in the setting August sun.
Two stones collided, sparked. India began to burn.

II

At Mahatma Gandhi's prayer meeting,
under Asoka's wheel on the tricolour,
the air intoning religious verses,
a man stood in the scabbard of the crowd,
a machine gun at the tip of his zealous tongue.
What well-tutored doves the politicians
had released into the skies above Delhi
had already blackened with the soot
of communal hatred. The air chanted
the Bhagvat Gita, the Koran and the Bible.
Gandhi nodded, warmed by his goat's-milk diet,
a Moses and a Mohammed thinned
to the bones of a self-denying innocence,
mild as foam on the tortured crest of his
people's violence, straight as a walking stick
on the savage contours of his country.

Gandhi was assassinated when he was coming to his prayer meeting not during it as Part II of this poem might suggest—Zulfikar Ghose: notes on the Poems, *Selected Poems,* Karachi: Oxford University Press, 1991.

When the bullets hit him, his body was cut
into the bars of a jail he had never left,
his stomach shrivelled in another hunger fast.

III

A boy in the street, sulking in his boots,
kicked at stones and pouted his lip at crows.
There was the shade to retreat to, the doors

to be behind. But the pride of mountains
annoyed him, the neighing peaks loud
with thunder exhaling the smoke of monsoon clouds.

His nostrils twitched like a cow's when a fly
sits there. For the sea air of Bombay was
salt, dry. And how could he describe his loss?

How desperately calm the landscapes were!
His heart, become a stone in the catapult
of his mind, could have struck the foolish adult

passions where murder and faith excluded each
other. Though eagles still hung like electric fans
in the sky and the rocks suggested permanence,

the blood in the earth was not poultry-yard slaughter.
The boy cushioned his heart in the moss
of withdrawal for his India and his youth were lost.

The Alien

There's an empathy between the trees
and me in England, an air between
us that's constantly beneficent.

With a look, the English transplant me
elsewhere, though their civil tolerance
permits the air of drought between us.

I frequent deserted common-land
where I'm friendly with sightless things, most
of all the community of grass.

The Water Carrier

A man the colour of dry earth, a stone
tied to the air with a loin cloth, carries
his goatskin bag of water like an oversize
wart permanently growing from his back:

a floating oasis in the Saharas
of thirst, the liquid shadow of a palm tree:
the water carrier slips through the empty
afternoon streets like an underground stream.

Where the sun drives him like a mule
towards the troughs of the horizon's haze.
And the stars at night which are also always
maddeningly hot like the eyes of women.

Quite in order, then, that man should be
an itinerant element, a water
cloud moving over the earth, his feet on fire
as they nibble the desert sands:

even if after his long-distance haul
the water carrier finds his own thirst
the greatest of all, a multi-tongued curse
in the saliva drought of unending desert.

On Owning Property in the USA

On my land in the middle of America the wind blows
through the cedar trees and the chickenhawks
stay up in the sky as if they were paid
an hourly wage and the hummingbird throws

its compulsive nervous body from the mimosa
to the wisteria and all kinds of other country
things go on and daily I walk on my property
to check the armadillo holes or close a

gap in a fence knowing what happens on this land
is my business with the free blue skies
over it and air that in California once
above an orchid's lip held a bee suspended

I've put down nasturtium seeds planted squash
okra and cantaloupe for this summer also
tomatoes and two rows of corn and some beans
and trimmed the camellia bush

and that's what you'd call pastoral or
bucolic or arcadian and in the nature
of things universal and eternal having
roots and the right kind of image in the lore

of the land that from Tennessee west
is strummed out on banjo and guitar
were it not for rattlesnakes and spiders
lying in the underbrush and you guessed

it mister I have extermination problems
and must simultaneously poison and preserve
such are the country's contradictions and
such the ambiguity of all dreams.

Lady Macbeth's Farewell to Scotland

I. The Shadow Woman

She haunted the street of the evil surgeons
and stared through windows at masked men
bent over bloody wombs. Large-bosomed nurses
held up gloved hands dripping red and the ceiling
light above them looked like a bleeding sun.
Women from the western isles, from their
stone cottages on shores where the wind was

always cold, chanted down the street their song
of ravens and of the deceptions of summer.
High-tech security sealed off the genetics lab.
Alarms were ringing, but it was only the guards
testing the system. Men moved with alacrity,
spoke to one another in code on walky-talkies,
video cameras scanned the environment, but

as the butterfly sucks from the milkweed a toxin
that keeps off predator birds so had she drunk
the shadow of the yew and become protected
from light. Though the island women stood blocking
the clinic of defunct genes, they could not stop
her. They held up their lanterns. A shadow fell
in a room where genetic engineers experimented.

IV. Exotic Nights

Ten thousand children were born in Dolores Hidalgo
between February and October. After the spring rains
the hot, dry months nourished the fields of sunflowers
and ten thousand flowers sprang up from each acre.
O Lady of Shadows, you were vilely illuminated!
The warrior on horseback had reached the shores of
that same lake where illicit lovers rented cabins

and pointed his sword at the water glowing pink
in the sunset. The medieval castle in the lake had long
been abandoned. Lady Macbeth roamed among the tall
sunflowers, throwing upon them the shadow of her
feverish head. There was a grinding noise in the air,
as of blades in a machine, a pulverizing of seeds, and
a bitter powdery dust floated across the horizon

where the evening's last flock of crows was falling
from the sky upon the silhouette of sycamores.
O Lady of Shadows, what source of light vexed you then?
You were crazed with the news of the ten thousand births
and began to trample the sunflowers. You spat out
the seeds. And when the sun went down and the light
turned grey you saw the crows rise up, applauding the night.

VII. Among Perfumed Landscapes

There is a continent of perfumed landscapes where hummingbirds
probe the throats of flowers for nectar and once annually
under a full moon an orchid blooms and pollinates.
O I've received a lot of information about the world!
The young outnumber the old there. Plastic surgeons
own islands with satellite dishes on hilltops and are tuned
to the planet's entertainment. Beauty is sculpted

in sterile rooms where women shed wrinkled skin.
Models parade furs in refrigerated salons, flaunting
long, tanned legs while tauntingly swinging mink and fox
at bejewelled old ladies pulsing with a cosmetic glow.
These are lands freed from memory. Ghosts of extinct
tribes go unnoticed here. Compulsively, in uncounted circles,
men walk in the squares at sunset, confused by the jasmine's

scent. The young throng the beaches and, stung
by desire, each sucks the venom from the other's flesh.
But these are also lands with perpetually frozen mountains.
I know I shall come to a valley with its white-crested river
of melted snow and discover the source of illusions.
There, I shall dream a life in which I walk like a somnambulist
in the unending corridors of the castle of the dead.

Kaleem Omar

Born in pre-Partition Lucknow, Kaleem Omar was educated at Sherwood in Nainital, Burn Hall in Abbottabad, and at London University. He started writing poetry in 1955. He describes Taufiq Rafat* as the mentor who helped him discover his voice and hone his craft. Kaleem Omar believes that the meaning of a poem at its first level should be very clear and maintains that although poetry must appeal to the mind's eye through imagery, it is principally for the ear. He writes with a consciousness of this vocal tradition which has seen a comparatively recent revival in the West, but has always been a part of Pakistan's literary life. The poets he admires, reads and memorizes are a legion ranging from the classic poets of the distant past, to twentieth century writers such as T.S. Eliot, W.H. Auden, Dylan Thomas, Philip Larkin, Richard Wilbur, Robert Lowell and Sylvia Plath. His work has appeared in prestigious local magazines, British and Commonwealth periodicals, and various anthologies including *Pieces of Eight* (1971), *Pakistani Literature: The Contemporary English Writers* (1978) and *The Worlds of the Muslim Imagination*. He edited the much acclaimed *Wordfall: Three Pakistani Poets,* consisting of work by him, Taufiq Rafat and Maki Kureishi*. All were considered Pakistan's finest poets at the time, though Omar's poetry was more political. Both Kaleem Omar and Taufiq Rafat held gatherings in Lahore to help younger poets such as Athar Tahir* and Shuja Nawaz*. This led to readings at the Quaid-i-Azam University and poetry workshops in various Lahore colleges. Kaleem Omar took part in poetry readings during the Islamic Summit in 1974 and did several poetry programmes for the radio while Shahid Hosain* was Director General; his work has been broadcast in the United States and India. He moved to Karachi in the 1980s and soon became a distinguished journalist. He often included poems in his weekly column for the evening newspaper *The Star*. He is now an editor at *The News*.

Trout

By first light we are at the river's edge,
unsnarling tackle. Hands, with a new day's life in them,
choose favourite spoons and pocket sweets
for the thirst that will come later. Spacing out
along the boulder strewn bank,
we agree to meet for lunch sharp at noon
and leave the beer in a safe place underwater.
I head for Cunningham's Pool,
eager for the big one that got away last year.

The rock that marks the place is wet and huge.
Grass, too rough to lie back on,
surrounds three sides;
the fourth juts darkly against the water.
Giving it the right degree of wrist,
I test my preparations and make a cast.
The line snaps out, sings thinly in coniferous air
and curves down short
of the far side. My arm feels good;

and breath steams with anticipation. The eyes
jump to the swirl where the sink goes in.
I wonder how big the big one will look
in a photograph. Will it
be a record for the valley? Will I be the only one
who does not have to lie? I reel in empty
and sense no presence deeper than this morning.
Sunlight creeps down the face
of the mountain opposite, tips the water

with the stirrings of a wispy sky. A fast cloud
darkens the river's surface,
cancels my shadow, moves away. A moment happens.
I lose a spoon, replace it with a fly
and watch the line more carefully.

It tugs—once, twice, again. I have a bite.
A good beginning. Hours later,
I am still doing all right. It is something to know
the hand retains its skill from other times.

I came here first with father. He is dead now.
The worms that hooked his flesh
no longer smell. He thought I was lost once,
on that first trip, and I heard his large voice
echo and call till I was safe. I have carried
the sound of those words for twenty years.
But I am blank now,
oblivious to everything except the need
to maintain silence, keep the tip in place

and wait, never knowing when the next one will come,
for the heart-stopping pull
that signals something alive at the other end.
It is time. The sun is overhead and the brown beauty
from last year has escaped again.
But there are others. I heft my catch
and trudge upstream, thinking of nothing much—
not a bad morning's work and a lazy blue
afternoon of love to look forward to.

Photograph

Bring her into focus, while the sun
is still in that quadrant of the sky
you wish the light to come from, and to be safe,
set the distance for infinity.
The country this encompasses between
that far horizon and the nearer green
will encompass her, and give you time
to fill the details in, to bring the scene
to the right moment at that aperture.

Tilt her face, ask her gently now,
ask that she hold still within
the stillness you demand, then watch her lean
against that castle wall of quarried stone,
where the gun suggests the picturesque
was once something else, and where the dead
were propped, and those trumpets blown.

The Hunters in the Snow

Ankle-deep in snow, they loom above the village,
their spears at slope, their thick bodies muffled
against the friendly cold, and swinging from their belts
the leashes of their dogs, lean animals who follow
closely at their heels, who do as they are told,
some tense with expectation from the hunt,
some drenched with blood, and some
too small to be of real consequence,
though trained to fetch a bone for these men
who have killed before, will kill again,
and make a feasting of it until the countryside
is as denuded as their hearts, as still
within the forest as it is outside.
But down in that village, there is life
busy with the citizens it sends across the ice,
a man with a fire-load of wattles on his head,
a woman with a pail, and on the frozen pond
the games of the children, a boy with a stick
raised above the ball he prepares to flick.

'Hunters in the Snow' is a painting by Pieter Bruegel.

Himalayan Brown

It wasn't much of a way to die
the way we got that old bear

smoking him out of the cave
he had occupied all winter

sighting down from a hide
halfway up the slope

our cheeks cold against the stocks
of our guns as we waited

for him to show.
We heard him well before we saw

that dopey looking head
clear of the smoke.

Every gun in the party
fired at once. No one

was taking any chances.
We had heard enough about bears

to know what could happen.
So we aimed

for the centre of the neck
not making the mistake

of thinking anywhere else
could stop him.

There was no time to notice
how bewildered he looked

in the chilly air.
We dropped him good and dead

and made a job of it.
Afterwards he just lay there.

Winter Term

There is early morning frost
in the quadrangle, and the wind
has chilled the bell
hanging from its swing.
The conker season is over,
winter is setting in.

I scurry into the common room,
where the year's trophies lie.
The clock on the mantelpiece
is in its usual place,
hour and minute hands have ceased
to work, no chime is heard.

The other boys are also here,
the magician's son, the school
yo-yo champion, the clever one.
They shift a little to let me in,
the ambit of their circle,
rearranged, says it is listening.

I have no glad tidings,
no good luck charm for anyone,
but still they look at me.
I am the weather man, I bring
the frost and gravel of the yard
into this room within,

and look again at the stairs,
the panelled walls, the names
a hundred scouting knives
have carved into the grain.
Cross this one out, and that,
because of news from home,

and let the rest remain
anonymous. The guns of forty four
silently proclaim
the term has come to an end.
Your pen-knife adds another friend
to its roll of honour.

The Fifteenth Century

They have set up a committee
to prepare us for our entry
into the Fifteenth Century.

I wonder what it will be like,
this era we are about to see.
Will printing be invented?
Will someone try to prove
the world is round and moves
around the sun? Will Galileo
be hung for his temerity?

Maybe I've got it wrong.
Maybe some of these
things have already happened.

General Ziaul Haq's Martial Law coincided with the turn of the fourteenth century AH. This poem was written in response to a headline in a national English daily.

I recall reading somewhere
that a couple of men had landed
in a shining module on the moon.
And any fool knows when that occurred.
So all I can say is that the Fifteenth Century
had better end, and soon.

A Troubadour's Life

I've known the highs and the lows,
Monsoon skies, perpetual snows,
Deserts that flame like lava flows,
Parched plains and old plateaus,
Mountain streams where mica gleams
Like fool's gold to tempt the senses,
Mocking all the mind's defences,
Steep tracks that wend their way
Through regions where, at the end of day,
Night falls like a sinking stone.

Mine has been a troubadour's life.
Tossed about this way and that,
A flurry of hopes set adrift
Upon a sea of ebbs and flows,
Where passion is the thing that goes—
A life of looking and not finding,
Or not looking and not minding,
Of seeking beauty for itself,
In pelting rain and searing sun,
Not much else have I done.

Age itself is a fearsome thing,
An inexorable diminishing
Of feelings taken for granted once,
Though, of course, I still pretend
It's made me wise in others' eyes,

As if pretending were enough;
And love weren't ephemeral stuff,
As easily brushed aside as moss,
As transient as candy floss,
Where did it go, whose is the loss?

Such twists and turns of destiny,
Such reckonings have I known,
A look here, a moment there,
Absences in autumnal air,
A memory of gilded wings
Flitting through a secret glade,
The feel of snow upon the face,
A kingfisher swooping down
Like iridescence upon a stream,
Places to lie back and dream.

Certainties come but once,
And destinations slip away
Like tumbleweed across the prairie,
Escaping into that canyon where
Hibernation has its lair—
A place of more shade than light,
Of wounded things that never again
Will soar as they used to soar,
A place where the familiar sound
Of laughter is heard no more.

Those days I knew still unwind
Like flashbacks upon the mind,
Tricking it into believing
There really were horizons once
Beyond which lay happiness,
That much mentioned commodity—
Days spent listening to the wind
Hissing through tall stands of pine,
Setting every needle aquiver,
Days of thinking they were mine.

And I have travelled far among
The words of poets through the years,
Plucking from the air the same
Evocations, the same songs,
Songs that haunt me even now
Like echoes from another world
into which the past's been hurled,
There, to disappear forever
As if it never had existed
And all of its happenings not been.

My thoughts recall misty eyes,
Sad cafes and empty piers,
Winter beaches stretching away
Beyond the point of no return,
Dark their sand, cold their spray,
Waterfalls and dragon cave
Going back to earlier times,
Heedless days spent on the run,
The distant sound of an ancient bell.
What it knows, it will not tell.

Night Music

Music from beyond the door
Envelops the moist night air,
Like a beloved's flair
For wreaking devastation
Once enveloped me.
From that recollection
To this place of disaffection,
The intervening years
Stretch like a renunciation
Eating into the soul.
Nothing else matters now,
No plan, no material goal.

A faint, descending note,
From a half-remembered tune,
Seeps, as if by rote,
Through the casual clatter
Of chairs scraping,
People chattering over dinner;
Someone arguing politics.
It lingers in the mind,
Burrowing into memories
Best left unexplored.
There is no serendipity here,
No happy song to sing.

Thinking of what has gone,
Fortuitous fireworks
Above distant hills
Steeped in local history,
The sharp surprise of sunrise
Transforming a dark waterfall
Into quicksilver, riches
Beyond human reckoning,
I think of how simple a matter
It would have been then
To disappear forever
Into that incandescence.

But one is never anywhere
One wants to be,
Always somewhere else,
With someone else.
Once, in the mountains,
In an all-encompassing valley
Redolent with the tang
Of approaching spring,
I thought I'd got it right,
Could almost sense an answer
Rising, taking wing.
Where it went, I don't know.

Now, in a very different time,
A very different place,
I sense something again —
An echo from the past,
Invading the mind,
Falling, fading, enfolding.
It speaks of love recalled
Years down the road.
This is another world,
Where even the wind keens
Like a lament for the dead,
The days that lie ahead.

So many I knew are gone,
Yet the sky tomorrow
Will be the same pristine blue,
As if nothing had changed,
And that woman I once saw
Walking a winter beach —
Her hair a dark tangle
Against the Atlantic wind,
Her eyes twin pools
Of unapproachable pain —
Were still walking there,
Headed for nothing, nowhere.

Is recollection, then,
The name of life's old game?
Is that all that remains?
Somewhere, in that beyond,
Rain is drumming on the roof;
Somewhere, bedtime stories
Are still being told,
Tales of pirates and treasure,
Sending delicious shivers
Down childhood's spine.
I try summoning it, forgetting
It is no longer mine.

What is that tune, that music
Behind that creaky door?
It's memory running wild,
That train whistling down,
Those shifting, whispering sands,
Seven days, seven days,
That river of no return,
Sometimes so peaceful,
Sometimes so wild and free,
The breeze and I, Rose Marie —
All songs from the past,
Words to break the heart.

Jocelyn Ortt Saeed

Australian by birth, Pakistani by marriage, Jocelyn Ortt Saeed was born in and educated in Brisbane. She was introduced to the poetry of Iqbal and Tagore by a group of Pakistani students which included her future husband, at the University of Queensland. She became a teacher and stopped in Pakistan on her way to do post-graduate studies in Germany and decided to get married. She did her teaching diploma in Language and Literature in Munich, however, before she started to live in a sugar-mill colony, with her husband on the edge of Pakistan's Thar desert: this prompted her poem 'Where No Road Goes'. In fact she started to write poetry to help her adjust to a new environment. Later, at Australia's Macquarie University she attended a poetry workshop conducted by Margaret Diessendorf, the editor of *Poetry Australia,* who also became a close friend. Her poem 'For Alys Faiz' the English born wife of the Urdu poet Faiz Ahmed Faiz encapsulates Jocelyn's multi-cultural, multi-faceted world. In Pakistan she has continued to work as an educationist, poet and an activist for women's rights and human rights. She is on the executive committee of several organizations, and was on the Commission for Peace through Literature for the 1996 EPRA conference in Brisbane. There her work was read on the radio and her poems are now on the internet.

She has participated in many other literary conferences, and has published several collections including *Selected Poems* (1986), which has an accompanying cassette. The poems reproduced here appear in both *Burning Bush* (1994), and her forthcoming collection *Accident at an Exhibition* (1997). She is also putting together a bilingual Urdu-English book of her verse.

FROM ***Burning Bush***

Where No Road Goes

I will go where no road goes
and the road will go with me.
I'll greet you in the sunrise
when the sunset sets me free.

I will dream in the fields of green
till their ears grow gold in me,
till you appear to harvest grain
grown in the desert sea.

I will sit by the hut of mud
till walls break down in me,
till new vines grow through memory
of flower and bird and bee.

I will climb the distant peaks
till the world turns pale in me,
till the lone bird of the wasteland
sings of spring in my withered tree.

I will sing till my song is sung
wherever you meet me—
on road, or field, or mountain,
in I, or thou, or we.

I will go where no road goes
and the road will go with me
to bring to you at sunrise
the now in eternity.

For Alys Faiz

The sky is a pale parchment.
The balcony pots
washed by drizzling
persistent rain.

I hear my Faiz tape,
hum Schubert Lieder,
read Ratushinska
and go over the hours.

Here's your piece for today
and your Human Rights' Letter.
We talk on the phone,
till I close up the house
and go with the wind to where you are.

In the gauze room we sit
drinking coffee and talking
how it was when I came
long ago to see Faiz.

We look through the gauze
to the garden of wings
where the scent of England's
in trees and shrubs.
And silence seems
for the sake of speech.

This speech is our hope
that we might be changed
and respond to the need
of fish beached on dry land.

Bapsi Sidhwa

Born in Karachi, Bapsi Sidhwa has spent most of her life in Lahore, which provides the backdrop to most of her fiction. She was educated privately at home, on the doctor's advice, after contracting polio as a child. Books, daydreams and story-telling became her great companions. Later she graduated from Kinnaird College, Lahore, did social work and represented Pakistan in the Asian Women's Congress in 1974. An admirer of Dickens, Tolstoy, and Naipaul, she started writing in her twenties, after her three children were born. She became a committed feminist while working on a novel which was later published as *The Bride* (1982) about a city-bred girl who is married into her father's tribe in the barren mountain country of Kohistan. However, it was Bapsi Sidhwa's first novel *The Crow Eaters* (1978) about the incorrigible Freddy Junglewalla and his outrageous mother-in-law which revealed her great gift for comedy. The book became the first major novel to be internationally published focusing on the Parsee community to which Bapsi Sidhwa belongs. She now divides her time between Pakistan and the United States, where she has taught at several prestigious American universities. She was a Bunting Fellow at Radcliffe and held an award from America's National Endowment of the Arts and received the $100,000 Lila Wallace-Readers Digest Award in 1993. Her third novel *Ice-Candy-Man* (1988), published as *Cracking India* (1991) in the United States, about Partition is her most important work to date and combines the humour of *The Crow Eaters* and the noise, colour and violence of Lahore portrayed in *The Bride*. The book was named Notable Book of the Year by *The New York Times* and won the 1991 Literature Prize in Germany. She went on to write *The American Brat* (1994) which follows the misadventures of a Pakistani girl in the United States. Bapsi Sidhwa has been showered with literary honours in Pakistan, including The Pakistan Academy of Letters Award, the Patras Bokhari Award and she has been decorated with the Sitara-e-Imtiaz (Star of Distinction). Her work has been translated into French, Russian, Urdu, and German. She was a Visiting Scholar at the Rockefeller Foundation in Bellagio, Italy. She is on the board of directors of *Inprint* in Houston. In 1997 she was appointed Distinguished Writer-in-Residence and Professor of English at Mount Holyoke College in Massachussetts.

Ice-Candy-Man describes the creation of Pakistan through the eyes of Lenny, a canny, endearing Parsee child with a leg paralyzed by polio. Lenny roams Lahore in her pram, accompanied by Ayah, her beautiful nanny and plays with Ayah's many admirers including the vendor, Ice-Candy-Man. The novel links Lenny's growing up with the changing political climate at the approach of Independence; the metamorphosis of Ice-Candy-Man from an entertaining street character into a thug, then a poet/pimp symbolizes the loss of innocence and the brutalization of society. The manner in which Bapsi Sidhwa describes the horrors of Partition, but never loses sight of human foibles, absurdities and qualities makes this a remarkable work. The linguistic strategy of Ice-Candy-Man is also a milestone for the Pakistani novel: it successfully employs an English narrative which captures the Pakistani sound: the English speaking Lenny incorporates both Americanisms and Indo-Pakistani phraseology and happily translates her multi-lingual world by converting Urdu/Punjabi/Gujrati conversations into English.

FROM *Ice-Candy-Man*

FROM *Chapter 1*

My world is compressed. Warris Road, lined with rain gutters, lies between Queens Road and Jail Road: both wide, clean, orderly streets at the affluent fringes of Lahore.

Rounding the right-hand corner of Warris Road and continuing on Jail Road is the hushed Salvation Army wall. Set high, at eight-foot intervals, are the wall's dingy eyes. My child's mind is blocked by the gloom emanating from the wire-mesh screening the oblong ventilation slits. I feel such sadness for the dumb creature I imagine lurking behind the wall. I know it is dumb because I have listened to its silence, my ear to the wall.

Jail Road also harbours my energetic electric-aunt and her adenoidal son…large, slow, inexorable. Their house is adjacent to the den of the Salvation Army.

Opposite it, down a bumpy, dusty, earth-packed drive, is the one-and-a-half-room abode of my godmother. With her dwell her docile old husband and her slavesister. This is my haven. My refuge from the perplexing unrealities of my home on Warris Road.

A few furlongs away Jail Road vanishes into the dense bazaars of Mozang Chungi. At the other end a distant canal cuts the road at the periphery of my world.

Lordly, lounging in my briskly rolling pram, immersed in dreams, my private world is rudely popped by the sudden appearance of an English gnome wagging a leathery finger in my ayah's face. But for keen reflexes that enable her to pull the carriage up short there might have been an accident: and blood spilled on Warris Road. Wagging his finger over my head into Ayah's alarmed face, he tut-tuts: 'Let her walk. Shame, shame! Such a big girl in a pram! She's at least four!'

He smiles down at me, his brown eyes twinkling intolerance.

I look at him politely, concealing my complacence. The

Englishman is short, leathery, middle-aged, pointy-eared. I like him.

'Come on. Up, up!' he says, crooking a beckoning finger.

'She not walk much … she get tired,' drawls Ayah. And simultaneously I raise my trouser cuff to reveal the leather straps and wicked steel callipers harnessing my right boot.

Confronted by Ayah's liquid eyes and prim gloating, and the triumphant revelation of my callipers, the Englishman withers.

But back he bounces, bobbing up and down. 'So what?' he says, resurrecting his smile. 'Get up and walk! Walk! You need the exercise more than other children! How will she become strong, sprawled out like that in her pram? Now, you listen to me…' he lectures Ayah, and prancing before the carriage which has again started to roll says, 'I want you to tell her mother…'

Ayah and I hold our eyes away, effectively dampening his good-Samaritan exuberance…and wagging his head and turning about, the Englishman quietly dissolves up the driveway from which he had so enthusiastically sprung.

The covetous glances Ayah draws educate me. Up and down, they look at her. Stub-handed twisted beggars and dusty old beggars on crutches drop their poses and stare at her with hard, alert eyes. Holy men, masked in piety, shove aside their pretences to ogle her with lust. Hawkers, cart-drivers, cooks, coolies and cyclists turn their heads as she passes, pushing my pram with the unconcern of the Hindu goddess she worships.

Ayah is chocolate-brown and short. Everything about her is eighteen years old and round and plump. Even her face. Full-blown cheeks, pouting mouth and smooth forehead curve to form a circle with her head. Her hair is pulled back in a tight knot.

And, as if her looks were not stunning enough, she has a rolling bouncy walk that agitates the globules of her buttocks under her cheap colourful saris and the half-spheres beneath her short sari-blouses. The Englishman no doubt had noticed.

We cross Jail Road and enter Godmother's compound. Walking backwards, the buffalo-hide water-pouch slung from his back, the waterman is spraying the driveway to settle the dust for evening visitors. Godmother is already fitted into the bulging hammock of her easy-chair and Slavesister squats on a low cane stool facing the road. Their faces brighten as I scramble out of the pram and run towards them. Smiling like roguish children, softly clapping hands they chant, *'Langer deen! Paisay ke teen! Tamba mota, pag mahin!'* Freely translated, 'Lame Lenny! Three for a penny! Fluffy pants and fine fanny!'

Flying forward I fling myself at Godmother and she lifts me on to her lap and gathers me to her bosom. I kiss her, insatiably, excessively, and she hugs me. She is childless. The bond that ties her strength to my weakness, my fierce demands to her nurturing, my trust to her capacity to contain that trust—and my loneliness to her compassion—is stronger than the bond of motherhood. More satisfying than the ties between men and women.

I cannot be in her room long without in some way touching her. Some nights, clinging to her broad white back like a bug, I sleep with her. She wears only white khaddar saris and white khaddar blouses beneath which is her coarse bandage-tight bodice.

In all the years I never saw the natural shape of her breasts.

Somewhere in the uncharted wastes of space beyond, is Mayo Hospital. We are on a quiet wide veranda running the length of the first floor. The cement floor is shining clean.

Col. Bharucha, awesome, bald, as pink-skinned as an Englishman, approaches swiftly along the corridor. My mother springs up from the bench on which we've been waiting.

He kneels before me. Gently he lifts the plaster cast on my dangling right leg and suddenly looks into my eyes. His eyes are a complex hazel. They are direct as an animal's. He can read my mind.

Col. Bharucha is cloaked in thunder. The terrifying aura of his renown and competence are with him even when he is without his posse of house surgeons and head nurses. His thunder is reflected in my mother's on-your-mark attentiveness. If he bends, she bends swifter. When he reaches for the saw on the bench she reaches it first and hands it to him with touching alacrity. It is a frightening arm's-length saw. It belongs in a wood-shed. He withdraws from his pockets a mallet, a hammer and a chisel.

The surgeon's pink head, bent in concentration, hides the white cast. I look at my mother. I turn away to look at a cloudless sky. I peer inquisitively at the closed windows screening the large general ward in front of me. The knocks of the hammer and chisel and the sawing have ceased to alarm. I am confident of the doctor's competence. I am bored. The crunch of the saw biting into plaster continues as the saw is worked to and fro by the surgeon. I look at his bowed head and am arrested by the splotch of blood just visible on my shin through the crack in the plaster.

My boredom vanishes. The blood demands a reaction. 'Um…' I moan dutifully. There is no response. 'Um… Um…' I moan, determined to draw attention.

The sawing stops. Col. Bharucha straightens. He looks up at me and his direct eyes bore into my thoughts. He cocks his head, impishly defying me to shed crocodile tears. Caught out I put a brave face on my embarrassment and my non-existent pain and look away.

It is all so pleasant and painless. The cast is off. My mother's guilt-driven attention is where it belongs—on the steeply fallen arch of my right foot. The doctor buckles my sandal and helps me from the bench saying, 'It didn't hurt now, did it?' He and my mother talk over my head in cryptic monosyllables, nods and signals. I am too relieved to see my newly released foot and its valuable deformity intact to be interested in their grown-up exclusivity. My mother takes my hand and I limp away happily.

It is a happy interlude. I am sent to school. I play 'I sent a letter to my friend…' with other children. My cousin, slow, intense, observant, sits watching.

'Which of you's sick and is not supposed to run?' asks the teacher: and bound by our telepathic conspiracy, both Cousin and I point to Cousin. He squats, distributing his indolent weight on his sturdy feet and I shout, play, laugh, and run on the tips of my toes. I have an overabundance of energy. It can never be wholly released.

The interlude was happy.

I lie on a white wooden table in a small room. I know it is the same hospital. I have been lured unsuspecting to the table but I get a whiff of something frightening. I hate the smell with all my heart, and my heart pounding I try to get off the table. Hands hold me. Col. Bharucha, in a strange white cap and mask, looks at me coolly and says something to a young and nervous lady doctor. The obnoxious smell grows stronger as a frightening muzzle is brought closer to my mouth and nose. I scream and kick out. The muzzle moves away. Again it attacks and again I twist and wrench, turning my face from side to side. My hands are pinned down. I can't move my legs. I realize they are strapped. Hands hold my head. 'No! No! Help me. Mummy! Mummy, help me!' I shout, panicked. She too is aligned with them. 'I'm suffocating,' I scream. 'I can't breathe.' There is an unbearable weight on my chest. I moan and cry.

I am held captive by the brutal smell. It has vaporized into a milky cloud. I float round and up and down and fall horrendous distances without landing anywhere, fighting for my life's breath. I am abandoned in that suffocating cloud. I moan and my ghoulish voice turns me into something despicable and eerie and deserving of the terrible punishment. But where am I? How long will the horror last? Days and years with no end in sight…

It must have ended.

I switch awake to maddening pain; sitting up in my mother's

bed crying. I must have been crying a long time. I become aware of the new plaster cast on my leg. The shape of the cast is altered from the last time. The toes point up. The pain from my leg radiates all over my small body. 'Do something. I'm hurting!'

My mother tells me the story of the little mouse with seven tails.

'The mouse comes home crying.' My mother rubs her knuckles to her eyes and, energetically imitating the mouse, sobs, 'Mummy, Mummy, do something. The children at school tease me. They sing:"Freaky mousey with seven tails! Lousy mousey with seven tails!" So, the little mouse's mother chops off one tail. The next day the mouse again comes home crying: 'Mummy, Mummy, the children tease me. "Lousy mousey with six tails! Freaky mousey with six tails!"'

And so on, until one by one the little mouse's tails are all chopped off and the story winds to its inevitable and dismal end with the baby mouse crying: 'Mummy, Mummy, the children tease me. They sing, "Freaky mousey with no tail! Lousy mousey with no tail!"' And there is no way a tail can be tacked back on.

The doleful story adds to my misery. But stoically bearing my pain for the duration of the tale, out of pity for my mother's wan face and my father's exaggerated attempts to become the tragic mouse, I once again succumb to the pain.

My mother tells my father: 'Go next door and phone the doctor to come at once!' It is in the middle of the night. And it is cold. Father puts on his dressing gown and wrapping a scarf round his neck leaves us. My screaming loses its edge of panic. An hour later, exhausted by the pain and no longer able to pander to my mother's efforts to distract, I abandon myself to hysteria.

'Daddy has gone to fetch Col. Bharucha,' soothes Mother. She carries me round and round the room stroking my back. Finally, pushing past the curtain and the door, she takes me into the sitting room.

My father raises his head from the couch.

The bitter truth sinks in. He never phoned the doctor. He never went to fetch him. And my mother collaborated in the betrayal. I realize there is nothing they can do and I don't blame them.

The night must have passed—as did the memory of further pain.

FROM *Chapter 11*

The April days are lengthening, beginning to get warm. The Queen's Park is packed. Groups of men and women sit in circles on the grass and children run about them. Ice-Candy-Man, lean as his popsicles and as affable, swarming with children, is going from group to group doing good business.

Masseur, too, is going from group to group; handsome, reserved, competent, assured, massaging balding heads, kneading knotty shoulders and soothing aching limbs.

I lie on the grass, my head on Ayah's lap, basking in—and intercepting—the warm flood of stares directed at Ayah by her circle of admirers. The Falletis Hotel cook, the Government House gardener, a sleek and arrogant butcher and the zoo attendant, Sher Singh, sit with us.

'She is scared of your lion,' drawls Ayah, playfully tapping my forehead. 'She thinks he's set loose at night and he will gobble her up from her bed.'

Sher Singh, wearing an outsize blue turban and a callow beard, sits up. Delighted to be singled out by Ayah, he looks at me earnestly: 'Don't worry. I'll hang on to his leash,' he boasts, stammering slightly. 'He won't dare eat you!'

I'm not the least bit reassured. On the contrary, I am terrified. This callow youth with a stem-like neck hold the zoo lion?

'What kind of leash?' I ask.

'A-an iron ch-chain!'

It's much worse than I'd imagined. A lion roaring behind bars is bad enough. But a lion straining on a stout leash held by this thin, stuttering Sikh is unthinkable. I burst into tears.

'Now look what you've done,' says Ayah in her usual good-natured manner. Gathering me in her arms and hugging me she rocks back and forth. 'Don't be silly,' she tells me. 'The lion is never let out of his cage. The cage is so strong a hundred lions couldn't break it.'

'And,' says Ramzana the butcher, 'I give him a juicy goat every day. Why should he want to eat a dried up stick like you?'

The logic is irrefutable during daylight hours as I sit among friends beneath Queen Victoria's lion-intimidating presence. But alone, at night, the logic will vanish.

Masseur and Ice-Candy-Man drift over to us and join the circle. Masseur is raking in money. He has invented an oil that will grow hair on bald heads. It is composed of monkey and fish glands, mustard oil, pearl dust and an assortment of herbs. The men listen intently, but Masseur stops short of revealing the secret recipe. He holds up the bottle and Ayah reaches out to touch the oil.

'Careful,' says Masseur, whipping the bottle away. 'It'll grow hair on your fingertips.'

'Hai Ram!' says Ayah, quickly retracting her fingers, and rolling her eyes from one face to the next with fetching consternation.

We all laugh.

Not to be outdone, Ice-Candy-Man says he has developed a first-class fertility pill. He knows it will work but he has yet to try it out.

'I'll give it a try,' offers the Government House gardener.

'Your wife's already produced children, hasn't she?'

'Tch! Not for her, *yaar*. For myself. I feel old sometimes,' confesses the greying gardener.

'It is not an aphrodisiac. It's a fertility pill for women,' explains Ice-Candy-Man. 'It's so potent it can impregnate men!'

There is a startled silence.

'You're a joker, *yaar*,' says the butcher.

'No, honestly,' says Ice-Candy-Man, neglectful of the

cigarette butt that is uncoiling wisps of smoke from his fist. He too will rake in money.

Masseur clears his throat and, breaking the spell cast by the fertility pill, enquires of the gardener: 'What's the latest from the English *Sarkar's* house?'

The gardener, congenial and hoary, is our prime source of information from the British Empire's local headquarters.

'It is rumoured,' he says obligingly, rubbing the patches of black and white stubble on his chin, 'that Lat Sahib Wavell did not resign his viceroyship.'

He pauses, dramatically, as if he's already revealed too much to friends. And then, as if deciding to consecrate discretion to our friendship, he serves up the choice titbit.

'He was sacked!'

'Oh! Why?' asks Ice-Candy-Man. We are all excited by a revelation that invites us to share the inside track of the Raj's doings.

'Gandhi, Nehru, Patel...they have much influence even in London,' says the gardener mysteriously, as if acknowledging the arbitrary and mischievous nature of antic gods. 'They didn't like the Muslim League's victory in the Punjab elections.'

'The bastards!' says Masseur with histrionic fury that conceals a genuine bitterness. 'So they sack Wavell Sahib, a fair man! And send for a new Lat Sahib who will favour the Hindus!'

'With all due respect, malijee,' says Ice-Candy-Man, surveying the gardener through a blue mist of exhaled smoke, 'but aren't you Hindus expert at just this kind of thing? Twisting tails behind the scene ... and getting someone else to slaughter your goats?'

'What's the new Lat Sahib like? This Mountbatten Sahib?' asks Ayah.

She, like Mother, is an oil pourer. 'I saw his photo. He is handsome! But I don't like his wife, *baba*. She looks a *choorail*!'

'Ah, but Jawaharlal Nehru likes her. He likes her *vaaary much!*' says Ice-Candy-Man, luridly dragging out the last two words of English.

'Nehru and the Mountbattens are like this!' the gardener concurs, holding up two entwined fingers. His expression, an attractive blend of sheepishness and vanity, reinforces the image of a seasoned inside tracker.

'If Nehru and Mountbatten are like this,' says Masseur, 'then who's going to hold our Jinnah Sahib's hand? Master Tara Singh?'

Masseur says this in a way that makes us smile.

'Ah-ha!' says Ice-Candy-Man as if suddenly enlightened. 'So that's who!' He slaps his thigh and beams at us as if Masseur has proposed a brilliant solution. 'That's who!' he repeats.

The butcher snorts and aims a contemptuous gob of spit some yards away from us. He has been quiet all this while and as we turn our faces to him he gathers his stylish cotton shawl over one shoulder and says: 'That non-violent violence-monger—your precious Gandhijee—first declares the Sikhs *fanatics!* Now suddenly he says: 'Oh dear, the poor Sikhs cannot live with the Muslims if there is a Pakistan!' What does he think we are—some kind of beast? Aren't they living with us now?'

'He's a politician, *yaar*,' says Masseur soothingly. 'It's his business to suit his tongue to the moment.'

'If it was only his tongue I wouldn't mind,' says the butcher. 'But the Sikhs are already supporting some trumped-up Muslim party the Congress favours.' He has a dead-pan way of speaking which is very effective.

The Government House gardener, his expression wary and sympathetic, gives a loud sigh, and says: 'It is the English's mischief ... They are past masters at intrigue. It suits them to have us all fight.'

'Just the English?' asks Butcher. 'Haven't the Hindus connived with the *Angrez* to ignore the Muslim League, and support a party that didn't win a single seat in the Punjab? It's just the kind of thing we fear. They manipulate one or two Muslims against the interests of the larger community. And now they have manipulated Master Tara Singh and his bleating herd of Sikhs!' He glances at Sher Singh, his handsome, smooth-shaven face almost expressionless.

Sher Singh shifts uncomfortably and, looking as completely innocent of Master Tara Singh's doings as he can, frowns at the grass.

'*Arrey*, you foolish Sikh! You fell right into the Hindus' trap!' says Ice-Candy-Man so facetiously that Sher Singh loses part of his nervousness and smiles back.

The afternoon is drawing to a close. The grass feels damp. Ayah stands up smoothing the pleats in her limp cotton sari. 'If all you talk of nothing but this Hindu-Muslim business, I'll stop coming to the park,' she says pertly.

'It's just a discussion among friends,' says Ice-Candy-Man, uncoiling his frame from the grass to sit up. 'Such talk helps clear the air…but for your sake, we won't bring it up again.'

The rest of us look at him gratefully.

(People start observing religious rituals more. Almost overnight Lenny becomes conscious of the fact that Ayah is Hindu, Masseur and Ice-Candy-Man are Muslim; while Lenny's Parsee family appears to belong to an irrelevant minority.)

FROM *Chapter 16*

We leave early. Master Tara Singh is expected to make an appearance outside the Assembly Chambers, behind the Queen's Garden. Except for Muccho and her children, who remain behind in the servants' quarters, our house is deserted. Mother and Father left before us with the Singhs and the Phailbuses.

There is no room for us in the Queen's Garden. Seen from the roof of the Falettis Hotel—the Falettis Hotel cook has secured a place for us—it appears that the park has sprouted a dense crop of humans. They overflow its boundaries on to the roads and sit on trees and on top of walls. The crowd is thickest on the concrete between the back of the garden and the Assembly Chambers. Policemen are holding the throng surging up the wide, imperious flight of pink steps.

There is a stir of excitement, an increase in the volume of noise, and Master Tara Singh, in a white *kurta*, his parted beard bristling on either side of his face, appears on the top steps of the Assembly Chambers. I see him clearly. He has a rifle slung from his back and his chest is swathed in leather bands holding bullets. Tight white pyjamas hug his ankles like bangles; bands round his waist hold a pistol and daggers.

He gets down to business right away. Holding a long sword in each hand, the curved steel reflecting the sun's glare as he clashes the swords above his head, the Sikh soldier-saint shouts: 'We will see how the Muslim swine get Pakistan! We will fight to the last man! We will show them *who* will leave Lahore! *Raj Karega Khalsa, aki rahi na koi!*'

The Sikhs milling about in a huge blob in front wildly wave and clash their swords, *kirpans* and hockey-sticks, and punctuate his shrieks with roars: *'Pakistan Murdabad*! Death to Pakistan! *Sat Siri Akaal! Bolay se nihaal!'*

And the Muslims shouting: 'So? We'll play Holi-with-their-blood! Ho-o-o-li with their blo-o-od!'

And the Holi festival of the Hindus and Sikhs coming up in a few days, when everybody splatters everybody with coloured water and coloured powders and laughs and romps...

And instead the skyline of the old walled city ablaze, and people splattering each other with blood! And Ice-Candy-Man hustling Ayah and me up the steps of his tenement in Bhatti Gate, saying: 'Wait till you see Shalmi burn!' And pointing out landmarks from the crowded tenement roof:

'That's Delhi Gate... There's Lahori Gate ... There's Mochi Darwaza ...'

'Isn't that where Masseur lives?' Ayah asks.

'Yes, that's where your masseur stays,' says Ice-Candy-Man, unable to mask his ire. 'It's a Muslim *mohalla*,' he continues in an effort to dispel his rancour. 'We've got wind that the Hindus of Shalmi plan to attack it—push the Muslims across the river. Hindus and Sikhs think they'll take Lahore. But we'll surprise them yet!'

'Hai Ram! That's Gowalmandi isn't it?' says Ayah. *'Hai Ram*... How it burns!'

And our eyes wide and sombre.

Suddenly a posse of sweating English tommies, wearing only khaki shorts, socks and boots, runs up in the lane directly below us. And on their heels a mob of Sikhs, their wild long hair and beards rampant, large fevered eyes glowing in fanatic faces, pours into the narrow lane roaring slogans, holding curved swords, shoving up a manic wave of violence that sets Ayah to trembling as she holds me tight. A naked child, twitching on a spear struck between her shoulders, is waved like a flag: her screamless mouth agape she is staring straight up at me. A crimson fury blinds me. I want to dive into the bestial creature clawing entrails, plucking eyes, tearing limbs, gouging hearts, smashing brains: but the creature has too many stony hearts, too many sightless eyes, deaf ears, mindless brains and tons of entwined entrails…

And then a slowly advancing mob of Muslim *goondas*: packed so tight that we can see only the top of their heads. Roaring: '*Allah-o-Akbar! Yaaaa Ali!*' and '*Pakistan Zindabad!*'

The terror the mob generates is palpable—like an evil, paralysing spell. The terrible procession, like a sluggish river, flows beneath us. Every short while a group of men, like a whirling eddy, stalls—and like the widening circles of a treacherous eddy dissolving in the mainstream, leaves in its centre the pulpy red flotsam of a mangled body.

The processionists are milling about two jeeps pushed back to back. They come to a halt: the men in front of the procession pulling ahead and the mob behind banked close up. There is a quickening in the activity about the jeeps. My eyes focus on an emaciated Banya wearing a white Gandhi cap. The man is knocked down. His lips are drawn away from rotting, *paan*-stained teeth in a scream. The men move back and in the small clearing I see his legs sticking out of his dhoti right up to the groin—each thin, brown leg tied to a jeep. Ayah, holding her hands over my eyes, collapses on the floor pulling me down with her. There is the roar of a hundred throats: '*Allah-o-Akbar!*' and beneath it the growl of revving motors. Ice-Candy-Man stoops over us, looking concerned: the muscles in his face tight with a strange exhilaration I never again want to see.

Ramzana the butcher and Masseur join us. Ayah sits sheathing her head and form with her sari; cowering and lumpish against the wall.

'You shouldn't have brought them here, *yaar*,' says Masseur. 'They shouldn't see such things ... Besides, it's dangerous.'

'We are with her. She's safe,' says Ice-Candy-Man laconically. He adds: 'I only wanted her to see the fires.'

'I want to go home,' I whimper.

'As soon as things quiet down I'll take you home,' says Masseur reassuringly. He picks me up and swings me until I smile.

Ice-Candy-Man offers me another popsicle. I've eaten so many already that I feel sick. He gathers the empty tin plates strewn about us. The uneaten chapatti on Ayah's plate is stiff: the vegetable curry cold. Ice-Candy-Man removes the plate.

'Look!' shouts the butcher. 'Shalmi's started to burn!'

We rush to the parapet. Tongues of pink flame lick two or three brick buildings in the bazaar. The flames are hard to spot: no match for the massive growth of brick and cement spreading on either side of the street.

'Just watch. You'll see a *tamasha!*' says Ice-Candy-Man.

'Wait till the fire gets to their stock of arsenal.'

As if on cue a deafening series of explosions shakes the floor beneath our feet. Ayah stands up hastily and joins us at the parapet. The walls and balconies of a two-storey building in the centre of the bazaar bulge and bulge. Then the bricks start slowly tumbling, and the dark slab of roof caves into the exploding furnace...

People are pouring into the Shalmi lanes from their houses and shops. We hear the incredibly prompt clamour of a fire brigade. The clanking fire engine, crowded with ladders, hose and helmeted men, manoeuvres itself through the street, the truck with the water tank following.

The men exchange surprised looks. Ice-Candy-Man says:

'Where did those mother-fuckers spring from?'

The firemen scamper busily, attaching hoses, shoving people back. Riding on the trucks they expertly direct their powerful hoses at the rest of the buildings on either side of the road.

As the fire brigade drives away, the entire rows of buildings on both sides of the street ignite in an incredible conflagration. Although we are several furlongs away a scorching blast from a hot wind makes our clothes flap as if in a storm. I look at Ice-Candy-Man. The astonishment on his features is replaced by a huge grin. His face, reflecting the fire, lit up. 'The fucking bastards!' he says, laughing aloud, spit flying from his mouth. 'The fucking bastards! They sprayed the buildings with petrol! They must be Muslim.'

The Hindus of Shalmi must have piled a lot of dynamite in their houses and shops to drive the Muslims from Mochi Gate. The entire Shalmi, an area covering about four square miles, flashes in explosions. The men and women on our roof are slapping each other's hands, laughing, hugging one another.

I stare at the *tamasha*, mesmerized by the spectacle. It is like a gigantic fireworks display in which stiff figures looking like spread-eagled stick-dolls leap into the air, black against the magenta furnace. Trapped by the spreading flames the panicked Hindus rush in droves from one end of the street to the other. Many disappear down the smoking lanes. Some collapse in the street. Charred limbs and burnt logs are falling from the sky.

The whole world is burning. The air on my face is so hot I think my flesh and clothes will catch fire. I start screaming: hysterically sobbing. Ayah moves away, her feet suddenly heavy and dragging, and sits on the roof slumped against the wall. She buries her face in her knees.

'What small hearts you have,' says Ice-Candy-Man, beaming affectionately at us. 'You must make your hearts stout!' He strikes his out-thrust chest with his fist. Turning to the men, he says: 'The fucking bastards! They thought they'd drive us out of Bhatti! We've shown them!'

It is not safe to leave until late that evening. As the butcher drives us home in his cart the moonlight settles like a layer of ashes over Lahore.

(Ayah's great love Masseur is mysteriously murdered; Ayah is kidnapped from Lenny's home by a mob led by Ice-Candy-Man; a maimed refugee boy, Ranna, comes from Pir Pindo, a village where Lenny once played and which is now across the border in India. This is his tale, told through Lenny.)

FROM ***Chapter 25***

No one realized the speed at which the destruction and the rampage advanced. They didn't know the extent to which it surrounded them. Jagjeet Singh visited Pir Pindo under cover of darkness with furtive groups of Sikhs. A few more families who had close kin near Multan and Lahore left, disguised as Sikhs or Hindus. But most of the villagers resisted the move. The uncertainty they faced made them discredit the danger. 'We cannot leave,' they said, and, like a refrain, I can hear them say: 'What face will we show our forefathers on the day of judgement if we abandon their graves? Allah will protect us!'

Jagjeet Singh sent word he was risking his life, and the lives of the other men in Dera Tek Singh, if he visited Pir Pindo again. The Akalis were aware of his sympathies for the Muslims. They had threatened him. They were in control of his village.

Jagjeet Singh advised them to leave as soon as they could: but it was already too late.

Ranna's Story

Late that afternoon the clamour of the monsoon downpour suddenly ceased. Chidda raised her hands from the dough she was kneading and, squatting before the brass tray, turned to her mother-in-law. Sitting by his grandmother Ranna sensed their tension as the old woman stopped chaffing the wheat. She slowly pushed back her age-brittle hair and, holding her knobby fingers immobile, grew absolutely still.

Chidda stood in their narrow doorway, her eyes nervously scouring the courtyard. Ranna clung to her shalwar, peering out. His cousins, almost naked in their soaking rags, were shouting and splashing in the slush in their courtyard. 'Shut up. Oye!' Chidda shouted in a voice that rushed so violently from her strong chest that the children quietened at once and leaned and slid uneasily against the warm black hides of the buffaloes tethered to the rough stumps. The clouds had broken and the sun shot beams that lit up the freshly bathed courtyard.

The other members of the household, Ranna's older brothers, his uncles, aunts and cousins were quietly filing into the courtyard. When she saw Khatija and Parveen, Chidda strode to her daughters and pressed them fiercely to her body. The village was so quiet it could be the middle of the night: and from the distance, buffeting the heavy, moisture-laden air, came the wails and the hoarse voices of men shouting.

Already their neighbours' turbans skimmed the tall mud ramparts of their courtyard, their bare feet squelching on the path the rain had turned into a muddy channel.

I can imagine the old mullah, combing his faded beard with trembling fingers as he watches the villagers converge on the mosque with its uneven green dome. It is perched on an incline; and seen from there the fields, flooded with rain, are the same muddy colour as the huts. The mullah drags his cot forward as the villagers, touching their foreheads and greeting him somberly, fill the prayer ground. The *chaudhry* joins the mullah on his charpoy. The villagers sit on their haunches in uneven rows lifting their confused and frightened faces. There is a murmur of voices. Conjectures. First the name of one village and then of another. The Sikhs have attacked Kot-Rahim. No, it sounds closer… It must be Makipura.

The *chaudhry* raises his heavy voice slightly: 'Dost Mohammad and his party will be here soon...We'll known soon enough what's going on.'

At his reassuring presence the murmuring subsides and the villagers nervously settle down to wait. Some women draw their veils across their faces and, shading their bosoms, impatiently shove their nipples into the mouths of whimpering babies. Grandmothers, mothers and aunts rock restive children on their laps and thump their foreheads to put them to sleep. The children, conditioned to the numbing jolts, grow groggy and their eyes become unfocused. They fall asleep almost at once.

Half an hour later the scouting party, drenched and muddy, the lower halves of their faces wrapped in the ends of their turbans, pick their way through the squatting villagers to the *chaudhry*.

Removing his wet puggaree and wiping his head with a cloth the mullah hands him, Dost Mohammad turns on his haunches to face the villagers. His skin is grey, as if the rain has bleached the colour. Casting a shade across his eyes with a hand that trembles slightly, speaking in a matter-of-fact voice that disguises his ache and fear, he tells the villagers that the Sikhs have attacked at least five villages around Dera Misri, to their east. Their numbers have swollen enormously. They are like swarms of locusts, moving in marauding bands of thirty and forty thousand. They are killing all Muslims. Setting fires, looting, parading the Muslim women naked through the streets - raping and mutilating them in the centre of villages and in mosques. The Beas, flooded by melting snow, and the monsoon, is carrying hundreds of corpses. There is an intolerable stench where the bodies, caught in the bends, have piled up.

'What are the police doing?' a man shouts. He is Dost Mohammad's cousin. One way or another the villagers are related.

'The Muslims in the force have been disarmed at the orders of a Hindu Sub-Inspector; the dog's penis!' says Dost Mohammad, speaking in the same flat monotone. 'The Sikh and Hindu police have joined the mobs.'

The villagers appear visibly to shrink - as if the loss of hope is a physical thing. A woman with a child on her lap slaps her forehead and begins to wail: *'Hai! Hai!'* The other women join her: *'Hai! Hai!'* Older women, beating their breasts like hollow drums, cry, 'Never mind us…save the young girls! The children! *Hai! Hai!'*

Ranna's two-toothed old grandmother, her frail voice quavering bitterly, shrieks: 'We should have gone to Pakistan!'

It was hard to believe that the decision to stay was taken only a month ago. Embedded in the heart of the Punjab, they had felt secure, inviolate. And to uproot themselves from the soil of their ancestors had seemed to them akin to tearing themselves, like ancient trees, from the earth.

And the messages filtering from the outside had been reassuring. Gandhi, Nehru, Jinnah, Tara Singh were telling the peasants to remain where they were. The minorities would be a sacred trust…The communal trouble was being caused by a few mischief-makers and would soon subside and then there were their brothers, the Sikhs of Dera Tek Singh, who would protect them.

But how many Muslims can the Sikh villagers befriend? The mobs, determined to drive the Muslims out, are prepared for the carnage. Their ranks swollen by thousands of refugees recounting fresh tales of horror they roll towards Pir Pindo like the heedless swells of an ocean.

The *chaudhry* raises his voice: 'How many guns do we have now?'

The women quieten.

'Seven or eight,' a man replies from the front.

There is a disappointed silence. They had expected to procure more guns but every village is holding on to its meagre stock of weapons.

'We have our axes, knives, scythes and staves!' a man calls from the back. 'Let those bastards come. We're ready!'

'Yes…we're as ready as we'll ever be,' the *chaudhry* says, stroking his thick moustache. 'You all know what to do…'

They have been over the plan often enough recently. The women and girls will gather at the *chaudhry's*. Rather than face the brutality of the mob they will pour kerosene around the house and burn themselves. The canisters of kerosene are already stored in the barn at the rear of the *chaudhry*'s sprawling mud house. The young men will engage the Sikhs at the mosque, and at other strategic locations, for as long as they can and give the women a chance to start the fire.

A few men from each family were to shepherd the younger boys and lock themselves into secluded back rooms, hoping to escape detection. They were peaceable peasants, not skilled in such matters, and their plans were sketchy and optimistic. Comforted by each other's presence, reluctant to disperse, the villagers remained in the prayer yard as dusk gathered about them. The distant wailing and shouting had ceased. Later that night it rained again, and comforted by its seasonal splatter the tired villagers curled up on their mats and slept.

The attack came at dawn. The watch from the mosque's single minaret hurtled down the winding steps to spread the alarm. The panicked women ran to and fro screaming and snatching up their babies, and the men barely had time to get to their posts. In fifteen minutes the village was swamped by the Sikhs—tall men with streaming hair and thick biceps and thighs, waving full-sized swords and sten-guns, roaring, *'Bolay so Nihal! Sat Siri Akal!'*

They mowed down the villagers in the mosque with the sten-guns. Shouting *'Allah-o-Akbar!'* the peasants died of sword and spear wounds in the slushy lanes and courtyards, the screams of women from the *chaudhry's* house ringing in their ears, wondering why the house was not burning.

Ranna, abandoned by his mother and sisters halfway to the *chaudhry's* house, ran howling into the courtyard. Chidda had spanked his head and pushed him away, shrieking, 'Go to your father! Stay with the men!'

Ranna ran through their house to the room the boys had been instructed to gather in. Some of his cousins and uncles were already there. More men stumbled into the dark windowless room—then his two older brothers. There must be at least thirty of them in the small room. It was stifling. He heard his father's voice and fought his way towards him. Dost Mohammad shouted harshly: 'Shut up! They'll kill you if you make a noise.'

The yelling in the room subsided. Dost Mohammad picked up his son, and Ranna saw his uncle slip out into the grey light and shut the door, plunging the room into darkness. Someone bolted the door from inside, and they heard the heavy thud of cotton bales stacked against the door to disguise the entrance. With luck they would remain undetected and safe.

The shouting and screaming from outside appeared to come in waves: receding and approaching. From all directions. Sometimes Ranna could make out the words and even whole sentences. He heard a woman cry, 'Do anything you want with me, but don't torment me...For God's sake, don't torture me!' And then an intolerable screaming. 'Oh God!' a man whispered on a sobbing intake of breath. 'Oh God, she is the mullah's daughter!' The men covered their ears - and the boys' ears - sobbing unaffectedly like little children.

A teenager, his cracked voice resounding like the honk of geese, started wailing: 'I don't want to die...I don't want to die!' Catching his fear, Ranna and the other children set to whimpering: 'I don't want to die...Abba, I don't want to die!'

'Hush,' said Dost Mohammad gruffly. 'Stop whining like girls!' Then, with words that must have bubbled up from a deep source of strength and compassion, with infinite gentleness, he said, 'What's there to be afraid of? Are you afraid to die? It won't hurt any more than the sting of a bee.' His voice, unseasonably light-hearted, carried a tenderness that soothed and calmed them. Ranna fell asleep in his father's arms.

Someone was banging on the door, shouting: 'Open up! Open up!'

Ranna awoke with a start. Why was he on the floor? Why were there so many people about in the dark? He felt the stir of men getting to their feet. The air in the room was oppressive: hot and humid and stinking of sweat. Suddenly Ranna remembered where he was and the darkness became charged with terror.

'We know you're in there. Come on, open up!' The noise of the banging was deafening in the pitch-black room, drowning the other children's alarmed cries. 'Allah! Allah! Allah!' an old man moaned non-stop.

'Who's there?' Dost Mohammad called; and putting Ranna down, stumbling over the small bodies, made his way to the door. Ranna, terrified, groping blindly in the dark, tried to follow.

'We're Sikhs!'

There was a pause in which Ranna's throat dried up. The old man stopped saying 'Allah'. And in the deathly stillness, his voice echoing from his proximity to the door, Dost Mohammad said, 'Kill us all…but spare the children.'

'Open at once!'

'I beg you in the name of all you hold sacred, don't kill the little ones,' Ranna heard his father plead. 'Make them Sikhs…Let them live…they are so little…'

Suddenly the noon light smote their eyes. Dost Mohammad stepped out and walked three paces. There was a sunlit sweep of curved steel. His head was shorn clear off his neck. Turning once in the air, eyes wide open, it tumbled in the dust. His hands jerked up slashing the air above the bleeding stump of his neck.

Ranna saw his uncles beheaded. His older brothers, his cousins. The Sikhs were among them like hairy vengeful demons, wielding bloodied swords, dragging them out as a sprinkling of Hindus, darting about at the fringes, their faces vaguely familiar, pointed out and identified the Mussulmans by name. He felt a blow cleave the back of his head and the warm flow of blood. Ranna fell just inside the door on a tangled pile of unrecognizable bodies. Someone fell on him, drenching him in blood.

Every time his eyes open the world appears to them to be floating in blood. From the direction of the mosque come the intolerable shrieks and wails of women. It seems to him that a woman is sobbing just outside their courtyard: great anguished sobs—and at intervals she screams: 'You'll kill me! *Hai Allah*…Y'all will kill me!'

Ranna wants to tell her, 'Don't be afraid to die...It will hurt less than the sting of a bee.' But he is hurting so much...Why isn't he dead? Where are the bees? Once he thought he saw his eleven-year-old sister, Khatija, run stark naked into their courtyard: her long hair dishevelled, her boyish body bruised, her lips cut and swollen and a bloody scab where her front teeth were missing.

Later in the evening he awoke to silence. At once he became fully conscious. He wiggled backwards over the bodies and slipping free of the weight on top of him felt himself sink knee-deep into a viscous fluid. The bodies blocking the entrance had turned the room into a pool of blood.

Keeping to the shadows cast by the mud walls, stepping over the mangled bodies of people he knew, Ranna made his way to the *chaudhry's* house. It was dark inside. There was a nauseating stench of kerosene mixed with the smell of spilt curry. He let his eyes get accustomed to the dimness. Carefully he explored the rooms cluttered with smashed clay pots, broken charpoys, spilled grain and chapatties. He had not realized how hungry he was until he saw the pile of stale bread. He crammed the chapatties into his mouth.

His heart gave a lurch. A woman was sleeping on a charpoy. He reached for her and his hand grasped her clammy, inert flesh. He realized with a shock she was dead. He walked round the cot to examine her face. It was the *chaudhry's* older wife. He discovered three more bodies. In the dim light he turned them over and peered into their faces searching for his mother.

When he emerged from the house it was getting dark. Moving warily, avoiding contact with the bodies he kept stumbling upon, he went to the mosque.

For the first time he heard voices. The whispers of women comforting each other—of women softly weeping. His heart pounding in his chest he crept to one side of the arching mosque entrance. He heard a man groan, then a series of animal-like grunts.

He froze near the body of the mullah. How soon he had become accustomed to thinking of people he had known all his life as bodies. He felt on such easy terms with death. The old mullah's face was serene in death, his beard pale against the brick plinth. The figures in the covered portion at the rear of the mosque were a dark blur. He was sure he had heard Chidda's voice. He began inching forward, prepared to dash across the yard to where the women were, when a man yawned and sighed, *'Wah Guru!'*

'Wah Guru! Wah Guru!' responded three or four male voices, sounding drowsy and replete. Ranna realized that the men in the mosque were Sikhs. A wave of rage and loathing swept his small body. He knew it was wrong of the Sikhs to be in the mosque with the village women. He could not explain why: except that he still slept in his parents' room.

'Stop whimpering, you bitch, or I'll bugger you again!' a man said irritably.

Other men laughed. There was much movement. Stifled exclamations and moans. A woman screamed, and swore in Punjabi. There was a loud cracking noise and the rattle of breath from the lungs. Then a moment of horrible stillness.

Ranna fled into the moonless night. Skidding on the slick wet clay, stumbling into the irrigation ditches demarcating the fields, he ran in the direction of his Uncle Iqbal and his Noni *chachi's* village. He didn't stop until deep inside a thicket of sugar-cane he stumbled on a slightly elevated slab of drier ground. The clay felt soft and caressing against his exhausted body. It was a safe place to rest. The moment Ranna felt secure his head hurt and he fainted.

Ranna lay unconscious in the cane field all morning. Intermittent showers washed much of the blood and dust off his limbs. Around noon two men walked into the cane field, and at the first rustle of the dried leaves Ranna became fully conscious.

Sliding on his butt to the lower ground, crouching amidst the pricking tangle of stalks and dried leaves, Ranna followed the passage of the men with his ears. They trampled through the field, selecting and cutting the sugarcane with their *kirpans*, talking in Punjabi. Ranna picked up an expression that warned him that they were Sikhs. Half buried in the slush he scarcely breathed as one of the men came so close to him that he saw the blue check on his lungi and the flash of a white singlet. There was a crackling rustle as the man squatted to defecate.

Half an hour later when the men left, Ranna moved cautiously towards the edge of the field. A cluster of about sixty Sikhs in lungis and singlets, their carelessly knotted hair snaking down their backs, stood talking in a fallow field to his right. At some distance, in another field of young green shoots, Sikhs and Hindus were gathered in a much larger bunch. Ranna sensed their presence behind him in the fields he couldn't see. There must be thousands of them, he thought. Shifting to a safe spot he searched the distance for the green dome of his village mosque. He had travelled too far to spot it. But he knew where his village lay and guessed from the coiling smoke that his village was on fire.

Much later, when it was time for the evening meal, the fields cleared. He could not make out a single human form for miles. As he ran again towards his aunt's village the red sun, as if engorged with blood, sank into the horizon.

All night he moved, scuttling along the mounds of earth protecting the waterways, running in shallow channels, burrowing like a small animal through the standing crop. When he stopped to catch his breath, he saw the glow from burning villages measuring the night distances out for him.

Ranna arrived at his aunt's village just after dawn. He watched it from afar, confused by the activity taking place around five or six huge lorries parked in the rutted lanes. Soldiers, holding guns with bayonets sticking out of them, were directing the villagers. The villagers were shouting and running to and fro, carrying on their heads charpoys heaped with their belongings. Some were herding their calves and goats towards the trucks. Others were dumping their household effects in the middle of the lanes in their scramble to climb into the lorries.

There were no Sikhs about. The village was not under attack. Perhaps the army trucks were there to evacuate the villagers and take them to Pakistan.

Ranna hurtled down the lanes, weaving through the burdened and distraught villagers and straying cattle, into his aunt's hut. He saw her right away, heaping her pots and pans on a cot. A fat roll of winter bedding tied with a string lay to one side. He screamed: 'Noni *chachi!* It's me!'

'For a minute I thought: Who is this filthy little beggar?' Noni *chachi* says, when she relates her part in the story. *'I said: Ranna? Ranna? Is that you? What're you doing here!'*

The moment he caught the light of recognition and concern in her eyes, the pain in his head exploded and he crumpled at her feet unconscious.

'*It is funny*,' Ranna says. *'As long as I had to look out for myself, I was all right. As soon as I felt safe, I fainted.'*

Her hands trembling, his *chachi* washed the wound on his head with a wet rag. Clots of congealed blood came away and floated in the pan in which she rinsed the cloth. '*I did not dare remove the thick scabs that had formed over the wound*,' she says. '*I thought I'd see his brain*!' The slashing blade had scalped him from the rise in the back of his head to the top, exposing a wound the size of a large bald patch on a man. She wondered he had lived; found his way to their village. She was sure he would die in a few moments. Ranna's *chacha*, Iqbal, and other members of the house gathered about him. An old woman, the village *dai*, checked his pulse and his breath and, covering him with a white cloth, said: 'Let him die in peace!'

A terrifying roar, like the warning of an alarm, throbs in his ears. He sits up on the charpoy, taking in the disorder in the hastily abandoned room. The other cot, heaped with his aunt's belongings, lies where it was. He can see the bedding roll abandoned in the courtyard. Clay dishes, mugs, chipped crockery, and hand-fans lie on the floor with scattered bits of clothing. Where are his aunt and uncle? Why is he alone? And in the fearsome noise drawing nearer, he recognizes the rhythm of the Sikh and Hindu chants.

Ranna leapt from the cot and ran through the lanes of the deserted village. Except for the animals lowing and bleating and wandering ownerless on the slushy paths there was no one about. Whey hadn't they taken him with them?

His heart thumping, Ranna climbed to the top of the mosque minaret. He saw the mob of Sikhs and Hindus in the fields scuttling forward from the horizon like giant ants. Roaring, waving swords, partly obscured by the veil of dust raised by their trampling feet, they approached the village.

Ranna flew down the steep steps. He ran in and out of the empty houses looking for a place to hide. The mob sounded close. He could hear the thud of their feet, make out the words of their chants. Ranna slipped through the door into a barn. It was almost entirely filled with straw. He dived into it.

He heard the Sikhs' triumphant war cries as they swarmed into the village. He heard the savage banging and kicking open of doors: and the quick confused exchange of shouts as the men realized that the village was empty. They searched all the houses, moving systematically, looting whatever they could lay their hands on.

Ranna held his breath as the door to the barn opened.

'Oye! D'you think the Musslas are hiding here?' a coarse voice asked.

'We'll find out,' another voice said.

Ranna crouched in the hay. The men were climbing all over the straw, slashing it with long sweeps of their swords and piercing it with their spears.

Ranna almost cried out when he felt the first sharp prick. He felt steel tear into his flesh. As if recalling a dream, he heard an old woman say: He's lost too much blood. Let him die in peace.

Ranna did not lose consciousness again until the last man left the barn.

And while the old city in Lahore, crammed behind its dilapidated Mogul gates, burned, thirty miles away Amritsar also burned. No one noticed Ranna as he wandered in the burning city. No one cared. There were too many ugly and abandoned children like him scavenging in the looted houses and the rubble of burnt-out buildings.

His rags clinging to his wounds, straw sticking in his scalped skull, Ranna wandered through the lanes stealing chapatties and grain from houses strewn with dead bodies, rifling the corpses for anything he could use. He ate anything. Raw potatoes, uncooked grains, wheat-flour, rotting peels and vegetables.

No one minded the semi-naked spectre as he looked in doors with his knowing, wide-set peasant eyes as men copulated with wailing children—old and young women. He saw a naked woman, her light Kashmiri skin bruised with purple splotches and cuts, hanging head down from a ceiling fan. And looked on with a child's boundless acceptance and curiosity as jeering men set her long hair on fire. He saw babies, snatched from their mothers, smashed against walls and their howling mothers brutally raped and killed.

Carefully steering away from the murderous Sikh mobs he arrived at the station on the outskirts of the city. It was cordoned off by barbed wire, and beyond the wire he recognized a huddle of Muslim refugees surrounded by Sikh and Hindu police. He stood before the barbed wire screaming, '*Amma*! *Amma*! Noni *chachi!* Noni *chachi!'*

A Sikh sepoy, his hair tied neatly in a khaki turban, ambled up to the other side of the wire. 'Oye! What're you making such a racket for? Scram!' he said, raising his hand in a threatening gesture.

Ranna stayed his ground. He could not bear to look at the Sikh. His stomach muscles felt like choked drains. But he stayed his ground: '*I was trembling from head to toe*,' he says.

'*O, me-kiya!* I say!' the sepoy shouted to his cronies standing by an opening in the wire. 'This little mother-fucker thinks his mother and aunt are in that group of Musslas.'

'Send him here,' someone shouted.

Ranna ran up to the men.

'Don't you know? Your mother married me yesterday,' said a fat-faced, fat-bellied Hindu, his hairy legs bulging beneath the shorts of his uniform. 'And your *chachi* married Makhan Singh,' he said, indicating a tall young sepoy with a shake of his head.

'Let the poor bastard be,' Makhan Singh said. 'Go on: run along.' Taking Ranna by his shoulder he gave him a shove.

The refugees in front watched the small figure hurtle towards them across the gravelly clearing. A middle-aged woman without a veil, her hair dishevelled, moved forward holding out her arms.

The moment Ranna was close enough to see the compassion in her stranger's eyes, he fainted.

With the other Muslim refugees from Amritsar, Ranna was herded into a refugee camp at Badami Baag. He stayed in the camp, which is quite close to our Fire Temple, for two months, queuing for the doled out chapatties, befriended by improvident refugees, until chance—if the random queries of five million refugees seeking their kin in the chaos of mammoth camps all over West Punjab can be called anything but chance—reunited him with his Noni *chachi* and Iqbal *chacha*.

Nadir Hussein

The son of a diplomat, he was born in Calcutta in 1939. Educated in London, Paris, Switzerland and the Philippines, he started writing poetry when young. His work was published in *Pieces of Eight* (1971). He was very well read, and had a rich and varied career as a journalist, cricket commentator and broadcaster. His special interest was astrology. He died when he was barely forty. He reputedly left behind many unpublished poems which have never come to light.

A Wedding

A tidal wave over-runs the island,
The young man adjusts his pliant turban,
His deathly pallor reflected in the sea
Of swirling faces round him, his brows lined
With the effort of trying to combine
The present with the future's mystery.

Escorted by a caravan of cars,
A strange and somewhat mournful procession,
He goes to claim his prize. Meanwhile the girl,
Wise beyond words, dressed like a party doll,
Bows her head in silent recognition
Of her destiny. With their unvoiced cares

The two sit side by side, the man, impatient
To drink from the ocean of her body,
The girl, unaware of his lust, too shy
To look him in the face. All is ready,
The deal completed, the glittering show
Over, the hosts relieved and complacent.

What of the two, no longer the centre
Of attraction? Dumb on another stage
Without an audience, the man, overwhelmed
By his manhood, in an uncontrolled rage
Over-reaches himself; the girl, condemned
To knowledge, moistly becomes his mentor.

G.F. Riaz

Ghulam Fariduddin Riaz was born in Lahore and educated there at Aitcheson College and Government College. He read Politics, Philosophy and Economics at St. Catherine's College, Oxford. On his return to Pakistan he joined the civil service but resigned in 1971. He did his Masters in the United States at the Fletcher School of Law and Tufts University. He now farms in Pakistan and is writing about rural life. He was introduced to Persian, Urdu and English poetry as a child and later read a lot of Dylan Thomas, Edna St. Vincent Millay and Theodore Roethke among others. He started writing poetry around 1970. His first collection of poems *Shade in Passing* (1989), was published by The Writers Workshop in Calcutta. Revised and enlarged for a new edition in Pakistan it won the 1992 Patras Bokhari Award given by The Pakistan Academy of Letters. He has also put together a second collection *Escaping Twenty Shadows* (1995).

FROM ***SHADE IN PASSING***

In Search of Truth at the Geological Museum

There's something of a place of worship
In a museum. The sapient ceilings reflect
The sombre sounds of reverence accrued.

Even the swirls of children scurrying in,
Ingest this and their scatter is muted.
Wonder tempers their ebullient pace.

Solemnly I stand before cages of glass
And learn that this febrile crust of earth
Is penny-stamp thin on a football globe.

The cake-layer crust is sliced, explained,
From ocean-brimming continental troughs,
Meeting the land's skinned desert hems,

Rising to the verdant renaissance of plains,
Gathering in upsurging snow-starched creases
In collateral quests, bristling with peaks,

Where the glaciers grown monstrously
Inch down, climbing one upon the other,
In laborious mating on haggard heights.

And the silver-sliver streams have trickled,
Three into two into one and disgorged,
Turbulent, thundering quick-viciously.

Cutting their diamond-stylus courses,
Through grey mountain sides and
Through black rocks and ochre and red.

The frothing water has forged through them,
And saddened grudgingly into a river,
Meandering into loops, wide and silted.

I stride defiant to the Earthquake Machine.
The calm of endless diagrams and charts
Belies the simmering chaos that churns beneath.

FROM *ESCAPING TWENTY SHADOWS*

The Silence

There were mountains in my past,
Where seasons met
In the layered cinema of leaves,
Where the swelling wetness
Of the boulders and tree-trunks
Gave shelter to our covenants.

Perilous crags escape the earth
Where once our foot-prints
Left pockets in the grass,
And the hawk clatters downhill
Along the contours of denuded hills.

The silence fluctuates grimly,
And questions turn darkly around
To ask who took what from whom
And who dwindles at the core,
Blinded by a collapsing sky.

Alexander Comes of Age

I hold the earth, you Zeus hold Olympus
Alexander's inscription on his statue.

He had not winced when the Sphinx made no reply,
The pangs of immortality were so acute, so manifest.
Fulfilling his destiny he strode across the earth,
And then as proof positive the late great Darius lay,
Finery in tatters, plumes awry, jewels snatched away,
Smothered in blood and sand, conclusively betrayed.

He relished the feast of Empire, single-mindedly,
As hosts of lesser Kings, Princes, Lords and Khans,
With impeccable traits of wealth and valour
Were brought to heel. Surely he had surpassed Achilles?

It was on Jhelum's banks the magic began to shred.
First, Bucephelas died. The horse-god with harness
And horns of gold, who was to gallop to eternity
On the evergreen flower-laden flanks of Olympus,
Ended inconstantly in the dust like any other horse.

Battered by wars, the Companions rebelled at the Beas,
Denying him the glory of standing on the edge of Earth.
In Multan an arrow struck deep into his chest, irreverently.
Piercing his lung, it gave him his first shudder of death.
The capricious sun to which he had so often sacrificed
Devoured his armies in the desert furnaces of Mekran.

In Hamadan, a passing fever killed his love, Hephasthion.
And not since he had killed Clietus in a drunken fit
Had he known such anguish. He wept inconsolably for weeks,
Adrift from life, away from Roxane, from touch.
Each day the wound worsened, festering in his mind.

After that he seldom felt like a god or even lion-like
And in intense moments of regenerate invincibility,
When he saw conquests ripened everywhere,
He would consider plucking Arabia, Africa or Italy,
But fell back to wearing Babylon like a stolen mantle
And drank himself, feast after feast, to oblivion.

He would not, could not remember how many corpses
Of nobles, captains, friends, devotees lay strewn
On random plains, in deserts, in forests and gorges,
In alleys and on the blood-stained walls of citadels,
Or drifted in steaming rivers, bloated, to the sea.

S. Afzal Haider

Born in Jhansi, Syed Afzal Haider migrated to Pakistan in August 1947. He grew up in Karachi, studied physics and chemistry at the D.J. Science College, and went abroad for further education. He studied electrical engineering, psychology and social work in turn and worked in those respective fields for ten years each. He started writing stories in the 1980s, some of which are very American and only hint at his South Asian background; others deal with issues of migration, identity and personal loss. He is co-editor of *The Chicago Quarterly Review*, and his work has appeared in various literary magazines and anthologies in America. He lives in Illinois and is married to a Japanese American.

From Brooklyn to Karachi via Amsterdam

My cousin Azra who lives in a basement apartment in Manhattan gave me a contraption for catching mice. It was a cardboard box which, when folded in the prescribed method, assembled into a miniature igloo with a single entrance. The inside bottom was covered with a thick, sticky, glue-like substance that shone like glossy polyurethane on a dark oak floor, rather like the one in the dining room of my own house.

I used the trap one time. I found the mouse still alive, anchored to the shiny floor just out of reach of the bit of bread I'd used for bait. It made desperate chirping noises as it craned its neck forward trying to reach the bread. I didn't like this method of entrapment, alive and stuck, nourishment just out of reach.

I put the igloo in a white plastic bag from Lucky's Grocery Store, tied it with a green wire twist and dropped it into the garbage can outside my house. I wondered how long it took a mouse to suffocate. They don't collect garbage until Thursday on my block, and it was only Monday.

It is Thursday evening, just before dinner. The six o'clock news flickers without sound as I learn from my brother through international telecommunication that Baba's ill health has taken a turn for the worse. Asif is a doctor, a professor of pathology. 'His mind is fine,' Asif tells me in his clinical voice, 'but he is refusing to listen, he doesn't want to eat or drink and he won't take his medication. He's going to slip into coma any time now.' Baba has been dying for over three years now. There is a tumour on his bladder which bleeds through a sore on his back.

Three years ago while visiting me in Brooklyn—his last visit—he saw a doctor at my insistence. He refused to have the recommended surgery. He did not like, he explained to me, the idea of the blood transfusion, his own blood mingled with that of strangers who might drink alcohol or eat pork.

I couldn't look him in the eyes. I growled, 'People are having heart transplants these days and you're worrying about a blood transfusion.'

He smiled and asked me to sit beside him on the bed. He kissed my forehead and rubbed his silver beard against my cheek and said, 'I would consider a brain transplant if necessary, but no thanks, I want to die with my own blood pumping through my own heart.'

Later in Karachi he refused the surgical treatment again, telling Asif that he couldn't bear the idea of being chemically put to sleep. 'What if the surgeon is having a bad day and performs a lobotomy by mistake while I'm out?' He added, 'A man dies only once. I want to die wide awake, with my eyes open.'

'If you want to see him,' says Asif, 'you ought to come immediately.'

I don't know what to say. I ask to speak to Baba.

'You should,' says Asif. 'He likes you better and he listens to you.' I want to protest but I know it's not the right time and besides, we both know it's true. There is a long wait while the phone is brought to Baba, a wait filled with the clicks and chirps of transcontinental communication. They are lonely sounds, unanswered in the vast impersonal distance that lies between the two telephones. I wonder if Baba really is going to die this time.

'How are you?' I ask when Baba comes on the line.

'Pretty bad,' he says. What I admire most in my old man is his courage, even when he is afraid.

'I hear you're not eating or drinking anything,' I tell him.

'Yes,' he answers, 'I cannot.'

'Why not?' I demand.

'My gums have shrunk and my dentures don't hold. I can't chew anything, I can't get up and go to the bathroom. I've been sick long enough. It's time to go.'

'Baba—,' against my own good rational sense, I am becoming angry.

'I can no longer paint,' Baba continues in the same soft voice, full of the calm of reason. 'I am tired of thinking about things I can do nothing about. All men die,' he says. 'All men die.'

'I'm going to leave tonight. I'll be there on Saturday morning,' I tell him with my voice breaking. 'I want to see you.'

'I want to see you too, dear boy, but I don't like being trapped in my own body, unable to move.' I remember the mouse. I plead with him. 'Please eat and take your medication. I still have a lot to talk to you about.' I always tell him that. 'I don't want to find you in a coma when I arrive.'

'I can't promise, but please come.' His soft voice is weak.

I hate overseas phone calls. They are always about bad news. When I return to the dinner table the six o'clock news is over and my food has gone cold.

'Did Baba die?' asks Sean as I carry my plate to the microwave.

I have been speaking in Urdu so the entire conversation has been lost to them—them being my Forest Park, Illinois-born oriental wife Virginia, our four-year-old son, Sean, and infant daughter, Sarina

Last year alone I travelled twice from Brooklyn to Karachi to visit my ailing father. At the end of each visit I wondered if I'd ever see him again, where I'd be when he died. My mother used to be big on weddings and funerals. 'Parents should arrange weddings for their children,' she said, 'and children should bury their parents.' I married a woman of my own choosing and missed my mother's funeral—the fate of the transplanted person. The least I can do is bury my father.

'Did Baba die?' Sean asks again.

'No,' I answer, 'but he may die any day.'

'What if Baba dies on my birthday?'

'Then we can celebrate a birth and mourn a death on the same day.' I sit down at the table again and look at Virginia. She is burping Sarina on her shoulder and she looks back at me, waiting.

'I am going to leave tonight,' I say. 'If I make the right connections, I can be there in twenty-four hours.'

'What if your plane crashes?' Sean asks.

I begin to put food in my mouth. I have no idea what I'm eating. My wife's excellent cooking is as devoid of taste as styrofoam. I reach over to tousle my son's hair. 'What if it doesn't?' I laugh.

'What if it does?' Sean insists. 'Planes do crash. I don't want you to die.'

'When I die, I shall be extraordinarily ancient with a long white beard down to here. You will be grown up with a family of your own and you won't need your old man anymore.' I look my son straight in the eye when I tell him this. I hope I'm right.

That night I leave for Karachi via Amsterdam. I am due to arrive in Karachi on Saturday morning. As I try to fall asleep on the plane, exhausted and tired, I think of Baba and how as a little boy I always hoped he would come home at night before I fell asleep; that I would be up in the morning before he was gone for the day.

Before my family migrated to Pakistan, we lived in a small town in India, on the banks of the River Jumna. In the summertime, early on Sunday mornings, Baba woke me with kisses on my forehead and a rub of his unshaven beard on my cheeks. Before sunrise, my mother, who prayed faithfully five times a day, went to *Fajr* (morning prayers), but Baba and I set out on our fish hunt. His gun in its case across his shoulder, his hunting bag secured to the rear carrier of his bicycle, dark hair combed neatly back, dressed in a loose white shirt and trousers, he sat me on the crossbar and pedalled the long uphill route with an urgency.

We always arrived at the bank of the Jumna just as the sun rose. Baba parked the bike carefully on its stand and began the ritual which never varied: the gun was removed from its case, the single barrel, ball and muzzle loader cleaned with a ramrod. Then black powder, a homemade lead bullet and a piece of rag were packed in. I would stand at the edge of the river, watching him aim at bubbles bouncing like pearls to the surface of the water. Baba would cock the gun, put a cap on the nipple, aim and fire. Then he would lay the gun aside, place his glasses carefully next to it, kick off his sandals and jump into the water. For a few moments it was as though the river swallowed him up. I would search the surface with my eyes, knowing he would appear again but anxious none the less.

Suddenly he would split the water with a great splash and climb the bank with a fish in his hands, the river streaming from his body, his brown face shining in the sun. My father was a sure shot. He thought there was nothing in life that couldn't be undone. With our fish filleted and packed in the hunting bag, we would sail downhill toward home, Baba smoothly pedalling the bike, a strong forearm on either side of me, his cool wet white shirt flapping against my head, to Mama's Sunday morning breakfast.

Baba was an art master at Sarsuti Part Shalla, the local Hindu high school. He made his living painting portraits of famous people and common folk. A Gandhi for a Mohan Das, a Jinnah for a Mohammad Ali, and someone's deceased mother when commissioned. He wore eyeglasses that he needed to take off to see what was directly in front of him. I would watch him for hours as, in slow motion, he observed his subject through his spectacles. When he was ready to paint, he took them off. 'People wear their lives on their faces,' Baba used to say. 'To see what a person has lived, you have only to read his face.' I saw a bit of his face in each portrait he painted. Sometimes I look into a mirror and see my father looking back.

Baba gave me the most he could. Unlike my mother, he hardly ever prayed, not even on big holidays, but he read the Koran every day. Upon my departure for higher education in America, he gave me his Holy Koran. 'Read it for peace of the soul,' he admonished. It sits on a bookshelf now, unread. Baba was a generous man, but he wouldn't permit me to wear his shoes, not even his house slippers. He was a complicated man. My mother would tell him about mischief I had accomplished during the day and he would reply that it was too late, I'd already done it. Knowing the pattern of my daily difficulties, Mama would inform him what I was about to do. He replied, 'It's premature, he's done nothing yet.'

During the British Raj, Baba shaved daily with a 7 O'Clock brand blade. He wore gabardine suits, silk ties and a grey felt hat. He smoked Passing Show cigarettes. On the package was a picture of a man with a brown face wearing a grey felt hat. Folks around us called him *Sahib*; his friends called him *Kala* (black) *Sahib*. *Kala Sahib* enjoyed good food, dressed well, and I, having read his *Kama Sutra*, could guess what he did for good sex. 'The art of loving is in knowing your own state of arousal,' he said. 'The cuckoo should not call before it is the hour.'

Flying against time, I arrive on Saturday morning at 11:05. When I step off the plane I collide with heat so intense it feels like violent physical assault. I have an instant of panic as I realize that my years in northern latitudes have finally robbed me of the ability to tolerate my native climate. A large delegation of relatives meets me at the gate. Even before we speak, I can see from the faces of Asif and my sister, Rashida, that I am too late.

I ride with Asif in his almond green Morris Minor, listening to Urdu songs on the radio. We proceed directly to the graveyard and Asif finds a bit of shade to park in near the entrance. As another car full of relatives pulls up next to us, I look around, stiff from travel and lack of sleep, enervated by the heat, and feel the smallest tugging lift of spirit.

I love graveyards in this part of the world. They are like a carnival or a baseball park during a game, alive and full of people. Vendors by the gates sell flowers, rose water, incense, Coca Cola. Inside, people are resting, reading the Koran, burning incense, chanting prayers aloud or praying silently. Asif buys a large bottle of rose water, a package of incense and a clear plastic bag full of red rose petals. My cousin Farook buys seeds to feed the birds. The three of us, along with Rashida and her children, Adnan and Naheed, and Asif's son Habib, named after our father, make our way toward the family plot. Farook rubs his eyes with his fists and says that Baba was more like a father to him than his own father.

At our feet is the new grave: my father, the brown face in the grey felt hat, *Kala Sahib*. Someone begins the prayers for the dead. I sit down between the graves of my parents, one smoothed and benign, the other, fresh, raw, a ragged wound that has not yet scabbed over. I'm wearing Levis, a western shirt and Adidas and I'm soaked with sweat. I listen to Farook chant *Sura Al Fatiha: 'Praise be to Allah, Lord of the Creation...King of Judgement Day.'* I pick at tiny clumps of dirt, crushing them with my fingers. My mother once expressed her fear that some day I would be unable to recite even a silent prayer for her. She was right: both my heart and my mouth are dumb.

Rashida sits next to me, holding my hand, sobbing openly. I want to cry, but I can't, or perhaps my whole body weeps as the salt of my perspiration pours out, drenching my clothes and hair so that I cannot tell the difference between my sister's tears and my own sweat.

'Tell me about Baba,' I say.

Rashida turns her face away from me and stares out at where her children are moving among the graves. She says, 'He was sitting up in bed when you spoke with him. He looked very grey. I wrung out a towel in cool water and bathed his face. Then I helped him to lie flat. He was shivering. That frightened me more than anything else, his shivering. The heat was really bad, worse than today. The floors were so hot I was afraid the children's feet would blister. And Baba lay there shivering.'

My sister closes her eyes and presses the end of her veil over her mouth. I look down at her hand lying in mine, the familiar structure of bone and tendon under rich brown skin, a delicate, fragile-looking hand, a lie of a hand, because it contains the strength to have done those things for Baba all alone when I was far away.

'I covered him up with a cotton quilt—the one printed with grey leaves and white flowers that you gave him the first time he visited you in America. He lay there quietly with his eyes open on the single bed, next to the bed where our mother slept. I'd been sleeping in it for the past week. I wondered what people think about when they are dying. I picked up his Koran and sat down next to him. I read aloud, you know, *Sura Al Rahman*, he always liked that.'

It is The Merciful who has taught the Koran. He created man and taught him articulate speech...which of your Lord's blessings would you deny? I remembered it well.

'Then,' Rashida goes on, 'he asked for *Sura Ya Sin*. His voice was very strong. Do you remember, *Ya Sin, I swear by the wise Koran that you are sent upon a straight path...*?'

I nod.

'I started to cry, but I wouldn't let myself. I finished: '*Glory be to Him Who has control of all things. To Him you shall return*. When I stopped reading, his eyes were closed. I knew then he was dying. He opened his eyes and looked up at me. ' "All men should be blessed with a daughter," he said.'

I squeeze her hand. 'A daughter like you,' I tell her.

She says, 'A tear rolled down my cheek and dropped onto his beard. I don't think he noticed. He was frowning as if he were trying to remember something, then his face relaxed and he smiled. At that moment, oh, I wish you could have seen him—he might have passed for his old self.'

Yes, I think, the man in the grey felt hat. In my mind's eye I see my sister's tear sink into Baba's beard like an uncut diamond into the fine ash of a spent fire.

'He said then, "Go now, please. I am ready to sleep." I kissed him and left the room.' There are a few moments of silence as Rashida labours for control. Finally she says, 'At dawn on Friday as you were somewhere over the Atlantic, I heard the muezzin call out from the mosque, "Prayer is better than sleep." Baba did not waken for *Fajr*.'

I close my eyes and continue to hold Rashida's hand. Baba died on *Al-Jumma*, the day of congregation, under the portrait of our mother he painted when she was a young woman. He had been bathed, groomed and wrapped in a white cotton shroud. After Friday congregation in the mosque, funeral prayers were offered. In one-hundred-seventeen degrees, he was buried the same afternoon.

Rashida gets up to join her children. I sit in silence as Asif scatters a handful of rose petals on Baba's grave. He, Rashida and Farook, my nieces and nephews, move on to the other graves in the family plot, chanting prayers for the dead. Habib sprinkles rose water, Adnan and Naheed cast rose petals. I turn to my mother's grave, thinking of Camus's Monsieur Meursault and his vigil beside his mother's coffin. I too do not feel any sadder today than any other day.

My mother has been here long enough to have a name plate. I gather a handful of the rose petals scattered by the children. They are already curled and fading. Dust blows in my face and I close my eyes. Even this hot breeze, a draft from some circle of hell where the rootless and homeless wander, feels good against my wetness. I see my mother's face, red in the sun, smiling at me. There is the mole on her cheek that I had forgotten. Silently I repeat the prayers for the dead. My brother lights a few sticks of incense. I stand up, easing the stiffness from my legs, rubbing the rose petals between my palms. I open my hands; the crushed petals and their wisp of fragrance fly away with the blowing dust.

As we drive through the noisy, crowded streets toward Baba's house, Asif tells me that one reason he never went abroad was to spare our mother the shock of losing both her sons. That was kind of him, I think, noble, even. 'Are you happy?' I ask.

'Am I happy?' Asif repeats. 'I am well accomplished. Daughters are happy when they become mothers. Sons always have to fight the battles of their fathers.'

I ran from my father's battles when I was eighteen, never to return to live with him, not even for high holidays.

The next morning is cloudy and dark, blanketed with heat and humidity. Perhaps it will rain, I think with hope, but by noon the wind picks up and blows away the clouds. The temperature climbs to one-hundred-twelve in the shade. I spend all that day and the next in Baba's room, cleaning out his closet, looking at his papers. There are awards and certificates (Drawing Master of Merit, Artist of Distinction), his membership in the Royal Drawing Society of London, yellowed invitations to high teas with dukes, banquets with shahs. I feel a swelling of pride and admiration: this was a grand man, my old man—my dead old man. Among his letters is a ribbon-tied bundle from an internationally renowned artist who lives in Lancaster, England. He had sought out Baba during his travels to India. There are also letters from Faye Dincin of San Antonio, Texas, a woman Baba befriended during his travels to the States after my mother's death.

Rashida wanders in now and then to bring me a cup of tea or merely to stare, as if to convince herself that Baba has not come back, as though he'd gone on a business trip to Delhi and might reappear at any moment. 'I knew he was going to die,' she says, not to me especially. 'I thought I was ready, but now that he is gone I still can't believe it.' The end of her shawl is wet from dabbing at her eyes.

The spare bed is covered with paint brushes, palette knives, tubes of paint, sketch pads, boxes of charcoal and pastels. The walls are lined with ranks of unfinished paintings. The fragrance of turpentine and linseed oil, a smell which in my childhood always meant Baba, hangs over everything.

I lie down exhausted on Baba's bed. I stare up at the blades of the ceiling fan. Despite the heat I do not dare to turn it on for fear of disordering the carefully sorted personal memorabilia and papers of no consequence to a dead man. Holy Jesus, I think. Rashida comes in to sit next to me on the bed. She fans me gently with a paper fan. 'Before I went to the States,' I tell her, 'I had an emptiness, a certain loneliness that I thought would pass with time.' I shift my weight and slip into the mould that Baba left in the polyfoam mattress. 'I thought it would be easy to leave it all behind.'

Rashida stares at me. 'You can never leave it all behind,' she says. 'A son is like a tree: the more branches it sprouts, the deeper grow the roots.'

I smile at her. 'And a daughter?'

She smiles back, a smile full of deliberate mystery and mischief, the smile of the child sister I left when I went to America. 'A daughter is like a river. Miles and miles it flows to merge with the sea, yet its banks remain unchanged.'

On Thursday, *Mamon* (Uncle) Majid, my mother's brother, dies unexpectedly of heart failure. It is as though the gods have repented making me miss my father's funeral and have kindly provided another in its place. After *Zuhr* (afternoon prayer) at the graveside, I see *Mamon* Majid's face for the last time. He lies in the coffin he brought back from his pilgrimage to Mecca, wound in a black sheet, only his face exposed. His head is bent slightly to the right, as though he died in the act of an ironic shrug. I bend over him and the pungent odour of camphor stings the back of my throat. He is pale, motionless, so very still, the way Baba must have looked. A big drop of perspiration slides off my nose, onto *Mamon* Majid's eyelid and rolls down his cheek. He looks as though he is crying.

The morning after *Mamon* Majid's funeral, Friday, the one-week anniversary of Baba's death, the sky remains dark with gusting winds blowing at near-hurricane force. Trees and utility poles are bent and uprooted, TV antennas blow like tumbleweed and billboards fly like pages of yesterday's newspaper. Half of Karachi loses electricity. Hail falls, giant frozen teardrops on the yellow grass. At last the rain comes in a great drowning torrent and the streets turn to rivers. Three members of a cricket team are electrocuted when their bus is stranded under a bridge and they walk on live power lines buried in the flood water.

As the lightning and thunder crash and the winds howl around the house, I pack for the return trip. Into my carry-on bag I put Baba's portrait of my mother and an unfinished self-portrait. I also take two of his books, a biography of Muhammad and the poetry of Ghalib, his silver betel tin, the letters of the renowned British artist and Baba's diary from 1930 to 1937. It is a thick black leather-bound notebook, with his name engraved in fading gold capital letters.

That evening, the weather calm once more, I leave on a non-stop flight to Amsterdam. At the gate, Rashida takes me in her arms and holds me for a long time. I feel her strength flowing into me, as though she is trying to transfuse me with it for the ordeal of my journey home. She tells me in a fierce whisper that she is afraid she will never see me again. I tease her, reassure her, make Asif promise to bring her when he visits me in New York next year. I think of what Baba used to say upon my frequent departures, 'Why leave if you are planning to come back?'

A bright sun shines over the clouds all the way from Amsterdam to New York. Virginia meets me at the airport, leaving Sean and Sarina with my cousin Azra, the one who gave me the mousetrap. Virginia kisses me gently, holds me close. 'I missed you,' she whispers. 'I'm glad you're home.' On the drive from Queens to Brooklyn, I watch a sunset dramatic enough for Hollywood: red sky, banks of purple clouds, radical oranges and violets dimming and drowning in the blackness which creeps from the east. On the car radio, Springsteen sings 'My Father's House.'

During the night, lying next to Virginia in the darkness that comes with sleep, everything becomes more real than waking life. It is sunrise and I am at the house on the banks of the River Jumna. Every door in the house is open, Asif's tricycle stands in the courtyard, the tea kettle on the stove has just stopped boiling. I walk from room to room. The beds are made up, covered with red, yellow and green quilts; Rashida's dolls sit on her bedroom shelf. I can sense them all there, the members of my family. As though they have just left each room as I enter it. I smell my mother's fragrance, the smoke of Baba's Passing Show cigarettes. I call out, but no one answers. I rush back into the courtyard and cross over to Baba's studio. The door stands wide and I find myself on the threshold of my own Brooklyn dining room. On the far side, across the gleaming expanse of dark oak floor, stands Baba, his back to me, working on a canvas. I feel a rush of indescribable joy. 'Baba!' I shout, and start across the room to embrace him. He turns to me, and there is a smile on his face of such ineffable love and sadness that I freeze in midstep. I call out again, but my feet are stuck, immobile on that fatal shiny expanse that stands between me and my father. It is only then that I see what he is painting: a self-portrait in a hall of mirrors, and the faces looking back at me from the canvas are Baba's, my own, and my son's.

Leaving the stranger who is my wife alone in bed, I sit in the living room of the unfamiliar house where my American children are growing up in a city as alien to me as the deserts of the moon. I drink coffee and chain-smoke, something I haven't done in years. I watch dawn come up over Brooklyn. One day soon, I tell myself, I shall write to the renowned artist in Lancaster, England, to Faye Dincin in San Antonio, Texas, and tell them that Baba is dead.

Talat Abbasi

Born in Lucknow, she grew up in Karachi, which she still regards as her home town, though she has lived away from Pakistan for almost twenty years. She was educated at St. Joseph's College, Karachi, Kinnaird College, Lahore, and The London School of Economics. She moved to New York in 1978, and has worked with the UN since. Many of her short stories have been broadcast on the BBC, and some have appeared in *The Massachusetts Review*, *Short Story International*, *Paris Transcontinental* and other literary journals. Her fiction has been included in various anthologies and college text books for literature students in the United States. She is very much a feminist and much of her work revolves around issues of class and gender. Most of her stories are set in Pakistan, but she has started to write more about Pakistani immigrants in the United States.

Simple Questions

But then I end up feeling sorry for her, for that ustaniji, that queer headmistress woman, for she's feeling foolish I know though it isn't my fault she can't answer a few simple questions. She's supposed to know everything, but she doesn't know what to say now to this poor illiterate creature who's right after all. So she's leaving in a huff and I'm running after her to see her off for she's a respectable woman, not a sweeper or labourer and she's a visitor though I never invited her. But by the time I reach the courtyard she's half out of the door already, ducking her head for she's taller than most men, poor thing. And the next moment she's gone, jumped like a man into her ricksha which she kept waiting in the lane. Barks something to the rickshawallah who nods quickly and starts his scooter. But I don't see more for I'm bareheaded, barefooted, running behind her like that. And there's quite a crowd collected there, gossiping with the rickshawallah, all wanting to know who's the visitor and why. And some of them are turning round and any minute they'll be poking their heads into my courtyard. So I quickly shut the door, leaning against it and smiling. Just a few simple questions and she vanishes like a genie! But then she really is strange after all which isn't surprising seeing there's no man, no children, and it just isn't natural. Then as the phut phut phut of the ricksha grows fainter I hear the baby cry so I run into the quarter, cooing na na na and take her from Wasima who's trying to quieten her. I hitch up my shirt but she's at the nipple even before it's bared. Her nails, which I haven't had time to cut, dig into my flesh for she clutches so hard like now she's got me she'll never let me go. She's going to be clever like Halima. But impatient. You can tell from the way she sucks, quickly quickly. But the poor thing's hungry, late for her feed, all because of that ustaniji. I stroke her head which is prickly like a man's chin. I shaved it soon after she was born to make the hair grow thicker and it's just starting to grow back. For a few minutes there'll be peace and quiet and I'm so glad for what a morning it's been.

The moment I wake up I know. I don't even raise my head from my pillow or throw off the sheet, let alone sit up and fumble for my chappal. No, I don't even turn toward the window to see if the sun is rising, is the sky pink or still dark. I close my eyes almost before they open and press my stomach. Not again, I'm begging, please God, not so soon, Munni's only five months. But I don't think more for suddenly everything inside me is rising to my mouth. I clutch the edge of the cot and just hang my head down and let it all come out. From the mouth, from the nose and even the eyes, they water, and it almost misses the spittoon which I remember to drag out quickly from under the cot. And while it's all coming out I'm feeling horrible. The taste, sour, of last night's dhal and then the yellow and green mess and red chili pieces whole. And even while it's all coming out I'm looking fearfully at him, lying in his bed which he has all to himself. He's turning over and pulling the pillow to cover his ears. And I'm trying to be as quiet as possible for I don't want all five girls to wake up. I hang my head over the edge of the bed and rest it on my arm till the wood seems to saw through my elbow. And quietly I stare at the spittoon, waiting to see if there's more. It's a cheap aluminium one, dented from being kicked around and it's all stained red with paan and here and there patches of white, from the lime. And the dhal is splashed into it and some on the floor. And I'll have to clean it up but it isn't such a mess after all. Thank goodness the spittoon was under the cot. And I wipe my forehead, which is wet, with an edge of the chaddar and my mouth too. And I spit some more into the spittoon though nothing comes out now. But I do it over and over for it's the taste I want to spit out.

If only I could get up and wash my mouth out but it's still dark. So I lie still as a corpse, almost falling off the edge. That's how I've been all night. Afraid to move because that baby'll set up such a howl. She's lying comfortable at last, tucked near the small of my back where she's slipped down from up near my pillow. Such a restless one this was, even in the stomach; I was sure it was a boy. And the rope of the cot's cutting into me and there'll be crisscross marks all over my back. But I daren't move for a man needs his sleep if he's to do overtime. And it's difficult enough with the old lady coughing and shouting all night in her sleep on the veranda where the doctor sahib said put her, she musn't be near the children at least. And until she's gone we need the overtime, every paisa, for there's doctors bills and medicine. And afterwards funeral expenses though she saved up enough for her shroud and bought it herself, while she could still hobble over to the government fair price shop. Bought an extra half yard for she said it'll shrink for sure, for it's bad cloth the government sells cheaply to the poor. And that was wise for the dhobi's going down into her grave to launder her shroud.

I don't tell him. I let him go off to work without telling him for I see he's in pain again, closing his eyes and passing his hand over his stomach again and again for that's where it burns like a bed of live coals. Milk, lots of it, says the doctor in the free government dispensary. Yes milk, but where from, Doctor Sahib, he wants to know, for it's easy to say milk, a seer of it, a day, no less, but does it flow in the ditches that a poor man can just bend down and scoop up a cupful? Next! shouts the doctor, who's next? So he never goes back but suffers in silence for he's a good man who never complains. Not once has he scolded me, it's only daughters you're giving me. It's the will of God, he says sadly every time. But he worries and worries I know for each girl's a fresh worry from beginning to end, and a man needs a son to share his burdens with. And what wouldn't I do to give him a son! I've cried at so many tombs there's not a saint I've left within a day's journey. And I give money regularly to a holy man. Not much for how much can I save? A rupee here or there. I see how much the others give. Not just money but ornaments. Silver, even gold. And I feel ashamed. Don't, it's not the money, says the holy man every time he takes it, for yes, you're right, it's little. But it's not the money at all. It's the sacrifice you make—and the bigger you make the better—that counts. But like he says sadly every time, it's God's will and so it's only girls and girls tumbling out so fast like they're just waiting in line inside me. So I look at him in pain turning away from the roti and tea Halima has brought him. He waves her away and reaches under his bed for his chappals. The tea, just the tea, I beg him, it's very milky. And I take it from her and blow on it hard to cool it for sometimes she makes it too hot. He smiles at me as if to say just to please you and takes a few sips before returning it. Then while he's buckling his belt—it's the last notch I notice sadly, that's how thin he's growing—I break the roti into tiny pieces and slip it into the bowl. He'll eat it if it's soft but I have to sit there and spoon it into his mouth as if he's a baby. And I make sure he finishes every last bite for he mustn't rush off on an empty stomach. Nothing's so bad, says the doctor. And as he opens the courtyard door, Halima races up from the kitchen with his tiffin. I lean against the door of the quarter for I'm feeling a bit giddy now. I call out to Halima did she remember to stuff the paratha with potato. Potatoes are soft and easy to eat. She nods as she hands him the box. He smiles at her in his tired way and pats her. Oh, he's a good father and fond of her as he would be of a boy. So I look at him in pain and not speaking of it and I think not today. It'll wait.

After he's gone I call out to Halima, come and massage my forehead. Yes, massage her forehead and crack her knuckles like she's some Begum Sahib, Rani, Mahrani! cackles the old woman and guffaws in her bed on the veranda. It's like that all the time she's awake. Begum Sahib, Rani, Mahrani! Like there's a parrot in a cage repeating the same words day after day. I've only to open my mouth and she's off taunting me so I'll come running out to fight with her. Always itching to fight for her breath may be going out but her tongue's still so sharp they could use her in a slaughterhouse. But I no longer reply like I used to. And today of all days I can't even think of Ammaji; I'm that upset with the midwife, dai Shakira. She said to me, don't worry, Halima's mother, it can't happen while you're breast-feeding. Never. Rest assured. But the lady doctor, I started to say. Well, go back to her then and let her tie you up. And now if you'll excuse me, I must rush over to Hanif, the tailor's, for his wife's in her third day of labour and bringing the house down with her screams. Shameless, letting the neighbours hear.

Shameless, I'm agreeing as I take the powder for the baby's gums and press two rupee notes into her hands. But all the while I'm thinking she's right, that's just what she said she'd do, that lady doctor. Tie me up. That's what she's been saying since the three died in the stomach, one after the other, after Haseena. Getting angrier and angrier and the third time so fed up she said she'd never see me again. She had to of course when Munni was born, for I'd have died if she hadn't cut me up and got the baby out. I was that sick. Even Shakira got frightened and said take her to the hospital. Now. Don't wait. And I don't want to be cut up and have the blood flow out of me again. Bottles and bottles they gave me but I'm still not the same. It's not my own blood after all. And sometimes I'm thinking I never will be, what with these headaches and eating less than a bird so poor Munni can't get enough milk. That's why she's so cranky. No, I don't want to be cut again, but I couldn't let her tie me up yet for next time it could be a boy. Yes, it could, she said, but you may not live to see him. And that frightened me but Shakira said don't worry, not every time. You won't have to be cut up every time. Make sure you feed the baby two years; that'll give you some time. And once you're strong again, yes, who knows, maybe a boy!

Halima comes immediately for she's a good girl, running out of the kitchen wiping her hands on her shirt. The tears sting my eyes now for the headache's that bad. My hair, which falls to below my waist, feels so heavy as if each hair is as big as a rock and they're all pounding against each other. I open my mouth to tell her leave the pots and pans for now, I can't stand the clatter, massage my head while the baby's asleep. But she puts a finger gently on my lips and immediately begins to massage my forehead, the dear girl. I press her hands softly to say God bless you child and lie back, giving myself over to the fingers. Soft as velvet, yet firm and cool like a splash of water putting the fire out. Harder, I motion, and her fingers rotate quickly on the temples. She remembers to dab oil on her palm before she begins massaging the scalp. Oh, she knows how to do it the proper way for I taught her myself, massaging my head and whispering a prayer, then blowing gently on the forehead. It's the only way it'll go. And Salima and Wasima both run in and settle down on either side of the bed and reach for my hands to crack the knuckles. And Haseena who's maybe only four, never to be outdone, skips in and jumps onto the bed. Ouch! My poor head as the bed shakes. But it's only to massage my feet with her tiny hands. And the tears sting again, but now they're tears of gratitude for such children even if they are girls. They make a poor woman a queen, so carry on with your Rani, Mahrani, old lady, you're not far-wrong. It's a queen lying in this sagging rope cot being soothed to sleep. And soon I really am drowsy for the fingers are drawing the pain out of my head and the pounding's still there, but it's coming from farther and farther away. And I must have dozed off for suddenly someone's saying, Amma, wake up! And I do try to open my eyes for I can hear clearly again, Amma, wake up! But it's like weights are placed on my eyes and waves of sleep are washing over me. Then someone shakes me by the shoulder. And this time my eyes open, and what I see gives me such a shock that suddenly I'm sitting bolt upright. Am I still dreaming ? I know I saw Shakira holding up a boy, saying didn't I tell you this time a boy? And he was fat as five girls too! So may be I'm still dreaming. I rub my eyes! No! Still there! Who's she? Where's she come from? What does she want? What's she doing here, this policewalli, for that's what she has to be, a policewoman. Tall and broad as a pillar,standing with legs far apart like a man, a khaki shalwar suit, dupatta not cast over her head but thrown over the right shoulder and knotted on the left side over the hip like a sash. She could be a bandmaster except there's no jolly smile and no music coming from her for I've done some wrong. Yes of course I have. Certain I have by the look in those eyes. Hard as nails, they're telling me, you lazy slut of a woman, lying back in this mess of a room on your bed having your head massaged and your knuckles cracked by these poor little girls when you should be on your knees scrubbing the floor. And I do know there's a smell of vomit but I did tell Wasima, clean out the spittoon and then wipe the floor. Remember the floor.

But she's not like Halima, none of them is, what can I do? And anyway, who's she to be standing there like I'm the trespasser in my own house?

Ustaniji, Amma, Ustaniji! My goodness! So that's who she is! That headmistress woman who sent that long letter. Both sides of the sheet it covered. I kept turning it over and wondering now who'd be writing to us and why. Ustaniji, said Halima's father when he returned at night and read it. Because Halima's dropped out of school and she wants to know why. Is it money, is it books? Can she help? She's ready to in any way for reading writing's important. Yes, even for girls and then Halima's one of the cleverest. It's a shame when the child herself's so keen. Send her back, you must! Oh, that's an order, is it, I laughed, and knew right away she was queer. But to turn up herself and stand over me, looking down like she's the Queen of England. And to look at Halima that's just what she is. Can't take her eyes off ustaniji, smiling and blushing and all excited. Fallen in love with ustaniji she has and how we all tease her. So this is ustaniji who's changed our life. Comb and plait your hair every day and your sisters' too, says ustaniji. So Halima must get up early for all this plaiting and combing for I said to her not me. I don't have the time, you tell your ustaniji that. And why they should plait it everyday I'm not understanding for where do they go? But ustaniji's word is law after all. And once a week at least it must be washed and checked for lice. Then all in a line they must sit in the sun with Halima bending over each, parting the hair and peering at their scalps and smacking them with a fine-toothed comb for they're dying to run away, the poor little ones. And last thing at night they must all be marched to the tap to clean their teeth again for you must do this twice a day, did you know. But you're allowed to use a stick of neem if you can't afford fancy tooth brushes as long as you keep them all marked and separate. And to all these things Halima's father says let her be, they're good things, don't object for they don't cost you a paisa, do they? But when I'm told don't wipe your hands on your shirt, keep a towel, wash it every day and, yes, all our clothes, everyday, if you please, then I say go ask your ustaniji if she thinks postmen are paid in soap cakes.

Sit down, Ustaniji, do! And I half get up as I point to one of the beds. But she shakes her head for of course it isn't proper to sit on beds. A chair then for ustaniji, Halima! Try next door first, otherwise the tea stall. Mind a nice comfortable one with arms. But it's no thank you to that too. Then tea at least. And I lift up my shirt and start untying the keys which I have knotted to the string of my shalwar. I have to for if I don't keep the sugar under lock and key the children's fingers will be in that box, the greedy things, and nothing left for Halima's father and he does like it with his yogurt. Yogurt's good for him, said the doctor. So I save everyone's ration for him. But it's no to the tea too. Well just as well too. I'm stingy with the sugar for a man needs to eat if he's to work. But what about paan, betel leaf, betel nut? I can make it right here for I keep the box next to me on the bed. First thing in the morning, last at night. I love it better than food, I tell you. My one luxury. And they're clean, the paan leaves. I wash them myself, trusting no one, not even Halima. Fresh too, for they're wrapped in moist muslin. See how they glisten, like it's just rained on them. And the betel nut's all cut and ready, the grains fine like sand. Just tell me how much lime. Everyone likes it different, some more, some less no one the same. It's the taste, so sharp. I myself—oh, so she hasn't come to eat and drink, isn't that clear? Can't you tell by now this is no social call?

Not at all. Why would a grand lady like you visit a hovel? Not for the enjoyment, that's plain. The flies for one are bothering you terribly. Excuse them, please, they think you're one of us. We're sorry there are so many of them today. It's because of that spot by the bed Munni's sleeping on. Wasima forgot to wipe the floor, but I'm sure you hitched your shalwar up to your knees when you had to pass by it. And I must apologize for myself too. Still in the clothes I slept in, not crackling with starch like yours. Hair streaming all over. I know you like it neatly plaited. But it's because of the headache, and that's returning as it always does when my sleep's interrupted which is what you've done. So I'll tie this rag tight round my forehead. Round and round like a clamp. And since this isn't a social call, I'll lie back, stop getting flustered, get her chair, get her tea, get her paan. But first I'll spread the lime on my betel leaf and put some betel nut on it, fold it and stuff it in my mouth, while I'm waiting for you to tell us why you've honoured us today. I daren't ask you for if I open my mouth too wide, you may see my teeth are all stained red with paan.

Why?

Paan's half way to my mouth when she raps it out, this why. And for a moment it remains held in midair. Then I stuff it in my mouth and chew slowly, looking at her wonderingly. Her hair isn't flying all over and she hasn't ripped off her clothes, but there's that look in her eyes which makes me think she's crazy. And she must be, to come barging into people's houses and demand why! Well? And now so impatiently like how dare I lie in bed chewing paan, not answering her questions! Like it's any of her business whether I send Halima to school or not for of course that's what she means by why. And for a moment I'm tempted to say why what? But she's a respectable woman so I say politely, because of Ammaji. Because of Ammaji doing everything on her bed like a baby if you let her for nothing moves but her tongue. And that never stops, not for a moment! Waking and sleeping she must shout out to all the passersby that I'm out to steal her shroud. Says she's heard me say aren't your daughters also your responsibility and where's the money for some dowry at least for though we're poor we're respectable and a girl can't leave her father's house empty-handed. And maybe I did say it, Ustaniji, for Halima's ten now, maybe eleven and I've got to start worrying. But God knows I'm not wanting Ammaji dead though everyone her age is gone now. Long since. And how much my girls and I do for her, Ustaniji, but she must still shout out to everyone to make sure she's not sent naked to her Maker. That's all she can think about. How they must wrap her in her shroud from head to foot, how tight it should be round the forehead so not a hair must be seen. Listen! That's her in her sleep: not a hair must be seen, not a hair—

… Halima. This girl. This child.

Sorry, Ustaniji, sorry! Like he says I do carry on! Of course it's Halima you've come to talk about. Halima. Not Ammaji.

And please don't get me wrong, Ustaniji. It's not that I'm against reading writing for girls if they're not needed at home. Why I'd even let the younger ones go if they wanted but they're not like Halima. Halima's clever and loves school like you say. How she cried when I said no more. Never asked why for she's a good girl. Just cried and cried till it broke her father's heart. All right, he says, when Ammaji doesn't need you anymore, you can go back. That's when I had to warn him, she'll be leaving your house in a year or two so don't you go promising her such things. You see, Ustaniji, he's soft. But as I said to him, don't take it so seriously, remember she's only a child. And you too, Ustaniji, don't worry so much about her, she'll get over it.

She will! That's the tragedy of it! Born in the darkness, dead before they can live. Like…like…a stillborn child! That at least I do understand!

Oh yes, Ustaniji, I do! Three died in the stomach you see, before Munni. That's her on the rubber sheet. And it's sad like you say, when they die like that. I cried every time till I was half blind and begged God to forgive me. I must have done some terrible wrong for two out of three were boys! Boys! Would you bel—

What! Finished already and fast asleep? Such an angel! And pretty as one, lashes long and curly. Silky too, my side of the family. Hey, Munni wake up! A bit more. Just a bit from the other breast. Tickle toes tickle toes. Yes, Haseena, you may tickle her behind the ears too. And the stomach. And under her arms. Everywhere. Fun for you but not an earthquake can wake her now. Well, sleep then and let's have peace while we can. Halima, put her on that bed. Oh, it's you, Wasima. And cover her face with the muslin. Can't you see the flies buzzing round her mouth already? Halima's locked herself up in the latrine. I know. I know. And crying her eyes out. I know. Salima! Get back. There's nothing to see. You leave her alone. And me too. All of you out. Yes, you too, Haseena. And shut the door. Thank goodness. Quiet at last. She's upset because I shouted at that woman. But I couldn't help it. You're not understanding, you're not, she's insisting, though I'm nodding at everything she's saying. And she has such a loud voice and Munni's stirring and my head's splitting and Ammaji's awake now and shouting visitors for Begum Sahib, Rani, Mahrani! All right, all right, I shout, take her back to school today. Now! But first you answer my questions please! Simple questions for I'm a simple woman but all the same I'm wanting to know a few things myself. I'm wanting to know just what good all this reading writing which I'm hearing about will do. Will it get her a husband I'm wanting to know. Will it get her a male child I'm wanting to know. Will it get her even a dowry I'm wanting to know. Come on then! Say it will! But she shakes her head for she knows I'm right. Oh, she does. I've never turned a page in my life but I'm not stupid, oh, not me. And still shaking her head, she pats Halima whose lip's already quivering and leaves. That's when I start feeling sorry for her for what's the use of all this reading writing if you can't answer simple questions like these?

ADRIAN A. HUSAIN

Born Syed Akbar Husain, he went to school in England and Switzerland, finally graduating from Oxford. While still at Oxford, his work caught the attention of Peter Jay, the editor of *New Measure*. He became part of a group, which included Gavin Bantock, Cal Clotheir, John Wheymar, and he won the Guinness Prize for Poetry. He was strongly influenced by The Confessional School of Poets, which he now believes hampered his development as a poet. He has since discarded that early work. He found his own voice in the mid-1970s by which time he had been back in Pakistan for some time and had begun to write about the environment around him. These poems merged his cultural duality, and were published in *The Encounter*, broadcast on the BBC and proved to be a turning point. He has steered clear of exotica however and says 'A poem should be able to work despite topography.' His aim, he says, is to write good English poetry which transcends time and space. In the 1970s he initiated a literary group 'Mixed Voices' which included Maki Kureishi,* Salman Tarik Kureshi* and Mansoor Sheikh*. The group advised many young poets, provided them with a forum and held gatherings where Urdu, Punjabi, Sindhi, Balochi and Pashto writers also read or translated their work. Later he did his doctoral thesis on Shakespeare, Machiavelli and Castiglione from the University of East Anglia. His poetry has been put together in a first collection, *Desert Album* (1997), and has also been published in two major Pakistani anthologies, *Pieces of Eight* (1971) and *The Blue Wind* (1984).

FROM ***DESERT ALBUM***

Crocodiles

From around the swamp
the forbidding vapours rise.
On one side, acacias shoot up.
The approach has been walled off.

Then in a sudden shaft of light
you see them: venerable,
weighted against the sand,
nursing their torpor.

Canines bared like tusks,
they lie
as though the swamp
had spewed them up.

You would think them
dead or asleep.
But each primitive lozenge
of skin is watching.

In each form
brooding on the bank
there flickers its instant
of ravenous lightning revival.

Margalla

Morning. Like my balcony
half of the hills
are in sun.

The light pauses
gliding effortlessly across
them. It has the forgetfulness

of fingertips
on a smooth table
as it rediscovers

how the land lies:
from the jagged rise
to the despondent

slump of Margalla.
The hills know
such ebb and flow

of light and shade—
desultory lifting
of film from diaphanous film—

hump and shaggy hollow
come casually into view
with a dried-up spring

as do the hills' summits.
Here day, fresh-settled,
glows. A thin group of pines,

gathering courage, climbs
gingerly up past
a stone ridge.

There are no other such trees.
nothing detracts
from this tremulous conquest.

Shrine

From its share of headland
it overlooks the sea,
the once plain mound
bearing up bravely

to the dour chafings of zeal:
death's rites: kiosks of incense
and roses, graves grazing like sheep
along the shrine's

sloped sides. At twilight in a huddle
you find junkies here: pilgrims
come to dribble
their own furtive requiems.

And beggars moth-hung around cars,
whose separate dusk you must
cleave to gain entry, pausing,
unshod, as you move to your tryst.

Portentous,
the garish dome
and cupola wait. A ceremony
of ascent and you are welcomed

to expiatory smoke, an intent
hum of voices: a diorama
wherein, somnambulist,
figures pace framing

rash prayers. Less sanguine, you too
track the saint with drapes
and rose petals, utter
a stumbling prayer, then stop

brought up short by a rustling,
a breath borne on the wind, faintly
crescendo—your own imagining
or at half-tide somewhere the real sea.

Landscape by Leila Shahzada

You have preserved
only what is essential: crags,
dun, flint-grey,
with a crevice between them.

Rising in the foreground
they scale a molten sky
where, announced by the hint of a moon
and sun cratered behind cloud,

by shifting hues and pale effusions of light,
day mutates into dusk.
But what are these faces
that peer out of the rock

or this rain of jewels
falling down the rockface?
Who are the king and queen
imprisoned here

and eyeing, a little sadly,
the slow cascade of topaz, aquamarine,
ruby, amethyst
and lapis?

Imagination's spendthrifts
locked fast in a dream:
of a rain that never fell,
a kingdom that never was.

The Music Leaves Antony

It was a maritime tryst,
the occasion of algae
and bilge: a muddied
iridescence.

The languors of Egypt
stole into him
with the licence
of soldiery:

carousals beckoned,
their genial fires
at large
beneath the palms.

impelled (if still not
hamstrung) by love
he sought respite
from conquest.

And would have
reneged on war
but for the humming
inside him,

a resonance barely
heard above love's
tumult. Or heard
receding. Oboe

and viol and systolic
drum put to flight
one evening past
a vigil of soldiers

till he awoke
to find, before Actium,
his courage—Hercules'
fine-tuned engines—gone.

For Srebrenica's Dead

Casualties of a somnolence,
you died
outside time,
your obsequies terse,

your graves a welter
of docile forms.
indifferent as they
who made them.

Today, that
murky bravura
recounted (no
detail too gross)

vouchsafe you
a name, a home.
While you, from deep chutes,
are brought up to air,

at last, with your
dressed taint—like
plankton, new-landed
and unblinking in the sun.

Srebrenica was the UN safe haven in Bosnia, where mass graves were unearthed in 1995.

Calvary Misunderstood
for Mir Murtaza Bhutto

Martyr to no known cause
(fumbling rebel, vague ideologue)
you went up no hill
but down a road

without a gradient—
deep, deep
into an inimical wood
dense with the shuddering

girths of guns. And there,
faith in your name's
talisman holding,
fondly stood your ground:

discovering later—
when the rabid bullets flew—
that from the place, noiselessly,
all of the tutelary gods had departed.

Out-Patient

I

Truant Visitor

An aimless clatter of stilletto heels
just before dark declares she is about,
preparing for some nebulous soirée.
By stages the dim corridor reveals
pale cheeks, stiff carriage and chromatic pout.
Her eyes by force of habit look away.

Mechanically, like someone in a dream,
pursuing the steep angle of her gaze,
she sits as though in an appointed chair.
Unless at times a comprehending gleam
of consciousness awakes in her, she stays
torpidly quiet, a smile half forming there;

and pulls on an obsessive cigarette.
Who is she dressed up for today in green?
And why the bouffant hair and manicure?
Her monumental fixity deflects
our cautious interrogatory routine.
We almost sense the truant visitor

beckoning as she wavers in the hall,
then stops and stares at us in prim reproof.
How shall we answer? What urbane regrets,
what brave assurances will serve to stall
her? How can we explain that time is proof
against suggestion—and is inveterate?

II

Tête à Tête

The woman reels
into the room.
Fifty? She could be any age
The flicker in her eyes congeals

as she enters. But for the lips
nothing moves in the face.
Slouched on the sofa
she strips

the door to a transparency
to smile
at someone
she can evidently see

and finds worth talking to
in snatches
(the other person
filling in as 'view').

To her right
her parents taper off
into their tide
of bedsheets.

On the scarped shelf
of their age
they barely notice
as the small voice laughs to itself.

Salman Tarik Kureshi

Born and educated in Lahore, Salman Tarik Kureshi has worked as a business executive in Pakistan and England. He has travelled widely in Europe, America, the Middle and Far East. His poetry has been published in various anthologies including *Pieces of Eight* (1971) and *The Blue Wind* (1984). He was a founder member of 'Mixed Voices' a multi-lingual forum initiated by Adrian A. Husain* for poetry and creative writing in the 1970s. He has now put together his first collection *Landscapes of the Mind* (1997).

FROM *LANDSCAPES OF THE MIND*

Winter Sunset

A ponderous
buffalo emerges, clambering slowly
from his mud pond; his flanks
steam blue into the yellow light.

His china-plate eyes are confused.
Fearsome muscles
twitch, shivering
at the needle touch of the air.

A little boy
cradles goose-pimpled feet
in his hands; his breath
hangs before his face.

The village houses huddle
like sheep without a fold
in the cold, golden light.
The air is sharp

with smoke of wood and cowdung.
The grey exhalations of the village
settle around
the silent tree trunks.

The buffalo's eyes glaze over,
pondering alternatives of comfort; he pauses
and settles back
into the warm, dung-richened mud.

The C Minor Prelude and Fugue being Played

I

First the affirmation:
A blossoming of tones
from great terraces of keys, pedals…

restrained it seems
by the mechanical reach of hands and feet,
by the bounds

of what the senses can encompass.
From these, this man proposes,
we aspire

II

He conjures enormous
vibrating columns of air,
piling beneath this cathedral

a mountain — from whose crest
it seems not possible
to clamber higher.

III

Each hand crafts
the succeeding steps
of a spiralling stairway of sound.

We are led past
the marble statuary,
the stained glass, through

the groins and corbels of the roof
on a relentless
helical track

that climbs, through sheer
fathoms of air, to penetrate
the fabric of the sky.

IV

We attain
a place
where planets are conceived,

where comets fatten and swing
outward, seeking
their appointed orbits.

V

And here all
is a complex
culmination of

tones, cadenzas,
sliding glissandoes…
sprouting about the hunched figure

hammering at the organ keys…
hammering at the iron
gates of Heaven.

The blind eyes
of angels, the pale
unfeeling eyes of God, regard him.

A Better Man Than I

Six Poems for Kipling

I

Your waistcoat pushes taut
against your watch chain. Your moustaches
execute a double curve above your lips.
Is that a smile
you're wearing, Rudyard?

You stare at me
from the end of the avenue that joins us.
Your eyes glitter with the confidence of your mission.

But tell me, Rudyard,
of the trip-beat hammering that grew in your chest
in the silent hours.
Of skin growing slippery with sweat of excitement
under a buttoned waistcoat.

Rudyard, tell me
what woad-daubed, hide-clad shaman
lurked beneath your skin?

II

I've seen monkeys playing wild
only in early childhood, in the mountains,
and I don't think I've ever seen an elephant outside the zoo.

But to you these things were ordinary. To you
they were the currency of your commerce,
your stock in trade, from which you garnered
your daily profit of words.

III

In your north, in Lahore,

> (where the subcontinent began; where invaders paused
> by the banks of the Ravi, assessed
> the kingdom's defences
> and leaped…
> Where the last invader found his way
> from the wrong direction,
> leaving the river unforded and the fort
> unalerted…)

In Lahore,
could the setting not be
resonant still?

Descendant of druids who ate raw beef
and roared for beer served in the skulls
of enemies—Rudyard—in Lahore,
Japanese cars with tinted windscreens and stereo sound systems
outnumber the tongas we knew.

And the Ravi itself runs lower.

IV

The Civil and Military Gazette was finally closed down
some fifteen years ago
but the gun you claimed for Kim
still stands at the end of the Mall Road.

Does your shaggy, blue-painted spirit wander that city,
carving runes of contempt
on the steps of the Engineering University, shaking
a rattle made from the skull of a sheep
in the middle of a scooter-thronged street?

V

Rudyard, where I live now—
this southern town of Richard Burton and Bartle Frere—
pulsates with the throb of a commerce
different to yours.

Its currency
is frozen prawns and colour television.

The noises and odours are not
of covered spice bazars
or bubbling samovars of jasmine tea.

The noise is of jet planes and motor cycles
and the clang of a bellbuoy on the swell;
the reek tells of diesel oil and the fish harbour
and food cooked in the shacks
of the poor.

This is a loud
city of palm and cactus,
where a beachless sea is shut behind
a wall of unrounded rocks.

VI

Below my balcony, flat land beyond three rows of houses
runs down to the sea.

A train is being shunted somewhere, bogies crashing
in detonations of sound. The salt flats,
beside which the track meanders on its way to the harbour,
drain dry in the outgoing tide.

In the distance, a ship's horn and the faint
faraway clang of a warner...
Far beyond the harbour lights

another spark of light: Manora lighthouse,
whose circling beam threw into relief
the fleet of buccaneer Napier
forging towards the lights on the shore.

It was destiny, you wrote,
your kind's appointed burden. But the tides changed.

The tides receded, leaving
empty shells and curious objects
for boys to ponder...

leaving finally
you, Rudyard,
and I.

As if these Clouds

As if these clouds
that hang so low and so heavy
could, in a moment's space, frost over...
crystallize, frozen in the sky. And the sun,
glimmering through their sudden translucence,
become iridescent—
broken into a million hues and sparkles, reflected
from facet to intricate facet
and down to me.
As if these trees were no longer green,
but a crystal aspect of brittle refracted colours;
so that one brilliant leaf
could splinter into shards and fall before me.

Tariq Ali

Born in Lahore, Tariq Ali was educated at St. Anthony's High School and Government College, Lahore. His political activities as a committed socialist had already earned the ire of the Government of Pakistan by the time he joined Exeter College, Oxford. Soon his name became synonymous with the student upsurge which swept across Europe in the 1960s. He served as a member of the Bertrand Russell War Crimes Tribunal, visited Kampuchea and Vietnam, was editor of two magazines *Black Dwarf* and *Red Mole* in the 1960s and 1970s respectively. He has also contributed political articles to various British periodicals and magazines and was an editor of *The New Left Review*. Although his political views have made it difficult for him to return to Pakistan, he has kept in close touch. His non-fiction includes *Pakistan: Military Rule or People's Power*? (1970), *1968 and After* (1978), *Can Pakistan Survive?* (1983), *The Nehrus and the Gandhis* (1985) and *Streetfighting Years: An Autobiography of the Sixties* (1987). He has said that his fascination with South Asian and Islamic history, as well as issues concerning universalist ideas, enlightenment and communism are very much a part of him, but after 1980 he moved away from active politics in Britain to pursue his creative interests. He gradually became a film-maker and set up his own company, Bandung, which produces programmes about the Third World for Channel Four. His first novel *Redemption* (1990) was a spoof on Trotskyism inspired by events in Eastern Europe. He went on to co-write a stage play with Howard Brenton, *Moscow Gold,* about Gorbachev, and has written television plays too. The Gulf War and the general ignorance being bandied around about Arabs and Muslim culture caused him to write a historical novel *Shadows of the Pomegranate Tree* (1992) set in sixteenth century Spain, the country which saw both the zenith of Muslim civilization and its obliteration.

Shadows of the Pomegranate Tree was published in 1992 to coincide with the 500th anniversary of the Fall of Granada. The novel follows the fortunes of a land-owning Moorish clan, the Banu Hudayl, after the fanatical and bigoted Queen Isabella has conquered Granada. Her confessor, Archbishop Ximenes de Cisneros, lets loose a reign of terror on the Moors, subjecting them to the Inquisition, burning their books and banning all Moorish practices. Some of the al-Hudayl family convert to Christianity, but Umar bin Abdallah remains true to his faith. While his daughters migrate and his younger son, Yazid, a child, remains with his mother, the elder son, Zuhayr, takes up the sword. The narrative uses the traditional Moorish names for cities which now bear Spanish names.

FROM *SHADOWS OF THE POMEGRANATE TREE*

(The scion of the Al-Hudayl clan, Zuhayr bin Umar, goes to Granada (Gharnata) accompanied by his friends, Ibn Basit, and Ibn Amin, to trap the Moors' great enemy, Ximenes de Cisneros.)

FROM *Chapter 11*

From the heart of the old city, Zuhayr and his comrades were walking towards the site of the new cathedral in an exaggeratedly casual fashion. They were in groups of two, tense and nervous, behaving as though they had no connection with each other, but united in the belief that they were drawing close to a dual triumph. The hated enemy, the torturer of their fellow-believers, would soon be dead and they, his killers, would be assured of martyrdom and an easy passage to paradise.

They had met for an early breakfast to perfect their plans. Each one of the eight men had risen solemnly in turn and had bidden a formal farewell to the others: 'Till we meet again in heaven.'

Early that morning Zuhayr had begun to write a letter to Umar, detailing his adventures on the road to Gharnata, describing the painful dilemma which had confronted him and explaining his final decision to participate in the action which was favoured by everyone except himself:

> *We will set a trap for Cisneros, but even if we succeed in dispatching him, I know full well that we will all, each and every one of us, fall into it ourselves. Everything is very different from what I imagined. The situation for the Gharnatinos has become much worse since your last visit. There is both outrage and demoralization. They are determined to convert us and Cisneros has authorized the use of torture to aid this process. Of course many people submit to the pain, but it drives them mad. After converting they become desperate, walk into churches and excrete on*

the altar, urinate in the holy font, smear the crucifixes with impure substances and rush out laughing in the fashion of people who have lost their mind. Cisneros reacts with fury and so the whole cycle is repeated. The feeling here is that while Cisneros lives nothing will change except for the worse. I do not believe that his death will improve matters, but it will, without any doubt, ease the mental agony suffered by so many of our people.

I may not survive this day and I kiss all of you in turn, especially Yazid, who must never be allowed to repeat his brother's mistakes...

Zuhayr and Ibn Basit were about to cross the road when they saw Barrionuevo the bailiff and six soldiers heading in their direction. Fortunately nobody panicked, but as Barrionuevo halted in front of Zuhayr, the other three groups abandoned the march to their destination and turning leftwards, disappeared back into a warren of narrow side-streets as had been previously agreed.

'Why are you carrying a sword?' asked Barrionuevo.

'Forgive me sir,' replied Zuhayr. 'I do not belong to Gharnata. I am here for a few days from al-Hudayl to stay with my friend. Is it forbidden to carry swords in the street now?'

'Yes,' replied the bailiff. 'Your friend here should have known better. Be on your way, but first return to your friend's home and get rid of the sword.'

Ibn Basit and Zuhayr were greatly relieved. They had no alternative but to turn around and walk back to the Funduq. The others were waiting, and there were exclamations of delight when Zuhayr and Ibn Basit entered the room.

'I thought we had lost you forever,' said Ibn Amin, embracing the pair of them.

Zuhayr saw the relief on their faces and knew at once that it was not just the sight of Ibn Basit and himself which had relaxed the tension. There was something else. That much was obvious from the satisfied expression on Ibn Amin's face. Zuhayr looked at his friend and raised his eyebrows expectantly. Ibn Amin spoke.

'We must cancel our plan. A friend in the palace has sent us a message. Ximenes has trebled his guard and has cancelled his plans to visit the city today. I felt there was something strange in the air. Did you notice that the streets were virtually deserted?'

Zuhayr could not conceal his delight.

'Allah, be praised!' he exulted. 'Fate has intervened to prevent our sacrifice. But you are right, Ibn Amin. The atmosphere is tense. Why is this so? Has it anything to do with the royal bailiff's errand?'

While they continued to speculate and began to discuss whether they should venture back to the street and investigate the situation, an old servant of the Funduq ran into their room.

'Pray masters, please hurry to the Street of the Water-Carriers. The word is that you should take your weapons.'

Zuhayr picked up his sword again. The others uncovered their daggers as they rushed out of the Funduq al-Yadida. They did not have to search very hard to find the place. What sounded like a low humming noise was getting louder and louder. It seemed as if the whole population of the quarter was on the streets.

Through the fringed horseshoe arches of homes and workshops, more and more people were beginning to pour out on to the streets. The beating of copperware, the loud wails and an orchestra of tambourines had brought them all together. Water-carriers and carpet-sellers mingled with fruit merchants and the *faqihs*. It was a motley crowd and it was angry, that much was obvious to the conspirators of the Funduq, but why? What had happened to incite a mass which, till yesterday, had seemed so passive?

A stray acquaintance of Ibn Amin, a fellow Jew, coming from the scene of battle, excitedly told them everything that had happened till the moment he had to leave in order to tend his sick father.

'The royal bailiff and his soldiers went to the house of the widow in the Street of the Water-Carriers. Her two sons had taken refuge there last night. The bailiff said that the Archbishop wished to see them today. The widow, angered by the arrival of soldiers, would not let them into the house. When they threatened to break down the door she poured a pan of boiling water from the balcony.

'One of the soldiers was badly burnt. His screams were horrible.'

The memory choked the storyteller's voice and he began to tremble.

'Calm down, friend,' said Zuhayr, stroking his head. 'There is no cause for you to worry. Tell me what happened afterwards.'

'It got worse, much worse,' began Ibn Amin's friend. 'The bailiff was half-scared and half-enraged by this defiance. He ordered his men to break into the house and arrest the widow's sons. The commotion began to attract other people and soon there were over two hundred young men, who barricaded the street at both ends. Slowly they began to move towards the bailiff and his men. One of the soldiers got so scared that he wet himself and pleaded for mercy. They let him go. The others raised their swords, which was fatal. The people hemmed them in so tight that the soldiers were crushed against the wall. Then the son of al-Wahab, the oil merchant, lifted a sword off the ground. It had been dropped by one of the soldiers. He walked straight to the bailiff and dragged him into the centre of the street. 'Mother,' he shouted to the widow who was watching everything from the window. 'Yes, my son,' she replied with a joyous look on her face. 'Tell me,' said Ibn Wahab. 'How should this wretch be punished?' The old lady put a finger to her throat. The crowd fell silent. The bailiff, Barrionuevo by name, fell to the ground, pleading for mercy. He was like a trapped animal. His head touched Ibn Wahab's feet. At that precise moment the raised sword descended. It only took one blow. Barrionuevo's severed head fell on the street. A stream of blood is still flowing in the Street of the Water-Carriers.'

'And the soldiers?' asked Zuhayr. 'What have they done to the soldiers?'

'Their fate is still under discussion in the square. The soldiers are being guarded by hundreds of armed men at the Bab al-Ramla.'

'Come,' said Zuhayr somewhat self-importantly to his companions. 'We must take part in this debate. The life of every believer in Gharnata may depend on the outcome.'

The crowds were so thick that every street in the maze had become virtually impassable. Either you moved with the crowd or you did not move at all. And still the people were coming out. Here were the tanners from the *rabbad al-Dabbagan*, their legs still bare, their skin still covered with dyes of different colours. The tambourine makers had left their workshops in the *rabbad al-Difaf* and joined the throng. They were adding to the noise by extracting every sound possible from the instrument. The potters from the *rabbad al-Fajjarin* had come armed with sacks full of defective pots, and marching by their side, also heavily armed, were the brick-makers from the *rabbad al-Tawwabin*.

Suddenly Zuhayr saw a sight which moved and excited him. Scores of women, young and old, veiled and unveiled, were carrying aloft the silken green and silver standards of the Moorish knights, which they and their ancestors had sewn and embroidered for over five hundred years in the *rabbad al-Bunud*. They were handing out hundreds of tiny silver crescents to the children. Young boys and girls were competing with each other to grab a crescent. Zuhayr thought of Yazid. How he would have relished all this and how proudly he would have worn his crescent. Zuhayr had thought he would never see Yazid again, but since his own plan of challenging individual Christian knights to armed combat had collapsed and the plot to assassinate Cisneros had been postponed out of necessity, Zuhayr began to think of the future once again and the images of his brother, studying everything with his intelligent eyes, never left him.

Every street, every alley, resembled a river in flood, flowing in the direction of a buoyant sea of humanity near the Bab al-Ramla Gate. The chants would rise and recede like waves. Everyone was waiting for the storm.

Zuhayr was determined to speak in favour of sparing the soldiers. He suddenly noticed that they were in the *rabbad al-*

Kubl, the street which housed the producers of antimony. It was here that silver containers were loaded with the liquid, which had enhanced the beauty of countless eyes since the city was first built. This meant that they were not far from the palace of his Uncle Hisham. And underneath that large mansion there was a passage which led directly to the Bab al-Ramla. It had been built when the house was constructed, precisely in order to enable the nobleman or trader living in it to escape easily when he was under siege by rivals whose cause had triumphed and whose faction had emerged victorious in the never-ending palace conflicts which always cast a permanent shadow on the city.

Zuhayr signalled to his friends to follow him in silence. He knocked on the deceptively modest front door of Hisham's house. An old family retainer looked through a tiny latticed window on the first floor and recognized Zuhayr. He rushed down the stairs, opened the door and let them all in, but appeared extremely agitated.

'The master made me swear not to admit any person today except members of the family. There are spies everywhere. A terrible crime has been committed and Satan's monk will want his vengeance in blood.'

'Old friend,' said Zuhayr with a benevolent wink. 'We are not here to stay, but to disappear. You need not even tell your master that you let us in. I know the way to the underground passage. Trust in Allah.'

The old man understood. He led them to the concealed entrance in the courtyard and lifted a tile to reveal a tiny hook. Zuhayr smiled. How many times had he and Ibn Hisham's children left the house after dark for clandestine assignments with lovers via this very route. He tugged gently at the hook and lifted a square cover, cleverly disguised as a set of sixteen tiles. He helped his friends down the hole and then joined them, but not before he had embraced the servant, who had been with his uncle ever since Zuhayr could remember.

'May Allah protect you all today,' said the old man as he replaced the cover and returned the courtyard to normal.

Within a few minutes, they were at the old market. Zuhayr had feared that the exit to the tunnel might be impossible to lift because of the crowds, but fate favoured them. The cover was raised without any hindrance. As seven men emerged from underneath the floor on to the roofed entrance to the market, a group of bewildered citizens watched in amazement. The men were followed by a disembodied weapon: Zuhayr had handed his sword through the hole to Ibn Basit, who had preceded him. Now he lifted himself up, replacing the stone immediately so that in the general confusion its exact location would be forgotten.

It was a scene that none of them would forget. They saw the backs of tens of thousands of men, women and children who had assembled near the Bab al-Ramla in a spirit of vengeance. This is where they had stood in 1492 and watched in disbelief as the crescent was hurled down from the battlements of the al-Hamra, accompanied by the deafening noise of bells interspersed with Christian hymns. This is where they had stood in silence last year while Cisneros, the man they called 'Satan's priest' had burnt their books. And it was in this square only a month later that drunken Christian soldiers had tipped the turbans off the heads of two venerable Imams.

The Moors of Gharnata were not a hard or stubborn people, but they had been ceded to the Christians without being permitted to resist, and this had made them very bitter. Their anger, repressed for over eight years, had come out into the open. They were in a mood to attempt even the most desperate measures. They would have stormed the al-Hamra, torn Ximenes limb from limb, burnt down churches and castrated any monk they could lay their hands on. This made them dangerous. Not to the enemy, but to themselves. Deprived by their last ruler of the chance to resist the Christian armies, they felt that it was time they reasserted themselves.

It is sometimes argued, usually by those who fear the multitude, that any gathering which exceeds a dozen people becomes a willing prey to any demagogue capable of firing its passions, and thus it is capable only of irrationality. Such a view is designed to ignore the underlying causes which have brought together so many people and with so many diverse interests. All rivalries, political and commercial, had been set aside; all blood-feuds had been cancelled; a truce had been declared between the warring theological factions within the house of al-Andalusian Islam; the congregation was united against the Christian occupiers. What had begun as a gesture of solidarity with a widow's right to protect her children had turned into a semi-insurrection.

Ibn Wahab, the proud and thoughtless executioner of the royal bailiff, stood on a hastily constructed wooden platform, his head in the clouds. He was dreaming of the al-Hamra and the posture in which he would sit when he received ambassadors from Isabella, pleading for peace. Unhappily his first attempt at oratory had been a miserable failure. He had been constantly interrupted.

'Why are you mumbling?'

'What are you saying?'

'Talk louder!'

'Who do you think you are addressing? Your beardless chin?'

Angered by this lack of respect, Ibn Wahab had raised his voice in the fashion of the preachers. He had spoken for almost thirty minutes in a language so flowery and ornate, so crowded with metaphors and so full of references to famous victories stretching from Dimashk to the Maghreb that even those most sympathetic to him amongst the audience were heard remarking that the speaker was like an empty vessel, noisy, but devoid of content.

The only concrete measure he had proposed was the immediate execution of the soldiers and the display of their heads on poles. The response had been muted, which caused a *qadi* to enquire if there was anybody else who wished to speak.

'Yes!' roared Zuhayr. He lifted the sword above his head and, with erect shoulders and an uplifted face, he moved towards the platform. His comrades followed him and the crowd, partially bemused by the oddity of the procession, made way. Many recognized him as a scion of the Banu Hudayl. The *qadi* asked Ibn Wahab to step down and Zuhayr was lifted on to the platform by a host of willing hands. He had never spoken before at a public gathering, let alone one of this size, and he was shaking like an autumn leaf.

'In the name of Allah, the Merciful, the Beneficent.' Zuhayr began in the most traditional fashion possible. He did not dwell for long on the glories of their religion, nor did he mention the past. He spoke simply of the tragedy that had befallen them and the even greater tragedy that lay ahead. He found himself using phrases which sounded oddly familiar. They were. He had picked them up from al-Zindiq and Abu Zaid. He concluded with an unpopular appeal.

'Even as I speak to you, the soldier who witnessed the execution is at the al-Hamra, describing every detail. But put yourself in his place. He is racked by fear. To make himself sound brave, he exaggerates everything. Soon the Captain-General will bring his soldiers down the hill to demand the release of these men whom we have made our prisoners. Unlike my brother Ibn Wahab I do not believe that we should kill them. I would suggest that we let them go. If we do not, the Christians will kill ten of us for each soldier. I ask you: is their death worth the destruction of a single believer? To release them now would be a sign of our strength, not weakness. Once we have let them go we should elect from amongst ourselves a delegation which will speak on our behalf. I have many other things to say, but I will hold my tongue till you pronounce your judgement on the fate of these soldiers. I do not wish to speak any more in their presence.'

To his amazement, Zuhayr's remarks were greeted with applause and much nodding of heads. When the *qadi* asked the assembly whether the soldiers should be freed or killed the response was overwhelmingly in favour of their release. Zuhayr and his friends did not wait for instructions. They rushed to where the men were being held prisoner. Zuhayr unsheathed his sword and cut the rope which bound them. Then he marched them to the edge of the crowd and pointed with his sword in the direction of the al-Hamra and sent them on their way. The incredulous soldiers nodded in silent gratitude and ran away as fast as their legs could take them.

In the palace, just as Zuhayr had told them, the soldier who had been permitted to leave earlier, assuming that his comrades would by now have been decapitated, had embellished his own role in the episode. The Archbishop heard every word in silence, then rose without uttering a word, indicated to the soldier that he should follow him and walked to the rooms occupied by the Count of Tendilla. He was received without delay and the soldier found himself reciting his tale of woe once again.

'Your Excellency will no doubt agree,' began Ximenes, 'that unless we respond with firmness to this rebellion, all the victories, achieved by our King and Queen in this city will be under threat.'

'My dear Archbishop,' responded the Count in a deceptively friendly tone, 'I wish there were more like you in the holy orders of our Church, so loyal to the throne and so devoted to increasing the property and thereby the weight and standing of the Church.

'However, I wish to make something plain. I do not agree with your assessment. This wretched man is lying to justify falling on his knees before the killers of Barrionuevo. Not for one minute will I accept that our military position is threatened by this mob. I would have thought that, if anything, it was Your Grace's offensive on behalf of the Holy Spirit which was under threat.'

Ximenes was enraged by the remark, especially since it was uttered in the presence of a soldier who would repeat it to his friends: within hours the news would be all over the city. He curbed his anger till he had, with an imperious gesture of the right hand, dismissed the soldier from their presence.

'Your Excellency does not seem to appreciate that until these people are subdued and made to respect the Church, they will never be loyal to the crown!'

'For a loyal subject of the Queen, Your Grace appears to be ignorant of the agreements we signed with the Sultan at the time of his surrender. This is not the first occasion when I have had to remind you of the solemn pledges that were given to the Moors. They were to be permitted the right to worship their God and believe in their Prophet without any hindrance. They could speak their own language, marry each other and bury their dead as they had done for centuries. It is you, my dear Archbishop, who have provoked this uprising. You have reduced them to a miserable condition, and you only feign surprise when they resist. They are not animals, man! They are flesh of our flesh and blood of our blood.

'I sometimes ask myself how the same Mother Church could have produced two such different children as the Dominicans and the Franciscans. Cain and Abel? Tell me something, Friar Cisneros. When you were being trained in that monastery near Toledo, what did they give you to drink?'

Cisneros understood that the anger of the Captain-General was caused by his knowledge that a military response was indispensable to restore order. He had triumphed. He decided to humour the Count.

'I am amazed that a great military leader like Your Excellency should have time to study the different religious order born out of our Mother Church. Not Cain and Abel, Excellency. Never that. Treat them, if it pleases you, as the two loving sons of a widowed mother. The first son is tough and disciplined, defends his mother against the unwelcome attentions of all unwanted suitors. The other, equally loving, is, however, lax and easygoing; he leaves the door of his house wide open and does not care who enters or departs. The mother needs them both and loves them equally, but ask yourself this, Excellency, who protects her the best?'

Don Inigo was vexed by the Archbishop's spuriously friendly, patronizing tone. His touchy sense of pride was offended. A religious upstart attempting to become familiar with a Mendoza? How dare Cisneros behave in this fashion? He gave the prelate a contemptuous look.

'Your Grace of course has a great deal of experience with widowed mothers and their two sons. Was it not in pursuit of one such widow and her two unfortunate boys that you sent the royal bailiff to his death today?'

The Archbishop realizing that anything he said today would be rebuffed, rose and took his leave. The Count's fists unclenched. He clapped loudly. When two attendants appeared he barked out a series of orders.

'Prepare my armour and my horse. Tell Don Alonso I will need three hundred soldiers to accompany me to the Bibarrambla. I wish to leave before the next hour is struck.'

In the city the mood had changed a great deal. The release of the soldiers had given the people a feeling of immense self-confidence. They felt morally superior to their enemies. Nothing appeared frightening any more. Vendors of food and drink had made their appearance. The bakers who had shut their shops and pastry stalls had been hastily assembled in the Bab al-Ramla. Food and sweetmeats were being freely distributed. Children were improvising simple songs and dancing. The tension had evaporated. Zuhayr knew it was only a temporary respite. Fear had momentarily retired below the surface. It had been replaced by a festival-like atmosphere, but it was only an hour ago that he had heard the beating of hearts.

Zuhayr was the hero of the day. Older citizens had been regaling him with stories of the exploits of his great-grandfather, most of which he had heard before, while others he knew could not possible be true. He was nodding amiably at the white beards and smiling, but no longer listening. His thoughts were in the al-Hamra, and there they would have remained had not a familiar voice disturbed his reverie.

'You are thinking, are you not, that some great misfortune is about to befall us here?'

'Al-Zindiq!' Zuhayr shouted as he embraced his old friend. 'You look so different. How can you have changed so much in the space of two weeks? Zahra's death?'

'Time feasts and drinks on an ageing man, Zuhayr al-Fahl. One day, when you have passed the age of seventy, you too will realize this fact.'

'If I live that long,' muttered Zuhayr in a more introspective mood. He was delighted to see al-Zindiq, and not simply because he could poach a few more ideas from him. He was pleased that al-Zindiq had seen him at the height of his powers, receiving the accolades of the Gharnatinos. But the old sceptic's inner makeup remained unchanged.

'My young friend,' he told Zuhayr in a voice full of affection, 'our lives are lived underneath an arch which extends from our birth to the grave. It is old age and death which explain the allure of youth. And its disdain for the future.'

'Yes,' said Zuhayr as he began to grasp where all this was heading, 'but the breach between old age and youth is not as final as you are suggesting.'

'How so?'

'Remember a man who had just approached his sixtieth year, a rare enough event in our peninsula. He was walking on the outskirts of al-Hudayl and saw three boys, all of them fifty years or more younger than him, perched on a branch near the top of a tree. One of the boys shouted some insult or other comparing his shaven head to the posterior of some animal. Experience dictated that the old man ignore the remark and walk away, but instead, to the great amazement of the boys, he clambered straight up the tree and took them by surprise. The boy who had insulted him became his lifelong friend.'

Al-Zindiq chuckled.

'I climbed the tree precisely to teach you that nothing should ever be taken for granted.'

'Exactly so. I learnt the lesson well.'

'In that case, my friend, make sure that you do not lead these people into a trap. The girl who survived the massacre at al-Hama still cannot bear the sight of rain. She imagines that it is red.'

Zuhayr bin Umar, Ibn Basit, Ibn Wahab. A meeting of The Forty is taking place inside the silk market now!'

Zuhayr thanked al-Zindiq for his advice and hurriedly took his leave. He walked to the spacious room of a silk trader which had been made available to them. The old man could not help but notice the alteration in his young friend's gait. His natural tendency would have been to run to the meeting place, but he had walked away in carefully measured steps while his demeanour had assumed an air of self-importance. Al-Zindiq smiled and shook his head. It was as if he had seen the ghost of Ibn Farid.

The assembly of citizens had elected a committee of forty men, and given them the authority to negotiate on behalf of the whole town. Zuhayr and his seven friends had all been elected, but so had Ibn Wahab. Most of the other members of The Forty were demobilized Moorish knights. Just as Zuhayr entered the meeting a messenger from the al-Hamra kitchens was speaking in excited tones of the preparations for a counter-offensive under way at the palace.

'The armour of the Captain-General himself is being got ready. He will be accompanied by three hundred soldiers. Their swords were being sharpened even as I left.'

'We should ambush them,' suggested Ibn Wahab. 'Pour oil on them and set it alight.'

'Better a sane enemy than an insane friend,' muttered the *qadi* dismissing the suggestion with a frown.

'Let us prepare as we have planned,' said Zuhayr as the meeting ended and The Forty returned to the square.

The *qadi* mounted the platform and announced that the soldiers were on their way. The smiles disappeared. The vendors began to pack their wares, ready to depart. The crowd became anxious and nervous conversations erupted in every corner. The *qadi* asked people to remain calm. Women and children and the elderly were sent home.

Everyone else had been assigned special positions in case the Christian army tried to conquer the heart of the city. The men departed to their previously agreed posts. Precautions had already been taken and the defence plan was now put into operation. Within thirty minutes an effective barricade was in place. The kiln-workers, stonemasons and carpenters had organized this crowd into an orgy of collective labour. The barrier had been constructed with great skill, sealing off all the points of entry into the old quarter—what the *qadi* always referred to as 'the city of believers.'

How amazing, thought Zuhayr, that they have done this all by themselves. The *qadi* did not need to invoke our past or call upon the Almighty for them to achieve what they have done. He looked around to see if he could sight al-Zindiq, but the old man had been sheltered for the night. And where, Zuhayr wondered, is Abu Zaid and his crazy family of reborn al-Ma'aris? Why are they not here? They should see the strength of our people. If a new army is to be built to defend our way of life, then these good people are its soldiers. Without them we will fail.

'The soldiers!' someone shouted, and the Bab al-Ramla fell silent. In the distance the sound of soldiers' feet as they trampled on the paved streets grew louder and louder.

'The Captain-General is at their head, dressed in all his finery!' shouted another look-out.

Zuhayr gave a signal, which was repeated by five volunteers standing in different parts of the square. The team of three hundred young men, their satchels full of brickbats, stiffened and stretched their arms. The front line of stone-throwers was in place. The noise of the marching feet had become very loud.

The Count of Tendilla, Captain-General of the Christian armies in Gharnata, pulled his horse to a standstill as he found himself facing an impassable obstacle. The wooden doors lifted from their hinges, piles of half-bricks, steel bars and rubble of every sort had raised a fortification the like of which the Count had not encountered before in the course of numerous battles. He knew that it would need several hundred more soldiers to dismantle the edifice, and he also knew that the Moors would not stand idly watching as the structure came down. Of course he would win in the end, there could be be no doubt on that score, but it would be messy and bloody. He raised his voice and shouted over the barricade: 'In the name of our King and

Queen I ask you to remove this obstacle and let my escort accompany me into the city.'

The stone-throwers moved into action. An eerie music began as a storm of brickbats showered on the uplifted shields of the Christian soldiers. The Count understood the message. The Moorish elders had decided to break off all relations with the palace.

'I do not accept the breach between us,' shouted the Captain-General. 'I will return with reinforcements unless you receive me within the hour.'

He rode away angrily without waiting for his men. The sight of the soldiers running after their leader caused much merriment in the ranks of the Gharnatinos.

The Forty were less amused. They knew that sooner or later they would have to negotiate with Mendoza. Ibn Wahab wanted a fight at all costs and he won some support, but the majority decided to send a messenger to the al-Hamra, signifying their willingness to talk.

It was dark when the Count returned. The barricade had been removed by the defenders. Men with torches led the Captain-General to the silk market. He was received by The Forty in the room where they had held their meetings. He looked closely at their faces, trying to memorize their features. As he was introduced to them in turn, one of his escorts carefully inscribed each name in a register.

'Are you the son of Umar bin Abdallah?'

Zuhayr nodded.

'I know your father well. Does he know you are here?'

'No,' lied Zuhayr, not wanting any harm to come to his family.

Don Inigo moved on till he sighted Ibn Amin.

'You?' His voice rose. 'A Jew, the son of my physician, involved with this rubbish? What is it to do with you?'

'I live in the city, Excellency. The Archbishop treats us all the same, Jews, Muslims, Christian heretics. For him there is no difference.'

'I did not know there were any heretics present in Gharnata.'

'There were some, but they left when the Archbishop arrived. It seems they knew him by reputation.'

'I am not here to negotiate with you,' began the Captain-General after he had checked that the names of every member of The Forty had been taken. 'All of you are aware that I could crush this city in the palm of my hand. You have killed a royal bailiff. The man who executed a servant of the King cannot remain unpunished. There is nothing unusual about this procedure. It is the law. Your own Sultans and Emirs dispensed justice as we do now. By tomorrow morning I want this man delivered to my soldiers. From henceforth you must accept the laws laid down by our King and Queen. All of them. Those of you who embrace my faith can keep your houses and your lands, wear your clothes, speak your language, but those who continue to make converts to the sect of Mahomet will be punished.

'I can further promise you that we will not let the Inquisition near this town for another five years, but in return your taxes to the Crown are doubled as from tomorrow. In addition you must pay for the upkeep of my soldiers billeted here. There is one more thing. I have made a list of two hundred leading families in your city. They must give me one son each as a hostage. You seem shocked. This is something we have learnt from the practice of your rulers. I will expect to see all of you in the palace tomorrow with an answer to my proposals.'

Having uttered these words, more deadly than any soldier's blade, Don Inigo, the Count of Tendilla, took his leave and departed. For a few minutes nobody could speak. The promised oppression had already begun to weigh heavy.

'Perhaps,' said Ibn Wahab, in a voice weak with self-pity and fear. 'I should give myself up. Then peace will return to our people.'

'What he said could not have been more clear. If we retain our faith the only peace they will permit us will be the peace of the cemetery,' said Zuhayr. 'It is too late now for grand gestures and needless sacrifices.'

'The choice we are being offered is simple,' chimed in Ibn Basit. 'To convert or to die.'

Then the *qadi*, who of all those present, with the exception of Ibn Wahab, had felt the blow most deeply, began to speak in an emotionless voice.

'First they make sure they are in the saddle and then they begin to whip the horse. Allah has punished us most severely. He has been watching our antics on this peninsula for a long time. He knows what we have done in His name. How Believer killed Believer. How we destroyed each other's kingdoms. How our rulers lived lives which were so remote from those they ruled that their own people could not be mobilized to defend them. They had to appeal for soldiers from Ifriqya, with disastrous results. You saw how the people here responded to our call for help. Were you not proud of their discipline and loyalty ? It could have been the same in Qurtuba and Ishbiliya, in al-Mariya and Balansiya, in Sarakusta and the al-Gharb, but it was not to be so. You are all young men. Your lives are still ahead of you. You must do what you think is necessary. As for me, I feel it in my bones that my departure will not be long delayed. It will free me from this world. I will die as I was born. A Believer. Tomorrow morning I will go and inform Mendoza of my decision. I will also tell him that I will no longer serve as an intermediary between our people and the al-Hamra. They must do their filthy work themselves. You must decide for yourselves. I will leave you now. What the ear does not hear the tongue cannot repeat. Peace be upon you my sons.'

Zuhayr's head was bent in anguish. Why did the earth not open and swallow him painlessly? Even better if he could clamber on to his horse and ride back to al-Hudayl. But as he saw the despondent faces which surrounded him he knew that, whether he liked it or not, his future was now tied to theirs. They had all become victims of a collective fate. He could not leave them now. Their hearts were chained to each other. It was vital that no more time was lost.

Ibn Basit was thinking on the same plane, and it was he who took the floor to bring the meeting to a conclusion. 'My friends, it is time to go and make your farewells. Those of you who feel close to our leading families, go and warn them that the Captain-

General is demanding hostages. If their older sons wish to go with us we will protect them as best we can. What time should we meet?'

'Tomorrow at day-break.' Zuhayr spoke with the voice of authority. 'We shall ride away from here and join our friends in the al-Pujarras. They are already raising an army to join in the fight against the Christians. I shall meet you in the courtyard of the Funduq at the first call to prayer. Peace be upon you.'

Zuhayr walked away with a confident stride, but he had never felt so alone in his entire life.

Muneeza Shamsie

Born in Lahore, Muneeza Shamsie (nee Habibullah) was educated in England, as was the family tradition. Her grandmother, Begum Inam Habibullah, a writer, a feminist and a politician in Lucknow, formed the women's wing of the Muslim League and Muneeza Shamsie grew up with a strong social and literary consciousness. From the age of nine to eighteen, she was at Wispers School where she did her A Levels; she went on to The Queen's Secretarial College, London, before she returned home to Karachi. She had wanted to be a scientist, but learnt that Pakistan offered few career opportunities for women. She has given much thought to issues of colonialism, culture, language and gender, which she is now addressing through fiction. From 1975-82, she taught music and mime as a volunteer at a special school run by The Association for Children with Emotional and Learning Problems (ACELP). She has been a regular contributor of features, interviews and book reviews for *Dawn* since 1982. She writes for *She* and *Newsline,* too. Her work has appeared in *Arts and the Islamic World*, *The Herald, The Muslim* and *The News*. She also wrote a weekly column in *The Star*. Her writing covers a variety of subjects, ranging from archaeology and architecture to development issues, but her main interest has remained literature and she wrote the monthly book page for *She* for many years. She was a delegate to the 1989 International Conference on English in South Asia at Islamabad and presented a paper on 'The English Novel in Pakistan.' She was the keynote speaker at a seminar on Toni Morrison at Karachi's American Center in 1994. Her fiction is appearing in various anthologies of Pakistani writing and in *The Toronto Review*. Her first short story 'Shahrazad's Golden Leopard' was written in 1992 after a three-day Creative Writing Workshop conducted by Dr David Applefield in Karachi. She is the founder member of a hospital, The Kidney Centre.

Shahrazad's Golden Leopard

'Shahrazad,' her mother cried impatiently. 'Hurry up.'

Shahrazad's mother stood over her in the cold, sunless dressing room. Shahrazad longed to please her mother; she looked more beautiful than ever at that early hour, her wavy black hair falling down her pale neck.

'I'll only be a minute,' Shahrazad said.

Shahrazad struggled with her cardigan. She had finally learnt to put it on without the help of Kishwari Bua, her matronly maidservant. She wanted to impress her mother with her achievement. Her mother had been brought up by countless slave-women in pre-independence India, until she moved to Pakistan at Partition; she could see absolutely no point in Shahrazad's small act of independence.

'You'll be late for school!' she cried.

Shahrazad and her brother, Shah Rukh, were among the first few Pakistani children to be accepted at Mrs Forrestor's School in Karachi; it was situated in the airy, colonial flat below theirs, on Clifton Road.

Shahrazad's mother seized Shahrazad and tried to yank her imported cardigan on, but it was too tight. Shahrazad, who had always been round and tubby, had put on more weight. Shahrazad's mother raged and stormed; Kishwari Bua muttered to herself and hunted for another, more suitable, cardigan.

Shahrazad edged closer to the large wooden cupboard with crystal knobs as her mother unlocked it. Her mother kept her French chiffon sarees there, but right on the top shelf sat Shahrazad's Leopard. Her Uncle Bunny had won it at a raffle in England. He had given it to Shahrazad on her birthday. But she wasn't allowed to play with it yet. Her mother said that she was only seven and much too young. Shahrazad could hardly wait to grow up and carry the Leopard under her arm. Sometimes her mother would allow her to climb up on a stool and stroke the Leopard's lovely golden fur, or stare into its eyes, which shone in the dark like a real Leopard's. At moments Shahrazad thought she loved it more than anything in the world, but she was immediately ashamed of her wickedness. One must love Mummy, Daddy and Shah Rukh first; even if Shah Rukh, had ripped her *Little Lulu* comics and beheaded her doll.

'Shahrazad was punished at school yesterday because she spoke in Urdu to Batool,' Shah Rukh said.

'You promised not to tell!' Shahrazad spun round. 'You promised!'

Shah Rukh, with his large and innocent eyes, continued combing his hair in the mirror, absorbed in his own reflection.

'Why did you speak Urdu?' screeched Shahrazad's mother. 'Don't you know you're at an English school? That we got you admission with difficulty? You're such a stupid, stupid girl. As for Batool. I don't know why you can't have any other friends but her. She comes from a second rate family with a second rate background. So *nouveau riche*.'

She pulled an appropriate cardigan roughly over her ungainly daughter. 'Your brother is two years younger than you,' she said. 'But he's always ready first.' She brushed Shahrazad away and hugged her sturdy son. 'Oh! You are the Light of My Eyes,' she said. She spoke in Urdu, the language she knew best. 'And you are the most precious gift that God could have ever bestowed upon me.'

Shahrazad tried to stop herself from trembling as she walked down the stairs accompanied by Shah Rukh. A manservant carried their satchels and thermos.

'Oh here's good old Fatty-Ma,' Malcolm Carter sneered at Shahrazad in the dusty school compound, which was shaded by two palm trees and a *neem*. Malcolm was a big red faced boy in Shahrazad's class. He was one of the few English children at the school whose parents knew hers. His father was a director in Read Chemicals where Shahrazad's father worked. That was why Shahrazad's mother had insisted on inviting him to her birthday party; and he had discovered that Shahrazad's middle name was Fatima. Considering her shape and size, he thought that enormously funny.

'Fatty-Ma. Fatty-Ma,' Malcolm led Shah Rukh and a chorus of children.

Shahrazad stumbled over a stone and almost fell, but her servant caught her and guided her to the porch. There were no classrooms at Mrs Forrestor's School. All the lessons were held in the long verandah. The pupils were grouped around six polished tables of various sizes, supervised by the galleon-like Mrs Forrestor and her thin, redhead sister, Miss Jones. Their private drawing room lay beyond the curtain flapping in the open doorway.

Shahrazad waved to lively, smiling Batool, her best friend in class and chatted with her until the bell ran. They were careful to talk only in English, although once or twice Shahrazad almost slipped into Urdu by mistake, as she had the day before

The bell rang. Children gathered for Assembly and then Miss Jones played the piano with gusto. She sang 'God Save The Queen' and 'Onward Christian Soldiers' along with everyone in her high, warbling voice. Shahrazad loved singing hymns and was enchanted by the photographs of the lovely new Queen of England, Elizabeth II and her sister, Princess Margaret, which gazed at her from the wall. She was equally overwhelmed by the print of the Great Queen Victoria receiving her Indian subjects.

'Shahrazad,' Mrs Forrestor suddenly bore down on Shahrazad and placed a freckled hand on her brown arm. 'I'd like you to move your books to the table where Jenny and Pieter sit.'

Shahrazad's large mouth twitched nervously.

She wondered why—and what she had done wrong.

Jenny, a sprightly girl, whom she greatly admired, was a whole year older than her. So was Pieter, a rather pallid boy from Holland.

'I've decided to put you in a more advanced class,' Mrs Forrestor's voice floated over her. 'Your grasp of reading and arithmetic is far ahead of children your age.'

Shahrazad had been so sure that Mrs Forrestor wanted to punish her that it took a little time to grasp that she was being given a double promotion! She was now in the smallest and senior most class. Jenny gave her a friendly smile of welcome and Pieter helped her arrange her books.

Shahrazad could hardly wait to tell her parents. She had forgotten that Uncle Bunny and his wife, Aunty SB (short for Shagufta Begum) were coming for lunch, because they were moving house.

'My God! She's put on more weight!' Uncle Bunny cried out in English, the moment she ran into the study.

Crestfallen, Shahrazad performed a dutiful *ad'ab* to her imposing Uncle, uncertain whether it was The Correct Thing to hang around or move away; it was not as if Uncle Bunny was any ordinary Uncle. He was a very important man. Uncle Bunny was The Secretary of Industries. He had shaken hands with everybody including The Quaid-e-Azam, Lord Mountbatten and The Queen of England. His stately, sophisticated wife Aunty SB had been at a finishing school in Switzerland. They had a son of ten, who was being brought up by his Anglicized grandparents in Surrey.

'Really Mehru,' Aunty SB turned to Shahrazad's mother. Her long manicured hands treated *chappatties* and *poories* as Europeans do bread, and she ate *kebabs* and curry delicately with a fork. 'You must do something about Shahrazad's weight. It's beyond a joke.'

Shahrazad's mother, Mehru, turned a pasty white.

Mehru took SB's criticism very personally. Bunny had been betrothed to her when he joined the ICS and left for Oxford in 1937. But he married SB whom he had met at a Commem Ball, while Mehru had to settle for Jo, his spineless brother.

'Shahrazad,' her mother snapped, her nerves at screaming pitch. 'Take those filthy ink stains off your hands, brush your hair and then come back to the dining table.'

Throughout lunch, Shahrazad kept trying to tell everyone about her double promotion. Each time she opened her mouth, the grown-ups started talking about something else. She decided to enjoy the meal, particularly since Ali Jan, the cook, had prepared all kinds of specialities for Uncle Bunny.

'Now look,' Uncle Bunny twitched a bushy eyebrow at her. 'Just look at her.'

He observed Shahrazad with revulsion as she reached for a sizzling hot, fluffy and fried *poori*. He and SB had come to the sad conclusion that there was something drastically wrong with Shahrazad. It was not that she was simply flabby and fat and had protruding teeth, held together by braces, but she twitched and rolled her eyes and didn't seem to understand a word said to her.

'Don't touch that *poori*,' Shahrazad's mother caught her by the wrist. 'It is very, very fattening.'

If the grown-ups could eat *poories*, why couldn't she? Shahrazad wanted to cry.

'Mehru,' Shahrazad's small, quiet father suddenly spoke from the other end of the table. 'It is not fair to put tempting things in front of the child and then expect her not to eat them.'

His wife's need to impress Bunny and SB enraged him. He was compelled to tolerate them due to the ties of blood.

'See,' Shahrazad's mother turned to Bunny. 'See. How your brother undermines my authority all the time.'

Silence fell.

Shahrazad's father concentrated on his food.

Shah Rukh decided he wasn't hungry and left the table.

'In England no child is ever allowed to leave the table without permission,' said Aunty SB.

Shah Rukh was promptly summoned back. He was ordered to eat the *poories* which he didn't want, while Shahrazad had to deny herself.

That evening Uncle Bunny and Aunty SB came back to have dinner with Shahrazad's parents. Just before bedtime, Shahrazad settled down to play with the large doll's house; it stood in the verandah, which had been partitioned to create the small study at the far end. She could hear the grown ups talking very clearly, but was much too absorbed in her games to listen. Suddenly she caught her name. She pricked up her ears.

'Jo,' said Uncle Bunny, 'I am not saying this to hurt you. But only in your interest and the child's. She's not just ungainly, but she doesn't seem quite normal.'

'What?' snapped Shahrazad's father. He was always so soft spoken that Shahrazad was surprised at his harsh tone.

'You must consider the possibility that she's mentally—'

'Rubbish!'

'Retarded.'

'She comes top of her class, damn you Bunny.' Her father's voice reverberated with hate. 'She comes first.'

Her father knew! Shahrazad realized with a shock. Her father knew she was clever.

'She's always buried in her books,' said Shahrazad's mother. 'That's her problem. She has no concept of being obedient, or looking nice. She only eats fried foods and sweets. She does no exercise. The children she wants to play with are riff raff. I really think she should be sent to a boarding school. Where the nuns can sort her out. Because I certainly can't. It is too much for me and my nerves.'

'Then I suggest Mehru that you try and control your fragile nerves,' said Shahrazad's father. 'I am not sending Shahrazad away anywhere.'

Shahrazad never knew how long she sat there, paralyzed, before she gathered herself up, with tears streaming down her face; she hid herself in the dressing room so that no one would hear her sobs. And then, as her eyes adjusted to the dark, she noticed through a wet blur, that the door to her mother's special cupboard was ajar. She could see the Leopard's shining eyes calling out to her. How beautiful the Leopard was! She felt her way around until she found a stool; she moved it to the cupboard so that she could stand up on it. The Leopard seemed to come alive when she put her hand on his head. She imagined herself as a pretty blue eyed and blonde princess, who lived in a crystal castle, high up on a snow clad mountain, guarded by her Leopard. He could read her thoughts. He understood her every word. He had the power to take away her pain.

'Shahrazad Bibi! Shahrazad Bibi!' She heard Kishwari Bua call. The maid servant's voice was tinged with panic. 'Shahrazad Bibi, where are you?'

Shahrazad clambered down, taking care not to fall. She rushed into the bathroom, where she sat down on the potty. She knew that Kishwari Bua would find her there, the moment she turned on the light. Of course it meant a scolding and a long, unnecessary interrogation to ascertain whether she had constipation, diarrhoea or wind.

The following day, Shahrazad followed her mother into the dressing room. With great anticipation, she watched her take out her key, but at that point Maulvi Sahib arrived, as he did three times a week, to give lessons in Urdu and the Quran. Both Shah Rukh and Shahrazad sat with him in the verandah. He told them fearful tales about the terrors of hell, while he adjusted his shawl and spat phlegm into his handkerchief. He then tested them on their prayers and made them read passages from the Quran, twisting their ears hard if either stumbled or made a mistake; and not even Shah Rukh dared protest. When Maulvi Sahib had finished with Shah Rukh's lessons he shaped a reed pen for Shahrazad and rubbed wet paste on the wooden *takhti* for her to write on. Shahrazad fashioned the thick and thin letters of the Urdu/Arabic alphabet with immense pleasure and concentration. Maulvi Sahib's eye fell on her copy of *The Arabian Nights*.

'*Nauzobillah*,' said Maulvi Sahib, flicking rapidly through the illustrations. 'It was sinful to own such books,' he said. 'Hadn't God declared that drawing the human form was forbidden —*haram*?'

Shahrazad was so distressed by this remark, that she insisted on telling her mother, before her afternoon nap.

'What absolute rubbish,' said Shahrazad's mother.

She had no choice but to tolerate Maulvi Sahib: he was the best, private Urdu and Quranic teacher she could find for her children.

'Kishwari Bua agreed with him,' Shahrazad said.

'Tell Kishwari not to be so stupid.'

'She says it's written in the Quran.'

'Shahrazad!!' her mother was really angry now.

Shahrazad couldn't sleep that afternoon. She slipped quietly off her bed; she went to the wooden cabinet where she kept her books neatly stacked. She examined each, one by one—*Winnie the Pooh*, *King Arthur and The Knights of The Round Table*, *Grimm's Fairy Tales*—and many others. Surely God didn't think they were all *haram*? She wondered what Maulvi Sahib would have said about *T'was The Night Before Christmas*? It was the first pop-up book she'd ever seen; it seemed almost like magic to her, the way all its pictures unfolded and stood up when she turned the page. She pulled the tabs which made Santa Claus go up and down the snow clad chimney; she could even move his sledge and reindeer right across the sky from one end of the page to the other.

Shafts of afternoon sunlight seeped through the wooden shutters and spread across the patterned floor tiles. Shahrazad didn't realize that Shah Rukh had woken up. His pudgy fingers suddenly clamped themselves onto the book and squashed the Christmas Tree. 'Now look what you've done!' Shahrazad cried. She tried anxiously to get the Christmas Tree to stand up again, but it kept falling on its side. Shah Rukh tried to push her away from the book. She clutched it to her heart. He embedded his fingers in her hair.

'Ow!' Shahrazad yelped. 'Let go!'

'Give me the book,' he said.

'No,' said Shahrazad. 'It's mine.'

'I'll pull harder. Then all your hair will fall out,' he said.

Shahrazad gave her brother a violent shove. He shot across the floor and crashed into the doll's house, taking a few strands of Shahrazad's hair with him.

'Mama! Mama!' He howled at the top of his voice. 'Shahrazad hit me.'

Kishwari Bua, who was snoring on the bedroom rug, woke up with a start. Shah Rukh ran out of the room, tears streaming down his face. Shahrazad fell into Kishwari Bua's comforting arms.

'Mama! Mama! I hurt my head, 'Shah Rukh told his mother. 'Shahrazad pushed me against the cupboard and pulled my hair out. And Kishwari Bua did nothing to stop her. Look.' He opened his fist to display a few strands. 'Just because I wanted to look at her pop-up book.' He started howling again.

'Well don't cry little one. I'll get another book for you.' His mother draped a cotton saree around her slender figure and admired herself in the mirror. She then put on some bright red lipstick and sucked in her lips to ensure an even gloss. 'Now go and get dressed for Malcolm Carter's birthday party.'

A short while later, she found Shahrazad slumped in the corner with her book. 'What? Still sitting there?' she said. 'Is that how you're going to go to Malcolm's party?'

Shahrazad could hear the clatter of the bucket and the splash of water coming from the bathroom, while Kishwari Bua was telling Shah Rukh in loud angry tones to keep still. He emerged a short while later, dressed in his new sailor suit. He smelt of baby soap and talcum powder.

'Oh don't you look lovely,' his mother gave him a dazzling smile. 'Unlike your sister.' She glared at Shahrazad. 'She just likes to wander around looking like a sweeper woman.'

'I don't want to go,' mumbled Shahrazad.

'What?'

'I don't want to go.'

'Why ever not?'

'I hate Malcolm.'

'Malcolm is a very nice boy,' said Shahrazad's mother. 'His parents are very important people. His mother recommended you to Mrs Forrestor's school. His father is taking over as the new Chairman. Your father's promotion depends on him.'

'Please Mama, can't I stay at home today?' whined Shahrazad. 'Just this once. Please?'

'Shahrazad doesn't want to go to the party because nobody likes her,' gloated Shah Rukh. 'They call her Fatty-Ma.'

'Well they're quite right. She is fat.'

Shahrazad ran into the bathroom. She was determined not to cry again. She would show she didn't care. And she knew she was better than Malcolm and Shah Rukh. She got higher marks in class.

'Shahrazad,' her mother called out after her. 'Why have you taken that book? You'll spoil it in the bathroom. Give it to Shah Rukh.'

'But he'll tear it!'

'Don't be so selfish,' reproved her mother. 'You had no right to hit your little brother and pull his hair out, because he wanted to look at it.' Then she added with venom: 'Someone should pull your hair so that you would know how painful it is.'

'I didn't pull his hair,' Shahrazad cried out. 'He pulled mine.'

'Now you've become a liar as well. How many times must I tell you that lying is a very low despicable habit, that only the servant's children pick up?'

Shahrazad wore a yellow satin dress with frills and bows and a pair of white shoes and white socks. At that hour of the day it was hot, even though it was November. Shahrazad longed for her comfortable cotton clothes.

'Now behave yourself at the party,' her mother said. 'Here is Malcolm's present. Don't forget to wish him Happy Birthday and say How Do You Do nicely to his mother.'

Shahrazad wondered what was in the enormous package for Malcolm. Malcolm ruined all his toys. She had told her mother so, over and over again, yet they always gave Malcolm such nice presents. Better than anything she had ever received.

Except for her Leopard.

Malcolm was always pushing her, spoiling her clothes (she always had to wear her best to visit him) but his ayah never said a word. His huge, blonde mother with her large hats and long white gloves, liked to dismiss his unruliness with the words, 'Boys will be boys.' Except once, when Malcolm had twisted Shahrazad's arm around her back, thrown her down and kicked her in the stomach. Mrs Carter had caught him and sent him up to bed. 'Never, never let me catch you behaving like that,' she reprimanded him. 'And don't ever hit a girl in the stomach.' But Shahrazad's mother had not been annoyed with Malcolm at all. 'I am sure Malcolm meant no harm,' she said to Mrs Carter with her sweetest smile. 'He is such a nice boy. Shahrazad must have provoked him.' Of course Shahrazad had protested. But her mother pinched her and scolded her and made her apologize to Mrs Carter and Malcolm. Mrs Carter had looked down at Shahrazad's nervous mother from her great height. 'Well I do hope Mehru, that Shahrazad will learn a little discipline from Mrs Forrestor's. And some good manners.'

When they got home, Shahrazad had been left behind with Kishwari Bua for being a naughty girl and a liar. Shah Rukh had been taken out for a drive. The mere memory brought tears to Shahrazad's eyes.

How she hated Malcolm's parties.

'Hello Malcolm,' Shahrazad alighted sedately from the car.

Malcolm lived in a rambling semi-detached house in Clifton, next to Jenny Mathieson, except that Malcolm's house was much bigger and had a lovely garden with huge trees and masses of winter flowers.

'Oh it's good old Fatty-Ma,' said Malcolm.

He was dressed in a cowboy suit and he slouched in imitation of the cowboy heroes in comics. Suddenly he whirled around, whisked his gun out of the holster and said, 'Pow you're dead, Fatty-Ma.'

Shahrazad looked around nervously. She wasn't quite sure whether to smile or not. Malcolm and Shah Rukh, his shadow, were both grinning at her. She longed to crawl back into the car and go home.

'Happy Birthday, Malcolm,' she said.

She gave him the present.

'It looks big enough,' he said.

Mary, his sari-clad ayah, carried the present to the lawn. Surrounded by curious children, Malcolm tore off the blue and gold wrapping paper. He wrenched open the lid of the cardboard box. He pulled out the tissue. Some of the children gasped. Shahrazad was aghast. There in Malcolm's large, rough hands was a beautiful leopard with dark spots and shining eyes. *Her Leopard.*

'It's a sissy toy,' snorted Malcolm and tossed him aside.

Malcolm was more interested in the bows and arrows that Jenny had given.

Shahrazad felt sick.

'That's a lovely present,' said Jenny. She picked up the Leopard and gave him politely to Malcolm's ayah to take upstairs with the other toys. 'Malcolm should have said thank you,' Jenny added.

'Doesn't matter,' mumbled Shahrazad.

She thought her heart would surely break.

She would never carry her Leopard under her arm now.

She could never show him off to her friends.

She could never talk to him again.

You can't have him! She wanted to cry. You can't have him! He's mine! Uncle Bunny gave him to me!

Shahrazad was so miserable that she didn't want to watch the magic show or sing Happy Birthday. She hardly noticed the cake, or the streamers, balloons and confetti. 'My dear I must congratulate you on your double promotion,' Malcolm's mother said in her loud booming voice. 'Mrs Forrestor told me all about it.' Mrs Carter was a personal friend of Mrs Forrestor. That was why Mr Carter had given permission for the school to remain in a building bought by Read Chemicals. 'Your parents must be very proud indeed,' Mrs Carter said. Shahrazad turned puce, to find herself the centre of attraction. She blinked and twitched even more than usual.

'Have you seen the absolutely gorgeous leopard that someone's given Malcolm,' she overheard a tall English lady say to another. 'I wish I could swipe it.'

Even the grown ups wanted her Leopard.

Malcolm decided to play Cowboys and Indians, after tea. Everyone wanted to be on Malcolm's side, the winning side, the Cowboys. So Malcolm made Shahrazad the Indian Chief. He delegated Jenny and a few children he didn't like to her side. Within five minutes, he declared that all the Indians had been killed, so they couldn't play any more.

'Oh he really is stupid,' said Jenny.

Jenny was lucky because her mother took her home, soon afterwards. Shahrazad sat out alone for the rest of the party.

'Why weren't you playing with the other children?' her father asked, when they came to fetch her.

'Oh she's always like that,' her mother said. 'She never makes an effort.'

'Malcolm's got my Leopard,' Shahrazad mumbled.

'Leopard? What leopard?' her father asked.

'The one Uncle Bunny got from England.'

'I don't remember it. But how did Malcolm get it?'

'Mama gave it to him,' Shahrazad accused. 'She wouldn't let me play with him. She said I would have made him dirty. I wouldn't have.'

'She is such a stupid girl,' her mother said. 'She wants everything to belong to her. I had to give Malcolm a nice present, but she doesn't understand the meaning of giving.'

Shahrazad gazed miserably out of the car window at the expanse of grey, low lying sand, interspersed with crystalline sea salt, which lay between Clifton and her home on Clifton Road.

'She's only a child,' said her father, parking the car. 'You can't expect her to understand these things. Never mind Shahrazad. You can play with it when you go to Malcolm's.'

'I hate going to Malcolm's. Besides he was my Leopard.'

'It was mine too,' said Shah Rukh.

'No he wasn't.'

'Now don't quarrel,' said their father. 'When Uncle Bunny goes to England again, I'll ask him to get you both a leopard.'

Shahrazad knew that he was lying.

Shahrazad had a terrible dream that night. She searched and searched for her Leopard but couldn't find him anywhere. And then, deep in the jungle, she met Malcolm mocking her, sneering at her. He set the Leopard on her. She ran and ran and ran, but couldn't run fast enough. She knew he was going to eat her up, while Shah Rukh stood by and watched, chanting 'Fatty-Ma, Fatty-Ma.'

She woke up, shaking with fright.

Suddenly, Shahrazad's bedroom lights blazed.

'Shahrazad,' her father's voice penetrated through to her. She was astonished to see her parents in their evening clothes, standing over her. 'I've just met Joyce Carter at dinner,' her father said. 'She tells me you've received a double promotion.'

'Yes,' Shahrazad raised a protective arm over her eyes and tried to adjust to the brightness.

Shah Rukh sat up and blinked.

'Why didn't you tell us?' her father said.

'You can't imagine how stupid I felt,' her mother's voice quivered. 'There was Joyce Carter congratulating me. And I didn't even know why.'

Shahrazad looked vacantly at her parents.

'It's all very well for you to be intelligent at school, but you ought to learn to be intelligent at home,' her mother pursed her lips. 'Otherwise people will think there's something wrong with you.'

Shahrazad sank into her bedclothes.

'Well, now that you've got a double promotion, I think you deserve a present, don't you?' said her father jovially.

Shahrazad didn't answer.

Her parents presented her with a big, illustrated encyclopedia the next day, but she hardly looked at it. Instead she invented stories about the Leopard and held long, imaginary conversations with him. Sometimes, she visualized herself with lots of little Leopard cubs, which she gave to her friends. Of course there were many moments when she almost told Batool, or Jenny or Pieter about the Leopard, but somehow she didn't. They would't really understand, though they lent her books, shared her sandwiches and agreed that Malcolm was horrible. That was why Batool and Pieter had refused his invitation and Jenny went there rarely although they were neighbours.

One night, Shahrazad dreamt that it was her birthday. All the children brought her lovely presents and Malcolm returned her Leopard to her. She held him tightly. 'My Leopard is back,' she wanted to cry, but couldn't. 'Wake up Shahrazad Bibi,' she heard Kishwari Bua call. 'Wake up.' Daylight streamed into Shahrazad's bedroom. She was seized with sudden panic. Where had her Leopard gone? Then she noticed that she was clinging to her pillow.

'Shahrazad Bibi,' Kishwari Bua scolded her. 'Don't waste time. You must change quickly.'

'But it's Saturday.'

'Saturday, Sunday, what difference does it make?' muttered the old woman. 'You still have to get up.'

'Where are we going this morning?'

'How should I know?' grumbled Kishwari. 'I only do as I'm told. You have to wear this frock.'

Shahrazad regarded the frock with suspicion. It was one of her best frocks, not a party dress, but the sort of dress that she wore when there were important visitors. Or when she had to visit Malcolm. Malcolm! She suddenly brightened. At least she would see her Leopard again. She could hardly contain her excitement or eagerness. She hoped Malcolm was looking after him properly. Yes, there he was sitting safely on top of a high shelf in Malcolm's nursery. He was even more magnificent than she remembered him to be. She longed to touch him, but could not reach up so high, nor did she dare ask. 'Don't you ever play with him?' she asked Malcolm in wonder.

Malcolm snorted.

'That? Only a girl would play with that, Fatty-Ma.'

Malcolm's mother had invited several other children over that morning for a scavenger hunt. But Shahrazad remained in Malcolm's room, on the pretext of a headache. She hardly noticed the noise and yelps of the other children, charging in and out of the house and the garden. She talked to her Leopard in a special, silent language. How she loved him! For the first time, she was reluctant to leave Malcolm's. She didn't even mind being called Fatty-Ma and would happily have played Cowboys and Indians and been killed off as the Indian Chief.

A few days later, Shahrazad caught flu. She was mortified that she couldn't accompany her mother and Shah Rukh to the Christmas Bazaar that Mrs Carter was holding in her garden.

'We played with the Leopard today,' Shah Rukh informed her when he came back. 'We had great fun.'

Shahrazad's insides churned with envy.

'What did you do?' she asked him.

'We played *shikaris* with him,' said Shah Rukh. 'We had a lovely time.'

Shahrazad could hardly wait to visit Malcolm again. No one invited her there, until one morning when her parents took her along to congratulate Mr Carter for taking over as the new Chairman.

Shahrazad could hardly bear the suspense while she and Shah Rukh had to converse with Mrs Carter. Shahrazad almost feared that she would have to leave, without as much as a peek into Malcolm's room. She didn't know how long it was before Mrs Carter finally sent for Malcolm and asked him to take the children upstairs. Shahrazad veered automatically into the nursery. But the Leopard wasn't there. Panic seized her. She must find him. She must. Where was he?

Malcolm was standing in the doorway, hands on his hips, grinning.

'I climbed a chair and took it down,' he said arrogantly. 'We wanted to play *shikar*.'

'Where have you put him?'

'There,' he pointed to a cupboard, crammed with toys. 'Look for yourself.'

Shahrazad lurched towards the cupboard. With frantic hands, she pushed away the pile of toy cars, aeroplanes, space ships, guns and headless robots. Underneath it all lay her Leopard, ruined. His tail was broken, his luminous eyes had been pulled out. There was a slit down the centre of his stomach; straw and stuffing were hanging out. *Her Leopard had been murdered.*

Tears welled up in her eyes.

'What have you done?' She turned on Malcolm in absolute fury. 'What have you done?'

He stood there, quite calmly, in the same mocking posture.

'We hunted, shot and were about to skin him, when we got bored,' he said.

'Oh, I hate you,' she screamed.

She leapt towards him, seized his hair, scratched him and kicked him as hard as she could. Shah Rukh fell on top of her and began to pummel her. Malcolm was much stronger than her, anyway. He soon freed himself. He slammed his leg viciously into her stomach and pushed her roughly away from him. She crashed into the pile of toys she had thrown out. For a moment she was completely stunned. She caught a glimpse of her brother chanting, 'Fatty-Ma, Fatty-Ma.' She saw Malcolm coming towards her, menacing and evil. Her hands fell on some hard objects. With all her strength, she hurled them at him, one after another. She wanted to punish Malcolm, to punish him for what he had done. 'I hate you! I hate you! I hate you!' she shouted hysterically.

Malcolm was coming nearer and nearer.

As her last defence, she threw the electric engine at his face.

Malcolm gave a howl of pain. There was blood everywhere. All at once everybody, including Shah Rukh, was screaming. Someone—a grown up—seized her arms and dragged her away. She struggled, crying out for help. But no one came to her at all. Instead, everybody surrounded Malcolm and kept asking him questions and saying how horrible Shahrazad was. Then her mother charged in and slapped her face, again and again. People kept rushing in and out. Malcolm was taken to hospital. His mother was crying.

'Everyone says you are a murderer,' said Shah Rukh.

Shahrazad had permanently blinded Malcolm in one eye.

JAVAID QAZI

Javaid Qazi was born in Sahiwal but spent most of his formative years in Lahore where he was educated at St. Anthony's High School, Aitchison College, and Government College; he was awarded two scholarships from the University of Punjab for his performance in his B.A. exams. Books had always been his refuge through family problems and he started writing short fiction. He went to the United States to do English Literature and soon academics took a priority over creative work. Between 1968-78, he was at the University of Missouri and the University of Chicago and did his Ph.D from Arizona State University, specializing in Shakespearean drama. Meanwhile his short story, 'Gloria Mundy and Other Depravities', won a literary prize in 1976; while 'The Beast of Bengal' received the second prize at the 1978 Arizona State University short story writing contest. His fiction, non-fiction and critical work has appeared in various literary magazines including *Chelsea*, *The Toronto South Asian Review* and *The Massachusetts Review*. He has written several articles on Thomas Pynchon and presented a paper 'Thomas Pynchon: A Study of Sources and Resources' at the 1978 Rocky Mountain MLA Conference. Later, he moved to San Jose, California, where he has worked as Technical Writer for the computer industry and taught English literature. He continues to write fiction, paints in water colours during his spare time and has translated Urdu short stories for two anthologies, *Contemporary Urdu Short Stories* (1991) and *Obscure Domains of Fear and Desire: Urdu Short Stories* (1992), both edited by Muhammed Umar Memon. His first collection of short stories is to be published soon.

The Laid-Off Man

Dev woke with a start and squinted bleary-eyed at the digital clock-radio on the bedside table. In the early-morning dark, glowing red numbers announced the time with pitiless precision: 5:55. As always, he'd woken up exactly five minutes ahead of the alarm. Alongside him on the double bed, Rushmi still slept soundly.

Then it occurred to him—he didn't have to worry about the alarm going off. He hadn't set it the night before. He was a laid-off man. He didn't have to get up early any more. A laid-off person has no job to go to, no need to get up, get dressed, swallow soggy corn-flakes and rush off to work.

He shut his eyes tightly, grimly determined to not think about being unemployed. If he could only sleep a little longer....But he couldn't. His heart had started to thump like a runaway drum solo and his brain was replaying every painful moment of his last day at Techware Solutions.

Techware hadn't been doing well for a long time. This much, everyone knew. In fact, all the local newspapers had been running stories for months on the 'meteoric' rise and slow decline of Techware. The editors who tracked high-tech companies were quick to assign blame. Some said it was the fault of the management, others the weak economy. Still others felt that Techware's products were out-of-date and lacked the nifty features offered by competitors for much less money. And then there were those who blamed Japan. In fact, blaming the Japanese had become very popular all over the country. As jobs vanished and the lines of the unemployed got longer and longer, everyone wanted a scapegoat.

For over six months Dev had been hearing rumours about a massive lay-off. But he didn't think Techware would fire him. Hell, he had seniority; he'd been with the company for over five years. Moreover, he'd been working on a high-priority project for nearly eighteen months. He was the only one who could wrap it up. He felt, more or less, secure.

But then everything changed one sunny day. Techware started chopping heads and Dev found himself among the casualties. Dozens of other employees also were forced to clean out desks and evacuate their cubicles. There were quick, embarrassed handshakes and farewell hugs on every floor. Tears in the parking-lot. Promises were made to stay in touch. Some left stoically silent. Others bitched about 'unfair tactics,' 'capitalism in action,' even 'blatant racism.' Before all the blood-letting came to a halt, even engineers who'd been with the company for over ten years found themselves pink-slipped and put out to pasture.

Dev blamed himself for this sudden reversal in his fortunes. Feeling guilty came naturally to him. His ethnic background and family influences had moulded him to always consider his own deficiencies when faced with failure, rejection and unsuccess. He must have some inherent flaw or shortcoming in his character, he reasoned. He must have done something wrong, or displeased his managers in some way. He must not have performed to the high standards that Techware espoused as a company. He must not have worked hard enough or fast enough. Perhaps he hadn't put in extra time at his computer. Or, (and this charge hurt most of all) he simply didn't have the smarts to be a Techware employee.

However, Bob Wilson, (another victim of the lay-off) refused to take the blame for Techware's decline.

'Look, man, we got lousy leadership,' Bob told Dev on the phone. 'We did exactly what they told us to do, but they never came up with a good strategy. Short-sighted planning and plain old greed, that's what got us into trouble. Instead of taking some of those earnings—all the bucks they made in the early years—and ploughing them into research and development, the top managers simply skimmed the profits and made themselves rich.'

'Oh well,' Dev sighed. 'Maybe we didn't work hard enough.'

'Shit, I gained one hundred pounds from sitting at the computer for all those hours,' Bob said. 'Don't tell me I didn't work hard enough.'

'I know. I know you did,' Dev murmured. 'But what can one do? We're just cogs caught in a bigger machine.'

'The hell we are,' Bob said with real energy. 'I'm not taking this lying down.'

'But...'

'I'm going to get even with these bastards. They can't use me and throw me aside like, like I'm some kind of garbage.'

'Take it easy, Bob,' Dev advised. 'Calm down. You'll find another job. Surely.'

Bob did have a point. Several of the top people had transformed themselves from ordinary, middle-class types into multi-millionaires in just a few years. The president and his chosen gang of vice presidents bought thousands of shares of company stock at a penny-a-share and sold it at over $50.00 a share. They made honey-sweet, barely legal, inside deals and awarded generous bonuses and dividends to themselves. But even as this gang of four or five got rich, Techware, as a company, dwindled and declined and slowly melted away like a popsicle on a hot side-walk.

Growing weary of tossing and turning and afraid of waking up his wife, Dev got up and headed for the kitchen. Rushmi needed her sleep. She worked long hours as a clerk at a nearby grocery store. They'd been married for a little over two years and only recently had she begun to feel secure enough to start talking about having a baby. He got along well with her, even though he hadn't known her before they'd tied the knot. Theirs had been an arranged marriage. Dev's parents had selected Rushmi and planned everything according to the customs of the Brahmin families of Rameshwaram, the little South Indian village where he'd grown up.

His American friends couldn't understand how he could have married a girl he'd never dated. They often teased him about marrying a complete stranger. But he'd smile politely and point out the high failure rate among typical All-American love-matches.

'You'd think these love-marriages which start so wonderfully, I mean, all the dating, etcetera—you'd think they'd last. But they don't,' he said defensively. 'Arranged marriages work well for our people. It's a matter of customs and traditions.'

'Hey, can you get me a mail-order bride?' Bob Wilson kidded him. Is there a catalogue or something—with pictures? I mean, how do you know which one to send for?'

'What if you end up with someone you just can't stand?' Ron Henchard wanted to know. 'Can you return the merchandise and get your money back?'

Dev did his best to explain how matches were made in India. He took pains to describe all the social nuances which governed the establishment of matrimonial alliances, all the delicate diplomacy and negotiations that went on between two families of equal social rank and similar cultural backgrounds. But his colleagues simply rolled their eyes and grinned and smirked. They had no interest in the traditions of India. The American way of doing everything was the best way. Right?

Dev made a pot of tea, (another cultural habit he had not been able to let go) and started looking over the morning paper. There might be an opening somewhere. Another company might be looking for a software engineer. Even though jobs had been few and far between lately, like a trained rat, he went through the ritual of looking every single day.

Suddenly, the name of his old company caught his eye. *Disturbance at Techware*, read the headline and the sub-head gave a few more details: *Disgruntled Ex-Employee Terrorizes Workers.*

Dev put down his cup and quickly scanned the story. *A disgruntled, ex-employee created a major disturbance at Techware Solutions on Friday afternoon. The company, which develops software, found itself under a virtual siege as the man roamed the corridors of the building, shouting insults and making threatening gestures. Responding to a 911 call, a SWAT team evacuated the building and arrested the man. The intruder, one Bob Wilson, apparently upset over being laid-off, decided to vent his frustration in a public display of anger. He was*

unarmed but appeared to be intoxicated. 'We're seeing lots of similar incidents lately,' Detective Sergeant Butkus, told our reporter. 'With the downturn in the computer industry and all the lay-offs, people are under a lot of strain. Some of 'em just can't take it any more. They flip-out—simply self-destruct.'
Dev put the paper down. His hands were shaking.

He could hardly believe his eyes. The Bob Wilson he remembered was a decent fellow, so bright, so witty, so cool-headed. He was a Computer Science graduate from MIT, for God's sake, not some wacked-out psycho.

Dev raced to the phone and started punching numbers feverishly. A couple of calls, and he managed to confirm the newspaper account. The most reliable source of information proved to be Janet, Bob's current girl-friend. She sounded relatively calm for someone whose boy-friend was in jail.

His parents are bailing him out, she said. The cops had charged him with disturbing the peace, unlawful trespass, resisting arrest, and being in possession of a contraband substance. They'd found some cocaine on him, she told Dev.

'I can't believe this,' Dev murmured. 'I never knew Bob took drugs.'

'Oh, well,' Janet said, 'he's not an addict or anything. I mean, who doesn't like to get high once in a while? Nothing wrong with that.'

'Oh?' said Dev.

When Rushmi woke up, he showed her the Bob Wilson story.

'The guy's gone crazy,' said Dev. 'I can't believe it. His cubicle used to be right next to mine.'

'I'm worried about you,' said Rushmi. 'Bob has a family here. They'll take care of him. You are alone. What are you planning on doing? We can manage on my salary for a while, but we'll have to sell the new car and cut back on extra expenses.'

'I guess we don't need a second car since I'm not working,' Dev murmured. 'I'll put an ad in the paper. We'll lose a ton of money since we've only owned it for a year, but at least we won't have this expense hanging over our heads every month.'

Rushmi nodded in agreement.

'I really don't understand this lay-off business,' she said. 'My father worked all his life for the Indian Railways. We weren't rich, but I don't think Daddy-ji ever worried about waking up some day and being without a job.'

'Nor did my father,' said Dev. 'Our family has been in the silk and coffee business for generations. Daddy didn't even know the meaning of not working.'

'I just don't understand this system,' Rushmi said. 'But I'm sure you'll find another job. However, when you do find work, I'm not going to let you rush out and buy a new car.'

Dev grinned sheepishly.

'I guess I was overly optimistic,' he said. 'I had no idea that this economy is flimsy as a house of cards.'

After Rushmi left for work, Dev paced around the small apartment like a nervous gerbil. The TV blared loudly with giggles and laughter and on-camera psycho-therapy sessions. Under the probing scrutiny of cameras, people seemed eager to reveal all sorts of amazing secrets about their private lives. Talk shows had turned the sacred rite of Confession into a public show. Voyeurism had become respectable. Not only had these people done nasty things to each other, but they had this inexplicable itch to get on national TV and wave their filthy laundry in front of a live audience.

Dev flipped the channels listlessly hoping for some news about India or some interesting report, but only found more meaningless chatter and sleep-walking soap-operas in which actors and actresses looked like embalmed corpses.

Seeking relief from the idiocy on TV, he went into the guest bedroom, turned on his computer and wrote a letter to his father. He made some general comments about being in good health and spirits but he didn't mention the lay-off. His parents wouldn't understand anyway. People in India looked upon the United States as some kind of magical Wonderland or El Dorado, where everyone had money and nothing to worry about. Besides, the exchange rate between the dollar and the Indian rupee was so lop-sided in favour of the dollar that his folks couldn't really help him money-wise. They had plenty of problems of their own to contend with.

Next he fiddled with his resume, updating it, adding information, formatting and re-formatting. Then, just for fun, he decided to write a letter to Meena, his little niece. He hadn't seen her since her Kindergarten days, but she'd grown up fast and turned into an articulate young person. Dev found that communicating with her was like establishing a link with his own lost childhood. She attended an Irish Catholic Convent School near Rameshwaram, where the nuns were teaching her English. She had developed into a pretty good letter writer and got a big thrill out of hearing from her 'American' Uncle.

But when he saw the letter he'd written, he grimaced. It looked so dull. The contents were cheerful enough, (he'd described a beach picnic Rushmi had organized a while back), but the printed words *seemed* so boring. Wouldn't it be nice if I could actually paint the scene, he thought, really capture the clouds, the ocean, the green grass and the tall, white lighthouse in the background?

On a whim, he decided to drive over to a nearby art supplies store and get some watercolours and brushes. He would decorate the letter with splashes of colour. He wasn't an artist by any stretch, but Meena would enjoy getting a letter filled with colourful illustrations instead of the usual, solid blocks of print he sent her most of the time.

He started to work on his project eagerly as soon as he got back to the apartment. And the more he sketched and painted, the more he wanted to keep at it. He found the process so absorbing that he even forgot about lunch. In fact, he wasn't even aware of being hungry, so enthralled did he become by the magical way in which colours mixed and blended and formed brand new hues as they flowed across the paper.

As the afternoon wore on, he realized that a very strange thing had happened. He suddenly found himself perfectly at peace with himself and the world. The nagging anxiety about finding a job, still lingered at the back of his mind, but all the black anger and bitterness that had whipped him up into a frenzy earlier in the day, seemed to have ebbed away.

Time passed imperceptibly. When he looked up from his labours, he was shocked to see that the sun was about to set. It was almost time to set the table and heat the food, pending Rushmi's return.

Dev couldn't remember having spent a more enjoyable day. He was thoroughly hooked on painting, he decided, no doubt about that. He couldn't wait to get paper specially made for watercolours, bigger brushes and more tubes of paint. It had never occurred to him that painting could be so relaxing, so satisfying and so much fun. It did not feel like work, something that fatigued and drained a person, but like a self-replenishing source of pleasure and energy.

Dev had always relished playing with computers and writing programmes, but that ultimately proved to be a frustrating and repetitive process. To do well in the profession, you had to keep the frustration in check and go on error-correcting and de-bugging the code until it behaved the way you wanted it to behave. You just had to be very meticulous and stay within a set of prescribed rules of logic and syntax.

But painting with watercolours required an altogether different approach. You did things instinctively, experimentally, unsure of what the end-product would look like. You had to be willing to accept random results, unpredictable consequences. You had to accept the treacherous machinations of gravity, the uncontrollable consequences of water and colour mingling on the porous surface of the paper. But all these chance developments and 'happy accidents' were a natural part of the process, a process through which a watercolour painting was not so much created as 'discovered.'

When Rushmi returned from work, tired and irritable, he proudly showed her the pictures he had painted.

'Very nice, dear,' she said dryly. 'But did you hear from any computer company? Did you send out any more resumes?'

'There is nothing in the paper,' he told her. 'The jobs have simply evaporated.'

'Keep looking, keep trying,' she said patiently. 'You can't just give up.'

'I know, I know,' Dev moaned. 'But all the companies are laying off people. The aeronautics industry is floundering. Semiconductors are sinking. And personal computers are in a real tail-spin.'

'Keep looking, sweetie,' Rushmi responded. 'You're too smart, too highly-trained, too young, to be wasting your life, sitting at home all day watching TV talk shows.'

'I don't want to be sitting at home,' Dev snapped back irritably.

And actually, he didn't. He didn't want to retire at thirty-five, not after spending years and years training and preparing himself to be a computer programmer. He had been the top student at the Computer Engineering department at Berkeley and also back at the Indian Technical Institute. How could he give all that up, just let go of his chosen career as if all his struggles, all that intense mental and physical effort that had gone into training himself—just didn't matter, had no value?

Over the next few months, Dev kept up his job search. He sent out resumes in response to ads in the paper, called his friends and acquaintances to let them know he wanted a job, and scrutinized the want-ads carefully. But at the same time, he kept on painting.

The painting proved to be a pressure-relief valve for him. He discovered a vast new source of creative energy within himself, an untapped reservoir that he didn't know he possessed. He bought books on art and on watercolours and began to teach himself how to sketch. With every picture he painted, he learned new tricks and techniques. With every picture, he got better and better, more confident of his skills, more knowledgeable about the medium.

As Summer turned into Fall, Dev found out about a Mrs Hammond, an experienced teacher, who gave lessons in watercolour painting. Mrs Hammond held classes in a large workroom behind the Artist's Supplies store where he bought all the paper and paint and brushes he needed. Dev signed up with Mrs Hammond and started attending a class which met on Mondays from 9 to 12. Rather nervous at first, he quickly shed his fears and began to pick up sophisticated techniques that seasoned professionals used.

Once in a while he'd go out on a job interview, but no one made him an offer. These interviews were like getting hit on the head with a sledge hammer. Again and again. You had to be a masochist to keep going through this futile and painful ritual. He got to feeling very discouraged and dispirited. But the joy he derived from his watercolours, kept him moderately sane and cheerful through this grim period of disappointment and rejection. With each passing day he could see improvement in his work. Even Rushmi noticed his progress and kept encouraging him.

Then almost six months into his lessons, his neighbour, Sam Samudio, offered to buy a large painting he'd done of a single yellow rose. Dr Samudio, a dentist by profession, also had a very artistic sensibility plus a love of classical music, expensive cognacs and fine cigars.

'What are you charging for it?' Dr Samudio asked.

'Oh, I don't know,' said Dev. 'I really don't know how much to ask.'

'Well, give me an idea.'

'How about a hundred dollars?'

'It's a deal,' said the good doctor and held out his hand, grinning happily.

Giddy with joy, Dev rushed into the house to tell Rushmi that he'd sold his first painting. Rushmi could hardly trust her ears. She'd heard so many stories of artists starving in garrets, or dying on the streets of Paris, diseased and neglected. She found it hard to believe that anyone could actually make money selling paintings.

As he got better and better, Dev began to seriously think about trying to make a living as an artist. He started haunting commercial picture galleries and talking to other watercolourists. But he soon realized that none of the artists he met were able to survive on art alone. They did other work to supplement their incomes. But the involvement with art enriched their lives. If he could sell just a few paintings a month, that would do fine. With Rushmi bringing in a small but steady pay cheque, they needed just a little bit more to make life comfortable. Later on, as his work started to sell, he would ask Rushmi to cut back on her hours and, ultimately, give up the job altogether. This was another one of his daffy dreams no doubt, but it felt good to be dreaming again, to experience the pleasure of doing rewarding work.

Bob Wilson, out on bail, called once in a while and talked about their job-related problems. Bob was also having a hard time finding work.

'How's Janet?'

'Dunno,' Bob said.

'Are you still seeing her?'

'Naaah,' Bob said. 'Can't afford her. Keeping her wined and dined and recreated got to be too expensive. I could spend bucks like that when I was bringing them in, but now—I'm barely able to feed myself and pay the rent.'

'I know,' Dev said. 'Same here. The only bright spot in my life is the watercolours that I'm painting.'

'I've gone golfing several times,' Bob said. 'But even that is more than I can afford.'

'Cheer up,' Dev told him, 'Things are bound to get better.'

He tried to inject a note of enthusiasm into his voice.' But he didn't think he sounded very convincing.

'Bye, now,' he said. 'Hope I'll be seeing you soon.'

And he did, but not the way he thought he would. Not many days later, Dev flipped on the TV and saw Bob's face plastered on all the local channels. Another crisis had erupted at Techware. Reporters were transmitting special reports from the company parking lot.

'Shit!' said Dev, sitting down in front of the set. 'I had a feeling this might happen. Even a brain-damaged donkey could have predicted this.'

Bob had, apparently, flipped out again. He had barricaded himself inside the building and was shooting at anything and everything he could see from his position. A dozen or so Techware employees were still in the building, being held as hostages. Dev heard the details repeated over and over again on TV. All the area TV stations had commentators on the scene, with the usual inane commercial messages.

Bob had gone back to Techware as though he were the Lord of Death. He had taken a duffle bag filled with automatic rifles, shotguns, pistols, hand-grenades, bandoliers of shot gun shells and bullets and even a machette. Cameras with telephoto lenses caught him as he walked past glass windows, dressed in camouflage fatigues. Bent on doing the Rambo thing, he'd even gone to the trouble of dressing up for the part.

The scene had an air of filmic unreality. Could the whole thing be a made-for-TV movie, featuring lack-lustre talent picked up at random from some street corner?

Television tended to make even serious situations look like staged events with make-believe car crashes and pretend death scenes. Sane people knew that once the scenes had been played out, the actors would get up, dust themselves, go take showers and sit down for dinners with family members.

But this wasn't a low-budget movie. His churning guts, sweaty palms were all the proof he needed. A friend and a colleague stood at the mouth of Hell. He could have already killed people—Dev had no doubt—and he wanted to be killed.

The minions of the Law, now encircling the building, were on hand to make sure that he got his wish.

Some workers had managed to escape, according to the TV commentators, but others were still trapped on the upper floors. A helicopter tried to land on the roof to evacuate them, but Bob fired at it from a balcony. The helicopter veered away sharply, started spinning out of control and went careening to the ground. Fire-engines and paramedics screamed towards the wreckage.

The TV crews were hard on their heels.

Dev wondered how long this would go on.

Professional negotiators had been sent for. Bob had asked for a TV newsman to come in and interview him so that he could tell his side of the story. For a doomed man to be so concerned that his final message to the world be reported right seemed rather odd to Dev.

Meanwhile, the SWAT teams busied themselves, positioning sharp-shooters and gathering, setting up all kinds of equipment to prepare for an all-out assault. Obviously, they wanted to get the 'situation' over with in a hurry. The longer the crisis continued, the more impotent and silly they looked. The matter had to be resolved, wrapped up, handled. The man had to be neutralized before the 5 o'clock news on TV. The forces of Law 'n' Order had to emerge as victors from this fracas.

Dev wanted to turn off the TV, to somehow stop the nightmare as it unfolded with its own slow but irresistible logic. But he couldn't. A sick curiosity, a ghoulish need to see blood spilled, held him in an iron grip.

He wondered if Bob would listen to him if he raced over to Techware, commandeered a bull-horn and begged him to surrender.

Bob, this is Dev, remember me? I had the cubicle next to yours. Stop this madness, Bob. Surrender. No matter how bad it is, I'm sure there is a way out. Please, Bob, listen to me. I beg you.

Or words to the effect.

Bob would probably respond with a volley of rifle-fire. Fuck off, he'd probably say. I'm sick and tired of being pushed around. I've had it up to here. I don't give a shit what happens anymore. I'm already dead, so what the hell. Take this and this and this, you lousy bastards. You aren't going to catch me alive.'

This is like the Wild West, Dev thought, like the pioneer days. The time-honoured tradition of dying in a hail of bullets. All we need is background music and this could be one of those Italian cowboy movies in which the slow-motion choreography of violence and death has a fateful inevitability.

By now the cops were lobbing tear gas canisters into the building. The SWAT team guys were running around in hideous pig-snout gas masks preparing to enter the building. Shots were fired at them from inside the building, but no one went down. Then, a kind of silence fell over the scene. Even the fire-trucks and ambulances stood silent, as if waiting for the next shot to be set up by the 'Director.'

With a supreme effort of will, Dev got up from the couch and turned off the TV. He'd seen enough. He already knew what would happen next. He went into the tiny guest bedroom which served as his studio and turned on the work-light. He knew what the guys in white coats would find when they entered the building after the tear gas had dissipated. They'd find an actor who had ben playing a role in a lousy movie. They wouldn't find Bob, his old friend and ex-colleague. Bob would be in some place faraway.

Dev took out a fresh sheet of watercolour paper and quickly drew a single rose on the white surface. Then he picked up a No. 8 sable brush and started to add colours to the sketch, blending them carefully, letting them mix here and there to form new tints, slowly filling the blank emptiness in front of him with the image of a flower that would never wither, never die.

Rukhsana Ahmad

Rukhsana Ahmad graduated from Government College, Lahore, did her Masters in English Literature from Karachi University and taught there. After her marriage, she moved to Britain. She started contributing articles to *The Asian Post* in the 1980s, but gradually moved away from journalism to fiction. Her commitment as a feminist and the politics of class and race permeate through most of her work, whether she writes about Britain, Pakistan or South Asian society. In 1984, she was among the first to join The Asian Women Writers Workshop. Her early stories appeared in the group's first anthology, *The Right of Way* (1988) and she co-edited their second collection, *Flaming Spirit* (1994). Her stories have also appeared in other anthologies. Her novel, *The Hope Chest* (1996), about mothers, daughters and marriage, links up the problems of a rich Pakistani girl, her servant's daughter and a British girl in Chelsea. She has been particularly prolific as a playwright. Her first play *Sepoy's Salt, Captain's Malt* (1986) about Indian soldiers in the First World War was commissioned by the Tara Arts Group. Her documentary drama, *Prayer Mats and Tin Cans,* based on Worcestor's local history won the Arts Council Commissions and Options Award. Her major drama, *Song for a Sanctuary* (1990), about a refuge for abused women, was staged on the London fringe, toured Britain and was adapted for radio and later published in *Six Plays by Black and Asian Women Writers* (1993). Rukhsana Ahmad's work broadcast by the BBC includes adaptations for the radio as well as original short stories and a full length play, *An Urnful of Ashes* (1994). She has translated Urdu feminist poetry into English, *We Sinful Women* (1991), and an Urdu novel, *The One Who Did Not Ask* (1993) by Altaf Fatima. Her story 'Confessions and Lullabies' was inspired by a documentary film about the lace-makers of Narsapur.

Confessions and Lullabies

Then there was the laying on of hands. Amy stood absolutely still, sensing the spirits fluttering in the hushed light of the hall. People with heads bowed stood still. Suddenly, but slowly, she began to move, like a Frankenstein struck by lightning, energized, charged, invincible. She left the hall before the others, putting an abrupt end to the healing session.

Her senses were heightened. Her mouth felt dry, her hands burned, her eyes smarted and blinked at the brightness of the Christmas lights and decorations which clustered the shops outside. Memories, people and spirits swirled inside her head so that it threatened to explode. She panicked at the extraordinary clarity that detailed everything around her. Why had she never noticed before the tiny grains of poison floating in every glass of water she filled from the kitchen sink? She washed the glass, ran the tap for hours and filled it again, and there they were, clear as daylight!

When she asked Mrs Friedman next door for a couple of jugs of water from her kitchen, later that day, she looked wary and suspicious.

'Don't you believe me?' Amy asked, slightly irritated.

'You may be right,' Mrs F conceded, the frown never leaving her brow, her eyes watching Amy intently as she filled the jugs for her.

Amy looked at the jug triumphantly. 'See, yours isn't poisoned, is it?' Mrs Friedman did not debate the point.

Amy returned to her kitchen to make herself some tea, her gaunt figure stooping in the dusk, the lines on her face deep with anxiety. She screwed up her eyes at the green mould on the bread. It appeared to move. She shuddered and put the bread down. She had difficulty drinking the weak tea that stood on the table.

Her eyes were held by the layers of browned grease on the stove. Each and every section of glass had been knocked out of the glazed door that divided the kitchen from the living room. The old green and yellow chintz curtains with their heavily stained frills looked strangely out of place, a forgotten attempt at home-making buried in the sea of neglect, the only reminder among the burnt pots and pans of better days. The chequered marble floor in the hall, dusty and cold, looked bizarre against the bald door frames. Amy dodged the heaps of black plastic bags which stood in the hall. She cursed inwardly. 'They keep bringing in the rubbish I throw out,' she had mooned to the sceptical Mrs F. In the bedroom webbed icicles hung on the window panes. The grand wardrobes looked haggard as they stood sentinel over her bed, their doors pushed ajar by the chaos that surged inside. She pulled the black quilt wearily round her shoulders, her head singing with the noises they made just to keep her awake all night. She couldn't sleep. Then she started looking for it: that creamy lace doily, turning sepia with age. That always worked. It sang her songs, told her stories. She held it in her tense, nervous fingers, listening to its gentle murmur. The tips of her fingers stroked it with the featherlight tenderness of an adoring mother.

'Here I am, across the black waters, with no hope. No hope of a return to Narsapur, the place of my birth. Miles and miles I've travelled, boxed, blindfolded. I shiver now, longing for the sun, in the musty stench and gloom of a battered old bedroom in this elegant suburb of London.

From an inert distance years-long I watched life, without being watched; dispassionate neuter entity, receiving comment without comment. Now memories keep me going, stimulate jaded consciousness. The past, rich with its pains and joys, shuffles before me, jolting the weary dullness of limp hours. I rejoice; I agonize.

Not many can remember what it's like pushing through the birth canal or the time of the pre-birth when a mere threat of demented, infinitesimal energy, wriggling to attain an identity, shoots, in blind passion, into the mother's womb. I do. Even the time before, when I waited, passive, inanimate, breathless, in *that colourless skein* that held me, waiting, for the quickening, in those far away, long, long summer days.

I see it clearly, a dusty little shop in Palakol where the whiff of the salt sea, when it blew, carried the tang of fish of an afternoon, reviving the villagers in the summer.

He had an enterprising gleam to his dark eyes, the tireless Mr Venkanna, who started his own lace business. He began exporting lace, then became a thread stockist, back in the thirties. He couldn't read or write so he got the village scribe to write to Messrs Coats in London, and became their agent. Now, fifty years on, it's a thriving business, a limited company run by his son. Venkanna Junior has something of a monopoly over the supply of thread in the area, which gives him lots of power and control over the lace business, even over the lives of the lace makers, all those women around Palakol and Narsapur.

Boxed and blindfolded we all arrived at his shop, fifty years ago. New country, new smells. India! Rich, strange and exciting they'd all promised it would be. 'Huh, books! They always lie,' I remember thinking, for I never really got to see much of the place except the dusty old shop, not for a long time, anyway, not until I was delivered into the convent in Narsapur.

Then it all changed, suddenly, remarkably, when she took me out of the cellophane wraps and held me in her warm, moist, square hands: Sister Josephine! Her memory still has such power over me as a mother has over the very thoughts of her babes. I can remember the living touch of her fingers, smell her breath, her body, hear her voice speaking, low when she remembered to lower it, loud when she forgot. Everyone knew she would never make it; she would have to die a 'sister,' poor thing. There is not enough self-discipline in her for one thing; much too much passion in her caring for humans. The only one who is late for prayers, meals, meetings, everything. She gets so involved in teaching the girls, sitting on the white-washed verandah, she forgets where she is. Or forgets to return to the cloisters like the others do, for the long afternoon siesta; stays out instead, enjoying the sea breeze and a little gossip about one of her old pupils in the cool shade of a tree. She has no ambition to pull herself together. Too happy, too content. Younger novices come to the convent, zoom past in their speedy spiritual progress, pursing their lips at her slipshod ways and her grimy habit, never quite as white as Mother Superior's, shaking their heads in guarded disapproval.

Adilakshmi adores her. She seeks her out with so many little excuses. Sometimes Mother Superior casts a frowning look at the pair of them. She sees the young girl, dark-skinned, bubbly, her vibrant youthfulness bursting out of every pore of her rounded body, and she worries. Then she looks at Sister Josephine's serious face, the single hair, now turning grey, that grows out of the mole on her left cheek, at her sagging breasts, her spreading middle, and decides to say nothing. 'If she hasn't learnt at nearly fifty, she never will,' she thinks. Sister Josephine learns all the time, from Adilakshmi, from Padmini, from the women who come selling the fish, and from Krishan who comes to deliver the milk. She chats with all of them, evading Mother Superior's frowns. Every week, she must offer the same confessions, the same penances. It doesn't bother her, she doesn't seem to learn.'

Amy's eyes were mesmerized by the drops of blood that dripped out of Jesus' heart. His fingers were long and delicate, and his face looked like a woman's. It was young and sad. The nails staked through his fine bones must hurt. She could see where they punctured the flesh, making it bleed. She clutched her little palms together and pressed them between her thighs. Her eyes were held by the drops of blood.

'Put your hands together, and pray,' her mother's voice whispered in her ear. 'God can see you wherever you are. He's always watching.' Amy brought her hands on to her lap.

It was hard to confess. She tried to find the words but they evaded her. Not the words so much as the sentences. Where was the sense in stringing sentences when all you had was the odd gasp of insight? If He's always watching then He must know. Nothing makes sense. Nothing hangs together.

Still, something akin to instinct brings her back unfailingly to the vast shell of the house that was her home. She clings to the stale odours of the house with a blend of fear and passion, like an abandoned cat still waiting for the owners to return. She waits for Leo to return to her, even though the outline of his face is blurred in her memory.

All she remembers is giving birth to the children. That is the cleanest memory of all. The pain, insistent, virulent, attacking her spine from inside. The nettles of pain clinging round her muscles, tautening and pulling her abdomen, ripping her open with an unimagined violence. She clutches the doily to her heart. Her palms feel sore as if nails had been hammered through them. In her dream she can see the drops of blood falling from Christ's heart on to her doily, muffling its voice.

'Adilakshmi is desperate to learn how to make lace so she rushes after the lessons, forgetting about lunch to find Sister. Adi loves beautiful things; she loves lace. She's seen her friend Geeta's new petticoat with a delicate lace edging. Maa's irritated with Adi when she asks her if she can make lace edging for her petticoat.

'Lace,' she says, 'is for people who live in big houses and dress in fancy clothes, not for people who live in mud houses. There's plenty to do here to keep the roof together over our heads, to keep the younger ones fed, the animals watered and your father happy.'

Then, noticing the tears in Adi's eyes, she says, 'Ask the sisters at the convent; they taught many of the women who know. Someone there will find time to teach you. You're old enough, Geeta's mother was only a girl like you when she learnt.'

Sister Josephine agrees to teach her. Adi is overjoyed, she doesn't know yet how happy these memories will become for her in the future that waits to mangle her vibrant youth, grind down the fullness of her body. Later on, she will remember with terrible yearning these hours spent under the old gnarled banyan tree in the courtyard of the convent.

Now she struggles, desperate to learn how to make a fine lace trim for her petticoat. Her fingers are clumsy, envious of the speed with which Sister Josephine can crochet. She finds it hard, very hard, to synchronize the movement of her young fingers with the eager lurch of the crochet needle as it plunges into the loops with hungry energy, using up the thread, using it up fast.... Using it up, as Deshu used her.'

The red carpet with its brave green and gold pattern camouflages the cigarette burns in its worn pile. It must be the darkest pub in Stepney. The wooden beams frown in the shadowy light sieved through the pink glass lamp-shades. Amy waits tensely for Leo to come, unsure of how he will react to her family.

He was fascinated by her adventurous tales of shoplifting and streetfighting as a child. Life in a flat above the pub in the East End with an unconventional mother and her gentle but unremarkable stepfather, Fred, had sounded quite unusual and exciting to him. He listens spellbound as he looks daringly at her grey-blue eyes, her blonde hair hugging her swaying shoulders, her long slender legs, omitting to censure the nose, a trifle too sharp, and the chin, a trifle too square.

When he visits that evening, the reality, no longer muted by its distance from the Chelsea School of Art, seems coarsely mundane. Amy tries to quash the word 'common' as it surfaces again and again in her head with reference to Mum's conversations with Leo. Her references to a prospective marriage become crudely obvious. Leo seems not to notice, thank God. Fred's grey mildness helps to alleviate the situation. Mum had always kept a sharp eye on Fred. She'd read *Peyton Place* more than once in her time. From the moment she noticed Amy's breasts developing under the blouse she kept a hawk's eye on customers and Fred alike. Amy was out in digs before the urge to leave home had even taken a clear shape in her head. Boldness rather than subtlety had been Mum's strength, and it had served her well enough.

Visits to the pub became fewer and fewer after the marriage. As time went on it was Leo who was confounded by the crudities of her family, and he went to great lengths to avoid seeing them. Christmas dinners inevitably ran aground over trivia, leaving a foul taste behind. It seemed kinder in the end not to ask Fred and Mum at all, rather than have them come and see them being ignored or, worse, snubbed over their ignorance. There were always tears at Christmas.

Amy stares sadly at the cigarette burns in the powder-blue carpet, angry with thoughtless customers for not noticing the ashtrays… It strikes her vaguely that the face peering at her is Benjy's.

'This is not the pub; I'm in my own home.' She tries to hold that fact in her fist as she looks up at her son's face, a little bemused by his anger. He towers above her, scowling.

'There's not a thing to eat in the kitchen. I got a take-away from the chip shop. There's a bit of saveloy and chips left if you fancy any, I wish you'd pull yourself together.'

'No thanks.' Amy tries to raise her head to show her gratitude but she feels faintly sick at the mention of saveloy and chips.

'Somehow, the paintings never turn out as wonderful as the image in my head, no matter how hard I try!' She is bitterly aware that the portfolio never added up to much. She looks bewildered as she explains to Leo what she was trying to express. He looks untouched. She can see the images so clearly in her head, but it is so hard to put them on to canvas, even harder to describe them. The holes in the powder-blue carpet don't make sense. She hides herself from those ugly holes in the soft, lacy comfort of the whispering doily.

'Years later, Adi looks at her crochet needle as it weaves the thread, using it up fast, and thinks how tired she is of Deshu and his demands. She can crochet faster than Sister Josephine, much, much faster, if only Sister could see her now.

In between feeding the baby and milking the goat, in between kneading the dough and preparing the vegetables, in between preparing the mixture for kallapi and main lunch, in between making cow-dung cakes for fuel and fetching the water, she picks it up for short snatches, fingers flying, and she can finish a couple of squares for a table-cloth, or a couple of rounds if it's only a doily she's working on. By evening her fingers ache and her nipples feel sore, her eyes hurt and her neck feels ever so tired. But doilies are easy to finish.

Doilies are small, insignificant things. They don't take that long. In the afternoon she gets a clear stretch of two or three hours if that monkey of a baby sleeps through. Small insignificant, I watch. It's a long weary day for her. She lies down at about eleven, bones crackling, muscles desperate to thaw into sleep, and then Deshu reaches out for her. A soundless sigh whispers to the darkness as she turns, unbuttons her blouse and pulls up her cotton petticoat. There's never time to make a lace trim for it. She's always behind with the orders.

The lace trim for her petticoat, that first one, took her hours and hours to finish. Three weeks to finish a metre of lace less than three centimetres wide! Years later she could do a bundle and a half in three weeks. She wouldn't have guessed that was possible when she started.

She struggles, putting a brave face on it. Sister Josephine applauds every inch as it grows, gently pointing out where the tension sags or has become too taut. I watch the struggle with amusement. It's fun watching things grow. Then it's time to move on and Sister teaches her how to make a lace doily.

'What do they do with these?' Adi asks, looking at the doily in Sister's hands.

Sister sneaks her round to the nun's parlour, points to the table in the middle of the room made from the best Godavri teak. It has a high polish on it. On top of it sits a little doily for the silver bowl of fresh roses that are replaced everyday.

'That is a doily,' she says. 'It saves the table from being marked. You can use it for drinks, ornaments, anything that goes on a polished table.'

'But we haven't a table like this in our house for which we could use it,' Adi argues. She wants to make a lace trim for her new blouse now, instead of a doily. Her mother would rather have her help with the baby.

'Still, you should learn how to make it. It may come in handy for a gift sometime. Or you could sell them as a set if you did enough of them.' Sister remembers all those girls who learnt from her. Some time in their lives it came in handy; got them a few rupees for rice, oil, lentils, whatever.

'All right, Sister, if you want me to,' Adi says dully. She knows Sister can be stubborn. 'But can I do a lace trim if there's any thread left, please, please Sister, for my new blouse,' she begs.

'Once you've done one of these,' says Sister, who knows about incentives.

That's how I came about. A doily without a polished table to sit on. The years I spent in a battered old trunk stored under the string bed in that crumbling, dusty hut, desperate for a whiff of fresh air and sunlight. Sometimes her mother would find a moment to rummage through before popping in some new-found treasure to save for Adi's marriage, and I'd draw in long deep breaths to revive my spirits while I lay dormant, dead to the world.'

Amy looks around her in horror. Benjy's asthma is frightening. Alone in India with two little children! 'Not quite alone,' Leo says, as he leaves, 'there's the ayah and the cook and the driver when you need the car. There's not a thing to worry about.'

He has to tour round all the manufacturing units, he tells her, to make sure they are keeping to the colours and the designs. Amy sighs in resignation.

'The dust doesn't help any,' explains the American doctor. 'The kids here develop immunity over the years. Our kids have a problem; they're delicate, they're not used to these conditions.'

The wheezing sounds dreadful through the night. Sophie whines for her attention, jealous of the cosseting being lavished on Benjy. Amy, exhausted and confused, worries about Leo and herself. His eyes are always evasive, his conversation vague. Where does he spend all this time away from home? Yet when he is near her she flits about nervously, fearful that he might tell her.

She looks at the architecture around her, the colours, the motifs, the landscapes, with longing. If only she had a moment to herself to subsume her experience, to see, to understand what was going on, to capture it all and put it on canvas. The pain inside her head grows and grows until it blurs the images. She walks round the beach wondering why beaches in England look so different?

She remembers walking on the pebbly, foam-grey beach at Brighton with her father and his 'woman' on those few but special weekends when she was invited. Her father steeped in alcohol and idealism would ramble about a Utopia which was near at hand. 'Huh, ideas are cheap,' Mum would comment cynically on her admiration for him, 'when's the last time he's bought you a pair of shoes? Don't you believe him, girl. You need a bob or two to get by in life, you take my word for it.'

Leo is the same. 'Without money you can achieve nothing,' he says. 'With money comes culture, the awareness of beauty, the avoidance of that which is ugly, cheap, coarse and shoddy. You like to surround yourself with beautiful things, don't you, Amy?' Amy twirls the stem of the crystal glass in her left hand thinking of Leo's family home where labels are sacrosanct, Hallmarked. Genuine. Real. 100% Pure—silk, wool, leather! Quality is underwritten by price. They all know it, accept it.

Everything is cheap in India. 'Is it tacky?' she wonders whenever she comes across something unusually beautiful. Enamelled boxes, hand-carved ivories, polished brass, engraved copper, inlaid marble: everything is cheaper than it is in Europe. India is too vast and frightening to comprehend. She longs for peace, struggling to pray in the tiny chapel inside the convent, but her mouth feels dry and her hands twist frantically.

Get a hold on yourself girl. Look at what you've got on! He'll leave you if you don't pull yourself together. Mum's greeting on their return to England haunts her. Leo is busy designing tiles for an upmarket company: the ethnic look is in this year.

Fear galvanizes Amy. She clings to Leo, the children, the house, their lovely home. Leo resents her clinging. He accuses her of perverse suspicion and jealousy. She tries to remain poised but panic besets her when she sees cold distance glaze his pupils. She longs for grace and dignity. Leo's mother is always elegant and calm in her world of mellow opulence, where the right balance of chintzes and lace, brocade and velvet strike the perfect note; ritual and decorum choreograph every move she makes. Amy tries to achieve that effect in her own home, uncertain of her own taste, after years of being 'just a housewife!' Nothing blends, nothing jells. Leo moves out even before the children decide to leave for universities in the regions, eager to get away from her.

She looks round. Now only the house remains, decaying and damp, but always there. She returns from her wanderings, wheeling her shopper crammed with her most precious belongings, and the house is still there. Suddenly she starts rifling through the shopper. *The lace, this time They've taken my lace away, just like They snatched Leo from me.* She rummages in the shopper and finds it; it is still there, gentle and reassuring.

'Adi, you must find time to work harder at your books,' Sister used to say.

Books! They don't seem relevant to Adi, years later. She remembers a sliver of a poem, stirring the onions over the fire or picking the stones out of the rice. Or some small detail from her geography lesson puckers the surface of her thoughts as she crouches over the lace, eyes screwed, back aching, and wonders if that can matter to her now.

If only I'd done some extra bits of lace and put them by instead of spending all those hours in those grim classrooms, learning, she thinks with some regret. Learning, for what?

She reckons if she had a few bundles of lace-work stored in her old trunk instead of just half a dozen silly little doilies and a couple of tablecloths she could be out of debt by now, forgetting that the money for the thread was always the problem then, as it is now. But the debt keeps multiplying, adding up.

Mind you, at least because of that bit of time at school I can work out my money better than Maa was ever able to. She lost money sometimes, poor old Maa, Adi reminds herself. No one can cheat me out of my due wages, not the sharpest agent in Narsapur or Palakol. They've tried hard enough, God knows they have. It's a small triumph but it keeps her going when times are hard.

Except that there was one occasion when she did get cheated but memory also cheats her now, not letting her recall that mistake, a little mistake that cost her quite a lot.

He looked nice enough, respectable. He had been at the shandy plenty of times before. She had seen him often enough, sold him stuff before. He paid her the right amount every time. Until that day when he fell for the bedcover. It was beautiful! It had taken her three months to finish. The thread alone was worth two hundred rupees. She borrowed to buy the thread at black market prices; Venkanna stopped selling it to the women when he had large orders himself. She hoped to make fifty or sixty rupees on it. He smiled when she asked her price, said nothing, and letting it drop back into her nylon basket, walked off. She saw him turn and leave but held herself back. She was going to hold out for her asking price. I applauded silently! Even twenty rupees a month was too little for the laborious hours she'd spent over the wretched thing.

He hovered round the other stalls. Adi stole a quick sideways glance, hoping. Not many enquirers. She needed money desperately. She decided to drop down to two hundred and fifty rupees.

He did come back, just as the crowd was thinning and the market looked about to fade. He didn't haggle.

'Look,' he said, 'I like that bedcover. You have a good hand. I like your work. It's tight and neat.' She tried to look cool and detached. 'I'll take it,' he said after a pause, quite decisively. Relief glowed through her body.

'I'm an exporter myself. I've got good links in Germany. I could probably order a few more of these if this goes down well.'

Adi's heart nearly missed a beat. She began folding the bedcover neatly, lovingly. He was pulling his wallet out.

'Oh no! What a shame! I'm not carrying enough cash!' he beat his brow in despair, and Adi's heart sank. 'Never mind. I'll take it next week.'

He seemed disappointed, 'Pity, such a pity! The German contact was going to be visiting my shop in the city. But, well, oh, never mind.'

Adi was more disappointed than he could have been. She looked at him helplessly.

'I hardly know you. I don't know if I should even ask,' he began delicately. 'There's fifty rupees here. I am a regular at this shandy, I know you know me because I've seen you myself before. Would you consider...?'

She did. Foolish reckless thing to do. He never showed up again. After the first four Wednesdays of desperate waiting, her hopes of his return grew dim. She didn't tell most people. No one would have sympathized: foolish thing to do, they were sure to say to her. She had to sell her only gold earrings to return the loan and the interest. Now she forgets; claims she has never been cheated. Women! So given to self-deception, so adept at it!

I'd say Deshu's cheated on her. You'll never catch her admitting to any such thing though. She tells everyone this story of how he really needed to go to Calcutta six months ago, in search of a job. She never remembers to say how he's been forgetting to send her money now for almost four months. He'd said he was going to find out about how to become a lace exporter. Only the exporters seem to have money round here, he'd reasoned. It may be he has found out. No one knows where he is now.

That was five years ago. She's still hoping. She sits, fingers frantically busy, lace table-cloth clutched between her knees, peering at it through her cheap spectacles, still hoping he'll return to her. Preoccupied. Not for him though, more with the anxiety of how she can concoct a meal for tonight from next to nothing in her meagre stores. She thinks of food, rich, spicy, warming, nourishing, with an intense longing. There is going to be a good Christmas dinner this week for all of them at the convent. A fabulous meal, fragrant rice glistening with oil, spicy yoghurt, curried vegetables, steaming, satisfying, filling. Thank God for Christmas, she thinks.

Unbidden, the 'Lords Prayer' echoes through her head: 'Our Father Who art in Heaven, hallowed be thy name. Thy Kingdom come, Thy will be done on earth as it is in Heaven, Give us this day our daily bread and forgive us our trespasses as we forgive those who trespass against us…' As always the words give her strength. A picture flashes through her mind of Deshu walking in through the door, his arms full of presents, his eyes penitent, begging her for forgiveness. Her eyes fill up with tears of compassion. She is ready to forgive him in that instant.

Occasionally she glances at the tatty curtain of sacking which acts as her door. Not much of a door to hold people in, or to keep intruders out, but then there is nothing much in here any one would care to steal. Nothing stirs outside. There is no sign of Deshu.

Perhaps he will come home for Christmas, she thinks. Her faith in Christmas is unshakeable. She has seen the glow of absolute faith in Sister Josephine's eyes, all those years ago, as a child. It is the love of Jesus that keeps the nuns in Palakol and Narsapur. She has seen miracles sparked off by prayers. She knows it was Our Lord's hand that saved her first baby when the doctor at the Mission had told her to prepare for the worst. She decides that she must buy some incense and a garland of marigolds for the crucifix that hangs on the wall of her only room before Christmas.'

Amy looks fearfully at the image of Christ, with his hand on his heart, on the chapel wall. She is relieved to see that it is a comforting picture, no blood, no nails. She steals a glance at Mary, who looks passive, unconcerned. She is discomfited by their indifference. She looks again but Mary still looks away from her, heavenward.

Suddenly the tears burst forth in a deluge of anguish. 'Dear Mary, don't ask more of me than I can give,' she begs.

But Mary looks blandly indifferent to her capacity for self-sacrifice, almost scornful at her outburst. Amy is unsure of what Mary wants of her, and of what makes her sob like this in anguish alone in the fragrant darkness of the chapel.

Outside in the cheerful brightness of the verandah a tiny crowd jostles round the convent's Christmas Fete. The smell of home-made cake wafts around, tempting the punters. Sister Josephine asks her how Benjy's asthma has been this week. Amy stands, pretending to be her normal self, answering her carefully. Then she notices Adi, whose eyes look appealingly at her.

'Lace, madam? All hand-made, all pure cotton. Want to see, haan?' Amy picks up a bundle of six doilies without thinking, and asks her, 'How much for these?'

The doilies capture her imagination. They suggest gracious surroundings to her. Far away from dusty Narsapur, she can see them breathing more easily in the clean, pure air of elegant rooms, sitting on polished sideboards or grand pianos, on white lacquered dressing tables and mahogany consoles. She can't put them down.

'Ten rupees only, madam.'

Amy wonders if she should haggle about the price. So often people tell her she must. So often it works. 'Isn't that too much?' she asks uncertainly.

'No, madam. All hand-made, very neat. It is fifteen rupees in the shops. You can ask anywhere. It is more in Delhi, Calcutta, everywhere.'

Amy hesitates. Adi looks keen on the sale, 'Take it please, madam. Good for Christmas present. And Christmas will be here very soon!'

Amy looks for the money in her bag, her eyes a little wary of Adi's confident smile. Adi is puzzled as she hands Amy the bundle wrapped in a piece of old newspaper.

'Happy Christmas,' she says reassuringly.

Amy nods as she leaves. She clutches the lace doily, stroking it with featherlight fingertips, and whispers to herself, 'Christmas will be here soon … '

Adi's voice, cheery, confident gives her new hope. She enters her front door breezily, light-footed, drunk on that renewed hope. 'Christmas will be here soon!'

There is no message from Leo. Ayah looks up with a suggestion of reproach in her glance as she walks into Benjy's room. He is listless and wheezy. Sophie has gone to bed without eating again. Amy's heart sinks as she wonders for the thousandth time that day whether Leo would be back before Christmas or not? She looks at the doilies sweating her hand now. Adi's voice sings out a miraculous message of hope once more, 'Christmas will be here soon ...' Amy shakes off the disbelief and listens to that voice, spellbound. Pressing the doilies to herself, she lies down on her bed, shutting out all else from her mind but the silent hum of that wild promise.

Outside her window, snowflakes silently fill the gaps between the laurel hedge and the brilliant green of the holly.

Song for a Sanctuary, a fictitious play, was developed through a series of workshops, after an Asian woman in Britain had been murdered at a refuge. The play deals with the psychological crisis faced by Sonia and Rajinder, both battered women; it also brings out tensions between Rajinder and the refuge worker Kamla, who belong to the same race, but a different class. Rajinder relates more easily to Kamla's colleague, Eileen. The story says much about Asian society and challenges British platitudes too. Rajinder is so shocked to learn that Sonia is a prostitute that she takes her children and goes back to Pradeep, her husband, only to discover that her daughter has been sexually abused by him for years. He in turn, cannot accept the finality of Rajinder's decision to leave and stabs her in revenge.
The extract reprinted here is from Act I.

FROM *SONG FOR A SANCTUARY*

Act 1

Scene 1. *Thursday morning. RAJINDER is unpacking in the refuge kitchen. She is lining shelves with sheets of old newspaper and wiping and scrubbing with dedication grumbling under her breath.*

RAJINDER: Hai, hai, ainna gund! You'd never guess how filthy it is inside, disgraceful .... Where is it now? I thought I had some Dettol here....

SONIA: (*enters*) Hello, there!

RAJINDER: Good morning.

SONIA: Welcome aboard! You've got into it nice an' early.

RAJINDER: Mmm... I came a couple of hours ago.

SONIA: Jesus! You've got loads of stuff there! I came with just one Tesco carrier bag.

RAJINDER: I don't like to run out of things at odd times... it's taken an hour to get the locker and shelves into order. Looks as though they've never been cleaned since they were put up.

SONIA: Possible. Good house-keepin' ain't a huge priority round these parts specially as you don't 'ave to bother with coffee mornings and ladies' lunches in 'ere.

RAJINDER: I don't do it for show. It's hygiene I'm worried about. Can you imagine all the millions of germs in here?

SONIA: Creepin' an' crawlin'! Ugh. Do I'ave to?

RAJINDER: There's bits of cheese and bread crumbs and stale chips everywhere. You can actually smell the fungus.

SONIA: Hmm, Not very nice at all is it?

RAJINDER: Just look at that.... that was a forgotten banana I think. It's got no business to be here in the first place.

SONIA: None at all! The locker on the right's mine if you've got some energy left when you've finished yours. It looks a treat already. *(RAJINDER only glares and turns back to her work)*

SONIA: Coffee?

RAJINDER: No thanks.

SONIA: I think it'll be good to introduce ourselves before we start rowin,' shall we? I'm Sonia.

RAJINDER: My name's Rajinder, Rajinder Basi.

SONIA: Hi, Rajinder, nice to meet you. You're goin' into the room next to me, aren't you?

RAJINDER: The room, at the back, on the ground floor.

SONIA: Yeah, that's the one. You got any kids?

RAJINDAR: (*nods*) Three. Two girls and a boy.

SONIA: Oh! Are they young?

RAJINDER: Fourteen, eleven and eight. Sanjay, my son is the youngest and I have two daughters.

SONIA: Oh, well, that's handy. They must be a help.

RAJINDER: They are, sometimes.

SONIA: At least they don't want feedin' in the middle of the night, like Barbara's little one. You can set your watch to his howlin', two a.m. every mornin' he starts.

RAJINDER: No. I've been through all of that. And how about you?

SONIA: I 'aven't bothered with any of that yet.

RAJINDER: Oh, really?

SONIA: It's hit me now you must be the lady who came on the inspection last week. So, you forgot to look inside the cupboards then?

RAJINDER: Is that what she called it, 'an inspection visit'?

SONIA: Well, you made history apparently; no one's ever done that before.

RAJINDER: I've always lived in a nice house. I thought it best to see the place beforehand, for the children's sake. I don't know why she got so resentful about that.

SONIA: Who did?

RAJINDER: Kamla, I think she said her name was. Indian name but she didn't look very Indian.

SONIA: Her soul's Indian I think.

RAJINDER: Do we have souls that are brown too, then?

SONIA: You are spoilin' for a row, aren't ya? Perhaps I sh'd take my coffee an' go to my own room?

RAJINDER: Sorry! I don't think I know what an Indian soul's really like.

SONIA: Unworldly? Committed, in some way...quite determined, maybe, like old Gandhi....bit like them Indian monks, you know, the ones who decide to give up the material world.

RAJINDER: I see.

SONIA: Oh, well. It was only an idea. (*pause*) Maybe we haven't got any souls anyway.

RAJINDER: I don't know that life's worth living if we don't.

SONIA: Yeah, you wonder sometimes if it is? Too heavy, all that for me this time of the mornin'. Got to get a move on. I do a Yoga class lunchtime on Thursdays. I think I need another coffee to get the ol' system goin'. (*SONIA winks at RAJINDER who looks unamused and concentrates on cleaning again. SONIA pulls up a chair, lights a cigarette and settles down to a comfortable silence with a newspaper and coffee.*)

RAJINDER: Have you been here long?

SONIA: Five weeks this time.

RAJINDER: So it isn't your first time?

SONIA: Oh, no! An' yours?

RAJINDER: I've been in a refuge before...couple of years ago, I went in an emergency situation, and it was a mistake. That's why I planned it all carefully this time. I think you need to.

SONIA: Maybe you'll stick with it better. I've been in an' out of here a lot. Gets up Kamla's nose. She doesn't like Returners, (*pause*) that's women who go back to their blokes.

RAJINDER: Doesn't she?

SONIA: I don't think she knows how hard it is to pull yourself out of it, for good. It's really tough.

RAJINDER: It's not easy when you go back either because husbands hate you so much for trying to get away, don't they?

SONIA: It's different I think with Gary. I'm not married, see, an' Gary, my partner, is actually quite nice for a bit when I go back to him.

RAJINDER: Not married!

SONIA: I think all men are different. An' he really tries to be nice when I go back, at least in the beginnin'; he'll get me presents, take me out for a drink, be quite lovin'. Then he falls into his ole habits. First it's a slap, and then maybe a fist or two, then a couple of kicks, until one day he has to let it all out on me. Last time he messed me up really bad....The worse it is the longer it takes me to get back to him, but I always do in the end. See my back?

RAJINDER: It looks dreadful. Five weeks, did you say?

SONIA: It doesn't hurt any more.

RAJINDER: (*Shakes her head in dismay*) You shouldn't go back this time. You're not even married to him. And it is so much...harder to leave, you know, once you have children, and then before you know it your whole life's gone. That is awful.

SONIA: He doesn't mean to be nasty or anythin' but you know what men are like. They only understand violence and they want to feel in charge, but me with my big mouth, I always slip out the wrong thing.

RAJINDER: (*Tries to distance herself a little*) They can't all be like that; my brothers are so good to their wives...Oh well....

SONIA: Lucky devils!

RAJINDER: God only knows what people do to deserve their luck.

KAMLA: (*Enters*) Hi. So you've met Sonia? I thought I'd come and say hello and get the papers out of the way.

RAJINDER: Sure.

KAMLA: Some details got left last week since you were in such a hurry.

RAJINDER: I only just made it in time. Pradeep got in a few minutes after I did.

KAMLA: That's okay. All I need is the names of the children here and your signatures.

RAJINDER: Savita, Bela and Sanjay.

KAMLA: Right, got that. Now, there's one other thing, would you mind running through...a few details with me... just a couple of questions about what happened? (*RAJINDER looks annoyed but says nothing.*) Have you taken out an injunction against him? Have you ever been to the police about your husband?

RAJINDER: Never. They open an inquiry and make your life hell with questions and questions and questions. The one who reports has to answer all their questions. They never catch the thugs; everyone knows that.

KAMLA: So was there an incident which made you leave?

RAJINDER: You're doing the same thing! I was told there would be no prying.

KAMLA: I'm sorry if it seems like that.

RAJINDER: This isn't easy for me, as it is.

KAMLA: Of course. Normally it isn't necessary.

RAJINDER: Then I would like to be treated 'normally,' please.

KAMLA: Trouble is you haven't been referred by any one, like a social worker or a doctor so, it is necessary. I'm sorry but resources are precious, we do need to prioritize in some way... to establish need.

RAJINDER: Do you imagine anyone would want to come to a refuge unless they needed to?

KAMLA: It's possible.

RAJINDER: Definitely not—if they've been in one before.

KAMLA: You may be right.

RAJINDER: I know I am right. It may look as though I have a choice, but I haven't really. I need to be two steps ahead of him.

KAMLA: Oh?

RAJINDER: I'm trying to escape from a man who's cunning, and strong, and tough as a bull; he can see through curtains, he can hear through walls. I am really frightened of him.

KAMLA: I'm sorry, I had to ask.

RAJINDER: It's all right. It's the haste of the young, isn't it? judging like that.

KAMLA: I'm not that young.

RAJINDER: You look very young to me. Where do you come from, Kamla?

KAMLA: South London.

RAJINDER: Oh, I see! (*pause*) Tusi Punjabi boalday o?

KAMLA: I'm sorry, I don't.

RAJINDER: It's....just, that I wondered about what other languages you spoke, if any?

KAMLA: Some French.

RAJINDER: Maybe I shouldn't have asked.

KAMLA: No, that was silly of me, I'm sure we can do better than this. Two grown women!

RAJINDER: Can we really?

KAMLA: Yes, I believe in friendship between women.

RAJINDER: I've heard about it, too.

KAMLA: This language thing, it's just that, it looks like an inadequacy and it isn't. Names are all they had left to them, in the Caribbean; to keep the languages going seemed a bit pointless in the end.

RAJINDER: So you're not from, India?

KAMLA: No, not quite. (*pause*) They struggled to make us Indian, in some sense. But it was hard; there probably isn't a lot we have in common.

RAJINDER: You're right, I'm sure.

KAMLA: It needn't be a problem though.

RAJINDER: I certainly hope not. (*Enter EILEEN*)

KAMLA: Hi, didn't know you were back! Rajinder this is Eileen, my colleague. She's been here since the refuge was set up.

EILEEN: Ages and ages ago! Hello.

RAJINDER: Pleased to meet you, Eileen.

EILEEN: Me too.

RAJINDER: Could I talk to *you*, if that's all right, about 'my case.'

EILEEN: Sure, whenever you like.

RAJINDER: Tomorrow, maybe? It seems I need to justify my being here.

EILEEN: You're welcome to be here if you need to, no questions asked.

RAJINDER: Thank you. I'm glad to hear that. Now if you'll excuse me, I must go. They get quite upset in the school if mums are late. (*Exit RAJINDER*)

EILEEN: Phew! Been stepping on toes, eh?

KAMLA: She would say nothing of her circumstances and she seems totally calm.

EILEEN: Could just be a layer, like her make-up.

KAMLA: Pretty thick layer, then!

EILEEN: Come on! There's nothing wrong with a bit of make-up, K!

KAMLA: Well...(*pause*) The thing is she looks able...and quite well-off. I have to ask, do people like her deserve to use up room?

EILEEN: I don't think anyone comes here, if they have a choice, Kamla.

KAMLA: Hmm. She did claim that she has no family here.

EILEEN: Exactly, and maybe no friends.

KAMLA: I dunno about that. I'd be very surprised! You become that smug only when you've got everything; and then, of course, good luck follows you wherever you go. You're never short of friends.

EILEEN: She's not your type, that's all.

KAMLA: No, she isn't. I wonder if she's using us, in some way, for some strange game of her own. She's not the kind who needs help!

EILEEN: Oh, Kamla, what's that supposed to mean? Stop being suspicious. How many times've you said yourself that class divides women, amongst other things. Don't let it do that to you now.

KAMLA: Just found her a bit...annoying....

EILEEN: Try to find the common ground, there must be some, somewhere within her, there must be the woman who needs help...I think you're being quite irrational about her.

(*KAMLA only shrugs. Exit EILEEN a little annoyed. KAMLA picks up RAJINDER's shawl and sits down on a chair. She opens the shawl and drapes it round her shoulders and walks slowly up and down the stage. She strokes the shawl and then lifts a finger to warn*)

KAMLA: You wrap it up carefully in old muslin if you can't find a polythene bag...you don't just leave good shawls lying around. Don't you know moths get at them if you're not careful? (*Carefully folds shawl and puts it back*) Oh, sorry I nearly forgot. (*Pause. Hums to herself, then tries to sing a snatch of an Indian song*) Aaj sajan mohay ang laga lo, janam safal ho jaai/'Any languages?' Riday ki peera, birha ki agni, sub sheetal ho jaai... Language classes, music lessons, dance lessons, they tried it all... it was no use to me. Who cares for all that crap anyway? (*Then she gets up and tries a few steps of Kathak holding her hands together in front of her looking stiff and awkward*) Tut, taa, thai, thai, tut, taa, thai, thai and now double (*faster*) taa, thai, thai, tut, taa, thai, thai. (*Enter RAJINDER*)

RAJINDER: I forgot my...shawl...oh?

KAMLA: Here it is. (*Exit KAMLA flustered*)

Scene 2. *Friday night; RAJINDER's bedroom in the refuge. The stage is in complete darkness. SAVITA has woken up after a nightmare. PRADEEP walks onto the stage and stands silently behind them. His shadow falling across them. Shuffles softly to her mother and whispers.*

SAVITA: Mummyji! Wake up, please Mummy!

RAJINDER: What is it, for God's sake, ssh quiet, Savita, you'll wake up the others. Hush, meray bachchay, you're shivering, what happened? (*RAJINDER moves and lights a lamp. A small spotlight comes on above them emphasizing the darkness*)

SAVITA: There's someone in here.

RAJINDER: Where? Are you crazy, darling! There's no-one here. Try to sleep, you'll wake up the whole house.

SAVITA: I saw him getting into the room. He broke in through the window.

RAJINDER: Who?

SAVITA: Maybe it was Papaji. I couldn't tell, his face was hidden in his turban, and, and he had his kirpaan, he was holding it like that, like a flag, above his head.

RAJINDER: Stop being so silly, Savita, there's no one here.

SAVITA: You know how he looked that day when he went mad 'cause you got back late...He just stood there, he was polishing his kirpaan...and his eyes looked strange...I really felt so terrified of him.

RAJINDER: Yes, I remember it.

SAVITA: And you know, that time...when he flung his plate at you, for talking back at him?

RAJINDER: Savita, stop it. I won't be able to sleep, don't stir it all up in my head at this time.

SAVITA: He wouldn't, he wouldn't force us to go back, would he, really, Ammah?

RAJINDER: I don't think so. Calm down, Savita. He can't find us here.

SAVITA: But if he does? Would he beat you in front of the other women here?

RAJINDER: He won't, he can never trace us to this place. Hush...

SAVITA: You can take self-defence classes at my school.

RAJINDER: (*Kisses her*) I'll think about it.

SAVITA: We could keep a hammer under the pillow. I kept Sanjay's bat under the bed, last night.

RAJINDER: Savita, what shall I do with you, my child, you're impossible....!

SAVITA: Ammah, I'm scared, don't laugh please.

RAJINDER: I'll cry if I don't.

SAVITA: Don't laugh, you sound strange. Why does everyone sound so different in the dark?

RAJINDER: Try to sleep, jaan. (*pause*) Hold on, what's that smell? Oh, Savita!

SAVITA: Ammah, I'm really, really sorry.

RAJINDER: Not again, I could kill you. All that washing it makes!

SAVITA: I never mean to. I don't know how it happens.

RAJINDER: Go and wash and then change your clothes. You're fourteen! What if someone finds out? (*SAVITA gets off the floor*).

RAJINDER: And just leave the wet things on the floor. I'll get up and rinse them out myself.

SAVITA: I *can* wash them out you know.

RAJINDER: I'll do it, then I know it's done properly and they won't smell. (*Exit SAVITA. Sound of a light switching on off-stage. Water running, then sound of a small baby crying*) Curse the day that brought us together, Pradeep! God forgive me, but I'll never let you find me ever again...I swear never to let you touch me again, Pradeep. (*Exit PRADEEP in silence*) Wash the bedclothes, your hands, your face, your body, once, twice, three times and pray for it to be cleansed. Then wash him off your body, Rajinder...and never let him touch you again... (*Light fades slowly on RAJINDER*).

Scene 3. *A bench in a park is set out at the front. RAJINDER walks on dressed for a walk. She sits down feeding the birds. EILEEN follows her and joins her on the bench.*

EILEEN: Mind if I join you? I saw you from the window and I felt like a walk too. We all stay cooped up indoors too much.

RAJINDER: Not at all. (*Moves to make room for EILEEN*) I love this half hour of peace and quiet, before the children return from school.

EILEEN: Look at that cheeky thing, they seem to know you already. D'you come out here every day?

RAJINDER: Just to get rid of the old bread and rice. I just collect it all from everyone. It's sinful to throw food in the bin.

EILEEN: Didn't I see you pourin' a pint of milk down the sink only yesterday?

RAJINDER: That was different...it...it got polluted.

EILEEN: Oh! (*pause*)

RAJINDER: I didn't mean to make a scene, but it matters to me, a lot. They don't seem to understand how much. How someone can just leave meat to defrost in a bag on the shelf, I don't understand...? The blood from it just dripped on to the milk.

EILEEN: Was only on the carton though, wasn't it?

RAJINDER: But still. It was... it is disgusting. It only needs for them to keep out of my bit of fridge and there wouldn't be a problem. Tell me how long have you been here Eileen?

EILEEN: Almost eleven years now.

RAJINDER: We must all sound the same to you!

EILEEN: Not at all. The situation is the same but women are so different. I'm not bored. No. A bit thrown by the enormity of it sometimes, but not bored, never that.

RAJINDER: You really care, don't you?

EILEEN: I think all of us do, in our own ways. Kamla does too, and the others.

RAJINDER: Maybe it's because you're older I felt I'd find it easier talking to you. I thought you'd understand more...than Kamla.

EILEEN: Perhaps I do, just a tiny bit more, an' that because I've been there.

RAJINDER: Meaning?

EILEEN: I came to this place for refuge myself, it was different then, a couple of women had set it up as a safe house. Then they gave me the job.

RAJINDER: I didn't know that. Do you ever get over it? I dunno if I should ask?

EILEEN: I don't mind talking about it now. It hurts, but I'm not bitter any more. I feel angry, more with myself for having stood it so long.

RAJINDER: You must have hoped he would change.

EILEEN: Yes, don't we all do that? I gave him a good ten years, and you? More than that, I s'pose?

RAJINDER: Fifteen. Sometimes people repent, they say.

EILEEN: I just couldn't take it any more. Bullyin', beatin', abuse and insults—an' he'd torment me over the money an' the housework. I became so nervous I'd be shakin' at ten o'clock when it was time for him to come home. He'd walk in and start pickin' on me. The night I left, he actually came at me with a hammer. I was so shit-scared I ran all the way to the police station in my slippers.

RAJINDER: How terrible! God, I can just imagine what you went through.

EILEEN: You know what the coppers did? Dumped me right back with him again. 'Domestic,' they said. I nearly died when he finished with me that night. That was it. I had to leave after that. I was too scared to go back.

RAJINDER: Hmm.

EILEEN: That was it.

RAJINDER: Yes. No one can really understand what it's like inside your four walls. (*RAJINDER is silent. Enter PRADEEP. Watches from a distance*) Do you have any children?

EILEEN: Two, they're grown now; wasn't much of a life for them I can tell you, all that bashin' an' terror day and night.

RAJINDER: It's the children you have to think of.

EILEEN: Are yours very disturbed by it all?

RAJINDER: Hmm.

EILEEN: For a long time I couldn't talk about it either. And for a long time, I never really felt safe. I'd be scared at night thinkin' he'd found me and was staring through the window panes.

RAJINDER: But he couldn't have, I suppose?

EILEEN: No. I'd put miles and miles between us.

RAJINDER: That means you can get away if you really want to. Can't you?

Shuja Nawaz

Born in Chakri Rajgan, near Jhelum, into a predominantly military family, Shuja Nawaz started writing as an undergraduate at Gordon College, Rawalpindi. He was introduced by Shahid Hosain* to Taufiq Rafat* and Kaleem Omar* who adopted him into their circle. Taufiq Rafat taught him the disciplines of writing and appreciating good verse. In 1972 he went on a fellowship to Columbia University, where he did his Masters in Journalism. He worked at *The New York Times,* became a newscaster and producer for Pakistan Television and, later, editor of the World Bank/IMF's quarterly *Finance & Development*. He has now put together his first collection of poetry, *Journeys* (1997). Last summer, he featured in the Miller Cabin Poetry reading series in Rock Creek Park, near Washington DC. He has translated Punjabi poetry into English, particularly by the Potohari poet, Baqi Siddiqui. He lives in Virginia and works as an IMF divisional chief.

FROM ***JOURNEYS***

Searching

Searching for a poem I wandered
among the debris of a lost war.

I did not find any word for death
among red-stained khaki and faces that mingled
with the dirt because their color was the same.

I did not find meaning in the imploded truth
a civilian's body told while a shattered mosque
raised fractured fingers at the silent sky.

I did not find rhythms in the whistle and boom
of artillery shells or the mad cackle of machine gun fire
at a thousand yards or more death has no rhyme or reason.

I did not find significant forms in the toting up
of casualties each day, ours and the other side's.
Who are the martyrs, who the simple dead? I cannot answer
I would need to ask the mothers, wives, sons, and daughters
silent in their grief. I will not raise this question, kill it
like a vanquished flag, wrap it up in history for our sons to ask.

Time will tell its own tale in words no man can articulate.

So I came back from the bloody earth, from shattered limbs
and shaken minds, from laughter of ignorant bravado and death,
for no bullet had my name written on it.

I came back into black-out days and nights. The full moon
had left us in mid-war and the sun was in mourning.

To windows clattering hysterically on empty houses with open
doors

open so that the weary, the wounded, and the dead could enter when they return.

The currency of words cannot buy back our losses
from the cold coffers of a possessive earth.

The Sarangi Player

Beyond this instant is leaf-fall
and a separation.
To carry my lament, I call
each errant note to its station.

But who will still the scream?
Deprivation
moves to memory's flashpoint of green
along strings alive in agitation.

I sing of places and recall
like a Persian wheel
an unending chain of memory that falls
away from me. I steal

tales from safe eyries
the years have built high.
For I have learnt from trees
height and distance hold the eye.

The song must end before
the pain, lest its impetus
be lost. I shiver more
from this than the coming frost.

Raja Bazaar

Rawalpindi, Pakistan

Someone has spread a sky
of tattered hessian
overhead.

The boy sells waist bands
of white cotton
curling

like edges of waves
foam-white snakes on
the shore

talks to a mullah
who argues about
the price

just an 'anna' or two
yet they bargain
money

jingles in coat pockets
warm and secure
unspent.

One vendor of old coats
meets relatives by chance
smiling
a broad clean smile
of uninhibited origin
washes

his dirty unshaven face;
the handshake and touching of
the heart

that small gesture suddenly
brings the whole bazaar
into my car.

The Initiation

From the day he could talk, the son asked
about his father and got no answer.
He learned to grow up alone and stood
by himself at prayers, solitary
as the heliograph posts in the Khyber Pass.
The high mud walls of his fort-like house
echoed the barren language of the hills.
And each year's questions were laid to rest
like a still-born child, unlamented.

Till at fifteen someone slapped his face
with word of his father's unavenged murder.
That night he took out the family rifle,
received blessings from his mother and left.

He saw the killers come as silhouettes growing
from the bank of a moon-lit field. Hurriedly,
he mumbled God's name three times and dropped
all three with a skill mastered over centuries

Next day, when the wailing rose from the other
village, the elders saw the rifle he carried
and pointed him out as Sherdil Khan's son.

Ozymandias II

Midnight
and time moves faster
than the Downtown Express.
Subway noise thickens
in the veins of the City.

He stands, skin
a paradigm of night
starless and dead
that drapes eight million
in a single shroud.

Furtive eyes scan
the next car for the cop
tired of Times Square.
A clammy hand feels
the spray can of paint, feels
the future, the tomorrows
that may escape

Under 'To do is to be—Nietzsche'
and 'To be is to do—Sartre'
and 'Doobee doobee doo—Sinatra'
in the Year of our Lord
Nineteen Hundred and Seventy Two
a new day's birth
witness the Black Proclamation
watch Egypt revive:
'Baby Face 125.'

TARIQ RAHMAN

Educated at Burn Hall in Abbottabad and at Peshawar University, Tariq Rahman joined the Pakistan Army and was an officer in the armoured corps. He opposed the 1971 military action in Dhaka and decided to resign from the army, although he was never posted to East Pakistan. His short story 'Bingo,' was written in 1974, much after the war. He has stated that it is entirely fiction and none of the characters ever existed. In 1978, he did resign from the army and went to Britain on a British Council scholarship for higher studies. He always wanted to be a research scholar and he has pursued an academic career since. He did his Ph.D. in English Literature from the University of Sheffield and an M. Litt. in Linguistics from the University of Strathclyde. Since then he has taught at various universities in Pakistan, was a Fulbright Scholar at the University of Texas at Austin and is at present Associate Professor of Linguistics at the National Institute of Pakistan Studies, Quaid-i-Azam University, Islamabad. He has published over 50 papers and several books including *Legacy and Other Short Stories* (1989), *A History of Pakistani Literature in English* (1991), *Work and Other Short Stories* (1991), *Language and Politics in Pakistan* (1996), *Zoo and Other Short Stories (1997).*

BINGO

It was miserable in the first term at the Pakistan Military Academy. They made us stand in the snow in underwear at night and I was given a cold shower and frog-jumps too. The Battalion Sergeant Major was a sadist. He made me hop around catching my ankles till I fell down and my legs ached like hell. But the cadets of my platoon were idiots. Each one of them broke the orders once and, lo and behold, we were all up to our neck in the soup. When I was the Senior Gentleman Cadet—the 'bloody SGC' as I was termed—I made them fall-in ten minutes before time. It's idiotic to be late. I made them double around as the seniors told me. Why should a chap be lousy when the staff and the seniors are all around to nab him by the neck and do the the dirty on him? So during my days the sergeant was pleased and the CMS ragged us only twice.

'You bloody jitter,' said my Cadet Corporal to me. 'You will be a good soldier.'

'Yes sir,' I shouted as he liked us to do.

The fellow beamed at me and omitted to make me front-roll when he left.

Tajassur, on the contrary, was such a fool, that the whole army spat on its hands and got down to the onerous task of making a soldier out of him. He didn't care. He let the cadets get late and stood like a statue who has had its behind kicked. He chatted around from room to room and didn't do his class work. He let us walk if he could help it. Naturally, whenever we were caught, Tajassur was the one who never heard the last of it. He gave away some of the articles of his FSMO and was the first one to be on restrictions. But he always walked around casually and smiled. It was foolish. The funniest thing was that he was my room-mate. It gave me the creeps to see him sleeping in the morning when I was almost in my shirt for the PT or the drill. He was a sub-human creature and knew no discipline.

Yet Tajassur had soft baby-looks and large black eyes. If one talked to him, he smiled and spoke nicely. The seniors called him a sissy and said he was fit to be a heroine in a Filipino movie. He often had one or two sadistic senior slave-drivers who delighted in punishing him or feeding him on sweets in the canteen. It was awful to be his room-mate. The seniors came into our room just to enjoy themselves by punishing him or talking to him—he was witty. 'Hey you heroine,' one would say. 'Have you got girl-friends?'

'No sir,' Tajassur would reply standing to attention. 'I don't know sir.'

'Get on your hands down idiot,' and Tajassur would fall to the ground on his hands and feet. 'And you too you priceless imbecile.'

So I, cursing the bastards, went into the same position. And the ragging would go on at my expense. Had Tajassur been less popular nobody would have bothered us so much.

I was good in drill and PT and Tajassur was lousy at both. Yet he managed to pass. In Map Reading the platoon mates often did his work. They enlarged the map for him and even found the grid reference of his own position. In exchange all the fellow did was only to tell them jokes. And in spite of his innocent looks, Tajassur knew jokes which could send the angels running after the chaste houris in Paradise. I like jokes but I detest stupidity. Of what use are jokes when the officers are just around the corner? All these immature things did make Tajassur popular but at the expense of his marks and position.

He was a Cadet Platoon Commander once and, at the end of the exercise, he brought us back in a truck. It was a big risk. We were supposed to have walked back twenty miles and there was a competition with the other platoons. And yet this grinning baby brought us back on this truck. Naturally we reached before midnight. So what does he do? He takes us to a hotel of all things and there makes us dance all night and eat and drink and have a rollicking good time. Oh boy, it was fun; but he could have been withdrawn if anyone had noticed. Well, we reached the Academy gates and were told that we were third. Tajassur seemed so tired that the cadet sergeant sent us to rest after the rifle cleaning. The fraud!

He passed out twentieth in the course. And, I bet, it was all because of his wonderful oral expression in English and wit. He read his lesson half an hour before the Model Discussion and gave cogent arguments. Besides, he was liked by our immature platoon-mates and they thought he was a good sort. He had given his water-bottle to thirsty people, who had been foolish enough to have wasted their supply in the exercise. He had cheerfully carried the Light Machine Gun—the most goddamnest pain in the arse—in the 'Initiative Exercise.' He had a smile for most of us and, in the Academy, chaps are nit-wits enough to get impressed by these kind of trivialities.

But just before our passing out, things were against him. He was a Bingo, you see. He belonged to Dacca itself and East Pakistan had begun kicking up one hell of a row to get separated from West Pakistan. We called him a 'Bingo' and a 'traitor' and Sheikh Mujibur Rehman's ADC. I went a step further and called him the 'Marshland Minion.' I told him, he would be the minion of old Mujib and since all his land was marshland so—the title!

But Tajassur kept quiet about these things. He was quite a kid and kids can't get serious about politics and such like grown-up things. So came the D-Day and we passed out. Tajassur had got many badges of rank, caps and stuff even from juniors. I thought it a shame to accept things from juniors and said so. He smiled sheepishly and told me that presents could not be denied. I told him he would bring shame to the army by being so unprincipled.

'I have my own principles, Safeer,' he replied gravely.

'And what damned lousy Bingo principles may those be sweetie?' I taunted him. I was getting angry.

'Look Safeer. They are not reasoned out. I just do what makes me happy and what makes people happy. And "Bingo" has nothing to do with it.'

'Happy,' I cried. 'That's a fat-headed thing to say and I will let you know it is. The sergeant would excuse us drill to make us happy. The soldiers should not kill the rebel Mukti Bahini to make them happy. And girls should get laid in order to please grinning morons. Happy—Oh now you know that's ungentlemanly and unofficer-like.'

'I am not much of an officer,' he rejoined.

'So much the worse for the army,' I replied.

Just then our bearer came in and Tajassur started telling him what to do with his shoes, once he left. The bearer goggled like a fish and seemed to relish the idea of laying his vile paws on those good shoes, coats and shirts.

I went into the Infantry and so did Tajassur. We got our regiments in the main dining-hall of the Battalion Mess. Whenever someone was assigned to Headquarters Eastern Command, a sibilant half-deriding sound came from the cadets. The Adjutant was terribly annoyed and threatened us with restrictions but the sound still didn't stop entirely.

'Sher Nawaz Khan,' called the Adjutant. '36th Cavalry, Kharian Cantt.' We all clapped. Sher got red in the face and sat down. 'Mohammad Adil Siddiqui, Daedalus's Horse. Report to Multan Cantt.'

This time the clapping was thunderous. Daedalus's was a much-coveted armoured regiment with aristocratic traditions.

'Ali Ahmed,' continued the Adjutant, '20th Baloch, Quetta.'

Applause greeted him also.

'Safeer Ahmed, 15th Punjab. Report to HQ Eastern Command.'

I sat down amidst a low hissing and the fellow on my right laughed mirthlessly. Then some people clapped. The Adjutant went red in the face. 'What's wrong with you buggers? Are you all yellow? I'll kick the whole lot out of here if I hear that damned hissing.' Then he went on with the names. Some people congratulated me on getting the Infantry. It was my choice.

'Tajassur Ullah,' said the Adjutant with a smile. The applause was thundering as he stood up shyly. He was blushing; the sissy. 'For the course favourite the GHQ decrees—report to HQ Eastern Command—15th Punjab.'

The hall went wild. There was loud hissing mixed with clapping. The Adjutant looked down and fumbled with the papers. I thought everyone made a fool of himself because

Tajassur was treated like a baby not like a grown-up man. I would have been ashamed to be in his shoes. But he sat down cheerfully and thanked the people around him with a bright smile.

We got only three days to report to the stations of duty. On the plane I met some of my course-mates. The rank of Second Lieutenant was new on our shoulders. It was fun to wear it. Very few people have the honour of being class-I officers of the government at the age of nineteen or twenty. We were among such lucky ones and I felt proud of myself and happy.

When we reached the unit there was an atmosphere of tension and hurry. The Adjutant was a certain Captain Maqsood Hussain. He told me to look sharp in my battle dress and to be fifteen minutes early for all parades. Tajassur also reported late that evening and Captain Maqsood ragged him a great deal for grinning like an ape. He seemed to be a strict Adjutant. In the evening we went to the mess on bikes. An old bearer served us soft drinks and we sat listening to the conversation. Then the Commanding Officer came and everyone stood up. He was a middle-aged man with a balding head, bushy eye-brows and a very serious grim face. 'Let me introduce, Second Lieutenant Safeer, to you sir,' said Captain Maqsood presenting me first since I was senior by number to Tajassur.

'How do you do?' said the CO. 'What was your passing-out number?'

'Fifth sir,' I replied.

'Good. The Punjab Regiment likes bright youngsters. Good.'

Then Tajassur was presented. The clown smiled even at the Commandant though the Colonel was as serious as church as he took his paw in his big hand.

'And what is your passing-out number?'

'Twentieth, sir,' he replied.

'Well, well. Work hard in the regiment. Your professional life begins here,' said the CO. I could see that I had given a good first impression.

The CO talked to the senior officers and we kept listening. Nobody addressed us again. Then the supper was announced and we moved to the table. The CO began talking about history.

'I admire the courage of John Nicholson and Sir Hugh Rose in 1857,' he said.

'Yes sir, the battle account is inspiring,' said Major Dost Muhammad the Second-in-Command.

'Sir, the Vietcong too are brave,' said Major Azhar Khan, one of the Company commanders.

'Yes, yes, that is wonderful,' replied the CO. 'Though they are a short-statured people. They don't seem to be a martial race.'

'I think there are no martial races,' Tajassur's voice startled me. Everyone turned to look at the man. The Adjutant was scowling darkly. Everyone seemed to have been struck by a bolt from the blue. 'People are forced to fight when they are exploited and transgressed against: and bravery is good only if it is used in a just cause. If it is used to oppress, it is evil.'

There was a pin-drop silence in the room. The CO looked as if he would have a fit. His face was red with anger. He didn't reply at all. Then the silence reigned in an ominous way and the meal came to an end. The CO left for his room and the Adjutant took us aside. He struck a cigarette and slowly turned to Tajassur.

'How dare you,' he hissed between clenched teeth, 'talk so insolently to the CO?'

'But I merely expressed my opinion, sir,' said Tajassur with genuine surprise.

'Blast your damned idiotic opinion, you bloody tit of a Second Lieutenant. Don't you dare utter a squeak when your seniors are talking OK. Do I make myself clear?'

'Yes sir.'

The Adjutant kept glaring at us. We kept standing at attention. Tajassur looked down.

'Seven days orderly officer duty for you, Tajassur. You will check the guard and report to me thrice every night.'

'Yes sir,' said Tajassur in a muffled voice. Captain Maqsood turned and stalked off. His boots crunched on the loose shingle. Tajassur stood completely humiliated. They had petted him and spoiled him at the PMA. I always had told him that the army was no place for suave young juniors, who didn't know how to respect seniors. Now he was crying. Oh God! I couldn't believe it. He had tears in his eyes. 'Don't be a sissy, Tajassur,' I said to him. It was most exasperating to see him disgracing our course like that. A most effeminate thing to do. He didn't reply. When I reached the room I found him asleep.

Soon enough Tajassur was in everybody's bad books. He got late for parades. He was too chummy with the other ranks and addressed the non-commissioned officers as if they were officers. He had, strangely so, no respect for the seniors. He contradicted them and thrust his opinion, as if he knew more than all those who had put in so much service. Everyone told me that the PMA was not training even the regular courses well. Even I was given long lectures when he did something wrong. As I had expected, Tajassur was a very poor specimen of an officer.

Then one day the CO called a conference and apprised us of the enemy situation. The Mukti Bahini i.e. rebel Bingo troops, had started playing havoc with our supply line. Since January Sheikh Mujib had become even more absurdly adamant about his 'Six Points.' I never knew what the damned Six Points were but anything coming from a loony like Mujib must have been crap. Tajassur kept sitting like a stooge throughout the conference. That evening we were supposed to crack down on a village where the bastards were in hiding. Tajassur had become quite glum.

'Hey Safeer, ready,' he said amiably.

'Yeah what about you?'

'OK.'

He sat down and started playing with my watch. It annoyed me. Goodness, wasn't he grown up enough to stop fooling with other people's things? It made a man sick to have such a kiddish roommate.

'Stop playing with it,' said I.

'What does it matter?' he replied. 'What does anything matter?'

'What matters now partner is that we had better roast your Bingo friends alive,' I said wearily.

'Why?'

'Why? What the hell do your mean why? Because they are Pakistan's enemies. Because they want to divide our country. Because they are Indian agents and anti-Pakistan. That's what we are being paid for. The CO orders us and we go. That's loyalty.'

'But where is your conscience?'

'My conscience tells me to rid Pakistan of its enemies.'

'Listen Safeer,' he said sitting on my bed. 'This is propaganda. Pakistan was not created to be a slave colony. Bengal was treated as a colony by the CSP officers. The army officers made fun of our men and beat them. Everyone took our wealth.' As usual his voice became choked with gushy tears. He clenched his hand. 'And now that we have risen against this exploitation, this tyranny, they are telling the army to shoot our people. The army has entered villages before and shot our innocent people. They've raped our girls. It's monstrous and unjust. Can't you feel it Safeer,' he caught my hands and his lips twitched and trembled. 'Can't you see that this lovely lush-green land is under hobnailed boots. Can't you hear the foul orders of those hate-filled fat men in Islamabad who are sending innocent boys to kill people they have never even met before. Come on Safeer where's your conscience?'

I shook him off. He was mad. I had never seen him so passionate. I was a little scared of him. These Bengalis were a treacherous race. Batmen had been known to have murdered their officers. This vile race knew of no loyalty nor even unit spirit. Nothing noble appealed to their conscience. 'Go to sleep. Go to sleep. Don't talk like that or you'll be caught you fool!' I muttered. In the evening the news shook everybody. Second Lieutenant Tajassur had deliberately become a deserter. They called his absence desertion straight away because his pistol was missing too and it was well known that Bingos took to their heels to join the enemy treacherously. I was surprised. He was too much of a sissy, I thought, to have dared to run away. It is risky after all.

We did roast the traitors in that village. First the troops surrounded it and then the machine-guns blazed away. The vermin came out and ever so happily the crack-shots took them on. It must have taught them a lesson not to hide the traitors any more. They took prisoners too who were handed on to the Intelligence Units. These Intelligence chaps knew how to get the truth out of stubborn Bingos for sure.

Days passed and I became a responsible subaltern. In March I did so well that I got recommended for the Commander-in-Chief's commendation letter. The GOC Eastern Command shook hands with me. In the Unit the CO called me, 'Hot-Rod Commando', and was very proud of me. Major Ali Ahmed was an expert in bringing in Bingos as a net brings in fish. We would shoot them slowly one by one. It improved my target practice a good deal. The bastards cried for pity and whimpered like dogs. I think this is a race of slaves. They look up at a person as if he were a god, and then they are so treacherous that they stab you in the back. We used to kill them whenever we got news that our brethren had been killed anywhere. It didn't compensate us for our losses, but it made one take out one's anger at someone. Some officers delighted in torturing the Bingos to extract information from them. In the beginning I thought it was excessive, but soon enough, I found out that these stubborn people didn't talk as long as you treated them humanely. Besides, everything is fair once your national integrity is at stake. However, the good old Second-in-Command was a playboy and all of us had laughs to think of the Bengali girls who came out of his room in the morning looking as if they had been ridden by a stallion.

I got my first girl too one day. Well it was a senior's order to celebrate my coming of age. I had been primed with whisky before I went in to her. The stupid wretch cried out in fear and recoiled from me as if I were a spider. This angered me and I had to slap her across the face before she became quiet. The rest was fun but she kept lying like a log. I was disgusted. I learned the rules of the game slowly and brown bodies became good to play with.

One day we were ordered to clear a village of the Muktis. I was incharge of a platoon and we moved off at first-light on jeeps. It was very clearly dawn when we struck. The scene was rather like some Second World War movie's, except that brown-skinned people ran out like chickens with their heads cut off. The Bingos are such cowards in front of soldiers, I thought, as I turned the machine guns on the main exit. The rush of the women stopped as many rolled in blood and confusion. Then hell broke loose. Our jeeps were hit by bullets and they swooshed and whistled past my ears. I heard the Company Commander yell the order to retreat. I jumped into a tree. But I managed to rush off in another jeep and got bogged down into their blasted flooded paddy fields. Frightful shapes advanced towards me and I was hauled out of the jeep. The pistol was yanked out of my hands and I was given a blow on the head which made everything go dark in front of me.

When I regained consciousness, I was in a little dark room. There was a window but, blast their treacherous brains, they had barred it with steel bars. I went around it once. Twice. This didn't happen. Officers of the Pakistan Army couldn't be caught like this by the Bingos. As I sat down trying to think some way out of it all, the door opened and a small mean-looking Bingo beckoned me to follow him. I did and was brought to a room in which a number of ragged ill-clothed men were sitting on cots. One of them was in uniform and he was sitting on a chair.

'Lieutenant Safeer of the 15th Punjab, I am Major Saif-ur-Rahman of the Bangla Desh Army,' he said in English, getting up to shake my hand.

I was stunned. There was no bloody Bangla Desh and no damned Bangla Desh Army, I was about to burst out. But then I remembered where I was and kept my mouth shut.

'Yes,' I said.

'Yes sir, Lieutenant,' replied the Major smiling impishly. I wanted to bash his ugly black Bingo mug in. But I had to be tactful.

'Yes sir,' I said

'That's better,' he replied.

The other Bingos shouted. Their faces were angry. They looked like animals. I had never seen men like that. Their animal faces scared me. This was not like war against a civilized army. These apes knew no Geneva Convention, nor did they know what an officer was. But this Major was more of a fellow officer. At least he knew these things.

He must have been in the Academy.

'You will be tried,' said the Major.

'What for sir?' I asked him.

'For killing innocent civilians. For butchering exactly twenty-two women, nineteen children and seven men of Bangla Desh.'

'I did my duty.'

'Which code of morals asks you to kill people at the orders of an unscrupulous government?'

At this the people raised a shout. They seemed to understand what was going on. I found out why this was so. An interpreter kept up a constant chatter conveying what was going on to the avid audience. My heart sank within me. These people were mad.

'I am defending my country against Indian insurgents and rebels. When the people hide them we have to take action. That's all.' I replied.

'And why do they hide them?' the Major's eyes were hard and glittering. 'Have you ever tried to get out of your propaganda and use your mind and eyes? They hide them because they love them. Because they are their own people. Because they hate you. That's why they kill you when you stray out of your little fortresses. But one day all your fortresses will vanish and we will be free—then you will be pushed out into the Bay of Bengal and the lotus will be out of your reach. You are colonists, like the French in Algeria and the Belgians in the Congo. Had you been as sensible as the British you would have withdrawn gracefully. But no. You'll get innocent youths fresh from PMA and open-mouthed recruits butchered first before your generals see any sense. You will have to be pushed out. You won't go.'

The room jeered at me. Their voices rose to a hysterical crescendo and the walls reverberated. Their voices had a ravenous hunger in it and the hope of life seemed to fuse in me. The bodies were brown and lean and naked, yet they were not in a cage where I could shoot them. They were not being kicked or raped. They were not pleading. There was a maniacal confidence in their eyes. They were not slaves it seemed. And looking around I felt my feet go cold. My throat was parched and I felt very weak. My heart was beating like mad.

'You will be shot in the morning,' said the Major.

I was taken back to my room. Its walls closed upon me and seemed to move physically. The light showed a star in the sky and I looked at it. The thought came and struck me like a blow in boxing—I wouldn't see it again. I wouldn't feel the wind on my face too. How wonderful was the Mess with the waiter bringing beer for you. How lovely the feel of the beer as it makes one light-limbed and heavy-lidded. And never would I feel that rising intoxication; nor would the black sky have silver stars again. I turned around and the hard damp ground resisted me. The soft skin of the girls was no more. I remembered the evenings of the PMA when we sat on the terrace of the cafeteria and looked at the green valley. Tajassur often treated me. He was so lively and soft-spoken. And tomorrow I would be dead. What was the use of it all? I would die and Bengal would live on. I don't know how many would die and then something would happen. But who was in the right?—And was there a right at all? I didn't know anything. I didn't want to think. It was agony to be alive.

I didn't know what time it was when I heard a knock. I was going to abuse the man so much that he would run way. It was bursting in me like a tidal wave. All the dirty words of Urdu, Punjabi and English were coming to my lips. I hated these Bengali bastards. I hated them all. I hated the army. I hated… 'Safeer, Safeer,' came a low soft voice.

'Yes,' I replied. It was a familiar voice. My ears were hungry for its melody. There was hope in its music. I liked that voice at that moment. It was Tajassur. I put my arms around his neck and almost stifled him. He was trembling. I too was trembling. I kissed him on the cheeks.

'Come with me,' he said in a low voice.

We stole out like shadows. The Bengali soldiers saluted him. He wore a Captain's rank and the same uniform I had seen on the Major. There was a jeep outside and in it we sped away from the loathsome house. We didn't talk. He took me to a house where a woman with soft eyes like Tajassur's gave me food. A girl brought me rice and cooked fish. It was excellent and I enjoyed it.

'This is my family, Safeer,' said Tajassur. 'You'll have to stay here till I can send you back to where you belong.'

'But Tajassur, why don't you send me soon? Now in fact.'

'It's impossible,' he smiled. 'Actually, this area is now under the joint command of the Indian and the Bangla Desh Army. The Pakistan Army is surrendering.'

'No!'

'Yes, Safeer,' he said and his voice was gentle and tired. 'The war is coming to an end.'

I lived there for three days and that soft-spoken family wafted me to states of mind I had never known before. A languorous peace filled me up as I drank milk and ate my rice, Tajassur's sister, Amina had a charming languor in her eyes which made me eat ever so softly. There was no hurry, no protocol and no friction. They had soft, cute, child-like smiles. They spoke a bit of Urdu and Amina knew a little English too. There was a warmth in their house which made me melt. It was lovely.

So when Tajassur came to take me to Dacca, I was sad at the parting. His mother put a talisman around my neck and his sister gave me chocolates, money and—a lovely smile! He took me out tenderly to a jeep. And I was about to get in when the deafening burst of a machine-gun rocked us violently out of it. We stretched out on the ground and I saw Pakistani Commandos enter the house. Tajassur leapt up like lightning but before he could shoot, he was bayonetted. I saw the bayonet go into his stomach and with a cry he fell back and the blood ran all over his belly and legs. The Commandos were in the house. I got up, forgetting caution.

'Hey, wait, wait. I am Lieutenant Safeer of the 15th Punjab,' I shouted like a madman.

'Thank God you are safe,' said an officer embracing me. 'We'll have to get away to Dacca. They've surrendered.'

I heard the meaningless words. What was surrender? It was all meaningless. There were commando soldiers. And inside the house were Amina and Tajassur's mother. And Tajassur lay dead in a puddle of blood and his guts had come out and sprawled on his thighs like snakes. He looked so boyish and lovely and young.

'What are they doing sir, your soldiers?' I cried shaking the captain.

'Let's go in and see,' he said calmly, loading his sten-gun again.

We went in. The world broke into mad patterns. Amina was naked, raped—dead? Stabbed! And Tajassur's mother was wild. She tore her hair. She flung things all around. She was frantic. I couldn't meet her eyes. I couldn't stand her grief. She was living in the agony of death. Her husband had died much earlier. I took the Captain's sten-gun and shot her—to end her agony with pity in my heart. She looked at me as if unable to believe the depth of human ingratitude. Then she fell down dead. I emptied the sten-gun on the ground. On the mud of free Bangla Desh.

'Bloody Bingos,' commented the Captain of the SSG.

'Let's go, sir,' I said. I felt like crying.

And we sat in the jeep and went away. Nothing mattered any more. Tajassur and his mother were no longer alive to accuse me. Bangla Desh was free and the Pakistan Army had surrendered.

Tahira Naqvi

Educated in Lahore at the Convent of Jesus and Mary, Tahira Naqvi graduated from Lahore College and went on to Government College, Lahore, to do a masters in psychology. In 1972 she moved to America with her husband, expecting to return after his post-graduate work, but they stayed on. After her third child, she enrolled into a masters programme in education and wrote her first short story—about Pakistan in 1983, during a creative writing workshop. She has continued to write fiction since. She has clung tenaciously to images of Pakistan and says 'My writing moves from my hyphenated, fractured, wonderfully kaleidoscopic immigrant world, to my world as a Pakistani in Pakistan, a role that relies greatly on memory. I am greedy with memory; I take everything it offers me and more, and I keep writing'. Her stories have appeared in *The Massachusetts Review, The Journal for South Asian Literature, Calyx* and other literary journals, as well as a text book and many anthologies. Her first collection, *Attar of Roses and Other Stories from Pakistan* (1997), will be followed by her second, *Beyond The Walls,* next year. Tahira Naqvi's extensive work as an English translator of Urdu fiction includes *Another Lovely Face: The Life and Works of Saadat Hasan Manto* (1985), and several books by Ismat Chughtai: *The Quilt and Other Stories* (1990), US edition (1994), *The Heart Breaks Free, The Wild One* (1993) and *The Crooked Line* (1995). As a visiting writer at Columbia University, she has taught a course 'Women Writers and the Urdu Short Story.'

Love in an Election Year

(1)

Benazir Bhutto has a notion she will win. The *mullahs*, their hands raised ominously, their eyes glinting passionately, are up in arms because, as they see it, a woman cannot, and if they can help it, will not, hold executive office. There are pictures in every newspaper. Pronouncements are inked everywhere. But the gaunt-looking young woman with large piercing eyes and dark sweeping eyebrows, seems determined to become our next Prime Minister. She reminds me of another woman who had, in a similarly brazen move, wished to be the president of the country her brother had helped found. That was many years ago. That winter, I was only fifteen and the *mullahs* hadn't been given a voice as yet.

Winter in Lahore was one's reward for having suffered through summer and having survived the ordeal. Friendly sunshine offering warm, tantalizing embraces, a furtive chill in the evening, lurking in the darkness, never threatening; plump, tangy tangerines that looked like balls of pure gold; afternoons of story-telling after school on the veranda where the bricks on the floor lit up with terracotta lights when the sharp, bright sun filtered through the holes in the latticed balcony; and Baji Sughra. Baji Sughra was in love in the winter of that year and I was her confidant and ally. Since she was twenty-one and I only fifteen, I had to call her *baji*, but the years between us were a mere technicality; we were friends. And it wasn't that we had become friends overnight. We have always been good friends, the way most cousins are; even when she and her family left for Multan and were gone for three years, we knew that as soon as we met again it would be as if we had not been away from each other. That's how it was with cousins—they were always there.

Within an hour of her arrival from Multan we were chattering without pause like two myna birds. Uncle Amin had been transferred to Lahore again, and until their bungalow in Mayo

Gardens was ready Baji was to stay with us. Although I tried not to show it, I was amazed, no, overwhelmed, at the change I saw in her. As if magic, by some process I had no wit to fathom, she appeared so beautiful. Like a sultry actress in an Indian film, like a model in a magazine ad for Pond's Cold Cream. Her hair, which used to hang limply on either side of her face in thick dishevelled braids, was now neatly pulled back and knotted with a colorful *paranda* into a long braid down her back, while little wisps danced on her wide, shiny forehead with wild abandon. She also smiled constantly, as if something was making her happy all the time, as if there was some joke she kept remembering, again and again. Her lips, which like mine, were once perpetually chapped and sallow, seemed fuller and soft. I could have sworn she was wearing pink lipstick, except that Auntie Kubra, her mother, would have killed her if she had. Lipstick was for secret dramas enacted in your rooms when the adults were having their conferences, or for when you were married. I think there was something the matter with her eyes as well. They twinkled and glimmered as if there were secret lights in them. As for the lashes, they were thicker and sootier than I remembered, while her eyebrows, without a doubt, were longer and darker. Later that day, when I found myself alone for a while in the bedroom I shared with my younger sister and now with Baji Sughra, I examined my own face closely in the dressing table mirror. Front, the sides, then three-quarter angles. Sadly, nothing I saw in the mirror was changed.

At first Baji and I cleared dust from old business. Cousin Hashim had run away from home twice, Aunt S was pregnant with her first baby, Meena was to become engaged to Hashim's older brother who was in medical school, and Aunt A's cold-blooded, unrelenting mother-in-law was a witch whom we would have all liked to see tortured, if not killed. I had seen *Awara*, the latest Nargis-Raj Kapoor film, and we, at our house, were all rooting for Fatima Jinnah, who was running against President Ayub Khan in the 1964 elections. As for the news about Multan, it was skimpy at first. Baji Sughra said the weather was dusty and hot as always, but she had made new friends in school, the mangoes in summer were sweeter and plumper than anywhere else, and yes, she too was rooting for Fatima Jinnah.

'A woman president for Pakistan. Can you believe it Shabo? And she's running against a general too. But she's so like her brother Jinnah, how can anyone not vote for her! She'll win.' Baji Sughra looked even more beautiful when she was excited. I wanted to ask her why she was surprised we might have a woman president; sometimes the finer points of politics eluded me. But I knew she had something important to tell me, so I let the query pass.

And finally, when the sun had settled beyond the veranda wall and we had been talking for nearly an hour, she broke the news to me. She was in love. With Javed Bhai, another cousin, a Multan cousin. If I had done my calculations correctly, he was three years older than she was, twenty-three. In his second year at the Engineering University in Lahore, he was one of our cleverest cousins, the one who showed the most promise, the elders had been heard to proclaim. On a visit to his parents' house in Multan, he and Baji Sughra met. It was at one of those family gatherings when the adults are too absorbed in conversation to keep an eye on what the children are doing, or even know where they are. Suddenly Baji and Javed, who weren't strangers and had known each other since childhood, felt they were more than just cousins. This rather overpowering revelation led to secret trysts on the roof of Baji Sughra's house while everyone was taking afternoon naps. Promises were extracted and plans made. Later, after he returned to Lahore, Baji wrote to him, but he couldn't write back for obvious reasons, she explained. I didn't ask her to elaborate; if the reasons were so obvious they would reveal themselves to me sooner or later.

'We'll be married when Javed gets his degree,' Baji Sughra informed me with her dimpled smile. 'In two years.'

I knew Javed Bhai well. He came to our house frequently as did other cousins, especially when they were visiting Lahore from elsewhere, or were students away from home, as Javed Bhai was. He was good-looking, tall, fair-skinned, with a windblown mop of hair, a few locks hanging carelessly over his broad forehead. A thick, black moustache jealously hugged his lips so you didn't see much of them ever. And what a voice he had! He sang film songs in a way that made you feel nervous and mysteriously elated all at the same time. He sang willingly, so we didn't have to beg and beg as we had to do with some of our coy female cousins with good voices, like Meena, for instance.

There was no reason to be amazed at what had happened. Baji Sughra and Javed were like Nargis and Raj Kapoor, like Madhubala and Dilip Kumar. They belonged together. I began to envision Baji Sughra as a bashful bride, weighted down with heavy gold jewelry, swathed and veiled in lustrous red brocade and garlands of roses and *chambeli*.

'He'll come to see me Shabo, so you have to help,' Baji Sughra held both my hands in hers.

'What can I do?' I said, excitement at the thought of secretly helping lovers, rising to form a knot in my throat. 'How can I help?' I repeated hoarsely.

'We'll be in your room upstairs and you just keep watch, make sure no one comes up while we're there.'

'But what if someone does, what will I say, and ...' I couldn't continue because all of a sudden I realized this wasn't going to be easy. I had to think. Baji Sughra and I had to make plans.

'Shabo, you have to promise you won't tell anyone about this, not even Meena, not even Roohi, promise.' Baji Sughra looked at me as if she were a wounded animal, and I a hunter poised with an arrow to pierce her throat. Her eyes filled with tears. I put my arms around her.

'I promise I won't, I won't tell, Baji, please believe me, I won't.' I hugged her, feeling older than my fifteen years, imbued with a sense of importance I had never experienced before. Perhaps that is how Fatima Jinnah feels, I told myself, empowered and bold, ready to take on not only a general but the whole world.

The rendezvous went smoothly. After lunch my parents, Auntie Kubra, and Baji's father Uncle Amin, left to go to our grandparents' room for their usual talks. I couldn't understand how their store of topics for discussion was never depleted. There was so much to say all the time. Politics, family quibbles, who was being absolutely, ruthlessly mean to whom, and who should marry whom and when. Well, finding ourselves alone, Salim (another cousin who had come with Javed Bhai that day, as advisor and helpmate, no doubt), Baji Sughra, my sister Roohi, and I, all took up Javed's suggestion that we play carom.

Four people can play at one time, so we selected partners and found we had one person left over—Roohi. She was the youngest in our group and hadn't quite grasped the intricacies of carom strategy as yet.

'No, no, Roohi can play,' Baji hastily intervened when I tried to coax Roohi into observing first and playing later. 'She can be your partner, Shabo. I'm going up to finish putting the lace on my *dupatta*. I'll be back soon and then Roohi can be my partner and Salim can watch.' Baji had instructed me that I was not to act surprised; assuming a rather nonchalant tone I was to say, 'All right, but hurry up,' which I did.

'Yes, I will, I only have one side of the *dupatta* to do.' She left quickly.

All of us sat down at the carom table which always remained in the same place on the veranda, right across from the windy gully separating the veranda's east and west sections. Even now, when it was cold, we kept the table there, because that was also the sunniest spot on the veranda. What was a little gust of bone-chilling wind every now and then when the sun was bright and warm on our faces?

Within minutes we had formed pairs. Quickly and expertly, Javed Bhai sprinkled some talcum powder on the board to make it slippery and slick, and Salim arranged the black and white disks in a circle. A large red disk, called the 'Queen,' resided safely in the centre of the circle. The Queen, over-sized and radiant, carried more points than its austere black and white companions.

I got the first turn. Slouching, my eyes narrowed, assuming the posture I had seen Javed and the other boys use, I aimed at and hit the striker, which was white and somewhat bigger in size than the other disks. I watched gleefully as it first hit and then scattered the other disks all over the board's sleek, yellow surface. Soon all the disks were darting frantically across the wooden board; some, under the expert hands of our male partners, fell into the snug, red nets hanging from the corners of the board, disappearing as if they had never been there in the first place. The Queen, everyone's target at one time or another, was waiting calmly for its turn to disappear. Finally Roohi was given the opportunity to 'push' it into the net.

The first game was over so quickly I began to feel apprehensive. How many games could we play? As Salim began rearranging the disks, Javed said, 'I'm going to run down for a pack of cigarettes. You people go ahead without me. I'll be back soon.'

Of course he was gone a long time. Roohi began to show impatience and said the game was no fun with only three players. She was learning quickly. Salim said, 'I think this is better, you can have more disks to hit. Javed was taking them all away from us.' Roohi gave him the look children reserve for adults when they think they're being duped. But, finding him placing the disks together with a solemn air, she turned to give me a stare, discovered I was gazing intently at the carom board, and gave up.

'All right, but where's Baji Sughra?' she muttered.

'She's in her room, where else? Now come on, pay attention.' I was getting irritated with her. If we had been in a mystery novel, she'd be the unwanted and unexpected interloper, and would have been knocked down senseless by now.

After a second game in which Roohi won because we more or less forced her to, I asked Salim if he would sing for us. He too, like Javed Bhai, had a strong voice and the uncanny ability to imitate Mukesh, my favorite playback singer. He put on his Raj Kapoor smile and nodded.

Awara hun, (I'm a rogue) he began after pausing solemnly for a few seconds with his eyes closed, his head tilted to one side. Before I knew it, he was also tapping the carom board rhythmically, keeping beat with his long fingers and the heels of his hands as if the carom board were a *tabla*. Roohi sat back slumped and sullen since she wasn't into film songs as yet. I could see she was getting more and more restless, and very soon she would offer to go and bring Sughra Baji down from her room.

'Well, what's going on here?' It was Sughra Baji. She silently made an appearance from the back of the gallery so we didn't see her right away. I was too engrossed in Salim's singing to hear her footsteps. 'And where's Javed?' she asked boldly, raising her eyebrows inquiringly without looking at any one directly.

'He went to get cigarettes,' Roohi said petulantly, 'and we can't play anymore with only three people. Why did you take so long?'

Roohi was still grumbling when Javed Bhai reappeared. Within minutes we were engrossed in another game of carom. Roohi won again. After two more games we decided to end the game; the sun had wandered off somewhere and it was getting chilly. I noticed Sughra Baji was flushed, and couldn't stop smiling, while Javed Bhai hummed and hummed. What was that song? They never once glanced at each other, except in the most indifferent, casual manner. Such subterfuge! I was impressed.

(2)

We were making streamers to decorate the front door and the areas along the balconies. The paper flags were twelve inches by six inches and the string was about twenty feet long. Aunt A, who was visiting, had cooked flour paste for us to use for the gluing; Cousin Hashim, after having run off a few times from home because of fights with his father over the subject of academic failure, was now staying with us for a few days to allow his father to cool off, and had been entrusted with obtaining twelve dozen, tissue-thin paper flags from a stationary shop at the corner of Allama Iqbal and Davis Roads. We were working feverishly so we could have the streamers ready that afternoon. One more day would be needed for everything to dry and elections were only two days away.

Our work wasn't going too well. After all, this was the first time we were making streamers ourselves. The idea was simple; apply the glue to the narrow white strip of the flag (which represented the minorities in Pakistan), attach it to the string, overlap part of the white strip over the string so it came over and deftly press the two edges together. But our hands were sticky, the tips of our fingers numb and caky from the starchy globs that remained on them and dried. The process was slow; we weren't going from one flag to the next as fast as was necessary to meet our deadline.

There was no shortage of help. Aunt A kept the glue coming, and when Abba came back from work in the afternoon, he too got his hands dirty stringing up flags. All this time Dadima and Dadajan watched us closely, she from her place inside the quilt, he from his easy chair, gurgling his massive, copper-based *hukkah*, occasionally twirling the ends of his large, white moustache between draws. Amma, meanwhile, was concerned mainly with how much mess we were making, and with the possibility that we might come to supper without washing our hands thoroughly first.

Suddenly, around three, there was a noise at the front door and I was surprised to see Auntie Kubra and her husband walk in with Baji Sughra in tow. They had moved to their bungalow in Mayo Gardens only a week ago, so why were they here today? True it was Sunday, and anyone could be expected to drop in for a visit. But I started like a guilty thief. I suppose scheming in secret makes you nervous. However, I was relieved to see Baji Sughra not worried at all and smiling. Soon I forgot my discomfort. When she joined us on the floor and told me to start handing her the flags one by one, began slapping glue on the flags with alacrity, handed them to Hashim so he could affix them to the string, I realized we had set up an effective assembly line. Now we were really moving with speed. We were having so much fun I even forgot Javed Bhai.

Then, just as we had almost ten feet of string ready and only ten more to go, Baji's parents, Abba, Amma, and our grandparents trooped out of there, one by one. They were heading for the room we used as a dining room and living room, which meant they were going to have tea and a conference. I didn't like the way they all went in together. If it was a dialogue about Fatima Jinnah's future they were planning, they would have stayed on the veranda and conducted the discussion right here. Allah Rakha, the houseboy, would have brought tea and *samosas* on a tray, and he would have also refreshed Dadajan's *hukkah* with fresh water and more coals. Obviously the elders had in mind some other topic, not suitable for our ears. Once again I was gripped by the same feeling of dread that first assailed me when I saw Sughra Baji's parents walk into our house this afternoon.

Cousin Hashim, perhaps anxious to run out for a quick cigarette, suggested we take a break. Roohi, her frock front soiled with a combination of glue and dirt, agreed; Sughra Baji said she had a whole batch of the party's pins for us, so we took the unfinished streamer up on the parapet to dry, and washed our hands. The pins were small, but the lantern, Fatima Jinnah's emblem, was clearly visible in all its detail. I had thought it odd that General Ayub's emblem should be the rose. A military dictator had little use for flowers. A sword perhaps, or a canon would have been a more appropriate symbol for his party.

'He's just trying to look benevolent, show people how gentle he is, how harmless, but it's just a front,' Sughra Baji explained when I took my puzzlement to her. 'But you see why the lantern is important? It's a symbol of light, of enlightenment. Also, the lantern is a poor man's source of light, so there are social implications too.' Sometimes Baji Sughra forgot I was so much younger than she and said things I did not grasp easily. But happy in the thought that she trusted my intelligence to address such complex matters to me, I often pretended to comprehend more than I actually did.

The streamer went up the next day with the joint endeavours of Cousin Hashim and Allah Rakha. It looked so short and inadequate at first, especially when you compared it to the rows and rows of ready-made flags, colourful banners and streamers that decorated shop fronts and other buildings up and down our road. But after a while we ignored its length. Filled with the satisfaction of having created it all by ourselves, we congratulated each other on a job well-done. Dadajan and Abba went further; they boasted about our endeavours to any one who came to visit. 'All done right here, they worked hard,' Dadajan told uncles and aunts whose visits were increasing as the day of the elections drew close. We were quite proud of ourselves after all.

Election day came and went. All night, as the votes were being counted, we stayed up. Even Dadima, who usually couldn't keep her eyes open after ten, huddled in her quilt, was awake late into the night, listening to songs, dramas, news bulletins, vote-counts. Roohi, stubbornly fighting sleep, was curled up under Dadima's quilt. We gathered around Dadajan's Philips radio, a small, plain-looking, unpretentious box on the surface, but of such immense import this night, holding so much excitement. Rounds of tea for the grown-ups were followed by milk and Ovaltine for Roohi and myself, and Cousin Hashim, in deference to his grey stubble I suppose, and because he was a guest, was offered tea instead. Aunt A had made thick, granular carrot *halwa* for the occasion, and there were bags of roasted, unshelled peanuts for all of us.

(3)

Fatima Jinnah lost the election. The voting was rigged in such clever and inventive ways that no one could prove it had actually happened, or how. There was a picture of her in the newspaper the next morning in which she looked sadder than any tragic heroine in any movie I had ever seen. She seemed to have aged twenty years. Her face had crumpled in one night, and in her eyes was an empty, faraway look. This is how Jinnah, her brother, must have looked as he lay dying, I thought, from a disease no one could cure.

Celebrations in the streets consisted of cars tooting their horns, tongas hitched with loudspeakers blaring away film songs and war songs, anthems about soldiers surrendering their lives for the motherland, paeans reeking of patriotic fervor. Young men on motorbikes, obviously elated by the victory of the handsome general, raced down the road in front of our house, in both directions, recklessly and dangerously weaving in and out of traffic that was frantic enough on ordinary days, and was tumultuous this morning.

A pall hung over our house. Dadajan had begun by cursing heavily, calling Ayub Khan names that made our ears burn, and then had lapsed into unhappy grunts as he rummaged through the things on his desk, going through the contents of his drawers as if he had lost something important. Dadima continued to mutter, 'She had no chance, the poor woman, no chance to begin with, ahh …'

Amma and Abba put up stoical fronts and went about their business with long faces and deep sighs, but no harsh words. As for me, I had a sinking feeling in my stomach, the sort of feeling one experiences after poor marks on a test or a disparaging remark from one's favorite teacher. I also wanted to take a club to General Ayub's head. Our sweeperess, Jamadarni, proclaimed angrily, waving her straw *jharu* before her like a baton, 'Someone should go and pull his moustache, the dog!' Roohi, a little overwhelmed by the expression of grief she saw around her, burst into tears. Cousin Hashim was restrained with great difficulty by Allah Rakha as he threatened to go out and cuff the man who was attempting to break into two a large, cardboard lantern that had adorned the entrance of the little tea shop right next to our front door. And so we mourned.

That evening Baji Sughra came to visit us with her parents. She wore a sad look, and seeing her face so pale and her eyes wet with unshed tears I thought how beautiful she was when saddened. I also envied her. She was feeling the same emotion I was, but she could feel more deeply than I and that's why there were tears in her eyes. She wanted to go upstairs, so after the preliminary *salaams* and what a terrible thing had happened, and may God curse Ayub Khan etc., etc., she and I slipped away, leaving the adults to their intricately philosophical analysis of Fatima Jinnah's crushing defeat.

No sooner had we entered my room than Baji Sughra fell on the bed and began sobbing. I was startled by this unexpected show of emotion and then, because I wasn't altogether stupid, I realized her anguish had its origin in something other than Fatima Jinnah's failure to rise to the leadership of our country.

'What's the matter, Baji?' I bent over her prostrate form anxiously. 'What's happened?' In my head, like words from a screenplay, a voice whispered warnings about love gone awry, my heart knocked against my ribs as if ready to jump out of there.

'Oh Shabo, my life is finished, I'm going to die,' she said brokenly. 'Abba and Amma have arranged a match for me, they had been making plans all this time and I didn't know. They don't like Javed, Amma said it would be a long time before he was ready for marriage, ohhh … what am I going to do?' She covered her face with her hands, flung her head down on her knees and wept as if her heart were breaking.

I was stunned. This was just like in the movies. Cruel society and equally cruel fate.

Taqdeer ka shikwah kaun kare
(Who can complain about destiny)
Ro ro ke guzara karte hain.
(I spend my life crying)

Lata's soulful voice ambled into my head so clearly I could even trace the musical notes. Ahh, poor Baji!

'But did you explain? Did you tell Auntie you love him and you can't marry anyone else?' I shook her arm.

'Yes, yes, but Amma said this was just foolishness, oh Shabo, she doesn't care about my feelings, no one does, and neither Amma nor Abba like Javed…I'll kill myself if they force me to marry someone else,' Sughra Baji wailed.

'But why don't they like Javed?' How could anyone not like Javed?

'He's too young, he has no means of supporting a wife as yet, such nonsense! And that bastard they've found for me, he's a businessman, he has a big house, he has a car, oh Shabo they think he's perfect. But how can I marry him? What about Javed?' A new wave of anguish swept over her; she smacked her head with her fists.

Frightened by her despair I said, 'Maybe we should talk to Dadima, she's the only one who can help, and she'll talk to Dadajan and no one can go against his wishes.' Suddenly I felt better. Dadima had come to my aid in moments of crisis many a time, and her influence over Dadajan was indubitable.

'They've already talked, they've discussed everything. Dadajan has given his approval. Oh Shabo, my life is over, I'll kill myself, I'll be a corpse instead of a bride, they'll see.'

'Don't talk like that Baji,' I said fearfully, visions of her dressed in her bridal garb and laid out like a corpse careening madly in my vision. 'There must be something we could do.'

'What? What can we do?' she asked, looking at me with pleading eyes.

'What about Javed Bhai? Why doesn't he come and beg, why doesn't he tell Auntie and Uncle that he loves you and he'll take good care of you and...' I realized how foolish my words must sound. If we were in the movies Baji Sughra would have indeed killed herself by taking poison which someone like me would have supplied to her, or she would have run away at the last minute, just as the *maulavi sahib* was getting ready in the other room to conduct the *nikah*. But this wasn't the movies, alas. And I was in no position to supply poison or any other form of assistance. All I could manage was unhappiness and tears. It didn't amaze me that in the space of one day I had experienced the urge to take the club to the heads of two men.

(4)

The wedding was grand. No one expected it to be anything less. Auntie Kubra and her husband had a very large circle of Railway friends and our aunts, uncles, cousins, second-cousins etc., didn't come in small numbers either. Also, this was the first wedding in Auntie Kubra's family. Baji Sughra's dowry was overwhelming. Thirty suits, nearly all richly filigreed and embroidered with gold, five sets of jewelry, furniture, carpets, cutlery, crockery, a television set—the list was endless I thought enviously.

Baji Sughra cried continuously, but only in front of me and our cousin Meena. She didn't want to distress her parents; they had enough on their hands already, and sending off a daughter is cause enough for sorrow, although joy has its place too on such occasions. Baji Sughra's tears went unnoticed. A sad bride is traditional, so that if anyone saw her in tears the only conclusion drawn was that the poor girl was weeping at the thought of leaving her parents' home. In fact, if you showed too much excitement at your wedding, you'd be accused of immodesty.

One evening, soon after all of Baji's friends and female cousins had finished applying *ubtan*, that foul-smelling turmeric paste which was supposed to make her skin glow for her husband, to her legs, feet, hands and face, she gestured me to follow her into the bathroom.

'This is for Javed,' she whispered when we were alone, handing me an envelope. 'You'll see him in a few days I'm sure, please give it to him. You'll take good care of it, Shabo, won't you? If it falls into the wrong hands, I'll be ruined.' She sniffled.

'Of course I'll take good care of it Baji, don't worry.' I couldn't bear to see her so sorrowful. My heart was wrenched at the thought of this tragedy. I hated tragedies. When I started reading a new novel, I'd check the ending first just to make sure it wasn't a tragedy. If it were, I didn't bother to read the book. Why waste your time with dead ends? But this was different, I told myself confidently. There was hope here.

In the days I waited to see Javed Bhai, the letter secure in my possession, I began listening to sad songs on the radiogram. Lata's melancholy melodies and the singer Talat Mahmud's sad laments drenched my spirits until I felt as if I were a part of Baji Sughra, a small, hidden component of her self. I even dreamt about Javed. In one disturbing dream he clasped me in his arms and together we ran across a heath; there was a mist, clouds and then a storm preceded by dark, billowing clouds and I lost him. He reappeared later, and we sat side by side on the veranda where we had played carom, right across the windy gulley, the sunniest spot on the veranda. He sang. In another dream, even more disturbing than the first, I saw Baji Sughra being laid out for burial. But she wasn't wearing the white burial shroud; instead she was dressed in her bridal suit, the gilt-embroidered, heavily filigreed *dupatta* covering her face, the long strands of the gold frill dangling limply from the *dupatta's* edges.

I protected the letter Baji had entrusted to my care with the utmost diligence. Afraid of leaving it in a place where Amma, Roohi or Aunt S or Aunt A might accidentally stumble upon it, I carried it in my bra, which was only a size 28 so that at first I had difficulty straightening out the bulge. Finally I found a corner below my armpit which held the epistle snugly. At night I took it out and slipped it under my pillow.

Javed Bhai was a long time in coming. He didn't show up until the night before the wedding. When he came, he brought with him a large basket of oranges for us, saying these had come from his father's orange groves near Multan. He explained to Dadima that he had been instructed to drop them off right away.

He looked like someone who had been living on the streets. A Majnu, the mad lover. His clothes were wrinkled and shabby, his hair tousled and uncombed, there were gaunt hollows in his cheeks, and his eyes were restless. He smiled when Dadima asked him about his parents, and inquired if they were planning to come to Sughra's wedding, but it was the smile of a man who had received a death sentence.

I slipped him the note, which was badly crushed by now and streaked with sweat, while he was talking to Dadima. She turned to push the heavy *hukkah* closer to her bed, was briefly engaged in a minor tug with the long pipe which had become tangled, and I swiftly transferred the envelope to Javed's hand. I had read the letter many times. Baji had instructed me to memorize the contents in case I had to destroy the missive and was compelled to give Javed her message verbally. The letter was not a coherent piece of writing and consisted of phrases like, 'Fate has played a cruel trick on us,' 'Don't forget me,' 'I was not unfaithful, you'll see,' Remember my love,' etc., etc. Certainly I would have worded it differently, especially when I knew it was to be a last confession, given it a literary twist, for after all, who knew where it might end up. Javed stayed for a few minutes longer afterward and then left. I will always remember the haunted look on his face as he walked out the front door.

The next day the *nikah* ceremony took place around four in the afternoon. The *maulavi sahib* asked Sughra Baji if she would agree to marry Salman Ali, son of Numan Ali with a *mehr* of fifty thousand rupees to be paid to her when she requested. You're not supposed to exceed the bounds of modesty and respond enthusiastically with a 'yes' right away; all brides must wait until the query is repeated for the third and last time and then, after a reasonable pause, come out with a demure 'Hmm.'

I was seized with a horrible thought. Was Baji Sughra planning to say 'no' in the presence of the *maulavi sahib*, the two uncles who were acting as witnesses, her own father? In one movie at least, I had seen a bride take to such recklessness. The huddled form swaddled in red and yellow *dupattas* was still. Oh God! What was going to happen now? My heart raced. *Maulavi sahib* was getting ready to present the question for the third time. The Koranic verses poured effortlessly from his mouth while he stroked his beard. Soon he asked, 'Do you, Sughra Bano Rehman, agree to marry Salman Ali, son of Numan Ali, for a *mehr* of fifty thousand rupees to be paid upon request?'

One of our aunts, Auntie Najma, who was sitting close to Baji Sughra, patted Baji with one massively ringed, chubby hand. Up and down the hand went, slowly, deliberately. 'Come on child, come now, don't be shy daughter.' She smiled with her eyes lowered as she whispered into the place on the *dupatta* behind which Baji's ear might be. There was a slight tremor in the bundle of *dupattas* and then we all heard a sound. It could have been a whimper. A sob. Even a whisper of protest.

'Congratulations!' The *maulavi sahib* said, turning to the men with a self-satisfied smile. Aunt Najma clasped Baji Sughra to her breast and started crying and soon there were cries of 'Congratulations! Congratulations!' everywhere.

Later, as every bride and groom must, Baji Sughra and her groom were sitting together on a sofa while everyone watched them. The bridegroom, contrary to my expectations, was neither short, stocky, nor bald. Most businessmen I knew were. This one, to my dismay, was tall, slim, sported a moustache like Javed Bhai's, and a crop of dark, wavy hair, all of which didn't make it easy for me to hate him. To make matters worse, he kept smiling in a rather delightful way. I felt guilty that I couldn't despise him immediately, and the sense of betrayal grew strong in me as I continued to watch him sitting next to Baji Sughra looking handsome and elegant in his cream-colored *kemkhab sherwani* and white and gold silk turban. Like a prince, I admitted to myself shamelessly.

I forced myself to look away and turned my attention to Baji Sughra. Tears trickled down her smooth, silvery cheeks as if moving along of their own volition. She was so pale and still, almost as if drained of life. I tried to get close to her, but the crowd of guests, women, young and old and children, especially girls, jostled and crammed and shoved for a place from which to view the bride and groom clearly. There was such laughter and giggling. So much free-floating gaiety. Everyone could dip into it without reserve.

Someone pushed me and I fell, my *dupatta* got tangled with a woman's stiletto heel, and before I could get to my feet and steady myself, Baji and Salman had been engulfed by the fervent throng of wedding guests.

(5)

The *valima*, the reception at the groom's house after the wedding, is an important event. The bride's parents get an opportunity to see their daughter in her new surroundings, shy and reticent still, but happy. However, happy was not a word that came to mind that evening for me. When we arrived at Salman's house my head buzzed with such horrible visions that I had difficulty concentrating on anything. I forgot to carry in Dadima's Kashmiri shawl from the car, left my own sweater with the mother-of-pearl buttons at home, and dropped an earring somewhere which made Amma lose her temper.

I knew Baji hadn't tried to kill herself, or we would have heard about it already and wouldn't be coming to attend the *valima*. But there were other possibilities I had entertained all night. She tells her husband the truth, thereby incurring his wrath; she tells him nothing but remains cold to his affections, thereby incurring his displeasure; she offers him her body but keeps her soul from him and he guesses there's something wrong and turns from her, rejects her in private, maintaining a subterfuge for the world in public.

We arrived to find Baji Sughra sitting on a bright red sofa, surrounded as every bride is fated, by women and girls. She was wearing a pink tissue *gharara* embroidered heavily with gold thread and sequins. The *dupatta*, this evening, only partially covered her face; and her hair had been swept back from her forehead, perhaps braided with a golden *paranda* and threaded *chambeli* buds. She looked lovely, like a fairy princess on a throne. I went up to her. At first she didn't see me because her head was lowered. I touched her hand.

'*Salaamalekum* Baji,' I whispered.

She immediately turned to me, and we hugged. I felt a lump in my throat, my eyes misted. As we embraced, the sharp gold edges of her long *kundan* earrings cut into my cheek. I looked at her face. Her skin was as pink as the pink of her clothes, her eyes were luminous, as if lit from within, her lips opened shyly in a smile.

'Shabo, my dear Shabo, how are you? I've been waiting for you.'

'I'm fine,' I said. 'I gave your letter…' I began.

'Shhh…' she cut me off urgently, 'we'll talk about that later.'

'So, are you happy?' I asked, a bitter note creeping into my voice as if she'd wounded my feelings.

'Yes Shabo, I am happy. Salman is such a wonderful man, he's so nice.' She spoke coyly.

Nice? What had happened to her? What was she saying? Nice? What about Javed? I wanted to ask her.

'There's something you must do for me,' she whispered when we were alone for a few minutes during dinner. 'You must get my letter back for me.'

'What?' My heart lurched. I felt as if she had slapped me. 'But Javed Bhai…' I tried to say, my eyes fixed on her face, her beautiful pink face.

'Shh, please Shabo dearest, just get it back, will you, please?'

'But why? And how…'

'Oh, you're such a baby Shabo, how can I tell you anything, you don't understand, do you? Please, my dear little sister, just do this last favour for me.' She held my hands in hers and for a moment I could have sworn I saw tears floating in her eyes. But it might have been an illusion created by the bright overhead lights in the drawing room and the dark *kajal* she wore in her eyes that evening.

I didn't appreciate being called a baby, and I wasn't keen on bringing the letter back to her. If I had any courage I'd have told her to do it herself. I was no longer her friend and ally, I'd have said. Anyway, even if I tried, I couldn't force Javed to return the letter.

'All right,' I said helplessly when she began to sniffle, and patted her small, thin, heavily ringed hand.

Of course, Javed Bhai refused to give the letter back. He cursed the whole world and said unkind things about Baji.

'She's false, inconstant, taken in by the highest bidder, so easily sold.' His words sounded like a dialogue from a film. Secretly I agreed with him.

'But Javed Bhai, she couldn't do anything, you know, what could she do?'

'She could have fought, she could have taken a stand, why didn't she?' He stared at me questioningly, but perhaps hit with the realization I was too young to give him a satisfactory answer, he turned away, biting his lips and shaking his head sadly.

'But the letter isn't important any more, why don't you give it back?'

I begged. At first he ignored my pleas. Some moments later he took the letter out of his shirt pocket and angrily tore it into a hundred pieces, his face contorted as his hands worked the letter into shreds. Then he flung the pieces over the parapet. Slowly the tiny scraps flew down and away, this way and that, scattered by the wind like eddying autumn leaves.

(6)

Time hasn't been very charitable to Baji Sughra. She's fat and dour. Yesterday, while I sat in the drawing room of her large, spacious bungalow and had tea with crispy, spicy *samosas*, she went on and on in a sullen, unhappy voice about the shortcomings of her female servant, complaining that it had become tiresome finding suitable help these days. Cutting short her impassioned discourse on the subject of female help, I asked her about Benazir Bhutto. Was she rooting for her?

'She's had plastic surgery, you know,' raising a plump, ringed hand, Baji Sughra offered in response to my question. 'And she's too much in love with that horrible husband of hers, that playboy. She'll never win.'

While Baji poured another cup of tea for herself, I thought about Fatima Jinnah. One could say the country at that time was young. That Fatima Jinnah was old and weary. That she reminded people too much of a past that needed to be put aside so the country could move forward unfettered. That democracy was a word with enormously complicated and rather foreign connotations. And so she didn't win.

'As I see it, Shabo, my dear,' Baji Sughra continued philosophically, 'she just likes to take risks. Why, she's always pregnant. What can she do if she's pregnant?'

'She's not crippled or disabled, Baji, pregnancy is not a debilitating illness.' I found myself using a tone of voice I had never used with Baji before.

'Well Shabo, she wants too much. Just think, you can either be a good wife and mother or a good leader. And she wants to be all three. Now, tell me Shabo, is that possible? How is that possible?'

'Do you ever think about Javed Bhai?' I asked.

Adam Zameenzad

Born in Pakistan, Adam Zameenzad spent his early childhood in Nairobi, where his parents were teachers. He came to love Africa and the African people through his male nanny and he still regards Africa as his spiritual home. When Adam Zameenzad was eight his grandfather died, leaving his lands to Adam Zameenzad's father, who moved back to Pakistan. Adam Zameenzad was a precocious solitary child who hated school and was educated at home instead, but he read voraciously and was befriended by poor tenants living in the nearby hutments. All his novels tell of 'the disadvantaged, the dispossessed and the outcasts of this world.' He finally joined a school in Lahore, graduated from Government College, did his Masters in English from Karachi University and became a teacher. He moved to Britain in 1974 and has lived and taught there since. His first novel, *The Thirteenth House* (1987) won the David Higham Award; it linked up the lives of a rich millowner's son, an impoverished clerk and a sinister holy man (*pir*) in Karachi. His second novel, *My Friend Matt and Henna the Whore* captures the enchantment and suffering of Africa, through the eyes of three children. Adam Zameenzad's ability to reach out to the truth through the eyes of the innocent is central to his sense of comedy and tragedy. His third novel, *Love Bones and Water,* revolves around the neglected child of a South American politician and his friendship with shanty town dwellers. The book is rooted in Biblical lore and the concept of redemption through suffering. In fact all his books have magic realist elements and a strong spiritual dimension. This is developed further in *Cyrus Cyrus,* a complex, original, bawdy and gargantuan book, about a man's search for dignity and salvation across three continents. He has written a fifth novel *Gorgeous White Female* (1995). In 1996, he was a VSO volunteer in Namibia and has wandered across North America and Europe extensively. He says 'My physical travels have been a part of my intellectual, political, and spiritual adventures. It is these that inspire me, and what I write about.'

Cyrus Cyrus is a magic realist tale of human aspirations, fate, migration, and many kinds of exile which incorporates the symbols of numerology, astrology, myth and lore. Cyrus is born an untouchable, a latrine cleaner—the lowest of the low. He is also pitch black, has disfiguring marks and is considered unlucky. Doomed to prejudice, he is frequently accused of crimes he hasn't committed. The novel contrasts his innocence with atrocities perpetrated by society, and contrasts him with the insidious blonde blue-eyed boy, whose image haunts him throughout the book and who becomes Jason, his stepson. Cyrus's misadventures lead him from Chandan in India to East Pakistan, America and Britain. Cyrus ends up in a British prison but disappears through the walls: the book consists of long dictation by Cyrus Cyrus to 'Adam Zameenzad, Man, Son of Earth.'

FROM *CYRUS, CYRUS*

Zoetrope: Reflections and Memories:

FROM *Part I: The Fulcrum and the Hub*

One Birth

One of my earliest memories is of being born. A hugely revolting and horrifying experience, ghastly and grotesque. In fact, a more ghastly and grotesque experience it is not easy to conceptualize. And I have had encounters with a kaleidoscopic range of ghastly and grotesque experiences, I can assure you. I know what I am talking about.

The wages of sin is birth.

One moment I was afloat in a sea of tempestuous peace—a throbbing vibrant peace: the only kind of peace which competes winningly with the challenges of war and for which it is worth forgoing conflict; the peace which does not suffer from negative growth rate, which does not engender boredom nor produce its own niggling second-rate protagonists. The next moment my sea is pulsating with agony, as if being boiled by Mephistophelean fires, rising to ebb away, dragging me along with horrendous force, ripping me from the comfort and security of my moorings.

Tearing flesh, gore and blood. Blood on my face. Blood in my mouth. Blood in my eyes.

How I fought and struggled. How I begged and pleaded. How I prayed.

In vain.

I resisted with every gene of my tiny being as I went through the terrorizing process of being pushed down, head first, sucked the wrong way out of the suffocating one-way passage, squirming, tortuous, oxygenless.

In vain.

I felt with appalling horror the searing pain I was causing my protector and sustainer as I tore through the centre of her body. I cried in empathetic pain, augmenting my own.

On how I cried.

In vain.

How I prayed.

In vain.

There I was, *plop*, in the middle of a world of which I knew nothing, and from which I wanted nothing; snipped in the bud, and knotted up.

How I cried.

How I prayed.

I could not understand why a hitherto loving and caring God had suddenly deserted me through no apparent fault of mine. The bitterness of His betrayal in my heart was worse than the bitterness of blood in my mouth.

I stopped praying.

I cried bitterly.

Mother wiped me clean, wrapped me in a clean shawl—it was a cold morning, being the first morning of the Year of Our Lord 1954—cleared up the mess, washed herself with Sunlight soap, dried herself with a tattered but clean blue-ribbed towel which had a lingering hint of musk on it, and went back to milking the goat.

The goat, pure white, with a strong lithe body which rippled under your hands, was the family treasure, the healthiest and best-fed member of the household. It was given to my mother by one of the local zameendars after he had raped her—raped my mother that is, not the goat, though I wouldn't put *that* past him either. Mother was really pleased. The goat was the best thing she had ever got after being raped. In fact it was the best thing she had ever got, after, during, or before *anything*. The worst, at least after being raped, was a black eye and three broken ribs. But then what could you expect from the local police chief? Mind you, my Aunt Verna did get more: two black eyes, five broken ribs *and* a broken nose. She looks like the world heavyweight champion to this day. At least she did the last time I saw her, which was some years ago. She fared better than my Auntie Neelum, who killed herself after she was raped. But she was only fourteen, and in love. Terrible thing,

love. Also, hers wasn't a normal rape. There were five of them, including two superintendents from Lucknow, the city of Mogul splendour about fifty miles to our north as the jet flies, come to our little town of Chandan to help the poor people after the rains brought many houses down. They were helping my Aunt Neelum get her charpoy out of the mess. A mud house can be very messy if it comes down in the rain, especially if it wasn't set up properly in the first place. Not enough straw and little cow dung, and you can be sure of saying goodbye to it sooner or later. But it isn't easy to come by cow dung if you haven't got cows, nor straw if you haven't got access to a field.

I must explain. All these rapes in the family. You must think we come from a very common lot. We do. We are Choodahs. In India, the lowest of the low, the shit cleaners. We survive in older, poorer parts of big cities, or in small towns; modern parts of big cities have modern toilet facilities, and people in villages use the open air, or have pits dug in the case of rich zameendar families. We are the most untouchable of the untouchables.

I don't suppose that explains too well, does it? If we are that untouchable, you might argue, how do we go about getting our mothers and aunts (to mention only the female side of the family) raped every other day, almost as a matter of habit, since the process must involve some form of touching by others and betters, however brief the carnal act? But you have to understand India a bit better to better understand, especially the India of villages and small towns. And don't tell me about the outlawing of untouchability. Try telling it to the people in our town, living practically on the banks of the Ganges and under the shadow of the holiest of cities, Varanasi, better known in the West as Benares. Try telling the British there are laws against racism.

Our untouchableness is absolute, but only in so far as we want to touch something we ought not to, or worse, someone we ought not to, someone better and superior to us in every conceivable way, according to our birth and the will of Brahma. It does not prevent our superiors and betters from touching us, if the fancy takes them, provided they wash in the Ganges afterwards; or, should the Ganges not be meandering close by to their rape location, at their water taps or hand-pumps; even the local canal would do, mud, urine, shit and all, provided they go to the temple to get properly purified afterwards. Mind you, many didn't bother with all that. Rape, and straight home to dinner, which is a shame. I believe there is a great deal to be said for tradition and ritual.

We got the brunt of the rampant cocks. We were the only Choodah family left in Chandan, so there wasn't much choice available. (Modern plumbing had started spreading its devious pipes round our little corner of the world forcing others of our kind out into bigger cities for employment of similar social orientation.) The peasants and other menial workers in our town had gradually become better organized and more difficult to deal with since one of them turned a Marxist, making it prudent to leave their sexually desirables alone, unless they happened to be too sexually desirable in which case it could be worth the risk. They got beaten up more often than us lot, though, and had more goods stolen. Goods that later adorned the local coppers' houses, or those of the landowners henchmen. That left only us for the naughties. The other families in the area were known and respected, some even feared.

Ours was a small—within a radius of about five miles—but important little town. It had its own railway station, and was surrounded by villages with very fertile land. All the grain and agricultural produce was first brought to our Chandan, to be later transported to places like Lucknow, the capital, Varanasi, the sacred cow of cities, and Allahabad, the famous University town, rival to Aligarh. We had our very own police station, controlling an area of thirty miles all around. Anybody wanted trouble, they had to send for our police lads. Not many small towns in India can boast of that.

The particular zameendar who indulged in my mother, the kind one with the goat, was a Muslim anyway, and Muslims needn't even bother with the post-untouchable-rape sex cleansing rituals. They have to have a bath, of course, as they do even after holy intercourse in marriage. But they do not believe in this untouchable nonsense. Neither do the Christians.

That is why our family, like many of the Choodahs since departed, had converted to Christianity years ago. Didn't help much. We were still treated as Choodahs; and what's worse, called Choodahs.

(Cyrus's father is falsely implicated in the murder of Cyrus's mentor, a Harijan doctor. The family flees to East Pakistan, but half of it is wiped out by flood, famine and grief after the 1970 cyclone. Cyrus's brother, Junior disappears. Meanwhile Cyrus has had his first encounter with the mythical Naga and tiger in a vision of divine love.)

FROM ***Part II: Along the Radius and over the Spokes***

First Love - Consummation Continuum

Junior did return, and with a boat. We ended up in Chittagong which was less than a hundred miles away and where most of the relief supplies were concentrated, apart from Dacca.

Once the waters had well and truly subsided, we built ourselves a little jhuggi at the lower end of the town, near the port—overcrowded, dirty, smelly, and dangerously close to the water should it rise again, but that was all we could manage. And to think we had got used to living in a proper house with proper rooms, three in all.

Junior and I fetched mud and straw and bamboo from wherever we could lay our hands on any, and Mother and Edwina worked at the structure.

Once it was ready, the first thing Mother did was to sell some of our food to buy a large wooden cross, which she hung in the centre of the main wall next to a picture of Mary and the baby Jesus. Then she bought an old rusty bucket from a tinker, rummaged through the city dumps to find a couple of brooms, and set to work. But not before going to the nearest church, and begging for forgiveness with all the eloquence and tears she could muster. She also managed to smuggle the bucket and brooms inside, by hiding them in a long, white, shroud-like chadar, in order to sanctify them. Edwina thought it was sacrilegious and would bring more bad luck, but Mother said it was all right since they had not been used, which was a joke for they had been used to death by whoever owned them before. But we knew what she meant.

I found work as an 'outside houseboy' and driveway cleaner-cum-gardener's helper in the bungalow of a local paper mill boss. My luck really had turned. Such good jobs were very hard to come by, and the competition was fierce. Millions of people lived in the city, and most were willing to sell body and soul to keep body and soul together. But it was hard work. The bungalow was enormous, and the driveway itself curved around for half a mile. By the time I had finished clearing all the leaves and rearranging the gravel if it got messed about a little, it was time to start again. And the boss was not the kindliest of men. Still, I was very lucky indeed.

Junior was lucky too. He got a job as a municipal road sweeper during the day. At night he hung around the grand hotels in the fashionable parts of the city in the hope of finding a white tourist or a local businessman looking for a young fat ass or a sturdy young cock; and often he succeeded in finding one. Or two. He had the advantage there in that, apart from being very appetizingly built, he wasn't ashamed to ply his trade with a certain brazenness which went down well with the punters; whereas the competition, of which there was plenty, both sexes, were careful not to be seen to flout the local morality codes. Of course he had to pay for his roguish panache by giving free fucks as well as a good part of his earnings to some of the more energetic and enterprising members of the local constabulary. However, by lying about what he made and by stuffing most of the higher denomination notes in a plastic bag and swallowing it before the officers concerned got to him, he managed to save a good amount on a regular basis. The only question was, how long would he last with that heavy a workload?

After all, there is a limit to how much a body can perform. In particular, a merely male body.

Junior was giving no thought to tomorrow as far as his body was concerned. As far as his life was concerned, he was full of tomorrows. He was hoping to go and settle in England, once he had the fare, and then call Mother and Edwina and me over as well. Mother and Edwina were really looking forward to it. I was the only one who didn't want to go. Can't say exactly why. Perhaps I just wanted to be different, as I often did. Strange that I was the only one who was destined to live, and die, in that country.

General elections came and went, 1971 came and stayed on. Political excitement in the country, already at maniacal pitch, continued to rise. Hope in a new, fairer future with democratic control over their own destiny in their own half of the country gave new vigour to the energetic Bengali people. Their own Bhasha would at last come into its own, with its own heritage of literature and music which permeated the very soul of its speakers, writers and singers—from the humble fisherman to the great Nazrul Islam, the true national poet and archetypal hero.

Our family, being neither Bengali nor Muslim nor really Pakistani, and certainly not political, could not possibly share the depth of feeling of the general population, but we too were quite excited about the excitement, and vociferously and heartily agreed with whoever expressed an opinion, however much that opinion differed from the one we had agreed with a moment ago.

For differences there were. Beneath the facade of unanimity, various beliefs and political propositions vied with each other for ascendancy: from the strongly patriotic and nationalistic vis-a-vis the cause of Pakistan and the nationhood of Muslims, to the strongly patriotic and nationalistic vis-a-vis the cause of a Bangla Desh separate from Pakistan and the nationhood of the Bengali people.

The divisions started to intensify, by the minute rather than the hour, as Islamabad began hedging over its avowed intention to accept the people's verdict and hand over power to the democratically-elected leaders. Sheikh Mujib's resounding victory and tough stand raised the spectre of secession even in the most liberal of West Pakistani leaders, such as Zulfikar Ali Bhutto; while at the same time the fear of perpetual 'colonization' of their homeland by the superior military power of West Pakistan began to haunt the minds of the Bengalis.

Bhutto asserted that just because the Bengalis were in a majority, that did not mean the rest of the country had to be subjected to their tyranny, for tyranny of the majority was the worst kind of tyranny. Mujib retorted with his tirade against the tyranny of the minority.

Divisions then started appearing within the electorate of East Pakistan itself. The Biharis and other Urdu-speaking people were strongly in favour of a united Pakistan with its centre of power in Islamabad; the Bangla-speaking people wanting the centre of power to move to Dacca. As tensions heightened, even those Bengalis who had previously been for a united Pakistan, allegedly including Sheikh Mujib himself, openly started voicing demands for an independent Bangla Desh. To some the motive force behind these demands was the upsurge of a long-suppressed love for Bangla Bhasha and all things Bengali; to others it was a CIA plot to break up Pakistan, with the help of Mrs. Gandhi of India fame: the always-on-time, greatly astute, true daughter of the very important Nehru; or the scheming, conniving, ruthless, totally opportunist and utterly frustrated wife of an unimportant Gandhi—depending on which side you were on.

Junior and I played our part in this passionate eruption of political awareness: joining marches, shouting slogans, carrying banners and placards, and pledging our life and limbs to the service of whichever party happened to be going our way. The Awami League and the Muslim League were the major ones, the PPP having completely failed to make its mark on the Eastern wing of the country.

Tempers and tensions reached breaking point when General Yahya Khan announced on 1 March that the Constituent

Assembly was suspended indefinitely. Sheikh Mujib spurned the invitation to come to Islamabad for talks, saying talks should be held in Dacca in the majority province of Bangla Desh, the newly fashionable name for East Pakistan. Bhutto declared it an outrage, and just stopped short of calling it an act of treason. Mujib retorted by calling a general strike throughout East Pakistan, Bangla Desh, and received unprecedented total support. Even those against him participated, some out of a sense of expediency, some out of fear for their lives. But there was no doubt that the vast majority was strongly behind him. Even the judges refused to acknowledge the authority of the President of Pakistan.

General Yahya's attempt to resolve the deadlock by a mid-March visit to East Pakistan proved worse than futile, and upon his return he declared Sheikh Mujib and his followers to be traitors. On 26 March Mujib announced a Unilateral Declaration of Independence for the new state of Bangla Desh. General Yahya immediately launched a massive military operation to 'recover' 'East Pakistan'. A full-scale war soon developed between the supporters of Mujib and the Pakistan armed forces, and although India did not officially enter the arena until the December of that year, its unofficial action was there for all, except the foreign press, to see. What the foreign press also failed to see was the massacre of the Biharis and the Urdu-speaking, pro-Pakistan citizens of Bangla Desh by the Bengalis, though it rightly saw and rightly reported the genocidal waves of attacks by the Pakistani Army upon the Bangla-speaking people. These were led by the notorious General Tikka Khan, even though it was his successor who was mainly responsible for the worst of the butcheries committed in those days of blood and sorrow. By this time Mujib had been arrested, and thousands of Bengalis were fleeing in terror to India on a regular basis as the 'Liberation Army' was forced to move out of Chaudanga, badly battered and in chaotic disarray. All this on top of the devastation wreaked by the cyclone of a few months before, and its horrific aftermath, from which the people had still not properly recovered.

The frenzy which seized the people of Pakistan, civilians and soldiers, was the frenzy of another 1947: the frenzy of the politically suppressed, the sexually deprived, the ideologically stuffed-right-up-to-empty-craniums-from-overflowing-colons. Inhumanity was matched with inhumanity, the Bengalis desperately trying to make up in depth what they lacked in scope and volume.

India made full and judicious use of the situation. Not even her best enemy could deny that she did her worst. Her propaganda machinery manned by people of far greater intelligence than Pakistan would dare employ proved that right was wrong especially if it was left. Indira Gandhi, like some wild maenad with Gorgonic hair and eyes and the blood of Salome in her veins, danced for the head of Pakistan, putting on rather than casting off veils. With foes like General Tikka Khan she hardly needed friends, but anyway found plenty in the West. Gloating over every murder, histrionically hysterical over each atrocity, she wept in public with artistic fervour and politicized passion. She lost no opportunity to preach, with smug nobility, what she had never practised—e.g. giving the majority their rights, as in Kashmir—nor had any intention of practising. She spaded in when the soil of Pakistan was wet with blood, sowed the seeds of war, and reaped kudos from the world. Her role as the instigator remained unrevealed, the reputation as a saviour established.

Patriotic Pakistanis were not to be outdone, and Mrs Gandhi's passionate hypocrisy was matched with awesome hebetude and breathtaking benightedness. Taxis and rickshaws owned by the faithful carried 'Crush India' posters stuck all over them like fake medals on a magician drowning to death in his own watery escape chamber. Unfunny clowns and intellectual dwarfs and moral freaks followed suit in their newly acquired cars, and it came to a point where you could not strip a good, solid, patriotic Pakistani, for whatever purpose, and not find a 'Crush India' poster sticking gracefully out of his posterior, so firmly and deeply entrenched as to deny any access to those parts of the said patriotic Pakistani that you might have intended to reach in the first place, not that I am suggesting you did. On the other hand, why else would anyone want to strip a good, solid, patriotic Pakistani? I wonder. Never Mind.

Jama't-i-Islami was not to be left behind, and turned its organized efficiency, developed at great personal and global expense by the Creative Insurgency Activators (known by some as the Criminally Insane Agitators, by others as the Confidential Insurrection Advisers: Capitalist, Ithyphallic and Armed) and meant primarily to prevent good, honourable Pakistani citizens from embracing the blasphemy of Marxism, was now put to excellent use, and overnight public and private walls were painted with 'Crush India' slogans. So much so that any time the self-same solid, patriotic Pakistani squatted to piss beside one, he was roused to fight by the spirit of Jihad while holding his weapon firmly by the hand, like a cannon that would blast the Indians right out of existence, and the rebellious Bengalis along with them for good measure; or like an inexhaustible fire hydrant that would flood away the enemy civilization in a manner to be remembered by the surviving world with the same holy awe as the rains in 'After the Rains'.

The results of all this political madness were manifesting themselves with stark horror all around us for anyone to see who had eyes to see. But did they! Had they! Why not? You may wonder. Does nationalism ever? I wonder. But whatever the reason, there you have it. In the meantime, death lived on.

I was without a job now. My employer, the paper mill owner, was a Panjabi—as indeed were most businessmen and industrialists, a major cause of the unrest and the uprising of the Bengalis—and had fled to Lahore at the first sign of serious trouble, along with his family and some chosen servants. His house was now occupied by some activists of the Liberation Movement, and the last thing they wanted was a houseboy with the appetite of a baby elephant. Used to wandering aimlessly, despite strict instructions from Mother to stay at or near home, one day I latched on to a wildly chanting Nazrul-Islam-songs-singing crowd of about fifty thousand, roaring through the heart of the city where some of the most popular cinemas and shopping arcades were located. Without any warning we were beset by soldiers in battle camouflage and fired upon with somewhat excessive zest. It was rumoured, by the pro-Pakistan lobby, still strong in some quarters, that three planeloads (or one or many, depending on the monger's imagination or knowledge) of injured and mutilated Pathans and Panjabis and Biharis had arrived at Karachi Airport the day before, and orders had come from above to take a thousand for each man, woman or child, but not to worry if the count was lost, and simply to start again.

It was a hot day, so humid that your sweat stuck to your body like motor oil. The blood ran freer. I just managed to escape slaughter by running with accustomed athleticism over the butchered remains of some faces I knew and others I did not that littered the road about me. I ended up in some squalid little street. I had no idea where it was.

It was nearly dark, getting darker. A strict curfew was being enforced, and apart from the heavy military presence, more sensed than seen, no one was about. Absolute stillness descended. Not a leaf stirred, or would have stirred had there been any around to stir. Not a dog or a cat dared put paw to tarmac, not a crow cawed over the deaths of the day. Feeling afraid, the type of fear you experience in an obsessively haunted house rather than in a ravaged land, I cowered into an alcove tucked away behind a sharp bend in front of a crumbling old house alongside many other crumbling old houses. I knew that I could expect nothing less than a bullet straight in the heart if a soldier were to chance upon me. I could hear the gruff whirring of a helicopter up above and flattened myself against the coarse wall.

My sudden scream cut through the air like a madman's axe through an infant's skull as my flesh was torn apart with the savagery of a madman's axe cutting through an infant's skull. I remained conscious until the very last morsel of my meat was devoured and the very last bit of my bone was crunched and the very last drop of my blood was lapped up by the tiger. The tiger lusted insatiably with the lust of the questing soul for *the* body and blood that would redeem its quest and let *its* body finally rest. In peace. In stillness, so that God could finally be God. So that God could finally be. That God could be. That God could. That God. God.

Even within the tiger's being, within the coiled lap of my Naga, there was no peace this time. No ritual, no rite, no ceremony. No holy temple, no maidens dancing, no choirboys singing, no acolytes carrying candles, no priest incantating. The Naga's infinite body twirled and swished restlessly with controlled rage infused with some uncontrollable passion which a mere mortal like myself could neither understand nor put a name to - except to say that its power seemed to rest in some form of a duality, like the duality of the Naga's own power, with its inbuilt, unresolvable conflict containing within itself the inbuilt resolution of the conflict. Both the certainty of resolution and the inevitability of conflict were equally valid and part of the same one and indivisible reality. This indivisible reality, as indivisibly reality, simply comprised the two, but as indivisible reality it transcended both with its own separate identity of being.

The Naga's skin of luminescent night shone with a blackness that could outshine the white heat of the sun and cast it into blinkered nothingness. Its rich body, formed of all the substances in Heaven and Earth fused and infused into one another with irrevocable creativity, which was the doing of being, writhed endlessly with the grief of a lover who has lost his love forever; and with the ecstasy of a lover in eternal union with his love.

This time its tongue was not going to lick my face with the gentleness of a mother. I could tell it the instant my troubled, half-open eyes looked up into its serene, ever-open eyes. I could not tell what it had in mind instead. I got no time to speculate.

Like lightning it lashed out with its fangs and buried them deep into the innermost recesses of my heart, introducing its eternal-life-giving poison into my mortal blood to flow in it forever more.

There was no ritual this time, no rite, no ceremony. Just the Eucharist, the ultimate communion. The consummation of love.

The consummation of our love.

And for as long as its poison remained the blood of my blood, which was always, the continuum of our love was guaranteed.

The man—I wasn't certain whether it was the Man or just a man—ran his fingers through my hair and peered anxiously at my face. Don't worry, child, don't worry, he said in a voice which could have been the Man's voice, you will be all right, I heard you screaming and pulled you inside before anybody could find you outside during the curfew. You are safe now. You must have had a fit. I can tell, my son used to have them. There is nothing to worry about. He died of one. You'll be all right. There is nothing to worry about. I'll get you something to eat. You look starved. There is nothing to worry about. You will be all right.

Epileptic fit! My apocalyptic foot!

I knew what it was. But I was not telling him, even though he meant well. Just like the Man.

I stayed with the man for the night. In the morning, when the curfew was over, he explained to me how to get to my house, having first made sure that I had one.

(Cyrus returns home to find his entire family senselessly butchered; the killers remain unknown. An American woman takes him to Shree Ramnath's ashram in New Mexico and he is almost the victim of a ritual murder. He escapes, inadvertently falls in with petty criminals and finally arrives in Britain as Daniel Prescott, using a dead man's papers. He encounters Jennifer and Ian at Southend Pier after saving their blond blue-eyed son, Jason from drowning.)

FROM *Part IV: Upon the Wheel*

Cyrus Cyrus

Ian drove me to Southend General Hospital after dropping his wife and son, Jennifer and Jason, at their house, which was only a short distance from the beach: I made a note of the street and the number. I went, remonstrating as politely as I could and struggling as gently as possible. On the outside. Inside I was struggling with all my might and screaming my head off. Just come from the United States, I believed a short stay in hospital, 'for observation only,' could mean you spending the rest of your life paying medical bills.

I remembered a Mexican fellow, not especially old, who had had a heart attack or a stroke or a fit of some sort at one of the Greyhound bus stations. Everyone looked at me like I was insane when I said call a doctor, as I'd heard it said in many a movie. No doctor came. Finally some paramedics arrived. They checked his papers and looked into his wallet to see how much money he had before deciding what to do with him. They made him walk through the crowds when the poor man could barely crouch. He kept mumbling something which I didn't understand. Another chap who spoke Spanish said he was worried about his wife and children and how they would get any money to pay his bills. He said if you were poor and fell ill you were better off dead, at least for the sake of your family. I had no family, and I did have Daniel's money, but this was not precisely the way I had in mind to spend it, if I spent it at all. Still, easy come easy go. There was nothing I could do about it. I was having difficulty even standing up.

I decided that in the circumstances the best thing to do was to uncoil my nerves and submit myself to the inevitable. Stretching myself in the back seat of the car, a taxi—Ian was a self-employed taxi driver—I shut my eyes and relaxed my breathing.

When I next opened my eyes I was in this white bed under a white sheet staring at a white wall with this woman in white standing over me. I couldn't possibly have died, could I? And gone to hell! I certainly felt cold as hell.

There, feeling better now, are we? said the woman in white, voice blander than the words.

I shut my eyes then opened them again in an attempt to focus my vision better. I wished I hadn't bothered. There was a policeman standing on the other side of my bed. He had an open notebook in his left hand.

I *was* dead. The day of reckoning was here.

I think you can talk to him now, Officer said the nurse. She retreated, the policeman advanced.

I was not dead. It was worse.

Delayed shock, said the nurse on her way out, managing a smile. More like I overdid my reduced breathing. I told myself as I returned the smile. Her eyes glazed over. The smile had not been for me.

Name? said the policeman.

Cyrus, I replied. The policeman waited, pencil poised on the notebook.

Cyrus what? he asked, mildly amused, mildly irritated.

I hesitated, nervous, unsure.

Full name, he said, slowly this time, and more loudly, though without really shouting.

Cyrus, I repeated lamely, Cyrus.

I was being forced to face up to my identity, something I had unconsciously avoided doing for the past many years.

On my passport my name had been put down as Cyrus Jagnath. The last was a combination of Jag from Jagdeep, who had adopted me, as it were, and Nath from Ramnath, whose patronage made it all possible. After escaping from the Ashram I had ceased to use that name. When I did my gardening in LA I got by with just Cyrus and was paid in cash. In New York I used the name David Mathias off a social security card from one of the wallets Suzi had pocketed. In Chandan I had been Cyrus Choodah; and in Bangla Desh, when we went Muslim for a time, I was Cyrus Khan. I had travelled to England as Daniel Prescott.

I was sorely tempted to go back to Cyrus Choodah, but decided against it. With the uncertainty I felt among the white British—friendliness and smiles one minute, abuse and mockery the next—I couldn't risk the contempt of any of my own people I might meet in the UK.

Confronted by the growing temper in the policeman's eyes, made more threatening by the cool of his stance and the utter stillness of his notebook and his pencil, one held at hip level in his left hand, the other slightly higher up in his right, I felt my own agitation mounting.

Cyrus, Cyrus…I stuttered. Shree Ramnath would have been most ashamed of me.

By that time the nurse was back. They have funny…(quick look at me)…some of them…their names don't always…not like ours…you know. She had the grace to go a trifle red.

So your name is, let's see…He held up his notebook in front of his face, about a yard away. Cyrus Cyrus. Is that it? Cyrus Cyrus! You could have cut through steel with the sarcasm in his voice. Let me make sure how you spell it. Is it an S or a C, a Y or an I, a U or an E or another I. Or is it KPLIGA or something like that, Sir?

The sonorous manner of his speaking gave me time to think. I remembered Father calling out to me, Cyrus, Cyrus, come here Cyrus, Cyrus…I remembered calling out to Father when I went looking for him in the woods. Father, Father, I used to call out, always hoping he would call back, Cyrus, Cyrus.

I remembered being with him in the caves of Ajanta and Ellora, in my dreams. I remembered shouting out my name, Cyrus, and the echo ringing back through the shimmering mist of their exotic antiquity and through the simmering passion of the erotic dancers carved into their walls, *Cyrus*. And thus it used to go on. Cyrus, *Cyrus*; Cyrus, *Cyrus*…

What better than to be called Cyrus Cyrus?

ALAMGIR HASHMI

Born and brought up in Lahore, Alamgir Aurangzeb Hashmi started to write poetry as a child, in both English and Urdu. Punjabi too was spoken at home but English became his dominant language at school. He received academic honours at Punjab University, from where he graduated. He did his doctorate in the United States and acquired more degrees in Europe. Poet, scholar, critic, broadcaster and a professor of English and Comparative Literature, he spent many years in the United States and Switzerland, writing and teaching. He now lives in Islamabad and has been a course director at the Foreign Service Training Institute. In the mid-1970s, he taught the only official Creative Writing Workshop in Lahore and compiled the first ever anthology of Pakistani Literature in English (1978). Later he put together other literary anthologies and published several scholarly books. His first collection of poetry, *The Oath and Amen* (1976), appeared in Philadelphia, while another, *My Second in Kentucky* (1981), won The Pakistan Academy of Letters 1985 Patras Bokhari Award. His ten books of poetry, include his collected works, *The Poems of Alamgir Hashmi* (1992), *Sun and Moon and Other Poems* (1992) and *A Choice of Hashmi's Verse* (1997). Memory, the sounds and smells of other countries, other places, are central to much of his work; he uses contrast very effectively to give his verse texture and richness; he sometimes draws on his tri-lingual background to create cross-cultural images. He contributes to a host of prestigious publications and is literary editor of *The Pakistan Development Review*. He has also been editor or advisory editor of many books and periodicals, ranging from the *Journal of English Studies in Pakistan* to *The Routledge Encyclopaedia of Commonwealth Literature, The Blackwell Companion to Twentieth Century Theatre* and *The Oxford Companion to Twentieth Century Poetry*. In 1986 he established the Jane Townsend Poetry Prize at the American Center, and was chairman of the Standing International Conference Committee on English in South Asia in 1989; he was subsequently advisor to the National Book Council of Pakistan for five years, became a member of the New York Academy of Sciences, was a 1994 Rockefeller Fellow and received the Roberto Celli Memorial Award that year. He was on the jury for the 1990 Commonwealth Writers Prize and the 1996 Neustadt International Prize for Literature.

FROM *THE POEMS OF ALAMGIR HASHMI*

Encounter with the Sirens
An Epic Poem in Miniature

Book I

Ulysses stopped his ears
with wax and had himself bound
to the mast of the ship,
though it was known to the world
that such things were of no help.

The song of the Sirens could pierce
through everything, and the longing
of those they seduced
would have broken far stronger bonds
than chains and masts.

But Ulysses trusted absolutely
the handful of wax and his fathom
of chain, and in innocent elation
over his little stratagem
sailed out to meet the Sirens.

Book II

Now the Sirens have a weapon more
fatal than song. And though such a thing
has never happened, someone might possibly
have escaped their singing; but
from their silence, never.
When Ulysses approached them,
the potent songstresses did not care
to sing. Surprised no doubt
they were by the bliss on his face,
thinking of nothing but his wax, and his chains.

Book III

Ulysses could not hear their silence,
and thought he alone did not hear them.
When for a fleeting moment he saw
their throats rising and falling,
their breasts lifting,

their eyes in tears,
and their lips half parted,
he believed
they were accompaniments to the air
which died unheard around him.

Codicil

So waving to them,
triumphantly he turned and sailed on.

Eid

Perhaps Eid is more than the vermicelli thing
I was spoonfed to believe.
In the mosque this morning
I promised God to bend my knees
another four times.
My fellow knee-benders raised offertory
to cushion the prayer-keeper,
so expiate the neglect he suffered
on the wooden bench.
Outside, the beggars buttonholed us.
Eid could not anchor in their corduroy cheeks.
How can these spindling shapes
be blotted out from the face of the morning?
I had left behind my blotting paper

Sweet vermicelli is traditionally eaten at Eid

the last day at school.
The masters said in holiday there was no danger
of staining. I was convinced.
But questions hovered like flies
over my plate as we began to eat. My
father said, Watch that!
I held the shining spoon to my mouth,
looking for my face in it.

Snow

The blizzard overnight.
We wake up
to crazy things:

the pine trees rinsed in ice,
their glass twigs shattered below.
Our brains like eggs scrambled,
after dim sleep and snow.

What can one make of snow
this late,
ice-filled
chrysanthemums
pinned to the window?

No thought in winter would
burn
itself to fragrance,
or summer wit.

In this ghastly white,
when I want to say I am afraid
and wordless,
I cannot breathe my breath.

I have seen it happen.
Once stealthily
as in the grey, white, off-white
hair in my father's beard
which the razor has never let
anyone see.

And the day
dazzled by the light of his commitment
he frowned—
it is not right
to be on the wrong side
of things—
he was already losing weight.
And two years later
two more wrinkles on the face
made him forever angry.

Here people talk like a Greek chorus.

As I eat in my thoughts
at breakfast
like the latent haze ahead,
I feel this morning's
three-inch ice
lapse underfoot,
and my eyes spill
with the salt sheet of snow.

Kashmir 1987

This is the blue-stone river
on whose banks the fairies danced at midnight.

The Neelam burbles through the city
echoing the language of undulate margins

which these valleys understand.
Its sound rationalizes even the mountains

and the pointed spires of land
reflect in its flowing photography.
The division of water is not
an issue here as down south,

for the Bald Mountain, discreetly snow-capped,
watches over the city and the country
holding right the balance of the deeds,
the annual cut of land against the water.

This is the blue-stone river
on whose banks the fairies danced at midnight.

The Neelam goes through the city
humming an old tune
that time can crack as fresh walnut,
while the valley's fruit collects

in wicker baskets and the cease-fire holds.
These houses are wingless words on the page,
but glow-worms
flitting in the breeze.

FROM ***SUN AND MOON***

Pakistan Movement

1

Movement, sure. Millions moving
from that side to this side,
from this side to that side, and back again sometimes,
across the thoughtful moment
wherein stood those who were undecided, and suspect,
like border-posts signifying the mid-century frontier.

The sultry summer—if you know what I mean—behind us.
The blistering journeys on foot, the grinding oxcart
expeditions, the slow, steamy railways
and their marauders behind us.
The slit throats of the nobility, the malfunctioning
desire, England's fond promises,
and snuffed-out love of the communal streets;
their moonlight shadows of lead, the changing of the colours
and '47's burning cities behind us.

Think this is where we wanted to be
from the beginning of our time;
a land as beautiful as a poet's dream;
or ever before he found it,
the Arab sailor's act of faith.

2

I have surely come across it before,
in one of the books, or what I imagined on an alien shore
perhaps appointed by time for a landfall.

That's my boat, these my oars; the sail's down.
The movement's upwards from the south
and the choice considerable,
for the compass might be affixed
by some dusky Eskimos. I can tent up in a high-rise,
wait out the passing plane through starlight, till dawn.
The sea-lions skid on imaginary ice, transfixing the world
with a new axis of summer, their eyes, turning, liquid, green.
The granary of the north gets a southward push,
into freedom, and feeds nearly everyone—
until the quaking elements rumble again in the earth's belly
and split the land beyond rejoining;
the furrowed fields like the cracks in time
scotched inside a number. A kind of fall;

but the people rising everywhere, free to grow
how they will, if they will.

3

It is the cyclical crops I was looking at—
and the interminable deltas of hope,
where the rivers are either in torrent or slow endless flow,
the past being a curious valley, the present tense.
Future's the only flower worth tending in this earth,
where I sow my words daily: and you know,
these good trees bear fruit round the year, discreetly,
moving along the waterways
and four seasons of the faithful sun.

Sun and Moon

(For Aniq—when old enough to read it)

1

Sunday was the best day
to play ducks and drakes
with one's spare time at riverside,
not so pink-hedged by the week-long thrift,
the water almost level with the land
and often kissing the lower bank mushroom
of every ten days ago
and its side gravel.

The resident brown snail there,
every Sunday, was seen airing slowly
his awkward opinions;
the TV antennae on his two-pin head transmit
the double-entendre
of the habitual wet's grouting
in the country's passhole.

One could also have one's lone sausage
with potato salad, or go Fanti
with one's girl and the self-made fire
from dry pine sticks.
Almost a perfect day,
instead of counting the blackshirts
that still lurk in the Alpine woods.

Could I then change places,
see that I may be becoming part of that
which is not part of me?
The trees around me dropped their leaves,
shook off their birds, and made
the autumn-beds of their brown leaves
often enough to make more autumn songs.
But I the same always; always the same;
too much the same.
The woman I loved was made of meerschaum
and one Swiss monsoon broke in two.
Love moved out; the tree-barks darkened in the face;
the river froze over;
the land sighed beneath the early snow
of its absences.
The world—its affairs, arias of intent,
offices—ganged up on me.

2

Sibelius, your seemingly silent bust in that other wood
is one with the snow and its wintry mind;
and in time is green, fernlike again
in the notes made of your country's air.
Yes, it is possible, elsewhere,
that an orchestral intention is realized
in being read so well by nature.
I am not promised any such nor have recourse
to what's in the ear but will not ring out

in the time that reamins.
Yet, strangely, as I write this,
tears come down like a rain that strings all instruments,
making new channels of grief in this poem
and across that continent of pain.

3

Is sadness a formation of land
across all waters,
in which the inland seas of joy and grief
mutate like Moving Rocks
to wash on an invisible shore?
Sadness is the only constant sun
melting on away;
each minute one gives up a bit more,
until the sun sets upon its own consequence.

How am I to change the laws of motion,
replace the continents into those symmetries
of love on which the moonlight
will not be a blemish;
hate not exceed love;
love's analogies not become its functions;
one's own life not stretch itself beyong one's gift?

4

Each day is a live wire
passing thought to the illogic of its conclusions:
a flame-tree's brilliant red or yellow flowers,
as if it were a sunset in the Margallas;
an image on which to fix myself
and, possibly, mint memory back into desire,
all my other coinage spent in Europe's shopping centres.

Son, when you were three
and one day your mother said 'You are my good son,'
you replied 'Not moon?' and laughed a knowing laugh,

as if the tangled planets and the stars over us
could hold the language for that one day
to a feeling that would stay,
meanings to remain for all just the same.
The family's language has changed in the meantime;
—you have lost your English and your Urdu,
and now you speak only German.
But you, to me, are still both: my son, my moon,
in this same sky arching

between places.
Life translates like that.
Time lapses but, somehow,
is always present to deal with.
In the house-garden here, a tall,
many-branched tree grows with fine leaves.
In the moonlight, with no one watching,
vagrants from the neighbourhood come around,
aiming their stones sometimes
to take from it what they can;
or smooching the pear-shaped fruit
ripe on its branch,
which surpasses all titular explanations
of the spring, its sovereign flower
in the sunlight gone,
transparent as Monday or Saturday,
both its timely announcements
pendulous on the stem.

Waqas Ahmad Khwaja

Born in Lahore, Waqas Ahmad Khwaja graduated from Government College, Lahore and did his LLB from the Punjab University Law College. In 1979, he was awarded the Rotary Foundation Graduate Fellowship which took him to Emory University in the US. He did his Ph.D in English Literature there and lectured for a year. His teaching career in Pakistan was subsequently divided between jurisprudence and literature at various universities and well-known institutions. Now a critic, poet, translator and fiction writer, he was among the founders of the Lahore's Writers Group in 1984 which encouraged creative work in English, English translations and brought out an anthology, *Cactus* (1984), edited by him. He also put together another anthology, *Mornings in the Wilderness* (1988), later reprinted in India as *Short Stories from Pakistan* (1992). He was a Fellow of the 1988 International Writing Programme at the University of Iowa about which he wrote a travelogue, *Writers and Landscapes* (1991). Meanwhile he gave poetry readings in both Pakistan and the US, and his work appeared in various literary magazines and anthologies. The several collections of his poems include, *Six Geese from a Tomb at Medum* (1987) and *Miriam's Lament and Other Poems* (1992). He also wrote a column for *The Frontier Post*, a weekly literary essay in *The News,* and was a practising lawyer for 12 years. In 1994 he moved to the United States to pursue a career in literature and is now a Professor of English at Agnes Scott College. His story poem reprinted here, 'The Legend of Roda and Jallali', has been developed from the essentials of a Punjabi folk tale.

FROM *SIX GEESE FROM A TOMB AT MEDUM*

April '77

The streets deserted in curfew hours are paced
only by marionettes, and the black scripts
await effacement. Over narrow lanes

buildings crowd in conspiracy emptying
their bowels in the city. The colours of spring
are bluff, and the bougainvillaea clinging

to walls brings blood in its veins. Only the khaki
and green are true—lords and fathers of institutions.
The butterflies between the brows have withered.

There is a cancellation in the alluvium.
Life falls short of its components, restricted
to isolated cells, and roads heavy

with steps release their burdens. One sits muted
at the edge of Ravi, and sluggish waters
flow into the mind.

Garlic and onions sprout through bodies and grow
through domes churning the sun, and jaggeried grain
is distributed among the city's poor.

Speech is the eel of comprehension, and what
is said ventriloquism, still cardboard men
communicate grappling with the differential

calculus of existence. She too has threaded
a noose of flowers and swollen rice for the saint.
But when words have failed, and the tracery of flowers

is laid on the grave, and the hungry gullets
of the poor have been fed, she sits cross-legged
on the terrace of Data Sahib listening

to odes recited with claps and harmoniums—
hour after hour held with a slowly strangled flock.
The shrine exhales its odium burrowing

its way through people swamped with attared
sweat, and the beating clock marks their path
through dust. Beneath phallic symbols

leaping to the sky children penetrate
patterns of cats cradle, nibble at spun sugar
and feel it melting in their mouths

in aftertaste. Frocked girls at hopscotch eye
the pickles at roadside cart-stalls
and whisper behind their hands among themselves.

The earthen jars and bowls lie open to
dust and straw and floating specks of horse-
dung. Boys wrestle on the balding turf.

A rumble scares them off. Soon
no more shouts. No laughter scatters
the air. Only armymen spawn on streets

spreading a terror through the stubble of heads.
Hands grope and part to uncover the sheath
and bitter seeds infest the wombs. When f(y)
approaches zero the city comes to a standstill.

F(y) is a mathematical term used to determine the value function of a sign under variable conditions.

FROM *MIRIAM'S LAMENT AND OTHER POEMS*

The Legend of Roda and Jallali

Among Burning Nettles

Go storm day with your shadow
Golden-maned steed,
Galloping, galloping without pause or rest,
Across oatfields and corn and wheat,
Past the shuddering, hollow-eyed hermit,
Trampling underfoot sun-fire, moon-dust,
Restless your hooves among burning nettles.

What pulls you short, as you snort and rise
On glistening hind-legs, hot with life,
Neighing your heart's rage, your lips pulled back?
So stamp and prance about on soft turf,
Softly all element yield under your hooves,
Your eyes shatter the sky's tinsel glass-box,
And a swish of your tail sweeps away stars.

And the woman, her dugs loose and pendulous,
Lurches with outstretched hands to touch it.
Trembling, steaming, it suddenly stands still
As over its wet body she runs her withered hands
Her grief flung to the wind's back,
The night's enormous skirt slipping from her,
an indistinct brown body swaying in the dark.

And wind keens about her thin sagging thighs,
Recoils in horror from the hoof-mark below her belly,
Sniffs her wrinkled elbows, her hairy armpits,
Fleeing, fleeing from her festering smells,
And trembling all the while the animal stands still,
Flicking an ear or gently swinging its tail.
And from its hide rises the warm stink of flesh.

Tightly she grasps a fistful of horse-mane,
And hoists herself up on its tall, broad back,
And it storms into night, storms across day,
Galloping, galloping without pause or rest,
Across oatfields and corn and wheat,
Past the shuddering, hollow-eyed hermit,
Charging day with the shadow of her dark hair

And a body glowing with youth.
In a field of burning nettles they come to rest,
In a stamping of hooves on soft turf,
And my mother's sister, the cursed one, old hag,
Is young with the fire that roars in her bones.
She leaps off her steed on wind-light feet
And surveys the twilight of a pining land.

Between burning nettles she quickly picks her way,
Her eyes restless, her limbs
Emptied of sand, supple, ripening;
Over the earth's rim rises the full moon,
And jackals cry and wail in the night,
A hungry wolf somewhere bays at the moon.

Indistinct shapes move about her on eager feet,
But the girl revels in her fire,
A wild upright thing striding unabashed,
The other sister, cursed to drift and wander
While her sibling raised a clamourous brood. Born again
Out of an unslaked desire
To discover the fish swimming beneath her skin.

Young and free now, cast off
From world of fret and reprimand,
Striding alone to the company of wolves
As they stretch their necks howling and bare their teeth,
Battering them under her feet,

Tearing off their thick furs with bare hands,
Pulling apart their jaws as red tongues go limp.

And the moon looks placidly from tree-tops,
The naked terror of beauty grown to fullness,
And eyes storming a desolate nightscape.

The Tribal Shadow

Bewildered passages of night:
she looks around for fern and leaf or life
to reunite herself to herself but
is now governed by impulses beyond
her diminishing arc of consciousness
disjunct from sap-root verb or fatal noun
inhabiting the texture of a dream.

So strand by strand she goes numb and fear
scrambles up her legs: in every shade she
sees turnfeet crouching in queer silence
ready to spring upon her, overhead
darkness mushrooms and faint leaf-shapes printed
on shadow move as they would speak to her—
the prepositional tissue fails her then.

Floating whites of eye hover about her
like arks adrift, bobbing and sinking in
underworlds of twilit sense where a torch
lifted suddenly above a herd of
black bodies throws about her its pale ring—
rags of autumn bronze are tipped across their
shoulders, fire ribbons flicker down their spines.

Shuffling about on splayed, uncertain feet,
piping whistles of reed or peepal leaves,
naked as night, freely before her they

display their nakedness, stick out their tongues,
blabber and bay and hop about closing
in all the time clapping their hands, leaping
through conjugations of an ancient rite.

A tribal shadow of the blood pounding
curse strikes her faultless isolation,
each adjective, each verb, each noun, the voice,
mood, number, case, the tense, the gender, each
is demolished, phrase and clause dismantled,
the grammatic code scrambled past repair.
Earth's greatest predators all work alike.

No, it is not rootless, this dialect
of myth, though randomness is not wholly
alien to it. All fabulous creatures
are mere gusts of air upon the tongue
incapable of tilting a candle
flame, they frighten no one, conjure up no
awe, till, yes, they quite topple off the edge

and roar across rough pathways and defiles
staggering through clumps of wood, through wastes of sand
and sea, howling in pain or mad with grief
or rage, or in a vivid moment finding love.

The Legend of Roda and Jallali

He found a heap of bones there,
bleached fragments lying with shrivelled
wolf-entrails and wolf-skulls,
smashed and shattered, some tangles
and masses of hair still rustled
in bush and grass. He wondered
what could have caused it and went
his way, but many years later

when he came back the place was
no more desolate, a bright
young woman sat skinning a deer
and children played around her
and all were naked as the day
that disclosed them. He addressed
the woman and attempted
to attract the children's
attention but no one looked
his way. When he pressed forward
the woman looked up abruptly
and there was such fierceness
in her eyes that he did not
dare a step further.
                    Later
he met a man coming through
dark columns of trees with
a bundle of sticks in his arms.
His back bore marks as if
the skin there was once split
and burned, as if giant
scorpions now lay embedded
there, and he too refused
to acknowledge his presence
or return his greeting.
                    We located
the place several years later
by certain marks and signs he had
left on dried goatskin—Madhu
had found it in the old
trunk the servants kept in their room—
they were great storytellers and possessed
all kinds of odd moments, little
icons of petrified wood,
strange stone shapes, limp, blackened
leaves between parchment covers,
about each of which they had

a tale to tell, and they claimed
to be the descendants of
that great traveller and hunter
who had first acquired them,
a protean figure who lived
to be a hundred and twenty—
but it was crumbling wilderness.

There was, however, a wild
tribe of short, curly-haired, dark
skinned people who lived nearby,
and they told us of the legend
of Roda and Jallali—
how low-born Roda was whipped
and branded by Jallali's father
and brothers, who were of
an ancient family of blacksmiths,
for the love he bore the girl,
and how he was quartered and thrown
to the wolves—Jallali lost
her mind, tore off her clothes
and roamed the forest by the river
bank, soon a wild and decrepit thing—
a crazy hag lurching and stumbling
under the trees.

In earlier
days she would suddenly appear
at her sister's door and make
pitiful efforts to befriend
her little boys and girls, but
they were all somewhat afraid
and recoiled from her. If men
were around they drove her
away with shouts but did not
harm her in any way.

As years
went by she ventured out
less and less and even travellers
through the woods seldom saw her.
Then one day she vanished
and tales grew about a mysterious
beast that had come and galloped
away with her in the night.

Some say they saw her return
young and lovely as she once was
and destroy with her bare hands
the wolves that had once devoured
her lover, but they also tell
that a tribe that holds the wolf
sacred then closed in upon her
and tore her to pieces.
Every
twenty-five years now, a black
storm hits the place and causes
great damage to men and crops
and cattle, and afterwards, some
report, one may come across
a young man with scorpion welts
across his back, carrying a bundle
of sticks in his arms as he
emerges from the dark columns
of trees, or by the door of
a solitary thatch hut
a woman may be seen, naked
as the sun, skinning a deer
while children play about her.

M. Athar Tahir

M. Athar Tahir was the 1974 Rhodes Scholar for Pakistan at Oriel College, Oxford, where he read English Language and Literature. Before his masters at Oxford University, he was editor of *The Ravi,* the literary journal of Government College, Lahore, where he also took part in poetry gatherings initiated by *Kaleem Omar and *Taufiq Rafat. Now a senior civil servant, he was the 1979 Rotary International Scholar at the University of Pennsylvania and read Comparative Religions and Muslim Architecture. He was awarded the Hubert H. Humphrey Fellowship to the University of Southern California. His critical and creative work and translations from Urdu and Punjabi have been published in both Pakistan and abroad. He has edited five volumes of Pakistani English poetry, *Next Moon* (1984), *A Various Terrain* (1985), *The Inner Dimension* (1987), *Silence on Fire* (1988), *Winter Voices* (1989); published a collection of short stories, *Other Seasons* (1991) and another of poems, *Just Beyond the Physical* (1991). His second volume of poems, *A Certain Season* is due shortly from London. His poems have been set as texts in secondary schools. His pioneering work on a nineteenth century poet, *Qadir Yar: A Critical Introduction,* won the Shah Abdul Latif Bhitai Award 1990 and the National Book Council Prize 1991. He collaborated with Christopher Shackle on *Hashim's Sassi*. He is an elected Fellow of the Royal Asiatic Society of Great Britain. He is the editor of a two volume anthology of fifty years of Pakistani creative writing in English for the Pakistan Academy of Letters.

Trolley Man

And when for hopes your hand shall be uncurled,
Your eyes shall close being open to the world.

Wilfred Owen

Ahmed Bux looked at himself in the small circular mirror on the cracked wooden shelf embedded crudely in the mud-wall. He was nearing thirty, with jet black hair, two dark eyes and a mouth that never knew distress. He had always been contented and even happy as far as he could remember. His parents had died when he was very young. He had no recollection of them. His uncle, who had left for the city with his family, had kept him until he had been fit to work. Good old man. He grinned showing a set of white even teeth.

He had a razor in his thick strong hand and sharpened it, on the strop suspended from the wall, with a wettish sound. Satisfied, he applied it to his face. It shaved off the short spiky hair with a scraping sound. There was still time before he was wanted at the station, so he took it leisurely enjoying each stroke. Life was pleasant for him. He had got this job at the station; he had friends; all the people liked him, for he was helpful. He was there at the ploughing, watering, sowing and harvesting. His strong lithe body could stand the long strain under the hot sun and when he would work endlessly on, the people just gaped at him. Once somebody had asked him:

'What do you eat? Almonds and lot of butter?'

Ahmed Bux had laughed in his usual engaging way and said: 'No, no, just ordinary wheat-flour chapatis and curry as you all do. I am not a jinn or something of the air you know. It's just that I like work.'

He had grinned again and begun to work. People called him 'a good simple soul' behind his back and he knew it. He was pleased. It was good to be liked.

'Thuck...thuckthuck...thuck.' The dull noise broke the stillness of his thoughts.

'Come in *bhai,* come in. The door's open.'

A man of large rough dimensions carrying a *hookah* came in. His was a swarthy face with yellow teeth, a sharp nose, a wide mouth and contented eyes. He was over thirty, married and a father of three, leading a quiet life.

'Salaam Ahmed Buxa.'

'Salaam *bhai* Jeero. How's your wife and children?'

'Fine, just fine. Thought I'd come here and then we'd go to the station together.' He was the signal man.

'I'm just finishing. Not shaved, these last two days, I had time to kill now, so…'

'*Aho,* a wise thing Ahmed Buxa, a wise thing.' He nodded his turbaned head philosophically.

They went out, and Ahmed Bux locked the room with a cylindrical key. The sun had just set, the scarlet clouds still stood against the vast mauve sky glowing with a last tinge of gold. Large groups of black crows flew across the sky, cawing, lamenting at the end of the day, to the trees on the left. A muezzin's voice floated up and far away with a strange restful quality of the serene sunset as it mingled with the open air. In the stillness, there was the faint buzz of the village bustle as rustics prepared for the night. Pairs of oxen that had turned the wheel endlessly at the well or dug the brown humid earth for the coming season were seen sluggishly making for the village. Farmers followed close behind sucking vigorously at bits of fresh sugarcane and occasionally urging the oxen on, with its other end. They walked through the fields, some bare and lined by the cut of the plough, others full and ripe for harvest. Their bare muddy feet briskly picked the way along the smooth uneven path as they talked about the health of Jeero's children, the coming harvest, the break-down of the tubewell that a Chaudhry had installed and Ahmed Bux's intentions of getting married.

The station was a small one and not all the trains stopped there. Only the slower ones did but for a very short while. It had one broken-down wooden gate which permanently stayed ajar leading to the platform, and two smaller brick rooms on either end. One was the Station Master's room and the other a spare room for equipment. The platform had a raised cemented dais with a corrugated zinc sheet for roof which housed levers for signals and changing tracks of trains. Only four men worked here: the Station Master, his assistant, Jeero and Ahmed Bux, the trolley man. They parted at the gate. Jeero went to the dais and sat on the concrete seat puffing at his *hookah* while Ahmed Bux went to the Station Master's room.

The Station Master's was a small white-washed room with one wooden chair, an equally old rickety table and a long - legged plank for a bench along the wall. On the table to the right was the black telephone of the late twenties. The walls had pasted on them, the time-tables of trains.

The Station Master was a short bearded man of forty odd years and said all his five daily prayers as there was nothing in this place to distract him. Perched on the tip of his nose were circular glass spectacles through which he goggled out, studying a few sheets of printed paper under the light of the hurricane lamp.

Ahmed Bux entered the room, salaamed with the flat palm touching his forehead and stood quietly waiting for orders.

'Hmm,' the Station Master looked up and salaamed. 'Ahmed Bux, today I'll have to go to the next village on urgent business, so get the trolley out. Here's the key.'

Ahmed Bux took the key and walked to the store. He unlocked the room and hurriedly dragged the trolley out on the railway tracks. He wiped it with the cloth, cleaned the seat and oiled the parts. His eyes glittered with pride. He so enjoyed clasping the bar in his hands and pushing the trolley, forcefully but lovingly, along the tracks. It needed force and he had it.

Presently, the Station Master came and rested his bulk on the trolley's seat. Ahmed Bux, glowing with pride, heaved and pushed it on. It began to gain speed as Ahmed Bux's sinewy legs moved faster and faster. His feet gripped the tracks with an earthy resolution, caressing them at the same time. The tracks slithered under his feet like an endless snake and beads of sweat began to ooze out of his body. He ran on with grave celerity, faster and faster. Oil-lamp lights vaguely appeared in the distance. The next village was approaching. The signal was down. He paid no attention to it and hurried on. Suddenly the tracks began to vibrate. A deafening sound followed. Ahmed Bux looked back and saw the glaring eye of a steel cyclops.

'Sahib, the train,' he faltered.

The Station Master had clambered out of his seat and jumped clear off the tracks with a speed amazing in a man of his bulk. He watched Ahmed Bux let the trolley go, his feet patter uncontrollably on the cool rails as he tried to stop himself, lose his balance swagger and fall, his head hitting a stone.

Ahmed Bux gained consciousness in a strange room with a throbbing head and a pain he had never felt before. The Station Master and a bearded local hakim looked anxiously on.

'He is coming round,' a hoarse voice declared. 'Send for a tumbler of hot milk. He needs rest.'

He slept, for he knew not how long but finally when he woke, the throbbing in his head was gone. He tried to move out of his bed. He could not. He threw the coarse blanket away. His left leg was cut off just below his knee. It was heavily bandaged. He stared blankly at it.

'Ahmed Bux,' the Station Master stood silhouetted in the door-way. 'Ahmed Bux…good to see you well.' The Station Master had lost the authoritative note. Ahmed Bux eyed him coolly.

'I forgot…to inform the station master of that village. I left in a hurry. It was time for the seven o'clock goods train. I tried to drag you away but it was too late. The driver did apply the brakes…'

Ahmed Bux understood.

'You won't…tell the folks…it was…my fault.' His look pleaded.

Ahmed Bux looked at him vaguely, then turned his face towards the wall.

When the Station Master had left the room, it suddenly

dawned on him that he would be a trolley-man no longer. He felt empty and sick in the stomach.

...But, I mustn't think of it now,' he resolutely brushed his thoughts aside.

Ahmed Bux had built a mud partition in his room, widened the door and now sat daily selling groceries to the villagers. His countenance betrayed no repentance or melancholy as he went about his work quite eagerly. Occasionally the local Chaudhry would call for him to supervise the harvest.

Now, as he hobbled on his way, his thigh resting on a horizontal wooden bit, clasping a long bamboo pole, the villagers eyed him with pity, admiration and awe. He was the current topic among women.

'*Behen,* Ahmed Bux is a good honest soul,' said one.

'*Aho,* and hardworking too.'

'*Aho,* but who would give his daughter to him now?'

'Tchk, tchk.'

'I heard Sughran was engaged to him.'

'*Aho, behen,* but Sughran's mother has not talked about it as yet.'

'Poor fellow.'

'I hear he is running a chilli-salt shop.'

'*Han, han,* the poor cripple. What else can he do now?'

'And he has to earn his living.'

'And that's the only way.'

'He has been granted a pension, sister.'

'Of thirty rupees.'

'In these costly days what is thirty rupees?'

'Nothing.'

'*Han,* nothing.' All the other heads bobbed up and down in agreement.

'But he has not lost his old cheerful self.'

'Always happy and whistling.'

'*Aho.*'

'Ahmed Bux, a good honest soul.' The heads repeated the movement.

Some weeks later when he had settled down with his new work, he thought of paying Sughran's mother a visit. It would have sounded too early if he had asked for Sughran's hand then, but now it seemed perfectly right. He would go and see her. He had a room and a shop, even if small. They could always add a few more rooms to it if need be. Besides that was basically a woman's job. Yes, the future sounded perfectly sound. He decided to pay her a visit the following evening, for she would be busy with the cotton-picking till the afternoon.

Sughran's dwelling was at the farther side of the village across a few fields. It was a sizeable house with a low mud wall enclosing a vegetable garden in the front. A pipal tree stood gaunt and large outside the wall. Under it sat a profusely oiled buffalo looking pensively at the surrounding, chewing the cud and whisking away the flies with its long tail. Near it a few chickens pecked at the ground as an old bitch sitting disinterestedly watched them with languid eyes. Sughran's mother had rolled up her sleeves and was busy collecting cowdung in a large heap. Then she made small cakes, added some hay and flattened them with her hand so that an impression of all her five fingers was left on each, plastered them on to the mud-wall. From far away, the wall seemed patched and marked like mosaic.

Ahmed Bux salaamed her, as she looked over her shoulder. She replied and told him to go on into the enclosure. He seated himself on the large charpoy under the shade of the wall. She appeared, her hands washed, her sleeves unrolled and seated herself opposite him.

'I had to clear up the mess before sunset,' she said pointing to the wall. 'It had been piled up for a few days. You know the cotton picking season.'

'*Aho*.'

'Everything's all right with you?'

'*Aho.*'

'Good. Do you hear from your uncle? A fine man he is.'

'*Aho.* They are all fine.'

'Now what will you have? A tumbler of hot, steaming milk? I have just finished milking the buffalo and it is being boiled.'

'No, *Bibi*, nothing.'

'But, you must.'

'No, no, really. I have just had something before coming. *Bibi*, I come to see you…ehm,' he cleared his throat. 'You know *Bibi,* I have not elders to send to you. So I thought I would remind you of the promise.'

'Oh, that…well, Ahmed Buxa, what to hide from you? I really have nothing against you, you know, but you do realize now, don't you?'

Ahmed Bux understood. He had expected this, hope against hope. He watched the chickens as they came into the enclosure and clawed the earth and pecked rapidly with almost mechanical movements. He lightly tapped the stick on the ground, made vague criss-crosses with it and stared at some point just above the ground.

'*Achha, Bibi*, Salaam,' he said at last as he got up.

'Salaam, son, salaam.' He could detect a note of pity and uncomfortable thankfulness in her voice.

The evening was dark and the new moon had appeared just above the horizon for a short while. The oil lamp was on the canister outside the mud-house near the wall. He, having had his last meal of the day, came and blew out the flame; wobbled to the bed he had earlier made and sitting on it put his stick along its side. It slipped and fell with a dull thud on the ground. It felt good to stretch oneself after the tiring day. He lay down flat. The stars were beginning to appear. Soon the whole sky was studded with them. He looked at the milky-way and silently followed its course from the horizon across the sky to where it just disappeared into nothingness.

FROM *JUST BEYOND THE PHYSICAL*

Border Line

An inkier blot against an inky sky,
spilling down the hillside, the town was littered
with lights, with animal eyes.
Bangle-like, a path clasped the rest-house in silence.

Leaning out into the wind howling
in the pines standing high to
outdo each other, we watched
the night fill hollows.

At the crossroad of sun and mist,
our eyes unearthed the separate holds
we had locked ourselves so firmly in.
So the parting: you down your track, I down mine.

Carpet-weaver

Between buildings which like beggar women
        squabbled for sunlight,
        I had, I think, lost my way
        when in a nook, I came upon him

huddled in an interior lit by black.
        His fingers blunt with wool
        labour at the ancient contraption
        to the scurry of a rat.

While he earns his bread
        by knots per square inch,
        only a muezzin*'s* call away
        at the shrine of the great sage

professionals extend their metal-bowls for food.
    Many well-beloveds of God
    with rice *dhegs* and strings of flowers
    come to thank this saint of the green dome.

Recommendations work even here.

This Sun is my Sun

No, not even the cucumbers smoothly
Sliced to greenness, nor the sherbet which
leaves its colour on the tongue can help.

And the eyes blinded
By the glare, which nothing smudges,
Roll inwards looking for shade.

To meet the challenge of the the sun
One must be baked to earth's brown.
This sun is my sun.

It squeezes everything out
Like a vendor of sugar-cane juice
And shadows cling close to walls and trees

The hibiscus hangs out its parched tongue.
Sweat forms on my skin
And slides down the spine like silverfish.

To meet the challenge of the sun
One must be baked to earth's brown.
This sun is my sun.

The tongue grates in my wooden mouth
As I retreat into
The sheltering tree of words

Seeking sanctuary from
The damnation of myself
And shadows, which are still hot.

To meet the challenge of the sun
One must be baked to earth's brown.
This sun is my sun.

Circles

The sky had come down
in patches on the watered field
and crows conspiring at their edges
shake the afternoon off their wings.
The light crawls up the poplars
but only when words cast

                    long shadows
does the mind begin to stir.
Sitting in a corner of myself
a little along the line-line
in the palm I mark off
my one and twenty years

                    and wonder
how much they weigh.
The question ripples the water.
Although I have driven into myself
to unlock the I and Me,
am still stranded between two circles

                    which do not intersect.
As old sugar turns bitter
so has the craving to fuse into another being.
And I sit and watch
a buddhist sun succumb
to the silence on fire.

Elegy

On the pipal tree sat
Five ugly scavengers, with bald heads
sunk between their wings.
Nothing escaped their eyes—
Not even the grass growing.
I sat huddled,
Holding myself to myself .

Silently one descended.
The sun turned black, effacing all beneath it.
Not a sound save the tearing of limbs.
Not a smell save that of blood.
Still warm but thick.
The air was dead; heavy
With the after-silence of conflict.
My shadow had shortened.

In the corner of the cafe seated,
In narrow chairs, still unconcerned,
These men smoke their past away
And sip their present hurriedly.
The future, they look for in their cups.
Only used tea-leaves stare back.
Outside, the ebbing day gilts the buildings,
But the walls in here are blank.
The scavengers are still there.

I know I must
Content myself, with a glass of water.

Brass Objects

At night, when only the light of the lamp
Keeps the aggressive walls at bay,
When a fly buzzes
In my ear and knocks against my face,
I sit alone, feeling the rattan of the chair.
In front of me, a medal hangs from a pin.
I dug it out with the broken handle
of a pan in my uncle's junkstore.

A piece of brass,
Stamped with an era long overthrown,
Waiting to be useful in the melting pot.
By one whose life was as heavy
As a single lead bullet, it was won.
Some great-grandchild, perhaps,
Was cheated for its weight in sweets
By the hawkers who prowl the narrow streets.

Restlessly, the blackout paper flaps darkness
And I become aware of the clock
Flanked by two unfired bullets.
For long, I had kept them live and dangerous,
Till I felt their weight, and with sweating hands
Poured out the gunpowder.
Mute, they stand now:
An image of their perilous selves.

In the distance, muffled,
As in some empty stomach the thunder rolls.
But the radio drones its
Long list of POWs. I wonder what
Their relations, huddled over their coals
In the late winter rain, are thinking?
Or those who at the Front are
Overtaken by nature's strange benediction?

Tomorrow, fresh medals forged in blood
Will pay off a debt.
But will they, as before,
Find their way into a junkstore?

Eid '75

The Pound fell to a new low today.
It has been falling steadily all summer
but with autumn everything
takes on a heavier shade.
Can I, then, think of you?

Fourteen weeks ago, I could stretch the sunshine
to where the map seemed greenest:
Cheltenhem, Salisbury and Hay
or north to Paki-populated Leeds and Bradford;
to York in white antiquity.

Fourteen weeks is a long time ago
with talk of sun on Cotswold stone
and feeding pigeons in mossy graveyards;
with silence-stained churches
and heavy creakings of oak doors.

Through winter branches
Eid, last year, slid away, but
nor it has limped nearer
autumn shades, with you
like virginia creeper's final red.

Moniza Alvi

Born in Lahore, Moniza Alvi moved to England when she was a few months old with her Pakistani father and English mother. She grew up in Hertfordshire and studied at the Universities of York and London. She now works as Head of the English Department in a secondary school in London. In 1991 she was the co-winner of The Poetry Business Prize. Her first full-length collection *The Country at my Shoulder* (1993) was selected for The Poetry Society's 'New Generation Poets' promotion. The poems in this collection referring to her Pakistani background are based on her childhood memories, family anecdotes and flights of imagination. Later, she made her first return visit to Pakistan and she went to India too: her impressions are at the heart of her second collection, *A Bowl of Warm Air* (1996). A very lyrical writer, she is now working on poems about the Asian experience in Britain, but considers work other than that about Pakistan to be equally important. She says 'When I started writing seriously, in my late twenties, I was reading Angela Carter's work and J.G. Ballard's science fiction. I consider that prose writers have influenced me as much as poets. I am attracted by fantasy and by the strange-seeming, and find there some essence of experience. I do feel an affinity with poets who have a multi-racial identity, for example Mimi Khalvati and Sujata Bhatt…I see my writing as a way of creating and recreating my life – extending its possibilities through the imaginative engagement with feelings and experiences.'

FROM *THE COUNTRY AT MY SHOULDER*

I Would Like to be a Dot in a Painting by Miro

I would like to be a dot in a painting by Miro.

Barely distinguishable from other dots,
it's true, but quite uniquely placed.
And from my dark centre

I'd survey the beauty of the linescape
and wonder—would it be worthwhile
to roll myself towards the lemon stripe,

Centrally poised, and push my curves
against its edge, to get myself
a little extra attention?

But it's fine where I am.
I'll never make out what's going on
around me, and that's the joy of it.

The fact that I'm not a perfect circle
makes me more interesting in this world.
People will stare forever—

Even the most unemotional get excited.
So here I am, on the edge of animation,
a dream, a dance, a fantastic construction,

A child's adventure.
And nothing in this tawny sky
can get too close, or move too far away.

Presents from my Aunts in Pakistan

They sent me a salwar kameez
peacock-blue,
and another
glistening like an orange split open,
embossed slippers, gold and black
points curling.
Candy-striped glass bangles
snapped, drew blood.
Like at school, fashions changed
in Pakistan—
The salwar bottoms were broad and stiff,
then narrow.
My aunts chose an apple-green sari,
silver-bordered
for my teens.

I tried each satin-silken top—
was alien in the sitting-room.
I could never be as lovely
as those clothes—
I longed
for denim and corduroy.
My costume clung to me
and I was aflame,
I couldn't rise up out of its fire,
half-English,
unlike Aunt Jamila.

I wanted my parents' camel-skin lamp—
switching it on in my bedroom,
to consider the cruelty
and the transformation
from camel to shade,
marvel at the colours
like stained glass.

My mother cherished her jewellery—
   Indian gold, dangling, filigree.
                    But it was stolen from our car.
The presents were radiant in my wardrobe.
   My aunts requested cardigans
                    from Marks and Spencers.

My salwar kameez
   didn't impress the school friend
who sat on my bed, asked to see
   my weekend clothes.
But often I admired the mirror-work,
   tried to glimpse myself
                    in the miniature
glass circles, recall the story
   how the three of us
                    sailed to England.
Prickly heat had me screaming on the way.
   I ended up in a cot
in my English grandmother's dining-room,
   found myself alone,
                    playing with a tin boat.

I pictured my birthplace
   from fifties' photographs.
                    When I was older
there was conflict, a fractured land
   throbbing through newsprint.
Sometimes I saw Lahore—
                    my aunts in shaded rooms,
screened from male visitors,
   sorting presents,
                    wrapping them in tissue.

Or there were beggars, sweeper-girls
    and I was there—
                    of no fixed nationality,
staring through fretwork
                    at the Shalimar Gardens.

FROM *A BOWL OF WARM AIR*

The Double City

I live in one city,
but then it becomes another.
The point where they mesh—
I call it mine.

Dacoits creep from caves
in the banks of the Indus.

One of them is displaced.
From Trafalgar Square
he dominates London, his face
masked by scarves and sunglasses.
He draws towards him all the conflict
of the metropolis—his speech
a barrage of grenades, rocket-launchers.

He marks time with his digital watch.
The pigeons get under his feet.

In the double city the beggar's cry
travels from one region to the next.

Under sapphire skies
or muscular clouds
there are fluid streets

and solid streets.
On some it is safe to walk.

The women of Southhall
champion the release
of the battered Kiranjit
who killed her husband.
Lord Taylor, free her now!
Their saris billow in a storm of chants.

Schoolchildren of many nationalities
enact the Ramayana.
The princely Rama
fights with demons
while the monkey god
searches for Princess Sita.

I make discoveries and lose them
little by little.
My journey in the double city
starts beneath my feet.
You are here, says the arrow.

The Wedding

I expected a quiet wedding
high above a lost city
a marriage to balance on my head

like a forest of sticks, a pot of water.
The ceremony tasted of nothing
had little colour—guests arrived

stealthy as sandalwood smugglers.
When they opened their suitcases
England spilled out.

They scratched at my veil
like beggars on a car window.
I insisted my dowry was simple—

a smile, a shadow, a whisper,
my house an incredible structure
of stiffened rags and bamboo.

We travelled along roads with English
names, my bridegroom and I.
Our eyes changed colour

like traffic-lights, so they said.
The time was not ripe
for us to view each other.

We stared straight ahead as if
we could see through mountains
breathe life into new cities.

I wanted to marry a country
take up a river for a veil
sing in the Jinnah Gardens

hold up my dream, tricky
as a snake-charmer's snake.
Our thoughts half-submerged

like buffaloes under dark water
we turned and faced each other
with turbulence

and imprints like maps on our hands.

The Colours of the World

It is time, almost time
        for her to leave her house.

It is not normally done
        for a woman to go out alone
except to the bazaar
        to buy rat traps or garlands.
She glows within her body
        like the model of the Taj
inside the Red Fort.
        She reads her sacred script
which flows like water,
        recalls her husband's words—
From my first wife
        there was no issue.
She yearns to place
        a block on cloth, strike it
with a mallet—one blow
        for each of her children.

She ponders the miniatures
        glimpsed in the museum.
The heroine watching
        violet, raging clouds.
Moghul ladies playing polo.
        While outside the rain falls—
the white, the sapphire,
        the blood-red drops
spreading into lakes.

She will leave her house.

She'll go to the bank
        and see for herself
how air-conditioning
        turns it into a palace.
She dreams the women
        are singing, bursting
in the red-light area, Hiramundi,
        while she rubs her face
against a map of the world.

She's a woman with modest dress,
        but when she goes out
the men will stare—
        she'll be conspicuous
like a Western woman.

The fullness of her clothes
        will swirl around her—
when the colours of the world
        rush out to meet her.

A Bowl of Warm Air

Someone is falling towards you
as an apple falls from a branch,
moving slowly, imperceptibly as if
into a new political epoch,
or excitedly like a dog towards a bone.
He is holding in both hands
everything he knows he has—
a bowl of warm air.

He has sighted you from afar
as if you were a dramatic crooked tree
on the horizon and he has seen you close up
like the underside of a mushroom.

But he cannot open you like a newspaper
or put you down like a newspaper.

And you are satisfied that he is veering towards you
and that he is adjusting his speed
and that the sun and the wind and rain are in front of him
and the sun and the wind and rain are behind him.

Hanif Kureishi

The son of an English mother and a Pakistani father, Hanif Kureishi comes from a family of writers, which includes Maki Kureishi*. He was born and brought up and educated in the London suburbs. At an early age he became aware of 'a whole range of exclusion' from subtle remarks to blatant racism and identified strongly with black American writers such as James Baldwin and Richard Wright. He read philosophy at King's College, London and started to write plays. In 1981 he won the George Devine Award for *Outskirts* (1981), about Asians in Southhall. He was nominated the most promising playwright of the year by the magazine, *Drama*, and was appointed Writer-in-Residence at The Royal Court Theatre. In 1983 he made his first visit to Pakistan, which was both new and alien yet helped him re-define himself and provided him with much material. He has recorded that experience and the difficulties of his childhood in a memoir, *The Rainbow Sign* (1986). This was published in a book with his famous screenplay, *My Beautiful Laundrette* (1986), which won an Oscar nomination. The film was directed by Stephen Frears and combined elements of a crime thriller with a serious comment on racism and unemployment in Britain; it also contrasts the attitudes of Asian Britons with their relatives from Pakistan. Hanif Kureishi has written several other scripts for film, television, radio and the stage. He made his debut as a director with the film *London Kills Me*. His adaptation of Brecht's *Mother Courage* was produced by The Royal Shakespeare Company and the Royal National Theatre.

He has contributed stories and articles to *Granta* and *The New Statesman* among other publications and is considered one of the best British writers of his generation. His first novel, a best seller, *The Buddha of Suburbia* (1990), about an Asian boy growing up in the London suburbs during the 1970s and seeking his future in the theatre, won the Whitbread Award for the Best First Novel and was made into a four part drama series for television. His second novel, *The Black Album* (1995), about the misadventures of Shahid, a young man of Pakistani origin at a London college, takes a look at Britain in the late 1980s and the rise of fundamentalism. He has co-edited the *Faber Book of Pop* (1995), is writing a screenplay, *My Son the Fanatic,* for the BBC, and has published a collection of short stories, *Love in a Blue Time* (1997).

My Beautiful Laundrette combines anger, violence and humour to makes a comment on the immigrant experience in Britain, as well as the brutal, acquisitive ethics of the 1980s. It provides a brilliant insight into the exclusion that young British Asians have to contend with while growing up in Britain; and it says a great deal more through its tense, tight dialogue and a myriad of cameo portraits. OMAR is the son of an impoverished, Pakistani, one-time journalist, living in London. He is given a job by NASSER, his amoral, prosperous, businessman uncle. OMAR re-establishes contact with the down-and-out JOHNNY, who moves around with a gang of white fascist thugs and was once OMAR's best friend. The bond between them proves stronger than the prejudiced world they live in. Together they transform NASSER's seedy laundrette and do battle against both the facists and a Pakistani gang of drug smugglers, which includes NASSER's friend SALIM. The screenplay, reprinted here was published in its original form, without incorporating any of the later changes made during the filming.

FROM *MY BEAUTIFUL LAUNDRETTE*

1. Ext. outside a large detached house. Day.

CHERRY and SALIM get out of their car. Behind them, the FOUR JAMAICANS get out of their car.

CHERRY and SALIM walk towards the house. It is a large falling-down place, in South London. It's quiet at the moment–early morning–but the ground floor windows are boarded up.

On the boarded-up windows is painted: 'Your greed will be the death of us all' and 'We will defeat the running wogs of capitalism' and 'Opium is the opium of the unemployed'.

CHERRY and SALIM look up at the house. The FOUR JAMAICANS stand behind them, at a respectful distance.

CHERRY: I don't even remember buying this house at the auction. What are we going to do with it?.

SALIM: Tomorrow we start to renovate it.

CHERRY: How many people are living here?

SALIM: There are no people living here. There are only squatters. And they're going to be renovated–right now.
(And SALIM pushes CHERRY forward, giving her the key. CHERRY goes to the front door of the house. SALIM, with TWO JAMAICANS goes round the side of the house. TWO JAMAICANS go round the other side.)

2. Int. a room in the squat. Day.

GENGHIS and JOHNNY are living in a room in the squat. It is freezing cold, with broken windows. GENGHIS is asleep on a mattress, wrapped up. He has the flu. JOHNNY is lying frozen in a deck chair, with blankets over him. He has just woken up.

3. Ext. Outside the house. Day.

CHERRY tries to unlock the front door of the place. But the door has been barred. She looks in through the letter box. A barricade has been erected in the hall.

4. Ext. The side of the house. Day.
The JAMAICANS break into the house through a side windows. They climb in. SALIM also climbs into the house.

5. Int. Inside the house. Day.
The JAMAICANS and SALIM are in the house now.

The JAMAICANS are kicking open the doors of the squatted rooms.

The SQUATTERS are unprepared, asleep or half-awake, in disarray.

The JAMAICANS are going from room to room, yelling for everyone to leave now or get thrown out of the windows with their belongings.

Some SQUATTERS complain but they are shoved out of their rooms into the hall; or down the stairs. SALIM is eager about all of this.

6. Int. Genghis and Johnny's room. Day.
JOHNNY looks up the corridor to see what's happening. He goes back into the room quickly and starts stuffing his things into a black plastic bag. He is shaking GENGHIS at the same time.

GENGHIS: I'm ill.

JOHNNY: We're moving house.

GENGHIS: No, we've got to fight.

JOHNNY: Too early in the morning.

(He rips the blankets off GENGHIS, who lies there fully dressed, coughing and shivering. A JAMAICAN bursts into the room.)

All right, all right.

(The JAMAICAN watches a moment as GENGHIS, too weak to resist, but cursing violently, takes the clothes JOHNNY shoves at him and follows JOHNNY to the window. JOHNNY opens the broken window.)

7. Ext. outside the house. Day.

A wide shot of the house.

The SQUATTERS are leaving through windows and the re-opened front door and gathering in the front garden, arranging their wretched belongings. Some of them are junkies. They look dishevelled and disheartened.

From an upper room in the house comes crashing a guitar, TV and some records. This is followed by the enquiring head of a JAMAICAN, looking to see these have hit no one.

One SQUATTER, in the front garden, is resisting and a JAMAICAN is holding him. The SQUATTER screams at CHERRY: you pig, you scum, you filthy rich shit, etc.

As SALIM goes to join CHERRY, she goes to the screaming SQUATTER and gives him a hard backhander across the face.

8. Ext. The back of the house. Day.

JOHNNY and GENGHIS stumble down through the back garden of the house and over the wall at the end, JOHNNY pulling and helping the exhausted GENGHIS.

At no time do they see CHERRY or SALIM.

9. Int. Bathroom. Day.

OMAR has been soaking Papa's clothes in the bath. He pulls them dripping from the bath and puts them in an old steel bucket, wringing them out. He picks up the bucket.

10. Ext. Balcony. Day.

OMAR is hanging out Papa's dripping pyjamas on the washing line on the balcony, pulling them out of the bucket.

The balcony overlooks several busy railway lines, commuter routes into Charing Cross and London Bridge, from the suburbs.

OMAR turns and looks through the glass of the balcony door into the main room of the flat. PAPA is lying in bed. He pours himself some vodka. Water from the pyjamas drips down Omar's trousers and into his shoes.

When he turns away, a train, huge, close, fast, crashes towards the camera and bangs and rattles its way past, a few feet from the exposed overhanging balcony. OMAR is unperturbed.

11. Int. Papa's room. Day.

The flat OMAR and his father, PAPA, share in South London. It's a small, damp and dirty place which hasn't been decorated for years.

PAPA is as thin as a medieval Christ: an unkempt alcoholic. His hair is long; his toenails uncut; he is unshaven and scratches his arse shamelessly. Yet he is not without dignity.

His bed is in the living room. PAPA never leaves the bed and watches TV most of the time.

By the bed is a photograph of PAPA's dead wife, Mary. And on the bed is an address book and the telephone.

PAPA empties the last of a bottle of vodka into a filthy glass. He rolls the empty bottle under the bed.

OMAR is now pushing an old-fashioned and ineffective carpet sweeper across the floor. PAPA looks at OMAR's face. He indicates that OMAR should move his face closer, which OMAR reluctantly does. To amuse himself, PAPA squashes OMAR's nose and pulls his cheeks, shaking the boy's unamused face from side to side.

PAPA: I'm fixing you with a job. With your uncle. Work now, till you go back to college. If your face gets any longer here you'll overbalance. Or I'll commit suicide.

12. Int. Kitchen. Day.

OMAR is in the kitchen of the flat, stirring a big saucepan of dall. He can see through the open door his father speaking on the phone to NASSER. PAPA speaks in Urdu. 'How are you?' He says. 'And BILQUIS? And TANIA and the other girls?'

PAPA: (*Into phone*) Can't you give OMAR some work in your garage for a few weeks, yaar? The bugger's your nephew after all.

NASSER: (*VO on phone*) Why do you want to punish me?

13. Int. Papa's room. Day.

Papa is speaking to NASSER on the phone. He watches OMAR slowly stirring dall in the kitchen. OMAR is, of course, listening.

PAPA: He's on dole like everyone else in England. What's he doing home? Just roaming and moaning.

NASSER: (*VO on phone*) Haven't you trained him up to look after you, like I have with my girls?

PAPA: He brushes the dust from one place to another. He squeezes shirts and heats soup. But that hardly stretches him. Though his food stretches me. It's only for a few months, yaar. I'll send him to college in the autumn.

NASSER: (*VO*) He failed once. He had this chronic laziness that runs in our family except for me.

PAPA: If his arse gets lazy – Kick it. I'll send a certificate giving permission. And one thing more. Try and fix him with a nice girl. I'm not sure if his penis is in full working order.

14. Int. Flat. Day.

Later. OMAR puts a full bottle of vodka on the table next to Papa's bed.

PAPA: Go to your uncle's garage.

(And PAPA pours himself a vodka. OMAR quickly thrusts a bottle of tomato juice towards PAPA, which PAPA ignores. Before PAPA can take a swig of the straight vodka, OMAR grabs the glass and adds tomato juice. PAPA takes it.)

If Nasser wants to kick you—let him. I've given permission in two languages. (*To the photograph*) The bloody's doing me a lot of good. Eh? bloody Mary?

15. Ext. Street. Day.

OMAR walks along a South London street, towards NASSER's garage. It's rough area, beautiful in its own falling-down way.

A youngish white BUSKER is lying stoned in the doorway of a boarded-up shop, his guitar next to him. OMAR looks at him.

Walking towards OMAR from on amusement arcade across the street are JOHNNY and GENGHIS and MOOSE. GENGHIS is a well-built white man carrying a pile of right-wing newspapers, badges etc. MOOSE is a big white man, GENGHIS's lieutenant.

JOHNNY is an attractive man in his early twenties, quick and funny.

OMAR doesn't see JOHNNY but JOHNNY sees him and is startled.

To avoid OMAR, in the middle of the road, JOHNNY takes GENGHIS's arm a moment.

GENGHIS stops suddenly. MOOSE charges into the back of him.

GENGHIS drops the newspapers. GENGHIS remonstrates with MOOSE. Johnny watches OMAR go. The traffic stops while MOOSE picks up the newspapers. GENGHIS starts to sneeze. MOOSE gives him a handkerchief.

They walk across the road, laughing at the waiting traffic.

They know the collapsed BUSKER. He could even be a member of the gang. JOHNNY still watches OMAR's disappearing back.

GENGHIS and MOOSE prepare the newspapers.

JOHNNY: *(Indicating OMAR)* That kid. We were like that.

GENGHIS: *(Sneezing over MOOSE's face)* You don't believe in nothing.

16. Int. Underground garage. Day.

UNCLE NASSER's garage. It's a small private place where wealthy businessmen keep their cars during the day. It's almost full and contains about fifty cars–all Volvos, Rolls-Royces, Mercedes, Rovers, etc.

At the end of the garage is a small glassed-in office.

OMAR is walking down the ramp and into the garage.

17. Int. Garage office. Day.

The glassed-in office contains a desk, a filing cabinet, a typewriter, phone etc. With NASSER is SALIM.

SALIM is a Pakistani in his late thirties, well-dressed in an expensive, smooth and slightly vulgar way. He moves restlessly about the office. Then he notices OMAR wandering about the garage.
He watches him.

Meanwhile, NASSER is speaking on the phone in the background.

NASSER: (*Into phone*) We've got one parking space, yes. It's £25 a week. And from this afternoon we provide a special on the premises 'clean-the car' service. New thing.
(From SALIM's POV in the office, through the glass, we see OMAR trying the door of one of the cars. SALIM goes quickly out of the office.)

18. Int. Garage. Day.

SALIM stands outside the office and shouts at OMAR. The sudden sharp voice in the echoing garage.

SALIM: Hey! Is that your car? Why are you feeling it up then? (*OMAR looks at him.*) Come here. Here, I said.

19. Int. Garage office. Day.

NASSER puts down the phone.

20. Int. Garage office. Day.

NASSER is embracing OMAR vigorously, squashing him to him and bashing him lovingly on the back.

NASSER: (*Introducing him to SALIM*) This one who nearly beat you up is Salim. You'll see a lot of him.

SALIM: (*Shaking hands with OMAR*) I've heard many great things about your father.

NASSER: (*To OMAR*) I must see him. Oh God, how have I got time to do anything?

SALIM: You're too busy keeping this damn country in the black.
Someone's got to do it.

NASSER: (*To OMAR*) Your Papa, he got thrown out of that clerk's job I fixed him with? He was pissed?

(*OMAR nods. NASSER looks regretfully at the boy.*)
Can you wash a car?
(*OMAR looks uncertain.*)

SALIM: Have you washed a car before?
(*OMAR nods.*)
Your uncle can't pay you much. But you'll be able to afford a decent shirt and you'll be with your own people. Not in a dole queue. Mrs Thatcher will be pleased with me.

29. Ext. Country lane. Evening.

OMAR, in the old convertible, speeds along a country lane in Kent.

The car has its roof down, although its raining. Loud music playing on the radio.

He turns into the drive of a large detached house. The house is brightly lit. There are seven or eight cars in the drive. OMAR sits there a moment, music blaring.

30. Int. Living room in Nasser's house. Evening.

A large living room furnished in the modern style. A shy OMAR has been led in by BILQUIS, Nasser's wife. She is a shy, middle-aged Pakistani woman. She speaks and understands English, but is uncertain in the language. But she is warm and friendly.

OMAR has already been introduced to most of the women in the room.

There are five women there: a selection of wives; plus Bilquis's three daughters. The eldest, TANIA, is in her early twenties.

CHERRY, Salim's Anglo-Indian wife is there.

Some of the women are wearing saris or salwar kamiz, though not necessarily only the Pakistani women.

TANIA wears jeans and T-Shirt. She watches OMAR all through this and OMAR, when he can, glances at her. She is attracted to him.

BILQUIS: (*To OMAR*) And this is Salim's wife, Cherry. And of course you remember our three naughty daughters.

CHERRY: (*Ebulliently to BILQUIS*) He has his family's cheekbones, Bilquis. (*To OMAR.*) I know all your gorgeous family in Karachi.

OMAR: (*This is a faux pas*) You've been there?

CHERRY: You stupid, what a stupid, it's my home. Could anyone in their right mind call this silly little island off Europe their home? Every day in Karachi, every day your other uncles and cousins are at our house for bridge, booze and VCR.

BILQUIS: Cherry, my little nephew knows nothing of that life there.

CHERRY: Oh God, I'm so sick of hearing about these in-betweens. People should make up their minds where they are.

TANIA: Uncle's next door. (*Leading him away. Quietly.*) Can you see me later? I'm so bored with these people.

(*CHERRY stares at TANIA, not approving of this whispering and cousin-closeness.* Tania *glares back defiantly at her. BILQUIS looks warmly at OMAR.*)

35. Ext. Nasser's drive. Night.

OMAR has come out of the house and into the drive. A strange sight: SALIM staggering about drunkenly. The ENGLISHMAN, ZAKI and SALIM try to get him into the car. SALIM screams at ZAKI.

SALIM: Don't you owe me money? Why not? You usually owe me money! Here, take this! Borrow it! (*And he starts to scatter money about.*) Pick it up!

(*ZAKI starts picking it up. He is afraid.*)

CHERRY: (*To OMAR*) Drive us back, will you. Pick up your own car tomorrow. SALIM is not feeling well.

(As ZAKI bends over, SALIM who is laughing, goes to kick him. BILQUIS stands at the window watching all this.)

36. Int. Salim's car, driving into South London. Night.

OMAR driving SALIM's car enthusiastically into London. CHERRY and SALIM are in the back. The car comes to a stop at traffic lights.

On the adjacent pavement outside a chip shop a group of LADS are kicking cans about. The LADS include MOOSE and GENGHIS.

A lively street of the illuminated shops, amusement arcades and late-night shops of South London.

MOOSE notices that Pakistanis are in the car. And he indicates to the others.

The LADS gather round the car and bang on it and shout. From inside the car this noise is terrifying. CHERRY starts to scream.

SALIM: Drive, you bloody fool, drive!

(But MOOSE climbs on the bonnet of the car and squashes his arse grotesquely against the windscreen. Faces squash against the other windows.

Looking out of the side window OMAR sees JOHNNY standing to one side of the car, not really part of the car climbing and banging.

Impulsively, unafraid, OMAR gets out of the car.)

37. Ext. Street. Night.

OMAR walks past GENGHIS and MOOSE and the others to the embarrassed JOHNNY. CHERRY is yelling after him from inside the open-doored car.

The LADS are alert and ready for violence but are confused by OMAR's obvious friendship with JOHNNY.

OMAR sticks out his hand and JOHNNY takes it.

OMAR: It's me.

JOHNNY: I know who it is.

OMAR: How are yer? Working? What you doing now then?

JOHNNY: Oh, this kinda thing.

CHERRY: *(Yelling from the car)* Come on, come on!

(The LADS laugh at her. SALIM is hastily giving MOOSE cigarettes.)

JOHNNY: What are you now, chauffeur?
OMAR: No. I'm on to something.
JOHNNY: What?
OMAR: I'll let you know. Still living in the same place?
JOHNNY: Na, don't get on with me mum and dad. You?
OMAR: She died last year, my mother. Jumped on to the railway line.
JOHNNY: Yeah. I heard. All the trains stopped.
OMAR: I'm still there. Got the number?
JOHNNY: (*Indicates the LADS*) Like me friends?
(*CHERRY starts honking the car horn. The LADS cheer.*)
OMAR: Ring us then.
JOHNNY: I will. (*Indicates car.*) Leave'em there. We can do something. Now. Just us.
OMAR: Can't.
(OMAR touches JOHNNY's arm and runs back to the car.)

38. Int. Car. Night.

They continue to drive. CHERRY is screaming at OMAR.
CHERRY: What the hell were you doing?
(*SALIM slaps her.*)
SALIM: He saved our bloody arses! (*To OMAR, grabbing him round the neck and pressing his face close to his.*) I'm going to see you're all right!

39. Int. Papa's room. Night.

OMAR has got home. He creeps into the flat. He goes carefully along the hall, fingertips on familiar wall.

He goes into PAPA's room. No sign of PAPA. PAPA is on the balcony. Just a shadow.

40. Ext. Balcony. Night.

PAPA is swaying on the balcony like a little tree. PAPA's pyjama bottoms have fallen down. And he's just about maintaining himself vertically. His hair has fallen across his terrible face. A train bangs towards him, rushing out of the darkness. And PAPA sways precariously towards it.

OMAR: (*Screams above the noise*) What are you doing?
PAPA: I want to pee.
OMAR: Can't you wait for me to take you!
PAPA: My prick will drop off before you show up these days.
OMAR: (*Pulling up Papa's bottoms*) You know who I met? Johnny. Johnny.
PAPA: The boy who came here one day dressed as a fascist with a quarter inch of hair?
OMAR: He was a friend once. For years.
PAPA: There were days when he didn't deserve your admiration so much.
OMAR: Christ, I've known him since I was five.
PAPA: He went too far. They hate us in England. And all you do is kiss their arses and think of yourself as a little Britisher!

41. Int. Papa's room. Night.

They are inside the room now, and OMAR shuts the doors.

OMAR: I'm being promoted. To uncle's laundrette.
(*PAPA pulls a pair of socks from his pyjama pockets and thrusts them at OMAR.*)
PAPA: Illustrate your washing methods!
(*OMAR throws the socks across the room.*)

42. Ext. South London street. Day.

NASSER and OMAR get out of Nasser's car and walk over the road to the laundrette. It's called 'Churchills'. It's broad and spacious and in bad condition. It's situated in an area of run-down second-hand shops, betting shops, grocers with their windows boarded-up, etc.

NASSER: It's nothing but a toilet and a youth club now. A finger up my damn arse.

45. Int. Back room of laundrette. Day.

OMAR sitting gloomily in the back room. The door to the main area open. KIDS push each other about. Straight customers are intimidated.

From OMAR's POV through the laundrette windows, we see SALIM getting out of his car. SALIM walks in through the laundrette, quickly. Comes into the back room, slamming the door behind him.

SALIM: Get up! (*OMAR gets up. SALIM rams the back of a chair under the door handle.*) I've had trouble here.

OMAR: Salim, please. I don't know how to make this place work. I'm afraid I've made a fool of myself.

SALIM: You'll never make a penny out of this. Your uncle's given you a dead duck. That's why I've decided to help you financially. (*He gives him a piece of paper with an address on it. He also gives him money.*) Go to this house near the airport. Pick up some video cassettes and bring them to my flat. That's all.

46. Int. Salim's flat. Evening.

The flat is large and beautiful. Some Sindhi music playing. SALIM comes out of the bathroom wearing only a towel round his waist. And a plastic shower cap. He is smoking a fat joint.

CHERRY goes into another room.

OMAR stands there with the cassettes in his arms. SALIM indicates them.

SALIM: Put them. Relax. No problems? *(SALIM gives him the joint and OMAR takes a hit on it. SALIM points at the walls. Some erotic and some very good paintings.)* One of the best collections of recent Indian paintings. I patronize many painters. I won't be a minute. Watch something if you like. *(SALIM goes back into the bedroom. OMAR puts one of the cassettes he has brought into the VCR. But there's nothing on the tape. Just a screenful of static.*

Meanwhile, OMAR makes a call, taking the number off a piece of paper.)

OMAR: (*Into phone*) Can I speak to Johnny? D'you know where he's staying? Are you sure? Just wanted to help him. Please, if you see him, tell him to ring Omo.

47. Int. Salim's flat. Evening.

Dressed now, and ready to go out, SALIM comes quickly into the room. He picks up the video cassettes and realizes one is being played. SALIM screams savagely at OMAR.

SALIM: Is that tape playing? (*OMAR nods.*) What the hell are you doing? (*He pulls the tape out of the VCR and examines it.*)

OMAR: Just watching something, Salim.

SALIM: Not these! Who gave you permission to touch these? (*OMAR grabs the tape from SALIM*'s *hand.*)

OMAR: It's just a tape!

SALIM: Not to me!

OMAR: What are you doing? What business, Salim? (*SALIM pushes OMAR hard and OMAR crashes backwards across the room. As he gets up quickly to react SALIM is at him, shoving him back down, viciously. He puts his foot on OMAR's nose.*

CHERRY watches him coolly, leaning against a door jamb.)

SALIM: Nasser tells me you're ambitious to do something. But twice you failed your exams. You've done nothing with the laundrette and now you bugger me up. You've got too much white blood. It's made you weak like those pale-faced adolescents that call us wog. You know what I do to them? I take out this. (*He takes out a pound note. He tears it to pieces.*) I say: your English pound is worthless. It's worthless like you, Omar, are worthless. Your whole great family—rich and powerful over there—is let down by you.

(*OMAR gets up slowly.*)

Now fuck off.

OMAR: I'll do something to you for this.

SALIM: I'd be truly happy to see you try.

48. Ext. Outside laundrette. Evening.

OMAR, depressed after his humiliation at Salim's, drives slowly past the laundrette. Music plays over this. It's raining and the laundrette looks grim and hopeless.

OMAR sees *GENGHIS and MOOSE. He drives up alongside them.*

OMAR: Seen Johnny?
GENGHIS: Get back to the jungle, wog boy.
(*MOOSE kicks the side of the car.*)

49. Int. Papa's room. Evening.

OMAR is cutting PAPA's long toenails with a large pair of scissors. OMAR's face is badly bruised. PAPA jerks about, pouring himself a drink. So OMAR has to keep grabbing at his feet. The skin on PAPA's legs is peeling through lack of vitamins.

PAPA: Those people are too tough for you. I'll tell Nasser you're through with them. (*PAPA dials. We hear it ringing in NASSER'S house. He puts the receiver to one side to pick up his drink. He looks at OMAR who wells with anger and humiliation. TANIA answers.*)

TANIA: Hallo.

(*OMAR moves quickly and breaks the connection.*)

PAPA: (*Furious*) Why do that, you useless fool?

(OMAR grabs PAPA's foot and starts on the toe job again. The phone starts to ring. PAPA pulls away and OMAR jabs him with the scissors. And PAPA bleeds. OMAR answers the phone.)

OMAR: Hallo. (*Pause.*) Johnny

PAPA: (*Shouts over*) I'll throw you out of this bloody flat, you're nothing but a bum liability!

(*But OMAR is smiling into the phone and talking to JOHNNY, a finger in one ear.*)

50. Int. The laundrette. Day.

OMAR is showing JOHNNY round the laundrette.

JOHNNY: I'm dead impressed by all this.

OMAR: You were the one at school. The one they liked,.

JOHNNY: (*Sarcastic*) All the Pakis liked me.

OMAR: I've been through it. With my parents and that. And with people like you. But now there's some things I want to do. Some pretty big things I've got in mind. I need to raise money to make this place good. I want you to help me do that. And I want you to work here with me.

JOHNNY: What kinda work is it?
OMAR: Variety. Variety of menial things.
JOHNNY: Cleaning windows kinda thing, yeah?
OMAR: Yeah. Sure. And clean out those bastards, will ya?
(*OMAR indicates the sitting KIDS playing about on the benches.*)
JOHNNY: Now?
OMAR: I'll want everything done now. That's the only attitude if you want to do anything big.
(*JOHNNY goes to the KIDS and stands above them. Slowly he removes his watch and puts it in his pocket. This is a strangely threatening gesture. The KIDS rise and walk out one by one. One KID resents this. He pushes JOHNNY suddenly. JOHNNY kicks him hard.*)

51. Ext. Outside the laundrette. Day.

Continuous. The kicked KID shoots across the pavement and crashes into SALIM who is getting out of his car. SALIM pushes away the frantic arms and legs and goes quickly into the laundrette.

52. Int. Laundrette. Day.

SALIM drags the reluctant OMAR by the arm into the back room of the laundrette. JOHNNY watches them, then follows.

53. Int. Back room of laundrette. Day.

SALIM lets go of OMAR and grabs a chair, to stuff under the door handle as before. OMAR suddenly snatches the chair from him and puts it down slowly. And JOHNNY, taking OMAR's lead, sticks his big boot in the door as SALIM attempts to slam it.

SALIM: Christ. Just go on one little errand for me, eh? (*He opens OMAR's fingers and presses a piece of paper into his hand.*) Like before. For me.
OMAR: For fifty quid as well.
SALIM: You little bastard.
(*OMAR turns away. JOHNNY turns away too, mocking SALIM, parodying OMAR.*)
All right.

54. Int. Hotel room. Dusk.

OMAR is standing in a hotel room. A modern high building with a view over London. He is with a middle-aged Pakistani who is wearing salwar kamiz. Suitcases on the floor.

The MAN has a long white beard. Suddenly he peels it off and hands it to OMAR. OMAR is astonished. The man laughs uproariously.

55. Int. Laundrette. Evening.

JOHNNY is doing a service wash in the laundrette. OMAR comes in quickly, the beard in a plastic bag. He puts the beard on.

JOHNNY: You fool.

(OMAR pulls JOHNNY towards the back room.)

OMAR: I've sussed Salim's game. This is going to finance our whole future.

56. Int. Back room of laundrette. Day.

JOHNNY and OMAR sitting at the desk. JOHNNY is picking the back of the beard with a pair of scissors. The door to the laundrette is closed.

JOHNNY carefully pulls plastic bags out of the back of the beard. He looks enquiringly at OMAR. OMAR confidently indicates that he should open one of them. JOHNNY looks doubtfully at them. OMAR pulls the chair closer. JOHNNY snips a corner off the bag. He opens it and tastes the powder on his finger. He nods at OMAR. JOHNNY quickly starts stuffing the bags back in the beard.

OMAR gets up.

OMAR: Take them out. You know where to sell this stuff. Yes? Don't you?

JOHNNY: I wouldn't be working for you now if I wanted to go on being a bad boy.

OMAR: This means more. Real work. Expansion.

(*JOHNNY reluctantly removes the rest of the packets from the back of the beard.*)

We'll re-sell it fast. Tonight.

JOHNNY: Salim'll kill us.

OMAR: Why should he find out it's us? Better get this back to him. Come on. I couldn't be doing any of this without you.

82. Int. Laundrette. Day.

The day of the opening of the laundrette.

The laundrette is finished. And the place looks terrific: pot plants; a TV on which videos are showing; a sound system; and the place is brightly painted and clean.

OMAR is splendidly dressed. He is walking round the place, drink in hand, looking it over.

Outside, local people look in curiously and press their faces against the glass. Two old ladies are patiently waiting to be let in. A queue of people with washing gradually forms.

In the open door of the back room JOHNNY is changing into his new clothes.

JOHNNY: Let's open. The world's waiting.

OMAR: I've invited Nasser to the launch. And Papa's coming. They're not here yet. Papa hasn't been out for months. We can't move till he arrives.

JOHNNY: What time did they say they'd be here?

OMAR: An hour ago.

JOHNNY: They're not gonna come, then.

(OMAR looks hurt. JOHNNY indicates that OMAR should go to him. He goes to him.)

83. Int. Back room of laundrette. Day.

The back room has also been done up, in a bright high-tech style. And a two-way mirror has been installed, through which they can see into the laundrette.

OMAR watches JOHNNY, sitting on the desk.

JOHNNY: Shall I open the champagne then? (*He opens the bottle.*)

OMAR: Didn't I predict this? (*They look through the mirror and through the huge windows of the laundrette to the patient punters waiting outside.*) This whole stinking area's on its knees begging for clean clothes. Jesus Christ.

(*OMAR touches his own shoulders. JOHNNY massages him.*)

JOHNNY: Let's open up.

OMAR: Not till Papa comes. Remember? He went out of his way with you. And with all my friends. (*Suddenly harsh.*) He did, didn't he!

JOHNNY: Omo. What are you on about, mate?

OMAR: About how years later he saw the same boys. And what were they doing?

JOHNNY: What?

OMAR: What were they doing on marches through Lewisham? It was bricks and bottles and Union Jacks. It was immigrants out. It was kill us. People we knew. And it was you. He saw you marching. You saw his face, watching you. Don't deny it. We were there when you went past. (*OMAR is being held by JOHNNY, in his arms.*) Papa hated himself and his job. He was afraid on the street for me. And he took it out on her. And she couldn't bear it. Oh, such failure, such emptiness.

(*JOHNNY kisses OMAR then leaves him, sitting away from him slightly. OMAR touches him, asking him to hold him.*)

Sara Suleri

Sara Suleri grew up in England and different Pakistani cities. After graduating from Kinnaird College Lahore, she went on to Punjab University and then the United States for higher education. She has lived there since and is now a Professor of English at Yale University. Her father, Z. A. Suleri is a well-known Pakistani journalist and her Welsh mother was a Professor of English at Punjab University. Her autobiographical book, *Meatless Days,* is a portrait of family life and its first chapter, 'Excellent Things in Women', won the 1987 Pushcart Prize. Sara Suleri is also the author of *The Rhetoric of English in India*, a scholarly dissertation on South Asian writers in English, and is working on a book about poetry and politics in British India.

Meatless Days is essentially a creative memoir, a collage about love, memory, exile and loss, crafted into chapters by metaphor. The basic structure revolves around human frailty and mortality, at the heart of which are the deaths of her mother and later, Ifat, her elder sister, both victims of hit-and-run accidents.

FROM *MEATLESS DAYS*

Excellent Things in Women

Leaving Pakistan was, of course, tantamount to giving up the company of women. I can tell this only to someone like Anita, in all the faith that she will understand, as we go perambulating through the grimness of New Haven and feed on the pleasures of our conversational way. Dale, who lives in Boston, would also understand. She will one day write a book about the stern and secretive life of breast-feeding and is partial to fantasies that culminate in an abundance of resolution. And Fawzi, with a grimace of recognition, knows because she knows the impulse to forget.

To a stranger or an acquaintance, however, some vestigial remoteness obliges me to explain that my reference is to a place where the concept of woman was not really part of an available vocabulary: we were too busy for that, just living, and conducting precise negotiations with what it meant to be a sister or a child or a wife or a mother or a servant. By this point admittedly I am damned by my own discourse, and doubly damned when I add yes, once in a while, we naturally thought of ourselves as women, but only in some perfunctory biological way that we happened on perchance. Or else it was a hugely practical joke, we thought, hidden somewhere among our clothes. But formulating that definition is about as impossible as attempting to locate the luminous qualities of an Islamic landscape, which can on occasion generate such aesthetically pleasing moments of life. My audience is lost, and angry to be lost, and both of us must find some token of exchange for this failed conversation. I try to lay the subject down and change its clothes, but before I know it, it has sprinted off evilly in the direction of ocular evidence. It goads me into saying, with the defiance of a plea, 'You did not deal with Dadi.'

Dadi, my father's mother, was born in Meerut toward the end of the last century. She was married at sixteen and widowed in her thirties, and by her latter decades could never exactly recall how many children she had borne. When India was partitioned, in August of 1947, she moved her thin pure Urdu into the Punjab of Pakistan and waited for the return of her eldest son, my father. He had gone careering off to a place called Inglestan, or England, fired by one of the several enthusiasms made available by the proliferating talk of independence. Dadi was peeved. She had long since dispensed with any loyalties larger than the pitiless give-and-take of people who are forced to live together in the same place, and she resented independence for the distances it made. She was not among those who, on the fourteenth of August, unfurled flags and festivities against the backdrop of people running and cities burning. About that era she would only say, looking up sour and cryptic over the edge of her Quran, 'And I was also burned.' She was, but that came years later.

By the time I knew her, Dadi with her flair for drama had allowed life to sit so heavily upon her back that her spine wilted and froze into a perfect curve, and so it was in the posture of a shrimp that she went scuttling through the day. She either scuttled or did not: it all depended on the nature of her fight with the Devil. There were days when she so hated him that all she could do was stretch herself out straight and tiny on her bed, uttering most awful imprecations. Sometimes, to my mother's great distress, Dadi could berate Satan in full eloquence only after she had clambered on top of the dining-room table and lain there like a little holding centre piece. Satan was to blame: he had after all made her older son linger long enough in Inglestan to give up his rightful wife, a cousin, and take up instead with a white-legged woman. Satan had stolen away her only daughter Ayesha when Ayesha lay in childbirth. And he'd sent her youngest son to Swaziland, or Switzerland; her thin hand waved away such sophistries of name.

God she loved, and she understood him better than anyone. Her favourite days were those when she could circumnavigate both the gardener and my father, all in the solemn service of her God. With a pilfered knife, she'd wheedle her way to the nearest sapling in the garden, some sprightly poplar or a newly planted eucalyptus. She'd squat, she'd hack it down, and then she'd peel its bark away until she had a walking stick, all white and virgin and her own. It drove my father into tears of rage. He must have bought her a dozen walking sticks, one for each of our trips, to the mountains, but it was like assembling a row of briar pipes for one who will not smoke: Dadi had different aims. Armed with implements of her own creation, she would creep down the driveway unperceived to stop cars and people on the street and give them all the gossip that she had on God.

Food, too, could move her to intensities. Her eyesight always took a sharp turn for the worse over meals—she could point hazily at a perfectly ordinary potato and murmur with Adamic reverence, 'What *is* it, what *is* it called?' With some shortness of manner one of us would describe and catalogue the items on the table. '*Alu ka bhartha,*' Dadi repeated with wonderment and joy. 'Yes, Saira Begum, you can put some here.' 'Not too much,' she'd add pleadingly. For ritual had it that the more she demurred, the more she expected her plate to be piled with an amplitude her own politeness would never allow. The ritual happened three times a day.

We pondered it but never quite determined whether food or God constituted her most profound delight. Obvious problems, however, occurred whenever the two converged. One such occasion was the Muslim festival called Eid—not the one that ends the month of fasting, but the second Eid, which celebrates the seductions of the Abraham story in a remarkably literal way. In Pakistan, at least, people buy sheep or goats beforehand and fatten them up for weeks with delectables. Then, on the appointed day, the animals are chopped, in place of sons, and neighbours graciously exchange silver trays heaped with raw and quivering meat. Following Eid prayers the men come home, and the animal is killed, and shortly thereafter rush out of the kitchen steaming plates of grilled lung and liver, of a freshness quite superlative.

It was a freshness to which my Welsh mother did not immediately take. She observed the custom but discerned in it a conundrum that allowed no ready solution. Liberal to an extravagant degree on thoughts abstract, she found herself to be remarkably squeamish about particular things. Chopping up animals for God was one. She could not locate the metaphor and was uneasy when obeisance played such a truant to the metaphoric realm. My father the writer quite agreed: he was so civilized in those days.

Dadi didn't agree. She pined for choppable things. Once she made the mistake of buying a baby goat and bringing him home months in advance of Eid. She wanted to guarantee the texture of his festive flesh by a daily feeding of tender peas and clarified butter. Ifat, Shahid, and I greeted a goat into the family with boisterous rapture, and soon after he ravished us completely when we found him at the washing line nonchalantly eating Shahid's pajamas. Of course there was no argument: the little goat was our delight, and even Dadi knew there was no killing him. He became my brother's and my sister's and my first pet, and he grew huge, a big and grinning thing.

Years after, Dadi had her will. We were old enough, she must have thought, to set the house sprawling, abstracted, into a multitude of secrets. This was true, but still we all noticed one another's secretive ways. When, the day before Eid, our Dadi disappeared, my brothers and sisters and I just shook our heads. We hid the fact from my father, who at this time of life had begun to equate petulance with extreme vociferation. So we went about our jobs and tried to be Islamic for a day. We waited to sight moons on the wrong occasion, and watched the food come into lavishment. Dried dates change shape when they are soaked in milk, and carrots rich and strange turn magically sweet when deftly covered with green nutty shavings and smatterings of silver. Dusk was sweet as we sat out, the day's work done, in an evening garden. Lahore spread like peace around us. My father spoke, and when Papa talked, it was of Pakistan. But we were glad, then, at being audience to that familiar conversation, till his voice looked up, and failed. There was Dadi making her return, and she was prodigal. Like a question mark interested only in its own conclusions, her body crawled through the gates. Our guests were spellbound, then they looked away. Dadi, moving in her eerie crab formations, ignored the hangman's rope she firmly held as behind her in the gloaming minced, hugely affable, a goat.

That goat was still smiling the following day when Dadi's victory brought the butcher, who came and went just as he should on Eid. The goat was killed and cooked: a scrawny beast that required much cooking and never melted into succulence, he winked and glistened on our plates as we sat eating him on Eid. Dadi ate, that is: Papa had taken his mortification to some distant corner of the house; Ifat refused to chew on hemp; Tillat and Irfan gulped their baby sobs over such a slaughter. 'Honestly,' said Mamma, 'honestly.' For Dadi had successfully cut through tissues of festivity just as the butcher slit the goat, but there was something else that she was eating with that meat. I saw it in her concentration; I know that she was making God talk to her as to Abraham and was showing him what she could do—for him—to sons. God didn't dare, and she ate on alone.

Of those middle years it is hard to say whether Dadi was literally left alone or whether her bodily presence always emanated a quality of being apart and absorbed. In the winter I see her alone, painstakingly dragging her straw mat out to the courtyard at the back of the house and following the rich course of the afternoon sun. With her would go her Quran, a metal basin in which she could wash her hands, and her ridiculously heavy spouted waterpot, that was made of brass. None of us, according to Dadi, were quite pure enough to transport these particular items, but the rest of her paraphernalia we were allowed to carry. These were baskets of her writing and sewing materials and her bottle of pungent and Dadi-like bitter oils, with which she'd coat the papery skin that held her brittle bones. And in the summer, when the night created an illusion of possible coolness and everyone held their breath while waiting for a thin and intermittent breeze, Dadi would be on the roof, alone. Her summer bed was a wooden frame latticed with a sweet-smelling rope, much aerated at its foot. She'd lie there all night until the wild monsoons would wake the lightest and the soundest sleeper into a rapturous welcome of rain.

In Pakistan, of course, there is no spring but only a rapid elision from winter into summer, which is analogous to the absence of a recognizable loneliness from the behaviour of that climate. In a similar fashion it was hard to distinguish between Dadi with people and Dadi alone: she was merely impossibly unable to remain unnoticed. In the winter, when she was not writing or reading, she would sew for her delight tiny and magical reticules out of old silks and fragments she had saved, palm-sized cloth bags that would unravel into the precision of secret and more secret pockets. But none such pockets did she ever need to hide, since something of Dadi always remained intact, however much we sought to open her. Her discourse, for example, was impervious to penetration, so that when one or two of us remonstrated with her in a single hour, she never bothered to distinguish her replies. Instead she would pronounce generically and prophetically, 'The world takes on a single face.' 'Must you, Dadi...,' I'd begin, to be halted then by her great complaint: 'The world takes on a single face.'

It did. And often it was a countenance of some delight, for Dadi also loved the accidental jostle with things belligerent. As she went perambulating through the house, suddenly she'd hear Shahid, her first grandson, telling me or one of my sisters we were vile, we were disgusting women. And Dadi, who never addressed any one of us girls without first conferring the title of lady—so we were 'Tillat Begum,' 'Ifat Begum,' 'Nuzhat Begum,' 'Saira Begum'—would halt in reprimand and tell her grandson never to call her granddaughters women. 'What else shall I call them, men?' Shahid yelled. 'Men!' said Dadi, 'Men! There is more goodness in a woman's little finger than in the benighted mind of man.' 'Hear, hear, Dadi! *Hanh, hanh,* Dadi!' my sisters cried. 'For men,' said Dadi, shaking the name off her fingertips like some unwanted water, 'live as though they were unsuckled things.' 'And heaven,' she grimly added, 'is the thing Muhammad says (peace be upon him) lies beneath the feet of women!' 'But he was a man,' Shahid still would rage, if he weren't laughing, as all of us were laughing, while Dadi sat among us as a belle or a May queen.

Toward the end of the middle years my father stopped speaking to his mother, and the atmosphere at home appreciably improved. They secretly hit upon a novel histrionics that took the place of their daily battle. They chose the curious way of silent things: twice a day Dadi would leave her room and walk the long length of the corridor to my father's room. There she merely peered round the door, as though to see if he were real. Each time she peered, my father would interrupt whatever adult thing he might be doing in order to enact a silent paroxysm, an elaborate facial pantomime of revulsion and affront. At teatime in particular, when Papa would want the world to congregate in his room, Dadi came to peer her ghostly peer. Shortly thereafter conversation was bound to fracture, for we could not drown the fact that Dadi, invigorated by an outcast's strength, was sitting alone in the dining room, chanting an appeal: 'God give me tea, God give me tea.'

At about this time Dadi stopped smelling old and smelled instead of something equivalent to death. It would have been easy to notice if she had been dying, but instead she conducted the change as a refinement, a subtle gradation, just as her annoying little stove could shift its hanging odours away from smoke and into ash. During the middle years there had been something more defined about her being, which sat in the world as solely its own context. But Pakistan increasingly complicated the question of context, as though history, like a pestilence, forbid any definition outside relations to its fevered sleep. So it was simple for my father to ignore the letters that Dadi had begun to write to him every other day in her fine wavering script, letters of advice about the house or the children or the servants. Or she transcribed her complaint: 'Oh my son, Zia. Do you think your son, Shahid, upon whom God bestow a thousand blessings, should be permitted to lift up his grandmother's chair and carry it into the courtyard when his grandmother is seated in it?' She had cackled in a combination of delight and virgin joy when Shahid had so transported her, but that little crackling sound she omitted from her letter. She ended it, and all her notes, with her single endearment. It was a phrase to halt and arrest when Dadi actually uttered it: her solitary piece of tenderness was an injunction, really, to her world—'Keep on living,' she would say.

Between that phrase and the great Dadi conflagration comes the era of the trying times. They began in the winter war of 1971, when East Pakistan became Bangladesh and Indira Gandhi hailed the demise of the two-nation theory. Ifat's husband was off fighting, and we spent the war together with her father-in-law, the brigadier, in the pink house on the hill. It was an ideal location for anti aircraft guns, so there was a bevy of soldiers and weaponry installed upon our roof. During each air raid the brigadier would stride purposefully into the garden and bark commands at them, as though the crux of the war rested upon his stiff upper lip. Then Dacca fell, and General Yahya came on television to resign the presidency and concede defeat. 'Drunk, by God!' barked the brigadier as we sat watching, 'Drunk!'

The following morning General Yahya's mistress came to mourn with us over breakfast, lumbering in draped with swathes of over-scented silk. The brigadier lit an English cigarette—he was frequently known to avow that Pakistani cigarettes gave him a cuff—and bit on his moustache. 'Yes,' he barked, 'These are trying times.' 'Oh yes, Gul,' Yahya's mistress wailed, 'These are such trying times.' She gulped on her own eloquence, her breakfast bosom quaked, and then resumed authority over that dangling sentence: 'It is so trying,' she continued, 'I find it so trying, it is trying to us all, to live in these trying, trying times.' Ifat's eyes met mine in complete accord: mistress transmogrified to muse; Bhutto returned from the UN to put Yahya under house arrest and become the first elected president of Pakistan; Ifat's husband went to India as a prisoner of war for two years; my father lost his newspaper. We had entered the era of the trying times.

Dadi didn't notice the war, just as she didn't really notice the proliferation of her great-grandchildren, for Ifat and Nuzzi conceived at the drop of a hat and kept popping babies out for our delight. Tillat and I felt favoured at this vicarious taste of motherhood: we learned to become the enviable personage, a *khala,* mother's sister, and when our married sisters came to visit with their entourage, we revelled in the exercise of *khala*-love. I once asked Dadi how many sisters she had had. She looked up through the oceanic grey of her cataracted eyes and answered, 'I forget.'

The children helped, because we needed distraction, there being then in Pakistan a musty taste of defeat to all our activities. The children gave us something, but they also took something away—they initiated a slight displacement of my mother. Because her grandchildren would not speak any English, she could not read stories as of old. Urdu always remained a shyness on her tongue, and as the babies came and went she let something of her influence imperceptibly recede, as though she occupied an increasingly private space. Her eldest son was in England by then so Mamma found herself assuming the classic posture of an Indian woman who sends away her sons and runs the risk of seeing them succumb to the great alternatives represented by the West. It was a position that preoccupied her; and without my really noticing what was happening, she quietly handed over many of her wifely duties to her two remaining daughters—to Tillat and to me. In the summer, once the ferocity of the afternoon sun had died down, it was her pleasure to go out into the garden on her own. There she would stand, absorbed and abstracted, watering the driveway and breathing in the heady smell of water on hot dust. I'd watch her often, from my room upstairs. She looked like a girl.

We were aware of something, of a reconfiguration in the air, but could not exactly tell where it would lead us. Dadi now spoke mainly to herself; even the audience provided by the deity had dropped away. Somehow there wasn't a proper balance between the way things came and the way they went, as Halima the cleaning woman knew full well when she looked at me intently, asking a question that had no question in it: 'Do I grieve, or do I celebrate?' Halima had given birth to her latest son the night her older child died in screams of meningitis; once heard, never to be forgotten. She came back to work a week later, and we were talking as we put away the family's winter clothes into vast metal trunks. For in England, they would call it spring.

We felt a quickening urgency of change drown our sense of regular direction, as though something were bound to happen soon but not knowing what it would be was making history nervous. And so we were not really that surprised, then, to find ourselves living through the summer of the trials by fire. It climaxed when Dadi went up in a little ball of flames, but somehow sequentially related were my mother's trip to England to tend her dying mother, and the night I beat up Tillat, and the evening I nearly castrated my little brother, runt of the litter, serious-eyed Irfan.

It was an accident on both our parts. I was in the kitchen, so it must have been a Sunday, when Allah Ditta the cook took the evenings off. He was a mean-spirited man with an incongruously delicate touch when it came to making food. On Sunday at midday he would bluster one of us into the kitchen and show us what he had prepared for the evening meal, leaving strict and belligerent instructions about what would happen if we overheated this or dared brown that. So I was in the kitchen heating up some food when Farni came back from playing hockey, an ominous asthmatic rattle in his throat. He, the youngest, had been my parents' gravest infant: in adolescence he remained a gentle invalid. Of course he pretended otherwise, and was loud and raucous, but it never worked.

Tillat and I immediately turned on him with the bullying litany that actually can be quite soothing, the invariable female reproach to the returning male. He was to do what he hated—stave off his disease by sitting over a bowl of camphor and boiling water and inhaling its acrid fumes. I insisted that he sit on the cook's little stool in the kitchen, holding the bowl of medicated water on his lap, so that I could cook, and Farni could not cheat, and I could time each minute he should sit there thus confined. We seated him and flounced a towel on his reluctant head. The kitchen reeked jointly of cumin and camphor, and he sat skinny and penitent and swathed for half a minute, and then was begging to be done. I slammed down the carving knife and screamed 'Irfan!' with such ferocity that he jumped, figuratively and literally, right out of his skin. The bowl of water emptied onto him, and with a gurgling cry Irfan leapt up, tearing at his steaming clothes. He clutched at his groin, and everywhere he touched, the skin slid off, so that between his fingers his penis easily unsheathed, a blanched and fiery grape. 'What's happening?' screamed Papa from his room; 'What's happening?' echoed Dadi's wail from the opposite end of the house. What was happening was that I was holding Farni's shoulders, trying to stop him from jumping up and down, but I was jumping too, while Tillat just stood there frozen, frowning at his poor ravaged grapes.

This was June, and the white heat of summer. We spent the next few days laying ice on Farni's wounds: half the time I was allowed to stay with him, until the doctors suddenly remembered I was a woman and hurried me out when his body made crazy spastic reactions to its burns. Once things grew calmer and we were alone, Irfan looked away and said, 'I hope I didn't shock you, Sara.' I was so taken by tenderness for his bony convalescent body that it took me years to realize yes, something female in me had been deeply shocked.

Mamma knew nothing of this, of course. We kept it from her so she could concentrate on what had taken her back to the rocky coastline of Wales, to places she had not really revisited since she was a girl. She sat waiting with her mother, who was blind now and of a fine translucency, and both of them knew that they were waiting for her death. It was a peculiar posture for Mamma to maintain, but her quiet letters spoke mainly of the sharp astringent light that made the sea wind feel so brisk in Wales and so many worlds away from the deadly omnipresent weight of summer in Lahore. There in Wales one afternoon, walking childless among the brambles and the furze, Mamma realized that her childhood was distinctly lost. 'It was not that I wanted to feel more familiar,' she later told me, 'or that I was more used to feeling unfamiliar in Lahore. It's just that familiarity isn't important, really,' she murmured absently, 'it really doesn't matter at all.'

When Mamma was ready to return, she wired us her plans, and my father read the cable, kissed it, then put it in his pocket. I watched him and left startled, as we all did on the occasions when our parents' lives seemed to drop away before our eyes, leaving them youthfully engrossed in the illusion of knowledge conferred by love. We were so used to conceiving of them as parents moving in and out of hectic days that it always amused us, and touched us secretly, when they made quaint and punctilious returns to the amorous bond that had initiated their unlikely life together.

That summer while my mother was away, Tillat and I experienced a new bond of powerlessness, the white and shaking rage of sexual jealousy in parenthood. I had always behaved toward her as a contentious surrogate parent, but she had been growing beyond that scope and in her girlhood asking me for a formal acknowledgment of equality that I was loath to give. My reluctance was rooted in a helpless fear of what the world might do to her, for I was young and ignorant enough not to see that what I might do was worse. She went out one evening when my father was off on one of his many trips. The house was gaping emptily, and Tillat was very late. Allah Ditta had gone home, and Dadi and Irfan were sleeping; I read, and thought, and walked up and down the garden, and Tillat was very, very late. When she came back she wore that strange sheath of complacency and guilt which pleasure puts on faces very young. It smote an outrage in my heart until despite all resolutions to the contrary I heard myself hiss: 'And where were you?' Her return look was fearful and preening at the same time, and the next thing to be smitten was her face. 'Don't, Sara,' Tillat said in her superior way, 'physical violence is so degrading.' 'To you, maybe,' I answered, and hit her once again.

It set a sorrowful bond between us, for we both felt complicity in the shamefulness that had made me seem righteous whereas I had felt simply jealous, which we tacitly agreed was a more legitimate thing to be. But we had lost something, a certain protective aura, some unspoken myth asserting that love between sisters at least was sexually innocent. Now we had to fold that vain belief away and stand in more naked relation to our affection. Till then we had associated such violence with all that was outside us, as though somehow the more history fractured, the more whole we would be. But we began to lose that sense of the differentiated identities of history and ourselves and became guiltily aware that we had known it all along, our part in the construction of unreality.

By this time, Dadi's burns were slowly learning how to heal. It was she who had given the summer its strange pace by nearly burning herself alive at its inception. On an early April night Dadi awoke, seized by a desperate need for tea. It was three in the morning, the household was asleep, so she was free to do the great forbidden thing of creeping into Allah Ditta's kitchen and taking charge, like a pixie in the night. As all of us had grown bored of predicting, one of her many cotton garments took to fire that truant night. Dadi, however, deserves credit for her resourceful voice, which wavered out for witness to her burning death. By the time Tillat awoke and found her, she was a little flaming ball: 'Dadi!' cried Tillat in the reproach of sleep, and beat her quiet with a blanket. In the morning we discovered that Dadi's torso had been almost consumed and little recognizable remained from collarbone to groin. The doctors bade us to some decent mourning.

But Dadi had different plans. She lived through her sojourn at the hospital; she weathered her return. Then, after six weeks at home, she angrily refused to be lugged like a chunk of meat to the doctor's for her daily change of dressings: 'Saira Begum will do it,' she announced. Thus developed my great intimacy with the fluid properties of human flesh. By the time Mamma left for England, Dadi's left breast was still coagulate and raw. Later, when Irfan got his burns, Dadi was growing pink and livid tightropes, strung from hip to hip in a flaming advertisement of life. And in the days when Tillat and I were wrestling, Dadi's vanished nipples started to congeal and convex their cavities into triumphant little love knots.

I learned about the specialization of beauty through that body. There were times, as with love, when I felt only disappointment, carefully easing off the dressings and finding again a piece of flesh that would not knit, happier in the texture of stubborn glue. But then on more exhilarating days I'd peel like an onion all her bandages away and suddenly discover I was looking down at some literal tenacity and was bemused at all the freshly withered shapes she could create. Each new striation was a victory to itself, and when Dadi's hairless groin solidified again and sent firm signals that her abdomen must do the same, I could have wept with glee.

After her immolation, Dadi's diet underwent some curious changes. At first her consciousness teetered too much for her to pray, but then as she grew stronger it took us a while to notice what was missing: she had forgotten prayer. It left her life as firmly as tobacco can leave the lives of only the most passionate smokers, and I don't know if she ever prayed again. At about this time, however, with the heavy-handed inevitability that characterized his relation to his mother, my father took to prayer. I came home one afternoon and looked for him in all the usual places, but he wasn't to be found. Finally I came across Tillat and asked her where Papa was. 'Praying,' she said. '*Praying?*' I said. 'Praying,' she said, and I felt most embarrassed. For us it was rather as though we had come upon the children playing some forbidden titillating game and decided it was wisest to ignore it calmly. In an unspoken way, though, I think we dimly knew we were about to witness Islam's departure from the land of Pakistan. The men would take it to the streets and make it vociferate, but the great romance between religion and the populace, the embrace that engendered Pakistan, was done. So Papa prayed, with the desperate order of a lover trying to converse life back into a finished love.

That was a change, when Dadi patched herself together again and forgot to put prayer back into its proper pocket, for God could now leave the home and soon would join the government. Papa prayed and fasted and went on pilgrimage and read the Quran aloud with most peculiar locutions. Occasionally we also caught him in nocturnal altercations that made him sound suspiciously like Dadi: we looked askance, but didn't say a thing. My mother was altogether admirable: she behaved as though she'd always known that she'd wed a swaying, chanting thing and that to register surprise now would be an impoliteness to existence. Her expression reminded me somewhat of the time when Ifat was eight and Mamma was urging her recalcitrance into some goodly task. Ifat postponed, and Mamma, always nifty with appropriate fables, quoted meaningfully: ' "I'll do it myself," said the little red hen.' Ifat looked up with bright affection. 'Good little red hen,' she murmured. Then a glance crossed my mother's face, a look between a slight smile and a quick rejection of the eloquent response, like a woman looking down and then away.

She looked like that at my father's sudden hungering for God, which was added to the growing number of subjects about which we, my mother and her daughters, silently decided we had no conversation. We knew there was something other than trying times ahead and would far rather hold our breath than speculate about what other surprises the era held up its capacious sleeve. Tillat and I decided to quash our dread of waiting around for change by changing for ourselves, before destiny took the time to come our way. I would move to America, and Tillat to Kuwait and marriage. To both declarations of intention my mother said 'I see,' and helped us in our preparations: she knew by then her elder son would not return, and was prepared to extend the courtesy of change to her daughters, too. We left, and Islam predictably took to the streets, shaking Bhutto's empire. Mamma and Dadi remained the only women in the house, the one untalking, the other unpraying.

Dadi behaved abysmally at my mother's funeral, they told me, and made them all annoyed. She set up loud and unnecessary lamentations in the dining room, somewhat like an heir apparent, as though this death had reinstated her as mother of the house. While Ifat and Nuzzi and Tillat wandered frozen-eyed, dealing with the roses and the ice, Dadi demanded an irritating amount of attention, stretching out supine and crying out, 'Your mother has betrayed your father; she has left him;

she has gone.' Food from respectful mourners poured in, caldron after caldron, and Dadi relocated a voracious appetite.

Years later, I was somewhat sorry that I had heard this tale, because it made me take affront. When I returned to Pakistan, I was too peeved with Dadi to find out how she was. Instead I listened to Ifat tell me about standing there in the hospital, watching the doctors suddenly pump upon my mother's heart—'I'd seen it on television,' she gravely said, 'I knew it was the end.' Mamma's students from the university had tracked down the rickshaw driver who had knocked her down: they'd pummelled him nearly to death and then camped out in our garden, sobbing wildly, all in hordes.

By this time Bhutto was in prison and awaiting trial, and General Zia was presiding over the Islamization of Pakistan. But we had no time to notice. My mother was buried at the nerve centre of Lahore, an unruly and dusty place, and my father immediately made arrangements to buy the plot of land next to her grave: 'We're ready when you are,' Shahid sang. Her tombstone bore some pretty Urdu poetry and a completely fictitious place of birth, because some details my father tended to forget. 'Honestly,' it would have moved his wife to say.

So I was angry with Dadi at that time and didn't stop to see her. I saw my mother's grave and then came back to America, hardly noticing when, six months later, my father called from London and mentioned Dadi was now dead. It happened in the same week that Bhutto finally was hanged, and our imaginations were consumed by that public and historical dying. Pakistan made rapid provisions not to talk about the thing that had been done, and somehow, accidentally, Dadi must have been mislaid into that larger decision, because she too ceased being a mentioned thing. My father tried to get back in time for the funeral, but he was so busy talking Bhutto-talk in England that he missed his flight and thus did not return. Luckily, Irfani was at home, and he saw Dadi to her grave.

Bhutto's hanging had the effect of making Pakistan feel unreliable, particularly to itself. Its landscape learned a new secretiveness, unusual for a formerly loquacious people. This may account for the fact that I have never seen my grandmother's grave and neither have my sisters. I think we would have tried, had we been together, despite the free-floating anarchy in the air that—like the heroin trade—made the world suspicious and afraid. There was no longer any need to wait for change, because change was all there was, and we had quite forgotten the flavour of an era that stayed in place long enough to gain a name. One morning I awoke to find that, during the course of the night, my mind had completely ejected the names of all the streets in Pakistan, as though to assure that I could not return, or that if I did, it would be returning to a loss. Overnight the country had grown absent-minded, and patches of amnesia hung over the hollows of the land like fog.

I think we would have mourned Dadi in our belated way, but the coming year saw Ifat killed in the consuming rush of change and disbanded the company of women for all time. It was a curious day in March, two years after my mother died, when the weight of that anniversary made us all disconsolate for her quietude. 'I'll speak to Ifat, though,' I thought to myself in America. But in Pakistan someone had different ideas for that sister of mine and thwarted all my plans. When she went walking out that warm March night, a car came by and trampled her into the ground, and then it vanished strangely. By the time I reached Lahore, a tall and slender mound had usurped the grave-space where my father had hoped to lie, next to the more moderate shape that was his wife. Children take over everything.

So, worn by repetition, we stood by Ifat's grave, and took note of the narcissi, still alive, that she must have placed upon my mother on the day that she was killed. It made us impatient, in a way, as though we had to decide that there was nothing so farcical as grief and that it had to be eliminated from our diets for good. It cut away, of course, our intimacy with Pakistan, where history is synonymous with grief and always most at home in the attitudes of grieving. Our congregation in Lahore was brief, and then we swiftly returned to a more geographic reality. 'We are lost, Sara,' Shahid said to me on the phone from England. 'Yes, Shahid,' I firmly said, 'We're lost.'

Today, I'd be less emphatic. Ifat and Mamma must have honeycombed and crumbled now, in the comfortable way that overtakes bedfellows. And somehow it seems apt and heartening that Dadi, being what she was, never suffered the pomposities that enter the most well-meaning of farewells and seeped instead into the nooks and crannies of our forgetfulness. She fell between two stools of grief, which is appropriate, since she was greatest when her life was at its most unreal. Anyway she was always outside our ken, an anecdotal thing, neither more nor less. So some sweet reassurance of reality accompanies my discourse when I claim that when Dadi died, we all forgot to grieve.

For to be lost is just a minute's respite, after all, like a train that cannot help but stop between the stations of its proper destination in order to stage a pretend version of the end. Dying, we saw, was simply change taken to points of mocking extremity, and wasn't a thing to lose us but to find us out, to catch us where we least wanted to be caught. In Pakistan, Bhutto rapidly became obsolete after a succession of bumper harvests, and none of us can fight the ways that the names Mamma and Ifat have become archaisms, quaintnesses on our lips.

Now I live in New Haven and feel quite happy with my life. I miss, of course, the absence of women and grow increasingly nostalgic for a world where the modulations of age are as recognized and welcomed as the shift from season into season. But that's a hazard that has to come along, since I have made myself inhabitant of a population which democratically insists that everyone from twenty-nine to fifty-six occupies roughly the same space of age. When I teach topics in third world literature, much time is lost in trying to explain that the third world is locatable only as a discourse of convenience. Trying to find it is like pretending that history or home is real and not located precisely where you're sitting, I hear my voice quite idiotically say. And then it happens. A face, puzzled and attentive and belonging to my gender, raises its intelligence to question why, since I am teaching third world writing, I haven't given equal space to women writers on my syllabus. I look up, the horse's mouth, a foolish thing to be. Unequal images battle in my mind for precedence—there's imperial Ifat, there's Mamma in the garden, and Halima the cleaning woman is there too, there's uncanny Dadi with her goat. Against all my own odds I know what I must say. Because, I'll answer slowly, there are no women in the third world.

Aamer Hussein

Born in Karachi, Aamer Hussein is connected to Sindh and Central India through his father and mother respectively and grew up in homes full of books, music and people who talked about them. He was educated at the co-educational junior school at the Convent of Jesus and Mary, but when he was thirteen his family moved to Britain. Aamer chose to join the Blue Mountain School in Ootacamund, run by his uncle. He arrived in England two years later. Books helped him cope with a sense of solitude, and alienation as they had in India. He started writing seriously in 1984. By then he had graduated from the School of Oriental and African Studies in London, with a degree in History, Persian and Urdu and he had travelled around Asia. He describes himself 'as a product of modern Asia with its Partition and post-national squabbles, not a child of Empire or English Literature' He has explored Urdu literature as well as that of Japan, Korea, Arabia and China, in translation, and identified with those traditions more than classical English texts. His first collection of short stories, *A Mirror to the Sun* (1993), about memory, displacement and exile, brings together a myriad of cultures, timeless tales and modern conflicts. His early work was influenced by the American writer, Eudora Welty. Then he began to read contemporary Urdu writers such as Intizar Husain, Khalida Husain and Fahmida Riaz. This had a very powerful impact on his English fiction. In some of his subsequent work he felt he was engaging in 'an imaginary dialogue' with his compatriots 'about writing and society and migration and history, past and present, voicing the ex-patriat's view.' This is very evident in *The Lost Cantos of The Silken Tiger*, (an abridged version of the original) which combines poetry with different styles of prose. Aamer Hussein is also a literary critic for *The New Statesman*. He has translated Urdu stories into English, researched the development of Urdu fiction with particular reference to women's writing, and lectured on contemporary literature in many countries. He teaches Urdu in London at The Languages Centre, SOAS.

The Lost Cantos of the Silken Tiger

Potiphar's Court

A stranger came to a strange new city, the most famous in a country that was only five years old. His name was Reza; they called him the silken tiger, for the verses he wrote were as smooth as silk, but had the soft-footed ferocity of a tiger's leap. Welcomed in every salon of the town, he purposefully made his way, however, to the court of the great and celebrated Minister of Culture, who was known as Potiphar for the powers and priveleges he enjoyed. His real name was forgotten; but not so that of his wife, the beautiful Aarzou, who was as famous for the beauty of her green eyes and golden hair as she was for the exquisite poems and songs she wrote.

This is how Reza arrived at Potiphar's court. Listen:

When Potiphar's wife heard that this bard and minstrel of the old country had crossed the border to find a home in the new land, she demanded that he appear in the court to engage with her in a battle of words. For she was well-known in the town as an incomparable poet among women; but none among the versifying men of the town had dared to pit his wit against hers, laughing behind their embroidered sleeves at the ignominy and folly of competition with a woman. In her presence, they only affected to praise the skill of her metre and the charm of her delicate images; but Aarzou was too clever a woman to believe that their flattery was sincere. Behind the veil of their compliments she discerned another veil, of mendacity; and behind that, too, a gossamer layer of jealousy and envy and fear.

As for the silken tiger, his reputation for romance and fearlessness had preceded him; he lived as he wrote and he wrote as he lived. Aarzou, at the ripening age of forty-three, longed for a true and vital rival. Not for her the sarcastic asides or the simpering similes of the city's court poets; nor the butterfly spin or homespun homilies of the court poetesses who, afraid to challenge their peers among men, stayed delicately confined in the verbal and visual decorum of inner courtyards.

So Aarzou summoned Reza to the outer courtyard of Potiphar's home. In those first years after ridding themselves of empire's yoke, the city's intellectuals were rediscovering, with fervour, their own heritage, and peasant craftsmanship, too; the white chambers of Potiphar's house were carpeted in straw matting and sparsely furnished, with mirrorworked cushions, some stools of straw and wood, a few patchwork seats, a single divan. Aarzou was dressed in a stark ensemble of black brushed with gold, cut daringly low on shoulder and bosom; its textures enhanced, with unerring brilliance, her brilliant colouring. Reza, dressed in white, his collar open at the neck, looked, with his unruly bright hair, as if he had just come in from the cricket-field. The stranger-poet, thirteen years younger than Aarzou, was also her rival in beauty; or, to tell the truth, her twin, for he like her was small and slight and seemed to be made of bronze and jade, and framed in spun gold. His hair, however, unlike Aarzou's unaided by artifice, was the colour of flame, and his narrow eyes showed traces of Tatar blood. Aarzou saw Reza as she saw her own reflection in glass, but while her mirrored image bored her for she had no true rival, the impact of her beauty stunned her when revealed to her in another's features and form.

Reza began the recital with a series of quatrains in traditional form; Aarzou responded with an elaborately asymmetrical composition in free verse, which had only recently become the mode among the literati, and was still disdained by many among the old guard. Reza dramatically raised a slender hand to his brow, and after a moment's pondering, improvised, in an identical rhythm, a verse permeated with gentle humour:

'Beauty's proud Queen mistakes a mirror for a lake
She needs love's sovereign to show her water's way.'

Aarzou responded with a few stammered and incoherent words, followed by a deafening silence. She was enraged, but her aesthetic discernment was pressing upon her to concede the victor's prize, when Reza heroically announced: 'Yours is the original; mine a mere imitation. To you, the victory of the beautiful word.'

To Aarzou, her victory tasted of defeat: she had not wrested it with her own artful strategies from the hands of the vanquished; it had been too willingly conceded. Her chagrin was aided all the more by the couplet that, before Reza's tribute to her, had welled up within her and frozen on her lips:

'O hunter in the night, you turn your back upon
my hapless love,
while I, your ardent prey, shed love's blood
in your way.'

But as these words—these naked, shaming words—began to play upon the redness of her lips and she, in her shame, was struggling to stop them from escaping the cage of her thoughts, Aarzou became aware of another burst of shaming red: the waterfall that, unbidden, had begun to flow, for the first time in three or four years, between her thighs. For like our mother Eve, who as a punishment for the sin of plucking the forbidden grains from the ear of wheat had known the pain of menstruation, the gaining of unlawful knowledge had caused Aarzou too, to bleed.

She determined to win and then break Reza's heart. But Reza's heart was there for the taking and the breaking: no challenge at all to the proud poet. And a tender companionship had grown between the young man and the powerful Potiphar; they would spend all their time together, comparing the verses of poets dead and living, for Potiphar, too, was a learned man. We would not be rash to assume that the silken tiger had crept into his master's chamber to leap and kill; but it was not the blood of Potiphar's heart that would slake his ardent thirst, only the melting of the icy orb of concealed desire in Aarzou's beautiful bosom. One quiet afternoon, the poet wept and declared his burning passion, and the lonely Aarzou opened to him the portals of her heart.

Aarzou lay in her lover's arms, sipping pale sparkling wine from fluted crystal, gold-tipped Sobranie between jade-painted finger tips in the splendour of her French boudoir (for Aarzou, the daughter of a Turcophile Prince and his exotic Turkish mistress, had early acquired a taste for things imported and

European, which was indulged, in the sanctity of the inner chamber where for many years she had slept alone, since her husband had long since expressed his preference for plump and very young pigeons of both sexes). She listened to his songs and sang him her verses, encouraged to be with him by her doting but negligent husband who (like Arthur in Camelot) wanted her amused while he occupied himself with state affairs. This ballad of desire and satiation was sung by the city's courtesans and minstrels, reaching on the airwaves the ears of other cities. And while the scroll of love unfolded, trouble was brewing in the country. The benign rulers of the land of the pure and the just had seen to it that the stalwarts of the honest bourgeoisie were permanently safe and protected, and that only such poverty persisted as allowed the less needy to perform their duties of almsgiving—for a structured society means a stable land. But the military had taken power, surreptitiously, and days, like prayer beads, were counted by the faithful who feared *a coup d'etat* and a subsequent takeover by the country's most powerful young general, a man whose regimental mind and puritanical spirit fascinated the mighty Potiphar, who believed—as he held that art and religion should be kept apart from state affairs—that might, right and order were synonyms, triple faces of one, omnipotent creator.

Aarzou, ever more keenly, listened, at the wrought-iron table in the glass-enclosed patio that served as their parlour, to her husband's confidences, imparted over crisp triangles of toast and marmalade (or home-farmed honey from her husband's country properties, her token concession to Potiphar's nationalist inclinations in this room which was, like her boudoir, furnished according to her pleasure). Potiphar's considerable verbal energies were at their most potent at this early hour; in the first years after their marriage, husband and wife had spoken of music and miniatures and verse, but now the duties of his calling burdened Potiphar with lethal secrets, which he shared with his wife—for silence is a sad state for a prolix man of high and fixed opinions.

'The General—let us not mention his name even *devant les domestiques*—is poised to coerce old Firaon into signing his resignation,' her husband told Aarzou. 'He will then persuade us to persuade him to establish martial rule to counteract disorder and chaos, for Firaon is still a much-loved man. After a decent interval, when army rule is dissolved, he will take the ruler's chair as the undisputed leader of our land.'

'And does this make you happy?' Aarzou asked, her alabaster brow furrowing, her green eyes narrow with concern.

'No—I think, for the moment, that we should let things ride; later, when the old man's ready to go, we can bring the General in with at least some semblance of democratic behaviour. But the General and the army are afraid of elections. What fools they are. Don't they know that no one—I repeat, no one—is prepared to offer their services to a position of absolute power? We all prefer to rule behind the scenes; we counteract the military's absolute influence by influencing the military.'

...Sated with loving, lips swollen like plums and green eyes shadowed with circles of tired green, tigerish limbs entwined with the limbs of her young tamed tiger in her purple-sheeted bed, Aarzou told Reza, three hours after her conference with Potiphar, of her husband's apprehensions. For she, a brave and brilliant woman held back by her sex in this land of patriarchs, trusted the finely-tuned judgement of the stranger-poet, who was an idealist and a pacifist. He would allay her fears. Or so she thought.

(The rest of this prose version of the story—if it ever existed—is lost. The above chapter was published in *Mah-e-Kamil*, the journal of the Circle of Luminaries, in the month of the cataclysmic events of which we are about to learn. But let us not race ahead of our tale. So. Listen:)

The Poet of the Many-Coloured Coat

Forty-three years later, a man, living in London, a cold city of the North, was struggling to complete the manuscript of a book about a group of poets in the then fair and self-regarding seaside city of Karachi, who styled themselves The Circle of Luminaries. Their aim was to dedicate their lives to art and only to art; their poems, novels and stories would eschew political comment; the journal of their glittering circle was called *The Full Moon*; they disdained the didactic pontifications of a rival group, The Association of Contemporary Writers, who believed in art for the sake of food, bread and a house for all, and admired Stalin and the Soviet Union. The Luminary-in-Chief was Agha Abdul Aziz, who wrote under the pseudonym of Abbas Zulfiqar, and even today holds a position of great respect in the annals of our literature. He is credited with having introduced Woolf, Joyce and Kafka to our prose writers, and Eliot, Pound and Rimbaud to our tradition-haunted poets. The man who aimed to be the chronicler of the Luminaries, our diligent researcher and would-be social historian—his name is Mehran Malik, and we can assume he is the chamber which contains the echoes of the many voices of this tale—discovered, during his researches, a strange, compelling fact, which created a hiatus, a missing chapter, in his book.

This is how it happened. Listen:

A famous revolutionary poet—who, exiled from our country for his unproved part in a famous early conspiracy, had for many years taught cultural history, from a neo-Marxist standpoint, in the west's leading academies—was persuaded to give a seminar on his verse, which he swore he had long since abandoned (with a brief, biting volume of poems in English, dissecting with bitterness his abandonment of the Soviet dream and his ideological Marxism). The seminar was part of a conference on Indic Literatures at the Academy of Oriental Studies in Bloomsbury. The occasion that had persuaded him to appear in an assembly of literatures was the publication of a slim volume he had authored, a memoir of mordant beauty tellingly entitled *Nights in Hell*, which told of his incarceration in Pakistan, release, exile, painful years of ostracism and penury in India, and eventual departure for the West. It was also a return—albeit in prose—to his long-forsaken mother tongue.

Our illustrious poet appeared in a suit of elegant cut and flamboyant fabric—grey silk, with crimson thread woven in imperceptible subtlety into the sombre texture. He was now an enlightened scholar of Islamic dissension, as famous for his philosophical diatribes against Said, Rushdie and Aijaz Ahmad as he was for his unconventional take on Islam. To hear him read was a great pleasure, for his poems, in our best twentieth-century tradition, took on political issues with grace, dignity, compassion and painful honesty. He had, however, requested that no questions be asked about his hurried and notorious departure from Pakistan—was it exile, or defection? He would also refuse to reply to queries about his part in the great communist conspiracy to assassinate the Prime Minister of the time and the leading General, in 1953.

He read with throwaway elegance, raising, from time to time, a slender manicured hand to his hair, which still bore the traces of its erstwhile flaming colour.

Then a request came, from the audience, for a love poem. The speaker who voiced it was a translator and budding feminist historian of our literature, Rubina 'Neeli' Raja, who insists on the quotation marks around her middle name, as a sign, she says, of the dialectic between the Self in its constant process of creation, and Family History. (She was in the habit of saying herstory, until Mehran, who was both a rival and a sometime fellow-traveller, pointed out that in the Latin origin of the word there was no gendered pronoun implicated, and in most romance languages 'history' was indistinguishable from 'story'. Now, since her discovery of Cixous and her own work-in-progress on Aarzou, the Luminaries' leading feminine constellation who was, according to La Raja, a great writer obscured by the critics only by her vast reputation as a paradoxical populist story-teller, La Raja speaks of my-story-pronounced-mystery; or Wombanview.)

But we wander from our story. So. Listen carefully:

When Reza Rizvi—for that is the name of our revolutionary poet and radical scholar—had finished reciting his tender and slightly lascivious love-poem, La Raja, dressed in turquoise sackcloth and polka-dotted flat crepe, her fine hair gathered behind her head into a variegated snood, stood up in the audience and declaimed: 'Is it true that this poem was dedicated to a character conspicuous in her absence from your book: Aarzou Baig?'

The septuagenarian poet flushed to his flaming roots.

'And to her husband, Agha,' he responded. 'And both of them are mentioned, in passing, in my very subjective and impressionistic memoir, which is exactly that and clearly not a socio-historical document.'

'But your political views were of a different colour from the Circle of Luminaries—what was your connection with Agha and Aarzou?'

'There are, in art, no sectarian banners or political colours. That is why I left the Contemporary Writers and refused to be part of any coterie. I abandoned poetry because my ideals told me the beliefs of my time and my commitment to art as a tool of protest were equally false...I recognized my failure to reconcile my goals. And only now, at this great old age, I can see, from my distance, the relative merits of my work, the intensity of my passion for medium and message alike, the articulation of my commitment to a common humanity, the only statement worth anything.'

'Have you read Aarzou's sequence of poems, *The Silken Tiger Cantos*?' La Raja persisted, to the chagrin of the session's chairman. 'Could you comment on her version of historically documented events? What gaps do you think it fills in for the layperson? And, finally, how do you feel abut her portrayal of you? For you are undoubtedly the silken tiger of the title. She hasn't even bothered to change your name.'

'Let our learned friend speak,' said the venerable Reza Rizvi to the irate and embarrassed chairman. 'Aarzou's is one version of history, her own version. I must have another: and there are too many unknown factors. History is one part myth and one part mystery; so if we choose to call the other myth, let's say I prefer to keep my story a mystery.'

The next day—the last but one of his stay in London—Reza Rizvi refused Mehran Malik the interview to which he had earlier consented; he cancelled it when he discovered that the younger writer was working on the lives and infamous times of messrs Agha and Baig. He was conspicuously absent from la Raja's presentation, entitled *Myth and the Feminine Mystique—Early Women Writers of Pakistan*, which she presented that day. Mehran, deprived of the opportunity to converse with a man whom he felt held at least one key to the mystery he sought so ardently to solve, decided to do a spot of sleuthing and see if the discussion would yield some fresh fruits of knowledge. After all, Aarzou, whom we now dismiss as typical of everything we disdain in the writings of romanticizing women, was for a time the Circle of Luminaries' leading luminary. But Malik had thought that it was her laconic grace and her ravishing, deliberately artificial beauty, crowned by her gilded hair and her position as Agha's wife, that made her so.

The Legend of Potiphar's Wife

'Do you remember?' Rubina 'Neeli' Raja said, shuffling her papers on the podium. 'Listen':

'After a long, long silence—of ten years or more, if you discount the embarrassing nationalist eulogies to which she lent her name during the '65 war—Aarzou produced the most splendid work of her career, the epic poem *The Silken Tiger*, a reinterpretation of Jami's Persian *masnavis*. She had already attempted a prose version of the story, of which one chapter was published as you have already been told by our learned friend Mr Malik, and as most of you will know, only three cantos of the verse version appeared in her lifetime; the fourth; which I am about to reveal to you today, was not only completed a mere four days before her death, but was not included in *Jaan-e-Aarzou*, the edition of her Complete Works edited, compiled and introduced by her grieving husband. It has so far only appeared in an avant-garde Karachi journal called *Today*, and in my translation in America.

'The poem is set in an unnamed land—reminiscent now of Turkey, now of Iraq and now of Southern France, but slowly, slowly unveiling the sea breezes, the burning sun and the outlying desert of her adopted city, Karachi—in a time which, we gradually discover, is her own, for among the Circassian handmaidens, haunted marble halls, ruby-studded lutes and star-spangled chiffon veils there are telephones, airplanes, gramophone records and highpowered political assemblies. Now Aarzou had always set her fictions in a romanticized Orient—and this, I will claim, was her husband's influence upon her or rather his editorial tyranny, because he did not believe in direct commentary or social realism. He was also afraid of offending the English, the militaries, and all men in boots. Aarzou's first novel, written in her own name when she was barely sixteen, is set in the first decade of our century, in a recognizable Hyderabad, the city she really came from. But editions now available, all of them reprints of a second edition, bear the signs of her husband's erasures; cities, names and dates are rapidly discarded. Agha also created the myth of Aarzou's exotic origins, hinting that she, like the heroine of her stories who was always called Tamanna Khanum, was the daughter of a high-ranking officer and his Turkish concubine. According to this legend, Aarzou was born in Istanbul, in a palace by the Bosphorus, and had grown up in Baghdad, where Agha, visiting the Orient's pearls on a literary pilgrimage, glimpsed her through a beaded curtain. That her father was a medium-ranking official in the Nizam of Hyderabad's employ is true, but her mother, to the best of my knowledge, was the daughter of a Sayyad cleric from Lahore. Her marriage to Agha resulted from an exchange of letters and missives, an outpouring of youthful poetry from her and dispatches of critical prose from him. Her caste-conscious parents only consented to this union with the much older litterateur because she was nearly twenty, a great age for a woman. She also flew kites, rode a motorbike, smoked black cigarettes and wrote very daring novels.

'Aarzou's later fictions are veiled in haziness—edited and censored, as my research among her manuscripts proves, by her husband, who nevertheless allows her the negative feminist endings which remain her form of radical protest against the stifling bureaucratic class, just one step below the nobility, into which she was born. Now we are all too ready to dismiss the lush romanticism and exotic locales of her work—but careful study will reveal to you that, in spite of Agha's tampering, Aarzou's is a powerful voice of protest, even a pioneering voice. In this great and graceful poem she tackles an even bigger problematic—that of the relation between art and politics in a newly created nation. Her writer husband, she prophetically casts as a bureaucrat—and that, of course, is what he later became, condoning and colluding with, by his deafening silences and his insistence on art for its own sake, the placing of clamps on the mouths of radicals and of women. Aarzou staged herself as Potiphar's wife—an early feminist struggle to present a woman mad, bad and dangerous, for hers is a story of revenge and betrayal.

'This is the last, lost canto of which I spoke. Forgive my clumsy English rendition of Aarzou's glorious lyrical diction, which derives its force from its radical combination of modernist form and traditional imagery. Let me read it to you.

Listen to the flute, as it sings its song of separation.'

The Lost Canto of the Silken Tiger

Seabirds stretch their wings,
   sheltering them from the
sun's heat. Sky and sea
   share a bed, are one.

The lovers ride the foam. Wave
   licks hoof: the black
horse falls. The seam of her
   man's brocaded jacket is torn.
I will mend it for you myself,
   she says. He blanches:
she will not let it go.

Hidden in its pocket's seam, she
finds the itinerary of her lover's
plan to kill the president and
his opponents, the military
leaders who are contemplating
a *coup d'etat*. So they would
rid their land, in one sharp
move, of its oppressors. He is
in league with a rebel group.
He believes in equality for all,
an end to exploitation by princes
and viziers. For he is a tiger
in disguise as a lamb, a renegade
and rebel, who receives instructions
from the land across the border, and
from another mighty, fire-breathing
empire.
The rain clouds swarm.

She cannot believe what seems to be
the truth—that her lover has used
her, without mercy, for his own needs.
Unwittingly she has served as a spy,
given away the country's secrets. She
has been a traitor to her high ideals
and her hopes of peace and prosperity.

Looking in the mirror she sees
the hollows and caverns beneath
the heavy paint on her face. She
is an aging woman looking for love,
deprived of love: only in her poems
has she ever fulfilled her deepest
velvet desires. On the parched desert
sand, the rain falls. It soothes the
sandstorm.

When he comes to her mirrored boudoir,
   she faces him with her new knowledge
of his treacheries. They encompass
   arson, gun-running, bombing and
the illegal possession of arms.

He tells her that he does love her,
   but this love he feels for her,
this consuming desire that inflames
   his entrails and his belly, must be
subjugated to a higher good.
   For there are torments in life
far greater than the agony of love,
   and greater bliss than the fevered
joy of union. Outside, the rain sings
   a relentless song. The wind howls.

She asks him to walk with her in
   her secret garden. She tells him
she will try to understand, to
   follow him, fulfil his dreams.
She will not heed the rain.

He says: You are only a woman, a
   mere feeble creature in spite
of your tiger graces. And when my
   chore is done, I will leave your
country for two years, to study
   in that great, great land where
visions of equality ad fraternity
   are realized. I will bring back
its grand and gracious messages
   to the oppressed of your barren,
                  rain-starved earth.

And Reza tells Aarzou: If
   in those years you read the

holy books of the prophets
of fraternity, you may be
redeemed, and survive in the
new order.

If not, you must go the way of
all oppressors, into the dungeons
where your kind have tortured,
imprisoned and tormented
the wretched of the earth.

But you are a singer and a poet,
she says, you are a man of dreams.
Where are those visions you showed
me of peace and happiness? Of music
and flowers, of miniatures and pastel
tapestries and verses of our restless
longings, painted in gold letters
on screens of white silk?

Peace can only be achieved after
struggle: blood must be spilt
to make a bed for rivers of milk
and honey. So the silken tiger
says. This is the only poem I know,
the only prayer I recite. All I said
before, the words I used to seduce
you, were trifles, gewgaws to bemuse a
vain and lonely woman. You call yourself
a poet? You sell your words, as a harlot
sells her flesh, for flattery.

His words pierce her bones and
the flute of her being. The hot
rain pours upon her, licks her skin
like a flame. The wind howls.

Poetry, she think, is the music
   of my soul. It is the cool air
I drink, the sun that warms my back
   and the soft rain that refreshes me.
It is the snow tenderly melting into blue
   waterfalls that flow from the mountain
of this land I love.

Poetry is my being, the God himself
   who in His glory, lives within
this altar of my body and my breasts.
   Poetry is the blood that flows from
my belly, and runs down my thighs.
   And who called forth the blood from me?
Reza, my twin, Reza, my Adam, my
   peacock, my snake, my Satan. Who pierced
my wood like a flute, in the agony of
   separation? But I was mistaken. He never
was my reflection, I was his. (I lost
   myself, a willing wanderer, in the mirrors
                                        of his love.)

And if the mirror breaks, where
   will my love go? And if my blood
ceases to flow, how will I compose
   my songs? For the music of my words
is his love. Allah! A string breaks.
                                        My voice dies.

He walks away from her as sunset,
   like a wild duck, spreads its
wounded wing. Alone, she wanders
   in her ornamental garden. White
geese float on its mirrored pond.
   Hibiscus petals fall gently on
her bowed golden head. She crushes

underfoot the bruised bodies of white
blossoms. The cruel scent of frangipani
fills the air.

The wild duck cries: I am forgotten.
A wild boy has wounded my wing with
a stone from his slingshot. My mate
left with the north-bound horde,
and I'm left broken on a burning beach.
The sea boils.

She stays there as the night turns
from stone to water and then to
black glass, reflects the jade pendant
of the moon, surrounded by a thousand
jewelled candles. Now her flaming tears
have turned to anger's ice. The moon
flees. The flute is silent now.

Dressed carefully for the occasion
in unadorned black, with only a single
thick silver bracelet on her wrist—a gift,
bought for her by Potiphar from a peasant's
market, she hitherto disdained—she goes to
her husband: reveals her infidelity,
says she will pay the price of her betrayal.
She unveils each detail of the plan her
faithless man has concocted with his companions.
She begs him to commend the conspirators to
justice and retribution: despatch them to Hell.
Outside, the drums beat and the rain sighs.
The scent of cruel frangipani fills the air.

Potiphar is grim-faced, silent. He looks away
from her. He cannot meet the candour of her
green eyes. He orders an investigation: the
grave and terrible work of justice and

retribution will, at his command, be done.
Then, Pilate-like, he rinses his hands.

The conspiracy is uncovered, the conspirators
disbanded and disembowelled. But then, how
strange! Potiphar relents. Perhaps the strange
poison of a fledgeling love, a bird fallen
thirsty from its fragile nest, beseeches him.
He pleads for the silken tiger's life.
But before they exile Reza from the land,
the masters leave their fatal mark. They
castrate him with red-hot coals, make a
limping travesty of the silken tiger. His
flute is broken now: its voice dies. It
is midsummer and the clouds have burst.
The drums are silent now. The wind sings
its ballads and the sweet rain falls.

Aarzou, like a masked Noh dancer or a
dirge-singer in Muharram, mauls
her face with her long nails. She
tears her hair. She damns herself
for her deed. Allah, you break my
strings and no one hears. The beads
of my prayers are scattered now. I
must calculate the days of separation
on the phalanges of my fingers till their
lines rub out. But then when I meet Reza
in heaven, he will turn his face from me.
So let me rot in hell. And if God is
forgiving, paradise a dream, then let me
be without rest, let me sleep without dreaming.

Her blood cries. She hears its last flow.
It tells her it has ceased forever.

'It is one of the most powerful and moving portrayals of a woman's rage turned inwards in ours or any other literature,' La Raja concluded. 'And it gains its strength because—more than any other work by this fabulist who is also a deeply autobiographical writer—this is a memoir, a testament, a calling to witness, a proud confession of sin—a mistresswork of my-story that uncovers one of our time's greatest mysteries: allegorizes and rewrites the destiny of a nation, how it is subverted by a woman's powerful passion and revenge.'

Reza Tells his Stinging Tale

'Methinks the lady doth protest too much, and I'll tell you why,' said Reza Rizvi to Mehran Malik, two days later. He had changed his mind about the interview; he had rung Malik at his office and told him it was merely a dental appointment that had caused the cancellation of so pleasurable an encounter. They could now meet, he said, the problem of the plaguing tooth being temporarily resolved. They were sitting in the salon of a dignitary of the Pakistan High Commission, over tea in fragile porcelain, fritters and tiny cucumber sandwiches—for we have forgotten to mention that Reza Rizvi, in these changed and newly democratic times, was now welcome to visit the land of his abandoned dreams whenever he so chose, and this embassy dignitary was his sister's son.

Reza ran his hand through his flame-and-grey locks. 'Aarzou Khanum's poem is autobiographical,' he said, 'except for one detail. Of course, Aarzou—the Lord rest her fantasizing soul—has exaggerated everything. Poetic license, we could say. I never was as much of a didactic Marxist as she makes out in her poem; certainly never a Communist or as pro-Soviet as those Luminary bastards would continue to write about me in their pretentious pseudo-philosophical treatises on our culture. More of an anarchist, really; I still am. Food and justice for all, but I like my champagne and my cigarillos, and never denied that my old man was a landowner, though once I went with some of my mates to create some mayhem in our own country house, smashed a chandelier, stole some silver, wrecked an amethyst fountain. And as for verse—I don't want to flatter myself, and old Agha's already taken enough credit for moulding Aarzou as the Embodiment of the Feminine in our collective soul, but I saw the potential for true greatness in her as soon as we met. In return, she helped me with my verses too, told me how to soften the crudeness of my message with the poetry of word and sound: statements were always clearest when understated. And I also have to say that she had the most beautiful style in the business. You should see the effect it had when she lent it, anonymously, to the speeches the revolutionaries made. I never, never jeered at her verse—only told her she should be less raw and painfully ingenuous in the expression of her pain and her beliefs. Even then I understood too well the hazardous, tightrope walk of polemical art. And you can see from the Reza and Aarzou poems how well she learnt the ploys of her craft. The rhetoric of revolution she attributes to Reza has all the bejewelled lavishness—and some of the self-indulgent bombast—of our youthful utterances. But if any one was a true revolutionary, she was. Yes, my boy, we were fellow radicals, co-conspirators. And she was closer to the edge of the precipice than I; she knew about plans and projects that I, who was ten years younger and a relative newcomer to her city, could only guess at.

'She was never the vain pleasure seeker that Aarzou occasionally appears to be in the poem. No hedonist, certainly; even in moments of love, Aarzou Khanum talked about the Golden Age of equality still to come, the earthly paradise of sorority and liberty; the peaceful, permanent Revolution. Her calculated appearance was just a gilded theatrical mask. And much of the money from those novels—she was a big seller at the time—came to our cells, paid for rescue operations. So when I was caught—and forced to take the rap for so many others, though I knew less than most of them—I protected her above all others. I rotted in solitary confinement in Lahore Fort for three months. If it hadn't been for old Pandit Jawaharlal getting me off—owed my father a favour, you know—I'd have been flayed. Her husband came to me in my cell before I left. It was there that he told me how his wife, in a moment of fear for herself, had betrayed me: and I wondered how much she knew, and how she could have known anything at all, because I never had carried a list of conspirators, and there were things that I did not know and would not have told her, in fear for her, if I did. So I thought that she perhaps had always known more than I; and, worse still that she may have been a spy all along.

'And then, all those years later, she writes this poem, telling this story, absolving herself of everything and dumping all blame on me. I could still hardly believe that she—she—would turn me over to that sleazy husband she'd hated after the first years of their marriage, who had forced her to churn out romances and turned her gems into sawdust or tawdry tinsel. And deny her own part in the struggle, her dreams and dawning visions. To turn so viciously against a man who had loved her almost as much as his life and their dream of revolution.

'But it took me years to unravel the mystery. Put this all in your book, for Aarzou's gone and very soon old Agha will be dead, and as for me, my months in prison have ensured that I have nothing left to lose. Shame, honour, home, dreams; I shed all hope's burdens years ago. Yes, put it in your book, and perhaps you and that bright young critic who interrogated me at the Academy should join forces. Your diligence and her ferocity, combined, might produce a worthy book.

'So let me tell you the truth of the last canto of Aarzou's poem. What she may have written, if she'd seen the truth. Maybe she did: only history will reveal that to us. Or maybe she herself destroyed what her intuition must have told her, erased for ever what she finally wrote. More probably, the Agha did it for her.

'But. Let me face you with my version of the story, in dramatic form. I leave it all to you, and time, to judge. So. Listen:

'Three years ago I decided to accept the government's invitation to come home—though Pakistan hardly was my home, for I didn't live there for more than six years, but I have no other, either. I was feted, lionized, received with acclaim and even love. And then one day old Potiphar—it is the best name for him, I have to admit—turned up at my door. He had once, though somewhat stout, been a fine-looking man; now he was a sickly white, fat as a frog, and walked with an ivory-headed stick. I greeted him with as much courtesy as I could muster.'

AGHA (muttering): I owe you an explanation.

REZA: We have no debts to settle. Your wife saw to that.

AGHA: Forgive an old man's impatience. But it was my jealousy, my impotence, my fury and my fear for my wife—whom I loved, because she was the Aphrodite who had risen from the foam of my literary dreams, in many ways my creation—that led to your downfall. It was I who found the plans for the assassination. Her name and yours were on a list of intellectuals with Marxist inclinations, Soviet sympathies and shady contacts. She denied nothing; not her wanton fornications with you, my friend and protegé; not her wild revolutionist dreams. Not even her betrayal of the aesthetic I had so painstakingly created for her. But how she begged me to let you go! She even said that she would take the punishment for your deeds. And I told her that after a required punishment I would arrange for your release. Silence—her eternal silence—was what I demanded for the favour. I would save you if she never dabbled with the politics of the revolution again.

She was merely a messenger. A cog in the wheel. But you, with your tiger's eyes and your snake's ways, you crept into my life, availed of my genius, cavorted with my wife: ah, my friend and my adversary, my rival in life and art, I hated you. I swear, as much and more than I loved you. I wanted you dead; then eventually I realized it was not your death but the living corpse of your shame and exile, dragged through the streets of our city tied naked to a packhorse, that would satisfy me. I wanted, with your admirers, to smell the stench of your defection. So that I could feel the triumph, then, of being your benefactor, the supplicant for your release, the release of a traitor to the nation. The worst crime in our country's eyes. To see you flee, a dissident and defector, into the arms of our enemy. I arranged the evidence which revealed the insignificance of your involvement. I could have destroyed her, too, along with you, but you realize that any word of her involvement in your subversions would have spelt the end of my prestige. I had to protect her to protect myself, and the price I paid her was your freedom. Also, she was my way of living. She was a wonderful writer, as her last verses prove, far greater than you or I. Can you imagine? What a fine reversal! For of course it was I who had the connections—I who betrayed you, but she had the last, dark laugh. She maintains her silence but tells her tale of sorrow and vengeance; steals my victory to take revenge; reveals her adultery in the bargain, shames my manhood, and damns herself as a traitor to love, which she never was. After all, she was my student; and she learned, though painfully, that the end of an old story can never be changed, and life, however dramatic, must be betrayed to create true art. Reality can never yield the joys and sorrows of a life lived intensely, moment by moment, on the virgin page. So in the end, my dear Reza, she cheated us both in her fidelity to her art. Kill, lie, maim, steal, even give up living, as she did: but serve the masterwork. That's all there is to live for.

REZA: But why the revenge on me? We were collaborators. Travellers on the same road. Our desire for each other was incidental. We saw the same visions.

AGHA: Because I told her you were involved in the assassination plans, of which, I discovered, she knew nearly nothing…and then I told her of the plot—which, of course, I invented—masterminded by the Russians and the Indians, to take us over…

REZA: But she has Reza castrated in the story! So heavy a punishment for a secret kept from a woman! I remember well the innocent machismo of those days, in which even the most dedicated revolutionaries, if they were women, were not entrusted with certain secrets…

'So you're admitting that you were involved in the conspiracy?' Malik was incredulous.

'I'm not admitting or denying anything,' said the poet. 'Let's just say I knew more than some and a lot less than others. But you are taking us away from my story. Listen:

'I said to old Potiphar:

'But castration!'

And he responded:

'Oh. My fault, I'm afraid. For I also told her that you were a double agent, who had sold our secrets to foreign powers, and then relented and confessed your plots to me. I said, too, that you had toyed with my great love, just as you had trifled with her heart. You should have seen her face. The man for whom she had humiliated herself before the husband she had grown to despise; for whose wretched life she had even been prepared to sacrifice her freedom: Reza, the traitor, not only to his land but then again to the cause she had thought he represented. Then perhaps her fears for your life and safety really did turn into a desire for revenge: and she, too, wanted to reveal your ignominies to the world. And so she settled her scores with the two of us: the one she thought had betrayed and sold her dreams, and the one who, by revealing what she thought was the truth, revealed her beloved to her as a traitor.'

I lunged forward; I wanted to hit him, but then it occurred to me that he may even, in the end, have tampered with the climatic verses of Aarzou's masterwork, just as he interfered with our lives and our dreams and with history itself so that he could get her to write the book he wanted. The old devil. She surprised even him. Somehow these thoughts made me laugh, and then I was laughing at the wretched waste of our lives and our passions, and what a great, great comedy of waste it seemed, how we'd grown older and learnt almost nothing, and I was still laughing when the old man went out silently, like the withered phantom of the past that he was.

'Does my tale,'—said Reza, relighting his cigar—'answer some of your questions?'

Hina Faisal Imam

Hina Faisal Imam has pursued two parallel careers as a writer and business administrator. She was born in Lahore and educated at The Convent of Jesus and Mary, The Cathedral School and Kinnaird College. She went on to the University of Michigan, Ann Arbor to do her B.A. and M.A. She joined Packages Limited in Lahore, worked there in various capacities, took part in many management seminars and programmes and is now Director, Dane Foods Limited, but she has continued to write throughout. Both careers have been strongly influenced by her commitment to women's rights. She asserts that women can no longer 'be brow-beaten into subjugation or bondage' that they 'have a voice and a claim, and must have the confidence to know their worth.' As a poet she gives voice to issues concerning women, including motherhood. Her poems, and her articles on literature, have appeared in various publications including *The Journal of South Asian Studies* and *The Journal of Commonwealth Literature*. In 1985 she won the Spring Summer Poetry Award, and she presented a paper on 'Women and Literature in Pakistan' at the Second National Women Studies Conference, University of Washington, Seattle. Between 1985 and 1992, she was editor of *Inspirations,* a journal of poetry funded by the Quaid-i-Azam Library, Lahore. She has published two collections of poetry, *Wet Sun* (1982) and *Midnight Dialogue* (1991).

FROM ***MIDNIGHT DIALOGUE***

Motherhood and Frustration

Babies make their own time
in computer terminals
and fear nothing.
A scream, a bursting cry
halts and changes any schedule.
The bundle of love grows
in my eyes.
I love her crawl,
imitate her baby talk but I
will never be a baby again.

And she feeds on my writing time,
plays into the chain of my thoughts
with 'Aa ja, Aa ja.'
Her clear water eyes
and her one tooth smile
makes me forget what I was writing.

I am mothered by guilt,
the negligence of wanting time
for myself for being so unlike
my mother,
for trying to write with
her in my lap.

Babies are unique,
their approach to discover life, original
and I find what I have
forgotten in the serious
shadows of my slide and merry-go-round rides.
I never played with dolls
because I was afraid of being a child
and spent the years in growing up like

an amateur adult.
I learnt to survive in competition
because I had to prove it to myself
and to others.

Crying hurt my eyes, they swell
and you noticed.
Anger pulverized me
and I could not speak
because I thought of all those times
when I was accused of being selfish—
all those times when I was just being myself,
but how would you know?

The politician pleases everybody,
and words expose everyone
at the same time
I will burn my lamp,
oil it with words
and you will never
know the difference
because everyone eats
dinner and praises
your expert hand.

The Road

The road opened
on sand dune curves
mounting truck pressure
while girls sang popular songs.
Their voices drift into
the wilderness of my dreams
where everything mystifies.
In the middle of the song,
I saw her walking into the happiness

of the past, where a smile or a fleeting
glance held her,
and left her free
to freeze somewhere
in her mind
beyond circumscribed space.
The accelerator pressed down
held the Pajero on a steady course
to Multan and
driving along Jahania
in the heart of green wheat fields,
I ran away,
I could not stop the jeep
or myself—but I ran—free.
A phrased tradition,
took root in loneliness.
Eggs make good sandwiches
for other people to eat,
just to fill a mental space
where I want my time.
Feudal marriages fit woman
into a house to hold fort
and give courage to men
who live apart in understanding
that women will be there to fulfil
their needs and show undemanding, virtuous
and traditional respect.
Mango orchards, rice, and cotton fields,
godowns for rain shelter, tubewells—all
tell a story of what man has grown,
bought and sold.
Women secure gold and dress for status.
They have nowhere to go
and everything to hide.
The soil has bound them like pillars
in the haveli courtyard to eat, sleep
and talk as the sun rises and sets on

blank faces
staring on solid protecting, empty
unyielding walls.
Tears fall on dust floors:
no one wipes them clean
from a pretty face
that mends loneliness
in the bathroom.
Peace lingers for a universal containment.
I have brought part of it—sharing—
my hands are empty again.
The cycle must go on
and I have
stitched peace into the sleeves of my heart
but a knock, a phone call, a long dinner
conversation rips whatever I had sown quietly.

Solitude

I plant signs and go between words,
a cascade flattened by sand
on the morning shore of
seedless waters.

The day travels with the sun
in jasmine flower deserts
fishing for ideas in barren wells
abandoned centuries ago in
muted silence.

My scorched lids see darkness
emanating from streams
in clover nets caste across the moon,
returning into the Earth's soul
for a second idea.

I ran into the screeching street
of night
and the stars gleamed into
the silent sea of yesterday's
beginnings.

And I wrote each word in
the lamp of magical dreams.
Recycled water rises in the flood
of your eyes and drops on
the brick floor of my experience.

Childhood Musician

A little girl sat on a stool
striking black and white keys
to find herself sadness
in the music masterfully
created by Beethoven and Mozart.

The room in the colonial house
in Mayo gardens was dimly lit
and an old grey haired teacher
watched her play with satisfaction.
Jingle bells in cold unsnowy
winters and the bombs at night
have frightened away the smile
and curiosity of peace in Palestine.

Come and sit beside me if you
wish to know time's power
rising from the sun. In
clove-leaf mountain streams
untie the night of trees and water
makes its own music on rocks and
stones brought from distant mountains.

and I look at her epitaph:
She dreamed of playing in La Scala
and the chords snapped. The wind
blew her to far away tombstones

An unfulfilled musician, can her
soul rest in peace?

Mansoor Y. Sheikh

Mansoor Sheikh studied pharmacy and business administration and organized poetry readings and workshops in Karachi, where he lives. He was a founder member of 'Mixed Voices' a multi-lingual forum for poetry and creative writing in Karachi during the 1970s. He published his first collection *In Search of Form: Poems* (1978). His poems have also appeared in *The Blue Wind* (1984), an anthology of five poets.

Shalimar

What abandon
filling these pools of stone
where jewelled fingers
once caressed their own reflections:

moon-bathed pavements
where you can still
sense a footfall
or an occasional sitar crescendo

from the bedchamber.
Yet they do not take you
through the inflexions of time
to where the music swells and nights falter.

Poem

There is a silence that delves for pain,
sounds that float around us
aching to be words
to be music.

This summer
gul-mohur flowered
before time.

Shrubs curl backwards
for shade.

Across the burnt grass
there is a dried pool
and beside it:

a small wooden bench
where we sit
grafting our silence
on each other's thoughts.

For Lowell

Death's not an event in life, it's not lived enough
Robert Lowell

Today your sobriety
distracts mermaid and dolphin alike.
They are looking at you
your women, your words
waiting to be recompensed.
I know that life is bitter
and *antabuse* worse
but if not—breathing in a taxi cab
meant death, we are all undead.
Sometimes I go to a fishing village
and watch the sun
setting through dripping nets.
As each moment dies into another
and each square
barbs and skews
to fetter the light.
I suddenly falter for space
and squares like thoughts about thoughts
cut through me.

antabuse: a drug administered to chronic alcoholics.

Qaisra Shahraz Ahmad

Born in Pakistan, Qaisra Shahraz Ahmad went to England as a child in 1967. She did her MA in English Language and Literature. She has been writing for 15 years, while bringing up her three children and working as a lecturer in Adult Education in Manchester. She teaches English as a second language, is head of the department and also contributes to the fiction component of creative writing courses. She visits Pakistan regularly and has written short stories about village life, but the most common themes in her work include her own background as a woman dealing with cross-cultural issues. Her short story 'Perchanvah' was shortlisted for the *Acclaim* magazine's 1991 Ian St. James Award and two of her stories are included in the English Literature syllabus. Her fiction has appeared in several anthologies in Britain, two of which, *Invitation to Literature* 1990 and *Writing Women* 1991, were published in Germany. She was a UK delegate at the 1995 International Writers and Intellectuals Conference in Islamabad. She has written articles, stories for children and also a stage play.

THE VISITING GRANDMOTHER

Rabia Bibi sat in an infant school hall, celebrating Christmas with the school children and their teachers. Rabia's eyes followed the prancing figure of her granddaughter Roxana, round the large noisy hall. Roxana worked as a reception teacher at this school. She had taken her grandmother to the school party, to show her how English children celebrate Christmas at their schools.

The music was on, and the Christmas games were in full swing. Giggles and squeals of laughter from the young children echoed round the hall. For the last game the children held each other's hands and under the guidance of their teachers made two circles. Then they moved round the hall with the music. One minute they twirled round, the next wriggled their bottoms to the beat of the music, almost squatting on the floor, and then rising up and jumping in the air. The teachers did the same.

Rabia Bibi stared hard, amused and bemused at the same time. It was all new to her. She might as well have landed from another planet, for all the affinity she had with her present surroundings, she felt so alone and miserable. She tried very hard to locate the whereabouts of her granddaughter. For Roxana was the tangible link between this world and that of hers, in Pakistan. Yet Roxana seemed to have blended well with this world. She felt tears creep up into the corners of her eyes. She brushed them away with the edge of her head scarf, *dupatta.* She wanted to cry not only because she couldn't identify with this environment of the school, but also because she was mourning the death of her cousin, Noor Begum. The latter was Roxana's other grandmother. She had died a fortnight ago. If only she was in Pakistan when Noor had died. She hadn't seen her since she arrived in England eight months ago. And now she would never see her again, and had missed out on the mourning period.

Mrs Johnson, the headmistress of the infant school, passed by the benches, where Rabia and other parents sat. Bending her head in acknowledgement here and there, she spoke to some of the parents. Rabia dreaded the headmistress's approach—Roxana had introduced her grandmother earlier in the afternoon to the headteacher, and had especially schooled her to say 'Hello' and 'How do you do?' and to flash a smile, a 'plastic' smile that the English people were very good at. They always seemed to smile at you, whenever they caught your eye. Rabia didn't know how to react. She couldn't very well smile at any *Nethu Pethu,* at any Tom, Dick and Harry.

Mrs Johnson's gaze encompassed Roxana's grandmother. She summoned a special smile to her lips, she had wanted to make her feel at home. Earlier she had spoken to her at length, although she knew Rabia wouldn't have understood a word. The grandmother had appeared so lost and harassed and cut a sorry figure, as they trailed silently behind her granddaughter, nodding her head dumbly as she was introduced to the other teachers. In reciprocation, the muscles of Rabia's face worked in an attempt to force a semblance of a smile to her lips. It was too late. Mrs Johnson had already passed on. Rabia was disappointed.

She looked around at the other people sitting around her. With the exception of one or two older English women, most of them were mainly young. There were a couple of young Pakistani mothers, but they sat at the other end of the bench. They were too far for Rabia to speak to them. She so much wanted to speak to someone who spoke her language. She had eagerly caught their glances once or twice and smiled at them. Rabia glanced again at the older women. She was interested in them because they were of the same age as herself, and yet between them lay an ocean of difference. They must be grandmothers or great grandmothers of the children attending this school. Rabia drew her *dupatta* over her head. It had fallen on the collar of her coat, no one else had their head covered—she was the only one.

The old woman, with the red hair glanced in Rabia's direction and catching her eye, smiled pleasantly at her. Rabia warmed to it, and nodded her head in acknowledgement, letting her face break into a smile readily. Like most of the other older English women that Rabia had seen, this woman had very short cropped hair and it was all curled up around the crown of her head. She wore make-up too. Lipstick!

If she had cut her hair short as that (like a man's) or wore make-up, she would be the butt of ridicule, and become a laughing stock in her community in Lahore, in Pakistan. People would laugh and exclaim, 'What has happened to the old woman?' 'What does she think she is doing tarting herself up like that?' 'Shouldn't she be looking her age?' 'She should be ashamed of herself!'

It was just another way of life, another perspective, she argued with herself. English people's culture was very different from hers. In the eight months she had been in England she had learnt so much about the English people, their culture and their habits. She was fast becoming attuned to life in England. When she first arrived, she was aghast at what she saw of the 'decadent' and 'permissive' west. Coming from a Muslim country, the contrast was especially piquant.

She had asked her daughter-in-law, why English women exposed so much of themselves, their legs, their arms, and sometimes almost the whole of their body, clad only in two scraps of material. Her granddaughter had told her in reply, that the English people in their turn, were similarly surprised at their way of dressing. They had asked why Muslim women covered their body and hair?

Rabia Bibi would never forget that day, however, when she was confronted by two bikini-clad young women on the beach at Blackpool. Never had she felt so embarrassed before in her life, as she did at that time—with her son by her side, she felt so ashamed. She hadn't known where to look, at the voluptuous curves of the young woman or the donkeys prancing on the sand, with children on their backs. How could they do it? She asked herself aghast. Later she shook her head. Who was she to judge them? She told herself unconvincingly. That was their way of life.

For the same reason, she daren't watch television when everybody else was watching. You could never trust the English

TV programmes. One was never sure when men and women on the screen would begin to kiss and cuddle one another, or get into bed together. Every time such incidents flashed on the screen, her cheeks would begin to smart from the heat, from embarrassment. In order to rid her discomfiture she would begin to talk about any topic, about Pakistan, and about their relatives and friends. She would look anywhere but the television, yet her grandchildren carried on watching nonchalantly as if nothing was the matter!

Parents began to clap their hands to the beat of the music. Rabia Bibi too joined in the clapping, opening wide her palms and fingers, as she always did at the *Bhangra* dance in Pakistan. She caught sight of the bulky figure of an elder teacher, waving and shaking her arms over her head, like the children, and then wriggling her bottom from side to side vigorously. Fancy an older woman making a fool of herself like that in public. Hadn't she herself, however, taken part occasionally in wedding ritual dances at the hen party, she conceded. She too, probably according to the on-lookers made some ridiculous looking movements. Her granddaughter was imitating the same movements; her hair flying out behind her, joining in the laughter of the children.

The music stopped; the clapping ended, and the hall grew quiet. The children sat on the floor in lines. Roxana sat with the other teachers on the chairs. The headmistress stood at the top end of the hall and made a speech. 'School' and 'Christmas' were the only two words that Rabia Bibi understood.

When the speech ended, it was time for the children to return to their classrooms to tuck into the party dinner. Under the guidance of their teachers, children filed themselves in neat lines. The children then left the hall, class by class. Roxana was almost going to leave the hall, when she remembered her grandmother. Locating her amongst the parents, and with a reassuring smile on her lips, Roxana beckoned to her grandmother to follow her.

With a beating heart and feeling very awkward at having to leave her seat while everyone else was seated. Rabia got up with her *shalwar* making a rustling sound round her ankles. She followed behind Roxana's class into one of the classrooms, dotted down the school corridor.

Rabia hadn't been in this room before. She stood in the doorway and watched in wonderment. The room looked so lovely. It was decorated with children's pictures, paintings, and Christmas cards, pinned to the display board. Tissue streamers criss-crossed across the room, from wall to wall. In the middle of the room, six tables were laid out with large pieces of coloured tissue paper covering their tops. The tables were laden, with plates, bowls, containing food.

Roxana placed a chair in one corner of the room for her grandmother, and asked if everything was OK. Her grandmother uttered the word 'Yes.' Satisfied, Roxana returned to her class, the children having already been introduced to Miss Gulzar's grandmother, who spoke in a funny language. Some Pakistani children in the classroom had heard and understood what Miss Gulzar had said, but were too shy to acknowledge that they had.

Wearing their funny looking tissue papered hats, the children began to tuck into the food. Sandwiches were passed around. Orange juice was poured into small plastic cups, and crisps and cakes were plucked by eager infant fingers from the school's Pyrex bowls. Roxana took a plate of sandwiches to her grandmother and offered them to her, speaking in Punjabi.

'Lay lo, Ama Ji.'

'Bethy, kya hey?' 'What is it daughter?' she asked, looking suspiciously at the plate. Then she shook her head. A glimpse of something creamy and green oozing out of pieces of cut bread didn't appeal to her. She wasn't sure whether it would be *halal.* There was probably *churbee,* animal fat in it. Roxana returned the plate to the table. Taking one sandwich, she munched away, apparently enjoying it very much. Sometime later she returned with a glass of orange juice and a bowl of crisps. These her grandmother accepted readily. She knew these two items. She had eaten them before, although the flavour of the crisps was different from the ones she had last time.

Roxana watched her grandmother and smiled reassuringly at her. In the hall, she had looked so lost and so abandoned. Love welled up inside her for her grandmother. But then what did one expect? School was such an institution, that it even reduced English parents to a state of nervousness. Let alone, her grandmother, who had come from another country, another way of life, and another culture. She just wished that her grandmother would attempt to smile as much as she could, rather than looking so glum.

When the school bell was rung, parents were already waiting outside the classroom to collect their son or daughter. After the children departed, Roxana, with the help of another teacher began to clear up. Her grandmother got up to help too. She was good at tidying up places. She just needed to be told what to do, and where to throw the used paper plates and cups. Rabia mused over her predicament. While in Lahore, in her household, she was the mistress, giving advice, instructions and orders to her two daughters-in-law and her granddaughters, here she was at the receiving end of instructions.

Her mind dwelt on her two sons and their families in Lahore. They all lived together in a large house. There was always a lovely, happy and merry atmosphere around the place which was sadly lacking in her son's family in Manchester. Here everybody always had something to do. The children, if they weren't doing their homework, they were either reading newspapers or watching television, or speaking to each other in English. She didn't have the same rapport with these grandchildren as she had with those in Pakistan, she was just the visiting grandmother. The one they saw for a short space of time, after a number of years, and the one who was staying with them temporarily. Her elder granddaughter, Roxana, and her daughter-in-law were the two who made a special effort to make her feel at home, to see to her needs.

With the place tidied up and having said goodbye to the other teachers, grandmother and granddaughter left the school. Roxana felt high-spirited and buoyant and she and her class had enjoyed themselves thoroughly, although her bones ached after all that running around in the hall. She wondered whether her grandmother had enjoyed herself too, and she asked if she had.

After a slight hesitation, Rabia nodded her head, more for Roxana's sake. She knew Roxana had enjoyed herself, but then she was part of this world and would do so anyway. As for herself – well that was another story. It had been one of the worst moments of her life and she had never before, felt so lonely, so alienated, surrounded by complete strangers, and had never before experienced the feeling of timidity and helplessness. Above all, the day had stripped her of her personal dignity and self-confidence—she had, for the first time, come across the real England, not the one, in the safe confines of her son's home.

When they reached their house, Rabia looked around the room with renewed interest. Today she viewed it as a sort of haven. It was familiar, warm and cosy, containing people she knew, loved and held dear. Ironically, it was only yesterday that she had felt suffocated in this small enclosed house. She was used to open surroundings, open courtyards, a large house with large airy rooms.

Later in the evening, her son asked her jokingly what she thought of her visit to the school. She listed the things she had seen and marvelled at, and the people she had met. She omitted to say how she had felt during the day. No one would understand her. Above all, she said, she had a taste of the life that her granddaughter lived day to day at her work. She marvelled at Roxana's ability to weave in and out of the two worlds, cultures, languages and identities. What alternative did Roxana have anyway? She had to.

All of a sudden she recalled the subject which had made her cry in the school hall: the death of her cousin, Noor Begum. Cautiously she brought up the subject of her return to Pakistan, while her son was in a good mood.

'Son, I have been here for the last eight months; I think its time I went home.' She wasn't talking in vain, there was a determination in her voice. Her son noticed this.

'Mother, stay for two more months, then you can go,' he rallied. 'Your visa doesn't expire until four months later.'

He didn't relish the thought of sending his mother away, it had been great having her around the house. There was a special merry atmosphere in his home since his mother had arrived and his family had revelled in it.

'No, my son, I must go. I must get back to Pakistan, before the end of the mourning period and the fortieth day prayer gathering of the relatives for Noor Begum, your mother-in-law.'

'But that's only in two weeks time, you can't possibly go so soon?'

'I must. I can't miss out on that gathering. What will our relatives say about my absence? Anyway, I want to be there. I must represent my family, otherwise your younger brother will have to take up all the responsibility and he is so busy as it is, and anyway, I feel so redundant here. I know you all want me to stay, and love me very much, but there is nothing much for me to do. In Pakistan I have so many jobs to do, and so many responsibilities which all keeps me healthy and busy. It is also getting very cold here for my bones and I am getting too old. I don't want to die here, one never knows when one might die—I want to leave England a live woman, not a corpse in a box.'

'Oh, mother, don't talk about death. You are in the best of health. We need you so much.'

'It happens my son. What happened to Noor Begum? I left her a healthy woman and now I have been deprived of seeing her face before she was buried.'

'OK mother, as you wish,' her son said quietly. It would make a hell of a difference in his household when she went. He would miss her cooking too. He couldn't keep her against her will, however.

Rabia Bibi's heart began to thud with excitement. She was going! And so soon. As she had to be there at the fortieth day prayer in honour of Noor Begum's soul, it looked as if she would reach her destination in a week's time. If she delved in her heart she knew that she was using Noor Begum's death to leave England. Only yesterday she had resigned herself to stay in Manchester for another three months.

For the most part she had enjoyed her stay in England. She had seen so many places and met so many people. She had made so many friends. She had been pampered and made to feel very special and cherished. Her son, his wife and her three grandchildren had showered love and presents on her as she never envisaged. So many dinners were given in her honour. She had gone on *Hajj,* the Muslim pilgrimage to Mecca in Saudi Arabia, three months ago.

There was so much to do if she was going to Pakistan next week. Rabia Bibi got up with renewed energy; she must sort out her clothes, the presents she was going to give her grandchildren and her three children. She had been saving them for the last few months. She left the room a happy woman. Her son was already on the phone enquiring about plane tickets to Pakistan.

A week later, as Rabia sat on the plane to go to Pakistan, she was overcome by a mixture of feelings. She was sad at leaving her son, her grandchildren and all the friends she had made. Would she see any of these people again? Yet she was so happy at going home, her 'home'.

As she looked down through the plane window at the cottony clouds as London disappeared below her, she fully accepted the fact that she was actually leaving.

Her mind switched to Pakistan. A poignant thought occurred to her. Did her grandchildren living in Manchester have the same thoughts and feelings when they said goodbye to Pakistan and returned to England, 'their' home?

Did her son, too, who was born and bred in Pakistan, regard England as his home and have the same feeling for England as she had for Pakistan? For the first time in the last twenty years, Rabia had an insight into the mind of her son. The son who over the years had become a stranger to her. He had settled in England since his early twenties, and in the last twenty years had made four short visits with his family to Pakistan. With a sinking heart, Rabia realized that the son was lost to her. She couldn't deny the loss any more.

Rabia brushed these thoughts away determinedly. She wasn't going to become morbid. A week of excitement lay ahead of her. Now, who would be there at the airport to meet her? They would all be there, every one of them. They would flock to Lahore Airport from towns and cities. Her relatives and she had been to *Hajj* and was now a *Hajen* twice over. A special car would be hired for her, a special feast and...

The pretty Pakistani hostess passed by and enquired of Rabia, addressing her as 'mother' as was the custom for older people.

'Ap theek hey, Ama Jan?' (Are you all right?)

Rabia nodded her head and smiled happily.

'Ji han, beithy. Meh apney ghar jathi hue.' ('Yes, daughter. I am going home.')

The hostess passed on.

Rabia closed her eyes, lost in her thoughts of England, and the family she had left behind in Manchester.

MOEEN FARUQI

Moeen Faruqi was born in Karachi and has lived there for most of his life. He went to America for higher education and graduated from the California State University, Fresno, in Physics. Later he got an M.Ed. degree from the University of Wales, Cardiff. He is now an administrator of a private school in Karachi. He has also taught Computer Science and English. He has written research papers on education for academic journals; and he contributes articles, particularly on education and art, for newspapers in Pakistan. His first poem was published in *Orbis,* a literary magazine in Britain, and his work has appeared abroad in *Verse, The Rialto* and *Cyphers*. He started writing poetry very early, but he regards painting as his first calling. He believes that visual art and literature are intimately related and his paintings tend to be narrative in nature. His work has been strongly influenced by a sense of alienation and loss from living in a large, difficult metropolis which has seen constant change.

Partition

In that year
they left the old house
taking the odour of clothes
and souls.

We replaced the trees and crows,
and planted fresh birth sounds
and sleep sounds.
We changed nameplates.
We changed the street.

Even now when the pot boils
on the old stove
making tinny sounds,
it is the noise of the morning women
restless, and the men
demanding bread.

There is cement on sandstone,
concrete on the ground
where the sleeping desert
once swam.

But from the cracks in the wall
the house speaks.
There is breath
coming from the black loam
around the rose bush.

The ants speak.
The wind that slaps the west wall
speaks.

I can smell the master's dream
in his old white vest,

soiled and tattered,
holding the bricks of the wall.

Shadows of bones walk
in the night.
The house bares its soul
with each monsoon drop
on the windowsill.

The Crows

In the mango tree in the backyard
she planted when she was just married,
there are crows cawing, crying for blood,
calling, calling.

Mother never cried,
though her tears were moist foliage.
The crows were never hungry;
she fed them meat and bread from our mouths
as sacrifice.

In the heavens there was a blue temple
she called to. The temple spoke;
there were comforting voices for her.

I thought I saw ice on her lips
when they showed her death face.
The crows flew overhead in droves.
They cried for her;
they paid homage.

The day she went we buried the world
and inscribed the dead sun on her gravestone.

Letter from Home

Even now, so far from the heat
and steam of the pot
endlessly simmering,
Mother's voice is in the wind
and the light.

Her face, playing hide-and-seek
behind sheets drying in the desert wind,
now emerges from the washer's black bowel.

When Hampstead trees are cold as steel,
the mist in the leaves
is incense from the mosque
of her prostrate body,
a soft prayer on naked feet
following
        following.

Each wrinkled aerogramme
brings with it
exhalations of a life
silent as stone,
outside on the porch,
packaging memories for the
fragrant sarcophagus.

I wait. I wait.
The old woman with power over souls still reigns.

The Return

After washing Paddington loos
and scrubbing Hampstead streets
I returned to my piece of the Punjab

bought the 26 acres they took
from my father,
dry, hot land
that stopped giving birth to dreams the day
he died in a London hospital, his lungi
covering up his bony face till eternity

Now the land is giving birth again
it cries every season
with new voices, and the stars
rain down white light again
  but the men still come
  looking for Kafirs,
                unbelievers

Two days ago another died
they called Kafir
(My old man said to me:
'I can see, but I am willing to be blind')

On nights when the air is choking with dust
and heat
I close my eyes and place
my hand on the soft, pregnant
belly next to me
and I remember the green hills
of *Inglistan*
  and the boot steps that
  one dark night followed me
  in a dark and sour London alley
  calling

Kafir! Kafir!
(And my old man said to me:
'I can see, but I am willing to be blind')

Perveen Pasha

Born in Karachi, Perveen Pasha was educated at Trinity Preparatory School, St. Joseph's Convent and St. Joseph's College. She did her Masters from Karachi University in English Literature and later, in history. She was encouraged to write by her literary father. She is one of the very few English poets who has concentrated on political concerns. Her poems about Bosnia, South Africa, Kashmir and Karachi or the plight of women in Pakistan, are essentially concerned about the larger issues of displacement and oppression and the struggle for freedom. Her political poetry was published in the daily newspaper, *The News* and provides the backbone of her first collection, *Shades of Silence* (1996).

FROM ***Shades of Silence***

A Tribute to Mandela

More to him, his cell
a visionary with
surges of freedom
in his soul; the
horizons come.
Not to resist, but
to live life as it
should be—
the cold bars that lock out life
warn the spirit
of its proud heritage
of freedom.
With faith and hope
all there in the waiting…
for some truths
there are no compromises
no shelters; the soulless
find alternatives.
In the distant echoes
of evensong, shifting in the cross-winds of time
a number of nameless hungers
blaze out of the calm sun.
A strong beautiful wanting
crying its want; caught in
a prism of word echoes.
The sun burns its gold
in a moment of irradiated light
men pay with their lives to be
free; to have freedom
by never walking away.
We must disenthrall our soul.

Beyond the Veil

Never to him come
never hear the cries of those
creatures of light; who paint
arabesques of faith, hope, tenderness,
yet, sequacious follow
the mindless tyranny
of insensate beings—
which is a death
beyond the veil.
A lone face, calm in her grace
she sat,
while skeined transparencies
of thought traced
fire-patterns in her being.
A legacy of humiliations!
sully her soul,
rived flesh, bared to the indignities
of human callousness.
Let us talk of bondage to
enlightened man.
Let us talk of slave-trade,
of inequality—of being cast aside
in the emptiness
of the night.
Let us talk of the
despair in her eyes!
The hand that lit the lamp
rough with labour
her callused soul
What of the hope
in those henna'ed palms
raised in prayer—
to die, yet many deaths
await the desecration
of the inner-most sanctuaries
of her mind.

Moazzam Sheikh

Moazzam Sheikh was born in Lahore, a city he associates with cricket, jasmine, dust, and the 'Marquezian, streets' of Samanabad and a people burdened with great sadness. He left for higher studies in the United States in 1985. Having been educated at Urdu medium schools in Pakistan, he had to work hard at improving his English. As he started to understand the language more, he became aware of the moral and political issues of American history, and of the downtrodden and dispossessed everywhere, which impelled him to write. His work has appeared in several literary journals and anthologies including the *Toronto Review*, *Mobius* and *The Adobe Anthology*. He is now working on a novel and translating the Urdu writer, Naiyer Masud into English.

Rains of the Monsoon

The early shadows of the monsoon had struck the night before with full rage; soon, the streets of Lahore would become rivers in August, carrying mud and filth. The frightening thunders were heard up till the end of the night, and the single wooden window and the back door in his room, which opened to the balcony, seemed already wet and swelled. Masud paced back and forth in his room, impatiently and nervously, like a caged cat. His face was dark and beaten, eyes small but deep, restive, and shoulders bent as if an invisible weight rested on them. If one looked harder, one saw a little cut under his pointed chin which he was in the habit of rubbing occasionally. He stopped for a second next to the table and lit another cigarette, staring at the Urdu newspaper folded on the table; the desire to read the paper had left him. She had been very punctual, he cogitated, for her survival depended on it, but now, as it continued to pour buckets outside, she was more than an hour late.

He stopped pacing and, looking out towards the balcony, saw the dark, vicious clouds which filled the frame his balcony door had created. The wind caused the rain to fall at an angle, away from the balcony door; the rain water was running aslant on the balcony floor to a hole in one corner, falling on the muddy sidewalk like a fall. He went out to the balcony and stood under the tin roof, resting his hand on the metal grille, looking out to the back of her house, the pale, yellow wall being whipped by the merciless rain. From four stories up, he could look at her window which opened into the back alley, but now was shut tight. It would remain so throughout the monsoon. The rain fell on the tin roof like an unpleasant, out-of-tune melody of a *sitar*, and, feeling irritated, he stepped back in. He sat down on a chair, jumpy, his legs shifting positions, his feet shaking slightly, and every time he moved, the chair squeaked because of its loose joints. Now, he was aware of the emptiness that suddenly gripped him.

Smoke rings drifted from his lips while his eyes raced all over the wall and its cracked surface. He needed her; the monsoon, the smell of the earth in the air, the subdued noises of the human beings out on the street, soaked and hurrying, the howling of the wandering dogs, and the solitude within him made him ache for her company. The comfort of her flesh. Was he addicted to her? He could not answer. She had never skipped a work day, he reflected as he paused again, even when she had a light fever three weeks ago.

He decided on impulse to walk to her house and inquire what stopped her today. Or, perhaps, it was the crying rain that called him out to see her naked misery. He grabbed his umbrella and, putting on his rain coat, walked down the dirty, old stairway which stank with such severity that it reminded him of rotten flesh every time he came out to the stairs. He could arrange for someone else, he thought as he descended, but, no, he enjoyed her presence. Was she on her way? He might even run into her on the street; the thought pleased him momentarily.

Masud Sheikh lived in a decrepit building, one of the remains of the British rule, the red, thin-tiled building with the Victorian facade, and its landlord rented out the rooms, because of their small size, to bachelors or married men, and some women too, who came to Lahore from other places to find work. But he had lived all his life in this city, in the old city encased behind thirteen decaying gates and, unlike others, rented this place quietly in order to forget his past.

At the foot of the building were five shops: a bakery, a laundromat, a grocery store, a hardware store, and a barber shop. It was at the barber shop that people gathered and sat, listening to the radio tuned to Lata's or Noor Jahan's voice: or to Ishfaq Ahmed's Hidayat Allah every evening at seven: or once in the morning to the Radio Pakistan, Lahore and once in the afternoon to Akashwani (All India Radio); also playing cards, drinking tea, and gossiping all day long. Jumma Khan, the barber, was the fulcrum of information and subject matter to these gossips; he was how the stories really spread.

It was Jumma who, one afternoon, out of consideration, had suggested Masud hire a cleaner, a sweeperess, one of the Christian women from the nearby slums.

'*Ar-rey*, Masud *Sahib*, you should get a sweeper for your room. It keeps the place clean,' Jumma had said, looking at him in the stained, warped mirror, his scissors dancing clip, clap.

'Do you know any, Jumma, whom you can trust?' he had asked with the same subtlety, looking into the mirror.

'Not at the moment, Brother *Ji*,' Jumma had said, gripping Masud's hair between his fingers and pulling it up, 'but I will certainly keep my eyes open and let you know.' And Jumma had smiled into the mirror, becoming a secret sharer.

Masud remembered the conversation now as he climbed down the last steps out to the street, into the rain, breathing hard. Having come out in the open, he felt a nakedness creep into him as he faced Jumma, who knew every *terra incognito* a heart could know and every truth hidden behind a pair of eyes, light or dark. The news of his desperation, he feared, would spread now among the card players, the indolent tea sippers, and then the other neighbours. Masud saw Jumma Khan from the corners of his eyes and hurried his steps.

'Ah-ha, Masud *bi-raa-der*, where to, in this rain?' Jumma's voice replaced the thunders of the monsoon; mostly to annoy Masud, he liked to enunciate the word *biraader* by breaking it into its paused syllables.

Masud stopped under the umbrella, the rain beating as hard as possible to subdue any sound. 'To the post office, Jumma *Mian!* How have you been?' waving his hand. He moved on without waiting for Jumma's answer, but he heard Jumma Khan exclaim, *'Al-hemdo-lil-lah!'* in Arabic, followed by a spiteful laughter. And it was then he remembered, annoyed by the laughter, that the post office was in the other direction. He felt a shrinking sensation as he walked away from the building.

There was a sense of panic on the street, he noticed. He had become deaf to every sound except that of the rain. Turning right from the Pakki Thatti *sherbet* shop to the Chora *basti*, he walked three streets south, along the meat market, and faced the wall with the big hole: there were advertisements painted on the wall on each side of the hole. People went through this hole instead of going half a mile farther to the iron gate installed by the city municipal corporation. He ducked his head down and came out the other side, having closed and reopened his umbrella. He stood in the neighbourhood of the servant class people, mostly the dark Christians who were, as some believed, the crop of British seed and fertilizer. After the masters had vanished, the leftovers from the British domain had become the rags of this society, a society which claimed human equality its basic pillar. At the corner of the two extremely narrow alleys to his left he saw a small *paan* shop: a small boy squatted behind a box and empty cold drink bottles. A tin shade jutted out from above giving shelter to two skinny men, standing, drinking their tea. The men gave Masud a curious look, then laughed and went back to their conversation. It was windier on this side of the wall; he tightened his grip on the umbrella. He noticed, as he walked on, the children of different ages, though mostly boys, some naked and some in shorts, running in different directions, playing the rain games. Sheltered underneath his umbrella, he examined the houses to the right and the left, registering the paleness of the walls and the doors which hung askew even when they were chained and locked. It was a long row of small, one room houses, huddled together as if scared, often without an alley between their walls or a verandah in the front. No tree grew on this street.

Here, the rain water in the middle of the earthen street was already a few inches deep. He walked on the slim muddy and slippery sidewalk. He made out her house and halted in front of its soaked, uneven wooden door, from which a lizard-like chain dangled. As he decided to strike his knuckles against the door, an unknown fear surrounded his innards and he felt weak in the knees; his fist remained suspended in the air. The frost of his breath came out in rapid successions. Closing his eyes, he jangled the chain. He looked to the street where the lean children played with an old tennis ball, throwing it to each other with loud, shrieking sounds, jumping up and down into the brown water. Though he could hear their sounds, it seemed that the yelling and shrieking did not reach his ears but his heart, piercing to the middle. Suddenly he reacted, as if caught off his guard, to the creaking door and its rusted hinges, and turned his head with an inward fright to face the skeleton, emerging from the dark room, who grinned at him without his front teeth, perplexed and scared.

Masud saw the two morbid looking eyes flicker in the old man's sockets. Though the intensity of the man's face softened, his gaze now showed contempt and subjugated hatred. The old man's stare penetrated Masud's vision, and the man's face fell out of focus for a moment. It was then that he felt guilty of some inexplicable crime and thought that he, in fact, had something to do with this man's fate, his skeletal existence.

After an awkward silence, the host, moving aside, motioned Masud to step inside, having guessed who he might be.

'Come in from the rain,' he said. 'Nasima is home.'

Masud stepped in with hesitation, folding his wet umbrella and shaking the drops of water onto the dried mud floor. He tried to adjust his eyes to the darkness of the room. Inside the room burnt a stove which made the room smell of kerosene oil. He made out the figures of a woman and two children standing next to the stove to stay warm; the flame cast a faint, dancing light on them. The woman's face was struck with surprise. The old man closed the door.

'*Salaam-alaikam*,' the woman mumbled.

'I thought you might have hurt yourself,' he said to Nasima.

The water dripped from the ceiling into a tin bucket, tip, tip, tip, in the middle of the room, with equal intervals, splashing out onto the mud. The sound of the leak inside, suddenly, seemed to grow louder with each silent second like an explosion.

Coming to the centre of the room, a little closer to him, beside the bucket, she said, 'It's been hell here, Masud *Ji*, the leak and the children and....' but her voice trailed off when she saw his uninterested face. His prolonged silence made her uneasy; however she managed to speak again: 'I thought you would not mind my not coming in the rain today.' Her voice sank into the sound of the water dripping, tip, tip...

Masud saw her lips moving, but did not hear what she said. His mind was somewhere else: in his mind he was back in his room, saw his empty bed, and was reminded of his loneliness. He looked at her husband, who stood crossing his arms to hide his naked chest, and the old man smiled faintly upon meeting Masud's eyes. Behind the skeletal man, just above his head, on the wall, Masud noticed a calendar with *Hazrat* Jesus nailed to the crucifix. Masud looked away to the flame in the stove, and cleared his throat.

'I have invited,' Masud began slowly, his voice deep and needy, glancing back to Nasima, 'some friends tonight for tea. If you could come for a short while?' His eyes rested, briefly, on her intimate breasts, obscured behind the shirt she wore of thin material, before moving his stare back to her face.

'Yes, yes, why not, Nasimey?' the old man's voice startled Masud. 'Go, go and do a quick sweeping, why not?' and at the end of his words he coughed, pushing his chest against his arms and bending forward, as if in obedience. A child stepped forward to the old man and grabbed his *dhoti* cloth.

Nasima moved to leave, staring at her children, and leaned to pick up her *dupatta* from the string bed. Masud thought of Jumma Khan and his cunning laughter, and halted at the door, the old man freezing behind him. 'You don't have to come with me. I have to run an errand on my way home, so wait about half a hour and then come.' Masud opened the door.

Holding her *dupatta*, Nasima nodded and then looked at her husband, who was looking at the rain falling on the brown bed of water.

Opening his umbrella over his head, Masud hurried out into the rain. Walking down the street, he felt his insides filling with rage, and as he approached his neighbourhood, sneaking through the hole, he did not avoid the puddles, his shoes becoming drenched and muddy. He took quick steps and his heart beat faster. He spotted Jumma, from a block's distance, sitting under the shade that jutted out from the building's facade.

'*Wah*! *Allah's* blessing is this rain, Masud *Sahib*, the crops are thirsty and waiting, and here God is ever merciful. I wonder what happened to Nasima?' Jumma took a deep puff from his Kashmiri *hookah*; water in the bottom of the *hookah* gurgled angrily. But before Masud could answer, Jumma cackled, 'Those lazy Christians. Those damn *Farangees* should have taken their filth back to *Inglistan* I say.' He shook his head as if with disappointment and disgust, but Masud knew it was more with malice and mockery.

'Jumma *Ji*,' Masud snapped, 'who would clean our Muslim toilets then? Who would wash our arses?' Leaving Jumma stunned with the tip of the *hookah's* mouthpiece hanging in his grip, Masud leapt inside.

With his head encased in his palms, leaning, he sat motionless, feeling nauseated, weightless; he tried to clear his mind of thoughts, but they kept crowding his head. He should not have gone, he reflected bitterly, a man could lose all his decency faster than any other thing he possessed: money, health, love.

He came out of his doldrums, on the verge of having drowned, on hearing the door creak; he looked up and Nasima was halfway in the room.

She stood staring at him, the rain drops sliding from her body.

'So when are those guests of yours coming? In this rain?' She asked, smiling, a bit teasing, a bit sarcastic.

He just stared at her.

She shivered with cold and squeezed the wetness on her arms with her hands. It took a while to register, but then he got up quickly, grabbed a towel, and extended it to her. He then changed his mind and began drying her hair, shoulders, arms, and the rest of her body himself. She stood there, staring at the ceiling, later at the lizard which stared back at her. He suddenly kissed her lifeless lips with the ferocity of the monsoon rains, escorting her to his *takht-e-shahi*, to his Taj Mahal.

Soon he crumbled to the side, breathing heavily, eyes closed, relieved. She kept her eyes open, but covered them with her elbow. He felt he was slowly sinking, like a stone, into the depths of an immense ocean. The numbness in his body made him alienated to his surroundings. The constant fall of the rain and the unvarying sound of it seemed to dull his sense of desire now. The silence started to cut into his heart. He knew he had to speak or else he would become a reef.

'Who was he?'

'Who? My husband?'

'Yes, the old man. Does he know?' he asked, feeling the bitter taste of his own words; acknowledging his own defeat.

'Yes, he knows. They all know…'

He wanted to know who they all were, but he did not. He longed for a trace of emotion in her voice, an inkling of compassion, sympathy, or even pity, but her tone fell flat. Suddenly he remembered the old man's sickly stare, glowing beneath the ashes of his life. The burning, coal-like eyes of the old man now moved closer and closer, thrusting inward, pushing against his own eyes, his brains. It felt as if two red hot suns had gotten inside his skull, and his face would melt any moment. A scream came to his throat, but got stuck inside his mouth. Then he heard Nasima's husband crack with laughter, 'Yes, yes, why not, *Sahib*. Why not?'

The anger rose inside him, and he wanted to break something, smash something, a pot, a picture, a memory; he wanted to scream aloud, 'pimp, rascal, coward,' but deep down he grew angrier at himself, feeling an urge to curse his own loneliness.

She raised her elbow and turned to look at his face. He looked to her. 'You should get married,' she said. 'Even when you are with me, you remain sad. Even when you are caressing me, your eyes remain sorrow-soaked. That is not good.' They both smiled an unexpected smile, their dark-rimmed, lifeless eyes becoming alive for a moment, glowing like dying cinders.

He began kissing her, and then his hands caressed the inviting curves of her body. He felt the lack of the same feeling on the other side. He thought of asking her to respond the way she would to her husband but then he forcibly stitched his lips. Perhaps she does not love him either, he thought. To his surprise, she squeezed him, wrapping her arms around him.

'Nasima,' he hissed.

'What?' she hissed back.

'Marry me.'

'Silly man; I am married,' she answered, laughing.

'Then run away with me.'

'I have children.' She looked into his eyes and her grip around his body relaxed. After a very short silence, she held him tighter with an unknown cruelty, digging her nails into his shoulders.

'Your husband is too weak—sick,' he said.

She moaned, as if in response.

'He is a guest of a few more days,' he whispered.

Her body stiffened. 'What? What do you mean?' Her voice grew in fear. 'Why do you talk like that? Because you can pay me?'

She trembled with emotion, pushing him away with her palms, and started to sob, shaking with sudden jerks. He felt miserable, angry, and he heavily moved to his side, feeling impotency settle in him, his own existence shrinking and shrinking, disappearing into a dark cloud.

He wrapped a white sheet around his waist, like a *dhoti*, and pulled another over her. She had, however, stopped sobbing and was quiet.

'I am sorry, Nasima,' he said, failing to meet her eyes.

'Don't say that again,' she murmured, as if talking to herself. She did not look to him either. He stared at her naked feet.

She sat up on the *takht*, her legs dangling, and put on her brassiere. He grabbed his wallet and took out three ten rupee bills. She had already gotten ready, and now turned to say farewell, seeing his extended hand with the money.

'This is too much,' she said.

'That's okay, I mean…' he replied with wandering eyes. 'And…take, please, two or three days off. I will be all right. You know *Ramazan* is approaching too.' He forced a smile.

She seemed to be lost in thought, but then she snapped out of it and said, '*Shukria*,' gratefully, and rushed out, shutting the door behind her. His hand reached for his cigarettes. A spider slowly began to crawl around his heart.

Three days later the rains still had not stopped, and the streets were like rivers; the wheels of the horse carriages turned in the water slowly, scooping up water on their wooden spokes and pouring it back on the street; occasionally the winds blew, angling the rain this way or that way; at times rocking the windows and doors fistfully. Here and there a wall collapsed or a roof caved in. Masud remained inside his room, going out only to buy milk for tea or *chappatis* at the *tandoor*. Masud tried to not think too much of Nasima, of her not being here, or her husband. Or his voice. But once in a while the old man's ghost appeared before him, mocking slyly, 'So, *Sahib Ji*, am I a guest of how many days? Going to die? So soon?' He tried to dismiss the ghost as fast as possible. 'Ha ha ha! I am going to die, and you can have Nasima all to yourself. But do not forget my children, Masud *Sahib*! Hee hee hee!'

One day as he sat in his chair, smoking a cigarette, reading the *Akhbar-e-Jahan* weekly, a sudden knock at the door jolted him. He felt a tinge of uncertainty and, nervously, stood up and opened the door, imagining it to be Nasima. With that conjecture, his longing for her exploded. But, to his surprise, a young woman of no more than eighteen, stood at the door.

'Yes? *Bolo!*' he asked her, confronting her silence.

'*Salaam Ji*,' the young girl's voice trembled, as she tried to smile.

'*Salaam*! Yes?'

'Nasima will not be able to come for a few days; I thought you might need...a sweeper.'

He wanted to tell her to go away, but he ended up saying: 'Huh...oh! come in, yes. I...'

Perhaps he felt a wave of pity rising inside him. A young, beautiful Christian woman fresh like a flower; poverty and the need to prostitute her body, he thought, would turn her into a skeleton of tired bones in less than ten years. He noticed the broom in her hand. She walked in after him and placed it against the wall, closing the door behind her.

He discreetly observed her small but firm breasts. He sat down and lit another cigarette. Putting out the match, he inhaled the smoke and breathed out a huge silvery cloud. He crossed his legs. His eyes fell, through the obscurity of the smoke, on her feet, and the sight perplexed him. Her *shalwar* had slipped from her waist to the ground, covering her feet. He lifted his head and found her absorbed in unbuttoning her shirt. For a second he thought he was dreaming, the smoke distorting his sense of vision, but then a sudden rage overpowered his calm.

'What are you doing?' he shouted.

'*Sahib Ji*,' she shuddered, like a scared child.

'Yes, I asked you what you are doing!'

She spoke reluctantly: '*Sahib Ji*, that Jumma Khan has sent me up here.' They looked at each other, speechless, as if two statues placed behind glass in a museum.

Masud saw her naked legs, smooth and innocent, like running water; then her half-revealed breasts, offering solace; then her dark eyes. Masud felt his anger being subdued by a familiar sense of weakness; desire began to burn inside his veins, his limbs trembled and ached.

The woman was nervous at first, but she regained her composure. 'The other sahib,' she spoke with a soft voice, 'who lived in the next room paid me five rupees...every time I came to clean.'

The smoke clouds had dissolved into the air; holding the open collar of her shirt she took a step closer.

He lay on his *takht*, next to her. Looking at her, he tried to catch the disappearing warmth of her young breath. His thoughts flashed to Nasima and back, and he realized that anyone could replace the sense of comfort Nasima brought. He felt happy and light. And yet sad. Somewhere down on the street a radio played a *ghazal*, the sound rising to his balcony like smoke.

He stood in the balcony door, and she, now sitting up on the *takht*, hooked up her brassiere, bringing her hands behind her back. He looked at her back, shiny and smooth like a bathed *neem* leaf, stretching and contracting, the bones of her young spine stacked neatly on top of each other. On her waist he looked for his finger prints.

She got up and put on her *shalwar* and shirt, rolling her shoulders, adjusting the cups of her brassiere. She caught him looking, and smiled at him.

'You have a sick husband?'

'*Naa, Sahib Ji*, I am not married,' she answered with a short giggle, 'but I have a sick father with TB and my mother lost her legs years ago,' she said quickly, without emotion.

He took two ten rupee bills out. Giving them to her, he said, 'Come back tomorrow if you can.' She took the bills and tucked them inside the elastic of her bra. But as she put the money away, she stopped, remembering.

'Oh my God! I forgot to tell you, my bad memory,' putting the top of her fingers to her lips.

He stared at her.

'I forgot to tell you that Nasima's husband died last night...too much cough and fever.'

Masud knitted his brows, relaxed them. It became difficult for him to breathe. He felt dizzy and held on to the back of the chair. The old man's face appeared and disappeared from his sight.

She grabbed her broom and said, '*Shukria, Sahib Ji*, I will see you tomorrow,' and left the room.

Masud felt suffocated. He walked to the balcony, looked at the back of Nasima's home. He slammed the door shut. It was as he turned he noticed the rain had almost stopped. But the dark clouds hung on the outskirts, threatening to come back and drown the city with their rage.

SORAYYA Y. KHAN

The daughter of a Pakistani father and Dutch mother, Sorayya Khan was born in Europe. She moved to Islamabad in 1972, and was educated at the International School there. She graduated from Allegheny College in Pennsylvania, and did her masters at The Graduate School of International Studies, Colorado. She had wanted a career in Third World development and worked with the UNCHR and the World Bank for a while, but decided that through fiction she could best contemplate issues such as 'the interconnectedness of the world' and 'bridges between East and West'. She believes that her dual cultural heritage is pivotal to her as a writer. In 1995 her novella *In the Shadows of The Margalla Hills* won the First Novella Prize in the Canadian literary journal, *The Malahat Review*. The story is part of a work-in-progress. Her other fiction has appeared in the *Kenyon Review* and the *North American Review*. She lives in the United States, has participated in 'Resetting the Margins,' a national reading tour organized by the Asian American Writers Workshops and worked as Technical Writer to Atlantic States Legal Foundation.

FROM *IN THE SHADOWS OF THE MARGALLA HILLS*

In November Sadiq invited his son, Haneef, to visit him in Islamabad. It was the middle of the school year in Lahore and under normal circumstances Sadiq would not have permitted his son to miss school. But he was alarmed at the message he had received from his wife. She described how unwell Haneef seemed, and how he had lost interest in everything except for the latest news broadcasts and his prayer rug. Three months earlier, on brief leave from his job as servant in our house, Sadiq had spent time with his family in Lahore and noticed changes in his son. Haneef, who was named for a famous Pakistani cricket player, had never been able to resist the temptation of a cricket bat and ball. Suddenly, Haneef had become sluggish and slow on his feet, and the only time he seemed at peace was when he sat on his prayer rug and communed with God. Sadiq said that his son was only suffering from growing pains, like any child, and that in a month or two, or three or four, he would again be the happy child he had once been. Sadiq's wife did not believe this. Even as she repeated her suspicions in her recent message, Sadiq had difficulty imagining them possible.

Haneef had been only two years old during the 1971 war when East Pakistan was lost. But he claimed to remember hearing the swearing-in-ceremony of the Prime Minister a few days later. This was impossible and Sadiq said so many times. 'How can you remember the words when you did not even speak then?' Sadiq thought that if his son remembered anything it was the excitement in the neighbourhood, the fire crackers and balloons, and that the special occasion called for the distribution of sweets. They were poor people and the Prime Minister's campaign of *roti, kapra, aur makan,* promised what they had little of: bread, clothes, and shelter. The campaign slogan was attractive, but it did not change Sadiq's opinion of politics, that government was something better resigned to than fought for and, as a consequence, it was difficult for him to take Haneef's interest in the Prime Minister and his political party seriously. He assumed that Haneef merely mimicked what he heard in his neighbourhood.

Sadiq's wife lived with Haneef and had her own opinions. The day after his eighth birthday, when the Prime Minister was ousted by the General and his army, Haneef fell on his bed and wept at the news. He clutched his new race car to his face and his tears ruined the engine. Eight months later, when the Prime Minister was sentenced to death by the highest court in the land, she watched Haneef lay down his cricket bat forever and give his favourite ball to eager friends. She witnessed Haneef's will to live diminish with the sinking fortunes of the Prime Minister. As absurd as it may have sounded to her husband, she believed the two facts to be so intertwined that when she sat on her prayer rug to offer her daily prayers, she prayed for the Prime Minister as though her own son's life depended on it.

Haneef's stay in Islamabad passed quickly. Sadiq did everything within his means to make him happy. On Friday, his day off, he took his son on a bus ride from the corner of their street into the Margalla Hills beyond. They got off the bus thirty minutes later, at a stop called Viewpoint, and sat at the edge of a parking lot drinking a bottle of 7-Up from two straws. Sadiq was encouraged that his son asked questions about the mountains in the distance and laughed when Sadiq explained that the white cloak on the top was winter snow. Haneef had never travelled beyond Lahore. Although he read in school books about places that were different, he was unprepared for the hills and mountains and the long and uncrowded streets of the man-made capital below. He spent most of his days in Islamabad in the back yard, where he played with a new soccer ball and chased the resident mongoose from one side of its shallow tunnel to the other. Whenever possible, he accompanied Sadiq on his errands. They walked to the market when laundry detergent was needed or to the post box on the far corner of their street to mail a letter. When they went to the vegetable *wallah,* Haneef sat on the handlebars of Sadiq's heavy black bicycle and, when they returned, he balanced a packet of vegetables on his lap.

In the ten days of Haneef's visit in Islamabad, there was only a brief mention of the Prime Minister. Haneef asked to see the jail eight miles away where the Prime Minister was locked in a cell without light or food. The request came at the beginning of his visit, and was not made again after Sadiq ignored it. In fact, Sadiq was happy with how infrequently politics made its way into their conversations.

Two days before Haneef was due to return home to his mother, Sadiq's brother, Yunis, arrived from Lahore to accompany his nephew on the trip. Yunis worked in my grandfather's house in Lahore as a sweeper. He made the bus trip to Islamabad once or twice a year to visit Sadiq and give him news of his family. Yunis was responsible for securing Sadiq a job in our house and whenever he visited he was reassured by my parents that they had made the correct decision.

Late in the evening, Yunis and Sadiq sat on the patio outside the servant quarters of the house in Margalla Road and commented on Haneef's obvious improvement. Both were pleased that Haneef's attention seemed less focused on politics, each for his own reasons.

Yunis had spent the thirty-one years since Partition, when the English had dissolved their Empire, recording the misfortunes of the country on pieces of crumbling plaster of Paris. After all the crowded columns of notches, Yunis felt that he could say what he did. 'The country is greedy,' he said, 'It only takes from us.'

Sadiq believed his son's preoccupation with someone so distant as a Prime Minister was fruitless. 'Why should we bother about a government that does not bother about us?' Sadiq said to Yunis.

Together, they marvelled on how ten days in Islamabad had virtually wiped the thought of the Prime Minister from Haneef's mind. Before turning in for the night, Sadiq told Yunis of the only other time Haneef mentioned the Prime Minister and his predicament.

On the morning of the previous day, Haneef awoke to the smell of *halva* and *pooris.* He jumped from his mat, washed his face, and dressed in clean clothes. He sat on the *charpai* next to Sadiq who was preparing a special breakfast. There was a glow to Haneef's complexion that Sadiq had not seen in a long time, and he could not resist asking him how he felt.

'I'm happy,' Haneef had said. 'The Prime Minister will not die. He will live a life as long as mine.'

Yunis, like Sadiq, took Haneef's new found optimism as proof of how successful his visit had been. Sadiq told Yunis to tell his wife not to allow herself to be carried away by exaggeration: their son was going to be fine.

The night before Haneef and Yunis were scheduled to return to Lahore, they made a quick trip to Aabpara market. Earlier, Sadiq had asked Haneef if there was anything he wished to have before he returned home. Haneef said nothing, but when he was asked again, he expressed a wish for tennis shoes. Everything was more expensive in Islamabad than in Lahore, and Sadiq knew it was more sensible to give Yunis the money to purchase the shoes there, but Sadiq was so thrilled with the hint of his son's recovery that he jumped at the opportunity to please him. After dinner, they took a minivan to Aabpara and visited several shoe stores until they found the canvas shoe that best fit Haneef's feet. Sadiq emptied the front pocket of his *kurta,* unfolded a roll of rupees, and paid the shopkeeper. The shoes were very expensive and the change returned to Sadiq was too little to pay for their bus fare home. At the bus stop, a minivan was coming to a halt, Yunis reached for his money. When he could not find it, he remembered putting his money aside for the trip the next day, and then realized he had forgotten to retrieve it before leaving for the bazaar. Without enough money between them for bus fare, Yunis, Sadiq, and Haneef began the long walk from Aabpara to Margalla Road.

It was a black evening. As always, the street lights were not working, and the few vehicles making their way on the streets had their headlights set on high beams to compensate. But the headlights of cars and trucks and buses did not illuminate the street. They came and went in blinding flashes that sent Yunis, Sadiq, and Haneef scurrying toward the farthest edge of the road. As they left the bazaar behind them, the traffic lessened and the walk became more comfortable. Yunis and Sadiq walked steadily and quickly, but Haneef, with his shorter legs and smaller heart, lagged behind. Every so often, bicyclists passed them on the other side of the street, punctuating their own conversations with ringing bells.

By the time the blinding headlights appeared, all three of them were relaxed and comfortable with their stride and did not move to the side of the road as quickly as they might have. But even when they scattered for the edge of the road where it broke into a field, the car swerved toward them. Yunis shouted. Sadiq lunged backwards for Haneef, but in the blackness missed and did not see him until it was too late. He saw Haneef's face in the split second between when the headlights fell on him and when the car struck him. Haneef did not make the slightest sound. There was the thud of a body on steel, the shriek of desperate brakes, the sound of a package of shoes falling to the side of the road, and before the car started up again, the silence of disbelief.

Sadiq fell to the ground. He crouched over his son, softly speaking to the crumpled body as if it could still hear and see and feel. Yunis threw his fist against the trunk of the car. He walked to the passenger's side and tried to open it. He kicked the wheel, and the engine that had died with the shriek of brakes came to life again.

'Tehero,' he shouted, beseeching the driver not to leave. But almost as quickly as the car came to a stop, it screeched forward, leaving a dead body and a trail of dust on the shoulder of the road. Yunis looked at the car as it sped away. A small bulb lit up the rear licence plate and, before he looked at Haneef, he was struck by the colour and numbers of what he saw.

Yunis touched Haneef's foot, the only part of the boy that Sadiq seemed unable to gather inside the hunch of his body. Yunis collected the package of shoes where they had fallen and, side by side, they walked the mile and a half to the government hospital at the corner of two busy roads. Along the way, a car slowed and the driver offered them a ride. Neither Yunis nor Sadiq, overtaken with grief, answered. The driver, a man Yunis' age, shouted, 'Who did this to your son?'

Inside the emergency room, after a brief examination in which he held the boy's hand in his own and searched for a pulse, the medical attendant pronounced Haneef dead. After Yunis recounted the accident, the attendant jotted down a few illegible words on an unofficial piece of paper, declared it the death certificate, and handed it to them.

Sadiq lifted his son from the stretcher on which he lay and cradled him in his arms as though he were a baby rather than a nine-year-old boy. Yunis hailed a taxi, but when it came time to descend the few steps of the hospital building, Sadiq could not put his son in a stranger's car. He clenched Haneef's body deeper into his chest and began walking along the shoulder of the road. Yunis ran after him, begging Sadiq to leave the body, assuring him that they could return with a vehicle to fetch it. But Sadiq would not give up his son. The walking was slow and cumbersome and he did not allow Yunis the comfort of helping him. The weight in his arms grew heavier as the house neared and, by the time they turned on to Margalla Road, Sadiq was barely on his feet. He stumbled from one side of the road to the other as though he was its sole occupant, oblivious of the traffic that wove around him.

My father awoke to the sound of Yunis' knock on the bedroom window. He put on his robe, opened the back door, and heard the news. He followed Yunis into Sadiq's room where Haneef lay on his father's bed. Even from a distance in the poor light of the room, it was clear that his body was bent in places it should not have been. Sadiq sat on the floor and held his son's hand tightly in his own. When my father spoke to him, Sadiq said he remembered nothing of the accident. Yunis answered my father's questions quickly. The car was large and white, the licence plate was yellow, and Yunis recalled the numbers printed on it: AD 64 31. *'Amriki?'* my father asked. Yunis repeated the numbers he had seen, the yellow colour of the licence plate. Then my father left to make a telephone call.

Early the next morning, long before the winter sun began to rise, Yunis and Sadiq left Islamabad for Lahore with Haneef's body in a rented minivan. The driver was fast and reckless on Trunk Road, but that did not frighten them. On another occasion, Sadiq would have prayed for God's mercy to complete their journey safely, but he sat in the seat in front of where his son's body lay and asked for nothing. He believed that if he was meant to arrive in Lahore safely, he would; if not, he would be with his son sooner than he expected.

Sadiq's wife waited. She had received word of Haneef's death in the middle of the night when a phone call was made from Islamabad to Lahore and a messenger on a bicycle brought her the news in a telegram. Friends spent the night with her and early in the morning they began preparations for the funeral. They rolled and patted dough into *chappatis* and *pooris*. They laid out sweetmeats on trays in neat rows of plump balls and silver-laced rectangles and squares. Sadiq's wife pointed neighbours in the right direction and answered questions for her company. She was as composed as possible until she heard the minivan wind its way into the *muhallah.* She gripped her neighbour's elbow with one hand, her shoulder with the other. In the distance, she watched Sadiq and Yunis emerge from the van with the broken body of her son clasped between them. Their hold on each other was fast and, as they neared the gate, they did not disentangle themselves and give each other up. They turned sideways and entered the door in a makeshift single file. The sight of them in her home sent Sadiq's wife careering backwards. She fell against the far wall, where fire rose from a hole in the floor and boiled a kettle of water. She did not feel the heated water scorch her skin. 'What have you done with my son?' she screamed at Sadiq.

Long after the funeral, Sadiq could not bring himself to tell her how wonderful Haneef's visit had been, how colour had returned to his face, and how a few hours before his death he had asked for tennis shoes. But it did not matter because Yunis had told her all this and more. When Sadiq returned to his job in Islamabad, and she was left with an empty house and the memory of the son who had once filled it, Yunis sought to comfort her. He did his best to remember everything he could about Haneef on the last two days of his life. As hard as Yunis tried to make her believe that her son was happy when he died, she refused to believe it. In a final effort to convince her that her son had been cured of his obsession for politics, he told her of the last time Haneef had spoken of the Prime Minister.

'I'm happy,' Yunis recalled Haneef's words. 'The Prime Minister will not die. He will live a life as long as mine.'

Sadiq's wife listened carefully to the words and then looked at Yunis incredulously. She could not believe that her brother-in-law was so naive he would mistake innocence for optimism. She alone understood the words of her son. Haneef was dead. The Prime Minister would follow. She was as certain of this as she had been of Haneef's spiritual association with a leader who had done nothing for him. She stood and walked to the side of the room where Haneef once stored his cricket bat and ball. She tore the poster of the Prime Minister from the wall and threw it into the flame underneath the kettle.

In Islamabad, a police report was filed. The hit-and-run car was easily traced. As the licence plate claimed, it was the car of a USAID employee. Within a day or two, the security officer at the American Embassy supplied the terms of the settlement. My father read them aloud to Sadiq. A sum of one hundred thousand rupees would be deposited at a bank for him. Sadiq's mouth fell open, first because of the amount of money involved and then because of the suggestion that money could compensate for life.

'Paisa?' he said. Then he told my father he did not need money, he needed his son.

Eventually, my father convinced Sadiq to take the money for the sake of his wife. In the future, he suggested, there might come a day when the money would make a difference between life and another death. Medical treatment, hospital bills, unforeseeable emergencies.

My father wished there was a way to bring the driver of the car to trial, but there was not. The driver was foreign, protected by diplomatic immunity from the smallest to the largest of any number of crimes.

Sadiq, on the other hand, was not concerned with retribution. He hid his face in his hands. *'Allah ki murzi,'* he said, attributing his son's death to the will of God.

My father embraced him. He left the room a few minutes later. Before he closed the door behind him, he discovered that Sadiq remembered more from the accident than my father suspected.

'A woman killed my son,' he said.

II

On the day Anne Simon drove her husband's long white Buick into the side of the road and accidentally killed a young boy, she began her morning by writing a letter to her mother in upstate New York. In it, she declared the date, the day before Thanksgiving, as marking the completion of seven weeks in Pakistan. Until that day, the weeks since her arrival had passed quickly, accompanied by the vague and uncomfortable feeling that she was living a life that was not hers. She moved into a house provided by USAID for whom her husband, Jack, worked as an electrical engineer. The house came with several servants, two of whom shared the name Mohammed, addressed her as Madam, and did all the housework, from dusting and cooking to making beds and ironing. The house was furnished with dark and heavy chairs and sofas and thick curtains that blocked the plentiful sunlight. Anne spent the first weeks after her arrival sewing cotton curtains for all the rooms of the house on the sewing machine she had bought for herself the day after Jack made his decision to accept his new posting in Islamabad.

Before moving to Pakistan, Anne Simon's life, forty years of it, was restricted by winters that lasted six months, springs that were unremarkable except that they promised summer, and spectacular falls that claimed all the colours missing in seasons passed. The entries and passings of the seasons were familiar to her and, although she complained of their roughness, she believed they hinted at the rhythm of her life. Her daughter, Beth, was born to the cries of cicadas in the summer. Her sons, Andrew and Anthony, arrived minutes apart in between the yellows and purples of fall. And she met Jack when the earth was still frozen and wrapped in snow.

Anne and Jack were newly married. They had met the previous year, during the spring blizzard of 1977, in the hospital in upstate New York where she worked as a nurse. He was in the middle of his only break in his career schedule with USAID, the two years he spent in America undergoing treatment for a cancerous tumour in his only kidney. She worked on his floor during the several months of his stay and learned that he had elected to have chemotherapy treatment administered in the hospital in his home town against the advice of his doctors in Washington DC. They came to know each other slowly. Their acquaintance began the night of the blizzard when Anne opted to work an additional shift so she would not have to drive home on roads piled high with snow. Jack prolonged her stay in his room beyond the routine blood pressure and temperature readings by pointing to the window, from which they could see cars and buses sliding from one side of the road to the other, and telling her how long it had been since he had seen the earth covered in white. Much later, they confided in each other as friends and she shared news of her children and the small city world that extended beyond his hospital bed. Finally, after they came to know each other beyond nurse and patient, he asked her to marry him. It was the fourth day of July and his birthday, although she did not know yet that this holiday of flags and independence coincided with his private celebration. 'Why, yes,' she said, even though until then she had not considered that the man she was leaning down to kiss for only the third or fourth time was someone with whom she might spend the rest of her life.

Driving home from the hospital that night, she reconsidered his question from behind the steering wheel of her old and rusted car. She suspected she had answered his unexpected question so quickly because she wanted to spend her life with him, but also, perhaps, because she did not expect him to live long enough to exchange marriage vows. The prognosis for his survival was scribbled across his charts, and once she had even heard the doctor mumble that Jack's life was running out with every heart beat he survived. She decided against telling her children of his proposal, resolving that they would only be told that the man who was already part of their dinner conversations might fill a larger part of their lives when and if his health improved. That time came a month later when Jack surprised Anne again, more astonishingly, when the tumour in his body collapsed from the size of a grown man's fist to the size of a quarter, no longer touched the kidney, and could be successfully removed. When the hospital released Jack with a bill of health as clean as it could be after fighting cancer, and the doctor who had been sure of his death stored Jack's shrunken tumour in a jar for a research project, she made Jack promise not to mention her commitment to him until her children came to know him better. Finally, when it seemed possible that the children might accept him into the family, she gathered them into the living room for a meeting and told them of Jack's proposal.

'If you like him enough, I might marry him,' she said and studied their faces.

She had not meant her feelings for Jack to sound as though they were subordinate to the concerns of her children. But in the six years since she had become a widow and assumed sole responsibility for the lives of her children, it was they who filled her life with meaning, and it did not seem unreasonable to ask for their permission to expand their family to include a father. For a moment, she considered that it may be unfair to them to marry someone whose chance of dying within the year was higher than any of theirs, but she did not dwell on this. Years earlier, when their real father, lying next to her in the middle of the night, had stopped breathing and every explanation that was given to her seemed impossible, she was forced to accept that her own life and all the lives of those whom she loved were bound to end one day. In this light, it hardly mattered that scores of doctors and specialists had calculated the odds of Jack's surviving the year.

They married in spring, during the one month the harsh winter paused, ice and snow melted, and the abundant lakes and rivers swelled. Jack was still on medical leave when he was contacted about a new posting to Pakistan and, after little deliberation, he signed the contract. He had dedicated his working life to the development initiative of his government in countries more needy than his own. He had never expected that his life would be divided into three or five-year increments that took him from country to country or that his life would be compact enough to fit into cardboard boxes at the end of each assignment. In college, he had wanted to be a surgeon, like his parents. But he spent the year before he planned to enter medical school hitchhiking through Asia, seeing a world he had never imagined, understanding for the first time what a privileged life he led as the child of two orthopedic surgeons. He embarked on this trip with the intention of laying to rest his interest in travelling, but when the year was over and his money had run out, he had not rid himself of the itch to see more. The poverty he had seen had amazed him and, although he had been protected from poverty at home, he had the intuitive sense that what he saw on his travels was substantively different, and he found himself overwhelmed by a sense of responsibility for strangers. On the flight home from Istanbul to New York, he changed his mind about attending medical school, convinced that he could make more of a difference in an unfair world by building bridges and designing irrigation systems than by setting broken bones. He went to graduate school to collect tools to enable him to meet his new goals and, when he graduated with top honours and a degree in electrical engineering, he rushed at the opportunity to be part of his government's development mission abroad.

When Jack first explained his work to Anne from his hospital bed in upstate New York, it had been almost impossible for Anne to accept that there were places in the world where electricity had yet to arrive, and for several days after that she made mental notes of all the electrical appliances upon which she depended. But now that she had arrived in Pakistan and seen how poor people seemed, she developed an appreciation for Jack's work that she had not had. Every so often, however, she felt some resentment toward Jack that, in their move overseas, she was left to consider her life while his life and work continued uninterrupted.

That morning, while she sat at the solid desk in the living room and composed a letter to her mother, she felt distant from Jack. For one thing, she had not realized how little time he would spend at home, and she had not grown accustomed to how often his work required him to travel. She spent much of her first seven weeks alone in Islamabad, trying to accustom herself to a house that was not hers, in a country whose name she had not known until Jack spoke it some months earlier. Her children were preoccupied with their new school, the American International School of Islamabad, and before she knew it the twins were hosting slumber parties and her daughter had set aside her dolls for her brownie troop. In the beginning, for lack of knowing what else to do, Anne had spent afternoons reclined on a chaise next to the swimming pool at the American Embassy compound a few miles from her house. She gave up on that pastime soon after, when she decided she could no longer bear the pretence of being somewhere she was not. At the poolside, the voice of a prerecorded disk jockey announced the dates and times and temperatures of American cities many miles away, and in the snack bar and dining rooms uniformed servants served her a wide list of items, from hamburgers to hot dogs, all of which she might have found at any restaurant back home. She remembered her mother's response when she was given their address in Pakistan. 'But this address is in Washington, DC,' she had said, unaware of how the diplomatic pouch worked. That morning, she wrote to her mother that in the confines of the embassy compound she felt sometimes that she had never left America. She closed the letter without relating her first argument with Jack that took place the night before and was the main reason she felt sad and distant from him at that moment.

Before they moved to Pakistan, Jack insisted on purchasing a new car in New York and transporting it to Islamabad. Anne did not believe that his long white Buick, designed to be driven in a right-hand-drive country like America, was meant to be driven in a left-hand-drive country like Pakistan, and the argument had begun when she told Jack this. 'I bought it for you and the children,' he had said, indicating that he would never have indulged in the luxury of such a big car if he had been unmarried. But as far as Anne was concerned, Jack should not have bothered: the Buick was not meant to be driven on the left side of the road. She told him that she did not feel comfortable driving the car and he said that she could elect to use their driver instead. Finally, he said what he had taken to repeating since their arrival. That she would get used to it, that things like this took time. She fell asleep angry with him and, when he awoke early the next morning for his trip, she pretended to be asleep when he kissed her and promised to call her that night.

Anne was in bed, wallowing in the warmth of sleepiness and blankets. She was waiting for Jack's promised telephone call, their argument all but forgotten. The telephone rang, but it was Beth, her daughter, instead. She was at a friend's party on the embassy compound and needed a ride home. Anne had made it a practice not to drive at night, but Jack was not in town, the driver had the night to himself, and Anne had no choice but to get into the long white car in her driveway and pick up her daughter.

Light rain fell with the breeze through the open window onto her clothes. It felt warm and she unrolled the window further. She guessed she would have driven the two miles to the embassy compound with her window down even if the defroster in the car had been working. The windshield wipers were on low, flattening the rain on the window before pushing it away. Every so often she wiped the film of condensation from the window with the palm of her hand, curious at how it managed to reappear in spite of the constant breeze. She drove slowly and hesitantly, reluctantly overtaking bicyclists and pedestrians. There were no functioning street lights on any of the roads and, as always during the night, she was unnerved by the blinding headlights of the oncoming traffic. She had been told to flash her headlight beams in immediate response by Jack's boss' wife during an informal orientation her first week in Islamabad, but Anne needed both hands and all her fingers to maintain her grip on the steering wheel and manoeuvre the car away from the oncoming one.

Her hands were tightly wound around the steering wheel during her return from the embassy, while Beth sat next to her describing in detail the events of her friend's birthday party. Later, Anne thought she might have become distracted when Beth mentioned that her friend's birthday cake reminded her of the cake her grandmother had baked for their goodbye party. A car rushed toward them with beaming headlights and, in place of the sheer blackness in front of her, she saw an image from the good-bye party, the farewell scene that followed the cake.

The momentary blindness passed with the car, and she would not remember if it was just before or just after, but she felt the impact of something slight hit Beth's side of the car. The slight, uneven mass was crushed by the weight of the car, but it remained whole enough to lift one of the rear wheels off the ground as the car rolled over it.

'Mom,' Beth screamed.

Anne stopped the car, instinctively turning off her lights and, because there was no oncoming traffic, the windshield framed a blackness quieter but less complete than a moment earlier.

Before she could pull the parking brake, the car shook with the fists and feet of an angry person beating against it. She heard someone lift the handle of Beth's door and then kick it when the safety lock prevented him from opening it.

'Mom,' Beth said again, only this time it was in the same tone of voice she had used when she discovered her father's body, cold and still, underneath two layers of blankets on his side of the bed. Anne's thought was death, then, and she knew absolutely that she had killed someone. She withdrew her hand from the parking brake and restarted the car. She looked out of the window as she turned onto the road and, because she was on the wrong side of the car and the headlights of oncoming traffic illuminated the scene, she could see what was behind her. A boy was lying crumpled where her car had hit him. A man was hunched on the ground next to him, arms wrapped around the crushed parts of his body, as if to restore to him shape and life. One man was hollering abuses and punching dents into the moving car.

She knew, even as late as that moment, that she should stop. Climb out of the car and drive the crumpled boy and the two men to the hospital, the voice inside her said. But she did not because she could not. The child in the car, sitting next to her, was hers. Beth's skin was so fair it burned in the rays of Islamabad's winter sunshine. Her hair was so blonde, almost a different colour from Anne's own light hair, that people only believed it was her natural colour because Beth was barely nine. In the end, it was the thought that they might have hurt her daughter, put their hands on her, that forced her to tear her eyes and face and body from the scene, find the accelerater, and drive home.

Later that night, the embassy had been able to locate Jack. The ambassador gave him the details and assured him that Anne and the rest of his family were safe. Jack rushed home on the first flight the next day, arriving in time for what would have been their Thanksgiving meal. The twins were at a friend's house and had not been given any reason for the silence that had overtaken their home the night before. Beth was in her bathroom, surrounded by all her rediscovered dolls, running her third bubble bath of the day. Anne was upstairs when Jack walked into the house, sitting on the easy chair in the bedroom, knees pulled up to her chin, arms sealed around them. The colour was drained from her face, from her hair, from her eyes. Had she not been in their bedroom, he might not have recognized her as his wife. There was a gray about her, the shade of low rain clouds whose shape and form promise moisture, but conceal much.

'Christ,' Jack had said, dropping on the floor beside her and sliding his knees underneath her chair, 'Annie.' He repeated her name again and again as if the repetition of her name would restore the woman he thought of as his.

She could hardly bring herself to say it. She felt Jack's breath on her face, the circle of his arms enveloping her folded body, but the cold-board stiffness of her bent knees and wrapped arms and bowed back persisted. 'I killed a boy,' she said, hearing these words spoken for the first time, in a tone so pale she might have said the most ordinary thing. Jack knew, but still he thought he misheard her. The focus of his vision tunnelled, and there was Anne and the words she had spoken filling the space in front of him so completely he thought it might burst with the pressure.

She told him the story. Halfway through, when she was describing the man beating on the door of her car, pulling up the handle to Beth's door, Jack pulled his knees from under the easy chair, regained his balance on his feet and lifted Anne's rigid body from the chair. He put her down on the bed, where she sat in the same position, half on his lap and half on their bedspread. When she reached the end of the story, he curled his body around her, kissing her fingers until they unlocked and her arms relaxed. He did this with every part of her: her knees until they loosened, her legs until they stretched, her chin until she lifted her face and the stolid mask cracked slightly and he could see again the dimple in her chin.

Afterwards, Anne saw the boy everywhere. She gave the crumpled boy, whose face she had not seen, black hair and eyes, a rounded nose, broad cheekbones, a shapely forehead and average lips. It was the hills, the swollen mounds of rock and brown that stood guard over Islamabad, that provided her with the details of the boy's face.

When her family had arrived in Islamabad, Jack and the children were immediately enthusiastic about the Margalla Hills. They planned hikes to uncover hidden waterfalls and took bets on how long it would take them to walk to the first ridge and then the second and then the one after that. In contrast, Anne was unable to take the Margalla Hills into her life, unable to relinquish what she was accustomed to: the green rolling hills of upstate New York that rose and ebbed like a gentle wave before falling in the long and flat lakes. When Jack asked her what she thought of their surroundings, all she could bring herself to say was what she missed. 'No water,' she had said and stopped, interrupted by her children's disappointed exclamations. Over the next several weeks, her impression of the hills did not change. Their exacting presence disrupted the landscape of her vision and returned to her a fear of closed spaces that she thought she had overcome years ago, when she moved her family out of a city apartment near the hospital into the country fifteen miles away.

On her first venture from the house after the accident, she drove with Jack to the embassy in the early evening, when the unblemished Islamabad sky began to surrender to the night. She tried not to look at the Margalla Hills, but she saw them anyway and, in the shape of their outline against the dusk-driven sky, she saw the profile of the boy. And while the setting sun thrust the shadows of the Himalayan mountains onto the city, she felt the presence of the boy she had killed fall toward her with the shadows, as if his very being had not already turned the substance of her into unfathomable pain. *Our Lord who art in heaven,* she prayed, but her prayer did not change what she had seen buried in the highest ridges of the hills.

Anne knew nothing about the boy she had killed except what the legal affairs officer told her during their meeting. The boy was an only child, ten years old, underweight, and attended the third grade of a government school. She had nothing to do with the settlement that was drawn up, the legal document that promised the boy's family an equivalent of $10,000 as compensation. She struggled to repeat the figure when the officer read it to her, but she could not.

'A year?' she asked instead, and withdrew her hand from Jack's when the man sitting in front of her corrected her.

'One-time payment,' he said. In an attempt to comfort her, he translated the sum of dollars into rupees. '100,000,' he said and, without being prompted, he began to tell her what that sum of money could buy in Pakistan.

A car, she heard him say, a house, bicycles enough for many a lifetime, but when he said 'lifetime' she felt the impact of the boy's body against the car, and she pressed her foot on the carpeted floor of the office as if she were manipulating the brake pedal. Jack reached for her hand again, drew it toward his thigh and placed both of his hands around it, unaccustomed to the coolness of her flesh. He could not have known that the recent cold of her hand was there to stay, that it would not be coaxed away, even if it were held, as it would be, above the gas flame in the kitchen, or if it were placed directly on the burning rocks of their patio in midsummer. This was not a seasonal cold that went with the melting of icicles and snow. It was a chill that moved into her as if it owned her.

Anne was not in the room with the legal document anymore, she was deep in her own thoughts of reprimand and torment. She knew from experience that no amount of money could fill the cavity of death, that a legal settlement such as the one awaiting her signature was print on an eight-and-a-half-by-eleven piece of paper and nothing more, that had someone taken her child away from her, by accident or not, she would have killed them. It was the knowledge of this last fact that haunted her, forbade her to venture out of her house behind the wheel of a car again, and required her husband to hire another *chaukidar* for the back of the house where the shrubbery could easily conceal the shape of a person harbouring revenge.

In the months ahead, Anne spent so much time thinking about the child she had killed, that the fact she did not know his name was unimportant. It seemed that she spent all her time contemplating his short life and for the moment it pushed her own children and husband into the background. She wondered, incessantly, what the boy had been thinking or feeling or seeing, the night she swerved the long white car into his body and took all of this away from him. Sitting in a hot bath at the end of the day, trying to coax feeling into her numb toes, she concentrated on the face that she had given him, the boy he had been. But she could not imagine what scenes might have flashed before him as the outline of his life sketched itself into the one-hundredth of a second before life became death.

Tariq Latif

Born in a small village, just outside Lahore, Tariq Latif spent his childhood on his grandfather's farm and moved to Manchester with his family in 1970. He graduated from Sheffield University in 1984, with a degree in Physics, has worked in a Cash and Carry, Fashion Shops and as a part time roadie. He is now self employed and runs a labelling business in Manchester. He started writing in his late twenties and soon put together his first collection, *Skimming the Soul* (1991). His poetry both reclaims the people and life he knew in Pakistan and describes immigrant life in Britain and all its cultural conflicts. He says his poem 'From Symbols to Components' from his second collection, *The Minister's Garden* (1996), harmonizes different aspects of him: scientific, literary and religious: each line, including the title has a syllabic count of seven, a particularly significant number in Islamic numerology.

FROM *SKIMMING THE SOUL*

Masunda

This is no holy land.

These walls of streets
that sprawl and the dank rooms of homes
are made out of straw grained mud
hand smoothed by our grandfathers
blessed holy with their hot breath

but this is no holy land.

There is a thin bone bagged dog
slurping his own faeces.
A fat grimed carcass festers with flies.
There are the open sewers
thick with slime, and
littered with sleeping mosquitos.

The old women drabbed in grubby saris
sit in the cool yard
smoking a cigarette, chatting, cackling
dreaming of a holy land.

Night falls and the mud walls dissolve.
A dog yelps at the golden moon.
Some prowling mosquitos stop
to sip my blood. The old men resting from the toils
in the field, talk and laugh, and share a pipe.
The hooka smoulders a sugar layered
dry cow dung.

This is my holy home.

Water Snakes

In this mud dank room
In the mixed smell of straw and oil
The huge wheels of the tube-well
Spin, belts turn
Pipes suck water
From the black ocean underground.

Outside, in the huge trough
The tube-well's mouth bursts
With bright waterfalls
Thunderous water
Crashes onto walls
Drowning air that surges about sea foam.

I can see

Water-snakes
Cascading into the trough.
They guzzle the air
Spit out rainbow sprays

I leap

Into the trough
Water crashes about my
Porous body of clay.
My head overflows with
White pearls, lapidated
By the watery fangs
Of the water-snakes

I could almost
Slush away
Down muddy waterways
Enter the paddy fields, where

The water-snakes ripple
Along green stalks—leap out
To invisibility, leave behind white seeds.

My body water dissolves this rice.
An invisible cord snakes
Out of my navel.
If feeds me soft tissues of manna.

FROM *THE MINISTER'S GARDEN*

From Symbols to Components

My father is deep among
Circuit diagrams, looking
For familiar symbols.
'Diodes will allow current
To flow in one direction
Only; like some passages
Crammed with pilgrims in Mecca.'

He locates the connections
Of the switch from the map
To the electronics. Test wires
Loop between my fingers like
Veins. I follow instructions
And make the link between two
Points; 'This part of the circuit

Is fine.' 'Try the one marked six.'
'That's it, this one is faulty.'
I unscrew the switch, hand it
To my father who whispers
A short prayer, then opens it.
After much thought he decides
To turn a plastic grub clock-

Wise by ninety degrees. I
Reassemble it and make
The relevant connections.
My father says Bismillah
As I plug the machine in
And the main fuse does not blow;
So far so good. We have faith

In electronic diagrams
Symbols and components and
Something beyond. I have some
Knowledge of electronics but
None of the Koran and its
Beautiful verse; the letters
Are symbols; complex diagrams

Of the soul. My father can
Read a little of both. Just
Then the machine fails and we
Go back to the diagrams
Running short of ideas and
Hope, but with our faiths open
Unshaken and connected.

The Chucky

My grandmother straddles
Around the chucky. She funnels
A handful of maize into the hole

Then she turns the upper slab
Clockwise, just as her mother used to.
Sometimes she feels the grainy texture

Of her grandmother's palm, sometimes
The flexible and awkward energy
Of young eager hands. Once

Light spilt from between the slab
Of the chucky and the mud dried room
Filled with the spirits of all our mothers

Voices spoke, voices hummed, voices
Sang of lush gardens, wonderous
And rich, of undying streams

And fountains that poured clear honey.
But usually all she can see
Is her aging hand, all she can feel

Is an aching absence. My mother
Has a Philips grinder and my sister
Knows how to change the fuse.

And when they make maize roti
We always have it with spinach
And lots of butter. Sometimes the scents

Swivel my grandmother's elbow
Before our eyes and we recall
The story of how our mother

Ran in with dad to tell
Her mum of their plans to go to England
How the grinding stopped and the flour

Spilt and the sudden silence
Was interrupted by a gust
Which shut the door on the light.

Harris Khalique

Born in Karachi, Harris Khalique was educated at the Cantonment Public School where the medium of instruction was Urdu. He went on to the DJ Science College and graduated in mechanical engineering from the NED College in 1990. He has been working as a social development worker and human rights activist since. His first book of Urdu verse, *Aaj Jub Hui Baarish*, appeared in 1991, and the second, *Saray Zurori Thay,* is under print. He contributes freelance articles in English to magazines such as *Herald.* In 1995, he started writing English poetry on themes where he found he could express himself better than Urdu. *If Wishes were Horses* (1996), is his first collection in English. The poems were written in England, Poland, Nepal and Pakistan over a period of one year.

FROM *IF WISHES WERE HORSES*

The Retired Old Bureaucrat, Next Door

At dusk
He appears on the by-lane we share
Expecting the visitors
Who once came

Closely shaved, soberly dressed
Allowing himself to wear
Just the right amount of perfume
He reminds me of an old house
Renovated and restored
Bit by bit
His smile is made of tinted glass
Not letting anyone see through
His manners smell of fresh paint
Mildly irritating but assuringly neat

When the night takes over
And darkness reigns supreme
He goes to bed
In his flannel night suit
Stitched when he was young
To dream of a thousand mourners
And an impeccable funeral.

In London

Defiant flirtation
Never puts me off
But when she said
'Bright South Asians
Have always struck my sight
I've never been close to one
What are you doing tonight?'
I felt like an ethnic top
To be worn once and thrown away
A balti dish never tried before
From the newly opened Indian take-away.

Nadeem Aslam

Born in Pakistan, Nadeem Aslam grew up in England. His first novel *Season of the Rainbirds* (1993) was published when he was 25. Subsequently in was shortlisted for the Whitbread First Novel Award, the Mail on Sunday/John Llewelyn Rhys prize; it won the Author's Club Best First Novel Award and the Betty Trask Award. The story, about a small Punjabi town in the 1980s, is written with great subtlety and filled with many vivid, beautiful and poetic images; its slow build up of tensions makes its sudden violence all the more effective.

Season of the Rainbirds is designed at two different levels: one describes the narrator's cocooned and magical childhood then the loss of innocence, and uses that as a foil to the main story about ordinary people changed by a climate of bigotry and terror. A mail bag lost in a train accident 19 years ago, suddenly turns up. The town's corrupt Judge Anwar is murdered. Azhar, the Deputy Commissioner, offers to investigate. He is in love with Elizabeth, a Christian girl, which upsets his community and hers. The local politician and strongman, Mujeeb Ali later uses this for personal revenge. Everyone is caught up in these events, including the school teacher Mr Kasmi, his friend Yusuf Rao, and the gentle, humane and elderly cleric, Maulana Hafeez.

FROM ***SEASON OF THE RAINBIRDS***

Fish.

The cook lifts the damp dark-red cloth to reveal a row of quicksilver fish, overlapping each other like fallen dominoes. Wherever we are, whatever we're doing, we leave the blinding white light of the summer day for the gloom of the kitchen. The rumpled cloth has fallen to the floor. We hold our breaths as the cook picks up the serrated knife – the knife we are forbidden to sharpen pencils with. Could this be it? Our chins tickle as the tip of the knife is inserted below a fish's mouth. Then the cook makes a rapid stem-to-stem tear and splits open our stomachs, pushes in two large fingers to uproot our guts and, without looking, hurls them into the bowl set beside her on the table. Still dizzy from the sunlight, we dip tentative fingers into the grisly mess and feel for shahzadi Mahar-u-Nisa's diamond ring. No, this was not the fish that swallowed it. We wait for the next fish to be opened. Our fingertips are coated with pink tissue fluid.

But the cook asks us to leave; the knife is raised in the air—a gesture reminiscent of early April when we enter the kitchen to steal aambis. Then, a ladle—a triangular plume of sweetly scented vapour attached to it—might be raised in the air. The cook bears provocation patiently but doesn't like us inside the kitchen. She doesn't flinch from tasting half-cooked dishes to check if the salt was remembered. If she thinks something is worthless she calls it 'the ash of seven ovens'. Not only is it worthless, there is also so much of it! We time our raids well: we sneak in when water is being added to the chaval. A specific number of glassfuls has to be added and the cook cannot turn around without breaking her concentration. She is tense as she counts: '...three...four, get away from there, five...six...you'll make me, seven...lose track, eight...eight, eight...nine.' Once free, she comes to the door and shouts across the courtyard, 'You'll all die of yarkan and I'll get the blame. No more aambis.'

Men with black beards are to be avoided; while those with white beards are kind and gentle. We hide under the bed and, through the serpentine curves of the bobin lace, listen to Mother and Uncle Shujahat talk to each other in raised voices. Uncle Shujahat has a black beard; it reaches down to his navel. Mother says, 'You're using religion as an excuse to withdraw from the world. You're running away from your responsibilities.' Uncle Shujahat says, 'We were not brought up to talk about God-Prophet in this manner. If only Father-ji could hear you.' Mother shouts back, 'Father-ji was religious but he kept things in proportion. He even sent me, a girl, to Lahore to get a university degree. He didn't mind my living away from home. And that was twenty years ago.'

Uncle Shujahat doesn't like toys. He takes our dolls and masks from us, breaks them in two, and then hands them back. He says images of God's creations are not allowed in the house, not while he's visiting.

The servants arrive for work in the middle of the morning. The homes where children don't have to be sent to school—and, therefore, the day's chores can begin immediately—are dealt with by them before our house. The first sounds of the day have vanished by this time: the bell of the candy-floss maker, Bibi-ji, reciting the Qur'an on the veranda, the 'aa...aa...come...come' of the dove-fancier who waves a bamboo pole, with its red ribbon, at his doves. Bibi-ji has long since harvested today's motya blossoms—before the rising sun could take away the fragrance—and fastened them into a garland for her hair.

With a pack-animal-like stampede, the servants begin their work; putting us to flight with the merciless swish of the linen, the beating of the rugs, the arcs from the hose-pipes above our heads, the spreading—like a flapping of wings—of the mats for preparing vegetables, the stubborn dusting and the obstinate sweeping. The air becomes charged with violence. The legs of the rope cots are taken out of the bowls of water—dead insects float on the surface of the stale water—and the milky fishbones are collected from the rims of last night's dinner plates.

During the afternoon hours the women sit on the cool screened veranda and talk amongst themselves. A young mother asks what the scarlet pimples on the newborn's upper arms could be. Smallpox, replies the eldest, and advises that the child be put in quarantine. The cook explains how to catch out a vendor who is trying to pass off tortoise's eggs as hen's. Someone else instructs that vegetables that grow beneath the surface of the earth should be cooked with the lid on; and those that grow above, with the lid off. While they sit on the darkened veranda, we swim about in the sunlight of the courtyard, burning with magnifying glasses the insects that have been sucked into the pedestal fan. Occasionally, we have to stop and look up: the adults are referring to our world: which one of us had smiled at nine weeks old, under which bush a dead yellow-striped snake was found one winter, the story of a schoolboy who got left behind, locked in, in his school over the summer holidays; how he ate chalk and paper and left tearful messages on the blackboard; and what happened when his body was discovered in September. We move closer to the veranda, pretending all the while to be interested only in our games—busy examining the pieces of coral trapped inside the marbles, waiting for the rosebuds inside the old necklace beads to open, discussing the inverted tears floating in the paperweights stolen from the study to add to our collection of glass spheres.

With the first call for the afternoon prayers this lazy calm comes to an end. The house is plunged once again into energetic activity. With an 'up, O mortal' each, the women pull themselves upright and disappear into the rooms. It's time for us to walk the two blocks to the mosque for our Qur'anic lessons. Beads and sticks and dolls are taken from our hands and we are coaxed into remembering where we left our scarves yesterday.

The street is still shut when we step into the molten-gold atmosphere of mid-afternoon. The houses face each other across the passages like armies on an ancient Arabian battlefield. The hot air carries the noise of inaudible rattles. We narrow our eyes against the glare. Beating their wings, the birds too are leaving the trees for the mosque. The leaves hang like limp hands from the branches. We try to think of the cool blue river and, turning around, glance towards where the river wets the horizon. But the river, too, seems helpless before the insanity of the sun, lying like an exhausted lizard at the end of the street.

We walk past the house with the blue door. It has been made clear to us that we are to walk quietly by this house, never accept an invitation to step inside, never return the smile of the woman of the house, nor glance at the old man who sometimes looks out of the upstairs window; at our peril are we to be tempted by the flowers lying under the eaves, or by the figs that the storms shake loose. But our shadows dare each other. One of them is foolish enough to climb on the doorstep but is pulled away just before it can reach the door bell.

And what might the penalty be for disobedience? We round the corner and fear all but suffocates us, an intense streak of fear that it is not easy to extirpate. Recumbent under the arch of a portico the blind woman takes her siesta. Wrinkles gouge her face and rags of every colour are wrapped around her body. Her eyes, though bereft of vision, radiate a feral inhumanity. A gnarled right hand, palm upward, lies on the cement floor, while the other rests—permanently, we believe—on the shoulder of a little girl. The girl's thicket-like hair stirs and her eyes watch us vacantly when we enter her field of vision. Set alongside the air of limitless danger that attends the old woman, the girl appears helpless—as helpless as the sparrow's bote that fell out of its nest last spring. All day long the girl guides the old woman through the streets, begging. We drag our inquisitive shadows towards the mosque, eyes downturned. A kite wails overhead.

The dangers of the street are counterpointed by the calm firefly-like presence of the cleric's wife. Her smile casts a delicate spell. She sits before us and we recite for her from our Qur'anic readers. Each reader is one-thirtieth of the Qur'an. The language is alien to us—we have not been taught the alphabet—but we have learned the shapes of the words by heart. The cleric's wife gives our old readers new shiny greeting-card bindings. We wait by her side as she stitches a tattered reader inside a camel-and-bedouin-beneath-a-crescent Eid greeting, or inside a pair-of-doves wedding invitation. Sometimes she polishes her wedding ring with ground turmeric.

On the wall behind her is a calendar which shows the whole of Ramadan in red and both the Eids in gold. Next to the calendar is the pendulum clock; it is as ornate as a woman's brooch. We wish for six o'clock never to arrive, for it never to be time for us to leave here.

Perhaps if we pray hard enough...

The clock strikes six, the hands divide the clock's face into two half-moons. The cleric's wife offers us one last exultant and forgiving smile. We kiss our readers and slip them into satin envelopes. Our shoes are set in rows at the edge of the vestibule, like boats at a Bengali ghat. The streets are full of inky shadows. But before we leave there is a quarrel. A combed-out flourish of the cleric's wife's hair has been found on the floor and we have to settle who gets to keep it between the pages of their reader.

FROM ***Wednesday***

Every day during the last hour before sunrise Maulana Hafeez went into the mosque to say the optional pre-dawn prayers. In the isolation and deep silence of the mosque he abased himself before God—bent his body at the waist, straightened and bowed. Afterwards, as sunrise and the time to make the call for the first obligatory prayers of the day approached, he rolled out the ranks of mats that stood leaning against the walls and, working methodically down the length of the hall, placed a straw skullcap and a rosary at the head of each mat. Not many men came to the mosque at dawn but Maulana Hafeez always spread out every mat, covering the entire floor of the hall, setting each place with meticulous care. At around eight o'clock, when the shops along the side of the mosque building were being opened and schoolboys in slate-grey uniform hurried down the narrow street, he returned home to breakfast and slept until noon.

Through the half-open door of his bedroom Maulana Hafeez could see into the kitchen across the courtyard. His wife—obscured by drizzle, faint as a watermark—was preparing breakfast. The house was connected to the mosque by a veranda and the two buildings shared a courtyard enclosed by some of the trees mentioned in the Quran—pomegranates and figs and the larger, more tree like, olives. Maulana Hafeez rose from the chair where he had dozed since his return from the mosque. It was a dull windless morning, clouds brushed low over the roof of the house. Maulana Hafeez knew that today he would have to forgo his after-breakfast sleep: there had been a death in town. Outside in the street a motor sounded—rising to a maximum and receding—accompanied by the noise of splashing water. The rains had broken at last. Maulana Hafeez draped a towel over his head and began carrying the flowerpots that edged the veranda to the centre of the courtyard. The day's rain would revive the tired foliage. After the flowerpots Maulana Hafeez took down the ferns hanging from the eaves and placed them in a cluster around the other pots.

When he came out of the drizzle his wife poured him a cup of tea—the second of many that Maulana Hafeez would drink during the course of the day. Maulana Hafeez dried his face and beard with the towel and took the cup.

'You were in Raiwind during the month of that train crash, Maulana-ji,' the woman said; she was thinking about the lost mail-bags. She was fair skinned, frail, and her abundant hair was as white as the stole covering her head.

The cleric made an effort to remember. On his forehead there was a small bruise, the size of a teddy-paisa coin, proclaiming the zeal of his obeisance in prayer.

'Nineteen years,' the woman said and rose to her feet. From outside she brought into the kitchen two chairs and set them with their backs to the fire. Over the chairs she spread the clothes Maulana Hafeez was to wear to Judge Anwar's funeral.

'I heard a papiha singing somewhere,' she said. 'It must be monsoon.'

Maulana Hafeez nodded. 'It's been singing since dawn.'

Resin sizzled, hissing angrily on the surface of the blazing wood; the fire burned, the flames horizontal against the base of the pan in which something fragrant simmered. Maulana Hafeez looked up at his wife and said, 'I do remember something about an infant surviving a train crash.' He searched his wife's face for confirmation. 'Was that the same accident?'

'You're right, Maulana-ji,' she said. 'Strange that you should remember that. A little boy *was* found under the wreckage, five days later. There was a picture of him in the newspaper.' Like everyone else in town Maulana Hafeez's wife addressed him as 'Maulana-ji'; she had never used the familiar 'tu'.

His wife came back to the stool and, removing the pan from the fire, got ready to bake chappatis. She tested the temperature of the baking iron with a pinch of flour—it turned brown immediately, the smell of singed starch spreading through the small room. She pulled out the wood to moderate the heat and, with rapid clapping gestures, began to flatten a ball of dough between her palms. Blue veins were visible beneath the skin of her knuckles. Maulana Hafeez looked out at the silent mosque—it looked like a collection of glittering vases floating in the drizzle.

'I still haven't announced the death on the loudspeaker,' he said.

His wife shook her head. 'There's no need, Maulana-ji,' she said. 'I'm sure the whole town has known about it since four o'clock.'

Azhar drew breath sharply as he entered the muddy street. A very fine drizzle was falling, its impact barely registering on the surface of the puddles; palls of dark clouds surrounded the sun. A small boy ran out of a house and headed, in front of Azhar, towards the judge's house. From inside the boy's home a woman's coarse voice shouted reproaches and threatened punishments; but the boy was out of earshot.

Azhar arrived at Judge Anwar's house. The talk became muffled and the crowd made way for him to reach the front door. Someone who was smoking a cigarette, and who exhaled smoke from his lungs fast as Azhar approached, reached out his hand and said 'They left without managing to take anything.' Azhar nodded without shifting his gaze, nor did he alter his precise pace.

The house was full of people, and here, too, everyone seemed in the middle of performing some important task. Two men had been to the mosque and borrowed the low wooden platform on which corpses were washed. All the rooms opening on to the courtyard were being prepared to receive mourners. Most of the furniture had been removed from these rooms—only the heavy beds remained, standing on their sides against the walls—and the familiar rooms appeared, Azhar noted, at once spacious and alien. White sheets covered the floors. Photographs and portraits had either been removed to other rooms or turned face to the walls. However, the framed reminders of the dead man's career had been left untouched: still crowding the shelves and mantelpieces were addresses, tributes and sapas-namas, each with the text printed elegantly between garlanded borders on shiny paper. Someone on his way out of a room stopped on seeing Azhar and said, 'The shotgun was a Lee-Enfield.'

Azhar stood outside the room and softly cleared his throat before entering. The lowing of the heavy door caused many women inside to look up. They sat on sheets spread over the floor; it was possible to tell from the faces distorted by interrupted sleep which of them had been in the house since dawn. They covered their heads as Azhar entered.

The body was laid out on a cot in the centre of the room. A length of white cloth covered it; part of one heel had remained exposed and its tough cracked skin seemed to impart a pink hue to the edges of the sheet. Flanked on either side by her two eldest daughters Asgri Anwar sat cross-legged at the head of the cot. Azhar uncovered Judge Anwar's face. The fabric resisted separation at the wound—the shot had obliterated the throat.

Dr Sharif entered the room. He had been sent for because one of the daughters had fainted earlier in the morning. As he advanced, the physician had to bend down several times and asked to be allowed through. The women shifted grudgingly. Because he insisted once a year on immunizing children against cholera and typhoid the physician was barred from many homes.

Many mothers did not want the limbs of their children 'turned into sieves.' Undeterred, Dr Sharif would drag inside any child that passed by the surgery and, pinning the kicking and screaming girl or boy to the floor with his knee, inject the dose.

'I sleep in the next room,' Asgri was telling Azhar. 'I heard nothing but the shot.'

Azhar looked about him uncomfortably. There was no air in the room. 'We'll get them, apa,' he said quietly. 'Whoever they were.'

FROM ***Thursday***

The sun was still low when Mr Kasmi stepped out of the house. The heat had not yet begun.·The streets were in shadow. Mr Kasmi set off slowly in the direction of the school. There had been just two prolonged showers in the previous two days, but already seeds were beginning to germinate along the edges of the streets and the lower parts of the houses looked as though they had been dusted in fine, green powder—the beginnings of what would become, within two weeks of the monsoon's arrival, a pelt of velvety moss.

Azhar was leaving his house. His recently washed hair was slicked back away from his forehead. He saw Mr Kasmi, and raised his hand and smiled. Mr Kasmi waved back from his side of the street. Azhar strode away in the opposite direction. Within the next few minutes Mr Kasmi could see the school, a charmless building. Ten yards further on and he began to catch whiffs of the penetrating odour that the newer parts of the building gave off in the rainy season.

Mr Kasmi had once taught here. In those days the school consisted of one room, serving as headmaster's office and staff room, and a walled-in strip of level ground where lessons were given by the three teachers to boys who sat cross-legged on the grass. Summer holidays would begin on the day a pupil passed out from the sun. Mr Kasmi's had been the first bicycle in town, and the sight of his gangling frame riding in through the gate the first morning had caused a sensation. The wheels left behind two wavy lines in the mud, like the path of two butterflies chasing each other in early March. Since Mr Kasmi's retirement, however, three new rooms had been added to the building. The pond behind the old room was drained and people were asked to dump their rubbish into the enormous crater left behind. Four months later cement was poured over the garbage and the new rooms were built.

Making unsuccessful attempts at breathing through his mouth, Mr Kasmi entered the small corridor at the end of which was the headmaster's office. Two classrooms faced on to the corridor. The headmaster was not in his office. Mr Kasmi dusted the moulded plastic chair and, propping his small zip-up bag against a leg of the chair, sat down to wait. Opposite him—through the open door and across the corridor—the teacher had returned to the classroom and the monitor, a pale-skinned boy with delicate gestures, was presenting him with the names of boys who had misbehaved in his absence. The monitor returned quietly to his seat, the bench nearest to the teacher's chair. The names were called out. Mr Kasmi watched, handkerchief pressed to his nose, as two boys got up and walked slowly to the front of the room. Before settling in his chair the teacher said something to the two boys which Mr Kasmi was too far away to catch clearly. They stood motionless for a few moments, facing each other. Then, prompted by a shout from the teacher, the taller of the pair reached out his hand and struck the other boys's face—the shallow arc of the splayed palm made a sharp sound on impact. Mr Kasmi stood up. The boy who had been hit swung his arm to catch the other's face. But the blow was foiled—the taller boy dipped his head sideways and, straightening, slapped the other boy's face once again. Mr Kasmi looked around; he had forgotten the bad smell. Another blow was struck and—perhaps Mr Kasmi had been seen—a boy walked up and closed the classroom door.

Mr Kasmi remained motionless for a few moments. Then, pressing the handkerchief to his nose, he sat down. He closed his eyes to calm his heartbeat.

'A new month, Kasmi-sahib,' said the headmaster. He stood in the doorway, smiling across the room at Mr Kasmi. Mr Kasmi returned the smile.

A wave of the foul smell rose from beneath the floor.

'You get used to it, Kasmi-sahib,' the headmaster said cheerfully, pointing at Mr Kasmi's handkerchief. He had walked around his desk and was settled in his chair. A little embarrassed, Mr Kasmi returned the handkerchief to his pocket. He unzipped his bag and took out the pension book.

As he handed the stamped book back across the desk the headmaster shook his head mockingly and said, 'I'm a generous man, Kasmi-sahib. I keep giving you all this money despite the fact that even with a double MA you don't know anything about literature.'

Mr Kasmi shut his eyelids and, raising a forefinger, whispered an 'ah'. He smiled. This was a long-standing but friendly argument. Mr Kasmi had always believed that Chaucer's *Squire's Tale* was based on a story from the *Arabian Nights,* taken to Europe by Italian merchants from the Black Sea. The headmaster never accepted this. He did not even acknowledge the similarity between the two stories. To back up his argument Mr Kasmi would bring back pages of notes every time he visited a city library. The headmaster would give them a cursory glance and say, 'No. Chaucer is far superior. Far, far superior.'

Stepping out of the office, Mr Kasmi strained to catch any noises coming from the classroom in front of him. Then he shook his head; there was no reason to suppose that the duel was still going on.

Mr Kasmi unhooked one leaf of the school gate and emerged on to the street. The sun shone oppressively, producing in the sky a glare so brilliant that it ate into the silhouettes, blurring their edges. The heat was beginning. The fortnightly queue of labourers was in place outside Mujeeb Ali's house, winding around the walls and stretching out of sight behind a cluster of trees. A few of the men had broken away and were helping to restrain a headstrong mare, kicking up dust. The others watched with interest, shouting occasional words of advice and encouragement. Mr Kasmi waited under a tree for the beast to be overpowered before resuming his walk towards the courthouse. He went along the riverbank, passing the bus station which was deserted at this hour. A bus remained in the shelter at all times, parked with its muzzle pressed against the posts. At seven o'clock every morning a busload of people, animals and birds, boxes and crates left the stand; to be replaced, an hour or so later, by the incoming service bringing the mail, newspapers, and school boys from the surrounding villages, as well as other passengers. There was another exchange in the evening.

Mr Kasmi went to Yusuf Rao's office. The small room stood away from the other buildings of the courthouse in the shadow of a dusty giant tree. The area around the giant tree's roots was overwhelmed by weeds that had run to seed and were turning yellow.

'Waiting for customers?' Mr Kasmi said into the office before entering. Above him hung a small, clumsily painted sign—

YUSUF RAO
Advocate, Notary-Public,
Non-Official Jail Visitor

The room was approximately twenty feet by ten; and pushed against the longer wall, behind the desk and beneath the only window, was a narrow rope cot on which Yusuf Rao was lying, his hands clasped behind his neck, his eyes closed.

'Of course.' Yusuf Rao opened his eyes. 'Lawyers are like prostitutes. If a customer comes we eat, otherwise we go hungry.' He swung his feet to the floor and felt for his slippers.

Mr Kasmi approached the desk. 'The courts are shut for four days in honour of the judge but I knew you'd still be here, waiting to pounce on some unfortunate passer-by.' Through the open window he could see the empty arches of the courthouse and, brilliant-white in the sunshine, the whitewashed bricks that lined the edges of the paths leading to various parts of the building. Yusuf Rao, because he had been the first lawyer in town, was the only one who had managed to build an office.

The three younger lawyers conducted their business from kiosks which stood beneath the trees. Their signs were chained and padlocked against those who would steal them for roofing material.

With an effort Yusuf Rao got to his feet and stiffly took the three steps to his desk. 'I'm an optimist. Anything's possible in a country where the land reforms are welcomed by the land*owners*.'

'And while we're on the subject of the rich,' Mr Kasmi said seriously, 'who do you think it was? About the judge, I mean.'

Yusuf Rao drummed his fingers on the desk. 'I don't know. He was a judge, corrupt to the core. *And* he was involved in politics. It could be anyone.'

Many years before, having just returned to the town of his birth to begin a practice, Yusuf Rao had soon understood that Judge Anwar of the Fourth Criminal Court put many obstacles in the way of justice. He had duly denounced the judge to the authorities in the capital, accusing him of failing to remand known criminals, even murderers, in custody and allowing them to intimidate witnesses; he had also given court credentials to some of the killers on the Special Commission's list.

'*And* he was rich,' Mr Kasmi said, unfastening his bag.

'Yes, but they didn't take anything. They must have come with only one thing on their mind.' Yusuf Rao touched two fingers to his right temple.

Mr Kasmi took out the jar of coffee

'Coffee!' Yusuf Rao exclaimed and finished taming his hair with the palms of his hand. He leaned forward and took the jar from Mr Kasmi's hand. 'Where did you get it?'

Mr Kasmi studied the pleasure on his friend's face. 'Burkat's wife brought it. She came to see me on Tuesday, wanted me to write a letter in English to her son.'

Yusuf Rao was drawing the smell of the grounds into his nostrils. 'Yes. I heard he was back from Canada.'

Mr Kasmi said, cautiously, 'She's Kalsum's sister. Did you know that?'

Yusuf Rao nodded without looking up. 'Yes, I did.' And replacing the lid on the jar he asked, 'How is that poor woman?'

'She gets by,' Mr Kasmi replied. 'After the boy died Mujeeb Ali went on paying her his wages. She's grateful for that.'

Yusuf Rao's head shot up. 'Is she, really?' He smiled with one side of his mouth. 'Perhaps someone should tell her that it was Mujeeb Ali who had her boy murdered in the first place.'

'There's no evidence for that. That is only your theory.'

Yusuf Rao ignored the interruption. 'A neat arrangement. I get my eighteen-year-old employee to fire at my political opponent at an election meeting. And to cover up I hire assassins to beat the boy to death after he has fired the shot. My opponent has a hole in his thigh, the boy is dead, and I get a chance every month to prove my generosity by giving money to the boy's mother. A very neat arrangement indeed.'

In the past on more than one occasion Mr Kasmi and Yusuf Rao had discussed this matter much more passionately, both men refusing to give ground. But today Mr Kasmi just shrugged. 'How is your leg, anyway?'

'The bones in my hip grind against each other like a mortar against a pestle.' Yusuf Rao had measured out two generous pinches of the coffee grounds on to a sheet of yellow typing paper and was wrapping it up, folding the paper into a compact diamond shape.

The sun was climbing fast. The patch of sunlight which was on the floor when Mr Kasmi arrived had crept on to the desktop, illuminating the crescents of dried tea left by cups and saucers. The heat in the small, cramped office was intense. The small pedestal fan set on top of the filing cabinet, its lead disappearing under the rope cot, spun noisily. Mr Kasmi wiped his brow. 'Not for me,' he gestured towards the coffee. 'I have to go to the post office before it closes to draw my pension.'

But Yusuf waved his objection aside. He walked to the door and shouted for the boy at the tea-stall across the street. He was supporting himself against the doorframe with one hand and brandished the packet of coffee above his head to attract attention.

After giving the boy detailed instructions on how to prepare the drink he came back and, with a grimace of discomfort, settled in the swivel chair. 'In 1951, the prime minister was assassinated in exactly the same way. The man who fired the shot was beaten to death then and there. The newspapers said it was the enraged crowd but the whole country knows that was not the case.'

Indifferent to the shouts of protest and working free of the arms that tried to hold him back, the old man detached himself from the group of men wedged in the door and entered the room. He advanced towards the desk behind which the overseer and the clerk sat and began cursing in a loud voice. The men behind the desk watched him calmly through narrowing eyes. The clerk folded his arms over the ledger. Ranged on the desk in neat stacks were coins and bundles of banknotes. The words *increase productivity* appeared on the coins and the notes of lower denomination.

'What's the matter?' The door at the rear end of the room opened and Mujeeb Ali stepped in, followed by Azhar. The crowd at the street door fell silent. Both the overseer and the clerk struggled to sit up straight.

The old man, covered in sweat, turned to Mujeeb Ali. 'I've been standing in the sun all day because he refuses to pay my wages,' he said in a gravelly voice. Beneath the wrinkles on his neck the cartilage rings of his windpipe could be made out.

'Wait for your turn,' Mujeeb Ali said. 'It can't be long now.'

'My turn has come and gone,' protested the old man. 'He says I'll be the last one to get paid because I'm impertinent.'

Mujeeb Ali glanced at the overseer. The clerk had turned back several pages and was searching feverishly for the old man's name.

The old peasant took two steps towards Mujeeb Ali. 'He didn't want me to sit in the shade. He said I'd ruin the grass in your garden. So I asked him if he thought I had a sickle for an arse. That's all I said.'

Azhar threw back his head and let out a laugh. 'Sickle for an arse. That's good,' he said to the old man. But the peasant, debilitated by hunger and the heat, stared in silence.

After making a thumbprint in the ledger and collecting his wages the old man went towards the door. At the threshold he stopped, took off his turban and wiped his face. A few dishevelled strands of silvery hair stood on his otherwise bald head. Then he turned and looked boldly at Mujeeb Ali. 'I've worked on your lands since the days of your grandfather,' he said and stepped out on to the street.

As the overseer and the clerk leafed back to their former place in the ledger, Mujeeb Ali led Azhar to the other end of the room. It was the only room in the large house that faced the street. The entire length of one wall was given over to the framed photographs, large and small, of several generations of the Ali family's male members. It was said that when Sher Bahadar Ali, Mujeeb's grandfather, died his two sons had divided the inheritance—silver and gold and money—using shovels and a balance from the stables. Mujeeb Ali and both his brothers had inherited the powerful shoulders and arms of their father. In several photographs Mujeeb Ali's youngest brother appeared, at various ages, with a bird of prey perched on a fist. And there was one photograph of the three brothers together, arms around garlanded shoulders, taken on the day following the last general election.

Azhar and Mujeeb Ali stood by the open window. Mujeeb Ali asked Azhar about the investigations into the judge's death. Azhar confessed that the police did not have a single piece of evidence which could suggest a line of inquiry. When the police were called in, shortly after dawn the day before, the inspector had stationed sergeants in all the principal streets; and at daybreak volunteers had combed the long approaches into the town, but the murderers had left behind no clues. 'Do you remember the murder last month when the woman's secret yaar broke in and killed the husband?' Azhar said, and without waiting for an answer continued: 'Well, last night the police inspector had to intervene when the judge's wife's brothers beat up a man who suggested that perhaps the two cases were similar.'

Azhar had, he said, appointed himself the examining magistrate, which meant that as well as exercising the familiar judicial prerogative of putting people in jail, he was responsible for collecting evidence and conducting investigations. In principle he had to gather all the facts relating to the death, weigh them up with proper objectivity, and determine whether a case should proceed. And he had decided to start by looking at some of the recent cases Judge Anwar had presided over, and interviewing the relevant people.

At the other end of the room the clerk had begun setting the desk in order. The overseer crossed the room towards Mujeeb Ali and Azhar. Mujeeb Ali took out a bunch of keys from his pocket, his thick index finger looped round the brass ring.

'Everyone in the world, it seems, is talking about the judge-sahib's murder,' the overseer said as he drew close, 'and those letters.' He carried a stack of ledgers, narrow and thick, balanced on the top of which were rolls of banknotes secured with orange rubber-bands and several packets of coins. Now that his task had been completed he appeared less tense. 'Most of these people'—he nodded towards the street door—'have never received a letter in their lives, but today even they mentioned them.'

Azhar turned his back to the open window. 'I have heard a journalist is coming from the capital in a day or two to write up the story of those letters.'

Mujeeb Ali and the overseer were walking away from him. The overseer said over his shoulder to Azhar, 'A woman whose son ran away from home twenty years ago says she dreamt last night that one of the letters is going to be from him.'

Azhar lit a cigarette and turned back to the window. He glanced across the vast backyard paved with chessboard tiles. The town was at the confluence of two of the province's five rivers and Mujeeb Ali's house stood in sight of the eastern branch. The interfluvial plain was considered the richest agricultural land in the country. And here most of it—orchards, vineyards, cornfields, rice-paddies—belonged to the Alis. On three sides, Mujeeb Ali had reminded a gathering during the run-up to the last elections, 'You are surrounded by water and on the fourth side is my family's land; so if you don't support us I will drive you into the water.'

Azhar flicked the cigarette on to the baking tiles and walked over to the other side of the room. The overseer and the clerk had taken their leave. Mujeeb Ali turned the key in the armoured cupboard embedded in the wall; a portrait of the Founder of the state hung above it.

'I'll start looking into the files when the courts open on Sunday,' Azhar said. 'I'll be away till Saturday.'

Mujeeb Ali accompanied him to the door. Azhar went towards the street where Dr Sharif lived to deliver a message from the judge's widow: the physician was to call at the house and collect any of the dead man's medicines he thought he could use. Mujeeb Ali watched him cross the street—as he stepped into shade the glare of his spotless white shirt was extinguished.

Glossary

aambis	unripe mangoes
aao	come
aap	you (formal term of address)
Abba	father
accha	all right
ada'ab	respectful salutation
ainna gund	so much filth
Akalis	Sikh warriors
akhbar	newspaper
Al-Andalus	Moorish Spain
Al-Hamra	the Alhambra (Moorish Spain)
Al-hemdo-lil-lah	God be praised
Al-Jumma	Friday
Allah-ho-Akbar	God is great
Al-Masiya	Almeira (Moorish Spain)
Al-Rahman	The Merciful: One of the Names of God
alu ka bhartha	spiced mashed potatoes
Ama-ji/Amma	Mother
angarey	burning coals
Angrez	Briton, British
anna	low denomination coin (now obsolete)
attar	perfume
awara	free, wayward
ayah	children's maid/nanny
azaan	the Muslim call for prayer
bab	gate (Moorish Spain)
baba	elder, father or (slang), man
baji	elder sister
Balonsiya	Valencia (Moorish Spain)
banya	shopkeeper/merchant
Begam/Begum	Lady
behen	sister
bety	daughter

bhai	brother
bhangra	a lively folk dance
bi/bibi	lady
biradari	fraternity, community
bolo	speak
bote	fledgling
burqah	veil and mantle covering a woman from head to foot
chacha	paternal uncle
chachi	paternal uncle's wife
chaddar	large wrap, or sheet
chambeli	jasmine
champak	white sweet scented flowers
chappal	slipper
chappatti	very thin unleavened bread
charpoy/charpai	string bed
chaudhury	village chief or landlord
chaukidar	nightwatchman
chicks	bamboo screens
chucky	flour grinder
churbee	animal fat
coolies	porters
Dadi/Dadima	paternal grandmother
Dadajan	paternal grandfather
dai	midwife
dall/dhal	lentils
deghs	cooking pots
dhobi	washerman
dhoti	loin cloth
Dimashk	Damascus (Moorish Spain)
duppatta/dupatta	long scarf or diaphanous cloth worn over the shoulders
Eid	Muslim Festival, celebrated twice a year: first after Ramadan, the month of fasting and later, to commemorate Abraham's sacrifice
Fajr	morning prayers

falsa	purple berries
faqih	religious scholar (Moorish Spain)
Farangan	Englishwoman
Farangi	English
fateha	funeral prayer
Firaon	Pharoah
funduq	hotel (Moorish Spain)
gharara	flowing skirt-like pyjamas
Gharnata	Granada (Moorish Spain)
goonda	thug
ghat	approach to river
hai	a general exclamation of woe
Haji	a man who has performed Hajj
Hajj	Pilgrimage to Mecca
Hajjen	a woman who has performed Hajj
hakim	a doctor practicing traditional medicine
halal	kosher
halwa	mushy milk and sugar based sweet
hamari gali	our lane
han/hanh	yes
haram	forbidden
haveli	house, large and spacious dwelling
Hazrat	term of deference and respect, used for a great man
holi	Hindu spring festival celebrated by the symbolic spraying of colours
hoka/hookah	
hukkah	traditional smoking pipe
ICS	The Indian Civil Service instituted by the British Raj
Id	Eid
Inglistan	England
Ishbiliya	Seville (Moorish Spain)
jaan	dear, darling
jagir	estate
jamardarni	sweeper woman
jehan	world

jharoo/jharu	broom made of long, fine twigs
jhuggi	a hutment
- Ji	a suffix, used as a term of respect
jihad	holy war
jinn	a spirit in Muslim mythology, made of fire
Jumha/Jumma	Friday
kajal	collyrium
kala	black
kamiz	long shirt
kapra	cloth/clothes
kazzaq	bandit
kemkhab	brocade
khaddar	hand spun cotton
Khaksars	a militant, revivalist peasant based movement
khala	maternal aunt
Khalsa	A council of Sikhs
khanum	lady
kirpan	a dagger carried by Sikhs
koel	a singing bird, belonging to the cuckoo family
kotha	roof/upper floor
kundan	traditional gold jewellery embedded with gems
kurta	shirt
kya	what
kya hey?	what is it?
lassi	a yoghurt drink
lathi	truncheon (sticks)
lay-lo	take
lota	vessel with long spout for pouring water
lungi	straight long skirt made of a single piece of cloth and tied at the waist
Mahasabha	A political party of extremist Hindus
maidan	open space, parade ground
makan	house
mali	gardener
mamon	maternal uncle
masjid	mosque

masnavi	literary composition
maulavi/maulvi *maulvi sahib*	mullah
mayun	a ceremony, prior to nikah i.e. wedding
mehr	sum promised by the bridegroom to a bride as her right, at the time of marriage
merey bachchay	my child
mian	lord/master/husband, polite form of address
mohalla	locality/neighbourhood
motia/motya	double jasmine
muhalla	see mohalla
Muharrum	month of mourning to commemorate martyrdom of the Prophet's (PBUH) grandsons
murdabad	Death to (slogan)
murzi	will
naga	snake/cobra, regarded sacred by Hindus, also the word used for ascetic or yogi
nauzobillah	God forbid
neem	The Margossa Tree
nikah	Muslim marriage rites
nizam	princely title/viceroy
O me kiya!	I say
paisa	money
pandal	platform
papiha	see koel
paranda	adornment for plaited hair
paratha	flat unleavened bread made in layers with butter and fried
pipal	a type of tree
poori	fried, thin rounds of flour
puggaree	turban
purdah	curtain; also used to describe women who observe the veil
Punjabi boalday ho?	Do you speak Punjabi?
qadi	magistrate

qalandar	mendicant/ascetic belonging to a sufi sect
Qurtaba	Cordoba (Moorish Spain)
Quaid-i-Azam	The Great Leader: title given to Mohammad Ali Jinnah, the founder of Pakistan
Ram	Hindu God
Ramadan / *Ramazan*	month of fasting
Raj karega Khalsa	Khalsa will rule
roti	a general term for breads
sahib	polite form of address, often denoting a person of some rank, or an Englishman in colonial days
shahbash	congratulations
shahzadi	princess
salaam aleikum / *salaamalekum*	peace be on you
salwar/selwar	baggy trousers
samosas	stuffed, fried tricornered savouries
sapas-nama	framed tribute presented to dignitary
Sarakusta	Zaragoza (Moorish Spain)
sarangi	a stringed instrument, peculiar to Iran, Pakistan and India
sarkar	lord, official
Sat siri Akaal!	seven-headed akaal
Sayyed	descendant of the Prophet (PBUH)
shaitan	devil
sherbat/sherbet	cold drink
sherwani	long formal coat with a high collar
shikar	hunt
shikari	hunter
shukria	thank you
sitar	string instrument
sufi	a Muslim mystic, or general term for the mystical orders of Islam
sura	a chapter of the Quran
tabla	a pair of drum-like musical instruments
takht	low platform, used for sleeping or sitting

takht-e-shahi	throne
takhti	a tablet to write on
tamasha	spectacle
tarikh	history
teddy paisa	popular name for lowest denomination coin
tehero	stay, wait
tiffin	midday meal, or lunch box
tonga	horse drawn carriage
tusi	you
ubtan	turmeric based body rub (usually used for brides)
Unionist Party	a political party of landed gentry, which was in power in the Punjab for many years prior to Partition
ustaniji	teacher
valima	wedding celebrations given by the bridegroom to indicate his formal acceptance of the bride
vida	departure of the bride from her parent's home
wallah	man/seller
yaar	pal/mate
yarkan	jaundice
zameendar	landlord
zenana	women's quarters
zindabad	Long live (slogan)
zuhr	afternoon prayers

Selected Bibliography

Ahmad, Rukhsana, FICTION: *The Hope Chest,* London: Virago, 1996; ed. with Rahila Gupta, *Flaming Spirit*, London: Virago, 1994. TRANSLATIONS: *We Sinful Women: Contemporary Urdu Women's Poetry,* London: The Women's Press, 1991; *The One Who Did Not Ask,* by Altaf Fatima, London: Heinemann 1993.

Ali, Ahmed, CRITICISM: *Mr. Eliot's Penny World of Dreams*, Lucknow: Lucknow University, 1941. FICTION: *Twilight in Delhi*, London: Hogarth Press, 1940; reprinted Bombay, London and New York: Oxford University Press, 1966, 1984; Karachi: Oxford University Press, 1984; Delhi; Sterling Paperbacks, 1973; New York: New Directions, 1994. *Ocean of the Night*, London: Peter Owen Ltd, 1964; unpublished revised version retitled, *When Love Is Dead,* completed in 1988; *Rats and Diplomats*, Delhi: Orient Longman, 1985; Karachi: Akrash Publishing, 1986; *The Prison House*, Karachi: Akrash Publishing, 1985. POETRY: *Purple Gold Mountain*, London: Keepsake Press, 1960; *Pupple Gold Mountain,* expanded version unpublished. TRANSLATIONS: *The Flaming Earth* (an anthology of selected Indonesian poems), Karachi: the Friends of Indonesian Cultural Society, 1949; *The Call of the Trumpet* (an anthology of modern Chinese poetry), unpublished; *The Golden Tradition: An Anthology of Urdu Poetry*, New York: Columbia University Press, 1973; reprinted, Delhi: Oxford University Press, 1991. *Al-Quran: A Contemporary Translation*, Karachi: Akrash Publishing, 1984; second edition 1986; reprinted, Delhi: Oxford University Press, 1987; revised definitive edition, Princeton: Princeton University Press: fifth printing with revision's, 1994: Book of the Month Club, 1994; third revised edition, Akrash Publishing, 1995.

Ali, Tariq, MEMOIR: *Streetfighting Years: An Autobiography of the Sixties,* London: Collins, 1987. FICTION: *Redemption*, London: Chatto & Windus, 1990; *Shadows of the Pomegranate Tree*, London: Chatto & Windus, 1992.

Alvi, Moniza, *The Country at My Shoulder*, Oxford: Oxford University Press, 1993; *A Bowl of Warm Air*, Oxford: University Press, 1996.

Aslam, Nadeem, *Season of the Rainbirds*, London: Andre Deutsch, 1993.

Baumgardner, Robert J., ed., *The English Language in Pakistan*, Karachi, Oxford University Press, 1994.

Dent, Peter, ed. *The Blue Wind: Poems in English from Pakistan*, Budleigh Salterton: The Interim Press, 1984.

George, Kadija, ed. *Six Plays by Black and Asian Women Writers,* London: Aurora Metro Press, 1993.

Ghose, Zulfikar, CRITICISM: *Hamlet, Prufrock and Language*, New York: St. Martin's, 1978; *The Fiction of Reality*, London: Macmillan, 1983; *Shakespeare's Mortal Knowledge*, London: Macmillan, 1993. FICTION: *The Murder of Aziz Khan,* London: Macmillan, 1967; *The Incredible Brazilian: The Native,* London: Macmillan, 1972; *The Incredible Brazilian: The Beautiful Empire*, London: Macmillan, 1975; *The Incredible Brazilian: A Different World*, London: Macmillan, 1978; *Crump's Terms*, London: Macmillan, 1975; *Hulme's Investigations into the Bogart Script*, Austin: Curbstone Press, 1981; *Don Bueno*, London: Black Swan, 1984; *Figures of Enchantment*, New York: Harper and Row Publishers, 1986; *The Triple Mirror of the Self,* London: Bloomsbury Publishing, 1992. POETRY: *The Loss of India*, London: Routledge, 1964: *Jets from Orange*, London: Macmillan,

1967; *A Memory of Asia: New and Selected Poems,* Austin: Curbstone Publishing Co., 1984; *Selected Poems*, Karachi, Oxford University Press, 1991.

Hamidullah, Zaib-un-Nissa, *The Young Wife and Other Stories*, Karachi: The Mirror Publications, 1958; reprinted 1971, 1987.

Hashmi, Alamgir, ANTHOLOGIES: ed. *Pakistani Literature: The Contemporary English Writers*, Islamabad: Gulmohar, 1987 (reprint of *The New Quarterly, Pakistan Literature*. Vol. III, No. 1 January 1978): ed. *The Worlds of the Muslim Imagination,* Islamabad: Gulmohar, 1986. CRITICISM: *Commonwealth Literature*: Lahore, Vision Press, 1983; *The Commonwealth, Comparative Literature and the World*, Islamabad: Gulmohar, 1988. POETRY: *The Oath and Amen*, Philadelphia: Dorrance & Co., 1976; *America is a Punjabi Word*, Lahore: Karakorum Range, 1979; My *Second in Kentucky*, Lahore: Vision Press, 1983; *This Time in Lahore*: Vision Press, 1983; *Neither This Time/ Nor That Place*, Lahore: Vision Press, 1984; *Inland and Other Poems*, Islamabad: Gulmohar, 1988; *The Poems of Alamgir Hashmi*, Islamabad: National Book Foundation, 1992; *Sun and Moon and Other Poems*, Islamabad: Indus Books, 1992. *A Choice of Hashmi's Verse,* Karachi: Oxford University Press, 1997.

Hosain, Shahid, ed. *First Voices,* Karachi: Oxford University Press, 1965.

Husain, Adrian A., *Desert Album,* Karachi: Oxford University Press, 1997.

Hussein, Aamer, *Mirror to the Sun,* London, Mantra, 1993.

Imam, Hina Faisal, (nee Babar Ali), *Midnight Dialogue* Lahore: Sang-e-Meel, 1991.

Kamal, Daud, POETRY: *The Compass of Love*, Karachi: published privately, 1973; *Recognitions*, Devon: Interim Press, 1979; *A Remote Beginning*, Devon: Interim Press, 1985; *The Unicorn and the Dancing Girl*: New Delhi: Allied Publishers, 1988; *Before the Carnations Wither: Collected Poems,* Peshawar: The Daud Kamal Trust, 1995; *Daud Kamal, The Selected Poems*, Karachi: Oxford University Press, 1997. TRANSLATIONS: *Faiz in English,* Karachi: Pakistan Publishing House, 1984.

Khalique, Harris, *If Wishes Were Horses*, Karachi: Irtiqa Publications, 1986.

Khwaja, Waqas Ahmad, ANTHOLOGIES: ed. *Mornings in the Wilderness,* Lahore: Sang-e-Meel 1987, (fiction section reprinted as *Short Stories from Pakistan*, New Delhi: UBS Publishers, 1992). POETRY: *Six Geese From a Tomb at Medum*, Lahore: Sang-e-Meel, 1987; *Miriam's Lament and Other Poems*, Lahore: Sang-e-Meel, 1992.

Kureishi, Hanif, DRAMA: *Outskirts and Other Plays*, London: John Calder, 1983; *My Beautiful Laundrette* and *The Rainbow Sign* (screenplay and memoir respectively), London: Faber & Faber, 1986; *Sammy and Rosie Get Laid*, London: Faber & Faber, 1988; *London Kills Me,* New York: Penguin Books, 1992. FICTION: *The Buddha of Suburbia*, London: Faber & Faber, 1990; *Black Album*, London: Faber & Faber, 1995; *Love in a Blue Time*, London: Faber & Faber, 1997.

Kureishi, Maki, *The Far Thing*, Karachi: Oxford University Press, 1997.

Kureshi, Salman Tarik, *Landscapes of the Mind*, Karachi: Oxford University Press, 1997.

Latif, Tariq *Skimming the Soul*, Todmorden, Lancs: Littlewood Arc, 1991; *The Minister's Garden*, Todmorden, Lancs: Arc Publications, 1996.

Naqvi, Tahira, FICTION: *Attar of Roses and Other Stories from Pakistan*, Boulder, Colorado: Lynne Reinner Publishers, 1997. TRANSLATIONS: *The Life and Works of Saadat Hasan Manto: Another Lonely Voice*, Lahore: Vanguard Books, Ltd., 1985: co-translator with Syeda Hameed, *The Quilt and Other Stories* by Ismat Chughtai, Delhi: Kali for Women Press, 1991; New York: Sheep Meadow Press, 1994: Karachi: Oxford University Press, 1996; *The Heart Breaks Free*, *The Wild One* by Ismat Chughtai, Delhi: Kali for Women, 1993; *The Crooked Line* by Ismat Chughtai, London: Heinemann International Press, 1995 and Delhi: Kali Press for Women, 1995, Karachi: Oxford University Press, 1995.

Nawaz, Shuja, *Journeys,* Karachi: Oxford University Press, 1997.

Omar, Kaleem, ed. *Wordfall,* Karachi: Oxford University Press, 1975.

Pasha, Perveen, *Shades of Silence*, Lahore: Sang-e-Meel Publication, 1996.

Rafat, Taufiq, POETRY: *The Arrival of the Monsoon: Collected Poems*, Lahore: Vanguard, 1985; *Taufiq Rafat : A Selection*, Karachi: Oxford University Press, 1997; TRANSLATIONS: *Bulleh Shah: A Selection*, Lahore: Vanguard, 1983; *Puran Bhagat by Qadir Yar*, Lahore: Vanguard, 1983.

Rahman, Tariq, FICTION: *Legacy and Other Stories*, Delhi: Commonwealth Publishers, 1989; *Work and Other Short Stories*, Lahore: Sang-e-Meel Publications, 1991; *Zoo and* *other Short Stories,* Lahore: Sang-e-Meel, 1997. LANGUAGE AND LITERATURE: *A History of Pakistani Literature in English*, Lahore, Vanguard 1991; *Language and Politics in Pakistan*: Karachi, Oxford University Press, 1996.

Riaz, G. F., *Shade in Passing*, Lahore: Sang-e-Meel 1991; *Escaping Twenty Shadows*, Lahore: Sang-e-Meel 1996.

Saeed, Joceyln Ortt, *Selected Poems*, Lahore: Nirali Kitaben. 1986; *Burning Bush*, Lahore: Stillpoint Books, 1994. *Accident at an Exhibition,* Lahore: Nirali Kitaben.

Said, Yunus, ed. *Pieces of Eight:* Karachi: Oxford University Press, 1971.

Shahnawaz, Mumtaz, *The Heart Divided*, Lahore: Mumtaz Publications, 1957; reprinted, Lahore: ASR Publications, 1990.

Sidhwa, Bapsi, *The Crow Eaters,* London: Jonathan Cape, 1980; *The Bride,* London: Jonathan Cape, 1983; *Ice-Candy-Man,* London: William Heinemann, 1988; reprinted as *Cracking India,* Minneapolis, Minnesota: Milkweed Editions, 1991; *The American Brat*, Minneapolis, Minnesota: Milkweed Editions, 1993.

Suhrawardy, Shahid, POETRY: *Essays in Verse*, Cambridge: Cambridge University Press, 1937; Dacca: Pakistan PEN, 1962. PROSE: *Prefaces: Lectures on Art Subjects*, University Press, Calcutta: (not dated); TRANSLATIONS: *V: Bartold: Mussulman Culture: translated from Russian*, Calcutta: University Press, Calcutta, 1934: co-translator with Liu Yih Ling, *Poems of Lee Hou Chu: rendered into English with Chinese text,* Bombay, Madras, Calcutta: Orient Longmans (not dated)

Suleri, Sara, CRITICISM: *The Rhetoric of English India*. Chicago: University of Chicago Press, 1992. MEMOIR: *Meatless Days*, Chicago: University of Chicago Press, 1989.

Tahir, Athar, ANTHOLOGIES: Lahore: Quaid-i-Azam Library Publications: *Next Moon*, 1984; *A Various Terrain*, 1985; *The Inner Dimension*, 1987; *Winter Voices*, 1989. CRITICISM: *Qadir Yar: A Critical Introduction*: Lahore: Punjabi Adabi Board, 1988. FICTION: *Other Seasons*, Lahore: Sang-e-Meel, 1990. POETRY: *Just Beyond the Physical,* Lahore: Sang-e-Meel, 1991. PROSE: *Punjab Portraits*, Lahore: Sang-e-Meel, 1993.

Zameenzad, Adam *The Thirteenth, House*, New York: Random House, 1987; *My Friend Matt and Henna the Whore*, London: Fourth Estate, 1988; *Love, Bones and Water*, London: Fourth Estate, 1989; *Cyrus Cyrus*, London: The Fourth Estate, 1990; *Gorgeous White Female,* New Delhi & New York: Penguin Books, 1995.

Journals

The Annual of Urdu Studies, No. 9, ed. Professor Muhammed Umar Memon 'In Memory of Professor Ahmed Ali', University of Wisconsin Madison: Centre for South Asia, 1994.

Frank: An International Journal of Contemporary Writing and Art, No 10, ed. David Applefield. Foreign Dossier: Pakistan, ed. Tariq Rahman, Montreuil, France & Lincoln MA, USA: Autumn 1988.

Inspirations, ed. Hina Faisal Imam: (a journal of poetry funded by the Quaid-i-Azam Library), Lahore: 1985-1992.

The Novels of Bapsi Sidhwa: South Asian Women's Writing ed R.K Dhawan and Novy Kapadia, New Delhi: Prestige Press, 1987.

The Journal of the English Literary Club, Session 1983-84, Peshawar: The Department of English.

The Journal of Indian Writing in English, 'A Tribute to Ahmed Ali,' Vol. 23, Nos. 1 & 2, ed. G. S. Galaram Gupta, India, University of Gulbarga, 1995.

The Review of Contemporary Fiction, Vol. 9 No. 2 'Milan Kundera and Zulfikar Ghose Number', Elmwood Park, Illinois, 1989.

Pakistani Literature, Vol. 3, 1994, Published by The Pakistan Academy of Letters.

Articles and Papers

Ali, Ahmed, 'English in South Asia: A Historical Perspective.' The International Conference on English in South Asia, University Grants Commission, Islamabad, January 4-9, 1989. Published in *The English Language in Pakistan*, ed. Robert J. Baumgardner, Karachi: Oxford University Press, 1993.

Choonara, Samina, 'Moving into Total Silence' (Interview with Taufiq Rafat), *Herald*, February, 1996.

Hashmi, Alamgir, 'Prolegomena to the Study of Pakistani English and Pakistani Literature in English'. The International Conference on English in South Asia, University Grants Commission, Islamabad, January 4-9, 1989,

Rahman, Tariq, 'Daud Kamal as a Poet', *The Nation* June, 19, 1989.

Shamsie, Muneeza, FEATURES: 'Do We Speak a New Variety of English?' (International Conference on English in South Asia) *Dawn*, March 3, 1989. 'Poetry in Isolation', *Dawn*, May 25, 1990; '1993: A productive year for English fiction and poetry in Pakistan', *Dawn,* January 23, 1995; 'Pakistani Literature in English in 1994', *Dawn,* 8th January, 1995; 'An Outpouring of Talent: Pakistani Novelists in English', *Dawn Tuesday Review,* July 11-17, 1995; 'Whatever Happened to Karachi's Poets?', *Dawn Tuesday Review*, July 11-17, 1995; 'The Melodious Poetry of Maki Kureishi', *Dawn,* December 15, 1995; 'A Productive Year of Accomplished Works: Pakistani Literature in English, 1996,' *Dawn,* January, 1997. INTERVIEWS: 'A Playwright from Britain' (Hanif Kureishi), *Dawn*, March 11, 1983; 'Through a Child's Eyes' (Bapsi Sidhwa), *Dawn* April 3, 1987; 'English is a Pakistani Language' (Alamgir Hashmi), *Dawn* May 25, 1990; Twilight in Karachi (Ahmed Ali), *Newsline*, October, 1990; 'Turning Reality Upside Down: Adam, Son of Earth' (Adam Zameenzad), *Dawn*, December 11, 1991; 'Publishing Pakistani Poetry from Paris' (David Applefied), *Dawn*, April, 5 1992; 'A Voice for Asian Women Writers' (Rukhsana Ahmad), *Dawn*, March 3, 1995 and 'Off One's Chest', *Dawn*, *Tuesday Review,* Jan 28-Feb 3, 1997; 'Controversial Comrade: The Life and Times of Tariq Ali, *Newsline*, August 1996; 'Mirroring Asia through Literature' (Aamer Hussein), *Dawn*, September 27, 1996. PAPERS: 'The English Novel in Pakistan', The International Conference on English in South Asia, University Grants Commission, Islamabad, January 4-9, 1989. REVIEWS: 'Faiz in English and Other Poems' (*The Journal of the English Literary Club*), 'Seasons in the Sun' (*Other Seasons* by Athar Tahir), *Newsline*, November 1990; 'Exile and Assimilation'

(*Selected Poems by Zulfikar Ghose*), *She,* March, 1991; 'Not the Queen's English' (*Pakistani English* by Tariq Rahman), *Dawn*, May 31, 1993; 'Not Derided any more as a colonial left over' (*A History of Pakistani Literature in English* by Tariq Rahman), *Dawn*, June 11, 1991; 'Distant Roots' (*Right of Way*), *She*, May, 1992; 'Our Man Adam' (Adam Zameenzad's novels), *Newsline*, May, 1992; 'Portrait of a Society' (*Work and Other Stories*, by Tariq Rahman), *Dawn*, April 3; 'A Cross Cultural Experience' (*The Poems of Alamgir Hashmi; Sun and Moon and Other Poems*), *Dawn,* October 2, 1992; 'The Prodigal Son' (*The Triple Mirror of the Self* by Zulfikar Ghose), *Newsline*, March, 1993; 'Monsoon Murder' (T*he Season of the Rainbirds* by Nadeem Aslam), *She*, June, 1993; 'The Eruditions of English' (*The English Language in Pakistan*, ed. Robert J, Baumgarner), *Dawn*, May 27, 1994; 'Remembering Professor Ahmed Ali', (*The 1994 Annual of Urdu Studies) Dawn*, July 22, 1995; 'Quilt of Cultures' (*A Bowl of Warm Air* by Moniza Alvi), *Newsline*, December, 1996.

Sidhwa, Bapsi, 'New English Creative Writing: A Pakistani Writer's Perspective', The International Conference on English in South Asia, University Grants Commission, Islamabad, January 4-9, 1989. Published in *The English Language in Pakistan*, ed., Robert J. Baumgardner, Karachi: Oxford University Press, 1993.

Acknowledgements

The editor and publishers would like to thank the following for permission to reproduce copyright material:

SHAHID SUHRAWARDY from *First Voices*, ed. Shahid Hosain (Oxford University Press 1965), reprinted with the permission of Oxford University Press. AHMED ALI from *Twilight In Delhi* (Oxford University Press 1984); poems from *The Purple Gold Mountain*, expanded edition; reprinted with the permission of Orooj Ahmed Ali. MUMTAZ SHAHNAWAZ from *The Heart Divided* (ASR 1990), reprinted with the permission of ASR Publications. ZAIB-UN-NISSA HAMIDULLAH from *The Young Wife and Other Stories* (Mirror Publications 1958), reprinted with the permission of Zaib-un-Nissa Hamidullah. MAKI KUREISHI, 'Day', 'A Christmas Letter To My Sister', 'Kittens', from *Wordfall*, ed. Kaleem Omar (Oxford University Press 1975); 'Curfew Summer', from *The Worlds of the Muslim Imagination,* ed. Alamgir Hashmi (Gulmohar 1986); 'Laburnam Tree' from *Pakistan Literature* Vol. 3 (The Pakistan Academy of Letters 1994); 'The Oyster Rocks', 'For my Grandson', from *She* November 1995; 'Snipers' from *The Far Thing* (Oxford University Press 1997), reprinted with the permission of Shireen Haroun; 'A Letter from Chao Chun', first publication by permission of Shireen Haroun. TAUFIQ RAFAT 'Circumcision', 'The Kingfisher', 'Return to Rajagriha', 'Arrival of the Monsoon', 'Wedding in the Flood' from *The Arrival of the Monsoon* (Vanguard 1985); 'To See Fruit Ripen', 'Poems for A Younger Brother', 'Lights' from *Half Moon*, reprinted with the permission of Taufiq Rafat. SHAHID HOSAIN 'Speculation' from *First Voices*, ed. Shahid Hosain (Oxford University Press 1965); 'Regarding the Appearance of Sir Laurence Olivier as Richard III in a Lahore Cinema' from *Pieces of Eight*, ed. Yunus Said (Oxford University Press 1971), reprinted with the permission of Oxford University Press. M. K. HAMEED from *First Voices*, ed. Shahid Hosain (Oxford University Press 1965), reprinted with the permission of Oxford University Press. DAUD KAMAL from *Before the Carnations Wither* (The Daud Kamal Trust 1995), reprinted with the permission of Parveen Daud Kamal. ZULFIKAR GHOSE from *The Triple Mirror of the Self* by Zulfikar Ghose, published by Bloomsbury Publishing in 1994, £6.99, © Zulfikar Ghose 1992, reprinted with the permission of Zulfikar Ghose and Bloomsbury Publishing; poetry from *Selected Poems* (Oxford University Press 1991), reprinted with the permission of Zulfikar Ghose. KALEEM OMAR 'Trout' from *Wordfall,* ed. Kaleem Omar (Oxford University Press 1975); 'Photograph', 'Himalayan Brown', 'The Hunters in The Snow', 'Winter Term' from *Pakistani Literature: The Contemporary Writers*, ed. Alamgir Hashmi (Gulmohar 1987); 'The Fifteenth Century' from *The Worlds of Muslim Imagination*, ed. Alamgir Hashmi (Gulmohar 1986); 'The Troubador's Life', 'Night Music' from *The News* 1996, reprinted with the permission of Kaleem Omar. JOCELYN ORTT SAEED from *Burning Bush* (Stillpoint Books 1994), reprinted with the permission of Jocelyn Ortt Saeed. BAPSI SIDHWA from *Ice-Candy-Man* (William Heinemann 1988), reprinted with the permission of Bapsi Sidhwa. NADIR HUSSEIN from *First Voices*, ed. Shahid Hosain (Oxford University Press 1965), reprinted with permission of Oxford University Press. G. F. RIAZ 'In Search of Truth' from *Shade in Passing* (Sang-e-Meel 1991); 'Silence', 'Alexander Comes of Age' from *Escaping Twenty Shadows* (Sang-e-Meel 1995), reprinted with the permission of G.F. Riaz. S. AFZAL HAIDER from *Sacred Ground*, ed. Barbara Bonner (Milkweed Editions 1996); reprinted with the permission of Syed Afzal Haider. TALAT ABBASI from *Feminist Studies 13*, no. 1, Spring 1987, reprinted with the permission of Talat Abbasi. ADRIAN A. HUSAIN from *Desert Album* (Oxford University Press 1997), reprinted with the permission of Adrian A. Husain. SALMAN TARIK KURESHI from *Landscapes of the Mind* (Oxford University Press 1997), reprinted with the permission of Salman Tarik Kureshi. TARIQ ALI from *Shadows of the Pomegranate Tree* (Chatto & Windus 1992), reprinted with the permission of Tariq Ali. MUNEEZA SHAMSIE from *Pakistani*

Short Stories in English, ed. Alamgir Hashmi and Shaista Sirajuddin, to be published by Oxford University Press; printed with the permission of Muneeza Shamsie. JAVAID QAZI from *Living in America*, ed. Roshni Rustomji-Kerns, (West View Press Inc., Boulder, Colorado 1995), reprinted with the permission of Javaid Qazi. RUKHSANA AHMAD 'Confessions and Lullabies' from *The Man Who Loved Presents* (The Women's Press, 1992); 'Song For A Sanctuary' from *Six Plays by Black and Asian Women Writers*, ed. Kadija George (Aurora Metro Press 1993), reprinted with the permission of Rukhsana Ahmad. SHUJA NAWAZ from *Journeys* (Oxford University Press 1997), reprinted with the permission of Shuja Nawaz. TARIQ RAHMAN from *Work and Other Stories* (Sang-e-Meel 1991), reprinted with the permission of Tariq Rahman. TAHIRA NAQVI from *Attar of Roses and Other Stories* (Lynne Reinner Publishers 1997), reprinted with the permission of Tahira Naqvi. ADAM ZAMEENZAD from *Cyrus, Cyrus* (Fourth Estate, 1990), reprinted with the permission of Adam Zameenzad. ALAMGIR HASHMI 'Encounter with the Sirens', 'Eid', 'Snow', 'Kashmir 1987' from *The Poems of Alamgir Hashmi* (National Book Foundation 1992); 'Pakistan Movement', 'Sun and Moon' from *Sun and Moon and Other Poems* (Indus 1992), reprinted with the permission of Alamgir Hashmi. WAQAS AHMAD KHWAJA 'April 77' from *Six Geese from a Tomb at Medum* (Sang-e-Meel, 1987); 'The Legend of Roda and Jallali' from *Miriam's Lament and Other Poems*, (Sang-e-Meel 1992), reprinted with the permission of Waqas Ahmad Khwaja. M. ATHAR TAHIR from *Just Beyond the Physical* (Sang-e-Meel 1991); 'The Trolley Man' from *Other Seasons* (Sang-e-Meel 1990), reprinted with the permission of M. Athar Tahir. MONIZA ALVI 'I want to be a Dot In A Painting By Miro', 'Presents from my Aunts in Pakistan' from *The Country at My Shoulder* (Oxford University Press 1991); 'The Double City', 'The Wedding', 'The Colours of the World', 'A Bowl of Warm Air' from *A Bowl of Warm Air* (Oxford University Press 1996), reprinted with the permission of Moniza Alvi. HANIF KUREISHI from *My Beautiful Laundrette* (Faber & Faber

1986), Copyright © 1986 Hanif Kureishi, reproduced by permission of the author c/o Rogers, Coleridge & White, 20 Powis Mews, London W 11 1JN. SARA SULERI from *Meatless Days* by Sara Suleri, first published in the USA 1989 by the University of Chicago Press, Copyright © Sara Suleri, 1989, reprinted with the permission of the University of Chicago Press. AAMER HUSSEIN 'Lost Cantos of the Silken Tiger', abridged version of the original, printed with the permission of Aamer Hussein. HINA FAISAL IMAM, From *Midnight Dialogue* (Sang-e-Meel 1990), reprinted with the permission of Hina Faisal Imam. MANSOOR Y. SHEIKH from *The Blue Wind* (Interim Press 1984), reprinted with the permission of Mansoor Y. Sheikh. QAISRA SHAHRAZ AHMAD from *What Big Eyes You've Got* (1988), reprinted with the permission of Qaisra Shahraz Ahmed. MOEEN FARUQI 'Partition' from *Verse*, v.9, no.2, Summer 1992; 'The Crows' from *The Rialto* no. 23, Summer 1992; 'Letter from Home' from *Orbis*, no 88, Spring 1993; 'The Return', from *Cyphers*, no. 40, Spring 1995; reprinted with the permission of Moeen Faruqi. PERVEEN PASHA from *Shades of Silence* (Sang-e-Meel 1996), reprinted with the permission of Perveen Pasha. MOAZZAM SHEIKH from *Adobe Anthology*,Vol.1 1993, reprinted with the permission of Moazzam Sheikh. SORAYYA Y. KHAN from *The Malahat Review*, Spring 1995, reprinted with the permission of Sorayya Y. Khan. TARIQ LATIF 'Masunda', 'Water Snakes', from *Skimming the Soul* (Littlewood Arc, 1991); 'From Symbols to Components', 'The Chukky' from *The Minister's Garden* (Arc Publications 1996); reprinted with the permission of Tariq Latif. HARRIS KHALIQUE from *If Wishes Were Horses* (Irtiqa 1997), reprinted with the permission of Harris Khalique. NADEEM ASLAM from *Season of the Rainbirds* (Andre Deutsch 1993), reprinted with the permission of Nadeem Aslam.

While every effort has been made to secure permission, we may have failed in a few cases to trace the copyright holder. We apologize for any apparent negligence. If notified we will be pleased to rectify any errors or omissions at the earliest opportunity.

INDEX